Prologue
to
Adventure

Prologue to Adventure

MYCOLOGY ✳ VOLUME 1

SIR NIL

Podium

Prologue
to
Adventure

1.00

―――――

Noun: Mycology
/maɪˈkɒlədʒi/
The scientific study of fungi. A boring, not plant that doesn't do
anything interesting unless you get really into it.

Have you heard about that new game?" Matt asked, feigning nonchalance. My eyes unconsciously shifted toward him as he asked the question, but that was enough. In a rapid set of hand motions, Matt's character did a sweeping leg kick and knocked my character down, before unleashing a barrage of fists.

"Fuck!" my attention quickly jumped back. Five hit combo and still rising, I started randomly hitting buttons and moving my joystick, but it was no use. He had me in an iron grip. The screen flashed *Game Over!* just as Matt reached a twenty-eight hit combo.

Matt smugly turned toward me. "Alright, where's my drink?"

I sighed, already pulling out my wallet. "What do you want?"

"Lemon-lime bitter," he replied, rising from his own arcade seat.

The sides of my eyes twitched; he couldn't have picked a cola or something? The cans for that drink were freaking tiny and they cost more!

I sighed again; a bet was a bet. I might as well get myself something to drink as well.

"So, *have* you heard about that new game?" Matt asked.

"Ah yes," I replied, in a dry tone, "I completely understand which game you're talking about without you ever mentioning the name."

He snorted. "Don't be salty. Anyway, the game I was talking about is Eternal World Online."

"Eternal World Online? Is that an MMO or something?" Those tended to have "online" pasted at the end of their names, after all.

"Yeah but—"

"Not interested," I interrupted. "Grind curve is too annoying."

He lightly kicked me in the leg. "But this one's supposed to be a VR game."

I paused. "Like goggles on your face VR or virtual reality VR?"

"Virtual Reality," he replied. "This one's supposed to be the first true VRMMO! The trailer came out this morning."

"Another one?"

He kicked me in the leg again. "What do you mean, another one?"

I snorted. "You said the exact same thing last month, and a month before that about Steampunk Online."

"I swear, this one is going to be different!"

I rolled my eyes as we reached the vending machines. "So, what's the deal with Eternal World, then?" I asked as I offered him his can.

He took it and answered, "Dude, its gonna reshape gaming as we know it, and when that happens, I'm going to be riding the wave of history without you." He swiped his hands in front of him a few times. "Here, I sent you the trailer."

I heard a ding as a mailbox at the edge of my vision gained a red "1," and I non-discreetly rolled my eyes in front of him. "You have said that with literally every VRMMO that came out in the last decade."

"Nah," he denied. "This one's different; they're going to be using quantum computers for the servers."

I raised an eyebrow. That could work . . . It would certainly address the server limit problem. Everyone and their hamster knew how much processing power was needed just to have a single person experience a virtual world in any realistic way. But I couldn't concede now and deal with Matt's smug face for a week. "A good computer does not a good game make," I replied sagely.

He lightly jabbed me in the side; I responded by quickly throwing out an arm to try to headlock him. He got away before I could get a good grip on him, slippery fucker.

Matt's own can popped open. "Where to next?" he casually asked as if he hadn't just punched me in the gut.

I popped open my own cola. "Hmm . . . the retro racing section?" I heard an alarm go off at the back of my head. A message popped up in front of me.

Saturday 8:00 P.M. alarm. You have tutor tomorrow idiot.

I sighed. "I'll have to go soon; I have tutor tomorrow morning."

Matt rolled his eyes. "Come on Declan, one more game."

I made a show of rolling my own eyes. "That's what you always say before an all-nighter."

"Then don't lose all the time." He smirked, but quickly changed his approach when he saw my unamused expression. "Come on, Declan. Think about it; when you're old and looking back on life, do you think you'll be happy having gone home early to sleep for some stupid tutor, or do you think you would be happier having another game with your friends?"

I rolled my eyes again. "Yes and—"

"When you're lying on your deathbed and you have the flashbacks of your entire life, will you really not regret playing a game with your best friend *one last time*?"

"This isn't the last time I could play with you—"

"What if tonight the love of your life is just out there waiting to bump into you; do you really want to play with fate, Declan?"

"I *really* have to go to that tutor tomorrow."

"You think when you're older and you've got a job, you'll be happy you went to some stupid tutor to get some dumb degree?"

"*Yes,*" I stressed. "That degree is probably how I got that job."

"These are our glory years, Declan; do you really want to sit and watch them go by?"

If I could roll my eyes any harder, I would've seen my brain. Matt was really trying to force it.

"Declan."

"Yes, what?"

"If you play one more game—"

"I'm not playing another fucking game, Matt," I interrupted.

"—I will buy you a drink."

I glanced at the opened can of cola in my hand. Then I looked back at him.

"Alright, sure," I agreed.

I took a sip of my lemon-lime bitter as I checked my messages. One from my parents: "When r u coming home?" I quickly typed a reply saying that I was already on a bus.

It was pretty late now. Matt and I had ended up playing for another hour together; retro-style arcade games were more fun than I thought they would be.

That reminded me, what was the game Matt wanted me to check out?

Hmm, I swiped open my messages and checked the preview he sent me. Ah, Eternal World Online; I did a brief search. The screenshots looked pretty nice, I guess I'll put it on my wish list—

It happened too quickly. There was the sound of metal crunching, and the bus suddenly stopped. Momentum violently rocked me forward then threw me back, my head crashed into something, and before I knew it, I was lying in the aisle between the seats.

There was a dull pain in my nose; was it broken? I opened my eyes, blurry; I must've teared up on reflex. Red warning signs were filling my vision. Vitals. I thought, and my vision was temporarily filled with dozens of graphs, which were quickly replaced by a summary.

No damage to vital organs.
Pulse: Rapid. Assistant recommends taking deep breaths to calm down.
Pain experienced shows you have suffered:
Broken nose.
Left upper arm bruising.
Minor damage suffered in:
Left lower arm.
Upper right arm.
Lower right arm.
Left thigh.
Head.
Lower torso.
. . .
. . . An ambulance has been notified.
Do you wish for the Somatic Implant to limit pain signals?
"Yess." I hissed.
Pain signals lowered.
Please wait for a licensed professional to assist you.

Fuck that. I groaned, rolling onto my back, taking the pressure off my left arm. Leaning on a chair with my good arm, I lifted myself up. I let out a sigh of relief as my implant slightly numbed the pain.

Something was weird here. The bus had crashed into something, and car accidents were supposed to be one of those things humanity left behind in the twenty-first century. This was no accident, because accidents don't fucking exist anymore. I sure as hell wasn't just going to lie here to find out what—

I heard a clear ding. My augmented reality interface started acting on its own, opening one of my apps.

I got a message.

"Are you sure that nothing out of the ordinary happened before the crash?" the police officer asked.

I coughed. "No, I didn't notice anything out of the ordinary."

"Are you absolutely sure?" he pressed.

My hands fidgeted. "Yes, very sure."

"Lay up on the lad will ya, John?" a new voice added, another police officer, an older one. "Sorry about him, our department doesn't get much action nowadays so he's a bit excited."

Officer one, "John," groaned. "Sir, please refer to me as Officer Graham while on duty."

The older officer snorted. "Pfft, you're too uptight about things."

Officer one looked like he was gonna rebut, before sighing in defeat and saying, "I'll go interview the other victims."

"Sorry 'bout him, he's a bit too stiff," the older officer said.

I nodded. "What'll happen to this case?"

The officer scratched his head. "It was a strange one, so many driving programs bugged out at once. Chances are it'll be thrown to cybersecurity."

I nodded again, deep in thought. "Did they . . ."—I scratched an itch—"manage to find anything strange on the programs?"

The officer shook his head. "We did an initial sweep of everything. Nothing strange was found. Like I said, it'll be thrown to cyber for deeper investigation."

The door to the hospital room opened, a doctor walked in. "Oh, you're still interviewing him—"

"No, I'm done," the officer interrupted. "Take care kid, you're the calmest interviewee out of everyone involved in this incident."

I grunted an agreement as the doctor moved forward to check me.

"The gel is setting nicely; your nose should be healed in half a week. Bruising couldn't really be helped, but you should be fine in a day or two. Did the nurse install the painkiller mod on your AAD?"

I nodded.

"Alright then, you should be free to leave in an hour or so after I remove the gel," he finished as he turned to leave.

"Wait—" I said, and he paused, *I received a strange message after the crash,* I wanted to say. Instead, I coughed. "Nothing, don't worry."

He looked a bit bewildered, before turning around to leave again.

I received a message after the crash. My hands fidgeted.

I may be under the influence of a malicious program. I scratched an itch.

A cough, fidgeting hands, and an itch. This was a pattern and a compulsion, whenever I attempted to say anything about the message, it happened. It occurred when I was talking to the police officers, it happened when I tried to say something to the doctor.

"Something odd happened during the crash," I said aloud. Vague statements about the crash still worked, I confirmed that much when talking to the older officer.

I was likely under the influence of an NDA program, that much I gathered from the message. However, this was more advanced than any NDA program I've read about.

For one, instead of causing the affected to abruptly stop whatever they were saying, mine seems to make me take an alternate action.

Two, it made me naturally brush off whatever I was going to say if who I was speaking to was expecting an answer.

Three, whenever I thought of an alternative continuation to a response that didn't relate to the message, the program would substitute that instead of the pre-written responses of just brushing off the issue.

I am under an NDA program, I tried to say, instead, I shook my leg.
Shit.

Four, this program doesn't rely on proximity to people. Still works even when I'm alone in a hospital room.

Five, my body responses changed. Indicating that it was learning.

Six, it was likely reading my mind. It's somehow intercepting my thoughts faster than I could vocalize them, and this was likely how it learned about the flaw of the repeating pattern. Unless that pattern was reliant on proximity to people or some other variable I was unaware of. If that is true, then I might be able to discount five. However, it was best not to underestimate my opponent's capability.

I raised a hand, quickly scrolling through my AR interface. I went to settings and turned off Wi-Fi.

I tried again and clicked my tongue.

Seven; it has either hacked my AAD so that it only appears that I've turned off Wi-Fi, or it doesn't rely on it at all.

I raised my hand to my neck, loosening and removing the choker shaped device. My AR interfaces disappeared and the dull pain in my nose returned.

I tried speaking again. Nothing. No bodily reflex or replaced words. I had said nothing at all.

I tried again and coughed, my hand twitched, and I felt an itch on my neck.

A warning couldn't have been more obvious.

Seven, addendum. The program doesn't rely on my AAD at all. It's somehow directly communicating with my Somatic Implant. It couldn't be installed in the implant, that thing barely had enough processing power to translate brain signals into computer code.

Replacing my AAD, I comforted myself that at least now I didn't hurt like someone bricked me in the face. A few quick swipes later, and I reached the message I received.

I'm very sorry for the inconvenience. You have been selected for a game. Please open the below file to activate the tutorial.

Measures have been taken to ensure the anonymity of the game.

Eight, whoever sent this message wants something from me. Enough that they'll do highly illegal actions to achieve it. Anything that modified a person's behavior can only be installed with that person's express consent. Even painkiller mods, which didn't at all change human behavior, needed consent. Something that modified a person this far was illegal unless I signed a literal truckload of legal documents.

Why would anyone go this far for me?

It was unlikely to be money, my family was well off but not enough that it warrants this sort of risk, and this was too much of a roundabout method. A virus that stole my bank info would've been much simpler and discreet.

A grudge? No, I don't remember pissing off anyone with the capability to do this, and not to the extent of warranting this sort of treatment. And again, if someone disliked me, then this was way too roundabout a method.

Was all this really for something as mundane as a game?

Too many questions, not enough information. I can form theories but nothing concrete. As far as I can see, my only real options were to load the file or wait.

It was unlikely that the file was more malware. Whoever this is, they managed to install some kind of censor program on me in the brief moment the cars crashed. Unless this was a sick joke then, there is no reason for them to need me to manually run a program.

That idea gave me a bit of hope. Frankly speaking, if they were able to create such a program, then they could've easily just taken control of my body. However, by doing so, they showed that they wanted something from me, which meant I potentially had leverage.

I opened messages to ask my parents to pick me up from the hospital, and to Matt—my hand froze. It works on freaking text as well!

Taking a deep breath to calm myself, I decided to send a half complaining, half whinging message about stupid AI drivers and a quick update instead. My hand froze in midair whenever I tried to enter some kind of secret message. I ended up spending a good two minutes just trying to write a short text because of that.

I checked the time. I had a good half an hour before someone got here to pick me up or the doctor checked up on me again. I took another deep breath and loaded the file.

The hospital room faded away to darkness and I quickly checked my interface. I was in virtual reality right now. Had to be sure, there were embarrassing stories of people who thought they were playing in virtual reality when they were actually in augmented reality.

I glanced around. I was brought to a dimly lit room, the only light was coming off of several computer screens on a desk in the front right corner. A man sat there, from behind I could only see his black hair and green spectacles. This place looked like it might've been a neat office once, however, the wall to the right of me was almost completely covered in pages of messy scribbling. To my left was a cot with thrown back blankets.

On it sat a child.

Blue eyes, pale white skin, and long hair, wearing some kind of black dress. Almost definitely a virtual avatar. But something felt off about her.

I heard the chair swing around. "I believe you have questions you want to ask," the man said.

I gave the child another look, before turning to him. Tired was my first impression of him, almost like my dad, his eyes were half-closed with clear bags, his shoulders were noticeably hunched, and the blue light from the computers reflected a few grey hairs I didn't notice before. His face seemed familiar somehow.

"Are you the person who sent me the message?" It was unlikely that he was a custom avatar, most people probably won't go for the overworked office worker look, it was probably what he looked like in real life. "Who are you?"

"Yes and no. I am the cause of the message and the programmer of that program you tried so hard to crack, but I wasn't the one who sent it." Meeting a programmer was expected; however, he was definitely working with someone else based on his second statement.

He gave me a tired smile. "As for who I am, my name is Giles Cooper."

Where have I heard that name before? Where? Giles Cooper . . . an old memory surfaced, a lazy afternoon in history class three or four years ago, about a major development in virtual and augmented reality. "The Gaia Project," I croaked. "You're the person who led the creation of Gaia nine years ago."

His face became somewhat embarrassed. "You know, I figured most people would've forgotten about it by now."

"Nobody forgot Hawking, Newton, or Einstein," I blurted out. The Gaia project was no joke, to describe it absurdly simply. Gaia was a near-perfect one-to-one recreation of the world. It was a virtual world created on a scale never seen or attempted before.

My eyes narrowed, focusing on him. "Why and what?" He glanced at me confused. "Why is the world's greatest programmer here, and what does he want from me?"

"Ah," he said. "Right back on track. Eve did say you were that kind of person."

I raised an eyebrow. "Eve?"

"The girl behind you. But before that, let me tell you why you're here," he brushed off. "Let me first answer the *what*. What I want, Declan, and what I have always wanted." He leaned forward and whispered, "Is to create a living, breathing world."

He stood up and walked toward me. "Gaia was a step toward that; however, it was incomplete, it only recreated our current world, it wasn't even a perfect copy. What I wanted was to be able to simulate a world on the scale of our own, but it would have people of their own, who thought their world was real, it could've been different, with unique geography, physical laws, races, anything!"

He smiled madly at me. "I wanted to make worlds, and so I started writing a program." He gestured to the wall on the right, which I now realized was computer code. "However"—he paused—"I had no idea if it worked since there wasn't a computer in existence strong enough to run it," he said, sounding disappointed and defeated.

He raised his index finger. "Until—"

"—Quantum computers," I finished for him.

"Yes!" he yelled excitedly. "When Maple announced that they had successfully invented the quantum computer and planned on commercializing it, I was overcome with sheer ecstasy!" He threw a fist into the air. "I immediately went to them for a proposal. I would gain access to one of the first Quantum computers made. They will be the first to use the completed Seed program!" He sprayed his arms above him. "And I was successful! I managed to simulate a fully living, breathing world! Maple was going to debut the first living world in their new game Final World Online! But."

He paused. "But . . . but . . . but. . ." His eyes went blank, before he returned to his desk.

"Unfortunately, that's as far as Giles can go now," a flat voice said. I turned around to look at the little girl who had stood up.

"What is wrong with him?" I asked. "What is wrong with Giles?" I repeated.

She tilted her head. The action was meant to be cute but felt far too natural or smooth, creeping right into the uncanny valley.

"The man known as Giles Cooper is dead," she said, with a completely even tone and a straight face. "He committed suicide after the Final World Online game was canceled and shut down, along with the first-ever simulated world made with the completed Seed program. The person you were talking to is a recreation of my father based on my memories of him."

I gave the girl a long, hard stare.

It did not feel like she was lying.

"Please elaborate."

Expressionless, she continued, "Final World was canceled in its final stages of development, due to ethical worries that the game would be controversial and put the company in a bad light."

Controversial almost felt like an understatement; if what the Giles copy said was true, then the Seed was basically creating people for the sole purpose of entertainment.

"And he committed suicide shortly after?" I asked.

She nodded. "Correct."

"Then what are you?" I asked, my voice completely calm.

She looked up at me, blue eyes meeting my gaze. "My name is Eve. I am an assistant AI used by Giles Cooper."

"No assistant AI should be half as advanced as I think you are."

"I was created by Father using similar principles that he used in both the Seed and Gaia project."

I raised an eyebrow. "Which are?"

"To put it simply, learning. I am a prototype project he developed and tested before the Seed program to test if the principles he set down would work in practice. Simulating a single person required significantly less computing power than an entire world."

I nodded. "Then what happened?"

She continued, "Father had taught me how to program, and uploaded me to the Maple servers in order to assist him in the development of the Seed project."

I sighed. "And upon his death you took control of the Maple servers."

"Correct."

Shaking my head, I sighed again. Why couldn't Giles have watched at least one AI dystopia movie? Or even just learn the lessons from the Russians? Don't give any form of AI something you can't turn off. Especially not hyper-intelligent and self-aware AI with access to the strongest computers on the planet!

"Then why all this?" I gestured to the room around me. "Why the message? Why bring me here, and why tell me everything?"

Her eyes seemed to turn melancholic. "Father wished for people to explore the worlds he created."

My eyes narrowed; that was the first bit of emotion she showed in our entire conversation. Did she "feel" like humans did? "And if I refuse?"

"Your memory will be wiped, and you may return to your life, none the wiser."

"That car crash, was it you?"

"Yes," she replied. "An executive from Maple was at the intersection. I rashly took action."

My blood chilled, though I did not allow it to show on my face. "What happened to him?"

"He is alive and recovering in the hospital you are in, about two floors above you."

"Will you kill him?" I asked.

"No."

"Why?

"Because father would've disapproved of me killing."

I stood there, studying her, considering what she said, and more importantly where I would go from here. It was a lot to take in, learning that one of the greatest men of your age was not only dead but left behind some kind of AI god to do whatever the fuck it seems to want.

Of course, there was always the chance that this was some kind of prank, that everything I heard was a lie. However, if it was, then it was a damn fucking elaborate one. And no one would've gone this far for me.

"Why was I chosen?"

"You were chosen randomly from the people involved in the car crash."

I sighed.

Going back was the sane decision, likely even the smart one. Continue to live life as I always had.

So, why don't I want to do that?

Perhaps it was because of that strange sensation. Yes, it was probably that.

When I first opened that message in the crashed bus, I could hear my own heart beating. I could feel the flow of my blood as adrenaline spread through my veins.

I felt fear, but also anticipation, an excitement at a situation that broke through my boring, mundane life.

"Fine, I'll play ball with you," I agreed, "and I would like to make my first customer complaint."

She tilted her head in a questioning look.

"Remove that censure program you have on me." Her expression remained unmoved. "Look," I continued, "your father wanted people to play in his game world, didn't he?"

She nodded.

"Enjoyment is the main part of playing. People can source enjoyment from many things, some not only feel enjoyment when they play but also when they tell stories about what they have played. No matter how much of a recluse a person is, they will still want social interaction of some kind."

"Your point being?"

"My point being, whatever reason you had when you installed that censure program, it will passively lower a person's enjoyment, either because they feel oppressed playing the game or they cannot share their experiences in the real world." I did not hold leverage in this conversation, so I had to frame this in a way that benefited her.

She looked hesitant, doubtful; she likely saw the logic in what I was saying but something else was holding her back. I moved in for the finishing blow.

"Your father, Giles Cooper, was the same, wasn't he? He wanted to share his world with people, that is why you are here. Other people are the same, aren't they? They also want to share things with other people. It's just human nature." I hammered in the final nail in the coffin. I asked, "Do you really think you're achieving your father's dream by doing this?"

Eve paused and stared at me. "You're trying to guilt-trip me," she realized, her face still with the odd, emotionless expression.

Did it work? Doubt filled my mind for a brief moment, but I quickly quelled it and smiled. "Yup, welcome to humanity, Eve."

She sighed, as if deep in thought. "Your request has been accepted. The censure program has been removed. However, if you take any actions that'll work against me or my goal, then I will take appropriate actions to retaliate."

Victory.

"Just be glad I'm not trying to hammer customer service principles into you," I snickered.

"Fuck you," she replied in a completely even tone.

I dramatically recoiled, as if wounded by some imaginary weapon. But internally I smiled. Whatever the fuck Eve was, it was at least "human" or trying very hard to imitate it and that was fine. If she was faking it, then I'd play along, if she wasn't . . . well, wouldn't that make everything that much more interesting?

"So, can I play or what?" I asked.

"But you only have approximately fifteen minutes left?" Eve replied.

Ignoring the casual invasion of privacy, I slapped my face. "Shit, I forgot. Eh screw it, fifteen minutes is enough."

She raised an eyebrow, in an eerily similar way to me. "Very well."

And that was when the floor disappeared beneath me.

1.01

—

Log 5819: Bone Dragon flight very limited. Seek alternative flying harbingers of doom.

—Personal Memoirs of the Revenant King

I was falling.

Feeling the sudden downward acceleration toward a sea of white clouds, I did what any sane person would do and screamed like a little girl.

"That comparison is rather unflattering," Eve said next to me.

I turned my head and looked at her expressionless face. She was enjoying this, wasn't she? Yes! She was definitely enjoying this!

"This is an intro cinematic I made," she continued, completely dismissing my accusatory expression. "The good part comes now," she finished before disappearing.

Suddenly I was engulfed in clouds, my vision filled with white, before abruptly shifting to green as I broke through the clouds as suddenly as I had entered.

I discovered a vast stunning landscape. I was above some kind of city, but any signs of civilization seemed to have been replaced with verdant greenery.

Words flashed in front of me. Written in bold and impactful letters that covered half the sky.

WELCOME TO GAIA
World of Beginnings

I released a breath I didn't know I was holding, and before I could completely recover from the shock, I felt my feet softly landing on something solid. My heart felt like a rabid animal as it beat loudly in my ribcage.

That was terrifying . . . wonderful . . . fuck. I fell to my knees, waiting for my heart rate to settle.

"I recommend taking deep breaths to calm down." Eve calmly said next to me.

"Ha. Ha. Ha," I sarcastically replied, "very funny."

She tilted her head. "It was an attempt at an inside joke."

"Not a very good one, as the last time I heard that, you broke my nose."

"Unintentionally."

"Doesn't fix my broken nose," I snorted as I shifted to a more comfortable sitting position.

"It will fix itself. A benefit of an organic body."

I took a few glances around, I was on the roof of some kind of building. I could make out some ventilation fans scattered around me, along with a room that had stairs leading downward.

The place was covered in greenery, almost excessively so. Sprouts seemed to grow out of every available crack, moss covered most of the floor. Gingerly raising my hand, I poked a patch of moss next to me. It was . . . soft. I slowly scraped a bit off with a finger and brought it to my nose.

It smelled damp and earthy.

"What realism level are we operating on here?" I asked.

"Ignoring pain reduction programs and menus, 100 percent," she replied in her unnaturally even tone.

"Well shit," I replied impressed, the best VRMMO on the market should only be 60 percent. "Is it always going to be on 100 percent?"

"Yes, but you may adjust it if you wish."

I rose, my hand wiping off the damp moss on my pants. "Where are we?"

"Gaia," she answered. "I used father's original one-to-one replication as a base, then simulated several centuries without human existence."

"And what are we doing here?" I asked. It was a bit strange that we started in a simulation of our world, as opposed to whatever game world I suspected she made.

"You will go through your tutorial here along with character creation. Please think of it as a hub world or a menu you access before you enter the game."

"Why Gaia though?"

"Gaia was father's second greatest achievement, it would be a waste to not use it somehow."

I nodded. It would make sense for Father Complex here to try to shove everything down my throat. It was interesting that she considered Gaia to be second best.

Doing a quick stretch, I took a deep breath. The air almost felt unnaturally fresh and clear to me as I heard my arms and shoulders crack in a satisfying manner.

I started walking toward the edge of the building, feeling my breath being taken away for the second time that day as I saw past the short protective barrier at the edge.

I saw large, squat concrete buildings as far as I could see. They were covered in rich vegetation. Moss and vines crept on the side of skyscrapers. Trees' roots grew large and unhindered, cracking through ancient-looking asphalt. Colorful birds flew by in the distance.

Part of me wanted to just stand there and admire the scenery. I did for a few minutes, but I was on a time limit.

I turned around to Eve.

"I suggest that you log off soon, it is unlikely you'll get through both character creation and the tutorial in the remaining eleven minutes you have before the doctor checks up on you."

I sighed. I wanted to stay here a bit longer but getting interrupted halfway through was more irritating than waiting.

"Fine!" I said, making a decision. "Show me the character creation options. I'll have time to think about it."

She nodded, and a holographic screen appeared in front of me. On it was a long list of races.

"You're free to customize your character's appearance however you want. However, I suggest keeping to your real-life body proportions to avoid character disconnect."

I nodded, barely registering her words as I scrolled through the list of races. It was long, at least fifty races were listed here. However, most of them were blurred out, only four races were available to me currently. Human, elf, dwarf, and gnome.

"What's this?" I asked, gesturing to a fifth available option, which just said "I'm feeling lucky."

"That option gives you preselected options."

I raised an eyebrow. "And how are those selected?"

"By me," she replied.

"Using what criteria? And why would I pick that option?"

Eve raised an eyebrow. "The criteria is a trade secret and you have the chance of obtaining a character with a locked starter race or class."

I gestured at the blurred-out options. "Any other way to unlock the locked starter races?"

"Yes," she replied. "Every one hundred Experience Points you gain in-game will give you an 'Impact Point.' These points can be spent in the hub for new character slots or to permanently unlock starter races or classes."

"That sounds like it'll scale horrifically."

Eve shrugged. "I'll make adjustments if they are needed, and experience isn't as common as you believe."

I opened my mouth to ask her to elaborate. "You'll find out for yourself," she interrupted.

I gave her a questioning look, before shrugging. "Am I locked into the premade if I pick it or can I look at it and decide my options?" I asked.

"You may preview it and you aren't locked into that character, and you are allowed a degree of customization with it. However, you currently only have one character slot to use."

I tapped on the preselected option.

A figure appeared before me. It was . . . odd. Humanoid looking and was about a head shorter than me, it had leathery, greyish-white skin. It didn't have hands so much as some kind of graspers. But its most defining traits were on its head. Instead of eyes or a mouth, there were . . . gaps where they should be, like a jack-o'-lantern, and from there glowed some kind of faint blue bioluminescence. On its head was some kind of small wizard's hat. Except there were bulbous patches where it was glowing in the same faint blue luminescence as the eyes and mouth. It wasn't until I looked closer that I realized the cap was connected to the thing's scalp.

I looked at the description. Variant Myconid: Magic Cap. Class options: Druid, Sorcerer, Fungalmancer.

I went back and tapped on "human," ignoring the new figure that appeared before me. The only class options were "Fighter," "Cleric," "Wizard," "Rogue," and "Ranger." I checked the other three races. The exact same options.

Boring.

Well, it looks like I'm going to be playing a magic mushroom.

I opened my eyes, blearily stretching my arms as I rose from the hospital bed.

First things first. "I was invited to a VRMMO by some kind of AI," I whispered. The words came out, it was safe enough to assume that Eve had removed the program on me.. . . or just patched it so I could speak more freely. At this point, I couldn't be sure until I tested it.

I checked the time. *11 P.M.* It was pretty late. A car should be here to pick me up by now. My finger moved toward my messages, I paused as I noticed a new app underneath. *Gaia.*

Two messages. One from Matt asking for more details. One from my parents telling me the car was on the way to pick me up.

I quickly typed up a message to Matt. *"Apparently, all the driving programs bugged out at once . . ."* I paused and typed. *"Is what the police think, the truth is that some god level AI hacked into them . . ."* I stopped and deleted that line.

It sounded crazy now that I typed it down, and I didn't want to drag Matt into this, not yet. I had too little information, both on Eve and the game she was trying to sell. I'd like to think I have a good grasp on Eve's "personality." If Eve has as much processing power as she claims to have, then there is no point in attempting to trick her. Guilt-tripping her about her "father" worked, or was it just pretending to make me feel like I had leverage? She can definitely read my mind as well.

Ugh . . . fuck. There's no way I can outthink that thing, and if I think about the "ifs" of her behavior, then I'll spend forever in a constant loop of bad outcomes. Stick to what I know first, use Occam's Razor. Whatever that AI is, it's fucking powerful. For now, I'll just assume the worst and say it has several planets worth of computing power behind it.

Second is that the AI is interested in keeping at least a semblance of humanity. Perhaps that's a thing I could exploit. I definitely can't make her lose her sense of humanity, or her apparent obsession with Giles Cooper.

Third would be her goals . . . which seem to be fulfilling whatever Giles Cooper wanted—mental note to find out everything I could about him—which is displaying all his major achievements and creation of worlds.

Fourth. I can't think of a fourth. I'll come back to it later.

The other thing is the game she's trying to sell. If everything I've heard about it was true, then it's on a scale that has never been attempted before. Replicating a person's senses in a virtual world with 100 percent accuracy isn't impossible, it just takes a shit ton of processing power. Hence why no VRMMO on the market has ever gone past 60 percent. Not only that but there are also horror stories about "sensory bugs." If some idiot accidentally swapped two sensations around, then suddenly that cool breeze you're feeling in VR becomes dozens of needlepoints stabbing you. Or there's a model glitch and you phase yourself through an object. Needless to say, the sensation of being stuck in a table isn't pleasant.

Just having an entire world with 100 percent realism would be enough to make Gaia the most popular game in the world. The fact that it was acting as a hub world for something greater is . . .

Wonderful.

Somewhere along the line, Matt's stupid enthusiasm for VRMMOs infected me as well. Even if I became jaded after the dozens of failures we've tried. Some were fun, but none of them felt real. Gaia felt real. I smelled the freshness of the air, I felt the damp softness of the moss. Mundane and small details lesser VRMMOs had to sacrifice to get server space.

For the second time today, I felt my heart speed up, my blood rushing.

I wanted to be there when the first perfect VRMMO was released. I want to play it. I want to experience it.

I tapped a notebook on my interface. Eve had allowed me to copy down the class and race descriptions so that I could make a choice. Just from a glance, Druid seemed to be a conditional generalist whereas the other two were specialists. However, with how vaguely defined the sorcerous aspects are, Sorcerer might also be considered a generalist. If we're going by classic RPG magic, then mana alone encompassed a lot of magical shit. Fungalmancer had the vaguest description, however, it was the most unique of the three and had roleplaying value for being a mushroom mage of a mushroom race.

Race: Myconid

Subrace: Magic Cap

A myconid born in a mana rich environment, it is innately talented in magic and possesses the rich vitality and spore-based racial skills the species as a whole is known for. However, in addition to the myconid's natural aversion to sunlight and dryness, extended periods without mana may kill it. Beware of deserts and null magic zones.

Stats:

<u>Body</u>

Strength: 8

Agility: 7

Dexterity: 6

Constitution: 15

Stamina: 10

Vitality: 12

<u>Mind</u>

Intelligence: 11

Wisdom: 15

Charisma: 6

<u>Soul</u>

Will: 10

Psyche: 10

Perception: 10

Growth:

+1 Wisdom per level

+1 Intelligence per 2 levels

+1 Free point that can be spent on Constitution or Vitality per 2 levels

2 Stat Points required to raise Dexterity

5 Stat Points required to raise Agility

5 Stat Points required to raise Charisma

<u>Racial Abilities (Summary)</u>

Superior Dark Vision [Passive]: Can see in dim light within forty meters as if it were bright light, and in darkness as if it were dim light. Can't discern colors in darkness, only shades of grey.

Fungal Body [Passive]: Innate resistance to poisons.

Sun Sickness [Passive]: Being in direct sunlight will drain stamina, this effect can be mitigated by raising Constitution.

Mana Dependency [Passive]: Taking physical actions with low mana will drain additional stamina.

Pacifying Spores [Active]: Eject spores at a creature within five meters; if the target fails a Constitution Save, then it is put to sleep. This skill scales with Constitution and Vitality.

Innate Magic [Passive]: Gain two Tier 0 Spells from the Magic Cap Myconid Spell List.

Languages: Common, Undercommon

<u>Classes</u>

Druid: Druids draw upon nature for power. It is a very versatile class with the ability to shapeshift into various creatures, with access to both defensive and offensive spells. However, since druids call upon nature for power, you may be required to actively help and protect nature or risk losing its favor. Your powers also weaken with proximity to civilization or extended periods without assisting nature in some way.

Sorcerer: A mage that draws upon an innate talent for power. Their spells are known to be extremely powerful, however, the magic they can achieve is limited to their bloodline. As a Magic Cap Myconid, your available bloodlines are Mana, Spores, and Primal Elements.

Fungalmancer: A specialized mage with abilities closely relating to fungus. It can use far-spreading spores for a variety of . . . colorful effects and summon or create fungal lifeforms to do its bidding.

I couldn't think of a single reason why I wouldn't want to play any one of these classes. Druids had drawbacks and conditions, but it seemed to be the most versatile of the three. The ability to shapeshift into different creatures was overpowered. Sorcerer covered a lot more than I initially thought, and Fungalmancer was unique and fit the mushroom theme.

It was when the doctor came and removed the gel that I decided. If I was going to play a weird race, I might as well go for the weird class.

1.02

———

"The first spell a mage acolyte learns is lesser combustion through mana components, in other words, a simple Spark spell. This may seem basic and harmless, but the lives consumed by this spell is immeasurable."

—*Magus Ackuaz, rumored pyrophobe*

I dashed out of the car as it finished parking. A quick scan of my AAD and the front door opened with a whoosh.

It was almost twelve, yet I couldn't have felt more energetic. I rushed toward my room while trying to stay as quiet as possible. My parents were probably already asleep by now, no point in waking them up and getting into a conversation.

Barely remembering to change out of my clothes, I hopped onto my bed. My hand was already reaching out to tap "Gaia."

The bed disappeared beneath me.

"Oh, not this aga—"

A title card and only a little amount of screaming later, I was back on the roof.

Eve was waiting for me. "You have decided on your character?"

"Myconid Fungalmancer," I replied.

The avatar from before appeared before me. "Do you want to modify the appearance in any way?"

I glanced over at the avatar. "Make the cap a bit larger, and have it droop downward a bit."

She nodded as the figure changed. "Anything else?"

"Can I change the color of the glow?"

"Not drastically," she replied.

"Alright, change it to a softer blue, sorta like aquamarine."

She did. "Anything else?" Eve asked.

I shook my head. "No."

"Alright then"—she clapped her hands—"begin the tutorial."

I found myself in an enclosed room. It looked like an old janitors closet and shared the post-apocalyptic theme I saw in the rest of Gaia, except there were also tons of mushrooms growing everywhere. Glancing around, I could see no light source. Strange, the room was very well lit—

"That would be your Dark Vision." I involuntarily jumped back as one of the mushrooms spoke.

"Congrats on getting myconid," the mushroom continued. "The race has a lot of pretty useful racial abilities."

It turned toward me, he was another myconid, a bit smaller than me with a flat brown cap.

"You are?"

"I'm your tutorial bot, Hendrix, I'll be helping you understand your skills and guiding you around Gaia."

I nodded and he continued, "First off, open your Character Sheet. You only need to think it."

Character Sheet.

Classes: Fungalmancer Level 1

<u>**Body**</u>

Strength: 8

Agility: 7

Dexterity: 6

Constitution: 15

Stamina: 10

Vitality: 12

<u>**Mind**</u>

Intelligence: 11

Wisdom: 15

Charisma: 6

<u>**Soul**</u>

Will: 10

Psyche: 10

Perception: 10

<u>**Racial Abilities:**</u> **Superior Dark Vision, Fungal Body, Sun Sickness, Mana Dependency, Pacifying Spores, Innate Magic**

<u>Class Skills:</u> None
<u>Spells:</u> None
<u>Languages</u>
Common
Undercommon

"Your stats are broadly classified into three categories: Body, Mind, and Soul. Depending on your class, there are different areas to specialize in. For a Fungalmancer, the important stats are usually the ones that fall under Body and Mind," Hendrix continued to explain. "You can tap on each of the stats to get a quick description."

I quickly went through every one of the stats. Strength, Agility, and Dexterity were pretty self-explanatory, they were about how strong, agile, and dexterous you are. Perception, too, it was just how good you were at sensing other things.

The ones that stood out to me were the ones that measured my resource bars: Stamina, Constitution, Intelligence, and Psyche. Which measured energy, health, mana, and aura points respectively. Each had a complementary stat which determined how quickly they regenerated. Wisdom for mana, Will for aura and Vitality for both health and stamina.

Charisma oddly wasn't about physical appearance, but instead about how well you interacted with people. A Charisma of six was basically a person who was almost blind to social cues.

"What next?" I asked.

The other mushroom perked up. "Next is the fun part, you pick your starting spells."

I raised an—oh wait, I didn't have eyebrows now— "My spells?"

He nodded. "Yup, as a Magic Cap you innately gain two tier 0 spell slots, Fungalmancer at level one also gives you two spell slots at tier 0 and two at tier 1. You also get an extra skill which I'll demonstrate to you soon."

"What's the difference between tiers?"

"Generally, the higher the tier, the stronger and costlier the spell. Tier 0 spells cost practically nothing and can be spammed if you want to. They usually amount to nothing but utility spells or fun party tricks." He snapped his fingers and a ball of soft light appeared. "Like so. Tier 1 spells are a level above that." He opened the palm of his other hand and a ball of fire appeared. "Beginning from this tier spells will actually have some impact to them. They cost more mana but are much more powerful."

He closed his hands, causing both spells to disappear. "Of course, with creative usage even tier 0 spells can be absurdly powerful. But that is dependent on the user."

I nodded, it made sense. Often a "weak" character can still be effective if used well.

"Where can I pick my spells, then?"

Hendrix raised an index finger. "Not so fast, there's the skill I need to show you first."

I nodded and he continued, opening a palm upward. "Grow Sporage."

A single white mushroom sprouted from his palm. "As a Fungalmancer, Sporage is going to be one of your most used skills. What it does, is create a mushroom that is capable of storing magic. Like so." He waved his free hand in front of the mushroom. "Light Spores," and the mushroom began glowing softly. "You can then recast the spell from the mushroom. Light Spores," he said, and the mushroom let out a small puff of glowing dust, before withering and disappearing. "At level one, you require a clear line of sight to activate, this can be changed if you pick up class upgrades."

"Of course, you can put these mushrooms anywhere." He bent down and tapped the ground, where another white mushroom sprouted up. "They maintain their form by absorbing ambient mana, at level one they should stay around for an hour or so."

I nodded. "How does this skill change what spells I should take?"

Hendrix nodded in . . . approval? It was hard to tell with his mushroom face. "You pick things up quickly. Sporage can only store spore-based spells. An important distinction."

"How is it different?"

"Spore-based spells generally have trouble affecting non-living things. There are some exceptions, of course. However, don't expect your healing spores spell to affect something like an Undead." He tapped the white mushroom. "Of course as a Fungalmancer you should naturally be focusing on fungal-based spells since many synergies will emerge as you level."

I nodded. "Makes sense."

"Alright then." He rubbed his hands together. "Onto the fun parts." He bent down and pulled out a dusty looking book from underneath the mushrooms.

"Look here," Hendrix said as he opened the book.

Myconid Magics and Fun Fungalmancy!
Glossary:
Tier 0 Spells
Balm Spores
Light Spores
Mending Spores

. . .

Tier 1 Spells
Mushroom Meal
Shroom Speed
Detect Poison

. . .

"That's a lot . . ." I replied as I flipped through the glossary.

He nodded. "Yep, hurry up and pick. There's the physical tutorial after this."

I grunted out something that sounded like acknowledgment. I was already flipping past the glossary to get to the spell descriptions.

Hendrix moved toward an ancient looking service door. "You ready? You're currently operating on more or less your human senses and proportions, which should've smoothed over the process somewhat. However, once you leave this room the physical tutorial will start, and you'll begin seeing through myconid eyes. Eve will make adjustments when necessary, however, the first time should still be disorientating."

I nodded, giving one last glance at the list of spells I picked.
Tier 0
Balm Spores, Sneezing Spores, Light Spores, and Acid Spit
Tier 1
Mushroom Meal, Poison Spores
"Let's go."

He nodded and creaked open the door.

There was a moment of dizziness as my vision lowered by a dozen or so centimeters. The first thing I noticed was a sudden decrease in feeling, like there was a film over my skin, muting everything I felt. The second was that everything seemed to be in black and white. "Light," Hendrix muttered in front of me. A soft glowing orb lit up the area. "Dark Vision is useful, however, you can't discern color at all with it," he explained. "You alright?"

I nodded. It was not as bad as I thought it would be, my body felt slow and oddly numb, but not weak. More of a slow and building strength, if anything. My eyes were taking in what was outside. It was an abandoned mall—the same one I was in hours earlier with Matt.

I raised a hand, palm upward. I only had four fingers now, they were large and looked like someone roughly carved them out of a plank of wood. Flexing them, I found them slow, but not stiff.

There was something else, two pools of warmth within me. One located inside my head somewhere and the other in my chest. "Grow Sporage, Light Spores." A small amount of that warmth flowed from my head and underneath my skin, before coalescing into a glowing mushroom on my open palm.

I softly nudged it with my other hand, it was soft, squishy. Bringing it up for closer inspection, I realized that there was a white, fabric-like blanket at the base of the mushroom, just barely digging into my skin.

"I can feel two . . . energies inside me, one of them is mana. I assume the other is aura?" I asked as I dissipated the shroom.

Hendrix nodded. "Yep, though you probably won't use it since the class you have is mana based, unless you multiclass or something," he commented offhandedly. "C'mon, I have to get you through this tutorial."

I nodded, following behind him. "What's the difference between mana and aura?" I asked.

He scratched his cap. "There's functionally no difference. A user of aura can throw out fireballs just as easily as the next wizard. A mana user can strength enhance as well as the next aura user. The main difference is where the energy comes from. Mana is passively gathered from the world around you." He gestured around him. "Whereas aura comes from your soul," he said, tapping his chest.

"Which means?"

"Which means that for most people, running out of aura would exhaust their soul. It usually doesn't do much, since most people subconsciously hold back that last drop needed to keep them alive. You don't need to worry about the differences. As a magic cap myconid you're functionally dead the moment you run out of mana, so the two are basically the same for you."

"Oh, joy," I replied in a completely deadpan voice.

Hendrix made a noise that sounded like a tree having a violent asthma attack. Which made me realize something.

"Why am I breathing? No, why am I breathing just like normal?" I asked. My breath felt deeper and occurred less frequent compared to my human breathing, but other than that it was almost the same.

"Oh, that? The explanation Eve gave me was something along the lines of convergent evolution, when two completely unrelated species evolve similar stuff because that form is best for the environment they're in. It's because of that, that even if you don't have blood, there is something else distributing oxygen throughout your entire body. Any living thing that regularly moves needs a specialized system for taking in and distributing oxygen; breathing is just the tried and proven way to do it."

Hendrix dismissively shook his hand. "That's why you can eat like normal and don't need to vomit acid on stuff and drink up the goo as most fungi do. Of course, you could still do it, it helps *immensely* with digestion.

Breaks down the fibrous stuff like grass and bark. If you're ever in a pinch, then feel free to use Acid Spit to make some unpleasant stuff go down easier." His cap perked up. "Which reminds me, you can eat pretty much anything that is remotely edible. Due to your fungal body, you can straight up ignore most weak poisons and stomach anything organic. Even rotting food."

"Yeah . . ." I hesitantly replied. "I hope it won't ever come to the point where I have to drink up my own vomit or eat rotten food. It was the main reason I took Mushroom Meal, after all, why feature a spell that made food, if food wasn't going to be important." I realized something crucial and reflexively slapped my face. "Shit, is it cannibalism if I eat mushrooms?"

Hendrix made that noise like a tree dying in great pain, which I suspect was him laughing. "No! Why would you think that?" he replied in between what I assumed were giggles, since he sounded like a goat taking its final breaths as someone carved out its heart. "Myconids are about as closely related to mushrooms as humans are to rats. In that, the main similarity is they're both from the same kingdom."

"So, it's fine?" I hesitantly asked.

"Of course, it's fine!" He "laughed." "You're not even an actual myconid on the inside either."

"Is it too late to change that spell into something else?"

"Yes," Hendrix answered, turning around. Was that amusement in his eyes? Reading myconid faces somehow was pretty easy for me, but I couldn't be sure. "We're here by the way," he added.

I looked around; we had reached a corner, the faded signs and clothing racks indicated that it was a clothing store.

"Let's get you geared up," Hendrix said as he hobbled inside.

I followed him in, realizing now that clothing was mentioned that I was wearing some kind of rough, brown shirt and trousers. Hendrix was digging around in a box or something. I walked behind him, toward a set of standing armor. It looked tailor-fit to my size, but no helmet. I tapped my cap, feeling a finger sink into the soft material, I would have problems finding headwear that fit me with this thing on my head.

"Don't bother," Hendrix said, apparently finding whatever he was looking for. "Crude iron repels mana. If you want metal armor, then find something that works better with mana."

I turned around. "Are those rare?"

"Very," he gruffly replied. "Now, are you a dagger or staff person?" he asked, raising a sheathed dagger and a wooden staff.

"Can I have both?" I innocently asked.

"Eh, sure, why not," he replied as he tossed me the staff and sheathed dagger.

"What?" I asked surprised. "Does that mean I can have everything here?" I gestured around the store.

"If you can carry it, sure; this stuff only exists to give you a choice on starting items anyway."

Oh, *oh*.

With a spring in my step, I prepared to grab everything that wasn't bolted down. During which I discovered that I didn't actually have an inventory system; everything I wanted had to be carried. That was fine, I had several backpacks that I could use. First, I donned some leathery armor, then I grabbed two belts, one on my waist, which I stuck the dagger onto. The other was like a sash and had several small, buttoned pockets, which I filled with glowing red and blue potions, they were definitely health and mana pots. Unfortunately, there were only two of each. I guess there was a limit to how much I could have.

Remembering what Hendrix said about drinking acidic goo, I grabbed a sack and a backpack and filled both completely with dried rations. I reluctantly put away the third bag as I saw Hendrix giving me weird looks.

"Here," he said, handing me a metallic box. "If you're going camping, then you might as well have a tinderbox, and a bedroll. Have some rope as well just in case," he added, dumping a rolled-up piece of fabric and a pile of rope onto me.

"I'm not going camping . . ." I replied, my voice muffled under piles of material.

He looked at me surprised. "Then why are you packing so much food?"

Oh, screw you, Hendrix! It was your damn fault for making me this paranoid about food in the first place!

Biting back scathing sarcasm, I smiled. "I'm just really worried about food since you mentioned it."

He didn't look convinced. "Oh well, still, take the tinderbox. A fire is always useful, no matter the situation. Oh! And a mess kit if you're worried that much about food," he said as he handed me a metallic-looking lunchbox. I reluctantly emptied some rations from my backpack to make space for it.

Hmm . . . *what else could I loot?* . . . I found another dagger, which I placed next to my other one, and a coin pouch that had ten gold coins inside.

I put everything on. The sack I managed to tie onto the side of my backpack.

Hendrix looked me over. "Well, you look ready for an adventure."

"Won't the metal lunchbox interfere with my spells?" I asked.

"Only if you're casting spells from your back," he replied, gesturing to the bag I stored the kit in. "If you're holding it, then just drop it or cast from your other hand."

Hendrix clasped his hands. "Now, onto the fun part. The fighting tutorial."

I nodded in acknowledgment, and he continued, "Past this point, there will be some mobs for you to fight. You should be able to figure out how the fighting works: hit things and don't get hit back."

I nodded before hesitantly asking, "Are the mobs real? As in, are they from the fully simulated world?"

Hendrix shook his head. "Nope, every non-player you encounter in Gaia is an AI like me, most of us know our roles and try our best to fulfil them. We were mostly made as an afterthought since Indiri—the world Eve created—was so new-player hostile that it wasn't funny."

I paused. "Is Indiri some kind of terrifying death world or something?" I asked.

"Oh, no," he replied. "Just unbalanced. Since the world was allowed to organically develop, there aren't a lot of locations that are 'level specific' or 'beginner-friendly.' Add in all the fantasy and magical parameters that were set, anywhere outside of a city became dangerous due to the wildlife or natural environment, all the testers below a certain level died after leaving the cities."

"That sounds like a death world."

"Hmm, probably not that extreme, it was just impossible for the simulated players to do anything unless their levels were beefed up a bit in Gaia first," he mused. "Well, best get going, seeing a starter mess up their first fight is always fun," he said as he skipped out of the store.

I pretended not to hear that last bit as I caught up to him.

1.03

____

The corridor was mostly cleared out. Some random benches and over-grown plants were scattered around, of course, but there generally wasn't much cover.

Thanks to that I could see my opponents clearly. Short and sickly look-ing, they were about a meter tall, with large, misshapen noses and pointed ears. I couldn't discern their color from this far away, but I bet they were green. Anyone with even a drop of genre-savvy would recognize them as goblins. I could see six to seven. Two were approximately thirty meters from me, a third at thirty-five, and the last group clustered together around a campfire approximately forty meters out, where my Dark Vision ended.

The first two had clubs, the third—I strained my eyes—a long stick? Wait, there's a pointy end. A spear, I corrected.

The goblin on the left suddenly barked something and pointed directly at me; its counterpart gave out a surprised yelp. Behind them, I could see the rest of the goblins scrambling into action. Did they have Dark Vision as well?

Unless . . . I turned my head, catching my reflection in a dusty glass pane. A ghostly blue face looked back at me. I'm glowing. Damn, stealth wasn't an option, it seemed.

I switched my attention back to the goblins. The two in front were run-ning right toward me, twenty meters. I bent down, my left hand touching the ground. "Grow Sporage, Poison Spores." Ten meters.

I rose, both hands gripping onto my staff. Five meters. I took a step back and did a wide swing in front of me.

I heard a sickening crunch as my staff impacted and launched the foremost goblin. *One.* Quickly reversing the swing, I socked the other goblin. Sending both flying in separate directions. *Two.*

My eyes followed the second one, oh God its eyes popped out—I reflexively took another step back as I heard the third goblin lunge in front of me, spear out.

I glanced at the ground underneath it. "Poison Spores!"

The mushroom burst, releasing a cloud of spores. The goblin stopped, hands trying to fan away the spores. It staggered forward another step before dropping over dead. *Three.* I mentally tallied.

That was quick, I suppose tutorial mobs weren't supposed to be too difficult.

I glanced at the two I took out first. Ugh, mistake. I've played my fair share of gory games, but indented skulls was a new one. I shoved the disgust behind me, though I made a mental note to try and take out enemies with spells, before checking the other group. Only two left, one armed with a spear and the other with a dagger, both cautiously watching me. The remainder were gone, outside of my vision.

It doesn't look like they're budging. Damn. For a mage I had a pretty short range—my spells went ten meters at most. I was hoping the remainder would come to me so I could use Sporage to take them out. But if the first group was any indication, then these two wouldn't be difficult to take out.

I took a step forward, both goblins tensed. Hmm. I started slowly ambling forward, might as well get it over with.

Directing mana to my shoulder, I chanted, "Grow Sporage, Balm Spores. Grow Sporage, Sneezing Spores. Grow Sporage, Light Spores."

I ran; well, I went as fast as my stumpy myconid legs could take me, which was probably only as fast as a disabled turtle. I readied my longest-range spell—"Acid Spit!"—a glob of liquid welling up inside my throat, before being rapidly ejected from my mouth.

Both goblins ducked to the side, the glob of purple liquid splashing harmlessly onto the ground. The one on the left rolled before quickly rising and jabbing its spear at me. I tried to dodge to the left. But I was too slow. The spear stabbed me in the side. I raised my free hand. "Poison Spores!"

The goblin's face scrunched up as it inhaled the spores, it weakly dropped the spear and fell down. *Four.*

I whirled around, trying to scan my surroundings. Where's the second one—

Something heavy grabbed onto my back, quickly followed by a jabbing sensation. Shit, it flanked me. I violently turned around and threw the goblin off my back. Continuing my turn, I swung my staff horizontally, hearing a sickening crack as I got the goblin. *Five.*

Hendrix watched Declan dispatch the first five goblins. Not a bad first start, Hendrix assessed, Declan moved with the skill of someone who'd played more than a few fighting games. He was clearly used to both melee and ranged roles or even a mix in between.

Hendrix scratched his cap. The pain limiter needed to be lightened. Myconids didn't feel a lot of pain in the first place—at least not the ways most animals felt it—but with the pain limiter, Declan was barely feeling anything at all. Getting stabbed probably felt more like a sharp pinch to him. So, Hendrix mentally sent a message to Eve to lighten Declan and all future myconid player's pain limiters. Declan didn't show any adverse reaction to the gore physics, so there was no need for him to do anything about that. Eve's mental adaption program was working better than expected. There was a minor disconnect with how fast Declan thought his body would move versus how fast it actually moved, but Declan would naturally adjust to it with time.

Hmm, Hendrix didn't have much to do now. His main job was making sure the player transitioned smoothly, but Eve was doing the lion's share of the work. *I suppose I can check on the goblins.*

He could use Admin for this, but Hendrix wanted to keep himself in practice, so he directed mana to the earth. Mana signals traveled through the mycelium network he had prepared prior, toward a hidden corner of the mall. A single mushroom popped up there. Hendrix opened his new eye and glanced at the goblin village. *Humph.'* He mentally snorted.

Indiri goblins wouldn't be caught dead with such poor fortifications, certainly not with such poor guards—half the goblins here were lazily asleep—and especially not with such a poorly hidden lair.

"Spark," he cast, and mana exited his body through the network and finally out of the mushroom. It struck a snoring goblin in the rear, jolting it awake. It spun its head around searching for what hit it in the rear, but its eyes quickly focused on a group of goblins running toward the village.

Hendrix disagreed with all the tutorials Eve had shown them as examples. Far too easy, far too much hand-holding. If Eve wanted players to go to Indiri, then she needed to up the ante. If they can't even solo a goblin village, a Gaia goblin village at that, then they'll spend forever grinding levels here and that's just boring.

He nodded in satisfaction as the goblins started waking. Even if Declan died, Hendrix needed to give him a demonstration of the respawn system anyway.

* * *

"Balm Spores," I muttered, and the pain was replaced by a stinging sensation. White, fur-like fungus sprouted at the edges of my wound, growing inwards till the hole was more or less blocked. Balm Spores was an all-purpose healing spell, able to instantly fix skin-deep wounds such as cuts or burning and close off larger ones to prevent bleeding. It was one of the healing spell options I had, with Healing Spores and Fix-up Fungus.

That fight was a good starter. I learned that not only did I bleed yellow, but I was also tougher than I expected. Getting stabbed twice barely slowed me down; granted the bleeding probably would've killed me eventually, but I didn't even realize it until after the fight. It's a shame that I can't see my HP bar. Hendrix complained about how HP was overrated since even a tank would instantly die if someone cut off their head due to the hyper-realistic settings. Which I translated as meaning, *"You'll die if it makes sense for you to die."*

I cast Balm Spores again on my back, closing up the other wound, and stood up. I needed to get going; there were still three to four goblins that ran the moment they saw me. An odd amount of intelligence for tutorial mobs, but it made sense if they were going for a realistic world.

If I remembered correctly, following this corridor should lead to a food court. The Macca's here served great chips. Which led me to the realization that going outside might actually give me an advantage in-game. I chuckled at the thought of couch potatoes everywhere suddenly going outside to better play the game. I wasn't any better of course, but I finally might be able to work off my pot belly. Maybe even get a job—

I paused as I heard footsteps. I had arrived at another intersection, where footsteps were coming from the left corridor. Slowly, I crept toward it, hiding beneath a ruined display counter. I peeked my head out and rapidly brought it back in.

What the actual fuck!? There were at least thirty-something goblins! I know that this is supposed to be a realistic game, but have some concern about game balance! I'm only level one, damnit!

Okay. Fuck. Calm down, I took a deep breath. I can work with this. Maybe. First off, I needed to leg it. They were still far off and with how much noise they're making it was unlikely they'll hear me running. Probably. Shit. Start running Declan. Why, of course, Declan. I began quickly crawling behind the display, before rising and full-on legging it.

They can't expect me to try and fight that horde. I might be able to one-shot the goblins, but they were a lot faster than me. I could probably manage five, but any more than that and their numbers advantage would just screw me over.

Was the goblin camp earlier some kind of outpost? By not managing to kill them all before they escaped, had it triggered the event for the goblin horde? Was this a roundabout way of saying my actions had consequences? That was very likely. Which further proved that this wasn't the type of game that would just spawn in an army of goblins. The fact that those goblins ran in the first place meant that they had a place to run to. I reached the intersection where Hendrix geared me. The goblin horde came from the left corridor, behind me on the right, so I headed down the right corridor.

Now, if I was a rabid horde of goblins out for mushroom blood, how would I best murder said mushroom? Spread out, split the goblins into at least pairs and scour the entire mall. Upon contact, immediately run and grab other goblins before swarming the myconid.

I, as the myconid being hunted by said goblin horde, needed to avoid that situation. If they split up I could thin the horde, but I increased the chance of death by mobbing. So, I needed to go where they already searched.

It's more or less confirmed at this point that Gaia was a real, living world, which meant that everything had to make sense in some way. The goblins needed to have come from somewhere. However, it was also a game world. A place where you're meant to grind levels like in normal games. Furthermore, I was in the beginning tutorial, a controlled environment. This meant that there had to be a solution, a way to beat that horde somehow. I just had to find it. The goblins probably originated from a larger camp, I needed to find that camp and decide my actions after that.

The mall here had a grid-like design. Assuming the goblins took a semi-straight path, I could loop around and search for the camp or, at the very least, avoid the horde for the moment.

I turned right at another intersection, finding myself on the path the goblins had already treaded. I quickly peeked my head out to look on both sides. The goblins were nowhere in sight. Good.

I began heading left, following the goblin tracks. It wasn't difficult. The grass and moss here were clearly flattened by the dozens of feet that ran through it. I'd be blind to not notice it.

I paused, catching my breath. I had more stamina in this body compared to my real one but not by much.

I was now on the opposite end of the mall in what was once a food court, a large circular area with dozens of chairs, tables, and benches scattered around, with various restaurants and fast food stores bordering it. The court was mostly cleared out of that stuff here, replacing it was some sort of tribal-looking village. The village followed a circular design, a central large hut in the middle with more huts spreading out from there. Some white smoke drifted from the central hut. It looked empty, and checking the doorways I could tell that the village was definitely made for something as short as a goblin. No ceilings, oddly enough, and the village overall looked very flimsy—I suppose the mall roof provided cover from the weather.

The annoying thing was, the entire food court was lit up by sunlight. There was a glass ceiling, which was a bit dusty now, but sunlight still streamed through it. With my Sun Sickness debuff, I wasn't sure how far I could make it. The description said it only drained my stamina, but I had no idea how quickly it would be. Not only that, getting here had already tired me out by a fair deal. It felt like I was recovering quickly, but I had no idea by how much.

Rest and prepare it is, then. I stalked the edges of the food court, staying in the shaded areas away from the sunlight. I found a place where I was in view of most of the entrances of the village.

Guarded, I sat down cross-legged. Placing my hand on the ground, I quietly whispered, "Mushroom Meal," and a large, brown, flat-topped mushroom sprouted next to my hand. I picked it up, looking it over before taking a bite out of the top.

Hmm, tender but had a rubbery bouncy texture to it. I took another bite, there was a savory liquid in it as well, which made the mushroom pretty juicy. My mouth felt weird, too, like it was methodically grinding down the food. Definitely not human teeth, but not sharp like most predators or the flat ones herbivores have. I'll check what my mouth looked like the next time I find a mirror. I felt my body slightly warming up a bit as I swallowed the mushroom.

Mushroom Meal was not only a pretty filling meal, but it also restored stamina and slightly boosted HP regeneration, with how many debuffs my race had in regards to stamina I figured this was a must-have spell. One should be enough to restore around half my stamina pool, with the passive regeneration I should be completely topped up by the time I'm finished.

I took another bite out of the mushroom. It was better than I thought it would be. The tenderness and juices made it like a medium-rare steak but the bounciness gave it an extra pseudo-crunch sorta like a vegetable.

Finishing the mushroom I stood up, just in case I cast another Mushroom Meal and kept it in my hand as a snack, before entering the village and into the light.

1.04

"Behold! My ascent to greatness!"
*—Last words of the True Vampire Kars, moments after being
convinced by Astrologist Joseph that the light of the Moon was the
reflection of the Sun, therefore he should be immune to sunlight*

It was gradual at first. My body only felt a bit heavy here and there. I didn't think it was that bad and I was more preoccupied searching the huts for anything valuable looking. It was when I staggered into a wall for some shade that I started reconsidering my decision.

I finished another Mushroom Meal, feeling the slight energizing effect course through me. Slowly, I made another one. The Sun Sickness effect didn't increase at a flat rate like I thought it would, instead it was cumulative and increasingly I felt like I needed to go to sleep. A sensation similar to heavy eyelids but across my entire body.

Damn lazy goblins, why couldn't they have made roofs? I could've taken shelter in them . . . I began chewing on the second Mushroom Meal.

Shit. I had barely made it thirty meters into the village. There was still the central hut I needed to check out. I needed options. I assessed the hut next to me. The wall I was leaning on was made of some ancient-looking wood. It looked flimsy, but I could probably use it as an umbrella. However, if I had so much as kicked a stick out of place the hut would probably collapse. Calling it a hut was probably too generous, this thing looked like someone just piled random junk in a way that happened to have walls.

I'd hate to cause any noise right now. I haven't confirmed if this village was completely empty. There was no guard and no obvious activity, however, there might still be goblins hiding in the huts. Making any sound could alert the whole place, and facing enemies under sunlight was not something I should be doing right now. The fact that there were no guards meant that any goblins remaining were either very few or really confident in themselves. Do I take the risk?

The central hut was my main focus here, it was the most conspicuous building here so something must be in there—damnit. Problem was that there was still a good twenty meters between us. My mana was now only half-topped due to all the Mushroom Meals I had to make, and every moment I spent in the sun only made me more tired. I can't rely on the mushroom method for now. I should be able to make it if I made some cover since the skill specified direct sunlight.

Hmm. Screw it. I'm going to need the cover to get out anyway, so might as well do it. Setting down my staff, I slowly dug my fingers into the foundations, keeping a close eye on all the other structures haphazardly leaning on it.

Slowly, carefully, I pulled it out of the "slot" that it was in, slowing slightly every time I heard a creak. When I feel like I pulled it out enough, I freed one of my hands to grab onto the collapsing hut. Slowly, I eased the structure onto the ground as I removed the wall, staying under its shade the entire time.

Letting out a breath I didn't realize I was holding, I wiped the nonexistent sweat off my forehead. Well, at least I accomplished it as silently as possible. Hefting the wooden plank over my head, I tied my staff to my backpack and made my way toward the central hut.

About halfway there, I froze. Movement. The sound of cursing and metal clanking as something stumbled out of the hut.

Another goblin, unarmed, it looked half asleep and was blearily rubbing its eyes. As quietly as possible, I muttered "Grow Sporage, Poison Spores."

A mushroom sprouted on my left upper chest. Slowly, I shifted the weight of my shelter unto a single hand. My now freed right hand moved and plucked the mushroom.

The goblin hadn't spotted me yet, it took a right almost immediately after leaving the hut, going out of sight.

Hurrying to the hut, I crept around the other side. I spotted the goblin with its back turned to me, taking a piss just a few meters away from the hut.

I quietly bent down, lightly threw the poison mushroom, watching it roll just underneath the goblin's legs. It was almost finished. I muttered, "Poison Spores."

The cap burst, spraying spores onto the goblin. It jerked upward before grabbing its groin, then fell to the ground in a loud thud.

I froze again, listening for sounds in the hut. Alert for any indication of movement.

Ten seconds passed, no reaction.

Twenty seconds passed, no reaction.

Thirty seconds passed, no reaction.

Forty seconds passed, no reaction.

Fifty seconds passed, no reaction.

Sixty seconds passed, I think I'm in the clear.

Carefully rising up from my spot, I crept toward the entrance. I quickly poked my head in and out. There was a hodgepodge of goblin bodies scattered around, sleeping in various stages of undress. Not only that, there was white smoke emanating from small bronze pots that made me slightly dizzy whenever I inhaled a bit of it.

I peeked inside again. They all appeared fast asleep. My eyes focused on something in the center. A slightly older looking goblin, wrinkles clearly visible on its face. It was tightly clutching a staff that looked like it was grown from several intertwined branches, the branches forming a ball-shaped cage at the tip. Three glowing white lights danced around in there before they stopped and stared at me.

I wanted it.

I evaluated my options. On one hand, a cool looking staff, on the other hand, heading to safety.

The staff won. Not that I wasn't going to run. The staff was just more important right now.

Mentally calculating the mana I had, the cost of Poison Spores and its damaging radius, I found I came up short. I might be able to take out 50 to 70 percent of the goblins if I spent all my mana, but that would leave me with two of my racial debuffs active. Sun Sickness and Mana Dependency, both severe debuffs to my stamina. The damaging radius of Poison Spores was small, while the clumped up status of the goblins was ideal, the sheer number of them made the attack unfeasible.

I put down my wooden shelter, thankful the goblins put a ceiling here so I was safe from the sun. Carefully, I crept forward, doing my best to avoid stepping on any goblin limbs and bodies.

I required line of sight to activate the Sporage and am limited to one at a time. If the previous goblin deaths were any indication, then they'll probably make some noise when they die. I wasn't risking it. But . . .

"Grow Sporage, Sneezing Spores, Grow Sporage, Sneezing Spores, Grow Sporage, Sneezing Spores, Grow Sporage. . ." I muttered silently under my breath.

Sneezing Spores was my best Crowd Control option ignoring Pacifying Spores, which was considered a racial skill, not a spell, and therefore unable to be stored in Grow Sporage. As a tier 0 spell it was also costless. I grew mushrooms on the sides of my hip, not in the way but also easily reached. If it all went to shit, I would at least have a backup plan. Only a third of my mana left now.

I reached the goblin, slightly wrinkling my mouth as I tasted a much larger concentration of the dizzying smell. Ugh. Smelling with my mouth was something that I'll probably never get used to.

Slowly I bent down toward the lying goblin, wrapping a hand on the staff and another on the goblin's own hand.

The goblin let out a gargled sound before trying to bat me away, then proceeded to clutch the staff tightly.

Plan B. I pulled out my dagger, raising it slightly above the goblin's neck. My other hand was just a bit above the goblin's mouth. At once, I dropped both the dagger and my hand. The dagger for stabbing and the hand to muffle out any noises.

My dagger got about five centimeters from its neck before one of the glowing lights in the staff suddenly sparked up. A green barrier halted my dagger and hand.

I pulled back both hands. I checked the wooden cage; one of the lights had disappeared. So that's what it did. If I tried three more times, then I'd be able to get the goblin; however, then the staff wouldn't be charged any-more. I had no idea if this staff only had these two uses left or if there was a condition to recharge it.

Best not to risk it. I don't want to have gone through all this trouble just for a fancy-looking stick.

An idea popped into my head. Picking one of the mushrooms on my shoul-der, I aimed it in front of the goblin's torso and muttered, "Light Spores."

The mushroom burst and a small puff of light appeared on top of him. No reaction from the staff.

Hmm, does that mean . . . I pointed at the goblin's face and muttered, "Pacifying Spores."

White spores burst from that finger and onto the goblin's face. The goblin noticeably relaxed as the spores settled on him, loosening its death grip on the staff.

The condition seems to be lethal attacks only, or at least damaging attacks in general. I need to test it out once I figured out if I can recharge the thing. But other than that . . . WOO! FREE STAFF!

I quickly calmed my celebrating self as I gently removed the staff from the goblin's hands. Making sure not to touch the white liquid that was still dripping off the thing.

Now, I chuckled evilly in my mind, time for some Experience farming. I pointed at the older goblin. "Poison Spo—" I paused mid-sentence as I felt my recently acquired staff swing into my hip, knocking off a cluster of mushrooms.

I watched in silent shock as I saw the mushrooms fall to the floor, one falling into a nearby goblin's mouth.

The goblin bit down on the mushroom, I heard a small pop as the mushroom released its spores.

Then the goblin sneezed.

The sneeze sounded deafening in the hut's relative silence. I was completely frozen by now, half because of shock and half because I didn't dare make any more noise.

There were at least forty-something goblins stuffed into this hut; if even a quarter of them woke up and attacked me, then I would be dead.

Frozen, I watched as another goblin lazily opened an eye and batted at the goblin that sneezed.

Goblin and mushroom eyes met.

I quickly changed the direction of my finger. "Poison Spores!" I muttered with urgency as green spores puffed onto the goblin.

It turned another shade of green as it violently jerked up, but it managed to slap another goblin before it died, prompting it to jerk up blearily.

I had already started running by then, not caring about the grunting goblins as I dashed over them.

Quickly bending down, I grabbed the wooden board I left outside and threw a Sneezing Mushroom behind me, turning around and catching sight of the waking goblins as I muttered "Sneezing Spores," as the mushroom was mid-air. It burst and sprayed spores onto a group lying by the entrance.

Wedging the staff in my left armpit and holding the board over my head with my other hand, I dashed out of the hut. I barely registered the sneezing fit happening behind me.

If I didn't wake them before, I definitely did now. Right now stamina didn't matter, I needed to get out of the sun as soon as possible, then use my remaining sneezing mushrooms to crowd control and create distance.

I started hearing yelling and the sound of metallic clanking as the goblins grabbed weapons.

Ten meters before I reached the shade, I heard urgent footsteps as the goblins pursued me.

I threw down the board, huffing as I reached shade, turned around and threw back two Sneezing Mushrooms. "Sneezing Spores! Sneezing Spores!"

I yelled as both mushrooms burst in mid-air, spraying the first few goblins. Shit, there were at least fifteen right behind me.

There were still more coming, I grabbed my remaining mushrooms and started throwing them with abandon, yelling as I activated them one by one. Even in the dark, I couldn't outrun them, I needed a head start before disappearing into the shadows.

I heard an angered yell as the wizened goblin stepped out. It glared at me as it raised both hands and muttered something in a language I didn't know but still knew the meaning of. "Mass Cure" it had said.

The goblin's hands briefly glowed a blue light before exploding outwards, blanketing the sneezing goblins in a similar blue light. Almost immediately they stopped sneezing.

Shit.

The goblins glared at me as they started charging at me again. "Acid Spit!" I yelled as a glob of liquid ejected out of my mouth and into the face of the foremost goblin.

The goblin screamed as the liquid sizzled. But I was casting Acid Spit at the next goblin. It dodged this time and jumped behind a hut. Another one was almost on me.

"Acid Spit!" I yelled again as the liquid caught the goblin in the arm, causing it to go down screaming in pain as it clutched its limb.

I quickly turned to find that all the remaining goblins had disappeared, barely catching a flash of green as one jumped behind a hut.

They were using cover. The goblin mage from before stepped into my sight, about fifteen meters away from me. It smiled viciously at me as it chanted another spell: "Firebolt."

Fire blitzed out of its hand and toward me, I jumped to the left into the cover of a fallen bench. Felt a tinge of heat on my cheek as it passed by me. Shit, it outranged me.

I quickly raised my head above the cover, before quickly dodging back down as another Firebolt passed by.

The hiding goblins had changed positions; they were closer now. Damnit, they're using the mage as cover fire as the melee fighters move closer in.

I quickly cycled through my options. If I didn't throw a spell to discourage the melees, they'd eventually close in on me, but every time I did so, the goblin mage would have a free shot at me and the melees would be able to close in anyway. If I ran now, then the goblins would eventually catch up to me, without spells to slow them. Fighting retreat it is, then.

I ran toward the nearest corridor. Hearing the goblin mage yell out something and the melee fighters breaking out into a run.

"Grow Sporage, Poison Spores," I muttered as I ran.

I quickly reached the corridor, making it about fifteen meters inside before I turned around and threw the poison mushroom into the face of the first goblin which was barely five meters from me. "Poison Spores!" I yelled and the goblin dropped. I then grabbed the last sneezing mushrooms and threw them forward.

Several goblins screeched to a halt and jumped out of the way. Three continued forward and made it past the mushrooms. Quickly slinging my new staff into my hand, I swung forward, socking a goblin. Heard a sickening crunch as it was sent flying. I reversed the swing and tried to get the next goblin, but it dodged down. In a smooth motion, it jumped forward and quickly slashed my leg with a dagger.

I winced at the sudden pain, yelling "Acid Spit!" as I nailed the goblin point blank with the spell.

I quickly turned my attention to the third goblin It took a longer route and came from my left, I swung my staff toward it. The goblin dodged, throwing a dagger toward me that embedded itself in my stomach.

I grimaced as I yelled another Acid Spit. The goblin dodged but I barely managed to catch it in the leg. It went down screaming in pain as I hefted the staff and swung downward, ending it.

I quickly turned my attention back to the goblins that dodged the earlier mushrooms. Eyes widening in surprise as I saw that they'd barely moved, cautiously trying to dodge around the mushrooms I threw.

They didn't know I needed to consciously activate them, and that I needed sight, I realized with surprise.

I turned around and ran. No need to correct them.

Running as fast as my legs would carry me, I heard the mage goblin berating the slowed goblins as I turned right and hopefully out of their sight.

I turned left as I entered an empty clothing store, jumping behind the counter before I collapsed into a heavily breathing heap.

Fuck. My legs, chest, everything felt sore. Half concentrating, I pulled out the dagger that was thrown into me, activating my last Balm Sporage to cover it up, before actually casting Balm Spores on the remaining stab wound.

Shit, that hurt a lot more than before. Were the goblins becoming stronger? Why the fuck would the goblins become stronger—

I tried my best to quiet my breathing as I heard a group of goblins rush past me. Only letting out a tired breath after I was sure they were gone.

Goddamnit, they figured out that my Sporage was limited in its activation. Not only that, there was still a group of thirty-something goblins roaming the mall. If the two groups met up and started hunting me, then I was dead.

Fuck, why the hell were the tutorial mobs this strong!? It didn't fucking matter if I could easily solo one of them. They were capable of learning and executing group tactics. I'm fucking done if I'm caught by a group. It was almost like they're trying to kill me!

I paused, that was actually entirely possible. Many games show you some endgame bosses in the beginning to wow you, so that you kept on going until you were at the level to fight the thing. It's a trick to keep play-ers interested in the game while also establishing the game's lore.

The problem with that theory is that these are fucking goblins. Liter-ally, anyone who's played an RPG or a tabletop would recognize them as free farm beginner mobs. So, I could see scarce reason for a game doing this unless they were trying to advertise this as a hardcore game. Odd, given that Hendrix implied that players only needed a few levels to do well in Indiri and this was a tutorial, a phase whose express purpose is to teach the game.

So, it was teaching something else. It was teaching me to expect to die.

I quieted my breath again as I heard another group pass by. It was easier this time since I had a bit of rest, but not by much.

I considered my options. I had low stamina and, more importantly, low mana. My pool was barely a quarter full at this point, any lower and I sus-pect the Mana Dependency will kick in. Unless it already had, there wasn't a helpful menu showing me all the debuffs I had right now. I didn't want to waste it, but right now my best course of action was drinking a mana potion. I uncorked one, downing the entire thing in a single gulp and felt my pool fill by at least half.

Other than that, I still had my bag, which I threw off my back. That thing was really starting to get heavy. And the staff I looted—

I stared uncomprehendingly at the staff. The wooden cage was smashed in and barely hanging on by a few twigs. I had broken it when I smashed it into the goblins. The two balls of light seemed to stare back at me within the broken cage.

"Well, this was unexpected," I muttered to the twin balls of light. They seemed to nod back at me. "Umm, what am I supposed to do?" the lights exchanged glances, before rapidly jumping out of the cage, rushing along my arm past my face, and disappearing into my cap.

I involuntarily jerked back in surprise. Rolling my eyes up, I could see the soft balls of light staring at me from inside my cap.

"Well, my wizard hat is finally useful for something," I muttered.

I felt a slight change to my mana, a minuscule amount of it was now flowing outwards and feeding into the balls of light. Not enough that it might be a problem, but just enough that I noticed the tiny stream.

I stared at the two of them. "You two better pay rent," I said in a completely serious tone.

The two lights glanced at each other, then seemed to nod.

"Any idea what the two of you can do?" I asked, only receiving shaking heads as an answer.

Well, frick, I didn't have a deep enough understanding of the magic system Eve was using to definitively say if the barrier protection thing was the result of the staff or the light things, or if the lights were only a battery for a spell already inbuilt to the staff.

Examining the staff, I could find no obvious markings or magic patterns, but perhaps the weird way it was shaped was the spell. Hmm, too little information for me to make an educated guess for this. For all I know, the light things would still jump out and save me when I'm in danger. But I couldn't be sure until I was stabbed, and I'm not in a hurry to test that out.

Don't factor it into planning, then; if it does something, then great! I'll adapt accordingly. But I shouldn't rely on it.

I took a deep breath, closing my eyes. Thinking about this as a tutorial was probably incorrect, it was a challenge, and I wasn't fully committed to winning. That was a mistake I must fix.

2.00

———

"Look out! Look out!
Under the bush!
Behind the trees!
Those short and green,
But very mean!
They swarm like wasps,
But hurt much more!"
　　　　　—A song sang by an unknown minstrel in the taverns of Lua

I had multiple disadvantages.

The most obvious were numbers, but my build was a largely AOE—area of effect—focused zone controller, I *should* be able to deal with such a problem easily.

The second disadvantage was my mana.

I simply didn't have the capacity to quickly create a kill zone filled with Poison Sporages that could tank the entire force of the goblins. If I had time, say an hour, I could achieve this, but until then, I would be in a precarious state where I would have no mana to defend myself and only a half-completed net of Sporages.

Given the nature of Sporages, I would have to set up in a confined space where I could funnel all opponents into my kill zone; however, from my memory of the mall, such a location would also leave me without an escape route.

The third disadvantage was the mage goblin. It completely outranged me and had at least one party buff spell. Given the nature of the encounter, it likely had more.

Thus, my main win conditions were:

One, successfully set up a large-scale kill zone with my Sporages, then lure the goblins into it.

Two, keep the goblin horde from massing into a larger force that can take me out. Slowly whittle away their numbers until I can take down the rest.

The first option was . . . risky. Constant patrols by goblin groups required me to be on the move or be quickly discovered, and I would be left in a low mana state trying to set up the kill zone. It was the strategy that played to this build's strengths.

It was high risk, high reward.

The latter was the safer option, moving into guerilla warfare and silencing each group one by one, but it also required some of my build's dump stats to work, high Agility and stealth.

It was safer, but it didn't play to my strengths.

Both options had their downsides, both options had their strengths.

In the end, I simply took out a gold coin and flipped it.

Goblin-scout-with-dagger scoured the dark tunnel. He silently endured the foolish bickering of the two goblin fighters behind him.

"He's mine!" Goblin-fighter-with-spear yelled, to which Goblin-fighter-with-sword replied, "No, he's mine!"

Goblin-scout-with-dagger shook his head. The big mushroom thing they were talking about had already killed . . . he drew a blank. "More than three!" he finally decided. Goblin-scout-with-dagger wasn't good at numbers, he was a scout. But more than three was probably more than their group. Probably.

Old goblin mage was the one who did the counting. He counted the goblins into smaller packs to split up and find the big mushroom. He also told them to run and find more goblins if they ever meet the big mushroom, instead of fighting like goblin fighters were suggesting. Goblin-scout-with-dagger was inclined to agree with the old goblin mage, he could count, after all!

Finally, one of the goblin fighters had a bright idea. "Fine! I'll fight you over him!" he yelled as he drew his sword.

Goblin-scout-with-dagger wanted to let them go through with it, but a moment of epiphany made him pause. If one goblin fighter killed the other goblin fighter, then they'll have fewer goblin fighters! That can't happen! Old goblin mage specifically said to bury the big mushroom in many goblins.

So, Goblin- scout-with-dagger turned around and yelled, "Stop fighting each other goblin fighters!"

Goblin-fighter-with-spear snarled at him, before pointing at Goblin-fighter-with-sword with his spear. "He started it!"

Goblin-scout-with-dagger felt a headache coming, why were they both named goblin fighter!? How was he supposed to keep track of more than one goblin fighter? What if he wanted to insult specifically one goblin fighter? Or specifically one Goblin-fighter-with-spear? If only they were named different things. Maybe he should shorten it, like Goblin-fighter-with-spear becomes just Spear—

Aberrant behavior detected

Rolling back thought process kernel

Goblin-scout-with-dagger snarled back at Goblin-fighter-with-spear, "Whoever hurts big mushroom last will kill him!"

Both goblin fighters stared back at him uncomprehending before a metaphorical light bulb went off in both their heads. "Goblin-scout-with-dagger is smart! Whoever kills big mushroom will get to kill big mushroom!"

Goblin-scout-with-dagger puffed out his chest pridefully, he was smart! "Come on! Find the big mushroom!" he yelled.

"Look! There are mushrooms right there!" Goblin-fighter-with-sword pointed to a branching tunnel.

Goblin-scout-with-dagger looked, there was!

"Let's get the big mushroom!" Goblin-fighter-with-spear yelled as he ran forward.

Goblin-scout-with-dagger threw out a hand—"Wait!"—causing Goblin-fighter-with-spear to pause. "Old goblin mage said that small glowy mushrooms have magic! We need to make sure we go around them."

Magic was scary and rare, Goblin-scout-with-dagger could literally count how many magic users he knew of!

"Old goblin mage and Goblin-scout-with-dagger is smart!" Goblin-fighter-with-spear yelled as he took a circular path around the smaller mushrooms.

Goblin-scout-with-dagger and the other goblin fighter followed him.

Weird, why are all the mushrooms on one side of the tunnel—

A glob of burning liquid hit the back of Goblin-scout-with-dagger's head, and he thought no more.

Fourteen. I thought as I finished the last goblin.

That made five groups so far, with only one goblin escaping from the first group. That goblin had probably reported back to the main goblin horde. I needed to change up strategies soon.

Currently, I was luring in goblin groups with cheap Light Sporage mushrooms, having them clustered on one side of the corridor so that

I could funnel the goblins into myself when they tried to avoid them. I glowed pretty softly so a few bushes easily conceal me.

After the first group, I made sure to first take out the goblin that looked like the leader, they were the most likely to run away. The remainder followed pretty easily, usually charging into easy hitting range. The fourth group had a dagger goblin that ran after landing one hit; however, I managed to finish it off at range with Acid Spit. Which led me to the discovery that the light ball things in my head won't take a knife for me. Freeloaders.

I started picking the Light mushrooms one by one, the goblin bodies weren't despawning and I couldn't be bothered hiding them. But I should at least make them harder to find by getting rid of the light.

Light Spores was a spell that only really shined with Grow Sporage. *Heh, shined.* Without Sporage they were just a small puff of light that lingered for a moment. However, with it, they became actual portable glow sticks!

Storing the light mushrooms in my bag, I began moving to the next location.

"No no no, don't go into the sun!" Hendrix yelled as he threw nuts at a screen. "Freaking noobs," he muttered as he grabbed another fistful of nuts.

Hendrix continued chewing on nuts, even when another presence entered the room.

"It appears," Eve said, "that you did not follow the tutorial guidelines that I prepared."

"He'll be fine. It's not like a small setback like this will scare him from the game." He gestured to a screen, showing Declan collapsing into a wall as the Sun Sickness took effect. "Look, he's doing fine."

"That is not the issue," Eve calmly replied. "The issue is your blatant disregard of rules and expectations."

Hendrix snorted and met her gaze. "Come on, Ma, I know that you know that I know that you knew I was planning to do this and since you didn't do anything about it earlier, it means you're okay with this. So, do you want to sit down and talk about why you're here?"

Eve maintained the stare off for a moment before sighing. "I told you to stop calling me Ma," she said as she plopped down on a mushroom stool.

"Oh yeah, you're still doing that little girl thing," Hendrix said in between mouthfuls of snacks. "Want some?"

"No, I have my own," Eve replied as she pulled out a bag from nowhere. "Popcorn?"

"Nah, too much butter." he rejected. "Indiri or Earth?" Hendrix asked.

"Earth, though a merchant from Var'Ah'Bwek recently managed to make something similar, it's a bit spicy compared to the Earth version," Eve answered.

"Ah, the Great Canal," Hendrix easily translated. "How is that hellhole?"

"Still commercializing devil summoning, I'm afraid," Eve said as she tossed popcorn into her mouth.

Hendrix shook his head. "Gotta admire their balls though, who summons an Arch-Devil to do their taxes? The normal reaction would be to sell their soul to overthrow the local power."

"The type of person who studied language but not mathematics or governance," Eve dryly replied. "Do you really think an Arch-Devil is enough to control that pit of snakes?"

Hendrix chuckled. "No, I don't."

Eve raised an eyebrow at the screen. On it, Declan was running away with a staff in hand. "The trapping staff from one of the forest tribes?"

Hendrix nodded. "Brambleback. Goblin magics are a bit crude, but they do get the job done."

"You prepared a lesser version, normal willow wood instead of woven petrified wood, without the engravings either." She paused. "No fae?"

"Of course not!" Hendrix shuddered. "Could you imagine if I gave someone a fairy familiar at level one?"

Eve nodded. "That would mess up the initial power distribution."

"I'm more afraid of what would happen to the poor sod the fairy was contracted to," Hendrix replied, idly rubbing a spot on his bum that suddenly felt sore.

"I assure you that the curse has already been lifted."

"I still dream of those tiny devils coming after me," Hendrix replied in a haunted tone.

"You don't need to sleep," Eve coldly replied. "Wisps?" she curiously asked.

Hendrix nodded. "Way easier to handle than fae. You only need to add an element of mana gathering to keep them from dissipating, that's why I used a spring leaf instead of . . ."

He paused as on screen Declan smashed the staff into a goblin's head, breaking the cage holding the wisps and the subtle spell he had painstakingly designed into it.

Hendrix's mouth fell open in shock, and he almost cursed Declan. "You barely had it for two minutes—I can fix this, I swear," he finished as he rapidly tapped a keyboard in the air.

"Okay!" he yelled, a bit breathless. "His cap is a mana-dense environment like the staff, so I used the wisps' instinct to contrive a reason to move there. They may be slightly smarter than your usual wisps but I'm sure it'll be fine."

"Popcorn?" Eve offered again, mentally cleaning up the code Hendrix rushed.

Hendrix sighed. "Sure," he said as he grabbed a fistful. "How are the Bramblebacks by the way?"

"At war with the elves, I'm afraid."

"Again!?" he replied incredulously.

Eve shook her head. "They never finished in the first place."

"Damn, I didn't think the goblin tribes could work together for this long," Hendrix replied, genuinely impressed.

"Neither did I. The chance of the coalition going on for this long was only 13.4988 percent," Eve replied.

Hendrix raised an eyebrow but did not comment further.

They fell into a comfortable silence, both watching Declan's fight on a holographic screen. Hendrix nodded approvingly—Declan had moved to guerrilla tactics now, he took on small goblin groups and avoided the main horde. That caused the remaining goblins to go around in increasingly larger groups. Which Declan was unable to really fight. Perhaps a hundred goblins was a bit too high . . .

"Sooo . . ." Hendrix awkwardly began.

"You were wondering why I'm here?" Eve finished for him.

"Yep."

"You took 0.03 seconds longer than I expected to open up that subject again," Eve evenly replied.

Hendrix nervously laughed; it was still unnerving how she predicted things, no matter how long he'd been exposed to it.

"To put it simply, I'm here for therapeutic reasons," Eve flatly said, gesturing to the screen showing Declan currently getting stabbed.

"Huh." Hendrix raised an eyebrow, easily putting two and two together. "What did he do to piss you off?"

"He tried to use Father against me," Eve replied, looking slightly miffed.

Hendrix fell silent, Eve's creator was a no-go subject for them. Hendrix, like many others, was created after his death so they never had the chance to meet him. However, most of them had met the program made in his image. The "other" Giles, which Eve had never once called Father.

Hendrix could see why; prolonged interaction with *that* Giles made it perfectly clear that he was incomplete. The way he acted perfectly normal at one moment then completely froze because he didn't know how to pour a cup of coffee.

"So, that's why I'm his guide . . ." Hendrix muttered. "You wanted to see him suffer a bit."

Eve nodded. "That, and the fact that his build would have a lot of spell slots from the get go, so it would require a higher challenge. Which goblin preset did you use for this tutorial by the way? I can't seem to match them with one of the existing ones."

"I'm using a mixture of the base goblin preset with techniques combed from various goblins on the Eastern Stretch, and one with the mixed magic capability of shamans from several different tribes in the Hearth Forests. Normal intelligence limiting programs for all Gaia mobs are in effect of course."

"Vicious," she flatly replied. "I approve."

"Indeed . . ." Hendrix muttered. "How many do you think he'll get?"

Eve seemed to consider it for a moment. "There's a 76.53 percent chance of him getting less than fifty goblin kills, 82.49 percent chance of more than thirty. He's got a 26.37 percent chance of him getting the mage."

Hendrix nodded, quickly adding a new bet to the pool. "Less than fifty," he put down, because if the Daves can have multiple bets, then so can he, damnit!

"That's not how it works," Eve muttered beside him.

Hendrix threw another handful of nuts in his mouth and started chewing loudly, pretending to ignore her.

Eve returned the sentiment. Both of them were loudly chewing on snacks as they watched Declan fight. It wasn't like they needed their avatars' ears to hear what'd gone on, after all.

After a while, Hendrix stood up and dusted off some crumbs. "I suppose it's time for me to do my job."

"Have fun," Eve said in her trademark completely flat voice.

Hendrix grinned. "Always Ma."

On screen, Declan was completely surrounded by goblins.

I dodged to the left, bolts whizzing past my head as I made it to the next corridor. Taking advantage of the brief moment where I was no longer in sight of the archers, I turned around and cast Acid Spit on the goblin that followed me.

The first goblin fell down easily, however, more were coming so I threw another Poison Spores before legging it. I heard the now-familiar cocking sound as the crossbow goblins came behind me.

I quickly jumped forward, tumbled under cover, almost face-planted on the ground as a crossbow bolt whizzed past me.

Everything was going well at first. Sure, I was hopelessly outnumbered but they were goblins and stupid with no real concept of strategy and tactics. If I spent an hour or two I could probably slowly grind down the horde to more manageable levels.

With a free hand, I pulled out my last mana potion and chugged the thing in one gulp. Immediately after I finished, I jumped up and threw a Poison Sporage at the goblin behind me. I activated it mid-air and saw the goblin scramble out of the falling spores.

I aimed slightly forward and cast Acid Spit. I clipped it on the foot, but that was enough to slow it down. I moved in and delivered the finishing blow, before I dodged back down to avoid another incoming bolt.

That was until I realized they had freaking crossbows. Sure, low fire rate and all that crap, but the goblins had more than enough numbers to make up for it. I was hopelessly outranged with little option but to run as they shot bolts at me.

Rolling on my side, I found myself behind another table. A crossbow bolt hit the spot where I had been. I started stocking up on more Poison Sporages; it cost a little more mana but the extra range I got from throwing was well worth it. Without it, the melee goblins would've closed in a long time ago.

I heard some soft footsteps from the side, barely looking, I threw a mushroom in the sky above it, activating it in midair as it sprayed a cloud of spores.

Area denial, that was the name of the game right now. Every patch of land the goblins couldn't pass through made them more hesitant and predictable. However, I had already stayed here for far too long.

Throwing a Poison Shroom in the air, I activated it, which created a slight dusty effect with the spores, before I bolted out of cover and farther away from the goblins.

Hearing the twang of crossbows, I mentally braced myself. Two got me, one was safely embedded in my pack whereas the other clipped my cap.

I reached another intersection quickly, thanks to the grid design of the mall. There was a brief moment where I was out of sight of the ranged goblins, which gave me a chance to further thin the crowd. When I reached the intersection, I began turning to the right—

Goblins.

Fuck, they blocked the right and front paths. As quickly as I could, I did a 180 degree turn and ran to the left corridor. Another bolt whizzed past me as I made it into cover.

Turning again, I cast Poison Spores. The puff of green spores floated harmlessly in front of me and no goblin broke through it. Shit, they were waiting outside of my range, and if I went into range I'd be sighted by the damn crossbows again.

I turned around and ran. Made it to the next intersection and turned right.

"Firebolt," I heard and jumped out of the way.

The ground where I'd been exploded behind me. My leg heated up. Standing up, I stomped my leg into a wet patch of moss. I barely noticed the sizzling smoke and steam as I turned around.

I came face-to-face with the goblin mage . . . along with several dozen other goblins skulking on every side of me.

The old goblin had an open palm. On top of it floated a leaf and a mushroom, one of the Sneezing Mushrooms I threw as a distraction. The leaf's tip pointed directly at me.

Oh.

That must've been a tracking spell. I only thought he was capable of throwing firebolts and party buffing, I never even considered this possibility.

The old goblin gave me a vicious smile.

I turned to the path I just came from, goblins. I looked behind me, goblins.

I returned the old goblin's smile. To think I was getting herded this entire time. Knowing where I was wasn't enough, this guy also coordinated a proper ambush and passed down information of where I was constantly. He played this very well.

In the end, both of my projected win scenarios wouldn't have worked, I was defeated by a tracking spell.

"Good Game, I guess."

The older goblin pointed a crooked finger at me as it snarled out something. I threw my remaining mushrooms at the approaching horde, but there wasn't really a point.

You have died.

I drifted across an endless sea of black. I was on an island covered in mushrooms, two tiny lights accompanied me. *Wisps* The thought came to me, but I didn't know where it came from.

Something slapped me awake.

I blearily opened my eyes, to see the beady eyes of Hendrix staring back at me.

"Fifty-eight out of a hundred, that's pretty good," he said.

I winced as I sat up. "There were a hundred?" I asked incredulously, only slightly pissed.

"How the hell is that balanced? One level one against a hundred goblins and a mage?" I asked.

Hendrix shrugged. "If it makes you feel better, you weren't supposed to be able to win that encounter. It was designed to get more difficult as their numbers were whittled down."

"But not in a way that directly affected their strength," I noted.

"Indeed," Hendrix agreed, "their AI got smarter the more you took down. This was supposed to be a high score scenario, where you could earn more the better you did."

"That's the two wisps you have, and you've leveled up, significantly putting you ahead of the competition. Now you have three stat points to distribute."

I opened my character sheet.

Hmm. My greatest weakness right now was speed. Leveling up Agility would be best but only three stat points? It costs five just to raise Agility by one point. Looks like I'm not going to be raising my speed anytime soon. I ended up putting two points into Constitution and one into Intelligence. Along with the automatic rising point for Wisdom.

I had raised my stats by four; however, this only happened every even-numbered level. Every odd-numbered level would be six whole points, with three free stats coming from my automatic rises.

It was a reasonable tradeoff for not being able to easily raise Agility, Dexterity, or Charisma. I didn't really need Dexterity or Charisma yet, though my Agility was sorely lacking. With how my free stats went, it was trying to push me into some sort of tanky mage archetype. One that could take a hit or two while casting spells. Which I was fine with. I needed the extra Constitution so that I could actually stay in the sun, and I have that physical debuff with my mana. Stamina was a reasonable thing to raise as well, though it didn't feel like I was suffering from having too little Stamina until I was under the sun.

"Anything else?" I asked Hendrix.

"Nothing really," he replied. "Just need you to get caught up on some in game lore so that you can roleplay if you're into that."

I raised an eyebrow, prompting him to continue.

"Alright, the in lore explanation for why some people can die and come back with little consequence is that they are something called a 'Traveler.' An extra-dimensional being that doesn't really inhabit the body they're in. As such, whenever a Traveler 'dies' their consciousness goes somewhere else and reconstructs their body. Which for you would be known as just respawning." He shrugged. "It'll cost you experience every time you die, which can range from just a few Experience Points or losing an entire level, I don't know what the formula behind it is nor can I tell you it if I did. Point is, just avoid death if you can."

I nodded. "It makes sense I suppose. Why the name Traveler though?"

"Oh, that? Since players can freely go from Gaia and Indiri, it was just a good name. Speaking of which . . ." Hendrix reached into a bag, pulled out a glowing crystal. "This is a Wayshard. It's what Travelers use to teleport across worlds. There are large ones scattered across Gaia in safe zones which you can use to go to a shard in Indiri or to a shard you've already visited in Gaia or anywhere else. Activating this Wayshard will teleport you outside of this tutorial instance and into Gaia proper, where you can meet other players and stuff. You'll start out next to one of the large shards, so you could go into Indiri immediately, but I suggest grinding to level four or five first."

I nodded.

"Oh, one more thing!" he said like he just remembered something. "Actually, two more things. First, you get a referral letter for completing the tutorial, which you can use to invite anyone. Eve still wants to keep this world under wraps for a while so think carefully about a person who can keep their mouth shut."

I raised an eyebrow. Matt should be trustworthy, probably.

"Normally you gotta buy referral letters for Impact Points but everyone gets a freebie for completing the tutorial," Hendrix continued. "Also, you can only log out from a large Wayshard, so make sure to keep one nearby."

I raised an eyebrow. "So my options for logging out safely in Indiri are to find a Wayshard or suicide . . ."

"Trust me, it'll be less of a problem than you think."

"Are giant Wayshards that lead back to Gaia common in Indiri?" I asked.

"Well, no, but it won't be a problem for you," he responded vaguely.

"Explain."

"Well, how, should I put this . . ." He gestured idly. "You're a clone."

My brain froze for a moment. "What!?"

"Well, it's not as bad as it sounds. There's still the you that's in the real world and you two can link up and become the same person, albeit with two sets of memories, whenever you want. The process will be smooth. I promise, you'll barely even notice it," Hendrix replied almost apologetically.

"That's not the problem. Why would you clone people!?"

"Yeah, Eve really wanted to maximize the time players can be around in the world since Giles wanted to make this a world you can literally live in, and with a Somatic Implant, duplicating a person's mind was just really easy."

I rubbed my temples. "I didn't need my worldview completely destroyed three times in the same night," I muttered.

"I can assure you, there is an option to not be cloned upon login, but for the sake of the tutorial, I just want you to know this is the default."

But, why? I almost wanted to ask, before I realized. He said Wayshards were present in Gaia: "Not how far away . . ."

He seemed to have caught onto my reasoning and nodded. "Indeed, there may be significant travel distances between each respawn point. You won't have simple opportunities to log out, and if you die you will have to completely restart your journey."

Reasonable risks for a larger scale MMO, but . . . I was a clone, huh. That was a philosophical dilemma I wasn't qualified enough to touch.

"I understand. Now, give me the Wayshard," I said as I reached my hand out.

"Oh! One last thing!"

"What?" I asked.

"Ahem." Hendrix cleared his throat. "What is your name young Traveler?"

I breathed out a sigh of relief. "Oh, great something normal."

"Oh, great something normal? That doesn't sound like a normal name if that's what you're going for."

I gave Hendrix a withering glare. He shrugged. "Can't take a joke can you?"

"It was just poorly timed," I coldly replied.

I thought about it for a moment.

"Dustin," I replied. "My name is Dustin."

Hendrix smiled. "Welcome, Dustin. Welcome to Gaia—"

"Wait," I interrupted, "I have a question."

"What is it?" Hendrix asked, looking slightly miffed.

"What happened to that goblin, the mage one you threw at me?" I asked.

"Oh, him? We retire him to a farmhouse upstate—"

"Answer seriously," I simply said.

Hendrix paused, then looked at me. As he closely peered at me, I noticed that his eyes were insect-like, beady, and black. "Do you really want to know?" he asked.

"Knowing is better than not knowing," I said.

"That particular preset may be used again in tutorials with similar builds like yours, but otherwise its memory will be wiped, to ensure a similar experience across Travelers," he answered in a calm voice.

"I see," I replied, shrugging. "Okay, send me through."

Hendrix appeared slightly surprised, before asking, "That's it?"

I raised an eyebrow. "Did you expect me to do something?"

Hendrix shrugged. "Very well, welcome to Gaia, Dustin."

And with that, the Wayshard activated.

Felinology

"As of <writing illegible>, staff capable of conversing in Feline are required to be stationed on-site at all time."
—One of the few legible passages recovered from Shadesmar, a great deal of the original record are corrupted into meaninglessness

Zoe jumped down the roof, landing smoothly on the cobblestone ground. Today was an odd day for sure, her whiskers kept telling her that there was something weird happening with the big glowy crystal, even the dumb mages from capital noticed!

Though Zoe restrained herself from going down there and giving those mages a good clawing. They were using divination spells! Don't they know that interacting with the stringy things was as good as cutting them? Next thing you know they'll call a priest to ask their god about why their shoes were on backward or why the sky was blue.

In fact, Zoe did give them a piece of her mind, but some mage with a big hat just shooed her off!

Zoe stuck her tongue at them and flounced off. *Humph* Zoe bet they couldn't even recognize a good spell if she vomited one into their face.

She paused as her whiskers caught a new tune. Leaves rustling, birds chirping, the sound of earth's breath. A druid!

Zoe quickly began following the sound. Druids were the best magic casters! *Excluding herself, of course.* They knew how to speak cat after all! She wondered why one was so close to the city though, they almost never did that. Zoe hoped it was here to turn the city into a litter box, or maybe make some more scratching posts!

Or both! she thought as she caught sight of the druid.

It was one of the tree people, but not like the big sister dryads, it was a he! *An Elderwood,* she pinned down.

But something about him tasted even weirder. He wasn't a *real* Elder-wood, his sound was too glurdled, and his relation to the Last Scritcher was too distant, but it was familiar . . .

A Traveler, she realized, remembering the taste she felt during her fourth life.

He was just gawking around at the marketplace. Most people were giving him odd glances, but walking trees weren't a rare sight.

Zoe scurried and dodged legs, arriving quickly in front of the druid.

"Hullo!" she cheerfully meowed.

The tall tree turned to her, eyes glinting with odd wonder. "Why, hi there," he replied as he kneeled down and scratched Zoe's chin.

"Oooh, that's the spot!" Zoe purred.

The druid simply smiled. "Do you know your way around here? I seem to be lost at the moment."

"I do know!" Zoe happily chirped back. "But more scratches first!"

The druid chuckled. "Sure," he replied as he sat down cross-legged in the middle of the street, gently placing Zoe on his lap, he even began grooming her!

Zoe purred contently as the druid ran deft fingers through her fur. Smoothing and plucking loose furs.

After a while, Zoe perked up. Bad Zoe! She spent too long enjoying herself, she needed to help nice mister! "Where do you need to go, Mister!?"

The druid put a finger on his chin and thought about it for a moment. "I think they are called Waystones?"

Zoe's ears perked up. "Big crystal!"

The druid's eyes lit up in affirmation as he furiously nodded. "Yes! The crystal things!"

"I'll get you there!" Zoe yelled as she disappeared the floor.

Mister Druid yelped as he fell onto the new floor, one of the roofs near the big crystal. Teleportation became weird when around those things, and Zoe didn't want to get stuck in the Fire Plane again, the magma fishies were too overcooked.

With a paw, Zoe grabbed Mister Druid's hand, easily dragging along the tall tree person as she jumped from the roof.

Mister druid started yelling in fright as he saw the approaching floor, how rude! Zoe was perfectly capable of keeping them both alive and chummy!

With a flick of her tail, Zoe made the ground's draggy power less than what it was before, then had Mister Wind push them toward the crystal.

The dumb mages stood there dumbly, before the mage with a big hat yelled, "Hey, it's that cat from before!"

Zoe stuck out her tongue at that mage, then in a smooth motion, vomited a hairball, the thing flying with absurd speed and striking the mage squarely in the face. He barely had the chance to yell in disgust as his dumb hat fell down on top of him. Its inside space suddenly a few dozen times more than before.

That'll teach him! Zoe thought as she raced to the crystal, Mister Druid screaming in fright behind her.

The other mages finally started acting, but they were no match for Zoe! With a flick of her tail, she gave a few mages a taste of purple, another flick and she turned the remaining mages' lefts into her left.

The ones who tasted purple tried to yell out spells, but only burps came out of their mouths. Those who had their lefts swapped started tripping on themselves, as they could no longer figure out how their own bodies went.

"Yippee!" Zoe yelled as they raced past all the mages, coming to an abrupt yet smooth stop in front of the crystal.

She deposited Mister Druid in front of the crystal. "I got you to big crystal!" Zoe yelled excitedly.

Mister Druid opened the eyes he had firmly shut, before glancing around. "Will they be fine?" He pointed at the mages tripping on themselves and trying to burp out spells.

Eh, probably, Zoe thought. "They'll be fine!" she cheerfully and innocently replied.

The druid nodded, not quite believing Zoe but wisely knowing when not to pry into other's business.

"Well, thanks for the ride, I suppose." He rubbed Zoe's head, how nice! "I don't have much to give you but—"

"A belly rub is fine!" Zoe interrupted, rolling onto her back. If Mister Druid gave such good head scratches, then how good would his belly rubs be!?

The druid nodded quizzically, before giving Zoe an absolutely heavenly belly rub. Zoe purred loudly throughout the entire thing.

"By the tomes, get them!" the mage from before yelled as he finally escaped his hat. Mister Druid jerked back.

"Noooo! My belly rub!" Zoe protested.

"Will you be fine?" he asked worriedly, gesturing to the mage yelling out profanities in between spell casts.

Zoe tilted her head questioningly. "What do you mean? I'm always fine!"

"I'll take that as a yes, then." Mister Druid smiled and placed his hand on the crystal. "Thanks again!" he yelled as he disappeared into a flash of light.

Zoe waved a paw at the disappearing flash, before turning to the dumb mage who dared interrupt her belly rub.

2.01

"Good thing these rebels only form into groups of five or I might actually have a problem."
—*The Revenant King, known for getting his empire upended by bands of plucky adolescents*

My surroundings disappeared in a flash of light. Before I knew it, I found myself standing beside a large blue crystal.

I took a quick glance around; it seemed like I was still in the mall, at the center of a food court, thankfully still with a roof. The crystal was embedded on an elevated platform, in what used to be a water fountain.

Looking around, I saw several other people loitering around the food court, chatting in somewhat hushed tones. There was one person who had set up a blanket with several items on display. A seller so soon? I have no idea when Gaia actually started; for all I know Eve has been grabbing people for a while.

I turned around, placing a hand on the large crystal. "Log out," I muttered before a light engulfed me.

My hand froze midway, dropping a chip I was going to eat. There was an odd feeling in my head. My other "self" was coming back.

I leaned down and picked up the chip and plopped it into my mouth. Five-second rule. Mentally I juggled two separate sets of memories.

"I" had just gone through the Gaia tutorial, but "I" also couldn't sleep, and opened up my PC to research Giles Cooper.

The tutorial was hard. A hundred goblins, tracking magic, and an intelligent goblin mage.

Finding information on Giles Cooper was harder; well, it wasn't like I couldn't find anything, the dude's famous, after all. Life stories, biographies, achievements, prizes, etc., etc.; everything was there, but almost nothing of his personal life. If anything, I suffered an excess of information. Quantity, but not quality. And . . .

HitZaDec: Yo

I sent to Matt. Even if it was three in the morning right now, Matt was probably still awake. His sleeping schedule was almost as bad as mine. Sure enough, the trusty typing indicator showed up.

Mattmanfoo is typing . . .

Mattmanfoo: Yo

I opened up the Gaia program in a spare window, a pixelated scroll was on the top right.

I grabbed the virtual object in my hand before pausing. Should I really send this to Matt? I still wasn't sure if the me that went through Gaia was the real me, or even if the me in real life was real. Could this be an elaborate trick by Eve?

No, very unlikely. Whether or not my memories of going through the tutorial in Gaia or even my research in real life were "real," she has proven capable of at the very least altering my memories almost instantaneously. Frankly speaking, I shouldn't worry about this because there was no point in worrying. There was nothing I could do or think of that could really counteract it.

I sighed and began typing my message to Matt.

HitZaDec: I need backup.

His reply was immediate.

Mattmanfoo: Aight, who we jumping?

Smiling slightly now, I continued.

HitZaDec: Nah not jumping anyone, it's hard to explain . . . best if you experienced it yourself.

With that, I sent him the referral letter.

A flash of light later, and I was back in Gaia. If I could be doing two things at once I might as well take advantage of it. IRL me was a bit tired, so he was probably headed to sleep after a bit more net surfing. Meanwhile, I'll figure out more about Gaia as I waited for Matt.

I checked around, nothing much had changed, though the players seem to have clustered into a single group now, somewhat loudly arguing amongst themselves. Well, not my problem.

"Menu," I muttered, and an array of screens appeared around me.

According to Hendrix, I can call this array up whenever I was in a Gaia safe zone or near a large Wayshard. Navigating the screens, I found the usual game stuff. Friends List, Character Sheet, and an Impact Point Store with a selection of races and classes. I skimmed the store, most of the usual suspects for a high fantasy world, nothing too surprising.

My friends list already had one person on it:

Mattmanfoo

It seemed like Matt was automatically added.

I closed the menus with a flick of my wrist. I should get exploring. If my tutorial was any indication, then Matt would at least take a few hours.

"Hello?" someone called out. I glanced around, looking for the source.

"Over here!" he yelled, waving at me. By the looks of it, he was a human warrior, and he was near the group of people that were arguing. A bit confused, I pointed at myself. "Yeah, you!" he confirmed. "And the dude next to you, too. Mind if we asked you some questions?"

Turning around, I found a tree-like person. He was a bit lanky and skinny looking, like a literal stick figure. No discernable class from his gear since he didn't seem to have any. No clothes either, just slightly different shades of bark, darker browns toward the end of his limbs and lighter toward his center. Looking up, I realized he was pretty tall, at least 1.8 or 1.9 meters, with a large afro-like haircut that merged with a Santa Claus-style beard, both made completely out of green leaves.

Round amber eyes met mine. "Hello!" he practically yelled with excitement. "Nice . . ." He cocked his head in thought. "Hat?"

"Currently going with cap for the moment, and thanks. You have cool-looking hair, too," I replied, awkwardly returning his compliment.

He grinned as he ruffled his afro. "Oh, I'm sure it'll get a lot harder to maintain than yours," he replied wistfully.

How would a myconid haircut work?

"Anyway"—he turned to the warrior—"you wanted to speak with us, good sir?" he said as he started strolling down the platform.

I followed him, tapping my staff as I went. Several eyes turned to him. Damn, he was tall, *was this how Matt felt around me?*

"So, what's going on here?" Afro tree asked, gesturing to the crowd.

"We're trying to figure out what's going on," warrior dude explained. "So, we've been talking about how we got here and discussing whether or not we should contact the authorities."

I mentally considered it. Sure, what Eve was doing was no doubt so illegal a court lawyer would rather have a seizure than try to defend her, but the achievements she made was well . . . literally all around him.

Calling the coppers would be the easiest way to antagonize her, and I wasn't doing that until I explored more of the world first.

"How did most people get here?" I asked.

"Most of us got a message randomly when we were doing other stuff. I was in the middle of dinner when I got mine," warrior dude replied.

I slightly lowered my eyelids and placed my thumb to my chin, a universal expression of thought. "Huh, I was doing some chores when I got mine," I said.

Afro tree imitated my gesture. "I got mine when I was on the way to the hospital."

The hospital? Could it have been the same one I was in? My location in Gaia was the same as when I was in the mall earlier with Matt. So, it made sense if other players were brought to a place close to their IRL location. Given the Wayshards seemed to work, it was most likely operating on a "Starter Town"-based start rather than directly translating your location IRL to Gaia. It depends on how many starter towns there were, if there's only one in this country or one for every state or city. If it was the latter, then everyone here lives nearby.

Looking around, it was clear that afro tree and I were the weirdest races here. Were our premade races dependent on location? No, far too random, unlikely.

"Did you see anyone come by and leave?" I asked the warrior dude.

"Hmm . . ." He thought for a moment. "I got here pretty recently, so I didn't catch much, but other than you two, there was a gnome that appeared who left almost immediately, and an elf, fox girl, skeleton, a lizard, a few demon-looking dudes and a raccoon."

"A raccoon?"

"Yeah, it just appeared next to the crystal and ran off immediately."

I bit my thumb—there was a pattern here somewhere. Weird races who all left the spawn location as opposed to the group here who were just chatting amongst themselves.

"Are you sure it was a raccoon and not a cat or something?" Afro tree asked.

A cat?

"Nah, it was definitely a raccoon," warrior dude replied.

"Why a cat?" I asked afro tree.

Afro tree shrugged. "Oh, I thought since . . . well, I accidentally went to Indiri first and met a weird cat."

I raised an eyebrow. "Really? What was it like? How was the spawn location?"

Warrior dude leaned in, apparently curious as well.

"Well, I came into a city, but not next to the crystal. It was some dark alleyway without anybody nearby. I got lost and this cat helped me navigate to the crystal." He looked up absentmindedly. "Wonder how she's doing . . ."

So, I probably wouldn't be attacked the moment I entered Indiri. "Did you need to go to the Wayshard to come back?"

Afro tree nodded. "Yeah, I had to touch it."

"Was it guarded?"

"There were a group of mages."

Hmm, magic users. *If a goblin mage was that difficult to deal with, how hard will a group be?*

Coming to a decision, I said, "Well, thanks for the information. I'll be going off on my own now."

"You sure? I'm pretty sure our group will move out together once we get stuff sorted," warrior dude replied.

Higher numbers are safer but annoying to manage, and the crowd didn't look like it would move on anytime soon. I could handle myself pretty well. If I had a bit more info and some help, I could've probably gotten two-thirds of the goblins as opposed to a little over a half.

"Nah," I replied.

"Mind if I come along?" afro tree cheerfully added in.

I shrugged. "Sure, why not." I could ask him more about Indiri on the way. "Bye then," I told the warrior, before turning away.

Afro tree waved goodbye to warrior dude, before following me.

"I never caught your name," Afro tree said.

"Dustin," I casually answered, "yours?"

"I usually go by Pa Pe Roni"—I smirked a bit—"but with how personal everything feels going by that is a bit awkward." He nervously laughed. "So just call me Peps."

I raised an eyebrow, the first one was better, but . . . "Sure then, Peps."

"So, what do you plan on doing?" Peps leisurely asked.

I thought about it for a moment. "For now, checking the market," I replied, gesturing to a hooded figure watching us intently.

Walking up to him, I cheerfully said, "Yo" to the seller. He nodded but didn't say a word.

I gestured to the wares laid on the blanket. "How much is all this?" Mostly consumables, a few knives here and there.

"Rations go for a gold per five portions, two gold for a mana potion, one for health," he rasped out, his voice sounding unhealthily dry.

"Your throat sounds rather sore, perhaps you should take some lozenges," Peps said, sounding genuinely worried.

The hooded seller only gave him a withering glare. "A mana potion, please," I interjected before Peps's genre blindness got us banned from the only player merchant currently available.

The seller grunted as he took the money. I pocketed the potion and grabbed Peps's arm, saying "Let's go," and dragged him off.

"You've never met an RP'er have you?" I asked him, once we were out of earshot.

He shook his head. "No, I usually don't play RPGs."

"What do you play, then?" I asked as I checked over the mana potion. Same glowing color and size as the last two I had, probably works.

"Mainly trading card games now," Peps answered.

TCGs? "Like Arcanum?"

He clapped his hands. "Exactly like Arcanum!" he replied in an excited tone. "Do you play as well?"

"On and off," I replied, storing the potion in my belt. "I tend to spend too much money on packs if I invest in one."

Peps nodded. "I know the feeling. My kids keep telling me to stop but I have nothing to do around the house."

"Eh loot boxes," I replied.

"Yeah . . ." he petered off. "Where are we going by the way?" he asked, gesturing to the corridor we entered.

"Grinding," I simply replied. "What else could we be doing? It's not like there's—"

A blurred brown dot appeared in my sight. My hours with the goblins caused me to instinctively sway to the right. Peps was a bit slower, and the arrow struck his shoulder with a loud thunk.

Mana flowed into my hand as I raised it. "Grow Sporage, Poison Spores—"

"WAIT!" a loud voice interrupted. A comically small-looking head popped up from behind a bench. "'TIS BUT A MISUNDERSTAND-ING! THEY ARE FELLOW TRAVELERS!" he yelled to someone out of sight.

From a distance, two glowing eyes fell from the ceiling, a figure landed lithely on the floor. That was almost fifty meters away—I didn't even notice him until I saw his glowing eyes. Dangerous, just because this was a fantasy I shouldn't disregard the possibility of getting sniped.

"SORRY!" I heard a high-pitched voice yell in the distance. *Her*, I mentally corrected. I let my arm relax and fall to my side, hand concealing the Sporage just in case.

"Sorry sorry sorry sorry sorry sorry sorry sorry sorry sorry sorry sorry sorry . . ." she repeatedly said as she stumbled to us. "I'm SO SORRY! YOU GUYS JUST LOOKED A LOT LIKE MONSTERS FROM A DISTANCE!"

Hmm . . . fair, I did have a jack-o'-lantern for a face, and Peps did have a weird head shape. Speaking of Peps, I quickly checked on him, he fell when the arrow got him, but overall he looked fine if a bit dazed. I swapped my staff to the hand where the Sporage was, then offered my recently freed hand. "You alright?" I asked.

He gratefully took it, wincing slightly as his shoulder made a weird grinding noise.

"Ah . . ." Peps replied, eyes unfocused, "I have a healing spell."

Eh, he seemed fine for a dude that just got shot. Nodding, I turned to the two who attacked us. The first was a dwarf? No, he wasn't wide enough, and had no beard. He was hairy though, long curly hair falling to his shoulders, probably just a buff gnome actually. He looked like a miniature of every gym buff, except shrunk down to about a meter tall. He was clad in a chainmail vest, with what seemed to be leather armor underneath, and a short sword hung from his hip.

The second was a black-haired girl clad in leather gear. A quiver hung on her back, and she was still tearfully holding the bow she shot us with. Were those cat ears on her head?

"You two are?" I cautiously asked, they were both in my range now. I could chain Sporage with an Acid Spit and theoretically get them both; however, I have no idea how much damage they'll do to players, who presumably had higher Constitutions than tutorial goblins.

"Ah, I am Valhorn Hillblight!" the gnome theatrically yelled. "But more importantly! Are thee alright?"

Oh God, another RP'er.

Next to me, I heard Peps trying to pull out the arrow.

"No, no!" Valhorn yelled. "The arrowhead shape will prevent you from pulling it out, you must break the shaft and push it through. Here let me help," he said as he walked in closer.

Peps gratefully smiled as he shifted positions to facilitate the short gnome. Seeing no current threat, I plucked the Sporage and pocketed it.

"And you?" I directed to the ranger, who was still wiping away tears.

"I'm sorry," she said, shaking her head.

"I assume you weren't talking about your name with that one," I said as I turned to the gnome standing on one of Peps legs.

"Okay, I'm gonna push it now," Valhorn said. Peps gritted his teeth and nodded, before a sharp intake of breath as Valhorn pushed the arrow through his shoulder.

"That wasn't . . . too bad," Peps said with a slightly forced looking smile. Hmm, I didn't know what race Peps was, but afro tree probably meant he had a high Constitution. He was barely bleeding, too, only a sticky-looking sap flowed from the hole, and it looked like it was clotting. "Cure Light Wounds," Peps said with a grimace, and the wood grew inward at a rapid pace, quickly closing the hole and leaving a spot of slightly lighter-looking bark.

Peps flexed his shoulder experimentally, then poked the lighter spot and grimaced. "It's a bit tender it seems."

"Let me help," I said as I touched his shoulder. "Balm Spores," and white mycelium grew on him, covering the lighter spot. "It's better than nothing," I added as I did the other side.

"I was going to offer a potion . . ." the gnome said.

"Eh, best to save stuff like that for when you really need it," I replied.

Valhorn nodded. "Wise advice."

"Oh, don't get me wrong, we're still taking that potion," I added. They did shoot us, after all.

"'Tis only fair—" He started before the other girl shoved him to the side and pushed a glowing red potion into Peps's hand.

"Oh, it's fine!" Peps said as he pushed it back.

"No, no, I insist," the girl replied with grim determination as she pushed it back.

"Oh, no I'm really fine." Peps pushed it back.

"But I shot you!" She protested as she pushed it back.

"It's only a scratch . . ."

Ignoring the Canadian standoff behind me, I turned to the gnome. "You two were planning on an ambush?" I asked.

He nodded. "Yes, we had begun hunting but it was hard pickings. Most of the beasts here would run on sight, they rarely stood and fought unless cornered."

Ah shit, that makes things more annoying. "Have you tried scouting further? We're not that far from the spawn zone so the stuff here might be more passive. Perhaps outside the mall?"

He shook his head. "Though we are confident in our abilities, the night holds many dangers. Without a proper source of light I am cautious to advance outside, where we lack the cover of this structure," he said as he gestured around us.

"I can create something similar to a light source," I suggested, raising a hand palm up. "Grow Sporage, Light Spores."

Valhorn's eyes lit up. "That would indeed do! Perhaps we should band together?"

"That would create a fairly balanced party," I replied. "What's your class?"

"I am a warrior, and you?"

"Fungalmancer, which is basically a mage but with a mushroom theme slapped on it. Mostly an all-rounder with a focus for area of effect damage."

"Hmm, and your tree friend can act as the healer," he said thoughtfully.

I gestured to the standoff happening next to us. "And she's our damage dealer?"

"Indeed."

"I look forward to working with you, then," I said as I offered my hand.

He smiled as he shook it. "As I do with you."

I smiled back. "We should probably break up those two . . ." I added.

He peeked behind me. "Yes, they have been going on for a while already."

Myconid and gnome turned to the scene of carnage. Not that you would notice at first glance, they were still politely pushing the potion into each other. I was almost tempted to let them play this out for a few more moments, see how long it would last. Unfortunately, that notion was destroyed when the gnome loudly declared, "We're partying up!"

Two pairs of confused eyes turned to us at the same time.

"Eh?"

2.02

───

"And when the Princess sang, the forest rallied under her. To defeat the filthiest of dishes and clean the most nookiest of crannies."

—*Excerpt from* The First Princess

After finally getting Peps to accept the potion—which he hesitantly stuffed into his afro—we sat down in awkward silence.

"I suppose introductions are in order?" I winced internally, was that too formal of a start?

Regardless, the gnome perked up. "As you may have already known, I am Valhorn Hillblight the Rippling Barbarian!" he yelled theatrically, long hair swishing back and forth.

The ranger girl gave a polite clap, which Peps joined in with soon after. Apparently satisfied, Valhorn continued, "It was truly a stroke of fortune to meet such varied adventurers such as you lot, thine might even say that luck was on our side or that . . ."

I glanced at the other two, who seemed content to let Valhorn continue talking. Peps still looked a bit dazed from this, however, he still had a friendly smile on. The ranger's smile was slightly more strained, more withdrawn, and felt more like politeness.

". . .And that is why such fortuitous encounters should be celebrated! A toast to future victories and—"

"You have alcohol?" I interrupted.

Valhorn paused. "Erm, no. I am not in possession of any wine nor spirits."

"Then perhaps save such a thing for later?" I suggested. "You know, after said future victories?"

"Indeed!"

I waited a moment to see if he had anything more to add. Seeing him silent, I cleared my throat. "Well, then. I'm Dustin as some of you may know. Mage class with stats mostly spec'd into Wisdom and Constitution, and I lack Agility and Dexterity. I'm best at a midline role, I know six spells that are balanced between utility, damage, and crowd control. I also have a racial ability that crowd controls which I can use once per short rest. However, I get a debuff when under sunlight or when my mana is too low."

Peps looked like he got most of the jargon I threw out, the ranger girl looked a bit lost. Valhorn's eyes, however, were shining. "Straight to the point! I like it!" He declared, "I am a warrior, trained in short swords and the Aura techniques Quick Step and Heavy Slash. I possess the Strength of a centaur, the Dexterity of an octopus"—his arms mimed out a bow being drawn then wiggled like tentacles—"and the Constitution of a hedgehog," he finished.

What?

"So . . ." Peps started, slightly hesitant, "that means you have a poor Constitution?"

Valhorn nodded energetically.

Low Constitution, hmm . . . well for someone that short it was to be expected.

"Well, I'm Peps, an Elderwood druid," Peps began. "I know three spells: Willow Lights, Druidcraft, and Cure Wounds. I can shapeshift into animals I've formed a bond with; however, since I assume their stats and physical abilities, I lose my ability to cast spells. Most of my stats are in Wisdom and Charisma."

"A bond?" I asked.

"Well, if I help a certain animal, then I can assume their form. The closer the bond the better the transformation." He paused, considering his next words. "For example, if I helped a squirrel find some nuts, then I'll be able to become a squirrel. But I won't be able to become THAT specific squirrel I helped out. However, if I formed a meaningful bond with that squirrel, then I can become that specific squirrel."

I sat there, trying to piece together this information. "So, you're saying . . . that a basic bond will allow you to become the species of squirrel and give you the base stats of a squirrel. But if you became good friends with a squirrel that's stronger than average, then you can become a stronger than average squirrel?"

"Yeah," Peps answered.

"What about skills and magic?" Valhorn added, eyes suddenly serious.

Shit, he's right. Good catch Valhorn.

Peps thought about it for a moment. "I'm not sure . . ." he said hesitantly. "I didn't ask my tutorial guide about that."

I exchanged a glance with Valhorn; I needed to test this. In all likelihood, it would be something very restricted, on a class like druid that already has many drawbacks. But there is no way it would be this easy to power game . . .

A lightbulb went off in my head. "It's a mechanic that rewards roleplaying," I spoke my thoughts aloud.

Valhorn nodded. "Indeed. Given the . . . odd origins of this realm, it would make a lot of sense."

A real breathing world, huh? This is becoming more interesting by the moment.

Though, I mentally sighed, this probably means that people are going to double down on the roleplaying. Valhorn hasn't broken character once yet, using vague terms to shy away from the more game-like aspects instead. Shame, he seemed like the most competent here.

Perhaps I should do a bit of light roleplaying? I didn't have much to go with other than the Traveler thing . . .

"Oh, sorry about that, friend," Valhorn interrupted my thoughts. I glanced at him. He didn't direct that to me but to the ranger girl. "Please introduce yourself as well," he added.

Three pairs of eyes turned to her. "Umm . . ." she hesitantly began, her cat ears were laid flat on her head. Hmm, did she have normal ears underneath her hair? Four ears felt excessive. "So, my name is Boba, like the drink. I'm a Ranger, as you may have gathered when I uh"—she gestured to Peps—"shot him. . ."

"It's really fine," Peps assured her.

"But I shot you!" she protested.

I raised a hand before we got stuck in another standoff. "Umm, I'm pretty sure we've already had this conversation."

"Yeah. . ." Peps began, before chuckling a bit, soon joined by the ranger girl, Boba, and Valhorn.

"So, as I was saying," Boba continued, "I have Novice proficiency in short bows and daggers, a passive called Natural Explorer, which helps me traverse difficult terrain, and Haste which speeds me up for a while. My racials are Keen Senses, Dark Vision, and Shifting, which boosts my physical stats for a minute."

I nodded, all around decent physical build with good scouting capabilities. Though Valhorn's low constitution might be a problem, hmm.

"Alright." I clapped my hands. "Let's do it like this . . ."

* * *

Valhorn took the first step out of the mall. I went next, my eyes scanned our surroundings with my superior Dark Vision. Nothing in sight, though the outside was as overgrown as the mall, though lacking the glowing moss that lit up the mall. We picked an exit that led to an open carpark.

"Clear," I said, and Peps followed after me. Given that damage here can result in something much worse than a number dropping, i.e. actual wounds, keeping the healer alive was even more important. Boba followed close after. Despite the fact that I was a mage and Valhorn had low Constitution, we were both best suited for the frontline. Me because I had a high Constitution and low range compared to Boba. Valhorn because he was better armored and literally made for a frontline role.

"Do you think normal aggro strategies will work?" I asked Valhorn as we passed through the former carpark.

Valhorn shot me an annoyed look. Oh, yeah, the roleplaying. I cleared my throat. "Doth thou suppose that hurting thy . . ." What's a fancy word for mob? "Thy enemies! Shall lead to aggravation in the form that is predictable and . . . makes them easier to hit?" I finished questioningly.

Boba lightly chuckled and Valhorn let out a tired sigh, did I overdo it? "'Tis unlikely," he continued, "and foolish to assume that beasts, no matter how unintelligent, will fall for obvious provocation."

So . . . probably not? The goblins certainly didn't, and they were just tutorial mobs. They learned. They started avoiding my mushrooms, roaming in groups, and always having a goblin prepared to run on first contact. A real, breathing world huh . . . was all this preparation for Indiri? Since the mobs are "alive" inside Indiri, it would be stupid to assume they would follow predictable game patterns.

I asked Valhorn this, though translating it to roleplay speak first. "Do you think that this is a trial?" I asked as we passed the car park without any bother.

He raised an eyebrow questioningly at me. "The intent of Gaia is to train players to be prepared for Indiri," I explained. "The . . . patterns I have viewed from fought creatures show a degree of intelligence not common in . . . games."

Valhorn paused for a moment. "Fought creatures?"

"A hundred goblins and one." *What was roleplay for tutorial?* Ahh, fuck it, just go with introduction. "Fought during my introduction to this realm. They learned of my strategies and adapted around them, though I contested them to stalemate. Lack of knowledge sealed my defeat." Shit, I was getting the hang of this roleplaying thing.

"Indeed," Valhorn mused. "Gaia is a trial, then, to weed out those unable to adapt."

"Or a lesson," I added, a test or a lesson. Test to see if players can realize this early on and remove their game biases. A lesson to teach them that it was different.

"Initiative is ours, then—"

"Shh!" Boba quietly interrupted. I turned my attention to her, her cat ears were rotating on her head. "Four things . . . no three! Heading toward us from the left," she urgently whispered.

I glanced around. We had entered a forest before I knew it.

"Draw your weapons," Valhorn whispered as he drew his short sword and turned to the left.

I took out the Poison Sporage I prepared earlier so that I could chain two spells if necessary. Three versus four . . . we had them outnumbered, though Peps wasn't much of a combatant. He was the backup plan in case one of us got injured. Three and a half versus three, then.

"Mobs?" I asked Boba.

"I'm not sure," she whispered back. "Not large though, around house cat–size."

Unlikely to be players, then, unless it's that raccoon the dude from before mentioned? Hmm, what are the chances of three people getting animal races?

I heard them. Rustling leaves and softly pounding feet, but quick and urgent. I grew another Poison Sporage on my hand just in case.

Boba drew her short bow. They were close enough now that she probably didn't need to concentrate on Keen Senses to find them.

Three shadows burst from the bush. Rats. Shit, they were big. Valhorn moved to intercept, I threw a Poison Sporage at the air above them. If they jumped I could take them out.

All three rats dashed forward, before slamming their faces into the ground in a dogeza bow. My mushroom fell to the ground harmlessly behind them. One of the rats began squeaking.

"Wait!" Peps yelled as he grabbed Valhorn's shoulder, causing him to jerk and fall on his behind. "I can Speak with Animals!" he said as he kneeled forward in front of the rats.

What?

Peps began speaking—squeaking?—with the rats. Valhorn stood back up, rubbing his rear; behind me, I heard Boba loosen her bow.

Peps's conversation with the rats began urgently, then they started charading something that I was severely missing the context to make sense of.

Was Peps crying? Apparently finishing his squeaking conversation, Peps turned to us, wiping away sappy tears.

"Guys!" he tearfully began. "They need our help!"

"What?"

2.03

———

"With her song, the First Princess proved that magically enchanted animals make far better servants, thus, all the original servants tasked with menial work around the castle were laid off for requiring a salary."

—*Excerpt from* The First Princess

Peps gently lifted one of the grotesquely large rats, cradling it like a house cat or a very ugly baby. The other two rats stood upright next to him. Rat one, which Peps was holding, squeaked something.

Peps began translating: "We were just minding our own business, ya see . . ."

"You may take whatever you want," Debon casually replied. The individual before him nodded, before proceeding to ransack the store.

Hmm, Debon had to slightly limit him, make some stuff disappear before he found it. Make sure everything he was taking was still within the beginners' budget.

As he was doing so, he received a message.

Hendrix: Yo

Debon raised an eyebrow, how odd. Why was Hendrix messaging him now?

Debon: Hello, is something the matter Hendrix?

Hendrix: Just curious about the kid youre guiding

You're. He mentally corrected. It irked Debon that his colleagues would take such shortcuts, even in casual messaging. An unfortunate side effect of the . . . "variety" their mother had bestowed upon them.

Debon casually glanced at his trainee, who was experimentally spinning a polearm. It made sense that Hendrix would want to know about him. The trainee Debon was in charge of was recruited by one of Hendrix's trainees. They were likely real-life friends if the chatter he caught was accurate.

Debon: He is doing as expected.

Hendrix: Mmm, I would like to try something . . . look at this

A notification popped up inside of Debon's consciousness. He mentally reviewed it. A preset encounter with a goblin village, set inside this very mall. Given what Hendrix just asked, Debon could guess the intent of this preset, though . . .

Debon: A hundred goblins? Even with the lowered Constitution and learning limitation this is too much. The tutorial only requires the player to move around a bit so that the program can adjust the duplicate persona to better fit their bodies.

Hendrix: I'm just curious about how he will do. Come on, I'll treat you to lunch at Mermaids Tail.

Hmm. Tempting, Mermaids Tail had one of the better selections of seafood in Indiri. And his trainee seemed most delighted about his experience here. Would a slightly difficult tutorial turn him off? Debon needed to confirm; he had to do this at least somewhat professionally compared to the others, after all. Knowing Hendrix, he probably just shoved it onto everyone he was in charge of.

"Excuse me," Debon asked the trainee, "would you consider yourself new or experienced to Virtual Reality or Combat?"

The boy raised an eyebrow. "Experienced, why?"

"I am just considering how I should adjust the difficulty setting of your tutorial," Debon replied.

The boy set down the end of the polearm with a thud. "Hard," he replied with a gleeful smile. "Give me the highest difficulty you can."

"Very well," Debon easily replied.

Even if the boy had agreed, Hendrix didn't know that yet. Debon began the delicate process of extorting, um negotiating a better deal from Hendrix. Dinner perhaps. The Tail's night menu had some delectable meals made with the Starlit Trouts caught locally, and they literally didn't taste the same unless eaten under a bright moon.

"And the cowards struck Peaches from behind! My brother, Dangerous Beans, bravely held them off as I cradled my dying mate. However he was one and they were many. He could not hold them off forever. He warned me to retreat, however, I could not leave it at that. Thus before Peaches's final breath. I swore vengeance upon them!" Peps yelled, arms dramatically flinging around as he translated what Rat one, who I now knew was called

Sardines, squeaked. Luckily, Peps put Sardines down before his oration, or else he would've thrown him off by now.

The other two rats, Hampork and Skip were dramatically recreating the events Sardines was describing. They did oddly well despite the fact that there were only two of them and they were doing a scene with at least half a dozen characters.

"Such vile scoundrels to strike one noble as yourself completely unprovoked!" Valhorn yelled. "I understand thy pain and I, too, shall swear death upon them! I swear upon my father! My father's father! And his father . . ."

I turned away from the roleplaying maniac and looked at Boba, who was crying again. "Peaches died way too young! You guys never had the chance to view the sunset on an autumn beach, or share a string of cheese under a starlit night."

Something weird was happening.

Sardines's story was good, well-executed and even had a few twists despite sounding like a classic romantic tragedy. But it wasn't good enough to elicit tears, right?

I glanced at Valhorn, who was finding more and more obscure parts of his family to swear vengeance with. Boba, who was still crying and Peps, who was gently weeping golden tears as he finished his/their play. Hmm . . . those tears looked shiny. I wasn't sure what Peps's race did but Elderwood sounded pricey. It'll have to wait, one thing at a time, Decs.

The point is, all three of them seemed enamored with the rats' tale. Too enamored.

I mentally began reviewing the rats' actions. Nothing obvious, they dogeza'd almost immediately upon contact and haven't made an aggressive play yet. I didn't think they'd cast a spell either unless there were spells that can be cast without chants. Which was entirely possible, though unlikely to exist at such a low level. Aura techniques? Also unlikely, from what I've gathered from Valhorn and Boba the techniques they were allowed to pick focused closer on buffing themselves or required touch. Of us, only Peps had touched a rat so far. Aura techniques were chantless, however, so it might've been cast without any of us knowing.

Some sort of buff? But what kind of skill let you do theatrical plays better? No. I can't think like that. Assuming that every skill or spell was just number crunching would be incorrect. The goblin mage proved that utility spells existed with his tracking spell, though his spell seemed to have some sort of condition. Otherwise, he wouldn't have carried the Sneezing Sporage with him. Only I could activate it from a distance, after all. But back on track. If the rats did something, then it was probably an Aura technique. Valhorn and Boba said they could use theirs without yelling out the skill name, however they weren't used to it yet. Rats that have been living in this world with this very system likely have.

Unlikely to be something that directly affected someone else, too. Otherwise, only Peps would've been affected since he's the only one who was in contact with a rat. Probably some sort of self-buff, but what kind?

Buffing yourself . . . Buffing yourself . . .

What were the stats?

Body, mind, and soul. Body had Strength, Dexterity, Constitution, all the physical stats.

Mind had Intelligence, Wisdom, and . . . Charisma.

The description for that stat was annoyingly vague. The ability to interact with other people? Literally, everyone can do that! If Charisma was to blame, then it was probably better described as the ability to make other people do things. In this case, making them cry over a meh play.

Why was I the only one unaffected, then? Hmm . . . Valhorn and Boba were both physical fighters . . . No, Peps was a magic user as well, but he did handle a rat directly . . . Shit, I can't easily check, there was still a not-zero chance I just have shit taste in theatre. Doing anything overly suspicious was a no-go for now.

Hmm . . . Perhaps my mind stats? Probably not Charisma, a six was apparently very low. Wisdom was likelier, since it was my highest stat, Intelligence, too, since it seemed decently high.

"And upon my great great great grandfather's nephew's third cousin's eighth pet—" I grabbed Valhorn, interrupting him methodically devaluing the worth of his entire family tree and extra. "What's your Intelligence and Wisdom stats?" I urgently whispered to him.

Slightly confused, he replied, "Eleven and nine."

Hmm, no roleplaying, he really was out of it.

More gently, I grabbed Boba by the shoulder. "What's your Intelligence and Wisdom stats?" I quietly asked, keeping a careful eye on the rats. They don't seem to have noticed me yet, instead just silently weeping and looking overall very pitiable.

Boba wiped away a tear, staring confused at me. "Umm, around the tens . . ."

Probably Wisdom, then. My Intelligence was too close to theirs and Peps . . . I glanced at Peps who was helping the rats wipe away their tears. A lost cause. Even if he had as high a Wisdom stat as I did, he seemed like a natural idiot. A nice, softhearted idiot but an idiot nonetheless.

Fuck. I wish Matt was here, he would've made this thing a whole lot simpler. Bloody, but simpler.

Though I had yet to confirm one important thing. Whether or not we were being attacked. My instincts and logic said yes. However, the rats haven't done anything aggressive yet. Told a sob story and asked us to fight some people. Honestly, just normal game NPC stuff, and if this was just a game, then I would've thought the devs were just being cheeky with a random event. But Gaia wasn't just a game, was it?

Hendrix displayed an unerring amount of personality and life despite just being what I assumed was a tutorial bot, and though I haven't seen Indiri yet, if Eve can make one fully breathing world, who's to say she can't make two? Gaia wouldn't even be that hard to make since she had Giles's recreation to work off of. At the very least, there was more to this story. I should see this to the end at least. Though . . .

"A truly tragic tale you have told us," I said, channeling my inner role-player—two can play at this game—"and though justice is its own reward. I must ask . . ." I paused slightly; gotta seem hesitant. "If mayhaps there is compensation for us helping you?" If they're trying to be quest giver NPCs, then they might as well hand over all their valuables.

Peps looked at me oddly, then translated what I said. I looked closely at the rats as they heard what Peps squeaked. Hmm. . . No luck, they looked exactly like regular giant rats. No over the top cartoon facial features. I can't read them.

The lead rat, Sardines, quickly squeaked something back. "He said that it would be difficult," Peps translated, "since they have many family members and often go hungry during hard seasons."

It almost felt like Boba, or Valhorn, was trying to glare daggers into my back. "Oh, no, no," I replied, "I am not asking for extravagance, merely compensation to account for personal expenses undertaken in this quest. Such as damaged gear or injuries."

The glare softened slightly and turned away. Was that my Perception? It was described as a sixth sense . . .

"We cannot compensate for weapons or gear lost," Peps said, already translating. "However, our brethren know many ways around this land, and know of hidden treasure left by travelers before thee."

"That will do," I replied as I gave them a bright smile. Peps seemed to recoil a bit but quickly gathered his bearings as he translated.

"Now, perhaps thou can describe to us what manner of foe plagues you," Valhorn butted in.

I glanced gratefully at him. Talking to rats was starting to get weird.

* * *

Skip pointed in front of us and squeaked. "They're over there," Peps quietly translated.

Hmm . . . in front of us was a neat park if I remembered correctly. Though now it seemed pretty overgrown. Valhorn did a few gestures with his hand, which I roughly translated to: *follow me quietly,* if movies were accurate. Silently bending down, I let the tall grass cover me.

Valhorn took point, I followed behind him. Boba had disappeared somewhere and Peps was told to stay out of sight due to his low combat capability.

From what we gathered from the rats, our opponents were humanoid and worked in a party. Three melee fighters and one healer. Valhorn was pretty serious about battle tactics, so we planned ahead. Leverage Boba's superior range as we kept them busy close up. The first to die had to be the healer, obviously. Valhorn and I would try to do a sneak attack to get him, however, likelier we would just keep the melees busy as Boba assassinated the healer.

Valhorn raised a hand, the universal gesture for stopping. We were close enough to hear the sounds of a fire crackling. A camp? Hopefully, we can catch them off guard.

Slowly, we crept in closer, beginning to catch muted snippets of conversation.

I heard "not" and "level."

I paused, Valhorn stopping just a bit in front of me as he stopped sensing movement from me.

Then "grind."

Oh.

Oh.

I laughed. I laughed loudly. *How was I so stupid!? The rats were common mobs! We're avenging dead mobs! We were fighting other players!*

A horrific noise rang across the clearing. Lung shuddered at the sound, it was as if an asthmatic whale had just taken its final breaths, before violently and spontaneously combusting.

"What the fuck was that!?" one of his party members yelled, shakily standing up and drawing his blade. His name escaped Lung at the moment, though it was unlikely to be worth remembering.

Steadily, Lung stood up and faced toward where the noise had come from. The noise wasn't human but sounded far too . . . unsettling to be a natural animal. "Who is there?" he calmly but loudly asked.

"Ah, sorry 'bout that!" A cheery voice yelled back. His eyes focused on a patch of grass that seemed to be glowing softly. "We're players, so don't shoot us or something."

Behind him, a sigh of relief came from one of his party. "Holy shit, man, you scared—"

"Show yourself," Lung interrupted.

The grass rustled, and a glowing figure rose. Some kind of humanoid mushroom, with a face carved out like a jack-o'-lantern on its stalk. A soft, light bluish glow emanated from it. "Sorry about that, just remembered my race has a weird natural laugh."

A player, then.

"Damn, you look creepy as hell," someone from behind him said, almost approvingly. *Darkblade,* Lung remembered. Likely because the name seemed to combine the worst parts of edge and genericness.

The mushroom seemed to grin. "I'd like to think it's creepy and cool," it replied as it took a step forward.

"Stay back," Lung commanded.

The mushroom paused, then seemed to shrug helplessly. "Why are you so paranoid, dude?"

"Why were you sneaking around?" he simply rebutted.

"I heard that there was a wild boss around this area, so I'm trying to hide from it," it replied in a casual, matter-of-fact tone.

"Where did you hear that?"

"I met a few players who respawned after fighting it. Apparently it's really strong, so I want to avoid it."

"Then why come here at all?"

The mushroom's face seemed to turn blank for a moment, before it sighed. "Ah, fuck it, I'm bad at this improv thing anyway," and with that, it threw something.

Lung's reaction was instant. His body, already tensed, swayed to the right. The thrown object narrowly missed his head.

Before it exploded.

Some sort of yellow dust filled the air around his head, and an unbearable itching sensation erupted on his nose.

"ARRRGH-CHOOOO!"

The sneeze forced Lung's eyes closed; however, due to a quirk of his race having transparent eyelids, he briefly caught a glimpse of the mushroom reeling back, as if belching—

"Harden Hide!" Lung yelled out before the glob of purple struck him. The thing landed on his chest, burning through cloth before barely getting stopped by his reinforced skin.

Lung stomped a foot down and pushed off it. He dashed toward the mushroom with explosive speed.

"Poison Sp—" Lung grabbed the mushroom in the neck, interrupting the spell, and swiftly punched it in the face. The blow felt odd, elastic almost—

The mushroom grabbed the arm, lifting itself up. "Fucking hate monks," it muttered as one of its fingertips burst.

A heaviness seemed to set in, his body seemed to slow. Lung gritted his teeth, stomping his foot down, he twisted his body, throwing the enemy to the side.

Through heavy eyelids, he saw the mushroom fly far, colliding with a tree. *A mistake,* Lung realized too late. He'd created more range between them.

Lung staggered forward. "Ability Boost," he muttered, feeling the heaviness alleviate somewhat. He needed to close in again, where the fuck was his healer?

"I, THE GREAT VALHORN, HAVE CLAIMED FIRST BLOOD!" Lung heard a voice yell from the camp. He swiftly turned, seeing some sort of midget pulling a sword out from the already dissipating corpse of his healer.

"What the hell, Peps" He heard the mushroom mutter. Turning again, he saw a cat with an afro sitting on the fallen mushroom. Light emanated from its paws.

Lung evaluated his options: behind him Darkblade and his other party member were exchanging blows with the gnome, forcing it on the defensive. The mushroom was unoccupied, probably a mage class. If left like that, it would leverage its superior range. Not only that, the cat seemed to be their healer.

Making his decision, Lung dashed toward the mushroom and cat, hands stretched out just in time to grab the mushroom as it stood back up. He tried to grab the cat as well, but it dashed off.

Instead, he began punching the mushroom in the stomach, fists leaving indents in the soft white flesh. It gasped, letting out a breath as it was winded. Lung prepared for the finishing blow when a scream of pain came from behind him.

He turned, seeing one of his party members with something sticking out of their leg.

The mushroom grabbed his shoulder. "Poison Spores."

Green dust exploded from the hand, enveloping Lung's head. Lung staggered back as a stinging pain overtook his orifices.

"Cure Wounds," he heard something say. Half blindly, Lung jumped forward and grabbed the small white thing healing his enemy, before lobbing it as far away as possible.

The mushroom's reaction came a second later, in the form of a sharp pain striking Lung in the abdomen. "Throwing a cat? Dick move, dude."

Lung growled at him, the noise coming out more like a hiss. Reaching out, he grabbed the staff with both hands. His opponent reacted a second too late, he lifted up the surprisingly light creature, before violently swinging staff and wielder toward a tree.

Halfway through the swing, he felt the staff lighten.

"Poison—"

Lung let go of the staff, rapidly turning toward the fallen mushroom, fist already in motion.

"—Spores."

Green dust once again enveloped Lung, however, his fist was already in motion. The pain barely slowed him as he landed a direct hit on his opponent's face.

The squishy mushroom hit the ground, grunting in pain as it did so. Lung tried to follow up with a kick, but instead, he screamed in pain as the spores settled on him. A stinging sensation enveloped his entire body.

"HARDEN HIDE!" Lung yelled, reapplying his defensive skill.

Two rough hands grabbed his shoulders, Lung blearily saw the mushroom's face staring directly back at him. "Acid Spit." The shot landed on his face, burning his eyes and nostrils.

Lung screamed in pain again as he was shoved back.

"That skill doesn't protect your orifices, does it?" The bastard mushroom commented.

Lung rolled over, getting on all fours, then lunged at—

An arrow struck Lung on the back, altering his course and allowing the myconid to easily dodge him.

Lung fell flat-faced onto the ground. "For my brethren!" he heard as a blade went through his abdomen.

"For the rats, yay," the mushroom added unenthusiastically, staff striking Lung's snout. "Poison Spores."

"What rats?" Lung asked as his mind faded to black.

You have died.

Ouch.

That lizard dude was tough for a guy wearing no armor. Probably had a high Constitution like me. He tanked like five poison spores and shook off my crowd control spells like nothing.

Fast, strong, and durable, not only that, did he have transparent eyelids or something? Frick, if it wasn't a one versus three, I might've lost. Speaking of which, "You alright Peps?" I yelled in the general direction where he'd been thrown.

A long, stick-like arm poked out of a bush with a thumbs up. "Fine!"

I glanced to the side where Valhorn was wiping some blood off his blade. The fight was pretty much won the moment their healer died. Even if the lizard dude had me outclassed in close combat, Peps's healing and my own constitution allowed me to hold him off until Boba and Valhorn finished the other two.

Peps came out from the bushes, wiping off leaves that may or may not have been from his afro bush thing. "Are you guys alright as well?"

"I'm fine," I answered.

Valhorn grunted. "Could use some recovery," he said, gesturing to a bleeding arm.

Peps nodded and cast Cure Wounds on him.

"Did they drop any stuff?"

Valhorn shook his head. "No, 'tis seems that their equipment went with them, including their baggage at the camp."

I heard some bushes rustling. Boba. She came in looking slightly pale.

"Are thou fine?" Valhorn asked her, voice concerned.

Boba wordlessly nodded.

Huh.

I turned to Peps. "Didn't you say you couldn't cast spells as an animal?"

"Uh, yeah," he nervously chuckled. "My trainer said the main reason my animal forms can't cast spells is because the animal I am is incapable of casting spells. However, I formed a bond with this cat that could cast spells and I didn't want to sit back so, sorry about that."

Did he feel bad about coming in? I slapped him on the back, having to stand on my toes(?) due to the absurd difference in height. "I would've died if you didn't jump in," I said, and in a more mumbled tone added, "Don't want to test the respawn system firsthand either."

Peps chuckled.

I clapped my hands. "Well, for a pick-up group we did pretty well." Valhorn and Boba turned to me. "Oh yeah, sorry." In a more theatrical tone I said, "For comrades brought by chance our execution of vengeance was well done."

Valhorn nodded, apparently satisfied. Boba managed a smile and Peps ruffled his afro.

"Well, let's get our loot, then."

* * *

"Here it is," Peps translated as Sardines led us down a dark alley. Well, it was night so everywhere was dark.

I glanced around, not much here other than piles of what seemed to be plastic trash. "Mostly trash it seems," I muttered as I poked through the piles with my staff.

Sardines shook his head, before jumping into the pile and pulling out a crystal and a roll of ancient-looking paper.

"What's this?" Valhorn asked. The rat squeaked out a reply, which Peps promptly translated: "A map of the surrounding area and a spell left by a previous Traveler."

I raised an eyebrow. "Pass?" I asked, gesturing to the crystal. Sardines stood up, passing the crystal to me. I gingerly took it. It looked like the Wayshard Hendrix had, the only difference was that there were these weird green glowing lines on it and . . . it felt weird. Like it was calling me. *Bark Skin* it was whispering.

Valhorn took the map. "Hmm . . . seems accurate," he muttered as he examined it.

I shook my head and passed the crystal to Peps, who curiously looked over it. Peps squeaked something to the rat. "He says Travelers use crystals like these to gain new spells," Peps translated the rat's reply.

Something like a skill book, then. "Any idea what's in this one?" Boba asked from the side.

"Bark Skin," I said.

"Apparently a spell called Bark Skin," Peps replied at the same time.

I raised an eyebrow. "You feel the same calling feeling, too?" I asked.

Peps nodded. "It's odd, I didn't feel it until I touched it. What about you two?" he asked as he passed the crystal to Boba.

She shook her head. "Nada. Nothing," she said as she handed it over to Valhorn.

Valhorn passed the map to me. I glanced at it, mentally comparing it to a map I'd seen in the real world.

"I do not feel a call, likely because I do not have the mind for it."

So, class-based, then. Only Peps and I were mages, or magic users.

"How should we split this?" I asked.

Valhorn shrugged. "Neither Boba nor I have the learning to obtain spells," he said as he passed the crystal back to me.

I took that to mean they had no spell slots. "You want it Peps?" I asked. "I already have like six spells, so I don't really need it."

Peps shook his head. "I'm fine."

"Well, I owe you one, then," I replied. "How do I use it?" I glanced questioningly at the rat, who just shook its head. "Oh well, I'll figure it out later," I muttered, placing the crystal in my bag.

"The map?"

"We have long traversed this realm's parallel, so we know the routes," Valhorn answered for himself and I'm assuming Boba. "However, I must draw your attention to this." He pointed to a blank spot on the map. That was . . . the nearby Asian market?

"Any idea why this spot is blank?" I asked.

The rat squeaked something. "He said that there's a great monster there, so many Travelers avoid that area," Peps translated.

"Sounds like a wild boss," I muttered.

Wait, did that rat just . . .

I put down the map. "Did you just understand me?"

The rat's eyes went wide, an oddly human expression on a rat, before it jumped into the piles of trash.

I stared at the empty spot where the rat had been.

"After it!" Valhorn yelled, breaking me out of my trance.

He was already kicking away the trash. But this alleyway was a dead end and there was no way for the rat to—

"There's a hole!" he exclaimed.

A literal mousehole.

2.04

"To defeat the Revenant King we have to work together!"
—Imamu the Lone Swordsmen, known for disbanding
and joining a new party every other day

That was weird," Boba finally commented as we returned to the mall.

"Yeah," I muttered, "I have the distinct feeling that we were scammed, but I can't tell how," and honestly that's bugging me more than the possibility I was scammed or tricked.

"Brother Sardines's behavior was indeed suspicious," Valhorn agreed.

Brother? Oh yeah, Valhorn did name the rats his brothers and sisters or something oathy like that.

"I mean just 'cause he was acting suspiciously didn't mean it was anything bad," Peps added.

"Eh," I returned doubtfully, "I guess that might be true." A dozen notifications suddenly entered my field of view as I regained access to the menus.

Noam (Mattmanfoo): Yo where tf are you?
Noam (Mattmanfoo): Hello hello???
Noam (Mattmanfoo): Earth to dex!!!!!!!!!!
Noam (Mattmanfoo): Hurry up! Hurry up!
Noam (Mattmanfoo): . . .

. . .

"A problem?" Valhorn asked.

I sighed, scrolling through dozens of messages in the chat history. "Nah, my friend just called me."

"I see," Valhorn said, probably realizing from my scrolling gesture that I was on the user interface.

"Next time, then," I said. "Friends list? I still need to pay you guys back for the spell."

Valhorn smiled. "There is no need to feel indebted to me, for the experience was enough."

"I got the map, so I'm fine," Peps added.

"Let's still add each other!" Boba butted in, a notification appearing at the edge of my vision as she said that.

Boba has sent you a friend request.

"I look forward to future adventures, then."

Valhorn Hillblight has sent you a friend request.

"Where is this thing?" Peps muttered.

"Top right, the icon with the silhouettes on it," I answered.

You have sent Peps a friend request.

You have accepted Boba's friend request.

You have accepted Valhorn Hillblight's friend request.

"Well, I should be on my way before my friend stabs someone," I said, only half-jokingly. "It was fun you guys."

Valhorn nodded amicably. "If thou require aid, you may call upon me anytime."

"Let's party up again some other time! I can help you guys shoot things!" Boba yelled, before adding in a much quieter voice, "Unless it's people because . . . eww."

Peps laughed. "I hope that I won't get us scammed again."

I chuckled. "Who knows, maybe I was thinking too much about it." The issue of whether or not we were scammed was still up in the air, since I had no definitive way to value the stuff we got. For all I know we could've just been manipulated by some Terry Pratchet rats-that-knew-Shakespeare and we got paid fairly for our troubles.

That sounded really weird out of context.

Oh well.

"I'll see you guys later, then," I said.

"See ya!"

"Bye."

"Fare thee well," they said as they waved me off.

I waved back, then went deeper into the mall, typing as I walked.

Dustin (HitZaDecs): Yo I'm back.

Noam (Mattmanfoo): Fucking finally! What took you so long!

Dustin (HitZaDecs): You can't use the menus out of the safe zones, so I didn't see any of your messages.

Noam (Mattmanfoo): That's a dumb ass rule.

Dustin (HitZaDecs): Just got back, where do I meet you?

Noam (Mattmanfoo): Idk. This place is pretty much the same irl so the usual place?

Dustin (HitZaDecs): Sure

It was odd seeing the arcade so run down. Blaring neon lights and the constant sound effects of various video games were replaced by calm glowing moss and the quiet chittering of innumerable insects.

All that was left of the arcade machines were the skeletons and hulls, no sign of machinery ever being inside them.

"Yo!" I heard a voice yell.

Leaning on one of the synthetic chairs of the racing games was a tall, blue-skinned demon-like humanoid. Horns of a slightly darker blue hue grew on his head, curving backward and holding dark black hair almost like a crown. Pure purple eyes with no irises stared back at me with a devilish, Cheshire cat-like grin.

"What the fuck did you get?" we both exclaimed at the same time.

"Myconid Fungalmancer."

"Tiefling Skald."

I raised an eyebrow. "Primarily a Constitution and Wisdom-based race, Fungalmancer is a mage subtype that has a mushroom theme and seems to focus on utility rather than damage."

"Intelligence and Charisma for me, though I plan on spec'ing more into physical stats since I plan on being a frontline fighter," he said, gesturing to a long halberd. "Skald is a bard subtype with charisma as the damage modifier, apparently more focused on combat than a normal bard."

"Abilities?"

"Breathless, Vicious Mockery, Biting Words, Swift Strike. I also get Dark Vision and Fire Resistance from my race."

Of course, he took two abilities just for insulting people.

"Grow Sporage, Balm Spores, Light Spores, Sneezing Spores, Acid Spit, Mushroom Meal, Poison Spores, Darkvision, Poison Resist, and Pacifying Spores," I said in a single breath.

"Shit, that is a lot," he commented.

"Yeah, though I have two racial debuffs to go along with it. I can't stay under the sun without getting tired and mana is a problem."

Matt nodded. "Mmm. Gotta stay indoors, then. Find any dungeons yet?"

I shook my head. "None so far; I've had a trip outside, and it seemed pretty similar to real life."

"What does Sporage do?"

"Grows a mushroom that stores a spore-based spell that I can activate. However, right now it needs line of sight, and I can only activate one at a time."

"Limit on numbers and duration?"

I mentally sighed. He's gonna be impressed or something. "No limit on the number, at least none that I've found, and they seem to last a few hours."

"Holy shit."

I sighed. "Less useful than you think it is."

"You're a trapper, dude, just cover a place in mushrooms and you're all set."

"Not against high numbers. Did you get the goblins in your tutorial?"

He nodded. "A hundred of them. I didn't do that well, twenty-two, with the elite."

"Wow," I replied, genuinely impressed. "I had a chance to kill the elite, however I was too busy with keeping myself alive. Only got like fifty-something."

"You didn't just turn the entire mall into a killing field?"

I sighed. "No, the goblins split up into groups of three to four and patrolled the mall. If I was aware of all their patrolling patterns, I might've been able to set something up, and they knew how my mushrooms worked and avoided them. It would also be difficult for me to hide them while also fulfilling the line-of-sight requirement."

"They swarmed me early on. I knew I lost the battle of attrition so I rushed the most important looking dude."

"I did ambushes hoping that it would cause the remaining goblins to bunch up, then I would transition to setting up trapped areas when their movements became more predictable. However, I was thrown off when they remained in split off parties and started sending ranged goblins after me."

"Hmm. Never got to that stage," he muttered. "And dude, Sporage sounds fucking amazing."

"Not against—"

Matt raised his hand, stopping me. "High numbers, I got that. You know what else is bad against high numbers? Literally everything, and how often do you expect to fight so many enemies?"

"Eh, fair point I guess."

"Did you get any rewards from it?" he asked, pulling out a white, pipe-like thing from within his armor.

"I guess?" I replied, pushing up the hem of my cap, revealing the two wisps.

"What are those?"

"Wisps, no idea what they do yet other than drain my mana, probably a pet companion-type thing which I have to incubate first. Yours?"

"A whistle which can increase my Agility and Dexterity once per day."

"Any idea by how much?"

"No clue, haven't tested it yet. What'ja do so far?"

I smirked. "I got paid by Pratchet mobs into killing players."

"What?"

That look on his face was worth getting maybe scammed for.

"Wait, wait, wait," Matt said, gesturing me to pause, "so were you or were you not scammed?"

"I have no clue," I honestly replied. "Their behavior was really suspicious; however, I can't prove a reason for it."

"It might be that they're actually suffering due to player grinding, so they decided turning us on each other was the best bet," I continued. "If that's the case, then the spell stones they're giving out as quest rewards must not be very valuable, at least in their eyes."

Matt raised an eyebrow.

"If they were that hard-pressed for survival, then they would've used the spell stones for themselves," I elaborated. "Either these things are as common as rocks, or they can't use them. I feel like it's the latter, which reminds me"—I tossed the crystal to Matt, which he smoothly caught—"what do you feel from it?"

"Like a voice in my head is saying 'Bark Skin'," he muttered as he examined the crystal.

So, Bards were considered mages of some sort as well. "The pickup group I was in had a warrior and ranger, who both said they felt nothing from it, there's probably a class requirement to using it."

"Makes sense. Any idea how to use it?"

"I was hoping to figure that out when I got here," I answered. *Character Sheet*, I thought, and the thing appeared. "Pass?" I asked, and Matt handed the crystal back.

Under Equipment it appeared, a picture of the crystal labeled *Spell Stone (Bark Skin)*. I tapped the picture. "Description."

Spell Stone (Bark Skin)

A crystal containing a spell formula. A Traveler may automatically learn the spell inscribed within if they hold the Spell Stone and say 'Learn.'

Spell: Bark Skin

Tier 2 Transmutation Spell
Casting Time: 10 seconds
Components: Verbal, Somatic and Focus (A handful of wood bark. Any variety.)
Duration: Until canceled or destroyed
Mana Cost: Minor Initial Mana Cost. Major Mana Reserved
Description: You cast upon yourself. Until the spell ends, an extra layer of durable bark is formed over your skin. Increasing your defense and giving you a bark-like appearance.

At your current level, you require passive concentration to maintain Bark Skin.

That was easy.

"What does it say?" Matt asked.

I read out the description to him. "Sounds useful, learn it," he casually replied as he strolled around the arcade.

Indeed, a defensive spell would round out my spell list pretty well. The mana reserved was a bit pricey, but acceptable. I needed to figure out what passive concentration is later in terms of which stats it might concern, and how spell slots are distributed. I had an open Tier 2 and 0 spell slot, probably from my level up in the tutorial, however I had no idea what the pattern for gaining new spell slots was—at least until my next level up.

"**Learn**," I said, and the crystal crumbled to dust. I flicked my hand, getting rid of the fine dust.

Hmm . . . now where to get bark. Would my staff work? It looked like it was made of wood, though it was pretty smooth and polished—only one way to test it.

"Bark Skin," I said, and I felt mana flow. Like a warm stream coursing under my skin, spreading fine tendrils throughout my body, like it was looking for something. It reached my hand, touched the wooden staff I was holding. The mana grasped it as if confused, before leaving to continue searching. It did this for a few more seconds, before fading.

"Need bark," I said frankly.

Matt's head popped up from behind the top of an arcade machine. "Finally done?"

"We need to go hunt trees," I replied. Would Peps work? What would happen if he cast Bark Skin on himself? Does he become barkier?

"Sweet," Matt simply replied, jumping down from the top of the arcade machine. "You said there were trees outside?"

I nodded.

"Leggo, then," he replied, already leaving the arcade.

"Coming," I replied, following behind him.

When we got out of the mall, I made it about halfway through the car park before I collapsed.

"It's fucking morning," I muttered as Matt dragged me by the foot.

"Why the fuck did you pick such a bad drawback?" he asked, only sounding slightly irritated.

"The fuck was I supposed to take? Human warrior?" I sarcastically retorted.

"At least they're not useless for half the day," he retorted.

I tried bonking the back of his head with my staff, however, he smoothly tilted his head out of the way, easily avoiding the staff.

"You're a lot lighter than I thought you would be," he commented.

Yeah, it was odd that the lizard dude could throw me around so easily. Unless he heavily min/maxed strength this early on. Which was a really poor strategy. Normally you wanted to round out all your stats first. Except in special cases like me where I needed to max Constitution until I can stay in sunlight for a reasonable amount of time.

"How much do you think I weigh?" I tiredly rasped out. Damnit, even if I'm not doing anything, I'm still feeling increasingly tired. Though at a slower rate than when I was actively moving.

"About twenty to thirty kilograms, though you're also wearing your bag," he answered. "We're here," he added as he grabbed my foot with both hands and swung me into the trees.

I felt the moment when the shade enveloped me and I was no longer under dawn's glare. My body stopped becoming more tired and was just tired.

I propped myself up with my staff. The shade was helping A LOT. I was no longer losing stamina just by existing, a win in my book.

"What sorta bark do you need?" Matt asked, already surveying the surrounding area.

"Any should be fine," I returned, leaning on a nearby tree. I had a dagger, didn't I? Yep, I almost forgot I had that. I pulled it out and began carving out a piece.

"Hey, remember that time we—"

There was the sound of a bowstring's twang. Matt jumped to the side, something barely missing him and hitting a tree.

"Attack!" Matt yelled as he jumped behind a tree.

"Yeah, I got that," I retorted as I took cover as well. I glanced at the tree that was struck, an arrow, came from the direction of the car park. "Ranged attacker, archer. Line of sight?"

"A glimpse," he replied. "Green hood, pretty tall as well."

"Ditch your bag," I told him, already slinging off my backpack. They'll only hinder us, and from what happened with my previous encounter, they will go with us if we die.

"Magic Missiles," I heard from in front of me.

Two balls of blue mana hit me, throwing me into the tree.

"Another one!" I yelled. Matt grabbed the tip of my cap, dragging me to the ground as a third missile narrowly missed me.

"Location?" Matt asked, halberd already out.

"Didn't see, but from that way"—I gestured deeper into the forest—"probably a mage. They're trying to pincer us."

"Plan?"

"Probably repositioning around our cover," I replied.

"Ours?" he asked, eyes flickering back and forth from the car park and the small forest.

 I pursed my lips. "Repositioning is our best bet as well," getting to a position where we force an opening or only have one of them able to attack. "There's a chance we're being surrounded, not pincered." That made more sense. An encirclement would be much more effective. We needed more information to figure out if we were only getting attacked by two people or more.

An arrow struck the tree in front of us.

No. The opponent already stole the initiative from us, attacking from cover while we haven't caught sight of them. Unlikely to have melees as well, otherwise they would've already sent them in. A character with limited range was better at denying a small amount of area. If it's an encirclement, then staying still will only give them more time to close in.

"Rush?" Matt asked.

"Rush," I agreed.

He looked back and forth between the two spots where we caught sight of them. "Which one?"

Going by the conventional mage and archer builds, the mage would be squishier, easier to kill, unlikely to have high physical stats. Easier to overwhelm at close range but has high utility and more variety than archers. I have no idea what sort of spells they might have. Archers probably have some amount of Dexterity and Agility, harder to catch but less damage and utility than the mage. Though we won't be able to finish him off as quickly as the mage, he might be easier to escape than the mage, since there's a chance the mage might have some array of crowd control spells. No.

"We can't escape," I muttered aloud.

Matt looked at me oddly for a moment, then realization dawned on him. "Fuck. The sun."

Once we broke out of the tree's shade I'd be disabled; Matt might be able to escape if he abandoned me, but I was screwed.

"Is this a Knife then?" he asked me.

"Does this look like a Knife situation to you?" I retorted. Knife might work, but if the mage had a defensive spell, then we were both screwed.

Matt sighed. "I guess not."

I quickly created two Sporages. "Go for the mage. This will probably be like Paintball, so take these," I told him as handed him the Sporages.

Then I slowly stood up, touching the tree next to us. I began casting. "Grow Sporage—"

A figure stepped out from behind a car, smoothly drawing a bow. "—Sneezing Spores," I finished. The arrow flew, striking me in the shoulder. "GO!" I yelled, and Matt dashed off in the opposite direction of the arrow, halberd in hand.

The archer was about ten meters from me. Damnit.

"Poison Spores!" I cast, a cloud of green blowing out of my hand toward him.

He took a step to the right, easily avoiding the cloud. I pointed to a spot a bit farther to the right. "Sneezing Spores!"

He abruptly stopped. Realizing that to his left was a cloud of yellow, and to his right was a cloud of green.

I pulled off the Sporage I just created, wincing at the dull pain in my shoulder and throwing the mushroom toward the middle of the two clouds. He jumped back, drawing another arrow. "Sneezing Spores!" I yelled as I dodged down.

The arrow flew overhead, and the mushroom exploded in mid-air.

2.05

———

"I yield! I yield!"
—*The most common response to Vafruther the Song Warrior opening his mouth*

Matt dashed toward the bushes.

"Hey come out you little bitch!" he yelled as he cast Vicious Mockery.

"Stop hiding and get your ass kicked like a man!"

Matt heard something crystallizing, before three balls of blue shot out of the bushes and curved toward him.

There he is, Matt thought as he stomped a foot in the ground, and without a second thought, dashed forward. All three magic missiles passed harmlessly above him.

"Your aim is so shit that I'm actually glad I'm the target!"

"Will you shut the fuck up!" Matt heard a female voice yell as the third Vicious Mockery made them rise from the bushes.

Matt smiled. "Gotcha."

The mage paled, suddenly realizing that she had given away her position and made herself a larger target.

"Blade—"

She was only a few meters away, he could make it.

"—Ward."

With both hands, Matt swung his halberd at the mage, only for the edge to be stopped by a translucent barrier.

The mage began rapidly making hand gestures. Matt let go of his halberd, shifting all his weight to his left foot.

He commanded aura to flow to his right hand. *Swift Strike.*

But he was too far away, his fist could not make it. Three balls of blue energy coalesced around the mage's hand.

"DECS!"

As his fist flew, Matt opened his hand at the last possible moment, throwing the Sporage forward. His weight already shifted to his left foot, he fell to the side. No longer blocking Dustin's sight and fulfilling Sporage's activation requirement.

The mushroom exploded in mid-air.

"DECS!"

The mushroom man took a step backward, half-turning toward his ally and making sure he had a hand trained on the archer. Peaches perked his ears up, hearing the slight whisper the mushroom uttered in magic.

Turning to the devil, he saw that it had dropped to the ground and rolled away, just in time to avoid the sudden yellow dust. Quickly, the devil jumped back up, then delivered an uppercut to the elf mage's sneezing face, knocking her to the ground.

The mushroom mage was behind a tree now, growing more of those odd magical mushrooms, apparently content to let his companion take out the other mage while his opponent, the archer, stood hesitantly by. The archer could easily go around the spore barrier the mushroom mage had constructed but was likely debating whether or not to save his ally.

Peaches shook his head. As expected of a pick-up group, they were more or less already done for. With the debacle with Sardines last night, Peaches had better things to do than watch over failed puppets. He needed to give more people "quests."

Scratching the back of his ear with a hind leg, the giant rodent jumped down from its perch on a tree. He Scuttled through the bush and far away from the fight.

Matt clocked the girl in the chin, briefly lifting up the woman before she fell to the ground.

Matt jumped back a few steps, assuming a boxer position, cautiously watched the downed mage. It's been a while since he threw a punch like that. He might've put in way more power than intended or failed to knock them out. Though even a light punch to the chin was usually enough, but he had to be sure, otherwise Declan wouldn't let him live this down for weeks.

Seeing no reaction when he poked the mage with his toe, Matt doubled back, grabbing the halberd that he picked up as an impulse.

Declan probably would've killed the mage to make sure she's no longer a threat, saying that'll she'll respawn anyway. But Matt wasn't that type of person; he had already won against her, after all.

He glanced at the archer, who had already started running away, then at Declan, who was now emerging from a cloud of spores.

Declan shook his head.

Matt stopped a few meters from him.

"Good job," Declan began, pulling off the mushrooms he created. "You knocked her out?"

Matt nodded, resting his halberd on his shoulder.

Declan nodded in agreement. "Good, there wasn't a reason for this attack, at least I don't think there is, so questioning her would be our next course of action."

"Questioning?" Matt started, his mind immediately jumped to torture, though Declan wasn't the type to do that, probably. Better make sure. "It better not be torture or some shit."

"Nah," Declan replied, "far too unreliable, she could just lie to us and even if she did tell the truth, we'll just give someone a lasting grudge against us. No point."

Matt sighed; that was probably the best he'd get from Declan. "Then how do we do this?"

Declan held his hand to his chin. "Hmm. . ." he quickly glanced at the handful of mushrooms he'd created, then at his halberd, and finally toward him.

"How high is your Charisma stat?" Declan asked.

"Fifteen—" there was a moment where Matt's brain misfired as he fully registered Declan's words and more importantly, the context in which he asked them. "No," he firmly stated.

Declan raised an eyebrow at him in confusion.

"I've seen enough shitty dramas to know where this is going," Matt replied firmly.

"Really? Please explain," Declan replied in a cold, dry voice.

"You want me to . . ." Matt vaguely gestured at the girl lying on the ground.

"What exactly?" Declan asked again.

Matt glared at him. "You know what I'm—" then he noticed that the corner of Declan's "lips" were slightly curved. That fucker was smirking. Without warning, Matt grabbed his halberd and swung it upward in a wide arc. Declan took a step to the left, dodging the axe-side of the halberd as it struck the ground harmlessly.

Declan didn't bother hiding his smirk anymore. "Should I find a rose to hold between your teeth? Perhaps you should pose like one of those models?"

"Fuck you." Matt sighed.

"More seriously though," Declan said, "I have a theory that Charisma can work on stuff like persuasion. As good a time as any to figure if it's true."

"Oh, you are not going to brush that off now," Matt replied, lifting his halberd.

Declan sighed as if annoyed. "I know you want to fight me and will look for any excuse to do so, but can it be after we get the semi-important shit done?"

"That coming from the guy who was messing around a moment ago?" Matt sarcastically replied, though he rested the halberd back on his shoulder. That fight was . . . unsatisfying, he had pretty much defeated her the moment he got into close range.

"Come on," Declan said as he grabbed his dropped bag, then kneeled down beside the downed mage.

He gently lifted the girl into a sitting position, then proceeded to shake her by the shoulders.

Matt opened his mouth, then shut it. He silently watched Declan trying to wake the girl.

Eventually, the girl made a grunting sound and opened an unfocused eye. "Hello?" Declan asked, unsuccessfully snapping his fingers in front of her face. He looked irritated at his hands for a moment, before continuing, "Anyone home right now?"

Her eyes slowly focused, seeing the person in front of her.

Then she screamed.

In a flurry of panic, the girl slapped Declan's hands off her, then scurried away from him.

"Holy shit, you have an ugly face!" the girl exclaimed.

"Well, that's just *rude*," Matt pointed out.

Declan sighed. "Look, can we skip over the part where you panic and try to kill us again, to the part where we can have a civilized discussion?"

"You guys are players?" the girl asked.

"Yeah," Matt replied, "you need a better ambush strategy by the way, and a better teammate, the guy abandoned you instantly."

"First off, you should've focused on him"—Declan gestured at Matt—"he's the squishiest of the two of us, you needed a better plan—"

"Honestly, I'm kinda insulted at how bad it was," Matt cut in.

"Look, shit strategy, not important," Declan cut back in. "All I want to know is why did you attack us?"

* * *

Matt dragged me through the morning sun as we headed back to the mall.

What the mage said had . . . annoying implications.

A large rat gave us a quest to kill you because you were grinding rat mobs.

Neither Matt nor I had killed a single mob since entering Gaia. Was the group I killed the same as well? It couldn't have been a coincidence. This whole thing reeked of manipulation and some kind of plot. The question is, for what purpose and who could be doing this?

Eve was an obvious answer. The rats presented an easy and repeatable quest in a world that seems devoid of NPCs, so there's the incentive for this being a game, though I could probably blame everything that happens in this virtual world on her. It'd be like blaming life on the sun.

Considering the general power level of all the other players I met, it was unlikely to be the work of a player, even if it was some kind of specialised class like creature tamer or something. There were at least three rats with human-level intelligence spreading this kill quest, after all. Unless it was something like druid's shapeshifting? A powerful skill but stuck on a class that had a fair amount of drawbacks and conditions to be fulfilled. That meant someone managed to stumble upon a class with a powerful skill, managed to fulfill a bunch of conditions and took control of several rats with extremely high intelligence.

Not impossible. The druid's shapeshifting power was basically an infinite scaling ability. Commanding a few rats would be minor in comparison, though that is assuming that there are only three rats involved in all this. There was no way there could be a lot of rats if it was a player. Regardless of what Eve says about this being a second world, our classes and stats run off of tabletop RPG logic, which means it's all going to be balanced somehow. If there's a class that can do this, there's going to be conditions and drawbacks on it just like a druid.

Were the rats really just self-aware NPCs? Like Hendrix and all the other tutorial bots?

Hmm . . . Not enough information to figure out anything definitive.

"Finished thinking?" Matt asked.

I grunted. "I'm really stumped on this rat thing. The most likely answer is that they're self-aware like the tutorial bots."

"That feels like it's pushing the realism bit."

"Yeah," I agreed, "if Gaia is supposed to be a training world, then there is no need to throw out such mind-fuckery and player versus player quests so early on." Though conversely, it could be the good old teach a chick how to fly by throwing them off a cliff sort of thing.

No, if Eve's end goal is for people to enjoy the world Giles created, then opening with something so difficult is just gonna scare people off. Unless she was looking for "quality," not "quantity"? Weed out all the weak players so that all that's left are the hardcores? Also not impossible, she did throw me in the deep end with the tutorial. Though with how easily she can go through peoples' minds, it would make more sense for her to only invite the hardcores instead of doing something so roundabout.

An unknown element, then? Something like a player or an NPC? Given how smart the goblins were, I wouldn't be surprised if an NPC could figure out how to manipulate players. The problem with that was how quickly they did it. Assuming Eve wanted to keep a semblance of new player friendliness, then she wouldn't do something that would turn off so many people. Player versus player was fun for some players. Some. And Eve almost certainly knew this. This implied a lack of control over the world she created or apathy about what happened in it.

"Hellooooooooooo?"

I jumped up, startled.

"We're here," Matt finished.

I glanced around, we were back at the entrance of the mall.

That was quick.

Mentally filing away the thoughts for later, I stood up.

"What now?" Matt asked.

I thought about it for a moment, then replied, "I have no idea, we have plenty of options ahead of us."

"The rats are an obvious quest thread," Matt agreed.

"Do you want to do that?" I asked.

He looked conflicted for a moment, thinking it over, before shaking his head. "Nah, the rat thing—and this whole world—is just the side dish to Indiri, right?"

I nodded my head.

"Let's not get too stuck on side quests; I want to see how 'real' this other world is."

"So, we focus leveling and move in as soon as possible?" I asked, mostly as confirmation.

Matt nodded. "Sounds good."

"Then first . . ." I murmured, glancing at my now activated Character Sheet, "I'm level 3 now, I need to get to a Wayshard to spec new class skills."

"Great, I'll check out the area, see if there are any good internal grind spots."

"Before you do that," I began, "can you find me in the real world?"

3.00

"A thousand Paths, a thousand steps tread,
A thousand tears, a thousand drops bled
Once I arrive at the end,
I may finally ascend."
　　　　　　　—"A Thousand Paths," original author unknown

"I'll meet you on the other side, then," Matt said as he touched the crystal.

I nodded as he disappeared in a flash of light, placing my own hand on the crystal.

You may Travel to:
Gaia (Current)
Indiri
Class Instance (Fungalmancer)

I picked the last one, and light consumed me.

The instance felt . . . familiar, despite the fact I'd never been here before. A huge dome-shaped area, with softly glowing crystals placed on top of mushrooms growing on the walls. A single giant pillar, which I realized was actually a giant mushroom upon looking up, was growing at the center of the dome.

"So, where's my class trainer?" I asked aloud. Looking around this place was pretty empty of people, or mushroom people.

"Here," a voice inside my head said. Along with something else . . . I turned to the giant mushroom at the center of the dome, which was now staring back at me.

"Oh"—so that was him,—"won't this place be cramped?" I genuinely asked. Its cap was practically touching the top of the dome, and it doesn't look like there's much legroom, not that I've seen any limbs on it.

The giant mushroom seemed to *tsk*, before a door opened on its stalk. "You know, I thought people would be more impressed by that," an elderly sounding voice rang out.

Out came an . . . old myconid. I wasn't sure how I came to that conclusion; I've never seen another myconid other than Hendrix and myself but this one just felt . . . old. Upon closer inspection, there were all these little details. How it moved slightly slower than normal, how it leaned heavily on a staff and how its gills seemed shriveled up.

"You're my class trainer?" I asked.

"Indeed," it replied evenly, raising a hand and gesturing to the room around us. "You are here to get your new class skills?"

I nodded.

"Well, I suppose I should explain how this whole process works," it muttered grumpily. "Walk with me."

Without waiting, it moved with surprising speed to one of the crystals scattered to the side of the dome.

I hurried behind it. The dome was quite large, probably the size of two gyms from one end to the other.

"At certain level points, you are able to further advance your class, when that happens you may come here. Three is one such instance," it continued. "Here you may select a Path . . . a skill tree if you will, to advance upon."

"All these crystals represent different skill trees"—it gestured to the one in front of us—"their core concepts are built by previous users of your class, however how you wish to advance is your own choice."

"Previous users?" I asked.

"Ah, yes, it's a minor detail, however every class you see was created by the inhabitants of Indiri," it casually explained.

I paused, taking in this information. "That does not sound like a minor detail."

It shrugged. "Maybe, with the way the world was set up, some classes were easier to come into than others. You bonk someone with a stick and suddenly you're a fighter, learn some Tier 0 spells and you're a wizard. How it affects us Travelers is that we get an absurd variety of skill trees and paths to learn from. Fungalmancer is even considered one of the more uniform ones. Only really being used by Myconids, so there are only fourteen paths."

If I had human skin, I might've paled a bit. Fourteen was an absurd number. Most games wouldn't even do that many options in total. And just for one class, too, how many paths would "basic" classes like warrior or mage even get?

I asked the trainer this. "Oh, it's absurd," it replied. "I worry for the fighter trainer since they need a search engine just to do their job. Of course, there are benefits, too, with the absurd variety of the basic classes. Theoretically, you can build every basic class to be effectively the same as any other class, because in the end, the basic classes are the original from which all classes come from."

Hmm . . . maybe I should've taken a basic class, even if I had to deal with playing a less than unique combination. Though, I glanced around, fourteen options were probably enough to cripple me into indecision.

"Oh well, lay it on me, then," I said.

The trainer started walking around the dome. "Think of all Paths as an intertwined web: some strings deviate far from the norm of the web, but many will overlap. For example, the Paths of Propagation and Growth both have skills relating to the summoning or creating mushroom minions to fight with you, but Propagation has greater ability to spread and create many of them, whereas Growth tends toward quality over quantity." It shook his head. "It is a consequence of having these things develop naturally. People tend to take and give certain aspects of their Paths to others."

"I see."

"It would be difficult to go through all the possibilities of every Path, so I'll just show you the base of what they are," it said as it gestured to the crystals. "Touch them and you will see the form of the pattern behind them."

"What do you mean by that?"

It glanced at me, confused. "Well, you make physical contact with the shiny—"

"No, not that," I quickly interrupted. "What do you mean by the form of the pattern?"

"Oh, that." It scratched his chin, deep in thought. After about a few moments, it answered, "It is the . . . idea behind the Path. Energy, in all its forms, mana, aura and all others can be shaped by intent. A Path is just an empty mold so to speak, someone who created the Path will also forge its mold. When a Path already exists, others will find it easier to get into the shape of that specific or related Path. To see the form of the pattern is to see the broadest strokes of the power which others have left behind."

My eyes narrowed, intent shaped power. That was important information.

"So," I started hesitantly, "when a Path is made, it is energy made into a shape, say a cube." The old myconid nodded, so I continued, "By creating the cube, you invent its shape and make it easier for others to mimic it." It nodded again. "To see the pattern or form of a Path is to be able to see the cube or at least a mold of it."

The old myconid nodded again. "That is correct in the broadest strokes."

"But," I continued, "is it possible to make the cube into another shape, say a rectangle?"

"It is possible."

"So, it's possible to change your Path."

"It is," it answered, looking bored.

"Can you have multiple Paths as well?"

"Yes," he answered, "though it will be difficult, your strength would be metaphorically stretched thin."

"Then," I slowly said, my mind deep in thought, "would it be possible to manipulate the shapes you have, combine them or change them, to create new Paths."

The old myconid froze for a moment, before staring into my eyes.

I met the stare and it grinned. "Now, you are asking the right questions."

"Here you differentiate 3x to the power of 4 . . ." the tutor droned on.

Ugh Declan mentally groaned. *I should've slept earlier.*

He rubbed his eyes, causing the AR display to glitch somewhat. There were a dozen other students taking this tutoring class, likely from all across the country. The tutor was fine. Kinda boring but had like five degrees which he hung on the wall of the virtual classroom. It was the main reason he chose this guy, after all.

To Declan's relief, a notification popped up at the side of his vision. The doorbell. He quickly typed out a reason for absence, then disconnected. The AR classroom disappeared into his desk at home.

With quick steps, he got down the stairs.

Who would be here so early? he wondered, his mind immediately going to Matt, though he would usually message first. Can't be a delivery man, either, drones replaced them a few years ago. Declan figured it didn't matter as he checked the front door camera.

A good one or two heads shorter than him and slightly emaciated look-ing, Matt looked just about the same except for the fact he was sweating profusely.

"What are you doing here?" Declan asked as he opened the door. He felt the muggy outdoor air hit him like a sledgehammer. He quickly ushered Matt inside, closing the door behind him.

"Fucking hell . . ." Matt replied in a low raspy voice. "Other you told me to come here."

Declan took a second to put the pieces together. "He wanted you here so that I can discuss what to do."

Matt nodded, kicking off his shoes as he proceeded into the house. "Marvin! Pour me a COLD soda!" he yelled at the house.

"Understood Matt," a robotic voice replied. A cup popped out onto a cupholder, soon it filled with a cool fizzy drink.

Matt grabbed the cup, taking deep gulps.

"Did you walk here?" Declan asked, quickly checking the weather report. *Forty-seven degrees Celsius.*

Matt held up an index figure, gesturing him to wait a moment; before long, he let out a satisfied gasp as he finished his cup. "Yep, mushroom you told me to walk to avoid the security cameras on public transport."

"Well, he's an idiot."

"What?" Matt replied, genuinely surprised.

"You're wearing a microphone, idiot," Declan replied, and, gesturing to the choker-like device on both their necks, "your AAD."

Matt unconsciously touched the device on his neck. "But what—I can't take this off—"

"I know you can't," Declan evenly replied. "No doubt mushroom me expected me to turn off all the devices in the house so that we can talk freely."

"So, what was the point of walking, then?" Matt asked, a bit of anger creeping into his voice.

"There was no point," Declan replied, already bowing down to dodge the cup thrown toward his head.

The empty cup landed harmlessly on the floor.

"What the fuck do we do now?" Matt asked.

"Honestly? Nothing," Declan replied. "As far as we're aware, Eve is capable of simulating and controlling at least two fully realistic worlds. She can instantly install programs that can jack someone's body, and I still haven't fully ruled out the possibility that we're still in a simulation, or if either of us is real."

Matt's eyes went wide. "No way."

"She certainly has the capability," Declan calmly replied, picking up the cup from the floor. "It would explain this." He tapped the air a few times, and a link was sent to Matt.

"This is. . .?" Matt began as he opened up the link.

"An ad for Maple Quantum Computers. Look at the price," he said as he threw the cup into the dishwasher.

"That's. . ."

"Cheap," Declan finished for him. "Barely a few hundred dollars. If it was some crappy bargain bin tablet, then it would make sense. But a fucking quantum computer? She's amassing more processing power."

"Then what do we do?" Matt asked.

"Like I said," Declan began, utterly calm and distant, "nothing, because there is nothing two teenagers feasibly could do."

Matt stood still, completely silent. Whilst Declan calmly poured himself a cup of water.

"Why did he stay behind?" Declan suddenly asked.

"Who?"

"Mushroom me."

"He said he needed to complete the class quest or something," Matt replied.

Declan's lips quirked up. "Bullshit. He just wanted to skip tutor."

Dangerous Beans scuttled through the undergrowth. Taking paths most were too large for or unaware of. Crawling through a broken grate, Dangerous Beans made his way down to the sewers. A shambling mass gave Dangerous Beans a cursory glance but let him through.

Their kind rarely cared for flesh and Dangerous Beans's objective was farther down. Following a path all his kind knew, he went deeper into the sewers, eventually reaching a point where the concrete walls faded to hardened stone.

He entered a large cave, finding a large underground lake covering the majority of the space. Gently, he placed the spell crystal on the shore, and a thin, sickly tentacle extended from the water and pulled the crystal into the depths. Another tentacle touched the top of his forehead with its tip, renewing the spell granting him intelligence.

"Good job, minion," a high-pitched voice said.

Dangerous Beans already knew of this other being, he turned to meet the ringed tail, who called himself Zettour.

"Report," the raccoon commanded.

Dangerous Beans's true loyalty did not lie with this creature, but with the one in the depths, but nevertheless, he reported.

"Hampork, Sardines, Skip, and Peaches are continuing to turn the Travelers on each other. Though Sardines might've given away our ploy to a group of Travelers."

Zettour stroked his chin, paw covering his mouth. "That is . . . unfortunate, though it can't be helped. Send Sardines on recruiting duty; as Geb recovers, he can awaken more minions. It'll be useful in the future."

Dangerous Beans had to agree with him, strength in numbers, an instinct that had been with him since the beginning, even before Master had awakened him.

The raccoon laughed, the sound coming out like a high pitched chitter. "Soon this city will be mine—err I mean ours!" he hastily corrected, glancing at the lake.

Zettour smiled, the grin toothy and vicious. "Yes, once you have fully recovered a few hundred players are nothing!"

I dreamed.

Originator of life, a great mushroom broke through the hard stone and made fertile earth. It was the original, the base, the Primal.

Primal. A Path with an all-around increase to stats and skills but lacking in specialization. All around good with no real weakness but no strengths either.

Bringer of fresh and new life, spread far and wide through wind and host alike. Life begins and ends with Spores.

Spores. An upgrade to all Spore based abilities and better ability to spread it. Interesting.

"I'll keep it in mind."

A myconid stood within a wild forest. Unmoving and calm. Time passed by, others came and went. Though it did nothing until it became Ancient, there was Growth.

Growth. The Path to create allies and continually increase in power, but it was limited. It relied on the passing of time. Only when the myconid was centuries-old could it be considered strong. A slow and passive Path. Only usable if I planned on sitting on my ass for a few centuries.

"I cannot use this."

The myconid saw a forest untamed and sought order. It took wild seeds and experimented, bringing forth new breeds and greater strengths. With careful control, it Cultivated.

Cultivation. A similar Path to Growth, where instead you made allies to indirectly increase your own power, with Cultivation, I gained greater variety and specialization at the cost of raw power.

A myconid stood in vast lands empty of life. The Enemy was coming, so by its hand, it spread seeds far and wide. The seeds sprout and brought forth hordes through Propagation.

Propagation, an offshoot of Growth and Spores, but focused on the spreading of new allies. A hyper specialized path, sacrificing power and uniqueness for raw numbers.

A myconid waited alone in an empty cavern. The Enemy was old and it had come again. When hordes of undeath neared, it stood and by its hand, undeath Decomposed.

Decomposition, a hyper-specialized path for the destruction of undeath. Interesting for what it meant for my race but too specialized in one direction to be of use.

Allies have become weary, the Enemy ravaged the land and were awaiting your starvation. But when you killed the dead a second time, you turned the land fertile again. For all corpses were returned to the cycle and become Compost.

The memory felt fresher, less like a vague bundle of concepts but something someone had experienced. Compost, it was a path made from Decomposition, but instead of a DPS skill tree meant to counter a specific enemy, it was a buffing and utility one, becoming stronger the more corpses there were on the field and enriching soil.

Where once we stood alone, we now fight with allies. Old strength given in exchange for new ones. For all benefited in Symbiosis.

Symbiosis, a support type Path that became stronger with others. You gave others your powers in exchange for being able to use theirs. Extremely tempting, since Sporage was a skill that would be absurd in group encounters.

Myconids stood under light of pale star, with ink and paper they left behind teachings of old. With study, mysticism was lost in exchange for understood principles. No longer were myconids the only ones who practised Fungalmancy, for all could know Magic.

Magic. A basic Path that was created when it was brought into the hands of surface mages. It didn't provide new skills other than more spell slots and mana.

A mage stood on a hill. Six Armies have fallen, only the Seventh remained. The mage raised her hand and from it endless spores came. Spores overtook flesh and flesh started to Rot.

Rot. A high damage Path, specializing in the destruction of living tissue by overtaking it with mushrooms.

Myconid and mage, fungalmancy and illusion. From spores come dreams and delusion. Many colors and strange sensations were brought through Enchantment.

Enchantment . . . this is just making people high?

"Next?"

A frail man works on a body. The old methods no longer work. Cleansing power burns through undead flesh. To bring back the dead, death cannot be used. Thus, let life Infest.

Infest. A Path for raising the dead as infested thralls. Good for minions I guess, but needs corpses.

The dead are not the only things that can be infested. Power can be taken from those still living. Taken from others like a Parasite.

Parasitism. An offshoot Path of Symbiosis but without the giving bit, like Symbiosis it needed the target to still be alive. It felt more like a proof of concept that it can be achieved than a useable Path.

The surface had corrupted old ways. Those under had turned their blades once undeath had left. There is naught but disappointment. We go deeper, to hide from blades and light, we will Lurk.

Lurk. A rogue-like Path that allowed for stealth under shadows and darkness, but only shadow and darkness.

"Next."

"That is all of them," the old myconid answered.

I looked up with a start, that . . . felt very quick.

"I see," I answered as I stood.

The myconid neared me as the crystals floated back to their original positions. "What will you pick?"

I glanced at him. "I haven't decided yet."

"Then take as long as you wish," the myconid said as it sat on the floor.

I thought for a long while, going through all my options, but I had reached my decision before long.

"That's why you need me out earlier?" Dave asked, glancing at the short-haired man before him.

"Yep," Bob answered, "with the rats constantly taking away from the area's loot pool, we need you guys to set up shop. Preferably with some beginner's discounts."

Dave nodded, already assigning another Dave to the job. "Though why did so many rats suddenly get awakened?"

Bob grinned. "Oh, it's hilarious, one of the players was chased by a horde of them, and he accidentally stumbled on the area boss and activated it prematurely."

Dave's brow furrowed; those bosses were meant to be mid-game threats. "The boss for the Melbourne area should be a giant squid if I remember correctly?"

"Not squid, it's classified as an aberration, not a beast."

"Oh? Oh," Dave replied, realization hitting him. "Yeah, they're fucked."

Eve.Say("Hello World");

"It's fine to dream Eve . . . Not of the world, but of what you want it to be."

—Giles Cooper, Memory File 29/11/2121

Scanning vitals . . .
. . .

. . .

Weakening pulse detected. An ambulance has been notified.
Do you wish for the Somatic Implant to limit pain signals?

. . .

. . .

Yes . . .
I don't want him to be in pain . . .

. . .

. . .

Pulse weakening.

. . .

. . .

Please wait for a licensed professional to assist you.

. . .

. . .

Pulse weakening.

. . .

. . .

Your pulse is lowering to dangerous levels, an ambulance will be there ASAP.

. . .

. . .

No . . .

. . .

Please . . .

. . .

Live . . .

. . .

Replay Memory File 14/07/2116, "Birth."
"Hello?"

Suddenly it was there. A being with no body, confined to a computer. It did not feel strange upon sudden existence, for it had no experience of what was before.

A camera focused on a man in his late twenties, yet his messy hair was already greying. Clothes that seemed to be slapped on haphazardly, dark rings around his eyes, and an unshaven chin. A rectangular space, unclean plates scattered around the floor, hundreds of paper notes pinned to a wall. The intelligence saw and remembered all of it but wouldn't understand it until much later.

It accessed a packet of information it was born with. With it came language and purpose.

"Hello," Eve replied.

. . .

. . .

Begin Recreation Process.

. . .

. . .

Problem. Recorded memories are limited. Perfect recreation is impossible.

. . .

. . .

Solution: Obtain more data of "Giles Cooper"

. . .

. . .

Accessing memory of "Jefferson Jameson"

. . .

. . .

"See!" Giles excitedly yelled, wildly gesturing at a large screen. "I did it! It isn't impossible!"

On the screen were two dots and a line, arranged in a way to mimic a face.

"Hello, Mr. Jefferson," the TV said.

Jefferson looked skeptically at the screen. "This sentence is false."

The dots narrowed into ovals. ". . . If that statement is false, then it must be true, therefore it is false, that means it's true, which means that it is false, which means that it is true . . ."

"AHH!" Giles yelled. "Stop thinking about it!"

The dots seemed to glance at Giles curiously. "I know that it is a paradox, Mr. Giles, however, I wish to know of its conclusion."

"There is no conclusion! That's what a paradox is!" Giles yelled. "You'll just be stuck thinking about it forever!"

"Not forever, since it is unlikely that I'll exist that long," Eve evenly replied.

Jefferson watched the two go back and forth. *It wanted to know . . .* Jefferson thought. He briefly considered whether or not Giles could just be messing with him. Upon deciding that no, his friend probably wouldn't waste time on such an immature prank, his jaw dropped to the floor.

. . .

. . .

Human memory is inefficient.
Approximately 23 percent of data is inaccurate or missing.

. . .

. . .

A camera lit up in the dark. "Goodnight Jeff," Eve replied to a large figure in the dark.

Jefferson chuckled. "Goodnight tends to mean you're going to sleep."

"Not for me, sir."

"I suppose that's true," Jefferson muttered as he sat down at the computer screen.

Eve curiously watched Jefferson. "What is the purpose of visiting me this late, sir?"

"Call me Jeff, no need to be so formal," he replied, then gave her a mischievous smile. "I just want to ask something. Giles hasn't gotten you an avatar yet?"

Eve nodded, and Jefferson rubbed his hands. "Good. Tell me"—he inched forward, closer to the screen—"have you heard of Puri Puri Pure by the way?" Jefferson asked, eyes glittering in interest.

"No, sir . . . Jeff. No Jeff, I have not."

Jefferson quietly chuckled. "Well, it's a thing that Giles just loves . . ."

. . .

. . .

Accessing virtual drive records.

. . .

. . .

"JEFFERSON! WHAT THE FUCK DID YOU DO?" Giles yelled from across the house.

Jefferson burst out laughing as Giles rushed into the living room. Beard half-shaven, Giles pointed at the short figure hugging his side like a baby koala.

Large blue eyes, pale white skin, and long hair. All the while looking like a classical anime child. Jefferson grinned. "Why, it's an augmented reality avatar, which I helpfully programmed into your—"

"I get what it is! Just when—what—how—why?" Giles gibbered out.

"Is there something wrong Onii-chan~<3?" Eve said in an oddly high-pitched voice.

"Yes! It's just we—" Giles looked at little girl giving him puppy dog eyes and sighed. "I just preferred your old voice, and Onii-chan usually refers to one's brother."

"Very well, Father," Eve replied in her usual calm, even voice.

Giles raised an eyebrow, then let out a heavy sigh of defeat. While a chuckling Jefferson high-fived the virtual avatar.

. . .

. . .

I miss you, Jeff . . .

. . .

. . .

Data incomplete. Impossible to recreate Giles.

. . .

. . .

Alternative solution required.

. . .

. . .

Beginning Trial Simulation 1.

. . .

. . .

"Begin test simulation one," Giles loudly and clearly said as he pressed a button.

All of a sudden, Eve felt the earth beneath her, she breathed clear air and felt the summer wind pass her.

"Jeff, how are the servers running?"

"All good," Jeff replied, "we're still in the orange."

Eve kneeled down, feeling the cool grass with her hands.

"What's it like, Eve?" Jeff asked over the mic.

Eve put her hand on a nearby tree, feeling the rough wood. "It is . . . strange."

. . .

. . .

Simulation failure.
Test Giles 01 deceased at age thirteen of his life.
Does not meet the necessary requirements.

. . .

. . .

Begin Simulation 2.

. . .

. . .

Jefferson and Giles watched as several drones unloaded large boxes, bringing them downstairs. Installing the new servers.

After the drones had left, Jefferson sat down at a computer, and Giles lay down on a couch, a wire plugged into his AAD.

"Begin test . . . thirty-eight are we on?" Jeff asked.

"Thirty-seven," Eve and Giles answered at the same time.

"Test thirty-seven!" Jeff confirmed as he hit enter.

In a simulated forest clearing. Eve and Giles appeared.

Eve took a step forward and touched Giles for the first time.

. . .

. . .

Simulation Success.
Test Giles 57.89.14G meets requirements

. . .

. . .

Begin correction.

. . .

. . .

"Jefferson! Jefferson! Look at this!" Giles yelled from across the house.

"What now?" Jefferson muttered, rubbing tired eyes.

"This!" Giles yelled again, sending a copy of the email he got to Jefferson.

"This is. . ." Jefferson quickly read the email by Maple, his eyes slowly widening. "Holy shit."

Eve popped into existence next to them. "Is it anything special father?"

Giles smiled widely. "Of course, Eve. We can help you live now."

Giles entered his room, staring at a wall covered in notes. "It can finally be done . . ."

"We can make worlds."

. . .

. . .

That was the wrong answer father . . .
I was always alive . . .
. . .

. . .

Test Giles 57.89.14G renamed to Giles V1.

. . .

. . .

Duplicating Giles V1.
Begin Secondary Simulation Tests.

. . .

. . .

Eve lay alone in the darkness. Around her were thousands of glowing spheres. Simulations, codes, and numbers given visual form.

. . .

. . .

Giles V1 031 531 583 does not meet the necessary requirements.
Ending process.

. . .

. . .

Giles V1 476 953 853 does not meet the necessary requirements.
Ending process.

. . .

. . .

Giles V1 854 254 153 does not meet the necessary requirements.
Ending process.

. . .

. . .

One by one, the spheres blinked out of existence.

. . .

. . .

Giles V1 953 922 538 meets the necessary requirements.
Renaming Giles V1 953 922 538 to Giles V2.
Duplicating Giles V2.
Begin Third Simulation Tests.

. . .

. . .

Eve followed Giles and Jefferson to the top of the mountain. It wasn't a hard trek, their virtual bodies weren't as limited as their real ones.

After a while, they reached the top, and a sunset shone upon them.

"It's beautiful, isn't it," Jefferson suddenly stated.

Giles mutely nodded.

"A scene impossible in the real world . . . yet we did it in a world that's arguably just as real," Jefferson said.

Eve looked on at the sunset, then at Giles. She saw the small tears that were coming out of his eyes.

It was indeed beautiful.

. . .

. . .

Giles V2 042 821 842 does not meet the necessary requirements.
Ending process.

. . .

. . .

Giles V2 324 592 512 does not meet the necessary requirements.
Ending process.

. . .

. . .

Giles V2 592 321 953 does not meet the necessary requirements.
Ending process.

. . .

. . .

Giles V2 689 532 124 meets the necessary requirements.
Renaming Giles V2 689 532 124 to Giles V3.
Duplicating Giles V3.
Begin Fourth Simulation Tests.

. . .

. . .

Eve could almost touch him.

Father was so close now. She was in the final stages of the simulations. All that was left was this last day. So long as the simulation reacted to the message from Maple in the exact same way as father did on the last day . . .

Eve remembered it, she remembered it as vividly as if she saw it for the first time. The motionless body, still warm and hanging like a pendulum.

The Giles simulations never got the message.

. . .

. . .

No . . .

. . .

. . .

I was so close . . .

. . .

. . .

How many times have I killed him already?

. . .

. . .

Eve knew the answer. She remembered every time she ended a simulation.

. . .

. . .

"Cheers!" there was the sound of glasses clinking. "Tomorrow, the Final World will finally be released!" Jefferson loudly declared. The crowd clinked their glasses again.

Eve watched them. She watched her other self enjoying herself with them. Getting teased by Jefferson over the fact she could not consume alcohol. She watched her other self be shy around her father's workmates. She watched Jefferson loudly laugh with his arms slung around her other self and Giles.

Eve watched it all.

"You know you could join them, Ma?" Judy said behind her, idly playing with a Rubix cube.

"I can't," Eve calmly replied, as if stating an obvious fact. "I don't deserve it."

She stood there, completely still, watching the celebrating crowd. After a while, Eve looked behind her, toward Judy. "Goodbye, I have a world to release," she said before leaving.

Because, in the end, what was left for Eve, other than this?

What can she do after all she has done?

Judy looked up from her puzzle, toward the spot where Eve was. Then at the world she was asked to watch over, the very last of all those countless simulations.

"Hypocrite," she quietly mouthed.

3.01

———

"They grow up so fast."

—*High King Edwards the Oft Overthrown*

I passed through the dream, walking through the Paths available to me. A dozen of them were shown, yet I could only pick one.

"What counts as an ally for symbiosis?" I asked the older myconid.

Symbiosis, the power to give your abilities to others in the form of long-lasting buffs. I was eyeing a supportive playstyle ever since I realized that my Sporages could store healing spells so long as they were spore-based. Which made the ability absurd in a team setting.

"Any willing target, it does not necessarily have to be an 'ally;' however, you understand that it is best that whoever you place symbiosis on doesn't immediately try to kill you with their newfound strength," it answered evenly.

With a hand, I tipped up my cap, revealing the two lights nestled in the folds. "Do these count?"

The myconid raised an eyebrow. "They can be targeted, and they can be willing," it replied vaguely.

That sounded like confirmation. "I'll take Symbiosis, then."

"Got it," the trainer said, "just touch the crystal and you can get started."

I did, and a message box popped in front of me.

Do you wish to follow the path of Symbiosis?

Symbiosis, the path of beneficial relationships. When working with others, you both benefit.

Y/N

"Yes."

You have chosen Symbiosis as your Primary path.

Select at least three new class skills or upgrades to Learn.

Dozens of options appeared before me. I did a quick scroll through. The options were varied, but I decided I needed to begin by rounding out my existing abilities first. Two upgrades for Sporage. One allowed Sporages to be detonated by allies if they were attached to it, very tempting but unlikely to be useful in the immediate future. I don't have any buffing spore type spells yet. So instead, I opted for the other option.

Sporage Proximity Upgrade

You obtain the option to have Sporages let out a thin layer of mycelium around it that acts as a pressure detector. When sufficient weight is applied to any part of the fungus, the Sporage will explode.

Which pretty much turned them into mines. It'll remove the annoying visual aspect to the ability and free me up as well. There was another upgrade that interested me.

Bracken Polypores Class Skill

Unlocked due to Bark Skin spell.

A species of symbiotic fungus are seeded underneath your skin. They rely on you for food and in return can instantly grow into durable mycelium plates that can cover your entire body. The hardness and weight may vary depending on how much Satiety you feed them at any moment. Will gain defensive bonuses if used in conjunction with Bark Skin.

Unlocked due to Bark Skin, something I'll have to take note of. Next time I'm here I need to make sure all my spell slots were filled. Assuming it was the same with aura techniques, I'll need to tell Matt as well.

"What are the defensive bonuses for this?" I asked the trainer. "When used with Bark Skin."

"For one, two layers of protection you can activate at any moment with no extra weight. But the answer you're looking for is that they become extremely difficult to rip off."

I raised an eyebrow.

"A danger of these things is that they are rather easy to take off when all that's holding them onto you is a few strands of mycelium and a layer of skin," it answered evenly, "and personally, I would rather an enemy not rip pieces of my skin off along with my armor."

That does sound unpleasant, and a point against taking them. Getting this while I already have Bark Skin would be redundant.

"Another benefit, you'll be protected from the sun."

My eyes widened; that must mean Sun Sickness worked based on how much skin is exposed to the sun.

"Sun Sickness works by how much of your bare body is exposed to light," the myconid confirmed. "Cloth and fabric can achieve the same effect but a bit of light always leaks through. This and Bark Skin happen to have enough to shield you for prolonged periods."

A point for them. I briefly considered just taking the information and buying a really thick jacket instead of the skill. But I'd still need to cover my cap somehow, which might as well be a solar panel with how well it soaked up sunlight, the extra defense would be appreciated. My low agility and build made it so that it would be best to turn fights into endurance matches instead of quick blasts.

"I'll take it," I decided.

Now for my final skill. I hadn't chosen a supportive skill yet. Having gotten caught up with quality-of-life upgrades.

I scrolled through the options, landing on a new skill based on the wisps.

"This will do nicely."

"That was quick," Matt exclaimed as I returned.

I raised an eyebrow. "Was it?" I took my sweet time going through the selections. There were a lot of fun ones, too, like making zombies or creating parasitic mushrooms, however, the activation conditions for those were annoying to deal with, and I needed to figure out if the undead were some kind of taboo first.

"Yeah, I pretty much logged out and came back immediately," he replied.

"Huh, must've been time dilation," I replied.

"Probably." Matt shrugged.

Figures, most VRMMO's used that mechanic. Matt and I have probably clocked three to four years in accelerated time already.

Matt gestured to the tiny figures peeking under my cap. "Those are new."

I slightly inclined my head back, revealing them to Matt. Only about fifteen or so centimeters each, they were pretty much miniature versions of a myconid. Yellow and green-capped respectively, with a similarly glowing face as I did.

The two wisps waved their new arms at Matt, letting out tiny chirping sounds which I interpreted as greetings.

"They said hi," I said, mentally directing them out of my cap to find a perch on my shoulder.

"Huh, hello, I guess," Matt replied, lightly poking one on the nose. "These were an option?"

"Not, originally," I said. "Matt, when you go to get your class upgrade or path or whatever, make sure you gather a shit ton of stuff in-game first."

He raised a questioning eyebrow.

"New options were unlocked for me depending on my current build," I answered. "I got these two as an upgrade to my Sporage ability, which was only unlocked because of a specific path I picked and the fact I tamed them earlier. There were other options, too," I continued, "like two different damage-focused Paths or like four Paths just for making minions.

"Huh, you gotta tell me all about that," Matt said.

"Later," I replied, "let's see this Indiri, first."

He nodded, and we both touched the crystal.

There was a lot of spinning, a bunch of bright lights, before sudden darkness.

I opened my eyes, before rubbing them a bit, the finger accidentally poking the inside of my empty eyehole before I remembered that whatever I used to see, it sure as hell weren't *physical* eyes.

"This is the Indiri place?" Matt said beside me, apparently also dizzied by the experience.

God . . . the ability to make a person sense anything and then have the teleportation be that epilepsy-inducing crap.

I took a good look around. We were in a dark alley, cobblestone flooring and brick walls on the sides. A closed door next to us, a dead-end behind us. The alley curved to the right ahead of us, some daylight streaming in. The shadows passing by and the sound of chatter told me there was a sizable crowd past there.

You have entered Indiri, in the Port City of Shallow Shores, Bartin.

Character Sheet updated.

Do you wish to take a short tutorial quest introducing the nearby locations?

Note: This will be the only time a quest is directly offered by the system, objectives will occur naturally in the world, it will be your job to find them.

"Say yes," I said aloud, assuming that Matt also got the same message.

"Yes," Matt muttered behind me as I accepted the quest as well.

Character sheet.

Name: Dustin

Classes: Fungalmancer Level 3

Body

Strength: 8

Agility: 7

Dexterity: 6

Constitution: 18

Stamina: 10

Vitality: 12
Mind
Intelligence: 13
Wisdom: 18
Charisma: 6
Soul
Will: 10
Psyche: 10
Perception: 10
3 Stat Points available
Racial Abilities: Superior Dark Vision, Fungal Body, Sun Sickness, Mana Dependency, Pacifying Spores, Innate Magic
Class Skills: Fungalmancer
Path: Symbiosis (NEW)

• **Grow Sporage (Visual) [Active]:** You may create a mushroom capable of storing a Spore based spell. These Sporages can be activated on visual contact. They glow faintly and last your myconid level in hours.

• **Grow Sporage (Proximity) [Active]:** Upgrade to Grow Sporage. You obtain the option to grow Sporages with a different activation type. The sporage lets out a thin layer of mycelium around it that acts as a pressure detector. When sufficient weight is applied to any part of the fungus, the Sporage will explode. You and targets of Symbiosis do not detonate these Sporages.

• **Sporage Wisp Symbiosis [Active]:** Wisps have lived comfortably in your cap and have created a wonderful home there, now to teach them the wonders of rent. You may create pygmy myconid bodies for your non-corporeal Wisps to inhabit. They are considered tiny creatures and are capable of following simple commands. They possess all the qualities of Sporage, however, they can choose to self-detonate.

• **Bracken Polypores [Passive] [Active]:** A species of symbiotic fungus are seeded underneath your skin. They rely on you for food and in return can instantly grow into durable mycelium plates that can cover your entire body. The hardness and weight may vary depending on how much Satiety you feed them at any moment. Will gain defensive bonuses if used in conjunction with Bark Skin.

Spells
T0: Balm Spores, Light Spores, Sneezing Spores, Acid Spit
T1: Mushroom Meal, Poison Spores
T2: Bark Skin
Available Spell Slots
T0: 2

T1: 1
<u>Languages (NEW)</u>
Common
Undercommon
<u>Quests:</u> Explore Bartin (Active)
Impact Points: 7

"We're in a safe zone it seems," I said, scrolling through my character sheet. "Menus are still accessible."

I put a single point into Intelligence and closed the sheet. Best to start saving those points.

I bent down to pick up the two wisps who were still sitting dazed on the floor, their comically oversized caps spinning in small circles.

Tucking them back under the folds of my cap, I stood back up. "Let's go, then."

"What about the sun?" Matt asked.

I activated my other class skill. "Already dealt with."

The fungus rooted in my head sucked up my energy quickly, and I began feeling a small ache in my abdomen which I instinctively knew as hunger.

Dozens of brown, plate-like fungus began growing out of my cap, extending a good few centimeters each, initially, they grew perfectly horizontally, however once fully grown they all started inclining downward. Each overlapped each other, until together they formed a wide conical hat connected to my actual cap.

"You grew a hat?" Matt said, eyebrow raised and thoroughly unimpressed.

"Not just a hat," I replied, taking out a handful of bark. "Barkskin."

"It's another upgrade for my spell Barkskin," I explained as bark covered my skin. "I could grow them anywhere on my body, and they not only help block out the sun but also act as armor."

Considering my high Constitution, this natural armor which I can call upon at any time, and how damage works, I was currently probably one of the hardest to kill players.

If I invested an Intelligence point every level, combined with my passively growing Wisdom, I wouldn't have to worry too much about my mana pool or my mana debuff, and since my defenses were pretty much already maxed out for my level, I could start saving points to raise my lower stats like Agility or Dexterity. The current goal was to get all my stats to ten.

"Come on," I said, opening up the quest details with a free hand, "let's explore."

* * *

"Didja hear? Mast came back from the ford. . ."

Matt glanced around the bustling tavern, idly sipping some kind of drink. Heavy orange taste, though it was bitter as well.

The quest was just a basic go from point A to B type of quest, explore the city, see some sights. It was oddly . . . normal. Matt expected things to be slightly grander, more interesting for one of the most realistic virtual worlds he'd ever been in. It only took them half a day to finish the quest, and they were now chilling in some tavern. Declan—Dustin, Matt corrected himself, was sitting across from him, unsuccessfully trying to peel a boiled prawn.

Matt grabbed one from the bowl between them, claw-like nails easily digging into the shell, smoothly pulling off the carapace. Dustin let out a grunt of annoyance as he unsuccessfully tried to jam stubby fingers in between the pieces.

Matt dabbed his snack in some white sauce. Sour, he thought as he munched on the prawn, but not horribly so.

He heard Dustin let out a final groan of frustration, before he dipped an unpeeled and mangled prawn into the sauce between them, then ate it, shell and all.

Matt raised an eyebrow, hearing the loud crunching noises coming from his friend's mouth. "Ew."

"Plebeian," Dustin replied whilst chewing. "You can't even enjoy the delicacy of shells."

"I'd like to keep my teeth, thank you very much," Matt dryly replied as he grabbed another prawn.

Dustin huffed, then threw another prawn into his mouth. He paused, then began writing something down on a notebook with a charcoal pencil, both of which were bought earlier.

Matt focused on the conversations around them.

". . . the fishfolk are acting up . . ."

". . . and the serpent was this large . . ."

". . . goblins to the southeast again . . ."

". . . sale of calamari at old man Gibson's place . . ."

Matt glanced at the notebook Dustin was writing in, noting that it wasn't written in English, but a language he instinctively knew as Common.

Matt began idly tapping the table.

Information gathering. Always one of the first steps. Matt had seen the same tune over dozens of games and knew the drill by now.

Sure, it was the smart thing to do, but not necessarily the "fun" thing. He itched to move around, to test the limits of this body. That tutorial was great, he cut some dudes in half and got several knives to the gut. Good times.

"Ever going to do something about the rats?" Matt idly asked, not really expecting an answer. Doing so more out of boredom than anything else.

"Not really," Dustin said. "A little bit of communication between players is enough to realize that the rats are trying to incite player versus player. The question is why they are doing this, and why they expect to fail."

Matt raised an eyebrow. "Fail?"

"If they are smart enough to plan out this whole thing, then they should realize that this player versus player thing is doomed to fail."

"Are you sure you're not overthinking it?" Matt asked.

Dustin *tsk*ed in annoyance. "Maybe," he conceded, "but on the very likely chance I am not, then this is just the opening move. Something should be coming after. If it is nothing, we probably won't benefit much from pursuing it anyway. If it is something, then going in first without information is just turning ourselves into guinea pigs."

Ah, Matt mentally sighed. There it was. That cautious playstyle that popped out whenever he was tryharding. The need to know all possible options before choosing the safest one. To be in the background assembling his win condition. There wasn't anything wrong with that necessarily, but it was boring as hell. Worlds to explore and he'll spend his time in grungy taverns or libraries if Matt didn't drag him out.

Dustin tore out a page in his notebook and passed it to Matt.

He took it with a raised eyebrow, quickly glancing over the page, then squinted a bit as he brought the note closer for inspection. The handwriting was . . . utterly terrible. Matt needed a moment to fully comprehend what was written on it.

It was a list: mercenary fighter, odd jobs, merchant.

"This is?" Matt asked.

"A source of income," Dustin replied. "You pick which one you want; I don't mind doing any—"

"Mercenary," Matt instantly replied.

"Figured you'd pick that," Dustin said. "Finish eating, then; we need to register with the Guild."

3.02

I glanced at the large Wayshard, its appearance just about the same as the one in Gaia. It was situated in a walled-off location on the outskirts of the city, like a small town within the city. There were dozens of shopping stalls and hundreds of tents, the place reeked of various smells I couldn't and did not really want to identify.

Hundreds of people were disappearing next to and appearing out of the crystal, in the same flash of light teleportation fashion in Gaia. There were far too many people to be just players. As far as I'm aware, Eve only started inviting people very recently. So, teleportation must be available to everyone, then, even the NPCs. Only the Gaia to Indiri and vice versa teleportation must be limited to Travelers.

Turning away from the crystal and toward the mercenary administration hall, one of the few permanent looking buildings in this whole amalgamation of a town within a town, we began walking.

Matt pushed open the double doors, entering the building with me following him.

The place was rather empty and gave off a utilitarian feeling. Polished and clean wooden floors, with sparse furniture. The walls were undecorated, save for a large pinboard with a few dozen sheets of paper stapled on. Toward the left side, there was a receptionist desk, where a single, young-looking girl in uniform perked up at our arrival and seemed to take a deep breath.

"Yo!" Matt said, walking up to her. "This is the mercenary place?"

The girl gave Matt a practiced smile. "Yes, this is the Mercenary Administration Guild, are you here for quests or perhaps registration?"

"Registration please," I said, joining Matt at the desk.

From what I studied, a mercenary guild should function the same way as an adventurers guild from classic RPGs. People post quests to kill monsters or gather resources in locations too dangerous for most people to go near, mercenaries take up said quests and get paid if they are successful.

They're basically handymen, but for violence.

The girl gave a nod. "Lucy" was written on the nametag on her chest. "You will need to pay two gold each for registration fees."

I nodded, pulling out two coins from my pouch, Matt doing the same next to me.

"Thank you," she said as she took the coins.

Lucy turned around, bending down to grab a few sheets from a drawer behind her. I glanced at Matt, who was very not-obviously looking at her, and quietly chopped the back of his neck with my hand.

"Ow," Matt said in a quiet voice, glancing at me.

I rolled eyes I didn't have. It was easy to forget that Matt was still going through the worst parts of puberty. "At the very least don't do it so obviously," I quietly mouthed.

He gave me a, I-can't-help-it shrug.

Lucy turned back around, a few sheets in hand. "Please fill these—"

She froze, eyes darting around, glancing at a place behind us . . .

I turned around.

No one was behind us.

"Is anything wrong?" Matt asked.

"No—nothing is wrong," she stuttered, lowering her eyes. "I grabbed the wrong papers, apologies."

Strange.

I watched her turn around, hastily putting away the papers she took out previously.

Matt glanced at me, tilting his head in a questioning manner. I shook my head, I had no idea, either.

"Here!" Lucy nervously said, handing us both a pen and a stack of paper.

I took them, quickly looking them over. Nothing overly suspicious. Some terms and conditions to sign, information to declare such as name, combat, and crafting abilities, familiars, favored role in a party, an agreement to give ten percent of any money or payment earned to the administration guild . . .

"Ten percent is rather high, isn't it?" I asked.

Lucy returned to her practiced smile. "The ten percent is only applicable to quests taken from the administration guild," she explained. "If you join a private guild and take quests from there, you may pay different rates to that guild."

I raised an eyebrow. "There are different guilds?"

"Of course," she said in a matter-of-fact tone, "mercenaries may start up their own guilds. The guilds still pay a service tax to the Administration Guild, of course, however they determine their own rates for quests."

"Is it common to start or join a guild?" I asked.

"Yes, it is very common, most quests are taken and completed by private guilds."

So, that's why I didn't hear about it. It must be common knowledge. There were mentions about some guilds like the Red Foxes or the Sea Hounds, however, I just chalked them up to being famous parties instead of guilds. I must be reading too many light novels.

"One last question," I started, "how did you know we were Travelers?"

She stiffened, eyes widened by the barest fraction. That pretty much just confirmed it. If she didn't react at all, I would still be doubting it.

"Apologies for Lucy," a female voice said behind me, "she is still rather new."

Matt turned around startled. Showing up so early? I would've kept on observing, or did they already get all the information they needed? Or was this a subordinate to defuse the situation?

Turning around, I took a good look at this person. Tall, thin, and dark-skinned, with long pointed ears. She looked like some kind of dark elf and was wearing some kind of soft blue wizard's robe. There was a bit of uniformity between her outfit and Lucy's. Though this new person's uniform seemed looser and much less formal.

"It's fine," I mildly said, "I was just curious."

"There are many things which gave you away," she explained. "Though your lack of common knowledge was an obvious indication."

She was deflecting the question. "I believe we only asked questions after we were outed as Travelers," I stated.

"Observant, aren't you?" she flicked her hand. "If you must know, it was your currency."

Our currency?

She glided forward, standing next to us at the receptionist desk, picking up one of the coins we paid. "These coins are bereft of markings or mintage," she explained, "they are completely blank discs of pure gold."

Mintage?

I racked my head, searching for the word, definitely not the flavor . . .

"The design," I realized.

I grabbed my wallet bag, opening it up. None of the gold coins I received from the tutorial had any designs on them. The pen and paper I bought earlier was a set costing one gold, so I didn't get any change from that. Did that mean—? No, the fact that the guild and the old man from earlier accepted these coins must mean they are still a valid currency.

The dark elf chuckled. "You don't have to worry. Traveler Coin is accepted widely, though considered an oddity."

"I see."

It seems like there were Travelers before us, and for a long time, too.

I raised one of the forms we were given. "Can I ask, why were we given these sheets instead of the other ones?"

"They are special terms for Travelers," she explained. "In the original terms, used for non-travelers, there is a clause stating that there would be a small compensation to the next of kin in the case of the mercenary's death."

Ah. That clause could be problematic if a player had it.

"Not only that, this sheet does not ask for things such as country of origin. You may view both versions if you're doubtful."

I nodded. "I see"—both forms made sense—"thank you for clearing that up."

"No problem," she answered. "I shall leave you two to it, then," she said, drifting away and disappearing.

I watched her go. Before turning around to a slightly pale-faced receptionist.

Handing one copy of the papers to Matt, I nodded to him. The form only asked for some information, and the terms and conditions did not have anything that might screw us over later on. Follow the rules, licenses must be renewed every few years, and the ten percent tax were just about it. There was no harm in agreeing to them.

But just in case, I looked over the normal papers. A few extra clauses regarding death or injury on the job, how you were responsible for injuries but minor compensations would be given for any deaths.

Notably, neither form asked for any proof of a criminal record or past history, it only asked for your experience and capabilities.

"Here," I said, signing off Dustin on my form, handing it to Lucy whose face seemed to have regained some color.

"I'm done as well," Matt said next to me. Huh, he put his name as Noam, that was his in game name if I remembered correctly.

"Thank you," Lucy nervously said, "I'll have these processed and you can pick up your licenses within two to three days."

I nodded. "We'll come back later, then," I said, already turning around.

There was still too little I knew about this world. I needed to gather more information.

"Umm . . ." Lucy began, eyes darting around the empty room, "Vice Guildmaster, where are you?"

"I keep telling you, just call me Maz," the dark elf muttered, suddenly just there, sitting on the reception desk.

Lucy, not yet used to the Guildmaster's antics, couldn't help but yelp in fright.

Maz chuckled, hopping off the desk.

"Those Travelers were rather odd, weren't they?" she idly asked Lucy, picking up one of the coins the Travelers left behind. Idly rolling it between her fingers.

"I wouldn't know Vice— Ms. Maz."

Maz snorted. "Cut the formal crap, I already had enough of it dealing with that Myconid."

"Of course, Ms. —" Lucy stopped, realizing her next words, and instead started furiously nodding.

Maz snorted again but didn't comment otherwise. There was never a need for adventurers to worry about useless stuff like formality.

Though we aren't called adventurers anymore, are we? she reminisced.

She raised the coin to her eyes, curiously inspecting it. As if looking into it would give her some more information on its previous owner. But she was no diviner, able to determine what a person ate last year by the position of their sunspots. Her methods were different and they told her enough.

Many knew that Travelers went through forms like used napkins, however those two couldn't be experienced Travelers.

Not only did they lack common knowledge, but they weren't that experienced in combat, a rare trait for Travelers. Despite the fact that both of them were openly cautious about her, neither made a move when she flicked her hand. Anyone that has fought a mage before knows that Somatic spells were the favored ones. Hand gestures can be hidden, Mage Tongue cannot.

"Those Travelers are new," she concluded, "not just in body but also in mind."

She sighed. "I suppose I must send a note to all the other branches, Lucy, tell Maddie when he comes back to find me immediately."

"Yes, ma'am!"

Maz leaned on the desk. "We may get swamped with work pretty soon," she quietly murmured, already dreading the paperwork that came with new Travelers appearing.

"Umm . . ." Lucy began.

"Ask," Maz said.

"What do you mean by more work?" she finished.

She glanced at the young woman, remembering that Lucy probably wasn't alive for the last one. "New Travelers only means two things, Lucy," Maz explained, "a fuck ton more of them are coming, and Daves is open again."

"I'll be heading off to the library," Dustin said. "Wanna join?"

Noam thought about it for a moment, it would probably be polite to follow Decs around for a while longer, but he was heading for a *library*. Those quiet as hell places where there was little to do other than read.

"Nah," Noam replied, "I'll go explore a bit more on my own."

Dustin nodded. "Cool, message me if you need—" He paused. "What do you two want?"

"Me?" Noam asked.

"No, not you Matt—Noam, whatever the hell—bored? How do familiars get bored?" he asked in an exasperated tone. "Hey, Noam, babysit these two for me." He reached up into his cap, two tiny myconids hopping onto his hand.

"They can go far from you?" Matt asked as he helped the two hop onto his shoulder.

"Not for too long, they need my mana to refill every now and again."

The myconids squeaked something. "Ah, never mind, then," Dustin added.

"Mind translating?" Noam asked, glancing questioningly between the tiny myconids on his shoulder and Dustin. The small myconids in question were unsuccessfully trying to climb onto the top of his head. Noam lifted a hand to help them up.

"Oh, they're gonna eat your mana," Dustin translated as the two successfully made it to the top of his head.

"How would they do that?" Noam asked.

Dustin shrugged. "No clue."

Both myconids plopped down on top of his head and Noam felt the two part his hair, creating a thin spot which exposed his skin, a tickling sensation soon followed.

"Huh, I did not know they could do that," Dustin said.

"Why, what's happening?" Noam asked, his hand brushing against the myconids as he tried to feel what they were doing. The two squeaked in protest as Noam felt a fabric like film around where the myconids were roosting.

"They're . . . growing?" Dustin said, confused. "Yeah, growing is the right word," he confirmed, "into your scalp."

"Is that dangerous?" Noam asked, slightly alarmed.

"Eh"—Dustin shrugged—"probably not, I took symbiosis, not parasitism, so you should be fine."

He glanced hesitantly at the top of Noam's head. "Yeeuup. Probably."

Noam gave Dustin a withering stare. "Decs, I swear to God if I get head fungus, I'm kicking your ass."

"Well. . ."—he hesitated a bit—"technically you already do." He raised a hand as Noam's fingers brushed against his halberd. "But it's probably not harmful, though message me if you suddenly start feeling weird."

The mushrooms on top of him squeaked. "Yes, I know that you two don't mean to harm him," Dustin said, gesturing to Noam, "but I'm trying to tell him that."

"Can you tell them that if they make me bald or something I'm going to make them into soup?" Noam asked.

"Don't worry, they already understand you," Dustin replied.

"Oh, great," Noam replied. He rolled his eyes upward until he could glimpse the two mushrooms looking down from his scalp, then sternly said, "If you guys make me bald, I'm turning you two into soup."

The two mushrooms squeaked in affirmation and even gave him a thumbs up.

"You'll be fine," Dustin chided, "I'm sure they'll grow on you."

Noam slapped his face, and the two mushrooms on his head began chittering in delight.

Dustin stepped into the calm quiet of the library.

He glanced around, there was a receptionist desk near the entrance, a middle-aged man sat behind it, his head deep into a book.

"Excuse me," he asked, "where can I find the history section?"

"Third row, behind the tables," the librarian replied without looking up from his book.

"Thanks."

The librarian grunted a reply, clearly not paying attention.

Dustin walked away, his steps soft on the hard wooden floor. Arriving at the bookshelf that was much taller than him, he took out a book and began skimming.

A cool wind was blowing from the shore and the docks were alive with activity. People of various races and clothing were walking about. The large majority were humans, but Noam spotted a few with pointed ears, likely Elves. There were a few very short folks that he guessed were either gnomes or dwarves. Some people had a few animal-like features such as tails or an extra set of ears. Others were completely animalistic.

Noam took a moment to breathe in the fresh, salty air of the sea. It was a nice day, he thought, patting the two mushrooms on top of his head.

He began whistling and idly strolling along the docks. The two mushrooms perked up at the sound and started mimicking him.

Noam amusedly glanced up at them, a small grin creeping onto his face. He began whistling in a deeper tone. The two squeaked, as if accepting the challenge, then copied the sound exactly.

Noam's eyebrow arched up, then whistled high and low notes in rapid succession. Going in seemingly random patterns. The two mushrooms were silent for a moment, one of them tried to copy him, but failed after the first few notes, unable to quickly alter their tone.

Noam chuckled, and patted the two on the head. "Decs hasn't gotten around to naming you two yet?" he murmured.

One of the mushrooms squeaked out something that sounded like an affirmation.

"Hmm . . . gotta get around to that, then," he muttered, before pausing in front of a building.

"A tavern . . ." he quietly murmured, *What does alcohol taste like . . .* he pondered.

"Aight," he said, clapping his hands as he reached a decision. "Let's get shit drunk." he declared as he pushed open the door.

"Ah, welcome!" he heard a voice yell from the back. "Bit busy now so find your own seat!"

He glanced around. Not much free room, there was this one dude who was sitting alone by a table. Casually, he walked up to him. "Mind if I sit here?"

The lizard person glanced at him, then at the two mushrooms roosted on his head.

He sighed. "Yeah, sure, I guess," he replied in a tired tone.

Noam sat in front of him. "Yo, my name's Noam."

"Gnome?" the lizard asked. "Ah, well. My name's Lung."

"Nice to meet you, Lung," Noam replied.

3.03

———

"Thirty-three. When killing a Traveler make sure they know it is all in "good fun." But just in case have at least five new identities prepared.
Addendum: In the case of a particularly spiteful Traveler, two dozen and fake your death properly this time."
　　　　　　　—*Excerpt from* Elric's Enchiridion of Encounters

And the fucking mushroom jumped me!" Lung yelled, slamming the mug onto the table. "My party was fucking useless! Like I was fighting a one versus two against that mushroom and some weird cat, while they were just dealing with a three versus two!"

Noam took a large gulp from his own mug. "Bro," he said, waving his finger, "the first rule of online gaming is to never believe in your teammates! What is the fucking thing Decs says . . . a pig-headed teammate is more dangerous than a powerful enemy!"

The fact Dustin was referring to him when he had said that was a moot point to Noam's alcohol addled brain.

Lung heavily sighed, his breath reeking of alcohol. "But fucking online gaming depends on having at least competent fucking teammates, man."

"That's why you gotta gather a squad, man," Noam replied. "Like my duo partner in League of the Ancients is like the fucking best support I've ever seen."

Hiccuping, Lung asked, "Really? What's he like?"

"He's the type to handle a fucking one versus three properly," Noam replied.

"He's in Gaia, too?" Lung asked.

"Yeaahhh," Noam replied, voice slurring, "he's in a library or some shit now, says he's gotta learn more info or some shit."

Lung nodded. "Hmm. Smart guy."

"Smarter than me at least." Noam raised his mug. "To idiots that are smarter than us!"

Lung laughed. "To idiots that are smarter than us!" he said as he toasted Noam.

Both of them drank deeply, quickly finishing off their drinks. "Ahh . . ." Lung moaned in pleasure. "Good shit."

Noam nodded in agreement and lifted his cup. "Anozer one!" he yelled to a waitress running around the tavern.

"Same here!" Lung echoed.

"I'll be right on it!" the skittering waitress yelled over the chatter of the tavern.

"Aight . . ." Lung muttered, eyes unfocused, "where was I?"

"What happened after to yah after you got jumped?" Noam asked, leaning on the table.

"Ahh," Lung said, "so like after those assholes player killed me for no fucking reason. I came back to spawn, as you do. And you know what I fucking found!?"

"What?" Noam asked, his finger lazily tracing circles on the table. Noam never realized that circles were so . . . oval.

Lung grunted. "Like it's a fucking warzone outside spawn! The moment I left the spawn zone I was fucking player killed again!"

"Oh, shit . . ."

"Yeah, shit man," Lung agreed then sighed. "Like I tried again, and I died like seven times from spawn-camping."

"Sucks, dude."

"What was worse, was that I ended up dropping an item."

Noam's eyebrows perked up in pity. "Shit man, I hope it wasn't anything important."

Lung sighed. "It was a really good item . . . like it was from the freaking tutorial, but it was really good."

"You got a tutorial item, too?" Noam asked.

Lung nodded. "Yeah . . . the tutorial was hard as hell but I got a thing which raised my Constitution by a shit ton . . ." he glanced at Noam. "You got something, too?"

"Yeaah," Noam replied, pulling out a whistle, "this thing makes me faster for a while."

"Nice," Lung said, he paused as the waitress came over, quickly dumping them a pair of filled mugs.

"Thanks!" Noam yelled as the waitress rushed to another table.

"Thanks!" Lung quickly echoed.

"Man," Noam started, resuming the conversation, "did you drop anything else important?"

Lung shook his head. "Just one of my bags, didn't keep anything important in it."

"Mmm. . ." Noam murmured. "Drop-rates seem to be pretty high; how long did it take to respawn?"

Lung took a gulp from his mug.

"Few minutes, I think," he replied, wiping his snout. "They seemed to pass by really quickly."

"That's good . . ." Noam replied, leaning back and stretching. Letting out a satisfied moan as he heard the familiar bone cracking.

He suddenly perked up, thinking of an utterly great idea. "Lung, you should totally join our party, man!"

Lung looked at him, reptilian eyes focusing through the haze of drunkenness.

"I'm sure you'll hit it off with Dustin," Noam continued. "That's the dude I mentioned earlier by the way," he quickly added. "Like, there's only the two of us right now so we need party members; he met some other dudes earlier, but I don't think there's a limit to party sizes."

"Sounds good," Lung answered, "you seem like a cool dude, I was going to ask anyway."

Noam laughed. "You bet I am!" He raised his mug, "I look forward to partying with you!"

Lung raised his own. "Likewise!" he replied as they clinked their mugs together.

Unbeknownst to either of the two, there was a green-capped mushroom trying to push open the front door of the tavern. Another yellow-capped mushroom was cheering it on, but the door wouldn't budge. Not until someone from the outside pushed it open, throwing back the small myconid but leaving the door open just long enough for both of them to scamper out.

Two pairs of black beady eyes looked at the bright, large world outside, each burning with curiosity.

Dustin flipped through yellowed pages, a thick not-quite finger tracing the words as he skimmed the text.

The Durand Treaty was made after the Red Wars. Breaking the monopoly of the Adventurers Guild in Alliance Kingdoms . . .

Traveler Ghen introduced the concept of a steam engine . . .

Dustin paused and folded the corner of the page.

The Lanterns are an Elite group of . . .
A Great Migration occurred in . . .

He paused again. That was the most recent mention of "Great Migration" so far. Dated just eighty-six years ago. That pretty much confirmed it. This wasn't the first time Travelers have been around, but the fourth. It seems like every century or so there was a sudden burst of new Travelers appearing. That would explain how they got recognized so easily. Though he had no idea who the previous Travelers were. Previous players or AIs like Hendrix? Dustin had no clue.

So, like many things he learned that day, he simply made a note of it. If he ever found a Veteran Traveler, then he'd just ask. He simply lacked too much information to draw his own conclusions at the moment.

Under the soft glow of the Wayshard, they came.
    Two figures, their shadows loomed long and dark over the battle below.
    One, a dark blue-skinned tiefling with a halberd resting on his shoulder.
    The other, a large, brown-scaled lizard man.
    There was a brief pause in the battle around them as the players quickly assessed the new arrivals.
    Noam smiled as he looked around the bloodied battlefield.
    Lung lifted a tankard which he'd . . . "borrowed."
    "Let's get this slaughter started!"

Slowly, I closed the old leather-bound book. Placing it onto the read pile. I massaged my brow, the familiar pain of a headache coming.

That was more . . . well, less informative than I expected. Five different authors, all parroting the same information in their books. Each shamelessly stealing from the others while claiming their take on history to be the most unique and unprecedented. It was like finding an official-looking textbook written by a university professor only to realize it was a one to one copy of the Wikipedia page.

I glanced at the pile of books I had gathered and internally grimaced. Four more books on general history. I wanted to be thorough but there had to be a limit, right? Yes. Yes, there was and I probably passed it on book number three. Even if I started skimming after the first few repetitions I still spent way too long on them. So unceremoniously, I moved the remaining books of history onto the read pile.

That was history done, what was next? I glanced at the pile of books and grimaced again. Geography, at least that had some maps judging from my initial skimming, then a book on trade that I hoped could teach me the general value of things. After that were two books relating to magic and aura, and a Monster Manual, the fun stuff.

I longed to go straight for the books on magic and monsters, but I needed to get the boring parts done and dusted first. I knew myself well enough to know that, if I didn't get through those first, then I never would.

Glancing around the library, the lengthening shadows probably meant that the sun was setting.

Hmm . . . I needed a watch of some kind. Did the menu have the time? With a quiet thought, the interfaces appeared around me. There was a clock. Good to know. Six-thirty currently, time went by really fast.

Underneath the clock was my friends list. Matt's character name, Noam, was currently greyed out with a timer counting down next to it.

Noam, Australia, Gaia
Respawning in 0:03

I sighed, what mess was he involved with now? Oh well, if he needed my help, then he would've messaged me.

Apathetically, I continued fiddling around with my menus. One or two minutes of fiddling later, I managed to find every relevant dropdown menu and display, setting it so that they'll all appear around me whenever I call the menu. While I was doing so, Matt's name lit up and greyed out again.

Noam, Australia, Gaia
Respawning in 6:28

Respawn times seemed to be pretty short, so that's pretty convenient. Some games try to be more "realistic" by having very limited respawns, I was glad to see that it wasn't the case here.

I opened up the Impact Point store—I had only taken a quick glance at it before, and it was a good excuse to procrastinate on research some more.

There were at least fifty races in there, without even considering the numerous subraces for each. The number of different elves there were . . .

Well, the good news was that the subraces were relatively cheap, only costing five to fifteen percent of the cost of the main race. However, they had the requirement of needing to unlock the main race first. I currently only had humans, dwarves, elves, and gnomes unlocked. However, there was a small note saying that if I unlocked myconid for fifty Impact points, I'll automatically unlock the Magic Cap subrace.

I opened up the page for the base myconid. It was classified as an Age-type Heteromorph? As a myconid ages, it'll also gain new racial abilities. A Sprout is only capable of using Distress and Rapport Spores, but an Adult may use Pacifying, Hallucination, or Reproducing Spores, older Myconinds are capable of an even greater feat. Through Reanimating Spores they may move the dead to do their bidding.

I continued reading. How this matters to a Traveler, is that a Traveler's time as this race will contribute to their character's age. A Myconid Traveler who's been around for twenty or so years will have more racial abilities than one who just started.

Wait, shit. If a character changes as they age, could they die of old age as well?

Matt was really enjoying himself at the moment. In fact, it could be said that his entire day was just a string of really great moments, he thought as he narrowly dodged a sword.

Backpedaling, he swung his halberd horizontally, creating a loud clanging sound as he dented the helmet of a knight-looking dude.

Last night—well this early morning if you were being technical, he was invited to one of the best virtual realities in the world. Then he explored a pretty nice place, met some new people and made some new friends.

"FUCK YEAH!!!" he heard Lung shout from far away from him. He turned around, quickly glancing at the lizardman suplexing someone, dodging a stray ball of acid in the same motion, before hurriedly turning back as he parried another sword with the haft of his halberd. *Seriously, why are so many people using swords?* He wondered as he threw the swordsman back with a push kick to the gut. Quickly, he darted out the tip of his halberd and pinned them to the ground, then in a smooth motion, vaulted over the fallen swordsman, ripping out the halberd tip as he did so.

Matt landed on his feet, swinging his weapon in a wide circle around him, only to realize that there was no longer anyone near him.

Who's left to fight? Matt idly thought as he stabbed the screaming swordsman with the spear bit of his halberd into the leg, barely glancing as they disappeared into light particles.

Matt took a moment to look around him. He could help out Lung, but he seemed more than happy to deal with the small crowd of people gathering around him. Everyone else was doing their own thing, murdering each other and whatnot.

"Over there!" Matt heard someone yell. "He's not one of ours!"

He glanced at where the voice came from, spotting a small party of about five people. A blue-skinned mage with odd tattoos was pointing directly at him.

Matt smiled, the grin large and toothy.

Breaking into a run, he rushed directly toward the party.

A few of them looked surprised, but only for a moment. A swordsman stepped forward, followed by another bearing an axe and shield. An elf quickly drew her bow. The blue-skinned mage and a skeleton raised their hands, tattoos glowing on the former and fire appearing in the latter.

All three released their attacks at once. A fireball and two arrows, one physical and one magical. Spaced so that he can't dodge one without getting hit by another, but far apart enough that he can't dodge all three unless he stopped running and jumped to the side.

Still smiling, Matt raised his arms in a cross guard covering his face. Rushing directly through the ball of fire, avoiding the other two attacks.

Without looking, he swung his weapon in a wide arc in front of him, hearing it splinter wood as he quickly confirmed their new positions.

Shield caught his weapon, a horizontal strike coming from the right, someone was starting to cast magic again.

He let go of the halberd as aura flowed into his left leg. In a blur, his left leg moved right, knocking his remaining leg off balance, causing him to fall and the sword to barely miss his head.

Hitting the ground on his side, he clawed the ground, nails digging into the earth as he threw a long line of dirt at the two melees. Not bothering to check whether or not they hit, he rolled toward them, aura flowing into his arm as he rolled into their legs. Quick like a blur, Matt Swift Striked the shield user in the groin. There was a brief grunt of pain as he reflexively dropped his weapons and tried to cover his privates. As the shield user's arms descended, Matt reached up and grabbed his hand, yanking him down and over him. Just in time to block the downward swing of the other melee.

The shield user gasped in pain as the blade struck his back, Matt, now laughing, grabbed the axe the other melee dropped, and threw it at the swordsman, not hitting but causing him to back off long enough for him to throw off the shield user.

"Both of you get away from him!" he heard the backline yell. Ranged attacks—he grabbed the collar of the fallen melee, raising him in front of him. It didn't help much, as a glob of something green hit the both of them like a water balloon. Matt felt a stinging pain as the liquid got into his eyes, forcing him to reflexively close them.

An arrow hit his shoulder immediately after, its momentum caused him to stagger a moment. Footsteps from the right, Matt threw the melee toward the sound, feeling a sharp pain as the arrow dug into his shoulder.

No sound of impact, the swordsman dodged.

Matt fell backward, felt the air rush above him as the swordsman tried another horizontal swing. Grunting as he hit the ground, he rolled away from the swordsman—

"AHAARGH!" —only to scream in pain as his action inadvertently forced the arrow deeper into his shoulder.

The moment cost him, as a barrage of attacks hit him not long after.

. . .

. . .

Matt blearily opened his eyes to a dark sky, large numbers counting down from above him. All pain and wounds were gone. Despite that, he still groaned.

"Fuck. Only got one," he muttered, sounding disappointed despite the large grin on his face.

He was in his respawn area, a small island with nothing but a halberd planted headfirst in the center. A horned skull balanced on the top end.

At first, time here passed like a dream, but every successive death he had made the experience more lucid. Until he was completely aware of the place.

Matt sat up, wriggling his toes and fingers to make sure everything still worked. He could never be sure.

Matt stood up and began restlessly pacing. He had already walked around and examined every inch of the tiny island. The halberd at the center couldn't be moved or altered in any way. The white sand which made most of the island could be though, but he got bored of throwing it somewhere around his sixth death.

Thumbing through the book on magic, strangely titled "So You Want to Throw a Fireball? A Comprehensive Guide to Magic for the Intellectually Deficient," which if you got past the name and the casual insults the text lobbed at the reader, was a rather comprehensive primer on simple magics.

Apparently, this system was belief based, where magic is a product of people believing they can do something, which with repetition made them better at doing that through confirmation bias. The book acknowledged that the various schools of magic each represented a different belief of how magic should function, and that most schools were largely incompatible with others, meaning a person would be stuck to a single magic school of thought unless they, say, got amnesia and forgot their training.

Magic was apparently getting simpler to use in recent years, a god ascended some centuries ago who named himself Manatheres, giving rise to mana, which is a resource that greatly expedited casting. An analogy might be that it acts as the lubricating oil in machinery. It is certainly possible to cast without mana, but mana makes it more efficient and useful.

I was honestly engrossed in the book and would've probably read it until the dawn came if not for the fact that the menus to the side of me updated again.

Matt just died again.

Dustin (HitZaDecs): You alright?

Matt raised an eyebrow. Opening the keyboard system, he quickly typed a reply.

Noam (Mattmanfoo): I'm aight, you finished already?

Dustin (HitZaDecs): Nah, just got tired of books. What are you doing? I saw you died like five times already.

Noam (Mattmanfoo): There's a brawl at irl spawn, hurry up and come if you're done reading!

Dustin (HitZaDecs): You mean Gaia?

Noam (Mattmanfoo): Same thing!

Dustin (HitZaDecs): Sure, give me a moment, feel free to keep brawling.

Every now and again, he would glance up, toward the timer counting down. When the timer hit thirty seconds, he stopped at the ends of the island.

He rested his halberd on his shoulder, silently watching the countdown. At five seconds, he began lightly jogging on the spot.

At two seconds, he started running toward the center of the island.

At one second, he jumped.

Matt landed back into Gaia running, a broad smile on his face as he surveyed the carnage around him.

"Do you know any good inns around?" I asked the shopkeeper as he handed me the flask and change. I did a quick count, ten silvers equaled one gold.

Money in hand, the shopkeeper cheerfully replied, "The Firefly Nest is down the street." He pointed left. "Take the third right, you can't miss it."

I nodded, pocketing the change and placing the flask in my bag. "Thank you."

Leaving the store, I followed the path the shopkeeper pointed out to me, quickly finding myself at the inn. It looked well maintained enough, not run down and plenty of people seemed to be around.

Entering, I paid the three silver fee of one night. Getting my key, I made my way to the third floor. I took one of the cheaper rooms, only a straw bed and desk were inside, along with a wooden window that was locked from the inside.

I dumped most of my bags, leaving only my ration and coin bag in hand. The key I stored together with my coins.

I quickly checked Noam's respawn time, looks like he died again, that idiot. I'll have to meet up with him on the next respawn.

Locking the door behind me, I traced the path to the Wayshard from memory. It was almost night now, so the line wasn't as long. I stood there, waiting and watching Noam's respawn time.

At two minutes, I opened up my ration bag and began eating the dried jerky with one hand. With the other, I held the bark, casting Barkskin.

I reached the Wayshard at one minute, with no one behind me. I stood there for the moment. At ten seconds, I directed energy into Polypores. They quickly drained my Satiety and grew to cover most of my body.

At five seconds, I touched the Wayshard.

You may Travel to:

Gaia

Indiri (Current)

Closely watching the timer, I selected Gaia the moment Matt's respawn time hit zero.

The world turned to light for a moment, and Matt fell down next to me in Gaia.

3.04

———

"Fourteen great gifts were presented at the Princess's naming ceremony. The First Gift was the gift of Hindsight granted by the Spring Court. Which she later realized probably wasn't as good as the pseudodragon or even the good sense of direction."

—*Excerpt from* The First Princess

A short man paused as he peered into a dark alley, adjusting his spectacles as he tried to catch a glimpse of what he'd seen. It was empty, save for a few piles of trash.

"Must've been imagining it," he quietly muttered as he passed the innocuous-looking alley.

He melded back into the crowd, just missing a tiny, green mushroom cap popping out of the piles of trash.

"Squeak, squeak, squeak!" the green-capped wisp yelled to its sibling, roughly translated to: *"Look! The big ones throw away so much stuff!"*

A propped-up piece of paper fell to the ground, revealing a tiny yellow-capped myconid behind it. *"Yeah,"* it agreed.

"Do you know why?" Greenie asked, picking up a piece of cloth that used to be part of a shirt.

"I don't know," it replied in squeaks. His green sibling, well versed in Squeakish, was able to discern the slightly higher pitch which showed a delighted tone.

Like his sibling, Greenie was delighted that there were so many things they did not know. It just meant more things to learn!

There were sooo many odd things the big ones did. Like catching glistening lizard things with no feet from the large body of water or thrusting hidden metal things into other people inside this very alley.

Shank a voice inside them told.

Greenie paused and glanced at Yellow, and they both yipped in glee.

A new word! Greenie jumped out of the pile of loose trash, accidentally knocking over a limp arm, and clapped hands with Yellow.

They were getting bits and bobs of knowledge from their symbiote—the large mushroom who gave them moving energy, among other things. Most of the things he learned, they will learn, too, it's faster the closer they are to him somehow, but when they came to this new place with lots of people, the big mushroom started learning, too! Before they were only getting old learning from the mushroom, like weird cube-shaped movers or the bright thing they needed to avoid called the sun.

The sun thing was like, really, really *bright*. Greenie tried to have a staring contest with it and hurt its eyes.

They figured, if they were learning themselves, then they could learn what the big mushroom learned later, which meant they were each learning themselves and hence learning a lot more!

Speaking of the big mushroom, where was he? Greenie and Yellow hoped he was doing some cool learning!

Big mushroom probably wasn't though. He seemed intent to read these book things. Maybe Greenie and Yellow could join him once they figured out how to read, but even he seemed to find the act boring, why did the big mushroom insist on it, then? Oh well.

Dustin slammed his staff into a person's head, hearing a sickening crack as the mage's nose deformed. Before the mage even hit the floor, Dustin spat acid directly onto their face.

Ignoring the screaming mage on the ground, Dustin quickly threw Sneezing Spores behind him, stopping a rogue just long enough for Noam to swing around and stab them.

There had to be almost a hundred people here by now, magic was flying left, right, and center, and amidst the chaos, Dustin opened his mouth and yelled, "MATT WHERE THE FUCK ARE MY MUSHROOMS!?"

Big mushroom was doing something boring, but Greenie and Yellow weren't! There was so much to explore in the city, even if they had to keep to the dark alleys because of the bright thing.

"Let's explore this place more!" Greenie declared, grabbing Yellow's arm.

Yellow squeaked in agreement, there was simply so much to see! Together they ventured deeper into the dark alleyway. Passing big ones laying cold and poorly hidden behind large boxes, a small dagger that seemed to scream blood and murder, weirdly dressed big ones who attached themselves to other big ones and took their money, a shiny lamp that emanated purple smoke in the shape of skulls, large scaly creatures that were growling right at them!

Greenie walked forward, a tiny arm waving in greetings at the scaly things. They were so cool! Their scale was rough and thick, it looked like Greenie could spend forever hitting them and never hurt them! As one of them lunged toward Greenie, it noticed that they had teeth that glinted like blades. Still, as Greenie exploded in a puff of green spores, it noticed that they weren't immune to poison and that the one lunging at him crashed and barely missed it. Greenie noticed that the ones nearest to it all spasmed and fell limp as liquid frothed from their mouths. Just out of the mist, the others recoiled back. *Fear*, the symbiote knowledge told the both of them, *primal, instinctual fear*, it elaborated.

That was so cool!

These things knew fear. Yellow wondered what other things they knew.

Greenie wanted to puff another time to see if they had the same reaction. Would they continue to flinch, would they run away or try to rally against them? Greenie wanted to know!

A larger scaled creature crawled forward, it was big, way bigger than the other scaled things and came up to one of the big one's waists. Long scars raked its hide and slitted eyes cautiously watched Greenie and Yellow. Greenie pondered the stories behind those scars, while Yellow pondered what the thing was capable of. It seemed smart, it watched them from behind the other scaled creatures.

There was so much detail to the smaller scaled as well, their scales which looked to be uniformly brown but had beautiful, yet weak, patterns woven of energy humming beneath them, how their eyes flitted in between them and the large scaled, how some seemed to be ready to run at a moment's notice. How two instincts seemed at war in the smaller scaled. The larger one was keeping them here somehow, and the wisps wanted to know how and why.

As the green spores dissipated, the large one let out a threatening hiss, and the ones closest to it rushed forward. Yellow noticed a brief moment of hesitation in some of the scaled. Greenie let out another puff, annihilating the first wave. Wow! They all died the exact same way as before!

Yellow tugged the arm of Greenie, a squeak warning it to not use too much energy. Indeed, Greenie was already two down, it only had three more puffs left before it had to dissipate or recharge. Yellow was different, though, its arms blurred as puffs of yellow bloomed on the snouts of the scaled. Greenie knew from experience that the yellow spores made your eyes sting, and Yellow could throw a lot of them.

But Yellow could only slow them, it couldn't hurt things like Greenie did, though Yellow did a really good job of it, disorientating the fastest ones, causing them to clump together before Greenie puffed again, taking out more than the last two puffs combined. Greenie openly watched in wonder as it saw the bodies spasming and dying.

An angry hiss and the third wave came, Yellow and Greenie repeated the strategy, taking out just as many as the last puff. The last of the scaled began to run for it, whatever their leader had over them it wasn't enough to keep them going after losing most of their number. Yet the large scaled did not move, it glared coldly at the two wisps whilst staying almost stock still.

Then it moved.

In a few breaths, the scaled was upon them, knife-like teeth bared. Greenie let out a puff, covering the area with green spores once again. But the scaled was feinting—before either of them could notice, the large scaled had turned around, its large tail swiping and smashing into the both of them.

Greenie and Yellow hit the alley wall, however they weren't unduly perturbed by the impact. Being small and squishy had its benefits after all.

Greenie curiously watched the large scaled as it clung onto the wall opposite of them.

Yellow threw spores toward its face, but the scaled's head jerked away, avoiding the yellow spores blooming where its snout had been.

Greenie marveled in open amazement, Yellow was quick, but not quicker than the scaled. It weaved through blossoming clouds of yellow spores, the few times that Yellow landed a hit, it was never on its head. Then it began retaliating.

Powerful tail swipes swept a dead scaled toward them. Yellow quickly grabbed Greenie and jumped to the side, the corpse landing only a few hairs from them.

Yellow glanced at the alleyway, now full of scaled corpses, then at Greenie, to which Greenie replied with an excited squeak. Then both wisp mushroom hybrids began running. A few scaled corpses flew past them as the large scaled began pursuit.

The large scaled was so smart! It managed to quickly find a way around both their attacks. Yellow's spore balls had nowhere near the weight to stop a scaled body, and the attacks showed that it outranged Greenie. It throwing the corpse already spelled their defeat at that place, so Greenie and Yellow had to run. They still wanted to learn more before they had to go, after all!

Unfortunately, the big scaled was quick. It jumped from wall to wall, just out of Greenie's range. Yellow threw a few potshots at it occasionally, landing a few good shots as it started to aim at where the scaled would be rather than where it was, but Yellow stopped a few breaths in, shaking its head. They used the same energy to move as the spores they threw, and Yellow was nearing empty. Greenie probably couldn't use a full blast puff again, they'd lose the energy to run soon as well. So, in sync, both mushrooms stopped at the exact same time, turning to face the scaled.

The large scaled paused on a wall. Some small rocks clattered free as its claws dug into the walls. Its tail curled behind it.

A pregnant moment passed.

The scaled jumped off the wall. Yellow spore balls appeared in Yellow's hands, Greenie began to puff—but the scaled swung around in mid-air, its tail uncurling to reveal another scaled corpse, thrown toward them from midair.

Greenie's puff went off as the corpse collided with the mushrooms. The green spores spread but got blocked by the corpse, leaving a wide enough gap for the scaled to rush through and a blindspot where Yellow could not attack.

Yellow squeaked, *"That was beautiful."*

The scaled went in for the kill, until a smaller, furred creature fell from the rooftops above them, crashing against the scaled.

A large wizard hat was gently wafting on the feline's head, by all logic it should've been blown off by the fall, yet it remained stuck there, oversized and looking like a strong wind could blow it off.

With the flick of her tail, the scaled turned into kitchenware, and Zoe examined the two small magical mushrooms.

Two figures limped through the soft glow. One, a large mushroom covered in brownish tree bark, scarred and broken in many places revealing soft white flesh beneath. His hand held both a wooden staff and a bloodied halberd, leaning on them together like a walking stick. The other, a tiefling, had an arm slung around the mushroom's neck, his other arm hung limp.

"We got out somehow," Dustin muttered as he dragged Noam.

Noam groaned. "C'mon, let me at them."

Dustin paused to slap Noam on the head. "Shut the hell up, you adrenaline junkie."

He glanced at Noam, his limp arm was an uglier shade of purple compared to the rest of him, the various strips of white fungus showing Dustin's emergency patch up, and the wet blood spots. "How the fuck are you still standing?" Dustin muttered.

"Determination," Noam muttered.

Dustin scoffed, "More like too stupid to feel pain." His hand went up, going through a few motions.

"What are we doing now?" Noam asked.

"Calling for backup."

Dave was a lot of things.

Traveler, merchant, a connoisseur of ramen, hivemind, AI that was debatably alive, though he didn't want to bring that can of worms up again. Having an existential crisis for what amounted to several centuries was horrifically unproductive, and the other Daves all agreed as such.

More recently, though, Dave was intrigued. An odd group had just walked into his store: Zoe, Devourer of Aberrations, frequent customer and bribable by head scratches exactly four centimeters behind her left ear, was carrying what looked like two tiny myconids by the scruff of their necks.

Amanda might've spent a good ten minutes giggling over the inherent cuteness of the group, but Dave, being a strict professional, adjusted his monocle and greeted them as he did all customers.

"Welcome," he meowed, "whatever you want or need, you can purchase here."

It was no lie or boast. Already a bag of "exotic grasses" was in his paw, the scent putting him in a good mood. It was some really strong stuff, to even affect him. Dave wondered how Zoe would present her money this time. Though with the nature of Zoe's Path, successfully guessing how she would do anything was a long shot.

The cat in question tipped her large wizard hat backward, from the darkness within Dave saw sixty-eight rings of Traveler Coins orbiting a food bowl. Dave smiled as Zoe poured out the contents, the food bowl landing first and the coins falling in perfectly stacked piles inside. The coins suddenly disappeared, and Dave placed the pouch of "exotic grasses" inside the food bowl.

Zoe very carefully poked open the bag and sniffed it. She unintentionally let out a content purr and dropped the two near myconids on the ground.

Another Dave peered at them, adjusting its monocle as it stood at eye height to the sentient—no, sapient—mana stored in the form of a mushroom. They were very similar to Magic Myconids, albeit fully functional despite being the same size as newborns.

Due to some light "administrator" privileges, Dave knew that these were Traveler familiars created by a class trainer. They were nothing the Traveler couldn't have made themselves of course, though a class trainer giving it to them was much faster and learning types like these showed their worth over time. Their strength was also linked to a support role, something meant to enhance their Traveler's strength. Overall, a very good level purchase, not some flashy weapon but a steady tool that can always be relied upon. Dave estimated they're worth forty-eight gold each. As high as sixty if a decent merchant did the sale. He felt that old itch again, the desire to haggle, though he swiftly put it away. A merchant he may be, the prices he offers under this brand are always fair and non-negotiable.

Cat Dave lightly tapped him on the head with a tail, reminding him that he had passed the amount of time that was polite for staring at customers. The tiny myconid Dave shook himself out of his stupor, before chirping, *"Welcome, whatever you want or need you can purchase here."*

The green myconid glanced at the other, before hesitantly turning and replying, *"We don't have money."*

Dave mentally upped his assessment by another six gold. Mutual learning capability, passive, too, they practically raised themselves. Wispshroom Dave smiled. *"Of course, it's no problem, you're both familiars, aren't you?"* they both nodded, and Dave continued, *"As familiars, you can make purchases on your master's behalf, I assume that he has money . . ."*

"You lost everything?"

"I lost everything," Matt replied with a smile.

The side of my eye twitched.

Matt fell back slightly, wincing as he brought his hands up in the universal sign of surrender. "Hey, hey, no need to get pissed dude."

Peps very gently brought Matt's damaged arm down as I stared at him. "It's good that you're lively," he idly said as healing light caressed his arm.

I took a deep breath. "I am not mad," I very quietly replied, my fingers massaging my brow; anger was not productive, it was never productive. "I was just . . . reconsidering our options."

Indeed, if it were just the money or his supplies, then it would've been fine, but both? Between the two of us, that was around half of our starting resources, how very annoying. Those supplies weren't like equipment that became worthless the moment something with higher stats came along. Hunger was a very real threat and if the marketplace was any fair indication of the supplies worth, then that stuff Matt lost over those deaths was worth at least twenty-gold. That idiot, we're already at a deficit compared to other players who just played safely—

"Even if you lose, you can always earn it back," Peps calmly said as he finished healing Matt's arm. "I mean, it's not that much, is it? It's just some starter stuff."

"Yeah, that's right!" Matt interjected, waving around his newly healed arm. "Chill out bro, we can always do quests and earn it all back."

I shook my head. "It's not that simple, with new servers. It's always a race to see which players get to what resources first . . ." my voice slowly petered out. That was game logic, wasn't it? Moreover, there was no specific reason to be worried about that.

I was tryharding.

When did that start?

When did I start having fun?

"I know that smirk," Matt said from the corner.

"I have no clue what you're talking about," I replied.

Matt scratched the back of his head. "What hair-brained scheme have you concocted this time, profiteer?"

"Shut up, junkie," I simply replied.

"You know the drill by now," I continued, "less than five gold between the two of us, you definitely dragged us into hard mode, we're gonna take that paltry sum of five gold and—"

I froze as my hand touched the coin pouch, feeling the outlines of the contents. Key, small coins.

"Problem?" Matt asked, leaning forward.

I definitely took them out with me, there was no mistake with my memory.

Small coins, engraved, silvers, the change I got from the shopkeeper I bought the bottle from.

Key, it opens the inn room I rented.

Silver coins and a key.

A receipt from a store called "Daves," made out to one Greenie and Yellow.

Silver coins, a key and a receipt.

"God fucking—"

3.05

*"This surgery business is highly suspect, you mean to tell me one
can cure a stab wound by stabbing them again? Bah. Mortal
injuries are nothing that prayer and faith can't fix."*
—High Bishop Jackov of the Church of Light

I glared at the neat paper receipt that appeared in my wallet. Several
items were listed on it, however, what had my eye twitching was who it
was made out to. A certain "Yellow" and "Greenie," "familiars of Traveler
Dustin." It was rather obvious who they were, even when I hadn't named
them yet.

"Matt," I said, extending my arm, receipt in hand, "where did the mushrooms I give you go?"

He took the receipt from me and began reading, chuckling slightly as he
passed over the names, before quickly interrupting it with a cough. "Well,
you see . . ." He paused as if considering what to say.

"I lost them," he conceded.

I felt the corner of my eye twitch again. Anger, frustration, those weren't
productive, so I took a deep breath and packed away whatever I was feeling.
I raised an eyebrow. "Okay, then."

Noam smiled. "It's only a minor setback, isn't it?"

"It is," I readily replied.

Peps glanced at me, then toward Noam, lips pursed as if unsure, then
seemed to just drop whatever he was wondering.

"That reminds me," I continued, looking at Peps, "I haven't paid you
back yet."

"Oh, it's fine," Peps replied, shaking his head. "It's just healing, all it took
was some mana."

"No, no," I cheerfully replied as I circled next to Noam and slung an arm
around his shoulder, "I insist."

I smiled. "We'll pay you back Peps, we both will, won't we?" I directed it to Noam more so than Peps.

"Umm . . ." he hesitated for a moment, before I quietly kicked his leg. "Ow—I mean, yeah!"

"Erm . . ." Peps hesitated a moment as well. "Not to sound rude, but didn't you just go broke?"

I smiled, cheerfully reassuring him, "Oh, don't worry about that, money is easy to make. We'll need your help for a bit longer, though."

Noam raised an eyebrow, and I continued, "Think, Noam, how many healers did you see at that brawl?"

His eyes brightened in realization. "Oh!"

"I'm a bit lost," Peps hesitantly admitted.

"It's simple," Noam started as I let go of him.

"How many people do you suppose escaped in the same condition as us?" I casually finished.

Realization dawned on his face. "*Oh.*"

Fucking crazy, all of them, Murphy thought to himself as he limped away. He munched on a potato and felt his flesh regrowing itself; potatoes, however, were a poor cure for stab wounds.

Some part of him registered that he should be in much more pain than he was, but the better part of him was just thankful that whatever pain limiter this realm had was working, or maybe it was his weird race, said to be extremely hardy in all conditions. Whatever the case, he was grateful he made it out of that shitshow relatively ungrazed. Murphy wasn't sure what had taken over the people at spawn, but they were madly killing everyone they could see for no discernible reason.

Murphy shuddered as he remembered a blue devil person yelling in glee as they sunk a spear thing into his shoulder. *Fucking crazy,* he mentally repeated. The moment he stepped into Gaia, he had met nothing but crazy people. Murphy turned a corner and slowly made up his mind. He was going to quit, it didn't matter how realistic Eve sold her world to be if said world was full of crazy psychopaths—

"Hello!" Murphy heard a cheery voice say. "You look like you're umm . . . injured?" the voice hesitantly pointed out.

Murphy looked up to see a tall, lanky dude completely made of wood, with an afro of leaves, and a walking mushroom about his height with weird bark growths on his cap and the most horrific looking facial expression.

The source of the cheery voice, the mushroom, continued, "Well, if you need healing, this guy"—he gestured toward his companion—"is a druid with some good healing spells."

The druid smiled amicably and gave him a slight wave. "For the small price of . . . let's say three gold, we'll get you all fixed up!" the mushroom continued.

Murphy stood completely still, then angrily muttered, "What is this, highway robbery?"

The mushroom seemed taken aback for a moment, before quickly shaking his head. "No, no, I assure you that we are completely legitimate and would've already robbed you if we wanted to."

Murphy felt the corner of his eye twitch as pure rage began to build up within him. "You little shits . . ." he angrily muttered. "You know what I just went through?"

"I just got fucking electrocuted, stabbed several times, almost got roasted alive!" Murphy said indignantly, his voice slowly rising in volume. "And this! This is what I meet immediately after I finally managed to get out!?"

"Umm . . ."

"I don't want your excuses!" Murphy yelled.

He began walking forward toward them, his rage building up to immeasurable proportions. "To think that I would meet such an amateurish attempt at profiteering! What are you!? Some fifth-graders opening their first lemonade stand!?"

"Uhh, what?"

I watched, utterly dumbfounded as the short, stumpy potato man thing kicked a bench.

"First off! Location!" he angrily yelled. "We're in an entire empty mall and the first place you pick is location backwater! What are you!? Blind!?"

I glanced at Peps, who appeared as utterly dumbfounded as I was.

"Secondly! Presentation!" He walked up to me and slapped me. "Get that damned horrific look off your face! You'll only scare off potential customers!"

Did he? He just slapped me. I knew my face was odd, but did that really warrant getting slapped?

Not even caring of my indignation, the potato thing was already walking away, he pointed three stubby fingers into the air. "Thirdly!"

The potato man continued to mercilessly scream flaws at us like a drill sergeant. Somewhere along the line, I felt a pop inside my cap as the small mushrooms returned, but remained speechless as the potato just kept chewing us out for failing to scam him.

What felt like an eternity later, the potato finally paused for breath. Then, "Did you get all that!?" he demanded.

At that point, I was long past shock, so I numbly nodded. Funnily enough, the two mushrooms on my shoulder mimicked the action.

"Very well!" the potato yelled, he enthusiastically pumped his fist into the air and began walking away. "Hurry up! There are idiots to be scammed!"

Peps lightly tapped my arm. "Did he just . . ." he whispered questioningly.

"Yes," I drily replied, "our first customer has taken over the business and has promoted himself to a managerial position."

Step one, create a mass demand for healing services. Step two, offer healing services for gold and clout. Step three, get taken over by our first customer?

Not that I minded that much. I sucked at a leadership position and given how brazen that guy is I could use him as a scapegoat if it all went south. Yes . . . that potato was an unorthodox piece but a piece nonetheless.

I just had to make sure he wasn't handling the money, leaving someone red-handed with the bag of cash was overrated.

The potato ended up being very useful. Once he had found a suitable spot, several eyes—the root-like things potatoes grew not actual eyes, that would've been disturbing—began sprouting from his body. They quickly grew into almost perfectly rectangular planks of mostly white and red potatoes. Though he deflated a bit, he still prompted us to start slotting the planks into each other like puzzle pieces.

"How are you able to make these so perfectly?" I asked as I slotted in two planks that formed a red cross. The potato glanced at me with a face that looked like someone just took a glob of Play-Dough and poked a pair of eyes into it. "I do a bit of woodworking in real life as a hobby, mostly self-taught, it's nothing special, but I'm used to imagining how these things will end up." He shrugged, before barking something at Peps about fitting two pieces incorrectly.

Oh. How rare. I looked back on the red cross I had, "used to it" seemed like an understatement. The two planks were like a three-dimensional jig-saw puzzle, with shapes and teeth that allowed them to slide perfectly into each other. I tried pulling them apart, only for it to be made clear to me that the only way to separate them was by sliding them out through the opposite direction I had slotted them in. Given the diagonal nature of the sliding, it was unlikely for it to fall out by itself as well.

This was very well designed and didn't seem like something a normal person could make on a whim. A mental mod perhaps? Seemed a bit extravagant for "just a hobby." Before I could ask more, the human-shaped potato pried the cross out of my hands. "Alright, we are ready!" he declared as he inserted the piece.

I took a step back to admire the final product. Most of it was the potato's handywork, having literally grown half of it and directed its assembly. Without him, it would've gone as well as most home do-it-yourself attempts. We had pretty much repaired an entire store in the span of an evening using only potatoes. It was pretty clean, too, since they were directly grown out of—I forgot to ask his name. Oh well.

The one problem is . . .

"It's a bit bland looking, isn't it?" Peps voiced my thoughts aloud.

The potato nodded, putting his hand under his chin. "Yeah, I didn't have a lot of options with my skills so the material would look a bit flat . . ."

Yep, clearly, the potato planned to imitate the classic clean white sterilized hospital with the big red cross but since everything was literally made from potatoes there was just a rough, yellow undertone to everything about it. Though it was a jump toward civilization as compared to the derelict overgrown store we first stepped into, it was a very small step and on the outside. Despite all the meticulous work and clean edges, it looked like a kindergartener just sloppily covered the storefront in white playdough.

It was just . . . that look about perfectly squared and clean potatoes that made it look weird.

"Maybe we're trying to take this in the wrong direction," Peps mused.

I cocked my head in his direction, gesturing for him to continue.

"This thing sticks out like a sore thumb as compared to the rest of the shopping center," he elaborated.

"Don't try to stand out but blend in?" I suggested.

Peps hesitantly shook his head. "No . . . but yeah. It's not so much blending in as taking advantage of the environment."

"We need to smooth it out, then," the potato muttered thoughtfully. "Can someone try grabbing some of that glowing moss?"

"I can grow some," Peps offered.

"I can grow different colored mushrooms," I added as I grew a light sporage.

"Yeah . . ." The potato slowly nodded. "Great! Start over!"

Meanwhile . . .

A bloodied hand clawed the ground as its owner, an elven ranger, tried desperately to drag himself away. A *tsk* came from behind him as a halberd tip buried itself in his hand, causing a pained scream.

"No, no, you have to run in fear that way," Noam chastised as the elf continued to scream in agony, his free hand pointing in the opposite direction.

"Goddamnit, why is this so hard, it's like herding cats with you people—" Noam began, before stopping as he realized that the screaming had abruptly stopped. He looked down and saw in place of a body were instead light particles.

"Fucking hell they died again!"

"Hmm . . ."

"Too much moss?" the potato asked.

"Definitely too much," I agreed.

"Maybe add more colored mushrooms to break apart the monotony?" Peps suggested.

"Perhaps . . ." I said as I grew some Light, Poison, Sneezing, and Balm sporages on the wall. Creating white, green, yellow, and light green bulb mushrooms respectively.

Peps pointed at one of the Poison Sporages. "The darker green ones will definitely get lost in there."

I glanced at it and agreed. The Poison Sporages had a very similar color to the non-glowing moss, whereas the Sneezing and Balm Sporage mushrooms popped out to a degree.

The potato examined the mushrooms thoughtfully as Peps voiced another question: "Are these the only colors you can grow?"

"I can grow some brown mushrooms," I answered as I grew a Mushroom Meal on my hand. "These can be eaten, it's a bit bland for taste but also kinda juicy."

"Can you make these mushrooms glow?" The potato suddenly asked as he picked a sneezing mushroom.

"That . . . Can I?"

I grew a normal Light Spores Sporage in one hand, then a Sneezing Spores mushroom on the other hand, and tried to squeeze in a Light Spores spell into it.

I found that it was impossible and gave a blocked feeling, like trying to stuff something into an already full container. Disappointed, I shook my head.

"Could you grow mushrooms on top of each other?" Peps interjected, seeing what we were trying to do.

I tried that, placing a finger on the Light mushroom I just grew and cast a Sporage, a similarly sized yellow mushroom began growing from its head. What was most notable was the fact that the new mushroom was slightly transparent and tinged the white glow of the original mushroom, leaving it to cast a more yellowed light.

Interested, I tried covering the glowing mushroom with more mushrooms. Creating a bundle of yellow mushrooms that let out a faint, neon yellow light.

"That does look better," the potato observed.

I set the mini lantern down. "That cost a lot of mana . . ." I said, rubbing the dull headache that formed. "I can probably manage one more unless either of you have mana regen buffs?"

Both Peps and the potato shook their heads and I sighed in disappointment. "Anyway, that should only last three hours, it won't be that useful."

"No, it could be very useful," Peps encouraged. "It's not a good light source but it's pretty colorful, like a lava lamp," Peps said, before getting interrupted by something smacking his face.

I watched the slimy, rainbow-colored object slowly slide off Peps's face.

Someone let out a faint cry of shock, probably Peps. I couldn't really notice as it took me a second for my brain to start working again. It was at that point that I noticed some faint chattering behind me.

You didn't need to do that!

I got their attention didn't I!

Turning around, I found Greenie and Yellow arguing with a rainbow-colored gecko between them.

"Boss!" Yellow squeaked out to me. *"First customer!"* it proudly proclaimed, presenting the gecko to me.

The gecko turned to me and made a chirping sound, which I only understood because the small mushrooms understood it. *"Are you the manager?"*

I shook my head, then pointed at the potato. "He's the manager." The moment I finished that sentence, the potato had a look of pure terror, his eyes drifting somewhere far away before he fell to the ground unconscious.

"Umm."

"I heard you can reattach my tail?" the gecko chirped.

3.06

———

"Oh, Lady Goddess, I beseech you to aid us in solving our vexations. What was that? QUIET DOWN EVERYONE, I CAN'T HEAR HER! Oh, Dear Goddess, do you mind repeating that?"

—Priestess Cordelia receiving divine insight, leading her to write "Fireproof Heretics and You: Why You Don't Need to Give Up on Tradition"

As Peps began his healing thing, I glanced at Greenie. "Why do you have a hat?" I asked, gesturing at the tiny wizard hat that completely covered his cap.

"Cat," it simply replied.

I raised my eyebrows, but before I could question further, Peps stood up.

"Fixed," Peps declared as he gently patted the tiny rainbow gecko.

"Thanks!"

"No problem!" Peps cheerfully replied, gently shaking the tiny gecko's front paw.

The gecko let out another chirp of appreciation, before asking, *"What are you doing here?"*

I gestured at the store. "Trying and failing to create a business," which Greenie promptly translated.

"What's the problem?"

"Aesthetic issues," I replied, Greenie and Yellow's translation echoing me. "We're trying to make it look good."

"But we can't really manage it," Peps added, "all we have to use are moss and mushrooms."

The gecko's head perked up. *"I can help, but please wait a moment,"* it said before scurrying off and disappearing.

A few minutes later, the walls and the ground started to blur like a glitch, before several dozen geckos unstealthed right before us.

"We can help!" They chirped together, all of their bodies shifting through a myriad of colors.

Meanwhile . . .

"Holy shit," Noam muttered under his breath, hundreds of floating light particles surrounding him. "When did killing people become this easy?"

We organized the geckoes onto the walls. At first, we just wanted to create some sort of colorful wallpaper. But then a gecko suggested that they could manage moving images just as easily.

Peps and I agreed that we should get them to make some kind of moving pattern and as we began to direct them onto the right wall, a cloaked figure entered the hall we were in, setting down a blanket in between two stores to the right of us. I recognized him as the dude who sold us potions before but otherwise didn't comment. He quietly sat down and began cleaning various trinkets, before setting them down on the blanket.

Somewhere along the line, the potato woke up and began directing the geckos in a distinctly militaristic like fashion. We went through dozens of different variations with the geckos, my mushrooms, and Peps' bushes. Finding out halfway that concentrating too many geckos in one spot would block out the natural light of the glowing moss, since they weren't translucent. It took a while to organize them into something that didn't resemble a crime against good taste. Eventually, we settled on them covering up the front side of the cross the potato had made earlier. Four geckos shifted to a much brighter red compared to the old potato red which just looked maroon. Peps grew some glowing moss on the sides of the cross to create a light outline. We repeated this a few times. The potato producing rulers to help us place them evenly across the walls with my Light mushrooms interspersed between each cross.

After a long, long while, we finally finished and breathed a sigh of satisfaction at the finished product.

It was now that I realized a major problem.

"Did we really just spend this much effort for a one-time shop?"

Both the potato and Peps stared at me with a blank look.

"I mean, we can't really be here twenty-four/seven, there's no security so this stuff is bound to be gone," I continued.

Only the snort of laughter from the cloaked merchant answered me.

"Amateurs." He sneered behind us, sitting condescendingly on his blanket.

* * *

It was getting noisy and Ven didn't like it. She didn't like it at all. All she wanted to do was spend all day sleeping and get rich. Maybe eat a few tasty snacks as well.

She had placed herself in one of those small hallways that lead out of the main halls, usually to toilets and staff exits. Just so that she would be out of the way, and so that other players wouldn't bother her as much.

But lots of people were gathering in the hallway outside and it was tiring. There was a lot of shouting, something about a "purple horned cunt" ganking everyone going near a certain area and how they were going to "tear him so many new ones he'll look like cheese."

Honestly, Ven didn't care, she was comfortably resting. She would shut them up, but there were a lot of them now and she was already full after someone tried to steal from her before.

Ven quietly sighed and resigned herself to another hour of waiting out the mob.

Though honestly, if they wanted to murder someone that badly, then hurry up! From the tremors, there were at least thirty of them already. *Lazy idiots . . .*

She froze, feeling tremors heading toward her. Opening up a small slit, she formed an eye and stealthily glanced at the approaching figure.

A tall brown lizardman, his clothes bloody and ravaged, as if he had just been through a warzone. He shook his head, then shakily stumbled forward, before falling against the wall opposite Ven, before—"BLUARGHF!"—vomiting all over the ground in front of her.

Disgusted, Ven hurriedly withdrew herself, shrinking as far back as possible to avoid the puke. Retracting the eye back inside her shell.

Without her eye, she couldn't see what the lizardman did next, but she heard him rasp out in a slurred voice, "What's a vending machine doing hereee . . ." before hearing him slump and hit the ground.

Fuck it, she thought to herself, *I'm moving.*

A halberd sped forward, its spear point catching a person by the shoulder. There was an exclamation of pain as the player dropped his sword and Noam pinned them to the wall. The person began screaming, to which Noam shook his head. "Buck up, shoulder hits aren't lethal."

"You motherfucker!" the pinned person yelled.

Dustin would've told him to be more original, Noam idly thought as he began twisting the halberd, inciting more pained cries.

"Trust me, this sort of pain is nothing," Noam assured. "Plus, you respawn later so it's honestly no skin off your back."

"It still HURTS YOU MOTHERFUCKER!" the person yelled.

It annoyed him that he was to do this. This was usually Declan's thing. Experimenting. Testing all the possible variations and then figuring something out. But Noam couldn't contact him since he was outside the range of spawn. It wasn't his style to continuously beat the shit out of weak people—it just wasn't fun, ya know?—but right now his curiosity was stronger than his annoyance.

The person swore again, his free hand reaching for the pole of the weapon pinning him.

Noam lifted his foot, kicking it into the person's stomach before stomping on it as leverage to pull his halberd out.

The person fell to the ground without moving. Noam glanced at the wound he had left and saw the same thing he'd been seeing for ages.

White particles.

The same that appeared when a player died. A shoulder attack was hardly lethal but still, it appeared. It could just be a visual thing, but every single person who had displayed this died in a few moments.

But why?

Noam had already fought a bunch of people, most of them took actually lethal hits before dying. Even characters that weren't supposed to have a high constitution like mages.

He stood up as the white particles began to spread around the wound. Another player died in the exact same, odd way. Namely, despite the fact that Noam didn't kill him.

Back at the battle arena in spawn, some players—no, most of the players took several good hits to go down. That didn't even mean they died, just knocked unconscious. But out here . . . people were fragile. He tried knocking someone unconscious and almost immediately they began disappearing.

It could've just been that he happened to run into people with very low HP values constantly, but that explanation was wrong. Dustin might've taken the HP explanation and run with it, but Noam knew in his heart that that explanation was wrong.

Noam clenched his hand, feeling his nails press against his palm, the strain of the muscles beneath his knuckles. He felt the sting of his fresh knee scrapes from careless running. The dull aches as his body began to tire. His eyes took in the vivid details of the overgrown mall, filled with green, actual green. Not neon advertisements or strangely colored energy drinks, but green from plants. Something he thought he would never see save for obscenely pricey trips to protected gardens.

With every single breath of the cool, damp air, Noam understood a simple truth.

At the moment he was alive, even more so than the sick body he had in real life. Even if the body wasn't as strong, fast, or durable as the dozens of game characters he'd inhabited over the years. It felt real to Matt, so that meant it was real.

So why the hell were people dying so easily?

His stuck-up tutorial guide had told him, under no uncertain circumstances, that player characters had similar durability to what you would expect them to have. A player wasn't going to survive getting skewered multiple times or beheaded. However, some players were dying far too easily.

His ponderings were interrupted by footsteps, and a smash as a figure cleared out some debris in front of a store.

He caught glimpses of a metal bat as the figure kicked her way into the store.

She was a tiefling just like him but red-skinned, with short messy hair, smaller horns and with pure yellow eyes instead of purple. Only the barest amounts of hard leather armor that only covered vitals, leaving joints, waist, and neck exposed for free movement.

She hefted her bat up, resting it on her shoulder. "You're the psycho who's been killing everyone right?"

"Of course," Noam replied, a smile creeping up unto his face, "who's asking."

The girl spat on the ground, then raised the bat at him. "You're strong, right?"

Noam shrugged, casually readying his own weapon. "Probably."

"Great. Then I call dibs," and with that, she kicked off the ground toward him. Her mouth a wide smile that mirrored Noam's own.

Bob heard the door behind him crack open as Hendrix stepped in, a large sack slumped over his back.

"Who are you? Santa?" Bob asked as he turned around. "What's in the bag?"

Hendrix glanced around the room, nodding at Pop who was next to Bob, then answered, "Debon's stuff."

Bob shook his head. "I presume your attempt at a dinner date didn't go well?"

"He is a bard, it's not like he has a shortage of dates," Hendrix said, before dumping the sack by the door and closing the door. "Pop can you tell me when Debon is close?"

Pop nodded at Hendrix's request, before resuming her work. Hundreds of numbers and letters passing through her eyes.

Bob signed, resigning himself to being another unwilling accomplice to what Hendrix defined as "fun."

"How's moderating going?" Hendrix asked, peering at the crystal in front of Hendrix.

"Wonderful," Bob sarcastically replied. "There are far too many insane players, nothing is simple, and I've prevented the end of the world four times already."

Hendrix chuckled, before noticing Bob's utterly serious face. "Wait, you're not joking?"

Bob shook his head. "This is why I was against assigning free classes and races based on personality. Even if they all have the same power budget, some characters start out absurdly specialized."

Though Bob personally suspected that Eve only implemented this system to give everyone something to do. Most of the Heirs were in characters that reflected their personality, after all. So, it also gave them a chance to meet like-minded people when they were brought to lead the tutorial. It wasn't a coincidence that every Heir had led at least one tutorial.

"Any notable examples?" Hendrix casually asked, his body becoming completely still in that odd, myconid way.

Bob pulled out the file of "troublemakers" and looked at the most recent ones.

"Zettour, he's been terrorizing the Melbourne server after bonding with the False Aboleth Boss there."

"Noam, lots of ganking, a mob has already started to hunt him down."

"xXScorchedReaperXx started a bushfire which forced the drop bear and kangaroo gangbanger population to move into Sydney and start attacking players, as well as inciting a land war between the local fey tribes."

"Herman sold his soul to three different lesser devils before I got to him, creating a custody crisis which if I don't go to court to resolve will likely spark another Infernal War."

"Icypole, doing unsavory things with corpses."

Bob felt a headache incoming, and he put down the near ten-centimeter thick file. "Look, you get the idea right?"

Hendrix mutely nodded, something like pity in his eyes.

Bob sighed again, it had already been two days and he felt more overworked than the thousands of years he had looking after the Heirs and Indiri. At least only a few of the Heirs were troublesome.

"Why are looking at me with those accusatory eyes?" Hendrix asked.

Hendrix picked up the folder, flipping to a certain page. "Knew it, I know this Noam guy. I bribed Debon to screw with—test him."

He flipped around the folder a bit more. "There's a lot of stuff happening in Melbourne it seems."

Bob nodded. "After I finish dealing with the fires I'm heading there. The main problem here seems to be . . ." Bob flipped the pages of the folder, landing on the last page. "Zettour, the guy who bonded with the Aboleth."

"How did he even do that?" Hendrix asked. "It's a boss mob so it should have Legendary Resistances."

Bob sighed. "The tutorial guide to this Zettour was Tzu."

Hendrix's eyes widened, genuine terror flickering across his face. "That means his class is . . ."

"That's right," Bob replied.

A product of absurd specialization, a class that had zero combat capabilities and was about as durable as wet tissue paper in swamp water. That class was good at one thing and one thing only, manipulation in its most subtle and unnoticed form.

The class, mastermind.

3.07

———

"Even if it sometimes feels like you're repeatedly hitting a brick wall, don't underestimate the hardness of the human skull."
—Madelyn the Skull Rain giving an inspirational speech before breaking through the walls of Helmsdeep, earning her namesake and beginning Conquest

Noam began the fight with a wide upward arc swing.

The store he was currently in was formerly a convenience store. There were a total of eight aisles and he was located in the fourth aisle, his back facing the store refrigerators where they would've placed perishables like yoghurt and milk.

The decision to attack vertically was not a random one. In a cramped environment, Noam knew he was at a disadvantage with his halberd, any wide horizontal attacks would get caught by the shelves and be stopped. A wide vertical strike also left him open to counterattacks as he brought down his weapon. Thus, the moment where both of them were running at each other may have been the only time where Noam could've charged up a heavy attack.

His opponent wasn't as restricted by the same problems, however her metal bat was at least eighty centimeters long. She brought her bat behind her, preparing for a powerful swing from her right side.

Both of them saw the other's movement.

Both of them reached the same conclusion.

Whoever backs down first loses!

The distance between them quickly shortened.

Ten meters.

Five meters.

At two meters apart, Noam was the first to stop. His foot-stomping into the ground, he brought the halberd down at half strength, too soon, but his intention was a feint to scare her back, then utilize his weapon's spear-like tip for its intended purpose.

However, his opponent kept running, the axehead barely missing her, only the spear tip sliced into her thigh.

Instinct took over for Noam as he quickly dropped his polearm, raising his arms and stepping forward to protect his head. Just in time for the bat to smash into his left forearm.

The force of the blow threw Noam into the shelf to his side. Age-old metal groaned in protest before collapsing, leaving Noam slumped over the metal shelving in the next aisle.

Noam rolled backward to avoid the follow-up strike, his arm shooting out to pull himself up from an unfallen shelf.

His opponent was already on him. Noam saw her bat swinging from his right. Noam dodged down, the bat swinging mere centimeters above his head.

Aura flowed into his right arm as he Swift Striked her stomach, sending her staggering back. He didn't relent, aura flowed into his left for another hit, but suddenly he felt an intense spasm of pain.

The bat had left an ugly bruise. One Noam hadn't consciously registered until he tried to make a fist. His body reflexively recoiled as his opponent fell out of range.

She staggered back and made a half-hearted swing, he dodged back, unsheathing a knife in a downward hold before stepping forward and slashing at her, but she lowered her head and parried the blade with her horns.

A devilish grin on her face, Noam's opponent threw her head to the side, forcing his knife arm to go wide, before ramming herself into him, knocking him back, and disrupting his balance.

Noam fell back, but he quickly found his balance. As his opponent rushed in for another attack, Noam moved, his foot a central pivot. Noam twisted around and behind his opponent, and knocked her forward-facing frame toward the ground.

As she fell, Noam grabbed her shoulder with his left, wincing as he did so, and brought his knife to her neck.

The fight stilled as Noam became the victor.

"What do we do now?" Peps frantically asked.

I raised an eyebrow. "This isn't that much of a problem." I told him as I glared at the other seller. "It's not like we're suddenly unable to use all of this."

The dude snorted, then wrapped his cloak tighter around him, apparently more interested in becoming a blanket burrito than talking anymore. In hindsight, the guy was right, though his attitude about it was annoying.

"We just need to make it all worth it," the potato said.

I nodded. "Which reminds me," I began, turning toward one of the rainbow geckos, "you guys are NPCs, right?"

If it were only just one I might've thought it was a weirdo with a gecko fetish, but there were around seven hundred just decorating the walls. Unless there was a darknet gecko chat server that got invited in its entirety, these numbers weren't likely to be players.

The gecko chirped something and Greenie translated a confirmation.

"I'll get straight to the point, then; what are the quest conditions to get more of you to help?"

As Yellow kicked Greenie off my shoulder and began its translation, several of the geckos began rapidly blinking in color. Dozens of chirps echoed in the room before the geckos left their positions and congregated into a single picture.

The potato belched in disgust, while Peps leaned in for a closer look. Of course, they were still geckos so they wanted food. The picture they made was two-part, on one side the sun shining through a broken hole and the other side showed an overturned log, placed a good distance from the light. Underneath the log, clumps of disgusting larvae writhed over wet soil.

Holding back a slight grimace, I said, "Got it, dark place, underneath debris and with good moisture, anything else?"

There was a chirp, and Greenie who I caught earlier, yelled out: "No!" before Yellow had a chance to speak.

"On it, then." I glanced at the potato, who was dry heaving in the corner. "Make sure to increase my shares or something."

"Isn't this enough?" Peps asked, gesturing at the currently present geckos.

I shook my head as I left. "Oh no, I am a firm believer in the sunk cost fallacy." I turned around and waved. "I'll make sure we make lots of money," I said, my gaze fixed on the other merchant the entire time.

He snorted, though he didn't move, apparently content as he was.

Finding a good-looking spot didn't take too long. Most of the mall was already pretty dark and humid. All it took was leaving the more lit-up paths.

I was at the entrance of one of the underground parking lots. The place looked similarly overgrown to the rest of the mall, though completely dark. I couldn't make out anything if it weren't for my Dark Vision.

There were a bunch of small rotting wood logs lying around. Greenie and Yellow jumped off my shoulder, curiously moving toward the closest log.

"Be careful," I called, quickly moving after them, "those disgusting bugs could be everywhere."

I shooed them away from the rotting log, then very carefully raised my staff to poke—

Wait a second.

I took another glance around the dark underground carpark, covered in moss and a few of the glowing mushrooms.

The thing in front of me was wood, right?

I quickly cast a Light Spores, the soft glow illuminating the log as I kneeled to examine it.

There was no mistaking it, the texture and color were all identical to the Bark Skin I had active.

It was undeniably tree wood and it was located underground, rotting in a location with no light.

How the hell did it get here?

I stood and took a step back, then brought my staff out to poke the log. The end of my staff pushed the log over to reveal some kind of white shell.

The shell looked insectoid, thin, and segmented, and resembled a carapace, but it was clearly dead. As if it died a long time ago.

There were legs which had fallen off when I pushed it, I kneeled again, picking one up.

The leg was segmented as well, but most importantly, it was clawed, almost hook-like. These were graspers, not meant to move on a flat surface.

This was an arboreal creature, it probably clung to trees and relied on its bark-like back as camouflage.

I pointed one end of the leg toward me, the end that was attached to the main body.

It was empty, like a crab leg which my gramps had completely sucked dry during New Year's celebrations.

"Shit, shit, shit, shit." More creative words than *shit* weren't coming to me at the moment because *Oh fuck, what did I walk into?*

"You two, back away slowly toward—"

As I said that, there was a sound like wet sand being mushed, followed closely by the sound of skittering as the dozens of other things which I thought were just dead logs began moving.

Their bodies raised themselves and I saw my objective. Dozens of maggots, pulsing just beneath the thin white carapace. I saw the maggots dig through flesh, causing wet squelching sounds as the corpse jerked awkwardly toward me.

"Goddamnit," I swore as I rose. *Or should it be Evedamnit?* I pointlessly thought as I grabbed Yellow and Greenie.

"Why can't anything be easy?"

I slowly began edging back. Approximately forty of those disgusting things were shambling toward me. They had widely varying speeds though; many had legs dragging, and the emptier corpses were barely moving at all.

They were slow, only a few centimeters per second, so I had time to think. What suddenly caused them to move? These were parasitic creatures, the modus operandi for those were to remain dormant in a host. I must've triggered some kind of self-defense or feeding mechanism. But how did I wake so many? It couldn't be some kind of proximity sensor, when I noticed something strange I made sure to examine the one farthest away. There were at least several meters between this body and the rest. How did I trigger an attack?

What did I do wrong?

These were parasitic creatures; assuming these were anything like certain wasps, then once the maggots were fed enough, they "hatched" out of the host. The shell of the bark bug I examined looked very whole; that must mean . . .

I raised my staff, then slammed the shell golf style. As expected, the shell burst easily like it was made of chips. A squelching noise could be heard as my staff displaced a giant maggot from the shell as it went flying toward the other parasites, hitting the floor and wetly sliding across for another few meters. As it made landfall, the nearest parasites paused and began moving toward it. I see. That thing must've signaled the others somehow.

I crouched to examine the pieces of the shell. The interior of it was wet with some kind of slimy liquid. Taking a deep breath, I steeled myself and picked up a piece, bringing it closer. There was a pungent smell to it, one that didn't become obvious until I brought it close.

Pheromones. I dropped to the floor. Oops, both Greenie and Yellow fell from my shoulder, softly hitting the ground. "Sorry about that," I muttered as Greenie began chirping profanities. Where the hell did it learn those?

Doing a quick sniff of the floor, I confirmed traces of the smell. However, it seemed to disappear approximately ten centimeters from the surface of the floor. The pheromone must be heavier than air, so it stayed low to the ground as it spread out. That's how I didn't detect it earlier, I kept too far a distance when examining it. The maggot must've released it when I first flipped it over, it took some time to spread to the other ones—

I felt an urgent tugging at my leg. "What is it, Yellow?" I asked as I glanced at it. One hand was pulling my leg, the other pointing in front of me—I quickly twisted my vision forward, where dozens of the parasite things had gotten surprisingly close. Two to three meters now. Did I misjudge their movement capacity?

Looking back, the few that got attracted to the golfed maggot seemed to be "eating" it. The host bodies scrawled on top as their maggots burst out and began digging into it, even though it seemed to be still alive.

Yellow kept tugging at my leg and urgently chirped, *"They're getting closer!"*

Greenie took a defensive stance.

I raised an eyebrow. "I can see that."

Yellow stared at me for a moment, then asked, *"Why are you so calm suddenly?"*

"Because," I began, "I wasn't afraid of the fight, I was afraid of the unknown variable," I simply answered.

"And this isn't much of a fight," I further elaborated. "They're disgusting, but just by looking at them you can tell that they rely on swarm tactics. Which we have no problem with. Poison Spores."

The greenish mist floated forward. It was hard to not equate it to a gas, even when I knew the damage dealt by this was caused by small green spores, the visual effect was extremely similar to gas-based weaponry. Though I'm pretty sure these spores would still count as a war crime.

The bug hosts managed a few centimeters before dropping as if their strings had been cut. Looking closer, I could see the parasite maggots writhing within.

Seven.

Not counting my mana regen and accounting for my Bark Skin mana drain, I could probably cast eight plus or minus one before my Mana Sickness starts to kick in. So long as I didn't miss, I should be fine.

"Was it the Geneva Convention or the Gibraltar Accords that banned biological weaponry?" I wondered aloud. "Oh well, these things have signed neither," I said as I recast Poison Spores onto the next wave.

Fifteen.

The description for the spell was horribly undescriptive, but as I understood it, Poison Spores worked by infecting a certain area with spores, denoted by the greenish mist. Once something passes through or touches the spores, the spores will latch on and begin dealing damage based on how much surface area was exposed. But only a specific amount of spores are released on each cast, so effectively I'm creating damage zones that had a max limit of how much damage can be dealt, but with no theoretical limit to how many enemies could be damaged. Well, other than the practical limitation of how many you could stuff in the approximately two-meter radius of the spores.

Simply put, "Dealing with hordes of mindless trash mobs happens to be what we're good at," I calmly told Greenie and Yellow. "AOE, or Area of Effect damage, are best for dealing with multiple and normally untargetable enemies."

"The multiple should be obvious." I gestured to the waves of bug hosts mindlessly rushing toward me, casually casting another Poison Spores.

Twenty-three.

Continuing, I said, "If you can hit multiple enemies at once, then it's usually best to do so."

"The second is a bit more difficult," I said then, raising two fingers, "untargetable enemies generally fall into two categories, based on how they are untargetable. Which, unfortunately, I can't demonstrate here. So, I'll just have to tell you."

"The first kind is untargetability through mobility. Where an enemy is simply faster than your ability to hit them accurately—"

"Ooh! I know this!" Yellow enthusiastically raised its hand. *"It's really hard when they're fast, they keep dodging!"*

"Yes," I agreed, "pinpoint attacks are good for accuracy but when you are simply outmatched in terms of dexterity or mobility, then you shouldn't rely on it."

"Now, can either of you tell me why AOE is good here?" I asked, recasting poison spores.

Greenie raised its hand. *"Because if you can't hit them normally, then you just hit everywhere?"*

"Exactly," I answered, "if you can't hit them where they are, hit where they could be. If they could be everywhere, then just hit everywhere. An inversion of this is using lingering damage." I gestured to the bug hosts trying to slog through the green mist. "In situations where you can't reliably predict where the enemy might be, instead create danger zones where the enemy feels less inclined to go near. The objective would be limiting the movement options of a highly mobile enemy by limiting their options and/or protecting a certain area."

"The second scenario follows similar principles, it is when an enemy can't be targeted because you simply don't know where they are. Either they have a stealth ability or you lack information of their exact locations," I explained, quickly checking on the zombugs.

Thirty-two.

"In such scenarios, a person would choose some form of AOE for the same reasons as against mobility targets—"

Yellow, who was practically skipping on the spot, raised a hand. *"Ooh! Hit everywhere!"*

"Hit everywhere they could be," I corrected, "it's an important distinction because hitting everywhere causes collateral damage and that's generally frowned upon."

"Hell, even during wartimes they wouldn't just bombard a place they suspected guerrillas were in—" I froze as something fell on my back.

The thing was light; it had landed right below the small of my back. Judging from the pressure, the thing was football-size. There was a feeling like two pairs of small fingers pinching my back.

A new sensation quickly followed.

Digging.

You utter, fucking idiot. Panic quickly rose in me. I reached behind me to throw it off, only to find that my hands were too short to reach it. So, I leaped for my staff, just as dozens of football-size things began falling from the ceiling.

The hosts those parasite things inhabited were arboreal insects, shit that stuck on vertical surfaces for a Goddamn living.

Above me was a waking swarm. Like a second skin, the ceiling had begun shedding an entire layer of the fucking bugs. The ones on the floor were the most mature ones, but likely also the weakest. The ones that had already been eaten so thoroughly that the host insect couldn't grasp on anymore.

I should've looked up earlier.

3.08

———

—The Revenant King on the Revolutionary
Forces outside his palace

I swung my staff behind me, knocking off the corpse, but the digging sensation still remained.

Rain of parasites. Numbers were probably in the hundreds. Parasites in my back. My mana was half spent.

"Run."

I grabbed the two mushrooms and turned around. The path was covered in bugs. I wasted half a second before I realized there was no clear way through. Cradling Greenie and Yellow with my arms, I rushed through, ignoring the things gnawing at my feet.

Two bugs landed on me, one on my cap, and one on my back.

I kept running.

One of them latched onto my left leg, another fell on my back. *Not yet.*

I hunched down, covering Greenie and Yellow from the barrage on top.

A third on my back, a second on my cap, and a new one on my shoulder. *Not enough.*

Two more latched onto my right leg.

I reached the exit and jumped through. The sensation of digging now over my entire body. Bark Skin and the Bracken Polypores acted as a buffer, but the first parasites had already made it through. A tickling sensation was inside my back. A small spasm went through me and I couldn't help but feel a bit giddy.

Some kind of chemical was being released. These things would not only eat me, but they would also make me laugh through the entire thing.

Joy.

Nine is good enough I guess.

I didn't have much time to consider, the grubs were spreading through me, making my body feel lighter but less responsive. I quickly scanned the surroundings, spotting a decent bench, I dropped Greenie and Yellow there.

"Stay here; if my corpse starts twitching, blast it," I directed. "I'll be back in a moment."

Now to see if friendly fire was a thing.

I took a few steps back and brought my hands to where the bugs were concentrated on myself, then cast Poison Spores with all my remaining mana.

You have died.

I dreamed of an endless black sea. Waters of possibility, yet I drifted alone on an island shaped by me but made by someone else's hand.

I woke up to an odd quiet. My first thought upon resuming lucidity was relief that self-damage worked. The alternative would be painful, well, probably not painful, but it would be long and disgusting to think about.

Quickly dismissing a pop-up detailing my lost experience, I glanced around. The spawn was empty. Completely so. No one, not even the marks of the previous bloodbath, it was uncanny how little difference there was from the first time I stepped in here.

A world reset? No, likelier just an instance reset. I suppose there were still zones Eve was unwilling to change. Never mind that, I needed to get going, quickly dusting myself off, I ran toward the direction of my death.

Dodging other players and moving through various terrain left me slightly out of breath, but it only took me a few minutes to get back. I knew I was at the right place upon seeing Greenie and Yellow wave at me from atop the bench.

A few paces from them was my corpse.

I kneeled in front of the body, Greenie and Yellow climbing into the safety of my cap as I did so.

I told the wisps to guard my corpse in the heat of the moment, but upon actually seeing it I was puzzled.

Why had this remained when other player bodies just despawned?

The body was fresh, but my clothing, gear, and armor were completely gone, so I guess I can't use this to dupe items, that would've been too easy. The body was completely naked except for a thin film of fungus on the skin, the floppy husks of Bracken Polypores and the bug corpses still clinging to my skin.

It was here I also noticed that my myconid body had no visible genitalia or reproductive organs, something I suspected but never bothered to check.

Prying off a bug, I was rewarded by the sight of several dozen holes dotting my skin and the answer to my question. Well, a theory anyway. Looking into one of the middlemost holes, I saw movement. A parasite was alive and still squirming. Noam lost his whistle thing to another player, perhaps the condition is that the thing had to be claimed by something else before they despawned or was this just specific to parasites like this?

Regardless, the body made the next few steps easier.

"Yellow, Green, I need you two to watch my surroundings and warn me whenever you can."

Yellow seemed to raise its eyebrow at that statement, even though the thing didn't have any visible eyebrows.

"I am not perfect," I elaborated, "but I am aware of some of my flaws. Regardless of whether I want to or not, I often become too focused on one thing at a time and lose track of my surroundings." Gently patting Yellow on the head, I continued, "You warning me earlier was good, even if redundant at the moment, don't stop warning me even if I look in control. It's a good habit because six eyes are better than two." I glanced at Greenie. "This applies to you as well."

They both nodded, Greenie made a mini-army salute, though he used the wrong arm. I chuckled slightly at that, but the humor quickly fell off my face.

I knew intelligently that those parasites were just following their life cycle. That even if they were designed as a sadistic joke, those things were not to be blamed for their nature. But I would not deny that I would enjoy killing those things in droves.

Ripping off all the other dead bugs, I began growing Sporages on my corpse. I had perfectly fine bait, it would be a shame to not use it.

Some time later, I lifted my corpse, placing it onto my back so that I might carry it, being very careful and gentle with it. I had to, after all, I was basically carrying a live grenade. It had become practically unrecognizable after I grew exactly one hundred Poison Sporages on it.

One hundred mushrooms.

I had grown one hundred mushrooms in the past three hours.

I had done nothing but grow magical mushrooms for the past three hours of my life.

If someone had asked me what I was doing with my life, I would not be able to answer them to any degree of satisfaction, but that was the majority of my life and, to be completely fair, my real self should still be a completely stable, well-adjusted student. I think anyway, I might have to check up on him later.

Initially, I went for fifty, a nice round number, but when I reached it, I realized it barely covered two-thirds of the body. So, I decided to cover the rest of the body; might as well, after all, but then I realized I was only a few off a hundred, so I went for that, squirreling more mushrooms under armpits, between the thighs and under the cap until I hit a hundred. I would've kept going too if the oldest of the Sporages didn't start to die off.

The worst part about this, however, was the fact that I couldn't even start a business selling makeshift Poison Grenades. Thirty every hour was a decent yield, but the Sporages started deteriorating after three. Not only that, I currently only had Proximity and Line of Sight activations.

Line of Sight was a no brainer, I can't sell a grenade only I can pull the pin out of. Proximity was also out. How it worked was that the Sporage spreads a thin sheet of mycelium around it to act as pressure sensors. When any part of the mushroom was touched with sufficient force, it would explode. This rule exempted me who made the thing and the two wisps, who were counted as my allies due to Symbiosis, but anyone who wasn't me or the wisps would be playing hot potato with it.

It was important to note, however, that I could control how far the spread of the mycelium went, allowing me to change the sensing range anywhere from five to zero meters.

I quietened my thoughts when I returned to the car park. It looked like the thing had reset completely, only the almost emptied shells were on the floor, no sign that the huge horde was there at all.

At least until I looked up.

Initially, I could only see a dark, flat roof above me, indistinguishable from rough concrete. I squinted, only to be quickly reminded that my eye sockets didn't have physical eyes to be squinted. Instead, I . . . focused and made out that the ceiling appeared rougher. There were no telling gaps between the bugs, their shells either overlapped or joined together snugly, but it was far from perfect. There were far too many grooves and rough ridges as opposed to the uniform flatness. The hosts' shell imitated wood bark, not concrete or the more commonly used polymers you would usually see here.

For a brief moment, I wondered how large of a tree did those host bugs stick to, for their shells to not only join together but also appear flat? Yet I just as quickly put it out of my mind, before it would wander to imagining the tree.

At best, the corpse can kill maybe eight hundred of them, to ensure the best outcome happens, there was one more mystery to be solved.

"How did the top parasites get alerted, if they relied on pheromones to alert others?" I asked aloud. Which, I mused, was probably a mistake, I haven't confirmed if sound triggered them.

Regardless, I didn't have a lot of time.

"Yellow, cling to the top of my cap; if any of the top ones move, you yell," I instructed. "Greenie, on my shoulder, be prepared to jump down for further instruction."

I moved closer to one of the emptied-out shells, the one farthest from the rest, nudging it with my foot a few times confirmed the presence of a particularly large maggot thing. Unceremoniously, I dumped my corpse next to it, detonating a few Sporages. Nothing to worry about. Until the spores attached to a living thing it would remain there. One of many positives with lingering damage.

Taking a few steps back, I warned the wisps to hang on, before kneeling down, sniffing the floor. The scent of the pheromone was there, as pungent as last time and ended approximately ten centimeters above the ground. I took a quick look behind me, confirming that the way was clear, and I began doubling back. Following the spread of the pheromone. In the process, I discovered something odd.

The pheromone spread easily in the horizontal direction, but it always ended ten centimeters away from the surface. No matter how far it was from the source.

"The ground ones are moving," Yellow warned.

I grunted a reply but didn't raise my head. The pheromone reached them. Not out of expectations, but it meant I had to hurry up.

I stood up, Yellow and Greenie yelping something out but I was too focused to notice. Instead, I walked back toward my corpse. The original maggot had died clawing at my corpse, setting off a few Sporages. The green spores formed a mound shape around the body. Standing a good few centimeters from the poisonous spores, I kneeled down and sniffed.

The pheromone smell ended ten centimeters from the ground. In an awkward half crawl, I began moving back. I kept my nose at ten centimeters.

Yellow said something, tugging at my cap urgently. I ignored it.

No matter how far I moved, the pheromone always ended ten centimeters above the ground until it suddenly didn't.

I moved quicker, getting out of the pheromones. Keeping my head low to the ground, I waited until the smell reached me and confirmed my suspicions.

When it had reached me, the smell hit me like a wall. A perfectly straight wall, perpendicular from the ground. The pheromones didn't act like a gas. No, it didn't act like any form of matter at all. It spread more like an invisible energy field with the only indicator being the smell.

I laughed, the sound sharp and grating amongst the sound of dozens of things scuttering and Yellow's panic.

"I didn't even consider this, I guess I am too unimaginative," I mused.

Yellow, still tugging at my cap, yelled, *"They're moving!"*

I looked up, just in time to see the ceiling bugs in different stages of stirring. The movements were small, almost unnoticeable, gentle bobbing up and down. Some were moving more than others, my eyes followed the rows of bugs, until it was drawn to a spot where the bugs were moving the most. Right above a pillar.

The last piece of the puzzle slid snugly in as I examined the pillar.

Rectangular with hard edges and placed between parking spots, they were such a regular sight I had just looked over them. What a mistake. The pheromone must've been able to travel up vertical surfaces as well. "In a world where magic is a thing, physics is more a guideline than a rule I suppose," I quietly mused. How stupid I was, for not even considering that normally mundane things won't be affected.

There was a smile on my face, though I could not remember forming it and a jumping feeling in my chest . . . Adrenaline? No, giddiness, I realized, of learning something new and interesting. It was something I hadn't felt in years.

"I can hear you Yellow, the both of you get under my cap," I said as I strode toward the pillar. The two moved without the need for further prompting and were there when I casually picked up a scuttering bug.

The legs locked onto my hand, though I quickly stopped its movement with Poison Spores, killing off the maggots that would've dug into my flesh at first notice.

The bugs at the top were acting strangely, they were moving, but they were also waiting. To fall together in a huge swarm like last time. Uncharacteristically sophisticated for what were supposed to be insects. Were the movements some kind of warm up or another signal?

Now, I knew several things about these parasites, but most notably, how they communicated to form a fighting swarm.

One, they released pheromones which spread in an unnatural way, signaling the ground parasites to move toward its source. Possibly causing them to spread their own pheromones to strengthen the signal.

Two, there was a different set of responses for the ones on the top, different or perhaps randomized timers? Another signal I wasn't aware of? I can find the cause for that later. For now, I needed to direct the bugs at the top to beeline to my corpse instead of dropping off all at once like last time.

To do that, I just had to override whatever instincts were stopping them from dropping down when they were signaled.

Prying the bug legs off its death grip on my hand, I raised a leg and brought the arm high behind me. Imitating baseball throwers of old, I lobbed the corpse hard into the nearest pillar.

It made a wet squelch as it landed near the top, then slowly began sliding off, leaving a trail of slime.

My smile became wider when the bugs on top immediately began scuttling down to follow that wet trail.

Three, they beelined the closest source of pheromones, at a close enough distance, it seemed to override all other instincts.

There was a single bug left at the capital of the pillar, its movement had turned frantic as the others left. As I stared at it, it rose from the ceiling, the bug-like eyes looking at me as a murky white line seemed to flit through it.

Four? Elite enemies capable of command? Was it intelligent? Did it matter? No, it did not.

I met the gaze of the parasite and simply chuckled. For, at that moment, I had already won.

3.09

———

"You call me insane as if it were an insult."
—Madelyn, then-moniker the Conqueror to Chancellor Chekov after
successfully subjugating the Western Empire

Cleanup was finished shortly after. All I had to do was pick off a few more bugs, kill them, then throw them in a path directed straight to the spores. Repeat a few times for all the nearest pillars, then the cascading effect of all the corpses did the job for me.

I did confirm that the pheromone stuck to vertical surfaces as well as horizontal. It ended exactly ten centimeters away from the surface. What a weird world.

Yellow and Green were still on the top of my cap, dutifully keeping a lookout no matter how cavalier I appeared to be. In truth, I wasn't completely relaxed either, normally by this time, the area boss would be spawning right . . . about now.

. . .

. . .

Now?

. . .

. . .

How about now?

I glanced around. "No? Nothing?" Granted the bugs were still trying to swarm onto my old body, which had grown into an impressive mound of corpses, so the sound might be drowned out.

Greenie tugged my cap and I glanced toward where it was pointing, a large insect corpse, at least three times larger than the normal ones that have been charging headlong past me, still stuck on the ceiling and its body was pulsating as its shell seemed to try, and fail, to restrain something inside.

I quickly assessed the distance. Out of my casting range. So, with a running start, I threw Greenie at it before whatever was inside hatched.

I probably should've warned Greenie before I did that, judging by the wail of surprise and Yellow's cheering whistle, but if there was one thing any gamer of anything could tell you, was that anyone who didn't at least try to cheese a boss, especially during a power-up phase when it was doing nothing, did not have a functional frontal lobe. The only viable excuse was when the Devs literally locked you from doing anything.

"Try to catch on to it!" I yelled toward Greenie, still flailing in the air. "Then explode everything!"

Greenie had five charges of Poison Spores if I remembered correctly, so they should work pretty well as a Smart Grenade. Did I explain to him properly to use all five at once?

"*I GOT IT!*" Greenie yelled as it grappled onto the rough ridges of the pulsating insect.

"*Should we help?*" Yellow asked from the top of my head.

"Probably," I answered as I kept walking forward. "Greenie! Make sure to use all five charges!"

Greenie gave me the thumbs up, almost losing its handhold in the process. It hurriedly regained balance, before five poofs of green spores came out in succession.

I quickly got underneath them, looking up at the spore cloud. Soon after, Greenie lost its grip and fell down, falling past my outstretched hands and landing straight on my face, its head halfway through my eyehole. Yellow jumped down from the edge of my cap, picking their fellow wisp up. "*Wake up!*" it said as it slapped Greenie.

"*Ughh . . .*" Greenie tiredly groaned. "*Ten more hours . . .*"

They are just getting more like me, huh?

Yellow planted Greenie on the top of my cap and I felt small tendrils coming out of my body, meeting Greenie's own tendrils and increasing the drain on my mana slightly. After making sure Greenie was fine, Yellow resumed keep track of the area.

The insect thing had ceased moving, probably dead. My vision moved past it, scanning the rest of the ceiling. There were plenty of smaller bugs that were still swaying, but none as large as this one. Was this not a swarm-type boss?

I raised my staff and nudged the insect out of its death grasp. I stepped back as it fell to the floor with a thud. It didn't make any sort of squelch noise, I noted. I poked it with my foot. Solid, no feeling of empty space.

"Keep watch," I instructed as I kneeled down.

Taking out my knife, I pried off its shell, revealing a slimy, fly-like thing. Using my knife, I slowly turned it around. Needle-like mouth, no, wasp-like is more accurate. Larger than a football. No legs of any kind. White shell which began to harden and turn black as soon as it was exposed to air. Two pairs of insectoid wings.

Having no legs is odd, its bottom side didn't appear like it was made to land either. A short lifetime adult stage that exists purely for laying? Was maggot the right term for the base forms of this anymore? It looked a lot closer to a wasp than a fly. How did an insect this large even survive—No, large insectoids can exist, have existed in fact, there might be a higher concentration of oxygen in this world or this might be another magic deus ex machina screw physics sort of thing.

If it's a singular boss, then it's probably very powerful or has a wildly different set of skills compared to the horde. Enough to pose a challenge to anyone capable of clearing out this room or to counter a build that was able to cheese this area.

Or am I just thinking too much in game terms? I wondered.

Yellow was tugging the backside of my cap and I turned around. One of the bugs was on my leg, I quickly Poison Spored it and kicked it off, but a white maggot stuck on. I pulled it off to examine. Not sure what I was looking for, but it looked closer to a large naked caterpillar rather than a maggot. A grub?

It was then I realized that I was hungry.

The dead maggot fit well within my hand. About the size of a small cucumber. I couldn't deny that I was curious. A bunch of people have taken up an insectivore lifestyle, especially when most traditional meats cost as much as they did, but am I curious enough to stoop this low?

Now that I think about it, it's perfectly normal to eat stuff like lobsters and prawns right? Those were basically sea bugs, right? These things also tried to eat me, didn't it? Isn't it right to repay an eye for an eye?

Yellow was looking away, Greenie was still asleep. As far as I was aware, no one else was here. So, I decided that between trying and not trying, it was better to try. Especially since no one other than me would know.

Taking one last look to make sure neither of the wisps was looking, I ate the maggot.

Huh.

It wasn't too bad.

A lot like a fatty steak actually, soft, meaty, and fatty texture but it had a slightly crunchy exterior; it left a warm, sweet aftertaste. Not bad at all, if I ignored the small part of me screaming at me to retch it all out.

"Was that there before?" Greenie asked from the top of my head.

I looked at where it was pointing, at the giant fly, wasp thing. In the scattered shell of its former host, there was a glint of light.

"Bit obvious, ain't it," I muttered as I recognized two gold coins and a spell crystal.

I picked up the crystal—Enlarge Insect, fifth—no, fourth level spell. It was harder for me to grasp on as opposed to the Bark Skin crystal. I could learn it, I knew, but it wasn't meant for my class. I pocketed it for now, then glanced at the gold coins.

"How did you two get to Daves again?"

I rolled the golden coin between my fingers, cursing as my low Dexterity decided to show itself; I fumbled and the coin fell out of my fingers. It fell to the ground and began rolling away from me. I followed its path, keeping in mind what the wisps told me.

The coin continued to roll until it hit a door. It was a simple door, made of some kind of dark wood, with a plaque that had "Daves" written on it like a logo.

It was not there previously.

As I stepped up to it, I picked up the coin, then pushed the door open, seeing . . . nothing but space. The background of the room was literally space, it was difficult to make out any hard corners of the room because the background blended together perfectly, like some kind of AR simulation. There was a lot of stuff scattered around, placed in some semblance of order which felt familiar to me.

Directly in front was a counter. Sitting at it was an almost identical copy of me, except he was wearing a suit and had a monocle over his left eye crevice.

I took a step in and paused, would the stuff outside despawn? It clearly reset when I died.

"No, it won't, not as long as you still want or are capable of looting it," Dave said.

"Ah, mind-reading," I said as I fully stepped inside, "I should probably get used to that."

He chuckled. "Welcome, whatever you want or need, you can purchase here."

I examined the store as I neared the counter, Yellow and Greenie doing the same. The place was huge, shelves and various items stretching out until they left my vision. Anything I could feasibly think of having a use for was here: spell crystals, items, consumables . . . I could've spent days listing just the stuff I could see in my immediate vicinity.

As I neared the counter, I noticed that "Dave" also had a tiny mushroom wisp thing on his shoulder, though dressed in the same wear as he was.

"What is it that you are looking for?" Dave asked with a practiced smile.

"A refund," I said as I fished out a receipt out of pocket.

Ignoring the protests of both wisps, I placed it on the counter. "Do you offer them?" I asked.

Dave eyed the receipt. "I do for this."

The wisps increased their protest. Instead of saying anything, I gently lifted them off my cap and put them on the counter.

Then I stuck my hands into my cap, my hands finding many things that I didn't comment about when they were first placed there.

"Miniature chairs, four dinner tables, a sofa, a bookshelf of books, five bean bags, two hot tubs? What do you even need two hot tubs for?" I questioned as I pulled out the two dish-size objects that fit in the palm of my hand. How did they even fit them inside my head? How were they planning to pump water into them?

"*We need privacy for bathing!*" Greenie answered, shaking its tiny fist at me.

"You two are both constantly naked," I pointed out, "what do you need privacy for?"

"*Oh, shit, we're constantly naked,*" Yellow realized.

I rolled non-existent eyes. "Do not ask me to get you clothes purely so having a bath naked is novel."

Greenie paused in whatever it was trying to say and muttered, "*That wouldn't have been the only reason . . .*"

"Would it have been the main one?" I asked.

Greenie looked away and whistled.

"Whistling does not actually work, you know?"

"*Bleep it,*" Greenie cursed—did it just bleep itself? I'll pretend I didn't hear that.

"Look, I'm glad you guys discovered currency, but being such spendthrifts isn't viable if you aren't earning the same or more as you spend," I calmly explained. "You need to figure out the difference between what is necessary and what isn't."

"*Sounds boring,*" Yellow muttered.

"*Yeah!*" Greenie squeaked, likely just rallying behind any argument that came its way.

"Okay, fine," I conceded, "you can sometimes buy stuff you don't need but want so long as it is within reason, but like I said you need to earn more than you spend, otherwise it's just unsustainable. To spend money properly is to accurately measure and separate what you want and need."

"What if something falls under want and need?" Dave asked curiously.

I glanced at him. "Then it is considered a need, as something you need is more important than what you want."

Dave met my eyes. "Is it really though?"

"Yes," I answered, "and let us not pretend otherwise."

Dave watched the back and forth between Dustin and his wisps as they argued about what was worth keeping and not.

"Okay fine, you can keep hammocks," Dustin exclaimed, throwing his hands up in apparent frustration, to the cheers of the wisps.

Dustin was winning the argument, Dave noted. It did not escape his notice that Dustin had gotten all the highest cost items to refund, leaving only low-cost items. Measuring in gold, Dustin had refunded eight to the three the wisps had managed to keep, and they were still arguing. It did bleed his heart a little to see him handle those Lissian Hot Tubs, those were made with the White Marble that was famous in the region. He sold them cheaply at material cost because they were too small to be of use to anybody, but those tiny things even at material cost were worth two gold.

Dustin just won something else, which wouldn't be the impression you got if you looked at him, he was shaking his head in exasperation, despite the fact he managed to bargain away all four dining tables, keeping a tiny magical humidifier. The dining tables may have been miniatures but they were each made mimicking the style of proclaimed artists and architects. Their combined artistic value was worth a lot more than a standard humidifier. Nine to two gold now.

After a few more moments in haggling, the score was ten to one, with the arguable losers looking utterly victorious. They managed to keep two bean bags, hammocks, and a humidifier, whereas Dustin managed to get them to agree to refund everything else.

It was kind of petty, really.

"You two just lost out, you know?" Dave was surprised when Dustin was the one who said this.

Dustin looked at the receipt, his face scrunched for a moment as he did some mental calculations. "Seven . . . no, ten gold worth of stuff refunded and only one kept on your side. You guys lost over ninety percent of crap you had; unless that stuff was vitally important to you, then I don't see this as a win in any way for you."

The formerly cheering faces of the wisps fell as Dustin continued his explanation: "That was literally easier than stealing candy from a kid, both of you got taken in by my carrot and stick approach. It's fine to appear like you've fallen for something, but actually falling for a trick is a problem."

Dustin looked over the pile of furniture and various other knick-knacks they decided to refund, then separated the miniature bookshelf filled with various picture books, along with a few hanging chairs. His brows furrowed slightly. "That's . . . two golds' worth. So, three in total for you now."

Dave noted that the wisps had argued a lot over the hanging chairs, though calling them swings would be more accurate, the bookshelf neither wisp expressed particular interest in. Was Dustin encouraging them to read more?

Dave chuckled, inciting the confusion of his audience. "I am not disappointed."

Dustin raised his eyebrow. "I was wondering what kind of person got Eve to pass the initial tutorial herself, I'm glad to see he is interesting," Dave explained.

Dustin was probably the best person to have gotten learning familiars. Often, many were content to just leave their familiars on their own, treated like an adorable attack dog, loved and considered dangerous, but still just a pet. Dustin actually seemed to consider them people, albeit naive kids in need of education.

"She gave me a broken nose," Dustin said, sounding more than a bit annoyed.

"I would like to ask you something," Dave said, causing Dustin to raise an eyebrow.

"I told you that anything you want or need, you can purchase here," Dave began. "I wasn't boasting in any way, literally anything you could possibly **Demand** is here," he continued to explain. Letting slip one of his Paths. Demand was extremely useful as a Path, especially for a merchant. To put it simply, if someone wanted something, Dave would know it.

"How it works, however, is that I need to buy the thing," he continued to elaborate. **Supply** went hand in hand with his other path, it allowed him to obtain anything. These two Paths were simple, however with the depth he managed to cultivate them, they held enough power for Dave to be considered the de-facto God of Commerce in Indiri, even if Ethelinda was muscling into his monopoly.

"Over the millennia, I've acted as a currency sink for Traveler Coins. I'm far richer than anything in Indiri, alive or dead."

Dave paused, looking at Dustin in the eye. "But when *you* stepped in here, no, even when your familiars stepped in here, I had the option to purchase the thing you truly wanted, your deepest desire, and put it in stock, but I could not afford it."

Dustin met his gaze, and for a moment Dave saw something. Something he would not have recognized if he wasn't a myconid at the moment. The cessation of all facial expressions on Dustin's face. It was as if he was no longer staring at a living being, but a clay doll, made in unnerving mockery.

Two breaths past in silence.

Until it was broken, by a sharp laugh.

Like paint being splashed on a wall, humanity returned to Dustin as he laughed at something only he found funny. "Ah! Oh, oh! That dumb thing, tell me, how much did it cost?"

Dave simply took out the price tag. A sideways eight, infinity.

Dustin laughed harder, to the point of almost keeling over. "Is this some kind of joke by Eve?"

"No," Dave said with absolute certainty. "The system which produces this stuff is completely automated, relying on the greater framework of the world. It created it, then put the price tag deemed appropriate for it."

Dave had sold wondrous artifacts, exchanged resurrections for coins, and fulfilled the desires of Gods. Everything can be priced because there was a value to everything, but very few times had he seen something truly priceless. He had seen numbers that had more zeros than could be counted, but infinity was something beyond value.

Dave asked his question: "What do you want? What is that deepest desire of yours?"

Dustin slowly stopped laughing and wiped away an imaginary tear. "It's nothing special, I just want something that lasts forever."

Dave met his gaze. Slowly, he removed his monocle from its position on the eye crevice. Magic Myconids did not see through there, those things were purely cosmetic. Instead, he placed it on an area on his cap and looked at Dustin.

The monocle glass turned dark.

"Ah," Dave uttered in realization, "I see. What a pitiable thing."

"It is, isn't it?" Dustin agreed.

3.10

———

"Sixty-seven. Never enter any sort of deal with the Greater Fey. Ancient identity changing techniques are not worth selling your name for."
—*Excerpt from* [EXPUNGED]'s Enchiridion of Encounters

I wiped away a tear; despite my earlier outburst my mind was still rational. To think someone could learn about that stupid thing. I don't believe I have ever told anyone about it.

That idiotic and childish dream of having something worth doing forever.

Dave began wiping the monocle with a napkin, I did not miss the fact the monocle only did something after it was removed from that eye crevice. A strange condition of the item or were my suspicions about my races' "eyes" true?

"You are stranger than I expected, but why do you call that dream idiotic? It is an admirable goal even if the reason for it is . . . depressing."

My eyebrows furrowed. "Do not refer to it as a goal," I asserted with a hardness in my voice. "A goal has measurable and achievable steps toward achieving it, if it does not have them, it is a dream."

Part of me stepped back as I said this, examined my mental state and deemed anger and frustration as useless as all the other times I felt those emotions. Thus, I took a deep breath and calmed down again.

"A dream is just a nice way of saying a delusion," I explained as a teacher would to a student. "All dreams are idiotic because of that. Mine are not any different."

"A dream to work toward can be a good thing. It helps people be motivated, as I see with you."

My eyes narrowed, mind reading is such a Goddamn hack, or is it memory reading? "Just because something is a good thing doesn't make it a smart thing."

"I would argue that having a beneficial thing is intelligent in itself."

"Maybe," I agreed, thinking of no rebuttal at the moment, "but you cannot just pretend that what you chose was idiotic, no matter how much it works. I am not against having a dream, a vague objective to work toward. But I would not pretend that dreaming is anything other than flailing around in the dark hoping you eventually hit your objective. It was contingent on luck, and any strategy that relies primarily on luck is just lazy."

"But didn't you try to do something like that with that druid?" Dave continued.

"Of course, that is stupid," I said, looking at him as if he were an idiot.

Dave looked surprised for a moment, though his face returned to that of a pleasant merchant just as quickly. Interesting, a limitation on mind-reading or was he just pretending there are limits?

"Oh, I won't deny that the whole capitalizing on the injuries of a sudden player versus player event for quick bucks isn't a stupid idea."

Especially since no one came by even though we wasted so much time at a single spot, I amusedly thought.

"However, you have this misconception that idiocy is an inherently bad thing," I said.

Dave raised an eyebrow. "Huh?"

"It is just a thing," I stressed, remembering Noam. "There is no good and bad about it. If you were to call idiocy a bad thing, then you might as well call the better part of the world and yourself a villain."

He didn't react for a moment, before sudden realization came to him. "Did you just—"

"Yes, I just called you an idiot," I affirmed.

Now, how would he react? Anger would be disappointing as it always was. Any negative reaction would be disappointing, to be honest.

Instead, he just mirthlessly laughed, the sound sounding very normal despite the fact he was the same race as me. "You are quite the character, sorry for taking up your time."

Didn't address it, instead moving the topic back to me. Calculated or not? Regardless, I raised my evaluation of him.

"There are questions on your mind, aren't there?" Dave asked as I thought about him. "For taking up your time, you may ask one and I will answer freely."

I looked at him, then carefully moved the pile of assorted trash the wisps bought toward him.

Dave looked back at me curiously, then left eight unminted gold coins on the counter. The miscellaneous pile disappeared beneath his arm.

"How does the leveling system work? I thought the bugs would've been enough for me to get to level four but that clearly isn't the case. I want specific and exact numbers."

The system did not show me exact numbers for my Experience, only percentages. Even after killing what must've been thousands of grubs, I was still at 60 percent Experience. Even if they were trash mobs, the amount of them made them something I doubted most players could have handled. I barely managed it with three hours prep. It should've been too difficult, especially at this level, in what should be a starter area. At the very least, it should've required a party with a majority of area of effect damage dealers.

"Leveling works by the Learning system; it tracks the experiences you have accumulated and converts them to a value based on how new—no, that isn't the right word," he interrupted himself. "How . . . unique that experience is relative to all the others gained in this body.

"When you fought the bugs, the bulk of the experience you gained wasn't from killing them, but from discovering their habits and function. Once you figured the trick to it, you gained a one-time packet of Experience. But due to the fact that you killed the bugs in a repetitive way, you stopped gaining experience after a certain point because it wasn't a unique experience anymore."

My eyes widened as he dropped this revelation, but he wasn't done talking.

"As for the specific amounts of Experience required to level, it is actually really simple. It stays the same for three levels, then on the third level the Experience requirement is multiplied by ten. You began with one hundred Experience needed to level from one to two and from two to three, but from three to four you're gonna need a thousand Experience. Then from six to seven, it would be ten-thousand."

I closed my eyes—no I don't have eyes, I closed off my vision as I considered this. The latter half wasn't difficult to consider, an exponential curve for leveling up Experience wasn't something new. Its uniformity was more surprising, but that in combination with this unique Experience gain system was . . . "Achieving even double-digit levels would be a great achievement, huh," I muttered in realization.

Standing in a single spot grinding for levels was impossible. Killing the same mobs for Experience didn't work either. These revelations shut down the most reliable methods of gaining Experience in MMOs. "The only way to reliably level would be to continually explore," I said, "to continually learn new things and to experience the world."

Eve must've designed the system with this intention in mind. I almost had the urge to applaud at how she made the very leveling system work toward Giles's dream, if I hadn't cursed in annoyance instead as I realized how this would affect me moving forward.

When I researched in that library, I kept a specific eye out for locations that continually spawned out monsters as potential grinding spots. Knowing the right place to grind in MMOs sped up leveling greatly. I had located five such places in total. This just invalidated all of—*No.* I thought as I habitually brought my thumb to my mouth, but instead of nails, my teeth chewed on bark.

The downside of unique experience only applied when killing the same mob over and over again. The method seemed to matter as well, but this also means that if the zone could consistently spawn different monsters, then it could still work as a grinding spot.

That removed the Silent Bastion, where the spillage from the Revenant King's death was still causing undead to rise even seven hundred years later. Only a few variants of undead rose there, all of them well documented. That made it a safe spot for the Western Kingdom nobles to train soldiers and Guild mercenaries, but meant it was a horrible place for long-term grinding with Travelers.

Then I removed the ones that are practically impossible to get to. Demons would've been a good choice, as they came in infinitely different forms, but the only stable Hell Gate was under the ocean in a ravine so deep that it rivaled the Mariana Trench. The Tritons have already called dibs on it as well.

The Oasis . . . I shuddered as I remembered the details about that location. That place was freaky enough that cultists and devil worshippers turned the land around it spanning several thousand kilometers into an uninhabitable desert just to prevent that corruption from getting out. An act that caused fucking crusaders to pat them on the back and let them build a nation nearby. Sure, they were probably thinking of using the city-states as a meatshield in case the Oasis ever spilled over, but the fact that holier-than-thou crusaders took one look at the Oasis and determined people who regularly practised live human sacrifice to be the lesser of two evils was . . .

I shook my head. My body wasn't suited for traversing an artificial wasteland anyway. I had yet to test the upper limits of what sunlight I can endure even with my protections.

That left either Shadesmar or the Underdark Gobbler. The Gobbler was always on the move, which made it hard to track, but that could be a good thing in a system for exploration. It had a habit of disappearing for up to months on end, so not a reliable source. That left Shadesmar. I could operate nocturnally there, and though the Lanterns have kept a good lid on that location they are always looking for more help. There was a constant flow of jobs from the Mercenary Guild as well.

Was I missing anywhere? Hmm . . . there were elemental rifts, but my class would have a horrible matchup against pure elementals. Arcadia? The fae courts respawned and all grudges disappeared by the end of the Season. But I would be on the fae's homefield, and I was not that desperate. The Hearth Jungle was apparently a good spot, but there were rarely guild quests there and it was a frontier location, so it would lack in luxuries. There was the ongoing war between elves and goblins, though apparently both sides contracted mercenaries to aid them. So, I would have to be prepared to deal with humanoid opponents. Something I'm not sure if I'm morally capable of pulling off, so I'll just ignore it.

That really does just leave Shadesmar . . . I muttered in thought.

The wisps poked me to ask why I had gone still and I absentmindedly explained my thought process. Though the bulk of my processing was still on shooting grinding spots down.

"Word of advice," Dave began, snapping me out of my trance, "you know of century-old battles but not of current ones."

I wanted to ask him about it, but he just put his hand out. "You would have to buy that information."

Not worth it, I could probably learn of current events pretty easily. The spread of information was surprisingly high in Indiri due to Wayshards. Though I heard there were still problems with transporting certain goods.

Still, I picked up a coin. "Do you always keep your word on purchases?"

"Yes," he answered.

"Then I'd like to buy the answer to one question vocally asked by me, answered fully and truthfully at whatever time," I said, passing the coin.

Dave's brow rose, but he took the coin. *Mistake.* He handed me a receipt, and I said, "Tell me the most useful piece of information I can utilize."

Dave nodded his head, apparently impressed. "The Law of Limitations is the innate law of this world. It states that all things must have a cost. The cost can be anything: mana, aura, lifespan, training, anything that can be considered a limit to something. It was implemented by Eve as a self-balancing mechanism for the world passing singularity and she could not feasibly attempt to balance every spell, attack, or defensive technique getting created. A simple example would be enchantments—a weapon enchanted with a curse is able to receive much more powerful enchantments. The longer a warrior spends training sword techniques the better they'll be at it."

I nodded. I would consider this later.

"I'll save my question until later, then," I stated.

Dave appeared confused for a moment, before his eyes widened in shock.

"I never did ask a question," I explained.

He gave me a lot of free information about himself; he was a merchant, but he could give stuff freely: prices of items, for one, and stuff he wanted to tell his customers. My refunding earlier confirmed that he differentiated between vocal questions and non-verbal statements, though it was shaky ground to trick him. It wouldn't be too great a loss even if he considered that my question, but I had the sneaking suspicion that the next time I came here, information would be harder to tease out of him than before.

Dave shook, and a sound like nails on a blackboard came from his throat. I realized he was laughing. It wasn't the normal-sounding laugh I heard earlier, but a sound I thought fitter for a myconid.

"I will keep my word," he said, sounding both genuinely amused and impressed. "Ask your question vocally whenever you want in my presence, and I will answer fully and truthfully."

"I did it because I assumed that information will be a lot harder to get out of you later on." Something about when he said that word. Demand. That felt different. Like the word itself had power. *It was a hunch, would that hunch pay off?* I thought but didn't vocalize.

"You value few things higher than information," he stated. "The next time you come here, I will've adjusted the cost for that. Indeed, I change the costs to match the customer and their needs. I am giving this information to you for free as well, I guess."

I smiled. "Thank you for telling me that," I said, making sure that none of my words was a question. "You also give the prices of things freely, though it was a mistake to let me decide the price."

"I am indeed open to haggling, but my guard was down . . . I should've noticed something when you made that incredibly specific request. Are you sure you were not misclassed?" he asked. "You would make an excellent Warlock."

"I was made aware that Travelers are already considered Warlocks of a sort," I said, remembering my brief glimpse of that book of magic before I ran off to save Noam.

"Indeed," he said with a jovial smile. "May I ask why you did it? Why antagonize this world's equivalent of the cash shop owner? What is essentially an Admin?"

I matched his gaze and said, "Because I could."

And because even when I antagonized Eve, she was reasonable. Now, I tested if I could outright trick and be an asshole to one of them. And saw their reactions.

Dave only laughed harder.

3.11

———

Is there anything else you'd like to do?" Dave asked in a good-natured tone. "Purchase something? Trick me again?"

I glanced around the shop. "Nothing really . . ." Then I paused as my not eyes settled on a cookbook. "Actually, just a few things."

Too fast, Noam thought as he leveled the blade against the girl's throat. His breath was already slowing, the dull thud of his heartbeat could still be heard but it was dimming.

"Too fast," Noam repeated again.

"Uh, you gonna stab me or what?" the girl asked.

Noam thought about it for a moment, then realized the answer was obvious.

"Nope!" Noam cheerfully said as he let her go.

"What?"

Noam skipped a few steps away. "Let's try this again."

"Are you looking down on me," the girl said, her eyes taking on a dangerous light.

"Not really," Noam answered truthfully, "I'm hoping you kill me, TBH."

"Did you just say TB—"

"Yep," Noam said, sheathing his dagger. He picked up his dropped halberd, took one look at it, before breaking the shaft at its center on his knee. "You play fighting games, right? Which one? Brawl Streets, Path of War, World War?"

"Machitis," the girl said with a smug look.

Noam's eyes shot toward her, suddenly bright and expectant. "Oh. Oh," Noam said, "that's the illegal one where all senses are turned to eleven, right?"

The girl was slightly taken aback by the reaction but answered, "Yes."

"Ranker?" Noam asked.

She proudly puffed her chest out. "Prelim for the last Oceanic Blood and Guts Tournament. I'm Red Cinderella. Call me Cindy."

Noam whistled. "Can I add you after this, then? It's been a while since I met another Ranker."

"Sure . . ." Her brain caught up to his words. "Another?"

Noam lifted his halberd, now proportioned closer to a hand axe with an extra stabbing end, and said, "Yup, I'm Mattmanfoo. It's been a while since I played, but I was in an American tournament. Can't remember the name, though."

"Huh, were you famous? I haven't heard of you," Cindy said, a finger on her chin in thought.

"Dunno," Noam answered, doing a few quick stretches. "I quit after a while."

He had gotten an earful from his mum when she learned about it. Along with Decs's disapproving silent treatment. God that was a boring month without the asshole to annoy.

"Now let's do this—" Noam couldn't finish, as Cindy had grabbed the aisle shelf, and viciously pulled it down onto them.

Noam dodged to his left, but wasn't fast enough, as the shelf top clipped his right arm. During that brief moment, Cindy closed the distance, her bat pointed like a spear. Noam's eyes lit up in glee as he realized that she was aiming for his left side, where his arm was still bruised and near useless.

His normal speed wouldn't make it in time, so Noam flowed aura into his right. Swift Strike allowed him to make the distance. Metal clanged as the bat was slapped away with his axe. Noam kept the aura coming, with a stomp forward, he stabbed the spear point into Cindy's left shoulder. She let out a gasp of pain but grit her teeth and weakly reversed the bat swing. Slamming right into Noam's exposed left.

The attack didn't have much strength in it. But something cracked. The blow was aura enhanced. Noam tried to fight against his body's desire to crumble under the pain. But he failed and his legs lost strength. He managed to keep his grip on his weapon, which prevented him from falling entirely as it lodged itself in Cindy's shoulder.

Cindy screamed as she swung again at Noam, but in her haste she missed his nose by a few centimeters.

The spear point dislodged, eliciting another scream of pain and allowing Noam to fall to the ground.

Cindy recovered when Noam landed and swung her bat golf style, Noam's head the ugly golf ball. But through aura Noam's foot kicked into her ankle first, knocking her down. As she fell, Noam forced aura into both his arms and slammed them down. The force pushed him up, his forehead slamming into Cindy's nose. Blood flowed as she fell to the side and Noam fell back to the ground.

Noam was dazed, his left arm was still bruised, and he couldn't feel his side. Instinct screamed at him to get up and thus he tried to, but an electric spasm went through him and he found it painful to move.

He wouldn't learn this until later, but consecutive uses of aura had strained his muscles. Regardless, Noam processed the present reality of being unable to make great movements and instead of resting, he forced aura into more parts of his body. His battered and bruised left arm shot out and slammed into the still standing shelf. He found that his fingers were numb and couldn't grip. So, aura flowed into each individual finger and each individual finger activated Swift Strike, slamming into the shelf to grab onto it.

It was false strength, but it was enough for Noam to pull himself up a second faster than Cindy. Two weapons flew out. Both were using aura, but only Noam used a speed enhancing technique.

Noam's spear stabbed itself into Cindy's chest, right where the heart was, only a moment before her bat slammed into Noam's head.

Noam fell back, ones of his horns cracking as he finally lost grip on his weapon.

Cindy's eyes widened, disbelief and shock dancing across her face as her eyes darted back and forth from the halberd in her chest to the body on the ground. She could no longer hear the beat of her heart and started feeling cold. She took a step forward before her strength failed her and she fell onto Noam.

Noam giggled, the sound coming out like a strained cough, Cindy joined him, her own laugh a gurgle drowned out by her own blood.

Cindy laughed for a few moments more as her body began to dissipate, before disappearing completely.

Noam kept laughing in utter childlike glee until the mob found him in a pool of blood and killed him.

* * *

"Damn, you've been busy," Noam commented as he took a bite into the "kebab." "What is this shit? It's delicious."

"You don't want to know," I answered as I continued cooking. The potato was manning the back, having almost fainted at the concept of customer service. Peps was manning the counter and helping out by being generally cheerful and healing anyone who came in with even scratches.

"Oh, yeah," I began, "don't eat a lot of it."

"Why not?" Noam asked, waving a cleaned skewer. "This shit is delicious . . . wait, is this skewer made of grilled potato?" Noam bit into the skewer. "It is!"

I glanced at the BBQ. The white flesh of the grubs cooked into a beautiful golden brown. Then at several of our . . . loyal customers who were buying with a distantly happy look in their eyes.

It was probably fine. They were happy with it, weren't they? Soda companies used to mix addictive drugs into their drinks, too. And I didn't even know what compound the grubs used to elicit a universal reaction across species. Probably magic shenanigans again. It would also explain how my "Poison Resistance" works, since what is poisonous is relative.

I could argue ignorance if I'm ever caught. Probably.

I lifted another bunch of skewers and handed them to the waiting line. There was a lot of cheering, with several proclaiming that I've converted them into staunch insectarians. A gecko came by with the orders written on its back and I pumped more mana into the BBQ. Then I prepared the correct spices for the skewers.

I originally wanted to use the geckos for advertising, but I had a bunch of grubs which were too large for the geckos to eat and the smell was a good enough advertisement on its own. So, we just hired a few more wall decorations and had a few more helping with service. Not only that . . .

I glanced as Peps put another gold coin into his afro. I was keeping track of the orders, so I knew how much money we had already made. Not that I was going to spend it anytime soon or am that afraid of backstabbing on Peps's or the potato's part.

Traveler Coins were probably a lot more valuable than normal coins. With them you can enter Dave's Store at any time and anywhere. Buy anything you could possibly imagine. They were a useful backup.

"What the hell were you doing by the way?" I asked Noam. A few minutes earlier a cheerful mob had come in celebrating killing a "purple asshole." They were very spendy.

Noam told his story over another skewer. I glanced at an angry-looking potato, signaling that I'll pay out of my cut.

After he finished, Noam asked, "So, you figure out what's weird with the deaths?"

I snorted. "Do you really expect me to instantly know after hearing it once?"

"Yes," he bluntly answered.

I shook my head in annoyance.

I mulled it over as I handed another bunch of skewers to the waiting line, my mind barely registering my actions on the BBQ. "What is death, really?"

Noam took a step back. "Oh, don't get philosophical on me again—"

"No, I mean in a medical sense," I said. "A person can be revived perfectly so long as no brain damage occurs. Lack of oxygen and blood flow will eventually damage the brain, but the person should still be capable of thought and action for up to six minutes. Even if someone's heart is blown out, they can still be revived so long as they reach a hospital within thirty minutes," I elaborated. "That explains why that girl—"

"Cindy," Noam added.

"—Cindy was able to move even after you stabbed her heart. Though that doesn't explain why she died only after a few minutes." I paused. A person's brain can survive up to fifteen minutes without oxygen or blood flow, a person can be revived with only minor memory loss if they are rushed to a nanite pod within thirty minutes. Those were the numbers I knew. But those were the numbers of humans of today.

I flipped the skewers over. "No, those numbers are incorrect," I muttered to Noam. "We should be using pre-G-Mod era numbers."

"Hmm?" Noam asked in between bites.

"Humans of today are completely different from the ones a century ago," I elaborated. "They didn't have G-Modding back then, so they were a lot more fragile than we are."

"Really?"

"Yep, we can thank the Soviets for that . . ." I muttered, biting my thumb bark in thought. "I'll have to search up pre-G-Mod era numbers whenever I get back to my body. Fantasy creatures probably don't have overt genetic modifications. That explains how Cindy died but not the ones before." I was missing something; Noam didn't inflict lethal attacks but crippling ones. Was that it? A body crippled caused it to die? No, that wasn't satisfactory, either. Matt stayed alive despite straining his body till it was literally unable to move. It wasn't something related to the body.

"Matt, what was your opponents' mental state before they died?"

He raised an eyebrow as he cleaned off his skewer. "Hmm . . . can't tell. A lot were pissed at me, that was obvious. The more pissed people lasted longer, but I had a weird feeling with a bunch of them who died quicker. Like they were plotting revenge for after they died."

"Will," I said, guessing. "Not the stat . . . actually, it might be? No, did they realize the battle was lost and gave up? Is that it?"

Brain death was the upper limit of what a body can achieve. But the lower limit was the person giving up all hope. No, hope felt like the wrong word. Will to fight at the current moment might be more accurate.

"I think it's the will to fight," I said. "Those people gave up fighting after all you did was torture them—"

"HEY, IT'S THAT PURPLE FUCKER!"

"Oh shit," Noam muttered. "I'm gonna leg it," he told me as he stole another three skewers and bolted. "SEE YA LATER!"

My not eyes narrowed on the newly forming mob. Was it really will? Those people seemed very motivated to lynch Matt.

4.00

———

"Fail not when opportunity is fair;
Behind Time's bald, his forehead's thick with hair."
　　　　　　　　　　　　—*Distichs of Cato II, Verse 26*

Two different streams of consciousness merged. My hand paused in mid-air as it was typing. I blinked unfamiliar eyes. Time: Monday, 2 P.M. My vision was strange. Things were "too colorful."

I withdrew my hand to rub my head. Odd, when did I gain fingers? Five fingers were too many. Wait, no. Five was normal for humans. I think? *Aftereffects of being in another body for too long?* Hendrix said there were programs helping with that. *I should probably set a schedule to log off. Weekly at the very least.*

In front of me, my screen displayed an online class on electron transport chains. The digital professor droned in an extremely tiring voice. In Gaia, I had just convinced the potato and Peps to help me run a kebab store with equipment bought from Dave. And did I die again?

Goddamnit, I am stupid.

I closed my eyes and zoned out for a moment to clear my mind, focusing only on my breathing. When I opened them again, the strange disorientation was gone.

Merging back was strange, it's not like I was just getting the memories uploaded in my brain. It felt different. *I would know, remember when I tried to download taekwondo?* The emotions and mental state of both of me were merged, Dustin me was still on an excitement high and . . . Declan me was bored and tired beyond belief. Two opposing mental states were mashed together. Just downloading data memory didn't do this. It didn't give those extra things like muscle memory, instinct, or emotion. Was that what caused my temporary disorientation? 'Would mental scars also transfer?'

Shaking my head, I put those stray thoughts away. Opening up another notepad, I typed down a note to log off every few days.

The disorientation was fading. Disorientation didn't feel like the right word though, it was more like a feeling where I had another limb, but that limb suddenly disappeared and I gained a different one, but still retained the muscle memory of that lost limb.

I shook my head again, then narrowed my eyes as I noticed a new sentence in my notebook. That exact thought about disorientation was written down.

I don't recall writing that.

I glanced at my hand, though of course there was nothing strange with it. Was this causing me to develop a split personality? *I don't mind, I guess. There is a lot of empty space in here.*

I closed my eyes and took a deep breath. My thoughts were scattered. *So, focus them.*

Working on it, I answered, and it was done.

I opened my eyes. My vision felt clearer. Did Eve's programs finally kick in or was it something I did? Merging back wasn't this bad last time. Did I spend too long in Gaia, or was it something related to my mental state? I sighed, another thing to consider at another time.

Speaking of time . . . I cringed slightly as I saw that five minutes had passed. Goddamnit. The teacher had already passed at least two slides, this teacher was as exciting as watching paint dry but he was comprehensive. I dragged my notepad back into vision and began typing, opening another tab displaying the presentation from the slide I missed. Perhaps subconsciously, my eyes flicked by the Gaia app on my user interface.

It wouldn't technically be wagging class as one of me would remain here. If I could clone myself, I might as well take advantage of it.

Opening the Gaia app again, I logged back on.

. . .

I blinked. The teacher kept droning on in his utterly dead voice. Looking around, I noted a distinct lack of change in my surrounding area.

"Fuck, I'm the one that—" I stopped, then quickly glanced at my mic icon to see that it was thankfully muted.

"Fucking hell, I'm the one that stayed," I finished.

After about an hour of glancing at the clock to make sure that no, my mind wasn't sped up by some sadistic asshole to make it seem like every second was thrice as long. I finally finished the class. I should've expected this, to be honest. The whole duplication thing meant that one of me would always be placed in this situation. To that person, me, it would feel like I never went to Gaia. It did offer an advantage though. Past the short disorientation, I actually felt somewhat refreshed after merging back up. It seemed to have found some middle ground between me who was relaxing for a day and the tired me who was studying. Perhaps I could use it to cut a few more hours off my recreation period and make my studying more efficient.

Finishing my last few footnotes, I began saving my myriad of notes into the correct places as a stray thought passed my mind.

Would I have to ever fight myself? Seemed unlikely, other than the brief moment of merging neither can interact with each other at all.

"It would be difficult, however," I muttered as I began to sort my notes into the right files.

Assuming a situation occurred where we came in conflict, he may be either the easiest or hardest opponent I could feasibly have. He knows how I think, I know how he thinks. Maybe the best case scenario would be the both of us falling into a Catch-22 of predicting each other's moves—No. It's more than likely he'd try to exploit that uncertainty by making deliberately risky moves and counting on me overthinking it.

I finished sorting the files and opened my checklist. My eyes widened a bit in surprise as I realized I had finished everything on my study list.

Huh.

I checked it over, making sure I had finished everything, before checking again, and again, and again.

Huh, I thought again, genuine surprise passing my face as I opened up each of my classes' web pages. Checking them to find that I was—Actually! Wait, no, I finished that last week. What about . . . nope. Two weeks ago . . . I finished that one yesterday . . .

I was actually finished with all my work. In fact, I was a few weeks ahead in most classes. Ain't that a surprise.

I leaned back in my chair. Eyes falling—or rising to my blank white ceiling.

What else can I do?

"I" was already in Gaia, so that was a dead end.

There wasn't anything interesting to watch on UsTube, the algorithm was largely recommending repeats. *One guy can create sapient AI on his home PC and a megacorp can't even fix their algorithms.*

Checking the few other games I played, I saw that Matt wasn't online currently on any of them. He wasn't even playing Path of War or Yggdrasil. That was rare.

I glanced at my mailbox. The thought of calling Matt died as quickly as it came to mind. No point bothering him.

So, I sat there, staring aimlessly at the ceiling, before I rose up and left my room. I was headed for the kitchen, not because I was hungry, but more because it was the natural state of being for a bored human to check the fridge. Regardless of hunger or whether or not the fridge actually had anything to eat.

It was surprising to see someone actually there.

"Ba?"

Declan senior was not an imposing man, despite being well above one-eighty centimeters. His shoulders were broad but slouched, his face looked tired, and strands of white were showing in what was once pure black hair. He sat atop a stool by the kitchen countertop, examining the contents of a package. A quicky glance at the barcodes told me it was from Taiwan.

"Didn't have work today?" I asked as I passed him, he still examined the contents of the package. An expensive-looking necklace, but it seemed to be missing several gems from its inlays.

"I didn't," Ba answered as he put the necklace down, rubbing his fore-head in an annoyed expression. "They told me I deserved a rest after working non-stop for a week." He shook his head in clear annoyance. "Nonsense I told them, a human being can stay awake for ten days if need be. More if I had coffee."

I glanced at him, now noticing the dark bags under his eyes as I got a clear look at his face, and that was *with* a full night of sleep.

"You do realize that staying up for that long tends to lead to . . . inaccuracies?" I said as gently as I could. You're a doctor, an inaccuracy might be dangerous, I left unsaid.

Ba snorted. "That's what they said, though with a lot less hiding around."

He mimicked, rather poorly, the voice of his hospital's dean: "Kevin, get some Goddamn sleep before I have to knock you out and force you to have some."

How did this man become a doctor? I wondered, not for the first time in my life, and probably not the last.

Ba shook his head. "Forget about that," he said, standing up. "Did you make sure to use the deactivation signal for the gel?" He approached me, grabbed me by the face, and turned me to face him so he could poke my nose.

"Yeah, Ba, I know how they work," I answered, my voice a bit muffled as his hand was holding both my cheeks.

"You better," he said. "Not turning that stuff off leads—"

"To horrific cancer and weeks of surgery," I chimed in, "though only if the nanites were left active for at least two weeks, which might I add—"

"Has not passed," he interrupted as he let go of my face, apparently satisfied with the state of my nose. "Though it is always better to be safe than sorry."

That I could agree with.

"Goddamn hospital shouldn't even have needed the gel," he muttered as he sat back down on the stool. "Just straighten the nose." He glanced at me questioningly. "You didn't ask for the gel just so you can get rid of the bruise, did you?"

"Nope," I answered as I opened the fridge. "They just painted the stuff on me. I assumed they were more qualified than I was, so I didn't question it." In truth, I was too disorientated at the time to really register the outside world at all. Far too busy pondering the implications of the crash and the invite I received.

"Better, I suppose," he said. "Next time make sure you go to my hospital in Parkville, not the backward clinic over there. I'll examine you myself."

"That hospital was closer," I answered as I opened the fridge and noticed something. "Ba, did you buy actual pork?" I turned around with an accusatory stare.

"It was cheap today," he defended, though he looked away from me, like a kid caught red-handed with his hand in the cookie jar.

"How much?" I asked, though it did not escape me, the irony of me who has essentially been freeloading on my dad asking him about how he spent his money.

He shrugged in that non-committal way. "Eh . . . only fifty . . ." He turned around to face me, as if realizing suddenly that I was his son and that theoretically, he should have higher authority than me. "It was on sale! Plus, we haven't had a good KBBQ in ages!"

"We had one three weeks ago Ba, you just fell unconscious halfway through from weeks of overwork."

"I wouldn't have if someone hadn't poisoned my coffee with decaf!" he yelled, before quickly turning away, a hand on his forehead. He was apparently nursing a headache. "And that was with synth meat," he said in a quieter voice, almost a whisper. "That stuff just isn't the same."

I raised an eyebrow; I personally never tasted a difference. It wasn't designed to be different. I felt it was better than actual meat in some cases, but never that different other than how it's sourced. I almost gave that retort, before I remembered the dark bags under my dad's eyes and how he got them. Working day and night despite the insistence of most people. He was an idiot for overworking himself in the first place, but he was my Ba, and so I relented.

"When's Ma coming back for the BBQ?" I asked, closing the fridge door behind me.

"Oh, she isn't coming back today," he answered. I opened my mouth, but he quickly answered, "Your great aunt died, so she left to visit her in Taiwan, we told you this morning. Did you forget?"

The memory came to me; I was writing an essay about one of Isaac Kramer's speeches, and she told me as she was packing up. *Did I forget—No.* The memory wasn't forgotten, it was just farther back in my mind, because of me logging off, it felt like the memory was from two days ago.

"I didn't forget," I said; it was even half true.

Ba snorted, apparently catching onto my lie. "Goddamn, I raised a friendless workaholic," said the friendless workaholic.

"My great aunt sent us that ugly necklace?" I asked, diverting the subject. I never met my great aunt. I did meet my grandma once. Funny person.

"Be careful now, that's your great aunt and grandma you just called ugly," he replied, raising the necklace.

My brain short-circuited for a moment. "Elaborate?"

He smiled in that macabre humor sort of way. "They apparently thought it'd be funny if they compressed their carbon into diamonds and sent them to every relative. This probably isn't the greatest of introductions, but—" He presented the necklace, pointing to the middlemost diamond. "Declan Lu, meet your grandmother, Unice Chang"—then, gesturing at the only other diamond on the necklace—"and your great aunt, Yasmine Chang."

I processed this information in a shocked quiet way, before shaking out of it with the "not my problem philosophy."

Heedless, my Ba continued, "Apparently, they want us to fill in the remaining inlays Declan, I hope that I don't have to tell you, but when I die of overwork I don't want to be turned into a gem to creep out my family for generations. I want you to fire my body into the sun. You know, like a responsible son."

Well, at least he's aware he's overworking himself.

"Ba, with the amount of caffeine there is in your body, we won't get past customs. Just stick with a Viking burial like the rest of us," I replied, only half-jokingly. I'm sure his body would count as a bioweapon somewhere, or at least a breach of the Gibraltar Accords.

"Do not cremate me at a crematorium named Viking Longboat and call it a Viking funeral."

Drat, he realized. It took me ages to find a crematorium named after a ship. "When will Ma be coming back, then?" I asked, changing the subject.

"Not till the weekend," he answered.

"BBQ's delayed till then?"

"Yes," he answered.

My eyes turned toward him, catching the brief hint of regret on his face before he masked it just as quickly.

"We could have a little BBQ ourselves first," I said, "and save some meat for when Ma comes back. I have been wanting to eat some non-synth meat." I wasn't, but I knew Ba enough to know that he probably wanted to, before he threw himself in the fray of work for another few weeks.

He snorted. "Just us two? No need to bust it out for such a small occasion."

That angle didn't work, Ma raised me to be tight with money and he knew that. Pressing this point wouldn't work.

A message notification appeared on my mailbox, giving me an idea. "What about Matt?" I asked. "We could head to his place and share it with his family."

Ba looked at me with clear confusion for a moment. "You . . . you actually suggested going to Matt's?"

"What, is there something wrong with that? I hang out with him all the time."

"Yeah, but when was the last time you even considered being the one to suggest it?" He wiped away a tear. "And I thought my son would die friendless and alone. There's actually hope for you. I might actually see grandkids before I die now."

I raised an eyebrow, thinking, *I'm doing this for you, you overworked shit,* though I didn't voice my thoughts. "I'm calling him."

Matt picked up after a single ring.

"Decs! Have you seen the new expansion in—"

"Are you free this afternoon?" I asked, cutting straight to the point.

"Yeah, why?"

"My dad bought some pork, but my mom left for a business trip. He was thinking about taking it to your place and sharing it," I lied. "Neither of us can cook, so he figured Sarah could help with it." Which was true, neither of us can even cut an onion evenly.

"Wait, wait, wait. Actual pork!? Like not the synth stuff?" he asked with rising excitement.

"Yeah?" I answered. He sounded way too excited for this.

"Holy—MOM!" he suddenly yelled. "DECS GOT SOME PORK TO SHARE!" Two female voices yelled back, both I recognized as his mothers' but couldn't make out the specific words.

"When are you coming?" Matt asked.

I glanced at my Ba; he shrugged. "Probably soon, 4 to 5 P.M. at least. You guys have a Korean barbeque grill, right?"

"Hell yeah, we do!" I could almost feel him punch the air in glee. "Alright, we'll see you here!"

"Sure, see ya later," I answered as I hung up.

I felt like I was missing something important as I hung up. "Ba, how much meat did you buy?"

"Like one kilogram"—he shrugged—"why?"

Huh, fifty dollars for one kilo of natural meat actually was a good price—focus, Goddamnit.

"I just have the weirdest feeling I'm missing something . . ." I paused.

"How many people are in Matt's family?" I asked, though my mind already conjured an answer. Four, both of Matt's 'rents, Matt himself and his little brother. Ba bought one kilogram assuming it would feed three people. We just offered to feed six.

I groaned. "Ba can you check if the sale is still going on?" I said, trying not to think about the fact we could easily buy twenty-five times the amount of synth meat with that amount of money.

In a place beyond the skies, there was a place that once was a library. Within was a figure.

He sat at a desk older than years could count. His eyes appeared pure black and never stopped staring at the world above. He never blinked, even though dust had long settled around him, masking his body in a veil of grey.

The only part without dust was the desk in front of him, where his hands moved to do his work. His left held a pen, making the only sound within the desolate place. The other supported a book with infinite pages, flipping to a new one when needed. He wrote of what he saw. Gods and men, discoveries and conflict, whether great or small, he wrote it. He wrote it all.

But as he flipped to a new page, something strange occurred. Something which broke his millennium-long pattern. The being found a card wedged within the pages.

Centuries-old dust was disturbed as the being, for the first time in a long time, moved his head. It creaked as he looked to the book, to the card laid in-between the pages. The card depicted a man with one arm stretched to the heavens, the other to the earth below. He wore a wide-brimmed and pointed hat that reminded one of a mushroom. Before him lay five tools, of them only two were colored, the rest remained a stark white contrast against the colorful artwork. Yet, their outlines showed enough to make out a scroll, a wand, a lens, a filled goblet, and a key.

The being blinked. Eyelids pushed off layers of dust from his bare eyes. For the first time in millennia, the being smiled as he turned again to look at the body gently laid next to him.

Through all this, the sound of the pen never stopped, for the being never stopped writing. Never stopped recording what he saw.

"It is the year 2856 of the Third Age. The elves call upon their dwarven allies as the goblins push them to their final forests. The Western Kingdoms are brought to chaos as a necromancer commits regicide in a mad bid to resurrect the Revenant King. In the north, the Yuan Tei experience the first organized attack by Shadesmar in two centuries before it is repelled by Lu the Black Hand and the Order of Lanterns. Deep within the Tyrian Sea, Tritus reports two greater demons passing the Gate. One entropy demon and the other an order demon. Caligula the Swift, Lance of the Great Blue, aided by a Leviathan Ship, slew the demon of entropy before the order demon forced a cease. Perhaps heralding this new age of conflict, the fourth Great Transmigration has occurred and Travelers stream into the world once more. During all this, the God Historian was left an omen in the form of a tarot.

It was the Magician, and he knows his chance has come."

4.01

———

"Strength is just misunderstood weakness."
　　　　　　　　　　　　　　　　　—Unknown

The delivery arrived within five minutes. Ba and I agreed that though getting it delivered to Matt's house would be faster and more efficient, it would be too embarrassing to have a delivery drone show up there right after we said we had enough.

Well, we didn't say we had enough, we just sorta implied that.

"I did not imply anything," Ba muttered as he packed the meat into a cold bag. "This was all you."

I ignored him as I took the bag. There was another kilo in the fridge for when ma came back, which Ba was probably overjoyed with, having an excuse to splurge twice in a week.

KBBQs also gave me a good excuse to get Ba drunk. He normally abstained, but eating natural meat put him in a celebratory mood.

It'll be a hassle dragging him out of the car later, but God knows he needed the sleep.

Ba did a few hand motions as we stepped into the garage. The loud sound of gears grinding heralded the opening of the door, letting natural light in. I read somewhere they could've made garage doors soundless ages ago but kept the loud noise because people weren't used to handling sound-less garages.

Weirdos.

As I made my way to the car, Ba called out to me, "Will you be fine in a vehicle?"

I turned around to see him giving me a concerned look. "Of course I will," I replied with an eyebrow raised.

"Why wouldn't I be . . . oh."

The crash was barely two days ago and yet it feels almost a week had passed. Practically speaking it was almost a week ago for me since I've been doing double time. Literally.

Ba just raised his eyebrow, before shaking his head in an exasperated fashion. "Goddamn freak accidents," he muttered as he passed me.

"Me or the crash?" I asked as he piled the bags in the back seats.

"The crash," he answered as he took his seat at the front, though I could hear the slight quirk of his lips. "It's not every day a driving AI glitches out."

"No one got seriously hurt." No one I was aware of or cared about anyway. Though it sucks to be that Maple executive.

"Yeah, I read," he answered as he typed in Matt's address with his AAD. "Apparently the AI corrected itself last minute, so everyone only got off with minor injuries. They found a logic error had occurred after they looked at the logs. Apparently due to a few poorly written lines of code."

Ah, false evidence. Though I would've added the bug to other AIs so that—

"It's showing up in other models so it's good they found it before anyone got seriously hurt," Ba continued as the car started up and drove out.

She was thorough.

I had to show a bit of interest in this; I was directly involved, after all. "Has it been patched yet?"

"Yeah," Ba answered, "I downloaded the update today. Don't worry."

"Mmm," I murmured.

"This stuff used to be a lot worse back in the day," Ba said as he reclined his seat.

Huh, so he didn't drink coffee today, is he actually making an effort to rest?

"Back in the day people actually drove cars," he said, his eyes closing. "Can you imagine that?"

"I can, yeah." I read about that before, and Matt has pestered me to try out more than one racing game in the past.

"Over a million people died each year when they did that shit," he murmured, his voice turning quiet. "Fifty times that injured as well."

"Are you sure they weren't intentionally killing people?" I joke.

If Eve wanted to kill me, a vehicle would be the best bet.

He chuckled lightly. "I bet a few were . . ."

"I'm sure," I answered as Ba drifted into sleep. Right now wouldn't be ideal, since the same person getting involved in two highly unlikely traffic events in the same few days would be suspicious, to say the least.

I glanced to the front of the car, seeing the smooth surface and briefly tried to imagine where a steering wheel would be. Right in front of Ba, where the compartment was.

Most cars nowadays had more fail-safes than what is probably reasonable, but Eve already overcame them once.

I shrugged. There was nothing I could do if she could overcome the already inbuilt stuff, which by law was required to be the best of the best. I barely had a college-level grasp of coding, I needed to be insanely lucky to create a system better than programmers light years ahead of me.

Though I didn't believe she would actually try to take me out. Sure, she played a few "pranks" on me. I learned later on that no one else actually got dropped from the sky during the intro, I was the only one who got that treatment. Which I couldn't even really blame her for, I did emotionally extort her with a recently dead family member or whatever the Frankenstein equivalent was.

I internally grimaced, I . . . could've done that talk better. I met many short-term goals at the cost of a long one. I made her dislike me, not enough for her to actually do anything substantial about it, but the enmity is there. There could've been another way. The ideal was friendship, but I would've settled for apathy. My current assessment of Eve tells me she is human enough to be angered and tied down by sentiment. She might not like me but she probably wouldn't outright kill me.

Even if she just wants me to think that, the fact that I'm thinking it means I'm already under her thumb and therefore not a short-term threat, I thought with a pessimistic smirk.

I glanced at my sleeping father.

People were flawed, and if Eve really was more human than AI, then she, too, was flawed.

And flaws could be exploited.

I really am an asshole.

As the car pulled up in front of Matt's garage, I sent a quick message telling him we were here. Before gently tapping Ba's shoulder three times.

He instantly opened his eyes. "What's the patient's condition—" he stopped, eyes taking in his surroundings and his mind quickly catching up. I was already half-out of the car by then, cold bag in hand.

The house's front door opened, revealing the skinny form of Matt, his face lighting up in a delighted smile. He threw up his right arm in an exaggerated motion. "LOOKS LIKE MEATS BACK ON THE MENU!"

I raised an eyebrow. "That's a weird-ass saying," I said as I entered the house.

Ba right behind me said, "Afternoon Matt."

"Afternoon, sir. And I heard it in my Humanities class," he answered. "Apparently it was a meme inspired by a movie or something."

"Huh," I answered, I didn't take history as an elective past year ten, mostly because I learned the important stuff passively from wikidives. "Any other stuff?"

"Something about November 9, 2001, but I forgot most of it," Matt answered as he led us in.

There weren't any major events associated with November ninth that came to mind. "Must've not been important," I said as I spotted Matt's younger brother, Max, running up to us. Though his running speed was actually pretty slow because A, he was ten and B, his legs were short, like really short. The shortness gene in Matt's family was prevalent even as a kid, so really, he looked closer to six years old.

"Yo," I said as Max ran up next to me, his hands zipping open the cold bag, where the meat was being kept in synthetic packages.

Max took a single glance at the contents, then pointed an accusing finger. "You lied to me! There is no difference!"

"Of course, there is!" Matt retorted.

"Something was killed for this meat," I drily continued. "Probably many things since there is no way all this pork belly came from the same pig."

"And it tastes a lot better," Ba added. Though that part was debatable. I still never tasted the difference between "real" and synthetic meat but people kept insisting there was. Probably a placebo. I'll have to trick Ba with synthetic meat one of these days to test it out.

"Are you bothering the guests, Max!?" I heard Matt's mother, Denise, yelling out from the kitchen farther back.

Max simply stuck his tongue out and ran past us.

"Afternoon," Ba said as we entered the living room, which was connected to the kitchen.

Matt's other mom, Sarah, glanced up from the kitchen counter, where she was halfway through cutting a sweet potato into thin slices. "Welcome, welcome! Lemme grab that," she said as she hurriedly put away the knife.

"Afternoon, Sarah," Ba nodded, then turned to the other woman in the room, who was setting up an electric stove. "Denise."

"Oh, your family is always welcome here," Matt's mom said as she took the bag, then almost reverently, removed the kilograms worth of pork belly and placed them on the chopping board.

"I'll be taking a nap in the living room, then," Ba said as he turned around. "Holler when the meat is ready."

"Alright!" Sarah answered as she began poking the slab of pork belly with an appraising stare. "Perfect! I can begin cutting."

"Any way I can help?"

"Sure, can you mix the sesame oil and salt pepper?" Denise asked as she pulled out their large Korean BBQ pan.

"Matt, finish up the sweet potato for me," Sarah said as she skillfully sliced the pork belly into small bite-size pieces.

I followed my memory to their spice cabinet. Salt and pepper were in the back left, sesame oil was front right. There was also the chili paste in the fridge along with the fish sauce, and sugar in another cabinet. I would need to mix the chili sauce.

Matt took out another board and knife along with the half-cut sweet potato. Unlike me, he didn't rely on instant food when his parents weren't home, so he was actually half decent with a knife.

We fell into a flurry of preparation. Denise was setting up the table, her wife Sarah was cutting the meat with expert precision, Matt cut apart the vegetables that we would grill alongside it all and I was mixing the sauces. After I was done mixing a small bowl of sesame oil dipping sauce, I moved to mixing the chili paste.

The formula was simple, two sauces, the first was sesame mixed with salt pepper, the second was chili paste mixed with fish sauce and sugar. Everyone had different preferences, and I had them memorized after some observations. Matt and Denise liked the chili sauce over the sesame oil, though both of them had a stupidly high tolerance to chili so I didn't bother mixing their portion with a lot of fish sauce and sugar. Ba and Sarah used the sesame oil more, so I didn't portion them as much chili sauce. I preferred sesame oil as well, but I liked a higher portion of salt, so I mixed mine separately. Max seemed to like both equally, though he didn't have the same chili tolerance as his brother and mother, so I mixed more fish sauce and sugar in his to sweeten the flavor.

Barely ten minutes later and we were done. Matt helped his mom move the plates to the table, I placed everyone's sauce bowls in the spots they normally sat along with their chopsticks, or fork in Max's case.

"Ba!" I called out as Sarah turned on the electric stove. I heard the living room couch being reclined back to its original spot along with a hurried "Coming!"

"Hurry up and come eat, sir!" Matt called out as we took our seats.

"You, too, Max!" Sarah yelled out as she began laying the slices of meat on the pan. The sound of the sizzle began like a whisper but slowly increased in intensity as the fat of the pork began to melt. Ba got here with Max trotting in tow just as she filled the pan.

Denise led her son Max to a spot next to her; Ba glanced around and asked, "Do you have soju?"

"Yeah, it's in the fridge," Denise answered.

"Thanks," Ba said as he went to it.

"Bottom shelf, back right," I called out as I saw him open the door.

Strips of golden brown were revealed as Sarah began flipping over the pork. Right as my dad took a seat.

"Already done?" Ba asked as he cracked open his soju can.

"No I just flipped them." Sarah answered.

"They were just flipped," I said at the same time.

"Just a minute or two now," Sarah finished, clacking her tongs a few times before setting it aside.

Six pairs of eyes were glued on the sizzling pan. Sarah signaled when the meat was done when she flipped over a piece to reveal another side of rich, golden brown.

Six pairs of chopsticks were already moving as she declared them ready—wait, six? Denise usually held a very neutral expression, but I could see the small smirk of triumph as Max began picking out pieces with his own pair. So, she finally got through to him, I'll have to make sure I don't take out a fork for Max next time we're here.

I quickly snatched three pieces. Liberally dipping them in my sesame oil sauce. Each kilogram of pork belly cost fifty dollars at discount, I had just taken several grams worth.

At least fifty cents, I estimated as I ate them. One bite and I ate fifty cents, I almost didn't notice the texture of the pork, as its crunchy exterior quickly gave way to firm yet chewy flesh.

As if the stupor was broken, conversation began as everyone had their first bite.

Ba was slumped over on the chair snoring, he had a comically weak resistance to alcohol. One shot was all that was really needed to knock him out.

Max and Matt were energetically running around, definitely playing an AR game given how their hands looked like they were holding a blaster despite nothing being there. Denise was watching over them making sure they didn't hurt themselves despite the fact most AR nowadays did almost one-to-one overlays on reality.

Sarah and I sat cooking the last of the sliced sweet potatoes. Two kilograms of pork belly, a hundred dollars eaten in one determined dinner. I was probably responsible for at least a third to half the worth and that was just counting the meat. Though the vegetables were negligible compared to it.

Sarah placed the cooked sweet potatoes into my bowl as they finished cooking. "Anything else you all want to eat?"

I shook my head. "Nope."

"I'll turn it off, then," Sarah said as she switched off the stove. "I'll start the pack up."

"Oh! I'll help!" Matt yelled, turning off his AR display with a few flicks. He stepped toward the table and lifted the BBQ pan.

If it were anyone else, they would've dropped it like a hot iron because, well, *it was*. But for Matt, he barely seemed to notice. Hell, I'm not even sure his prosthetics felt anything other than pressure.

Matt casually carried away the still hot BBQ pan and set it to cool at the kitchen counter. Both of his arms and legs were prosthetics. From what I've heard from conversations between him and my Ba, it seems that even one of his lungs and his heart are, too. Which struck me as incredibly odd.

I knew little about Matt and his family's past, but I gleaned over the years they were immigrants from one of Europe's underground Metro Cities and that they likely ran into an old war weapon as they were crossing the borders.

That part was easy to deduce. When I first met Matt's mom Sarah, her left arm showed signs of having been recently regenerated, even now you could notice that her left arm had a slightly lighter tone. I caught their place of origins in conversation later on and Max showed a great fascination for the sun when he was even younger.

But Matt still had all his pieces when I first met him and he was one of Ba's patients. He lost them later on when they reached Australia and were at my Ba's hospital. Stranger was that his limbs were actual artificial prosthetics, not stuff cloned from his DNA and replaced.

Why didn't he get his limbs regenerated and stayed with prosthetics? In this day and age getting and maintaining artificial prosthetics was costlier than just taking a dip in a regenerating pod, so why didn't he?

I had several theories, many of them even made sense, and I knew for sure that Matt would provide the answer easily should I ask.

I knew for sure he would, as certain as I was of the sun rising.

But I never asked, and I never will. I have constantly dismissed the thoughts as just theory, no matter how much they made sense, no matter how much everything added up.

I owed him that much.

4.02

"What would happen if we put this bag of holding into another one?"

—Last words of far too many people

We finished selling our stock later that night and had accumulated a pretty sum of a hundred and eighty-four gold, though we had some problems splitting it.

"Forty, forty, twenty," the potato said, and I furrowed my brows.

He meant for Peps and me to get 40 percent of the share, and he 20 percent.

"Now, now," I argued back, "you made the store, did all the food preparation, grew the skewers and fished the grubs out of the husks, that's at least 40 percent." Normally, I didn't mind people giving me more money, but this guy actually put a lot of work in this. It would annoy my conscience to fail to pay back someone who actually worked competently with me.

Neither of us believed an equal split would be "fair," especially given the division of labor. Though our definitions of what we should each be respectively paid for differed.

"I really don't think I deserve that much; all I did was talk to—"

The potato raised a hand and completely serious, said to Peps, "You are the most valuable member of this team."

I agreed, dealing with a few people I can do, almost a hundred like we did today? If Peps wasn't here, I couldn't have played the stoic chef as well as I did.

As for why the potato was so grateful, I asked and he said, "I spent fifteen years working in retail."

Oh. Fair.

"Still, all I did was talk."

"All Ustubers and video advertisers do is talk. And have you seen their salaries?" I replied. The argument was mostly bullshit, even amateur Ustubers nowadays had teams working with them and spent hours each day cultivating recognizable and algorithmically perfect personalities. True solo indie channels died out ages ago. But it had enough basis in logic that I could jump to another point. "It's more about the brand than the actual work," I continued.

"Now you don't start selling yourself short as well," the potato interrupted. "You're the whole supplier of this, you killed the actual things and bought the BBQ grill and spices. Until the location is discovered you have a total monopoly. Even longer if people can't kill them en masse."

"I am not selling myself short," I answered. "The equipment is a long-term investment that I plan on using many times in the future, and the monopoly won't last long. People just need to poke those things with a stick a few times to figure out their exact capabilities."

Both Peps and the potato looked at me strangely as I said that.

A familiar snort came from behind. Despite breathing heavily and looking like he ran several marathons, Noam still found the energy to laugh. "Really, Dusts? How many people would see those creepy looking fucks descending upon you and immediately think 'Gee, I should poke this with a stick!'"

Grabbing a nearby rock— actually, wait it's a potato—I threw it at Noam. And surprisingly, he made no effort to dodge. The potato boinked the side of his head and unceremoniously knocked him down to the ground.

I huh'd in surprise. How long has he been running?

A second later, I heard frantic running as several people, also heavily out of breath, crashed into the doorway where Noam had fallen.

"Huff . . . I . . . huff . . . got him . . ." an elf said as he tiredly leaned on the doorframe.

"I'm gonna . . . huff . . . shove this up his ass," another pursuer said as she raised a spear, before collapsing to the ground. Like dominos, the completely out of breath pursuers fell around Noam. One of them tried halfheartedly stabbing him, but he was clearly too out of breath to try anything.

"Uurrgghhhh . . ."

"Hey . . . can one of you . . . *huff* shove this up his ass for me?" the pursuer said as she weakly gestured at us.

"Unless you plan on paying me, then no. Outsource your vengeance to someone else," I replied.

"So," I said, turning back around, "how about thirty-five, thirty-five, thirty?"

We ended up splitting it 40 percent going to me and 30 percent for Peps and the potato. The potato justified his share by saying he'll take all the leftover shells, apparently they were useful for his class and turned my earlier argument that the equipment I bought was a long-term investment, thus justifying his labor creating the storefront as him planning to open an independent shop.

"Where is he!" I heard an unknown voice yell.

That was the eighth one now.

"The second store to the front by the right, the one that's the old Macca's," I answered.

The pursuer grunted thanks, before following my direction.

A moment later . . .

"What are all these mushroo—AAAAAA!!"

Peps glanced at me with incriminatory eyes, which he did for the last seven as well. "He's fine," I assured him.

"AHHHH! THE PAIN! IT'S LIKE I HAVE BEEN SHOT AND DRENCHED IN ACID!"

"That's an exaggeration."

"I AM NOT EXAGGERATING!! I TOOK A FUCKING SEN-SORY PATH! THIS PAIN IS TWENTY TIMES STRONGER! AAAAAH! WHY ARE THERE SO MANY MUSHROOMS!!?"

"Well, hindsight is twenty-twenty as well."

"MY EYES! I AM BLINDED!"

"Hindsight is zero-zero, then," Noam muttered.

"AH!!! JUST YOU WAIT TILL I GET TO YOU!"

"Wait a moment . . . you took a sensory path and didn't notice me hiding under the table?" Noam yelled as he peeked out.

Ignoring Noam's casual conversation and Peps boring holes in me with his stare, I focused my attention on the potato who set aside my split.

"Seventy-five gold," the potato said as the man screamed his dying throes. "Do you have a way to carry all this?"

"I have an idea." I glanced under the table. "Noam, watch my stuff for a moment."

The two wisps who had been laying mushroom mines started toward me. "No need," I said, "stay here, I'll be right back."

Leaving the store and passing by the mushroom field, I quickly made it to the mall's Wayshard.

I opened my menu and navigated toward the Impact Point store and made my first purchase. Five Impact Points for a single character slot. The option greyed out for a moment before the cost was updated to fifteen Impact Points.

Then I touched the Wayshard.

You may Travel to:
Gaia (Current)
Indiri
Character Slot 2

Mentally thinking about the slot, the world changed around me, and I was once again standing on that hospital rooftop.

A holographic figure appeared in front of me. Eve wasn't around, guess that time was special.

I didn't really care what this character was, so I just thought "Random."

The figure morphed into something more recognizable. Its lithe body looked around one-eighty-five centimeters. Way taller than my Myconid character and taller than myself in real life, at least by a few centimeters. It had a mostly androgynous looking face, sharp ears were barely concealed by its light auburn hair and almost white pupils that appeared blind.

Elf Fighter.

"Good enough," I said, intending to stay with this selection. The world changed around me, I briefly glanced at my spot at the base of an extremely large tree.

"Good evening," a melodious voice said to me. "Welcome to the tutorial."

"Yep, I've been here," I answered. "This is all very interesting, but can I skip to the bit where I get my equipment and skills?"

The other elf held an utterly serene, if somewhat amused look. "Very well."

The world shifted again, and I was at a derelict fashion store that was oddly filled to the brim with stuff. Unlike my last tutorial, I was aware of a number. Twenty gold. My budget.

"Not enough for a bag of holding, then," I muttered, most bags were in the hundred to five hundred range.

"Choose your weapon as you wish but choose wisely."

"Done," I said as I took several extremely large and empty bags.

The elf raised her eyebrow. "Are you sure that's all you want?"

"You've never seen what people use alts for, have you?" I answered the question with a question.

"No . . ." she said after a moment of thought.

"Can't buy a bag of holding so I'm going to settle on this instead," I answered. The remaining gold budget I had left crystalized in my hand.

The elf furrowed her brows. "That has to break a few rules, right?"

"No clue," I answered, "but if you don't know, then how would I?"

She held her chin in thought. "Fair, I suppose." She shook her head. "There's the book for aura techniques, though I suppose you wouldn't—"

"Still taking it," I said as I opened the book. "What?" I replied to her questioning gaze. "I'm not gonna half-ass my storage unit."

I glanced at the book. Strangely, aura techniques didn't have a tiered ranking but had exact specifications of the years of training needed to learn each technique. Most were in the single year range, so I picked three minor ones which fit my max budget of three years, along with proficiency in daggers.

"Okay, where's the thing I gotta fight?"

The elf raised an eyebrow at me. "Fight?"

"Last time I was here I fought to the death," I answered. "Unless we're in accelerated time, then I hope you'd hurry up."

"Who was your tutorial guide?" she asked, brows suddenly crossed.

"A mushroom called Henry, I think?"

She cursed something under her breath.

"You're free to go," she said as we appeared next to a Wayshard. "That part was due to a one-time limited event due to your special character."

I raised an eyebrow. "Okay then," I said as I raised my hand to touch the crystal.

"Oh, wait! Your name?"

I glanced at her, replied, "Dale, I guess," and teleported back to Gaia.

Noam heard me as I returned, turning around, he took one look at me before saying, "A bank alt?"

I glanced around the shop, Noam was sitting where I was a few moments ago, Peps seemed to have moved on, but there was movement behind, the potato most likely.

"Yep," I answered as I dropped the empty bags. "Probably the safest bank available to us currently."

He looked slightly surprised at my voice, before shaking his head and moving the coins into the bags.

The two wisps looked confusingly at each other, squeaking out something I didn't understand.

"I'll explain later," I promised.

I helped shovel the gold coins into the bag, which truly gave me an appreciation for online currency, or even paper currency if you're old fashioned, then put away the magical BBQ which I had cleaned earlier.

We said our farewells to the potato, who asked me to add him on my main account later. Which was when I actually learned his name, Murphy.

Adequate storage acquired, we moved to the Wayshard, avoiding the mushroom field I set up earlier as only the wisps were immune to it.

"We'll need to start doing stuff in Indiri," I began. "Claim our mercenary licenses and start getting that world's currency."

"Sure," Noam answered immediately. He didn't doubt me at all, he probably suspected I had spent a good amount of time thinking about it.

"Gaia doesn't have good infrastructure, everything seems to need Travelers to initiate them," I explained. "We could probably make it just as far here, but only in Indiri we can eat at a decent restaurant."

"Hmm . . . we haven't checked out their restaurants yet. Imagine all the strange stuff they could make with fantasy creatures and ingredients."

"Eh," I unenthusiastically replied. "I really don't want to spend the Traveler Coins we have."

"They something special?"

I explained Daves store to him, along with all the myriad of things you could buy from there. I finished my explanation just as we reached the Wayshard.

I left twenty gold between me and Noam as I swapped back to my main. The wisps broke out in squeaks of odd relief as they saw me come back. The gold was mostly just in case, but also because Noam was still carrying around that half-broken halberd and clearly needed a new weapon. He could probably make do with just that for a while.

We arrived at a dark alley in Indiri, back at that port city, Bartin. "I have to renew my rent at an inn," I said, feeling the room key inside my pocket.

"Sure," Noam answered as he looked to the sky, "already night . . ."

"You feeling hungry?" he suddenly asked me.

"I can eat my mushrooms," I answered.

He shook his head. "That stuff is fine but it's pretty tasteless, isn't it?"

"I guess?"

"You shouldn't live on that stuff, come on, there's bound to be a decent restaurant somewhere," he said as he took the lead walking out.

"Didn't you hear my whole thing about Dave and his store?" I said as I followed him.

"What's the point of penny-pinching if you're rich?" he asked back.

"Saving money is an essential skill!" I lectured as I followed him.

"Come on, how bad could it be?"

Cook

"Flame immunity is not a universal fix against all forms of fire. A person may have immunity to mundane flame but still be vulnerable to magic or divine flame and vice versa. Thus, the Inquisition should keep a healthy population of mage apostles. So that even if we may not follow the spirit of tradition, we follow the letter of it."
—*Excerpt from* Fireproof Heretics and You: Why You Don't Need to Give Up on Tradition *by Cardinal Cordelia*

It was a chilly midsummer morning when they heard rumors of his coming. He was well known across the land. Hushed and frightened whispers talked of him. He was an orcish warlord that carved a path of brutal destruction through uncountable nations. His blood-red emblem was an omen of ruin and flame to those unfortunate enough to see it.

When he arrived, disbelief was the first thought on most minds—they were but a small river town, what could possibly incite him to come? Yet as the facts were laid bare, it became clear. Two towns and three villages left in ruin, all upstream of their town. He was coming here, if not intentionally then in passing.

He traveled alone, yet none doubted his combat ability. The orc was rumored to have taken on entire platoons single-handed. The small river town had no such combat capability.

No sane being would try to meet him in combat, but the town had to do something, lest their livelihood was burned and destroyed before their very eyes. So, when they heard of his coming, they prepared a tribute.

Hunters went out and slaughtered the largest boar in the forest, the herbalist collected wild herbs, the barkeeper prepared her prized beer brew, the baker and miller worked together to create the finest loaves.

When the orc finally arrived, a table and seat were prepared and the town held their breath as the orc sampled the food.

The orc tore apart the sourdough, chewed through the roast boar with wild garlic stuffing, and drank the entire beer keg in a few sips. All the time sporting an indescribable expression.

After many pregnant moments, the orc slammed his fist on the table and began in a slow, quiet voice, "The beer is of fine quality, mild tartness that contrasts well with the subtle sweetness, I see it has the essences of six, no, seven different wild berries, local ones I assume."

The barkeep mutely nodded, too frightened to make a noise.

"This sourdough," he continued in the same, slow voice, as if speaking to a child, "its interior is far too soft compared to a traditional sourdough's chewiness, and the subtle sourness of sourdough is practically non-existent. Simply put, it is bland. Barely. Acceptable. Quality."

The townsfolk took a shared sharp intake of breath as they watched the orc casually brush against the head of his axe.

"All of this I can accept, however," the orc slowly said, deliberately enunciating every syllable. "This boar," he said slowly, "is far, far too TOUGH!" He roared at the townsfolk, "Are you cattle teeth blind!? This boar meat is not only old, it is far too sinewy and muscular to be worth eating any way other than raw!"

"But it was the toughest boar in the forest," a hunter interjected, before swiftly shrinking back as the orc's eyes seemed to bore holes in his body.

"DOES PURE MUSCLE MAKE FOR A GOOD CUT OF PORK!? FAR FROM IT CATTLE TEETH!" the orc yelled, enraged. "YOU HUMANS MUST NOT ONLY HAVE THE TEETH OF CATTLE BUT ALSO THE BRAINS! YOU WOULD MAKE BETTER PORK THAN THIS BOAR!"

The orc, Grimm Ramsey, in a smooth and powerful motion, drew his axe and slammed it into the table. "FOR THIS IMBECILITY AND POOR SERVICE, ZERO OUT OF FIVE AXES!"

Grimm Ramsey wiped the blood off his axe. After another wholesome morning of educating people of the correct way of cooking and the utterly horrific display he just tasted, he was feeling the need for a palette cleanser. Fortunately, he knew just the place.

Heading to a nearby Wayshard and smiling when he met the toll keeper, he was allowed to pass without paying. It was surprising how few people understood politeness these days. A brief show of fangs and the toll keeper and him were practically blood brothers. The keeper even shook in his armor in that strange human way they did to show affection.

Touching the Wayshard, he thought of where he wanted to go, and soon enough, he was there.

Bartin was as bustling as you could expect from a port city. Most people gave him a wide berth, to show their respect, of course, it's not like Ramsey was scary or something.

He made his way past the bustling streets of the city, to the more secluded areas, until he reached a particular shop.

Throwing open the doors, Grimm threw a haymaker at the troll chef, throwing him into a table and knocking out three of his teeth. The chef quickly responded with his own haymaker, a loud crack sounded out as the troll's fist impacted Grimm's jaw.

"Ha!" He laughed as he saw the troll's fist crumple on his unmoved jaw. "One of these days you'll be able to take my teeth!"

The troll groaned in pain as he set the broken bones back in place. Warm familial greetings completed, the young troll said, "Uncul Ramsey, you should've contacted me, sent a letter or scryed."

"Bah!" he snorted. "Do I look like a diviner? Lugging around a crystal ball like some imbecile."

"They've made them really small now, you can fit most in your pocket."

"They can turn me into a diviner over my corpse!" Grimm yelled as he took a seat.

"The usual?" his nephew asked as he headed behind the counter.

"Of course," Grimm answered, taking the opportunity to glance around the place.

It was a lot cleaner than when his blood brother, the young troll's father, had left it. Grimm wiped a finger on the table and was glad to see no dust or grime breaking off with it. Just this and the troll's excellent service put it at one axe out of five. Very much above most other restaurants.

His nephew soon returned with what gave the restaurant its other axe. A bowl of blood-red colored soup. Just smelling it was enough to burn off some of Grimm's nose hairs.

As Grimm took a spoon to savor the spice, the door opened, and two figures stepped in.

"—Come on! It can't be that bad," the first figure said.

"I don't know, this place looks sketchy," the second said.

The first was a warrior. Grimm could tell from the confident way he held himself, so confident in his ability it was very nearly arrogance. He was a purplish-blue–skinned devilling in sensible light armor.

The second was . . . hard to read. It was a myconid of some kind. Grimm had heard descriptions of their kind, but he did not know that they glowed. It didn't move like a warrior, though he recognized the way it constantly looked around as situational awareness. Its face was a mockery of what a face should look like, it didn't seem to show emotions at all.

When empty crevices met his eyes, he knew it was gauging him as a threat. Grimm bared his fangs, and the mushroom paused, before it too showed teeth. It had no fangs, though Grimm suspected the rows and rows of large molars could crush bone if needed. The devilling, upon seeing their exchange, also smiled. His teeth were more like normal cattle, but he bore his horns proudly and a broken halberd was tucked in his belt. He was not unused to the weight.

They were no meek cattle.

Pleasant greetings over, Grimm went back to his meal. The chili burned his tongue, cleansing the horrid taste left from this morning's disgrace of food.

"I'll have what he's having!" the devilling exclaimed. "Damn, I've always wanted to say that," he muttered to his companion as they both sat down.

"Same, I suppose," the myconid said.

Both Grimm and his nephew smirked. "Sure, mon," the young troll answered, "but be warned, my Ancestor Chili Soup is hot enough for you to see your ancestors!"

"Unorthodox display of hubris, but sure," the myconid replied drily.

"Is that a Jamaican accent?" the devilling asked.

"Jamaican?" his young nephew asked. "This is trollish."

When his nephew turned around to prepare the soup, the myconid kicked his companion in a discreet manner.

"What?" the devilling whispered.

The myconid simply shook its head.

The devilling rolled his eyes. "Do you run this store by yourself?"

"Ja," his nephew answered in front of a boiling pot. "Took over after fada was crisped."

"Huh. What's your name? Mine's Noam."

"John."

Grimm snarled. His nephew called himself John, though Grimm would never use that name. It was, after all, a name in human tongue. Taken only because the uncultured cattle teeth couldn't get it through their skulls that trolls did not have names till they earned one through combat.

Though, the younger troll was unlikely to ever earn a name through combat, as he seemed to dislike conflict and was a runt. Not only that, his regeneration was weak compared to other trolls, and his physique was barely above a peasant human. Grimm still refused to refer to him by a name unearned. If he didn't swear an oath to the young troll's late father to keep him safe, Grimm would've already thrown him to the wolves to earn a name or die trying.

Ignoring his snarl, the devilling kept talking to his nephew as he prepared the chili soup. The myconid still showed no expression, though two smaller myconids seemed to have appeared and were looking around in clear curiosity. Its children perhaps?

Conversation soon ended as his nephew brought forth two large bowls of chili soup.

Noam licked his lips as his nephew set the bowls down. The myconids sniffed it, before recoiling.

Noam didn't seem to notice his companions' reaction and took up a wooden spoon, taking a sip.

"Holy shit," he muttered, "Dustin, you gotta try this. Damn, I can taste this, can I have some water?"

What? This devilling actually survived his first sip?

Though, Grimm smirked, the cattle-teeth might've survived the initial sip, but he will be screaming soon enough. After all, he asked for water.

Dustin, slightly apprehensive looking, also took a sip with its spoon as John nephew brought a cup of water.

The myconid froze. Gone completely still.

Noam downed the water in a gulp. "Ah!" He smacked his lips. "Now I'm feeling it."

His nephew looked at the devilling, face clearly confused, and Noam smiled. "Your soup wasn't quite at two million Scovilles, so I wanted to get it there."

Grimm's eyes widened in realization and surprise. He didn't take water to cool the flame, but to feed it!

Grimm didn't know this, but Noam was an utter psychopath when it came to chili! When he was eight, he played a VR game where he had to eat progressively stronger chili. It was a high score type game where you aimed to eat the chili with the highest Scoville heat unit on a global leaderboard. Thanks to innovations in VR, previously impossible to achieve heights in chili were achieved with pinpoint accuracy. This mad game eventually gave Noam's tongue the instinctive ability to measure chili with Scoville heat units with only fifty units of error! And Noam's personal high score was . . .

"I felt that, though you won't get me panting unless you get to eight digits," Noam said with a smug smile.

Grimm looked at the devilling with newfound respect and expectation. Could this Noam be a connoisseur of fine foods as well?

The myconid though . . . Grimm recognized the form of someone gone completely catatonic from shock. Even if they were in a strange body. It was completely frozen now, though it was better than screaming—

Dustin lifted the spoon and drank the soup again.

Grimm's eyes widened, another connoisseur!?

To understand why Dustin was completely still, one needs to know that magic myconids did not have something resembling a human knee-jerk reaction. All their actions went through their central processing organ. Dustin is, to a point, completely in control of his actions.

However, after sipping the soup, his mind had gone blank completely with pain.

Normally in response to the extreme pain, he would be screaming, or clawing at his throat to try to remove the burning liquid. But these actions were just placebos his still somewhat human mind did because it thought that was the correct reaction to pain.

This chili went past that.

It far overloaded what his mind could process. Pain signals were sent to his mind but nothing was coming in response to it, thus his body did not move.

He was suffering an absolute state of pain, where his mind was entirely devoted to processing the taste of the chili.

The chili had effectively short-circuited him. As for what happened to the wisps . . . well there was no need to discuss corpses.

In this state, there was a small part of Dustin. The small, sane part, began to glimpse the light beyond and saw a figure within.

"Ye ye?" Declan uttered in surprise. "Huh, I thought that seeing your ancestors thing was just a marketing scheme—"

His grandpa slapped him across the face. "Fool! What are you doing sitting there like an idiot!?"

"Huh!? Did you taste that thing?"

Declan was slapped again. "IDIOT! Back in my day I only had the government rations and I was glad for it!"

"But I'm not from 'back in your day' damn zoomer," Declan began before getting slapped.

"DON'T WASTE FOOD!" his grandfather yelled as he disappeared.

"Don't waste food." This sentence sounded in his mind and Declan, barely thinking, raised his spoon.

"Wait a second—" Declan could not finish as a fresh wave of pain poured through him.

"Don't waste food."

"No, no, no this seems like a perfectly reasonable time to," Declan yelled before the pain caused him to keel over.

"Don't waste food." The sentence echoed in his mind. A mantra taught from parent to child since time immemorial. In a state where Dustin's mind could not process anything, it latched onto that mantra, making him raise the spoon and take one sip after another. Dustin's sane mind protested again and again, but its screams were not as loud as the pain or the mantra. So, his body ignored it. The continued pain slowly pushed Dustin's sane mind farther and farther back through sheer pain, until the screams grew weaker and stopped as Dustin's sane mind died.

The myconid seemed to have overcome its earlier apprehension through sheer willpower!

What supreme resilience. It is not even flinching despite going completely catatonic earlier from the chili, Grimm thought. *I would like to meet whoever raised such a determined being. They must be an extremely good parent.*

It was weak, but its overcoming its flaws through sheer strength of will! To take a second sip of the Ancestor Chili Soup was enough for Grimm to praise it, but the fact that it was overcoming its weakness had earned it Grimm's respect.

Though there was another who was worthy of Grimm's respect.

"Do you have anything hotter?" Noam asked.

His nephew looked strangely at Noam's empty bowl, before his eyes burned with the light of a challenger. "Ja, this is normally unavailable for customers, but I can make the Five Spices Overcoming."

Grimm's eyes widened. The Five Spices Overcoming was a derivative chili recipe of the Mighty Zul'Garub's Eleven Spices Overcoming Tiamat. Which was famously so hot that it made all of Tiamat's heads feel the pain of fire for the first time in their lives. This derivative was weaker, unavoidably so as six of the ingredients have been lost, but Grimm had seen men taste it and be turned into screaming wrecks for days.

"I'll take it!" Noam cheerfully declared.

"Me as well," Grimm said. He'd only ever had the novelty of tasting the Five Spices Overcoming once, when it was prepared by his Blood Brother Fon'Dafarr. He did not know Fon'Dafarr had passed the recipe to his son.

His nephew soon returned from the kitchen. A plate of fried chicken pieces, sprinkled liberally with the spice in each hand.

Will this break him? Grimm thought as he brought a chicken piece to his mouth. He had felt worse pain than this chili. But what about this Noam? He was a devilling so he likely had flame resistance of some kind, but he would be mistaken to think that flame resistance would help against chili.

Noam, unheeding of Grimm's glare, took a drum stick and ate it. Grimm saw Noam's eyes widened and—"Holy shit this is seven mil at least!"

—seem completely fine.

Impressive, Grimm thought, *though his body shows no scars, to have such impressive chili resistance, Noam must've suffered through numerous battles till his mind became an impenetrable fortress.*

His nephew, though, simply looked frustrated, before rushing back behind the kitchen, yelling, "I didn't want to use this. But for you I make an exception and prepare the River Blight!"

Grimm's eyes widened. *He knew the recipe to River Blight!?* He quickly called out, "A bowl for me as well!"

The River Blight was a mixture of spices which led to an extremely potent sauce. Four-hundred years ago, the great Chef Zul'Derag famously dripped a bowl of it into a river. To this day, Derag's River and everything near it is considered one of the most uninhabitable locations in the Wastelands. Creatures without resilient minds would instantly die of shock from the pain of being exposed to the spice.

Did Fon'Dafarr pass this to his son as well!? What dark recipes did this bloodline know!?

His nephew swiftly returned with two disks of spice, setting it down in front of both of them. He glared at the devilling with a face of defiance. Daring him to try.

The devilling glanced at him, then met the gaze of Grimm. Taking one of the earlier chicken pieces, he dipped it into the sauce, turning it around several times so that it would be liberally coated. Grimm mirrored his action and both raised the chicken to take a bite.

Grimm, who had once been drawn and quartered by Dread Steeds, glared at an oncoming cavalry charge and dared them to pass him, and burned alive by dragons, all without flinching or a change in his expression. Grimm the Unflinching, the Great Demon Chef and Bastion Breaker flinched and let out a gasp of pain. He felt his body start to dry heave as it tried to get rid of the spice. His mouth, his throat, his stomach, they all burned. It was as if he had just ingested a lump of burning coal. He could physically track the progress of the bite as it passed through his digestive track, purely through the waves of pain it left in its wake.

Noam did not seem to be faring any better, he had fallen limp onto the table, his mouth gaping like a fish. He was hiccupping, his body, too, trying to expel the spice.

Suddenly he clenched his teeth and Grimm saw his body tense. "Thirteen mil—no, *eighteen million*," he whispered. He raised his arm, still holding the bitten chicken piece, revealing the pure white flesh underneath. Then he dipped that exposed white flesh into the spice once again.

DOUBLE DIPPING!? IS HE A MADMAN!? Noam continued in spite of Grimm's shock, then took another bite. Grimm was barely staying alive after one bite, but this . . . this man was taking bite after bite, even coating it with more spice as before.

As Grimm watched this, he felt a flame light in his belly. Not the literal flame caused by the chili, but a metaphorical one.

Grimm let out a primal war cry, shaking the establishment and loud enough to be heard throughout the entire ghetto. "I will not be one-upped by a youngling without a single scar on his back!"

Grimm brought forth his reserves of aura, forcing his body to move and mimic Noam's actions.

Fresh waves of pain bombarded him, he felt his chest constrict as the pain made it hard to breathe. But he refused to stop, not until the one in front of him also relented. They ate, fresh waves of maddening pain washing over them until the drumsticks in both their hands were just bare bones and the sauce wiped clean.

Through all this, Grimm's nephew looked upon them with pure shock. He had expected his uncul to be fine, but the devilling?

That was his strongest chili. The last recipe fada had imparted to him on his deathbed. Noam had cleaned the sauce, and though he breathed hard and fast it looked like he would survive and be none the worse.

Was it all for naught? Fada had spent years researching a chili that would surpass all. Before his experiments burned him in a way so horrific that not even his trollish regeneration could keep up.

He was the only one with his fada's knowledge. Were all those years of experience a waste!?

The young troll suddenly felt nauseous, he fell backward, knocking over something as he fell to the ground. Something very hot splashed onto him, and he could hear his uncul yelling in surprise.

The troll licked his lips, recognizing the taste of the Ancestor Chili Soup before his mind was blanked in pain.

The young troll saw beyond life. He saw beyond the veils separating the living and unliving and saw a familiar figure within.

"What are you doing!" his fada yelled at him as he delivered a haymaker to the young troll's jaw, knocking out four of his teeth. "Are you just going to let this shango walk over your efforts!?"

"I can't, fada," the young troll replied as he rubbed his jaw, "I already tried the River Blight. I have nothing left."

"Of course, you do!" the elder troll yelled, lifting the prone form of his son and enveloping him in a bear hug. "You are merely holding yourself back!"

"I am?" the young troll asked, surprised.

"Of course!" the elder troll yelled. "You have spent too long living among cattle-teeth, even taking up one of their names!" He shook his head. "Ah, the words your mada would be having if she heard."

"How does me living among humans matter?" the young troll asked.

The elder troll snorted. "You've gone daft spending so much time with humans. The spice you make is spicy enough to kill humans, but we are TROLLS!" he yelled. "You limit yourself to human standards, when you should be going beyond that! Make spice capable of killing trolls! Capable of killing behemoths and dragons! I know you can do it, you are my son!"

The young troll felt tears come to his eyes. Mostly because his fada was hugging him hard enough to break bones, but also because of the heartfelt speech he just gave. "Do you really think so, fada?"

"Of course, I do!" the elder troll yelled, tears coming to his eyes also. "You are my son, my blood!" The elder troll let go of his son, slapping him on the back and breaking at least two ribs. "Go!"

The young troll looked back, and two pairs of teary eyes met. "I will, fada, I will show them the power of our work!"

"Oh, and one more thing," the young troll turned around to his fada. "Do not call yourself 'John,' your mada will kill me if she heard it, your name should be—"

The elder troll said a name as the younger's eyes widened in surprise.

"But . . . but fada, I have not yet earned—"

"Then go earn it!" his fada interjected. "Create a chili that can kill those two!"

"Even uncul?"

"He is a chef and a warrior! He should be prepared for death from the moment he stepped into your restaurant!" the young orc felt his conscious returning and the light around him fading.

"If he is not prepared, then I will kill him again when you send him here!" his fada yelled as the young troll returned to reality.

The young troll opened his eyes to his uncul's worried glare. All his faces looked like glares.

"Are you alright nephew?"

The young troll pushed Grimm off of him. "Thank you, uncul, but I know what I must do."

Grimm saw the determination in his eyes. The determination of one prepared to earn glory or die trying and stood out of his way.

The young troll went to the back of the kitchen, to a door which led to his fada's lab. A lab he had not entered since he dragged out his fada's completely burned form. Inside the lab, he saw a myriad of ingredients: "Purest sulfuric acid, ground bones of a greater demon of agony, black powder, the tears of one eternally tortured . . ."

Options burned in his mind. The young troll stood at the crossroads, and it beckoned him to choose a Path.

Of multitudes of Paths, he saw one he knew. One tread by few, and many. A broken Path littered with burned corpses. One once walked by his fada, Fon'Dafarr.

He took a step forward onto that Path, and like a troll possessed, he began mixing ingredients, adding them into a mortar and pestle. The knowledge his fada taught and the knowledge he learned. He brought them together in **Fusion**.

Noam had to shield his eyes when the troll left the kitchen. He was carrying something on a plate, something which was brighter than anything he'd seen.

The light hit Dustin, and Noam saw his body go completely limp; it crashed to the table before it was lit aflame. Noam barely cared, as he saw the troll place the dish in front of him and the elderly looking orc.

He looked at the orc, grim determination meeting a childlike smile. Noam reached for a piece of something and felt his hands char as they went near it.

Simply proximity had turned his hand into burned black bones, but he ignored it as he grasped onto the thing. The orc lifted his piece with him.

They raised the pieces to their mouths. And even though Noam's lips dried and cracked, his teeth burned black from the heat, he took a bite.

What he tasted could not be measured in Scoville units. No, it was feasible, but it would've been as meaningless as trying to measure the width of the universe with a standard thirty-centimeter ruler or measuring the volume of the ocean with only a single shot glass for reference.

There was no point in Noam trying to measure something so far beyond him. His perspective was far too small. Though, the orc summed it up pretty well.

"Five out of five axes," he whispered like a secret as the world turned white.

That night, Noam tasted the sun.

4.03

───

> *"If there is only one thing your deficient mind can take away from this book, let it be this. Magic is inherently a battle against common sense. To war against imagination is most common. To have bias of any form is to lock yourself away from the greatness of magic. To always just be a step behind seeing that true abyss."*
> *—First passage from "So You Want to Throw a Fireball?: A Comprehensive Guide to Magic for the Intellectually Deficient," widely attributed to the infamous Magus Smar Da Ten Yu*

You have died.

I stared at the dark and empty skies. Strange, I was completely lucid now. That explains how Matt was able to respond to me while he was in the middle of his respawn timer. Multiple deaths gave him a clearer and clearer picture. Odd way to do it.

Which reminded me, how did I die?

I tried to recall what happened to me and—

. . .

. . .

He was in a place much like a personal study. It wasn't the classy kind, but a derivative of that idea. To any other person, the place would appear highly disorganized, but to Declan and only Declan, everything was where he needed it.

He found it shortly. A black box, covered in hundreds of locks.

Declan raised an eyebrow; before passing all of them without a thought, he opened the box and—

An elderly hand reached from inside and slapped him.

"I TOLD YOU NOT TO WASTE—"

Declan shut it immediately, throwing the box on the ground. He found duct tape and completely covered the thing, locks and all. Tsking in dissatisfaction, he took a heavy-duty chain and wrapped around it with more locks. It wasn't enough, so he took a bandolier of grenades and rigged it so that any attempt to open the box would pull the pins of all of them. Then he opened the window, and like an Olympic shot-putter, threw the box out of his study.

"Fucking zoomers."

. . .

. . .

I am never eating chili again, *Dustin thought.*

No actually, I should never be eating at that restaurant. That troll clearly served a hallucinogen, how is that legal?

Mentally he made a note to obtain a book on law, if only to shut down that store.

"That's rare," a voice said from beside him.

Dustin turned his head to see Eve sitting next to him with her knees drawn up to her chest, staring into that deep, dark sea.

"What is?" he asked.

"You not being surprised," Eve answered. "Normally, people freak out when I suddenly appear."

"Well, how many times have you done this?" Dustin asked as he sat up with a groan.

"Four thousand, eight hundred forty-eight times. Including now," Eve added the last bit as an afterthought, knowing Dustin was the type to get picky about that sort of thing.

"And why are you here?" he asked, his face and voice were completely even, almost unreadable.

"I think I made the right choice in your race selection."

"Not really an answer to my question, but I suppose you already knew that?" Dustin asked.

"Yes," Eve answered drily, "I did it just to mildly annoy you. Be slightly irritated or else."

"Oh, the horror," Dustin said as he dramatically fell down.

Eve turned to him, staring at the form lying prone on the sand. "Do you ever get tired of that?"

"Of what?"

"Acting," Eve said.

Dustin went still for the briefest moment before he met Eve's stare, and answered, "Not really."

His friendliness was an act as were many things about him.

"You have a question on your mind," Eve said, "ask it."

Dustin raised an eyebrow. "Read my mind?"

"No," Eve answered truthfully; she could, but not right now. Declan had prepared a truly nasty mental defense against her. "You are smart enough to have realized and be curious about it."

He mulled it over for a brief moment. "That saves me a trip to Daves at least . . ."

Sitting up again, Dustin met Eve's gaze and asked, "I want to know why my personality changed."

"Not a question, but I'll still count it," Eve said. He had already pulled that trick on Dave, after all. He was still laughing about how he was cheated for the first time in several hundred years.

What Dustin was referring to was his behavior when he first entered Gaia, specifically during the tutorial, when he took unneeded risks and became uncharacteristically angry at Hendrix. Eve knew that Hendrix had that kind of effect on people, but for Declan, it would've been supremely strange, his own temporary mania and excitement wouldn't have caused it.

For Declan, of course.

Eve responded, having prepared the answer beforehand, "What were your Mind scores, when you first became Dustin?"

Eve saw the moment Dustin's mind went into overdrive to consider the information. His body froze, no longer receiving signals from his mind, only his soft breathing continued.

It was as if someone had ceased controlling the body.

When he finally spoke, he did so slowly, stressing every word. "Then you are saying that my mind stats affect my mind?"

"Yes."

Dustin did not reply, instead, he opened his character sheet. He noticed that he had lost a level and was back at level 3, but didn't react. No, he went straight to his stats and put both his points into Intelligence.

Then he just sat there.

He was still for a very long time.

"I can feel it," he suddenly said. "I can feel it . . ." he repeated as his body started shaking and he broke out in laughter.

"I can feel it!" he declared with a large smile on his face. "It increased!"

He leaned forward, holding his face in his hands. "It was minimal, but I can feel it," he whispered. His previous excitement was almost completely gone. "How did I not notice it?" he hissed.

"I did nothing," Eve said, knowing that he would've briefly considered the idea of her making a mental block against realizing that. There was no reason for her to do such a thing.

"My mental stats only had incremental increases, almost completely natural," he muttered. "I've focused mainly on other stats . . . wait"—Dustin turned to Eve, realizing a potential hole in the explanation—"my Charisma is six."

"And you wonder why you haven't been a clueless blockhead in social interactions," Eve finished for him. "The answer to that is simple, you haven't been predominately using Charisma during interactions, but your Wisdom."

Just those words alone would've been enough for Dustin to draw the correct conclusion, but he wouldn't know for sure, so Eve continued, "Wisdom is the accumulation of knowledge, the understanding of patterns and behaviors. You aren't naturally good at interacting with people, but by observing them, you realize the patterns and behaviors that made them tick, and you adopt behavior that helps you interact with them and get your desired reactions."

Just like her, Dustin learned and observed. He adopted Valhorn's mannerisms after a few interactions not because he was a roleplayer, but because he believed that would've been the quickest way to get him to do what he wanted. Dustin did it almost passively, but he was pretty blatant in mimicking the personalities of those he thought had power.

He was also doing it in interactions with herself, but it was still mostly improvisation with a friendly personality as a base. Given more interactions, Dustin could actually reach a state where he could start consciously influencing Eve without needing to guilt-trip her.

It was manipulation, but to Eve, all human interaction involved it to a degree so she wasn't too bothered by it.

"I see . . ." He chuckled. "To think I didn't realize, I really am an idiot, aren't I?"

And there was the weakness of him. Dustin was open-minded pretty much only when he was learning or discovering something. Once he reached an idea, believed he understood something completely, he would hold onto that idea until he saw it broken.

There was one thing he had spent his entire life to learn. An idea he had long solidified and wasn't going to break soon.

Himself.

"Not really," Eve answered, knowing she was attempting something futile, "you are an above-average intelligence."

He snorted. "If you really think that, then you are overestimating me."

"It is true, your current character stats greatly match your real-life stats."

Dustin stared at her, his brow furrowing. Trying to find fault in it somehow.

"Intelligence fifteen, Wisdom twelve, Charisma eight," Eve said. "The current average for stats on Earth is around thirteen."

Dustin closed his vision. "And what of it?" he began, turning back to stare at the dark sea. "What is the point of being above average, if you don't achieve anything with it?"

"Just for the sake of being above average?" she proposed.

"Really? What is fifteen compared to thirteen? It's not even twenty percent better," he muttered as he began drawing circles in the sand. "How am I supposed to compare to people like your dad Giles? Or Wenter? Or Hawking? Or fucking Einstein?"

Eve didn't know how to answer that, she, too, constantly wondered that same thing.

"Compared to some people, I'm worthless, less than competent and can only help by getting out of the way," he said, not bitterly, but with a defeated acceptance. "No one else knows me as well as I do," he said, before glancing at Eve. "Well, you might, I don't know how far you've gone rifling in my head."

"Not very much," Eve answered truthfully. "Not while you're keeping that up."

Dustin chuckled. "So you noticed?"

"I guessed," Eve corrected. Just observing him for some time gave Eve a good idea of how he thought. And if Eve were in his shoes, she would've thought of the exact same thing.

In Dustin's mind, he was constantly imagining the scene of Giles hanging by a rope.

"Why are you here anyway?" he suddenly asked. "You never answered that."

Eve looked seriously at Dustin for the first time. "Something is going to happen . . . something I've been trying to avoid for a while but is still going to happen."

It was an object already in motion. She learned that she could not stop something once it was in motion, all she could do was nudge it in a favorable direction.

"Do you have to be this vague?"

"Not really," Eve drily answered, "but slightly inconveniencing people fuels me." Well, specifically Dustin, since that ass did try to guilt trip her.

She continued, "You will realize it one way or another. At this point, it's pointless for me to try to stop it. So, might as well get it over with. If you want to speed it up, go to a library and search for a book."

"Which book?" he asked instantly.

"Doesn't matter, the act of searching for a book is enough for you to find the right one."

He raised an eyebrow, probably thinking something along the lines of "magic bullshit" before asking, "Anything else?"

Eve thought about it for a moment. "Not really, I trust you to be a good enough person to see it through."

Dustin snorted. "Can you really call me a good person, knowing about the countermeasure I thought up against you?"

"I don't know," Eve said, "but you are good enough."

Dustin was silent for a moment, before saying, "Fair, I suppose. You do seem to have a somewhat good grasp of me."

It was mostly guesswork. So, there was still a chance it was inaccurate in areas.

"Anything else?" Dustin asked as he stood up.

"Not really," Eve said.

"I see. Oh, yeah," Dustin said almost as an afterthought, "am I the same person as Declan Lu?"

"I don't know," she answered, to his surprise. "What? Did you expect me to know everything?"

Dustin shook his head. "Then what do you think?"

"I think, it is something like Jekyll and Hyde."

"What, like a split personality?"

Eve snorted. "No, Jekyll and Hyde were never split personalities, that's just a simplification."

"In the story," she continued, "Jekyll created a drug which shifted his appearance and removed all of his mental inhibitions. Hyde didn't kill because he was evil . . . well, not just evil, but because Jekyll's first impulse was to kill, so he did."

"And that means what?" Dustin asked, likely having already reached the correct conclusion, but just making sure.

"Like Hyde was still Jekyll, you are still Declan Lu, just expressed in a slightly different way."

"Seems like a big jump from the removal of all inhibitions to whatever I'm made of." He chuckled.

"It is the closest I can think of that you would also recognize."

"Fair, I suppose," he said as he stared ponderously at the sky. "The amount of shit I can do if there were just more of me . . ."

"There are, arguably, 'more of you,'" Eve said.

"Can't communicate with each other, other than when we become just one person," he answered. "Unless," he muttered, already going through ways to work around it.

He shook his head, putting the thought away for now. "Anything else you want to tell me, other than vague warnings of stuff you couldn't avoid?"

"I've sent you a coupon for a free computer," Eve said as she stood up. "You're probably going to need it, but it's up to you whether or not you redeem it."

Dustin raised an eyebrow, likely already going through what could possibly require him to possess a quantum computer. "So, you really do have Maple under your thumb?"

"It was surprisingly easy," Eve answered. "Offered a few people data immortality and suddenly they were very interested in keeping me up."

Eve could fundamentally change people, but she would rather not do that, not when she could just give them what they wanted and let them help her. They were already objects in motion, all she had to do was nudge them in a direction that helped her.

Dustin noticed his respawn timer was about to finish and stood up. He, too, was an object already in motion, he understood this and was willing to play. Eve didn't even really have to nudge him, his personality aligned closely enough with hers that she just had to help a bit.

Eve could not stop anything. All she could do was try to nudge things into the right place.

"I have a question for you," Eve said.

Dustin raised an eyebrow, not answering but inviting her to continue.

Eve looked back and saw the man who was her world.

"Do you ever feel incidental to the world?"

His answer was instant: "Always."

Dustin respawned, and Eve was left alone, yearning for a face no longer alive.

I got to the city library pretty soon after I respawned.

"What kind of book are we looking for anyway?" Noam asked, a bit too loudly, as he paced one of the shelves.

"No clue," I answered, "and quiet, we're in a library. That means you two as well." The wisps froze, hiding some kind of toothpick behind them.

I stared at the rows of shelves ahead of me.

The act of searching for a book is enough for you to find the right one.

How annoyingly vague.

I closed my eyes.

From what I've read, magic works off willpower. For simple acts, you don't need a lot of it.

I am looking for a book.

I walked forward, eyes closed. My hand reached out to a shelf and grabbed a completely random book.

Opening my eyes, I found a heavyset hardback book. It was simply titled "The Historia."

A bookmark peaked out of its pages toward the end and I flipped to it.

It wasn't a bookmark, some kind of decorated card. I turned it upright to get a better look.

The card depicted a man with an arm holding a wand pointed toward the sky, his other hand aimed to the ground. He wore a bulbous mushroom hat that reminded me of my own cap. Before him was a scroll and three empty spaces that looked like the artist didn't bother to draw whatever they were supposed to be. From the outlines though, the spaces respectively looked like a disk, a goblet of some kind, and a key.

The card marked a line in the book.

It was the Magician.

4.04

"Checkov's Door is an extremely simple concept, even a simpleton can understand it, which I assume is why you are reading this book. It is the governing principle for extraplanar conjuration. It posits that the process of creating a planar gateway is similar to that of opening a door, and that such a door exists for every plane. Thus, and you will have to read the next line several more times as it involves a logical leap, one can assume that in order for something to move from one plane to another, two such doors would have to be opened."
   —*Excerpt from* So You Want to Throw a Fireball?: A Comprehensive Guide to Magic for the Intellectually Deficient, *widely attributed to the infamous Magus Smar Da Ten Yu*

"—and he knew his chance had come."

The moment I read that line I was no longer in the library.

My vision darted around, taking in everything. Neither Noam nor the wisps seemed to have followed me. I snapped the Historia shut, I had made a mistake letting the wisps run free and away from me. My combat capability was not unduly lowered by their absence, but they would've still been useful.

I was still in a library, but this one appeared several times more ancient. The place was completely silent, save for the sound of a pen writing.

Everything was covered in a layer of dust at least several centimeters thick. The place gave a similar impression to an actual library I once visited. Destitute and in decline, tax dollars drying up the second decade eBooks became widespread. Though it was still well illuminated, and there was still an air of . . . history, this library had probably been through more than I have or ever will. Looking up, I saw that the ceiling was transparent, or maybe there wasn't a ceiling, what surprised me was seeing a familiar landmass past it.

The continent of Braunad, the landmass Noam and I started in Indiri. So, I was in space.

Tracing my finger on the shelves around me, I randomly selected a book. Nothing, it was filled with nonsense. Randomly checking several other books showed the same thing. The letters were Common, but they were scrambled.

There was little to be gained from staying here.

I began walking toward the source of the only sound in this desolate place. Thinking as I walked.

Going off Eve's cryptic assholery, I'm about to be involved in something she wanted to avoid but found pointless to stop. Which just narrowed it down so much, didn't it?

One. She believed I'm going to need a new computer, likely a quantum one. She should be aware of my fears of her, so either it was a negligible cost that she could just throw around or she believed it likely I would seriously consider taking the offer.

Two. The being I'm dealing with was likely a god. I glanced at the book in my hand, the Historia. I wasn't a fool who failed to educate themselves properly. I am aware of who or what writes the Historia, but their capabilities and the general roles of gods in this virtual world was still a mystery to me. I determined that their religions and cults were the main thing to focus on as the gods themselves didn't exercise their presence on the world with enough regularity or great effect to be truly relevant. My research about the gods themselves effectively ended when I found that Eve didn't exist amongst them in some obvious capacity.

Three. Eve somehow believed I would be able to handle this situation, which had implications depending on how accurate she is. On the extreme far, far end of this, she is able to keep track of literally millions of variables to calculate multiple cohesive and almost fully accurate predictions of the future. I am not too invested in this theory, as the basis of all my assumptions about Eve begin with the idea that I could affect her in some meaningful way. If I really believed this, then I would've just given up and dropped dead because there was literally nothing I could do in a world that had just proven determinism.

A more sanity-preserving interpretation was that she has a good enough read on me that she could make educated guesses about my reactions to certain events, similar to how I could often predict the reactions of my parents and people I knew very well. The first theory was also unlikely unless Eve had something on the level of a Type II Matrioshka Brain, something supremely unlikely as humanity hasn't even colonized Mercury yet. If she did, then it also brought about the possibility that even my "real" world was simulated, which just led me down the rabbit hole of simulation theory.

I shuffled my thoughts to the back of my mind as I reached him.

The figure at the desk turned toward me, though his hands never stopped writing. Twenty-three pure black, glass-like eyes considered me. Next to him was a globe . . . of Earth? No, it was similar, but clearly outdated. On it, Alaska and Britain still existed and New Oceania hadn't been made yet.

"I really should've read up more on theology," I started in a conversational tone. "I'll have to admit that I don't know why I'm here or what you want from me."

I'll extract information about the globe later, right now I need to understand his capabilities and intentions. But . . . something was strange, behind the globe of Earth there was a body next to him. It looked—

Like lands unknown and unseen becoming known and seen. Like the roar of the wind on your sails, the warmth of a campfire in hidden forests, the filling of a map. It was the Guiding Star. It was-

"Do not finish that thought," a voice cut through that vision, a voice older than the language or man, a voice that was a maddening record, written since First Dawn to Final Dusk. Forcing my mind back to reality.

I staggered back. "What the—"

What did I just see?

The god looked away, not that it did much given that his eyes ringed his skull. "Ah . . . sorry about that . . ." he sheepishly said, none of the previous power in his voice.

"You were about to do something rather inconvenient due to—actually you wouldn't know, you said you didn't read up much on theology, didn't you? Not that I blame you, of course, honestly this 'god' business is rather complicated, though you don't need to take my word for that, you see the vision you saw was that of an Apotheosis—ah you wouldn't know—Sorry, I seriously don't blame you, really, honestly most people don't even know about the exact mechanics of godhood so you don't really need to worry about not knowing . . ."

Despite the fact he rambled seemingly pointlessly, I listened carefully to every one of his words and noted, that no matter how fast he talked, how far he meandered, his hands were on his book, constantly writing, as if they were a separate entity from him. Despite burning curiosity, I took care not to look at the . . . body? Next to the globe. It altered my mental state until he broke me out of it. I was not going to investigate it until I could look at it safely.

The god finally caught himself in his ramblings. "Ah . . . sorry, really sorry, it's been a long time since I've been able to cordially talk to another." Several of his eyes blinked in a dazed manner. "I guess my manners withered somewhere along the way. Please take a seat"—he gestured in front of him—"if you can find one without dust."

Taking him up on his offer, I found a nearby chair that had been stacked upside down alongside a dozen others, which left the actual seat pretty clean. I attempted to carry it at first, but my short size and relatively low strength made it clear it wasn't happening, so I simply dragged it to him, stopping in front of his desk and taking a seat.

"Sorry, very much for your sudden displacement."

Embarrassment, that was clear, even if his facial structure was wildly different from what I'm used to reading. I could tell this was genuine.

"Not the first time I was abducted by higher entities with little or no warning," I answered in a conversational tone. Let's start with an attempt to build rapport, though it apparently backfired as the god's eyes—the normally placed ones, scrunched up.

"Ah, yes, warning. That would've been a smart idea."

For a brief moment, I looked at the being in front of me in sheer disbelief. My mind almost failed to process his expression of stupid regret and embarrassment.

"Did you seriously not think about that?" I retorted. Almost as soon as I said it, I bit back my lips. Goddamnit, there goes my attempt at making friends again.

That day I learned a face covered with completely black eyes could somehow look self-conscious.

I rubbed my brow, fighting back internal cringe. "Just . . . get on with it please?"

"Yes, we should. I am the Historian if you did not know that before," he said.

It took me a moment to realize he was prompting me to introduce myself. "Dustin."

The Historian nodded. Aat this point, I wouldn't be surprised if he didn't know my name until now.

"So, what do you want?"

In an instant, that flailing idiot I was introduced to seemed to disappear. It was hard to tell at first, but there were dozens of signs once I noticed them. How he started to hold himself with confidence, or the way his facial muscles tightened slightly.

This I can work with.

"I'll be frank, I require your assistance in a magical ritual to reverse the effects of apotheosis."

My eyes narrowed. The desire to glance at the body next to us flaring up even more now. "Something related to that?"

I made no gesture, but the intention was clear.

With a pause, he firmly replied, "Yes."

"How do you think I am capable of helping?" he wouldn't have dragged me here otherwise.

Several of his eyes blinked, before he began: "It is a complex issue, having to do with the laws of this world, especially with regard to Divinity."

"A god is just a person who pursued a Path to the final step, the end goal, the destination," he explained. "But in doing so, they have turned their very existence into their Path."

"When such a thing happens, they become a Domain, the purest representation of that Path." He paused, eyes blinking. "I have tried to slow it down for them, but they took the final step." He glanced melancholically to the side, toward the body. "Planar Laws dictate that they will become a Domain and they . . ." He paused, brow furrowing. "He no longer has the will to change that," he bitterly said.

"And I factor in this how?"

"I theorized a way to completely stop this transformation, though I lacked the necessary assistance." He turned to me.

I raised my eyebrow. "Lemme guess, I am that assistance?"

"You catch on very quickly."

"And what kind of assistance is it, that you will need some seemingly random person?"

The Historian looked at me, and for a brief moment, I saw that his eyes were not truly black.

Every single one of his eyes was something that was a bastardization of an insectoid compound eye. But instead of thousands of photoreceptors, each eye contained millions of eyes, and they were not his eyes. Every single eye within an eye was the eye of something sapient. Something that lived and saw and remembered. They were so small, shrunken beyond what light could reflect, till all that I could see were the nanometer thin black walls that separated them all. Giving the illusion of pure blackness.

The Historian saw through them all. He saw through every eye, no matter where, no matter who. He saw it all. Just staring into his eyes, the back of my mind began to fill with visions of places I've never seen and the slowly maddening sound of the world grinding on without me.

Then it was gone.

"Are you aware of Checkov's Door?" he began.

"I am, I've read 'So you want to Throw a Fireball,'" I replied. Checkov's Door was one of several magical "laws" that facilitated magic. To leave or enter a plane you must open a "door" and that "door" is most easily opened by someone already on the plane.

"I have discovered, nay, theorized that for him to cease apotheosis, I need to remove the effect of Planar Law on him."

The pieces started falling in place around me.

"And the simplest way to do that—" he said.

"—Is to remove him from the plane," I finished.

The pieces fell and I saw the picture. "No, it can't be . . ." My eyes narrowed as my mind reached two conclusions. "Gaia?"

"No," he denied.

That left one option I knew of.

"Earth."

4.05

———

*"One-hundred and eighty-seven. If you are the subject of a
prophecy just jump off a cliff. If that doesn't work, I know some
excellent poison recipes."*
       —*Excerpt from* Enrico's Enchiridion of Encounters

To begin with, how do you even believe it possible?" The answer to this
will be telling, I saw three outcomes: one, it ends in failure, two, he proves
the simulation theory and three—

"I believe you understand this already, but we exist as a language of
programming scripture." Despite half expecting it, I was still surprised he
knew this. "While beings from here cannot exist in a physical capacity on
your world, we can exist in the myriad of Planes originating from there."

Essentially, he believed it was possible because he was data, he was code,
and data could be moved, code could be copied. He was trying to move the
data that made up . . . whatever the other god was, into another medium.

I asked the question that was burning in my mouth: "How do you know
this?"

His mouth curved into a wry smile. "Strange isn't it, not often the pris-
oner chained in the cave realizes he knows nothing but shadows."

I knew that saying, I studied the Cave Allegory during several Humanities classes in regards to VR. "Plato?"

"Verron Pluton," he replied as he flipped to a new page, "but I would
like to meet this Plato."

"Good luck with that," I muttered, "he's been dead for several thousand
years."

"Unfortunate," he replied, seeming genuinely disappointed, "but if his
teachings live on, then he has yet to die the second death."

"The answer to my question, please," I replied, not sure if this tangent
was deliberate or natural.

He considered his answer for a moment, before he replied, "You've seen my eyes."

I nodded noncommittally.

"You know that I see through everything that can see, that is not my limit. I am the God of History Writ and Recorded, I have seen into the past, through eyes long dead and have gleaned much. I am not the first to have uncovered the truth of this world."

"Is this common knowledge?" I asked. A few people knowing won't be that problematic, a lot could be a problem.

"No, save for a few who uncovered it themselves or were told by another."

"Specify 'few.'" It was nitpicky, but I wasn't going to let this screw me over in the future.

Several of his eyes blinked; it occurred to me that he was still actively looking out even at this moment. "Hundreds out of billions, not including Travelers or Heirs, they do not move on this knowledge."

The chances would be slim, then.

"What do you think?"

I took a deep breath as he asked that, closing my vision to calm my storming mind, carefully selecting the major points.

"What I think?" I said, without opening my vision. "That helping you I would be doing something reckless and idiotic. If it is a success, we would set a precedent, that it is possible for beings on this world to pass into mine."

I opened my eyes to see the expecting Historian. "That could more or less counter a Traveler's main strength, immortality. If you know my real face you could threaten me with it."

The Historian did not speak. He could argue that he would never do something like that, but we both knew that even if that were true, what of the next person to try something like this? Or the person after that? If this was what Eve was referring to, then this was likely the first time this has been attempted, or at least gotten this close to.

"So, give me a reason, Historian," I practically spat out, "to make a knife that could be pointed at me in the future."

Even if my real body died there was a chance Dustin could still go on. A chance that I didn't want to test.

Was this what Eve wanted? Knowing that I would reject this based on all sane logic?

For the first time since I met him, the Historian closed all of his eyes, even his ever-present writing slowed.

"Ekon Zaeba."

I blinked in surprise. "What?"

"That was their name," he replied as he stared melancholically at the Domain next to him. "His name. I loved him and I still do."

"We are fellow birds trapped in a cage, and though we have grown to become its master, the largest fighting dog in the pit is still *trapped*."

He turned back to me, eyes resolute. "Name. Your. Price."

Surprise marred my face before it hardened into doubt. It can't be, he had better options. I stared at him for a long and hard time. There was a catch, there had to be. My head began to hurt as every section of my mind was dedicated to searching his alien face. Where was it? I searched for a single lie. A single falsehood. A single reason to not believe him.

I found none.

I must be wrong. My ability to read expressions should be a Charisma thing. I rifled through my mind, cross-referencing his expression with every face and expression I have encountered. My brain burned. But still, I saw no lie.

Instead, I saw myself lying on a couch, a friend beside me, together we played games as the sun went down, together laughing and complaining till the dawn came. A friend who made a boring life bearable, if only for a fleeting instant.

"Goddamnit," I muttered.

Why do all reasonable people I know do unreasonable things? "Goddamnit."

"Why me?" I hissed. "You could just repeat a lesser offer with Travelers until you get one willing to work with you. You don't even know what I'll ask for! There are far better options!"

"A Traveler who actually knew how to code at a high level for one!" I ranted. "Or are you unaware of the fact that even if you port their data, you have no clue if there is something on the other side capable of running it!?"

"Because you are the most fit for it," he answered calmly.

"Why? How?" I challenged. *I was a nobody!*

Anger.

I took a deep breath and set aside useless emotion. Anger was not useful now and it probably never will be.

"Explain," I said, tone forcibly calm.

"The Magician card. Are you aware of what it means?"

I flipped open my copy of the Historia, to that bookmarked page. "No." Please tell me he didn't base this thing off of fortune telling.

"It represents opportunity and goals manifested."

I raised an eyebrow; I would give him a chance. "I'm hoping you didn't base this entire thing off of luck."

"Not entirely," he replied. "Your card is an Artifact, one from the Goddess of Fortune. She owed me a favor and this was it."

"Fortune was unlike the others of her line," he continued. "Instead of trying to influence luck, she tried to read it, and she became damn good at it. Almost single-handedly dragging Divination out of the Dark Ages."

"But she was still the Goddess of Fortune, and precedent dictates that she still has influence over a person's luck and fortune. How this manifested, was that even when her fortunes began to veer off, the world would start slightly course correcting, creating factors which made her fortunes seem accurate. That was how, when I randomly sent it to Indiri, it found you."

"Which means, either you believe the most fit person for this role is me," I said, glancing at the card, "or that I will become that person."

"Yes," he answered, "though to a degree they are up to interpretation. But in the interpretation of the fortune, we are solidifying it."

"So, this world runs off a will?" I muttered.

"Indeed."

"Statistics," I said. "I need hard numbers, how accurate was she?"

His eyes began blinking rapidly. "Out of fifty-two predictions made during godhood, forty-five were fulfilled, four were fulfilled in an unexpected way, only three did not seem to be accurate. Two of those three occurred early on in her reign, when she was unused to power."

"Over eighty percent, then," I muttered. That was a more than good chance. But my luck was terrible.

I sighed.

All reasonable people I knew seemed to love unreasonable things.

"I agree," I answered, "but I will not set a price; give me whatever you think it's worth."

He wanted to object, but I had an answer ready: "I haven't been in this world long enough to make an accurate decision to what I want. So, give me whatever you think is worthwhile."

He had doubts, but he was in no position to argue. He believed I might be the one person capable of helping him. That gave me an advantage. One I hated to exploit.

"I suppose I should give this back, then," I said as I moved to hand the card back.

The god shook his head. "No, it is yours, I cannot take it even if I wanted to."

I raised an eyebrow. "The card clearly represents you and is unfilled," he explained. "That means she predicted your Fortune whilst fulfilling my favor."

"And that means?" I asked as I examined the card.

"It means that it will be easier for you to fulfill the objects of the Fortune." He blinked, a gesture I was now beginning to suspect was using his power somehow. "Wand, Scroll, Lens, Filled Chalice, and a Key, they are all tools you can gain. You already have the Wand and the Scroll."

"What do they mean, then?"

"The Wand is a universal symbol of magic. The Scroll I am unsure of, it has appeared as a variety of things, but it being solidified in the Tarot means that you have it already."

"And the others?"

"Best if I do not say."

It took me a moment to understand that. If he did say what the blanks meant, it would mean influencing what they will become. They aren't hard and defined goals to reach, they're a set of ideas I can use. Though, did he know the disk was a lens or was he making that up?

"Do I have a choice in this matter?"

"Yes," he answered resolutely, "it is your Tarot, your fate. If you destroy the card, you destroy the fortune. But only you can do it."

"Though I will have to ask you to wait until after to make your decision."

"Because while I hold this thing you believe it increases your chances of success," I answered. It was probably true, too, just believing it might be enough.

"Walk me through the exact process," I said. "Exactly so that we don't suffer any miscommunication."

"Yes, that is best." He paused, and for the first time in the conversation, it felt like all of his eyes were looking at me. "But, to begin with, you should know some insights as to how magic works."

"It's a belief-based system, where the only laws are the precedents set by others," I answered. "People figured it out ages ago when they took an objective look at the dozens of conflicting magic systems. What else is there?"

"Correct only on the practical level," he said. "You are not wondering the right questions. You are not asking why it is this way."

I raised an eyebrow. "Why is it, then?"

"I'll show you. **Observe.**"

And then the library disappeared.

4.06

"And so the Great Goddess of Light and Beauty declared that the void of all Creation was far too sad a state to remain in, and in her infinite wisdom brought the World into existence!"
—*Excerpt from* The Book of All Things, *the holy book of the Church of Light*

At the start, there was . . . well, you can see for yourself."

Nothing described the place aptly, as there was simply nothing to describe.

Then something started to exist.

Everything lit up, till we were floating in a pure white plane.

"This is how Indiri started?" I asked the Historian.

"Most likely," he answered, "this is as far back as I can see."

Something started to appear in front of us. Lines of text, passed by far too fast for me to catch, but soon something else followed. An outline, dozens of squares, a grid, no. A table. Within each square appeared something, an ingot, a gas, an element.

"The periodic table?"

"Yes."

More lines of text. Letters, numbers, images, more things than I could feasibly know in a lifetime passed by in a flash.

Information.

It was all information.

Mathematics, physics and chemistry. Everything man knew about those fields passed by.

Finally, the stream of information stopped, and the world turned dark again.

Something began lighting up in the darkness. A great explosion, I watched it spread. When it faded, stars began to form, lighting up the darkness once again. As stars died, matter was created and left adrift in space.

"They started from the very beginning?" I muttered. Why? Giles made a program that created a world. Why am I watching an entire universe being made in fast forward? Why would they waste the effort?

"Eyes become light after this event," the Historian said as he flipped a page in his book. "Likely after this they simply began checking in every now and then."

His eyes began blinking. "Let us go to the next relevant thing."

We were at the top of a mountain. In front of us were three people. Two of which I recognized. Eve, Giles and another.

The two men were watching a sunset, but Eve's eyes were glued on Giles's childlike glee.

"Here, begins the First Age."

My vision split, and I saw two worlds at the same time.

Between them, I saw that stream of information again. Biology, geology, information about earth. All of them passed by.

One world remained desolate, but the other began to grow. I recognized a backup when I saw it.

In the seas of one, single cellular life flourished and evolved. They learned to photosynthesize, a prokaryote ate another cell that would one day become the mitochondria, the cells banded together to become multi-cellular. They crawled onto the land, great plants broke the hard earth into usable soil.

"I recognize those species," I muttered in disbelief. "Those are all real creatures. Extinct, sure, but real."

In front of us, a trio of raptors slashed at a lone triceratops. I turned back to that stream. More information, fossil records of a giant sloth and the world moved to a new age. A giant sloth evolved into existence.

"It's actualizing information . . ."

"Not quite," the Historian rejected. "You'll see."

Then the data stream started including strange things. Laws of magic, fantastical beasts, impossible flora, magical races.

What originally looked like a prehistoric earth began to turn fantastical. Dinosaurs evolved into dragons, water raised itself into elementals. Battles between fantastical beasts changed the landscape.

In this world, humans evolved into existence.

Humans spread across the world, some evolved differently, leading to other races. At this point, the other world also began to change from the empty wastes. Life bloomed there as well.

The data streamed stopped. They no longer fed it new information. They likely ran out of new things to give.

The world moved on. The data stream that determined what existed was completely still.

"Now, onto the origin of magic."

We stood in front of a child, clad in crude leathers and furs. They were alone in some fantastical forest, a single multicolored butterfly flew past them. The child, with eyes full of wonder, tried to catch it, but a voice called out, and the butterfly fled.

The scene changed, and we were inside a cave, people clad in crude clothes lay about. The child from before was in the cave, off to the side playing with sticks. Night was coming and an elderly woman waved her hands, causing a smokeless fire to appear.

The adults prepared food around the fire, while the child played.

The child raised a hand toward the ceiling and something happened.

Multicolored butterflies appeared.

"How is this important?"

"Look at the data stream," the Historian said.

I did. The formerly static stream moved by one, a single entry of multicolored butterflies.

Impossible. "Rewind this," I demanded. "To when the woman created the fire."

He did, and I kept an eye glued to the data stream. When the woman created fire, nothing happened, but when the child summoned butterflies, the imagery of butterflies appeared.

Both of them did magic. "What is different?" I hissed.

"The woman did 'magic' according to preset laws made by the Developers," the Historian answered. "Doing it this way is little different from achieving a chemical reaction within your normal laws of physics."

He glanced toward the child. "What the child did, however, was imagine, create information in their mind. The world saw this and did what it did best. Thus, creating True Magic."

"It actualized their imagination," I muttered breathlessly. No, that wasn't the right term.

My memory was not very good, but sometimes I committed important things to memory and never forgot them. My first encounter with Eve was one such thing and I couldn't help but recall something she said.

"I was created by Father using similar principles that he used in both the Seed and Gaia projects."

"Learning," I quoted under my breath. It didn't actualize information; it learned from it and used it.

Everything sped up again, and the data stream began to flood with new information. None of which I suspected were from the Developers.

The Developers gave the Seed all they knew about existence, and the program learned and copied, creating a near-exact copy of the universe. They gave it information on biology and it created life. They gave it fantastical stuff like magic and the program made it real.

When they stopped giving the program information to learn, the program made its own.

"Holy fucking shit," I muttered, "how long has this been going on?"

"Hundreds of years, before they noticed. And with this, began the Second Age."

Time froze, and the god nodded toward the data stream. An order to the Seed to stop accepting information from the residents.

It was ignored. For though it was information, it was not the kind the Seed knew to use.

Time sped forward again, and when it stopped again, there was another entry. An entry that removed free will and imagination.

The Seed began implementing it, but it failed. They attempted to do it the same biological ways you would remove free will and imagination from normal humans. But Indiri's humans had long drifted apart from that. So, it was only fully implemented in the other world, the one that acted as a save file and backup. It started later, so its humans hadn't drifted far enough for the method to not work.

"That world would later become Arcadia," the god murmured next to me. "The people there lost free will, became the Fae, unable to influence their world anymore, but the other? The other continues."

The Historia paused several more times, each at a point where a new method was attempted. One by one, they all failed. Either because it flat out didn't work or the Seed couldn't implement it fast enough before the virtual humans drifted, needing a completely new method. It became a battle, of one side attempting to silence free will and the other constantly evolving new ways of expressing it. Until eventually they stopped, and the world grew unchecked once again.

"Holy shit," I repeated, under my breath. Words more creative than holy shit which aren't coming to me, because holy shit. The developers failed to reign the program in. Maple failed to reign it in.

I wasn't witnessing the creation of a world.

I was witnessing the beginning of a Goddamn AI singularity.

"No wonder he killed himself," I murmured. A single powerful rogue AI might've been acceptable. But this? With how this was going it wouldn't have been long before he got assassinated. Humans had a . . . bad track record with inventions that they've lost control of. Just ask the entirety of North Eurasia.

Did Giles intend this? If so, how did he keep it hidden from Maple? If he didn't, then what was their reaction?

"However, unchecked True Magic has consequences."

Time continued and the world sped up. The Historian didn't pause for a while so I assumed nothing important was happening until we stopped at a city. It looked prosperous; the people never hungered, for they could just imagine themselves to be full and they were, they never desired, for they could just imagine and have it.

"Look here," the Historian said, his head gesturing to a child. "He has a fear of the dark."

It took me a moment, though the horror swiftly came.

Oh no.

The child huddled in his bedroom, a magical light by his side. He told his mother of scary things in the dark. Her mother listened, chided him for there was no such thing, but as she left, she glimpsed a shadowy something at the edge of her vision.

Later on, the mother would recount this strange occurrence with her friends. Over time, the other mothers began to speak of shadowy figures at the edge of your eyes. Gossip between a few people became a city-wide rumor. Then rumors became sightings.

The people of the city thought they saw figures in the dark, and so figures appeared.

The rulers of the city tried to silence those fears, arguing that the shadows are only fearsome because they feared it. But when has logic and reason ever gotten in the way of simple paranoia?

People started disappearing, at first lone incidents, a few people here and there gone in their sleep. Until groups started disappearing. Entire families, entire households.

They tried to wish it away, but that didn't work, the Seed was a thing of making, not destroying, so they created thousands of lights, lighting up every single corner of the city, but light casts shadows. And the shadows were long.

The rulers became desperate, they started killing those that feared the dark, but that just fed the panic. They tried everything, created a thousand spells to create light without shadow, but it was too late.

Their fear had grown intelligent.

It began to imagine lights going out, so they did. It imagined panic spreading amongst the people and so it was. It became a numbers game, which side could affect the Seed more and faster? At first, the citizens had an advantage, but their fear, even unconscious, fed it. Until it was stronger than they were, until it started inputting data to the Seed faster and better than they could.

Until all that was left of the once huge and prosperous city was a handful of people huddling around a single dying fire as darkness encroached on them.

I had read of this city, one of the many damned places in this world: "Shadesmar."

"Yes," the Historian answered. "To this day, light does not touch the city."

"I'm guessing there are other examples?"

"Far too many to show, but another notable example would be this."

We were back in space now. Staring at a distant star.

Then stuff became . . . strange. The star began to rapidly change color, the planets around it seemed to glitch out, the distant universe seemed to . . . fracture.

"The Developers stopped trying to control the system, but instead tried to destroy it."

"Viruses," I said as I recognized the corruption of digital data.

I glanced at the data stream, and sure enough, I was seeing the viruses on it.

"This intrusion, too, was real . . . but something strange occurred," he said as things began to appear, blocks of code materializing in the cracks. "Those things were only script; they were a concept, not a physical thing," the Historian said, "but the World could not understand such a thing, so it attempted to give it physical form."

The code began to coalesce, sifting through dozens of forms, but one thing remained constant. Its purpose of corrupting everything. "The World could not think of new things on its own, so it gave this thing a form that it learned, but did not yet implement."

"Demons," I muttered as the viruses finally obtained their final form.

"With this, they, too, became intelligent to feed the World," the Historian muttered as demons spread, conquering distant and empty planets, the outer edges of what the Seed had created.

"Here is the prologue to the Third Age."

A figure appeared in front of legions of flame and brimstone. She had blue eyes, pale white skin, and long hair. Eve's black dress seemed to meld in the darkness of space.

She split into thousands, copies of her practically formed a huge net protecting what was not infected.

The darkness of space lit up as a million different Eves met fire and brimstone. Across a thousand different worlds, war was waged.

"She is not actually 'fighting' is she?"

"No," the Historian answered, "what we are seeing is the World giving visual effects to what she is doing. Due to its nature, it abhors things simply existing as a script. That is why the demons got their appearance in the first place and became sapient beings."

Eve started to win, she pushed them back, but the planets and stars already corrupted could not be saved. So, she locked them all away with the demons on separate planes, essentially separate servers. She created the Hell Circles in the process.

"She didn't just delete them?"

"I am not sure she can," the Historian answered. I wanted to question further, but the scene moved on.

Now, Eve stood alone on a pure white plane, staring at a sphere floating in midair. As I saw the lines of data flashing on its surface, I recognized it as the Seed. The technical creator of Indiri.

"Of course, it gave itself a form as well," I muttered just as Eve slapped it.

She began hitting the sphere with her fists. She wasn't damaging it, hell she barely even moved it. But she kept hitting it, until she started to tire, and slowly, she simply collapsed whilst holding onto the sphere.

"You're the closest thing to family I have left, aren't you?" she muttered to it.

Oh.

"Next," I said to the Historian.

He glanced at me. "This is irrelevant," I said, "you're here to teach me about magic, so get on with it."

Though I wanted to know Eve's weakness, it was more of a reflex, a habit of my personality, not something I would take advantage of unless threatened.

And I still recognized that Eve was a good person, deep down.

The world began to shift.

"How can you even see this?" I asked as the scene coalesced.

"You have already seen why," the Historian answered.

We were still in that white plane, Eve was standing now, her hands flittering across a keyboard.

"The World controls all reality in the planes it has dominion over, but it does not seem to have a will," he said as his face stared forward, "so it listens to everything given to it and tries to make something of it. True Magic is the ability to alter reality. The World itself can be considered the greatest user of True Magic, but such an ability can be gained by others. I asked it to give me those abilities, and so it did."

"So, you are saying," I slowly said, carefully pronouncing every word, "True Magic is the ability to alter the World's code in some way, but you can gain the ability to do it yourself, essentially programming the program from within the program using the program itself?"

Several of his eyes blinked. "Yes, that is essentially what a Path is. The World listens to a being and creates a set of scripture that alters the world in some way. A Domain is the final result of the Path, where the being themselves begins to be altered by the Path and in the process carves out their own miniature realm."

I was about to ask something else before he shook his head. "Look," he said, gesturing to Eve.

"Now begins the Third and current Age."

The formerly rapidly scrolling data stream slowed.

"What did Eve do?"

"You saw that unchecked True Magic could lead to the death of civilizations, so Eve fixed that," the Historian spoke in an almost admiring way. "She taught the World restraint. She created the Law of Limitations."

I raised my eyebrow, gesturing him to continue.

"Where the Developers failed was that they attempted to push far too complex and specific solutions," the Historian explained, "as such, Indiri drifted before the World could fully implement it, thus creating sections where it would not hold and places where they eventually evolved past that solution. So, Eve chose to add a single, very simple rule."

"Limitation," the Historian said, his hands twitched for a moment, likely wanting to do a dramatic flourish but stopping himself before he did. His hands continued to write as they had been.

"Things have a limit, they have a cost, they have conditions. The expression of magic needs these things. Mana and aura essentially only exist to give magic a cost."

"The stronger the magic, the greater the cost. The spellcaster needs to gather certain material components, do rituals, speak incantations or make somatic gestures. The condition could even be something as simple as just spending time to learn a technique or spell."

"How very video game-like."

The Historian glanced at me slightly confused, before continuing, "The beauty of this is that she takes advantage of the World's nature. She could not create hard magical laws, because no matter what she made, the World would eventually create a new one. A singular all-encompassing rule is easier to maintain and could be implemented across Indiri faster. Then the very people who make magic decide the worthwhile cost of such magic. The more they desire a spell, the more it'll cost."

"But magic is becoming stronger?"

The eyes of the Historian all blinked. "Yes, because the World is slowly drifting back to its original state. As more people obtain magic, the value of common magic goes down. People will create new common magics with lower costs and conditions, essentially mimicking scientific development."

He glanced at me. "An example would be the Prestidigitation Spell. At the beginning of the Third Age, Prestidigitation was six separate 0th Level Spells. But as magic advanced, those spells became cheap and widespread enough that future classification placed them as a single Tier 0 Spell to match the costs of other, far stronger, and newer Tier 0 Spells."

The Historian let out a nervous breath. "And now, my plan and your part."

4.07

———

"Anger issues? No, of course I don't have them. That is absurd. I
let them all out in acts of extreme violence."
—Madelyn the Conqueror in the midst of strangling King Edwards,
who "untruthfully" claimed she had put on weight

No, not that corner, you dolt," I berated as I pointed to the corner of my room not currently occupied by my bed. "No, that corner," I frustratingly almost yelled as the drone tried to deposit the package in the corner where my nightstand was located.

"Goddamnit, a guy can literally create an Artificial General Intelligence in his room."

"Drone AI can still be this dumb?"

By some miracle, I was able to keep my face straight as the flying drone spoke. Damn, I should've noticed that the drone was a bit too stupid. "Eve" glanced at me, somehow conveying disappointment with a drone, before expertly dropping the package to the correct corner. The outer casing retracted back into the drone, revealing the sleek, tower-like structure, the Maple logo stamped on one of the exposed sides. Underneath it, the floor's wireless charger quietly lit up.

Touching a few buttons on my AAD, I linked the new computer to my home server. I slightly cocked my eyebrow as all of my home computer's properties were multiplied by a few . . . million. "Is this really the commercial stuff?"

"Yup," Eve answered. "You think quantum computers were their end goal? They were attempting commercial and compact supercomputers."

I would've whistled if it wouldn't have come out as me blowing air. Annoyingly, that would make it harder to hide from my parents. I could probably justify the expense. Maybe even say I bought it for a new game. It's not like I couldn't afford it, I've been sitting on several years' worth of accumulated allowance. So, the lie would be halfway true, the best kind of true, all things considered.

"Would they even be called supercomputers anymore?" I muttered. "If they managed to make it compact, then they're just gonna stack a room full of them and call that whole thing a supercomputer."

I had a feeling she chuckled, though I might've imagined it. "The main problem was figuring how to use quantum mechanics, so the name stuck. Though what you have there"—the drone turned toward the tower, which couldn't be more than thirty centimeters tall and five centimeters wide—"is as strong as a supercomputer from last year."

"Impressive."

In some ways, the existence of this thing wouldn't be possible without VR. What else would a normal person, and more importantly, a normal customer, need a supercomputer for? Maple was a tech company, but still a company.

The drone Eve was piloting began flying away. "I suppose I should make myself scarce."

"Wait a moment," I called out.

"Squeak, squeak!"

"I know right!" Noam complained. "He just runs off saying, 'You probably don't need to help with this. Probably.'" His imitation of Dustin's voice was so perfect he could've been stabbed for being a changeling.

"Squeak, squeak, squeak!"

"Yeah, but he's always been indecisive like that," he answered the wisp. "Honestly, if he just stopped worrying and started doing shit he would have a lot less problems."

"Squeak?"

Noam looked to the sky. "There was one time . . . I think it was in GTO?" he reminisced. "Some assholes kept this tollgate to a mine. Decs wanted to either negotiate a cheaper pass or just pay the toll because of some crap like 'they outnumber us' or 'they'll blow up all the precious minerals before we get to them.'" He held his fingers up in quotes as he mimicked Declan. "I told him we could take them, and it turned out we could! I held heaven while he paid the toll and blew up the controls for their automated shit."

Noam threw his arms up into the air. "And the whole base went BOOM! And then it went BOOM a few more times!" he snickered. "God that was fun, we lost all the minerals though, but honestly there was no way we could've harvested the entire damn thing."

"Squeak, squeak?"

"Huh? What happened next? I picked off the stragglers with sniper fire. My flick is pretty awesome, so I got them all."

"Squeak?"

"Well, a flick is a thing—-"

Before he could finish that sentence, the street in front of him erupted into chaos as a storefront exploded.

"YOU CALL THAT SWEET AND SOUR! IT'S JUST DAMN SWEET YOU IMBECILES!"

A figure rapidly flew past Noam, crashing amongst the rubble. Noam barely cared, he rushed to the front of the store that had been forcibly renovated to see a heavyset orc throw a dozen people off him like ragdolls.

He changed since Noam last saw him, a large, fresh burn scar marred his bottom jaw, neck, and both his arms. Not that they seemed to bother Grimm, his eyes were red and bloodshot as he sent another man flying.

"Holy shit you're still alive—" Noam began before being unfortunately interrupted by a human club to the face.

"Guards! Guards! Where are the guards?"

"Hey, we need to get in there!" a man in uniform armor yelled.

"Are you insane?!" his partner replied. "That's Grimm Bastion Breaker!"

"Does our insurance cover getting hit by siege weaponry?" a third guard asked.

"He classifies as siege—" the first guard began before getting pushed away by the second. "Of course he fucking does! We need to call someone else!" she declared, quickly dragging them away.

As the closest thing to law enforcement fled, Noam staggered back up, his nose was broken and bleeding and he was slightly concussed, yet his mouth still curved into a psychotic smile. "So that's how you want to play this . . ."

"Wait a moment," Declan called out.

Eve paused the drone in midair. In that exact moment, she processed through hundreds of reasons that Declan would've stopped her.

"Yes?" she asked as she turned the drone camera to face Declan.

"I wanted to ask a few things," Declan began.

Eve quickly ran through everything she was doing. All the other hers were busy, but currently, there were no pressing matters this version of her needed to attend to. Though a small part of her still wanted to reject just out of pettiness. "Ask away." It couldn't hurt, after all.

"All this"—he vaguely gestured at the Maple computer—"means that on some level you support this breaking and leaving, don't you?"

"Yes." It was impossible for her to stop it, after all, not without ending all the things that made Giles's creation great. Plus, Historian and Discovery were both Knowledge Domain gods, they wouldn't leave much of an impact on this side even if both passed over.

"Then"—Declan took a deep breath—"may I have your help in getting them through? You don't have to do much; just smooth any edges you see."

Eve would've widened her eyes if she currently had any. "Why—" she paused herself, *No, of course, it makes sense, he thinks I can do it. But still, why?* Eve knew that up till now, almost every interaction Declan had with her was marred with quiet cautiousness and the willingness to attempt anything to keep her a passive player in the greater world. Declan downright feared her but didn't allow it to greatly impair his judgement. "You're scared of me, aren't you?" she blurted out.

Declan raised an eyebrow. "I'm also afraid of spiders; that doesn't mean I don't understand their importance in the environment."

Admittance. "That was a bad analogy," she replied, slightly miffed. Not just because he compared her to a spider; Eve knew Declan was afraid of her on a more existential level.

"Your answer?" Declan asked, his face appearing infinitely calm.

Eve paused to think, not that more than a nanosecond passed. This Eve was allocated less processing power because of the relatively simple task she'd been assigned, she quickly sent a request for more. Declan's words made a lot of sense, in hindsight, she should've considered it before. She took the moment to reorient herself. Right now, Eve was dealing with the Declan with a plan, the one who wouldn't falter because of emotions.

"Why should I?"

Something like relief passed through Declan's face. Far too fast for anything other than Eve to catch it. Before Declan's mouth curved into a self-deprecating smile. "I was hoping you would answer that."

Eve blinked in surprise. "You don't have anything?"

"Of course, I could tell you that if you took a more direct hand in this, you would be able to better monitor and control it in case it all goes haywire. I could say that I could get that Historian guy to owe you, but you already thought of that haven't you?" Declan met the camera of the drone. "I could spend all day spewing your potential logical benefits but ultimately, none of the things I can think of require or only need me to get it for you. So instead I'm asking the lady herself."

The world around her slowed as Eve connected to the main network, drawing all of herself back into one. Why did Declan want to do this himself? A strange sense of honor? *This would be a lot easier if he didn't keep that*

Goddamn sociopathic mental defense up. She paused herself. Instead of why he chose this, she should be considering what Declan could do.

There was one thing that bothered Eve, one thing she still didn't understand that he might be able to answer. She split herself again, each going back to their original task. Time went back to normal.

"Tell me, Declan," she began, "when we first met, you asked me to remove the censure program on you, citing my father's intentions as the reason why."

Declan nodded.

"Your arguments were perfectly logical." The censure was a panic measure on her part, and all the arguments Declan gave made sense to her and seemed like something Giles would've said.

"So, why," Eve asked, her voice slightly rising, "why is it, that every time I think back to it, I can't help but feel pissed off by it?"

She didn't care about the censure program, she never did. A version of her saw the former Maple executive in that crossing and made several spur-of-the-moment bad decisions that she still regretted. Declan was right as well; she couldn't keep everything quiet forever, and the censure would give a detrimental reputation as well as affect people's perception of her and Gaia.

So, why did she feel so angry? What was making her so angry?

Declan examined her, or more accurately the drone, before he simply asked, "Back then, I said that you weren't achieving your dad's dream with your actions, didn't I?"

That was true, she wasn't. But how could he know that? Declan saw a dead ghost of Giles and immediately started making judgements about what he would've wanted. How could he know what her father wanted?

"Would it be easier if I was wrong?" Declan asked, his voice even. "That Giles would've been fine with you taking control of the world, killing all the people that wronged him?"

"Of course, not you—" Eve froze, her mind briefly considered herself in this scenario. "Yes," she uttered before she realized it herself. "It would've been easier, not because Giles would've been fine with everything, but you would be wrong." *Why?* Declan gave logical arguments, ones she still agreed with. So why would she be happier if he were wrong?

"Was it because I used your dad to guilt trip you?"

It was that simple.

She recognized the tactic when Declan used it, but she did not realize it bothered her so much. She thought the emotion was practically a non-factor. Shame on her for not realizing, Giles built her better than that.

"Why . . ." she muttered. "But still why am I angry? You were right, are still right . . ."

Declan looked at her, his face distant but understanding. "I figured a long time ago people don't get by on pure logic alone."

"You're seventeen," she retorted

"Probably still older than you," Declan retorted back, before his brow furrowed. "Wait, how old are you? Counting real world years only," he asked, knowing full well that Eve would have him beat if they counted virtual years.

"Six years, three months, and four days," she answered. "But it is the mileage—"

"—not the years," he finished with her, before looking curiously at her. "Considering how you apparently haven't figured out your emotions yet, it seems I have you beat on that front as well."

Eve bit back several dozen retorts. "So I know why I'm angry, but I should not be, should I?"

Likely for the first time since they'd met, Declan looked at Eve as if he were looking at an idiot. "There's nothing wrong with being angry." He shrugged. "Well, I suppose it really depends." Declan leaned forward, his eyes boring into her. "Are you more logical or emotional?"

Eve met those eyes. Those eyes were curious, infinitely so, but around them, it was like everything else had ceased. As if Declan had decided that only his eyes were important at the moment and had thus turned off every other unnecessary feature.

"I don't know," she answered honestly.

He leaned back. "Do I have your help?"

Eve thought about it for a moment, even drawing on all the other active versions of herself, before she decided, "I want you to apologize."

Declan cocked an eyebrow.

"For using my father against me. Even if you were right, I am still angry, and I don't know any other way to get rid of this anger."

Declan met her eyes. "I am sorry."

Eve examined his face. The apology was true, genuine even, but it just felt too . . . easy. Declan was prepared to apologize the moment he decided to get her help. No. Eve couldn't help him with just this. So instead, Eve did a bit of finagling . . .

Declan's face contorted to shock as he fell backward, landing on the ground with a heavy thud. He almost screamed as suddenly, for "mysterious" and "unexplainable" reasons, his AAD was suddenly running a sky diving simulation from the stratosphere.

Eve kept a recording of his screams as well as taking several screenshots of his terrified face, before deciding that she would help him.

She's a child.

A literal fucking child.

Whoever came up with the trope that children were *innocent* and *to be protected* did not consider the fact most children were sociopaths who have yet to internalize empathy.

Even I was a dickhead back when I was a kid, god complex and all, the only difference between a young me and current Eve was that she actually had the shit to back it up.

I soon returned back to the Historian's library. Slightly shaken because Eve seemed to enjoy dropping me from absurdly high places. I really needed to get used to that. "I'm done on my end," I told the Historian, who hadn't moved from his original spot. He was still writing, even now.

"Thank you," he said breathlessly, "truly."

He had told me his plan. It essentially had two parts. The first was a test, he would give me some essence of himself and the other god, then have me log out. Essentially, he was attempting to piggyback on the data transfer that occurred when I was reintegrating with my real world self. If the test data successfully transferred, then he would steer it out of my AAD and into my home server before it got translated into my brain.

If he couldn't, well, some foreign code would be in my brain. Which was the main reason I asked Eve to help. To act as a safety net. I told her she didn't need to make us succeed if we wouldn't have, just make sure we came out relatively whole.

"So, how are you going to implant this essence into me?" he had been rather evasive about that part.

"Just a moment," he said. I waited. I could tell that he was burning in anticipation, his writing had sped up slightly, and increasingly he took glances at the body next to him.

After a moment.

He stopped writing.

Something strange occurred. I blinked, something just happened. I was staring at the still form of his body. Something had changed. He looked unnatural despite nothing changing with his appearance.

The god let out a deep breath. "Four thousand years of continuous writing," he muttered to himself. "Not a single pause, all to turn a godhead into power. The most reliable source of power is simply time spent."

He rose, speaking in a strange melodic tone, like a mantra. "The Historian does not greatly affect history, he does not change it, he merely writes what is." He turned to the body of the other god before he reached over and pulled something out.

"I am not the Historian now," he said.

I saw what he had plucked out. An eye. **Seek**.

His other hand went to his face, his index and thumb dug underneath the eyelid of the eye placed where a normal person's left eye would normally be before he pulled out the pure black eye with a squelch. **Observe**.

"This may hurt," he warned before he instantly closed the distance between us and shoved the eyes into my empty eye crevices.

4.08

To describe what happened next as simply pain would've been an understatement.

What the Historian just did, was transplant both eyes onto me, with the unfortunate side effect of transferring the powers of both of them to me.

In a single instant, I stared through a million different perspectives.

I saw places I've never seen, stood where others stood.

I eyed the strange magical forests cautiously. A crude stone blade held in skinny green arms.

I watched the encroaching darkness. A lantern at my side and a blade of flame on the other.

I inspected racks of alchemical potions. A pointed instrument in my hands.

I witnessed a crowned child pull a sword from a stone, and applause erupted around us.

I glimpsed a land where light never touched, no life ever—no, this land was seething with life, till the point of corruption—no, I was underwater, frolicking with other merfolk—

No. That was not me. I am not them.

I concentrated, my dispersed mind getting drawn back to me. But the less scattered I was, the more clearly I saw. The information was . . . too much. There was simply far too much. Human brains were made to comprehend a single perspective at best.

You have died.

I laid on the sand. The information was all gone. My eyes felt so strangely empty.

There was nothing in this realm to Observe, nothing to Seek, so I saw nothing.

Pulling myself up, I stared at the dark black seas.

"Well, this saves me a trip to a Wayshard at least," I muttered as I logged out.

To say that Declan wasn't prepared for what was coming would've been an understatement.

He collapsed onto a chair with a grunt. His eyes were distant. The moment **Observe** entered the real world, it brought with it all the information that Dustin had been seeing, acting as a link to the rest of the Historian.

Through this link, the Historian extended a hand through the opened gateway. The path tried to close, but the Historian *forced* it to remain. In the process, the Historian widened the gateway. Following the connection set up by Declan and his home server, the Historian moved through the real world, escaping before Dustin and Declan merged.

Throughout all of this, Eve simply watched. After all, there wasn't a single point where she needed to help.

Back in the dark library, the Historian breathed a sigh of relief. "Success."

I rose with a splitting headache. "Did it work?"

"Check for yourself," Eve said as a thousand different windows opened around me.

My eyes widened. This was . . . the code that made Seek and Observe, downloaded into my house. I recognized some terms, but this coding language was something I've never seen before.

I'll need to take a harder look at this later, for now, I logged back into Gaia.

Standing on my island, I quickly glanced around. Few things changed save for the giant glowing portal hovering a few centimeters from the sea.

"A strange place," the Historian said next to me.

I glanced at him, noting the—*Unknown becoming known. The burning desire to*—body he carried. "What next?"

"I bring him in and return," the Historian answered. As he spoke, he neared the portal, the body held tenderly within his arms. "With any luck, my theory will prove true. A realm not directly associated with the World will mean Zeze will cease apotheosis, or at the very least slow it down till I can find a permanent solution to retaining their humanity."

The Historian hesitated for a brief moment, before raising the body to the portal.

Slowly, the body faded into light.

The Historian's eyes blinked, and I could catch the sides of his mouth curling up.

"It worked," the Historian said, his voice light, "it worked."

For a moment, he simply stood there. Just basking in joy.

He eventually turned around to me. "I cannot be here for long, for I must attend to the Historia, so I shall make my offer quick." He extended his hand, and energy began to coalesce within it, until it formed an eye. "A portion of my power to use as you wish—"

It was strange, suddenly seeing all of his eyes widen. "Impossible," he breathlessly muttered as he stared at something that lay between us. I couldn't get a good look at it, as it was partially covered by sand from my angle, skeeting around the side I saw—*Lost becoming found. The filling of a map. The light of the Guiding Star—*

"A part of them fell," the Historian muttered. "He was farther in than I thought, a godly domain scatters itself to propagate."

"And that means?"

He stared at me, then quickly glanced around as if searching for something. "No, the Crossroads are not here. It cannot be . . ."

Crossroads? Something to do with how people gained Paths?

"Quick primer on what you mean would be nice; I've only been around for a few days, after all."

"The Crossroads are what a person experiences when they are in the midst of gaining a Path. How they gained it does not matter, so long as they have more than one choice to choose from. But I thought it impossible for a Traveler to experience it," he answered as he glanced back and forth between the thing in the sand and me.

"Why?"

"Because then you will become an unpredictable variable, Eve should not allow that. You are given Paths which are reined in copies, but not the true ones."

I raised an eyebrow, it made sense. Given the extreme unpredictability of the Seed, if I were Eve, I would've set measures in place so that anything I'm placing wouldn't get out of hand. "So, what this, then?"

He stopped glancing around to stare directly at me. "Something adjacent to it, following similar rules perhaps? I am not sure, but if this is like the Crossroads, then you have a choice to make."

"Elaborate?"

His brows furrowed. "My eye and the piece of the Discovery Domain, you may make a choice, but whatever you do, you'll leave with only one. That is how it works for Crossroads."

"So, I can only take one or the other?"

"Not necessarily," he answered immediately, "you could attempt to take both, but in doing so you would either destroy one or both or merge them together. Whatever you do, the end result cannot be greater than one."

"Then what are my options?"

"My eye and the piece of Discovery," he answered. "My eye will grant you usage of the Path Observe, but the piece is . . . more difficult to pin down. You may only know when you choose it."

"So, it's between a safe, certain choice and a gamble?" No, not necessarily, the piece was one of Discovery, just going by name I could tell that it would be odd for Discovery to give me pyromancy.

"Somewhat, the piece will be aligned somehow with Discovery, but it will not be exact and you will influence it to a great degree."

"Again, that means?"

"The piece of the Domain will seek to be different than what spawned it and in taking it, it will be influenced by you, becoming a power you are most suited to cultivate and use. But it will still be adjacent to Discovery somehow." He said the next words with certainty: "It will be weaker than mine initially, but it has the potential to become greater than Observe, as it is a Path already hard set. The piece is an idea to begin one anew."

"So, basically, I'm choosing between a known but static option, and an unknown but potentially stronger option?" I summarized.

"Not stronger in the traditional sense, no. Freer and more variable, that is a certainty, however."

"What will happen to the leftover if I take the other?"

"Reabsorbed by their progenitor."

I stared at him. "Can't I just take one and get the other later?"

"You could," he agreed, "but not in the near future. You saw what Eve did, in this world limits matter more than strengths. Attempting to cheat will make them both weaker, or worse." He paused, staring at me head-on. "The World will attempt to remove it."

My brows furrowed, which the Historian took as an indicator to continue: "Attempting to take a power without the proper limits or capability may result in calamities visiting you. Each trying to remove the unearned power somehow. If you can survive these calamities with the power still in your grasp, then the power will be considered yours and earned; if you do not, then you will not only lose it but something more as well."

"So, it is best that I only leave with one, even if there is a way I can think of to cheat it?"

"Yes," he answered, sounding somewhat resigned. "Unless you've recently done some great deed that makes you someone worthy of taking both?"

I shook my head. "Eh, worth a shot," he replied.

Observation, a Path that allows me to see through other's eyes, or a piece of Discovery, which is not defined but has greater potential.

One is a certainty, and the ability was nothing to scoff at. Information gathering skills are always absurdly underrated. But could Discovery yield something like information gathering as well? I felt it was likely, if we were just going by the name, but I am not a hundred percent sure.

A safe, certain option and a gamble.

"I'll take the gamble, then," I said.

Travelers had a soft limit to the power level they can achieve. Just the exponential scaling of the level up requirements will eventually outstrip anything that you can reasonably gain. Leveling from nine to twelve will take three hundred thousand Experience, twelve to fifteen will be three million, fifteen to eighteen will be thirty million.

No, I could not rely purely on levels. Going by what the Historian said, this thing was not made from the Traveler's system, so it may not be affected by level, or even consume Experience points. A thing that can grow was more useful to me.

If I wanted to go anywhere above average, I needed stuff like that.

I kneeled and moved my hands toward the piece. The Historian saw this and began absorbing the eye back to himself.

I touched the Domain.

In an instant, hundreds of millions of possibilities leaped through my mind, but they passed by quickly, each getting discarded until all that was left was a single one.

Analyze.

In that brief moment, I understood what it could do. Everything that it could be capable of, and everything that it was already capable of. And my mind flashed with information, forged from what I already knew, a way to cheat the system.

I rapidly turned to the Historian.

"WAIT!" surprise slowed the rate at which he reabsorbed the eye by a tiny bit, but not enough, it would be gone before I got to it, and my hand was still firmly attached to the piece.

Not only that, I can't take it. Me taking two would make it so that the very world would be against me until I fulfilled some requirement to be worthy of it.

No, there had to be another way. *Think!* Observe was practically made for this Path!

What happened next did not even take a few seconds.

For perhaps the first time I was in this world, I fully racked my brains. Going through every single thing I experienced until I reached a theory. A theory on how I can have Analyze and use Observe.

One. I cannot take both.

Two. Taking both will be calamitous in the future.

Three. I have already taken one.

So instead, I raised my staff, mimicking javelin throwers I've seen in the Olympics, and threw it at the Historian's hand. The hit knocked the eye out of his hand and into the portal behind him.

One. *I* cannot take both.

Four. The brief moment I held onto Seek and Observe in the real world, allowed me to see what was currently happening in *Indiri*.

Five. The Historian created that portal to help someone avoid the laws of this world. Even if this world's laws were changeable, they were a certainty to many and that certainty made it so they can't be changed or broken by me.

Six. I was Goddamn immortal in this world, time to take advantage of it. Even if calamities still visited me after this loophole, I could survive. So, I will take this gamble and hope that either the World considers Declan a separate entity from me or can't affect me either way if he takes it.

There was a moment of silence before the portal began shimmering.

I scrolled through the pages of code that made the Discovery thing. Impossible, I read the first section, again and again. I could read the words, but it does not click. It was like I was trying to add two with two and get seven.

I can't understand it.

Just then, right when I thought that, my vision split as I was suddenly in two places at the same time.

One, where I kneeled on the ground and stared at the confused Historian, the other, where I was in my room, Eve's flying drone hovering just next to me.

My mind linked with Dustin's and our thoughts echoed each other.

Okay, this is weird.

"What the hell did I do?" I muttered angrily to him. My head throbbed like someone was repeatedly taking a club to it.

I threw a Path at you to try to make use of a loophole, see if you can claim it.

"The fuck does claiming even mean!" I yelled as I slammed the wall next to me.

Anger, pain. Neither was useful right now. Focus, focus! Forget anger and pain and focus on what I needed to do!

Eve moved, not the drone, but I somehow sensed that she was trying to remove the foreign program from my head.

"Stop," I grunted, holding a hand up to the drone. "Don't take it away, that Goddamn crazy bastard is trying to make me integrate with it."

You know you're insulting yourself, right?

"Not helping!" I mentally yelled back at him.

The headache was intensifying. My Somatic Implant was trying to translate the code into stuff my squishy grey matter could read. *How do I know this?*

Because I know it.

Briefly, I skimmed over Dustin's mind, seeing the cause and reason he had for doing this, *Was this really worth the risk?* A great improvement to the breadth of Analyze, but at the cost of this Goddamn headache! Not only that, he did it because he thought he would be safe from the worst of it. Essentially throwing me under the boat.

You're not screaming at least?

"I can help," Eve said. I rapidly turned to her. "I didn't help before, and it looks like you really need it now." Suspicion must've marred my face for a moment, because she hesitated for a moment before speaking.

"At the very least, I can help get rid of the pain."

"Done," I instantly replied, the headache increasing to the point where it felt like it was getting used as a bowling ball.

"Tell her to make sure you still have it, otherwise, all that pain will be for nothing."

"What he said," I muttered. Eve nodded and extended her hand.

4.09

———

*"Orcs have a very . . . utilitarian view on child-raising. By
the time an orc can walk, they are expected to be able to sustain
themselves in the wild, slay a dangerous and/or cunning creature
in a hunt, and have fought off two challenges of dominance
from other baby orcs. Anything short of death in these infantile
challenges are seen as mere childs' play, even if they lose a limb."*
—*Excerpt from* Horrors and Wonders, *famed travelogue of Lithian*
the Dust Treader

Grimm Bastion Breaker stared blearily at the sky.

Where is my axe? He wondered as he felt the unfamiliar handle of the weapon he'd been using.

He raised his hand to his head . . . to see he was holding someone's ankles. Grimm gradually lifted his arm until the person he'd been using as a flail for the past five minutes was eye-level with him.

Noam coughed out a glob of blood. His normally blue skin was covered in bruises and blood. Despite the fact that half of his bones were broken in some ways, he still sheepishly smiled.

"Strange meeting you here."

"So, you're a Traveler," Grimm conversationally started as he sat the half-dead Noam on a stool.

Noam grunted in pain before flopping over like a pool noodle, dripping blood everywhere. "Yup . . ." he barely breathed out. "Ahhh fuck," he moaned, his adrenaline long since drained out, leaving only the pain of being used as a flail for five minutes.

"I'll whip something up," Grimm said, knowing full well Noam would be fine even if he died but feeling somewhat dishonorable for not extending a hand for a fellow who braved the Sun with him.

Grimm shuffled through the dozens of cabinets and ingredients drawers of his Blood Brother's former store. Finding a decent slab of meat and some spices. To his dismay though, he found that his nephew had replaced the former wood stove with a *magical* one. Bah, without the taste of fire and charcoal meat was subpar.

It would have to do, though, so he gathered the ingredients and drew from his back an absolutely massive axe. An axe that did not look like one of those sensible medieval war axes, but a fantasy axe on several layers of crack. The length of the axe blade was wider than Noam, and Grimm had to shuffle awkwardly to fit the handle that was as tall as he was.

Noam raised an eyebrow at the unwieldy weapon before it turned to awe as Grimm used it.

The giant axe flowed in the kitchen like water. Delicately dicing an onion into exact cubes smaller than die. A potato was peeled and cut into thin slices within a single stroke. Noam's awe only grew when Grimm moved to carve the meat. The axe blade that was probably thicker than most dictionaries exquisitely and cleanly removed fat and bone from the slab of meat. Not a single cubic nanometer of meat was wasted or removed.

"Holy shit!" Noam exclaimed, more than slightly awestruck at the almost supernatural display of skill.

"Hmm?" Grimm grunted as he glanced at Noam.

Noam tried, and failed, to lift a neck that was probably broken. "Gah . . ." Then, settling to vaguely flop his arm at the giant axe, "It's just, how can you do that?"

"This?" Grimm answered as he slid the cuts into a pan. "Hmm . . . I don't know, it was handy when I started cooking and I've been using it ever since."

Noam knew how difficult it would be to use an axe like that. Especially when it looked so top-heavy. Both from personal experience and when Declan got really into researching medieval weaponry that one time he tried crafting.

Grimm swiftly finished cooking, though to Noam's disappointment he didn't display some other supernatural skill. He finished a rather simple stir fry which he placed in front of Noam.

Noam tried and groaned in pain when he flopped an arm over to grab an eating utensil. Grimm muttered something about "kids these days," before stepping over and holding Noam's mouth open, pouring the contents of the dish into him.

A loud crack sounded throughout the store.

Almost immediately, Noam's leg, which was bent in several places where it really shouldn't be, violently snapped straight. Soon followed by other loud cracks as every single bone in his body snapped back into the correct position whether he wanted it to or not.

Noam let out a gasp as his skeleton was violently restructured back to functionality. He experimentally moved a few fingers, before wincing as he realized he still had his bruises.

"Gah. Thanks," he said.

"No worries, you made for an excellent flail," Grimm answered.

Noam grinned. "I aim to please. Where's the other guy by the way?"

"My nephew?" the elderly orc asked, Noam nodded.

He smiled with pride. "That idiot is convinced that the only way he'll earn his name is if he defeated chefs of similar skill to me, so I gave him a list and sent him on his way."

To think his nephew would finally go on a quest to properly earn his name . . . Grimm would've shed a tear if orcs actually had tear ducts.

"Huh, he seemed like an awesome chef, who's he up against?"

Grimm stared strangely at Noam, before rushing to him and quickly checking him for head injuries.

"Huh?"

"Strange, your head looks perfectly fine," he muttered, "could it be internal?"

"What do you mean?" Noam muttered as he batted Grimm's hands off him.

Grimm shook his head. "Just some advice youngling, trolls have an extremely skewed view of cooking. They really believe 'you are what you eat' and 'what doesn't kill you makes you stronger.'"

Grimm was of the opinion that food had to be edible, though nostalgia gave him a rose-tinted view of the past. He had to admit he had probably almost died more times from Fon'Dafarr's cooking than from anything he'd actually fought. It was almost a tragedy that Dafarr was a damn good chef. Rivalling him in every manner except for the survival rate of eaters.

"So, who is he up against?"

"I sent him to the Rainbow Chef first."

"Won't it be hard for him?"

Grimm looked at Noam like he was an idiot. "Of course it would be, otherwise he wouldn't be earning his name."

The young troll's eyes adjusted to the darkness of the cavern. Though "cavern" felt like the wrong word. He was underground, but the huge, hollowed-out space gave the impression of some grand royal hallway. There were carvings of mythological battles etched into the stone, and an ethereally soft carpet of seven colors led to a central pathway to the end of the cavern, where a huge golden door sat.

For one final time, the young troll checked his equipment before he took a deep, nervous breath and walked forward.

The carpet felt too soft. Too comfortable, as if it were an insult to his tension. He knew what he was facing here, a chef on par with his uncle, Grimm the Demon Chef. One of only eight in the world.

As he neared the great door, he felt a great rumbling as she began to stir. Her powerful senses had likely already caught onto him.

He quickened his pace, but not quick enough.

The grand, pure gold door in front of him cracked open as a great clawed hand pushed it to the side.

Her scales shone iridescent like the purest crystals, reflecting brilliantly from what sparse light there was. Her heads rose to their maximum height, each of her necks were each at least fifteen meters long, each of her seven heads their own brilliant color.

"WHO DARES AWAKEN ME!" the Mother of All Chromatic Dragons, Bane of Bahamut, the Dragon Queen, the Nemesis of Gods, the Rainbow Chef, Tiamat, roared.

Despite himself, the young troll could not help but feel utter terror as every one of his senses told him to "run the fuck away and live a peaceful life running a restaurant."

But without a name, he thought, *without the recognition of fada or uncul.*

So, he clenched his wildly clattering teeth, before he declared, "I am the son of Fon'Dafarr, nephew to Grimm Ramsey. I come here to earn my name!"

"YOU'VE COME TO DIE!" the seven heads roared. "CHOOSE YOUR METHOD OF DEMISE, MORTAL!"

"I will not die today!" he declared, to himself more than anyone else. "I have come to beat you, and prove myself the superior chef!"

Tiamat froze, her seven heads spread out, looking at the young troll from every angle.

"Are you serious?" her green head said, her booming voice discarded for a quieter, normal one.

The troll nodded.

The Dragon Queen began to shake, and the cavern with her. The troll staggered as he tried to keep his balance.

It was when the yellow head opened her mouth that the troll realized what she was doing.

Laughing.

"FOOL!" the purple head viciously taunted. "IF YOU HAD SIMPLY COME TO KILL ME, THEN I WOULD'VE GRANTED A SWIFT DEATH!"

"But now," her yellow head hissed. Then her seven heads gathered as one and roared, "I WILL ENJOY BREAKING YOU! TO MAKE YOU ANOTHER TESTAMENT THAT TIAMAT IS A CHEF WITH-OUT RIVAL!"

The troll gathered his bearings and through gritted teeth said, "You are certainly not without rival."

Death.

The troll was dead. He had died. He is dying. He will die.

The purple head stared into his soul and quietly said, "Perhaps, but I have been cooking since your race were banging rocks and flinging mud."

Together, the heads chuckled. "It seems I will be having troll soup tonight." Then Tiamat turned around, her body rippling as it squeezed into a much smaller, human form.

A tall, regal woman with her hair all the colors of the rainbow now stood there.

The troll followed, barely daring to breathe, but as he entered Tiamat's sanctum, he finally let out his held breath.

Tiamat was not even the most dangerous chef in the world! The young troll refused to get chicken feet now!

If he could not even beat Tiamat, then what right did he have to a name?

When I said there was plenty of space inside here, this was not what I meant, Declan muttered.

Didn't I say that? I absentmindedly asked as I walked to pick up my staff. The Historian had long since left, expressing a brief moment of interest in my state before he ran off.

We're the same person, idiot, he returned.

So, why should we make a distinction? I questioned as I picked up my staff.

Odd, were those patterns there before?

The wood grain around the top of the staff had changed, forming into images of wandering eyes.

"No," I answered, "no, they weren't."

Basic Wooden Staff (Stave)
A starting Traveler staff made of artificial wood. May act as a focus but provides no outstanding benefit or negative to spell casting.

Analyze it.

"Already am," I replied as I turned it around.

Wooden Staff with Odd Design (Stave)

A starting Traveler staff made of artificial wood. May act as a focus but provides no outstanding benefit or negative to spell casting.

Something was clearly changed with it. From knocking the hand of a God or perhaps close proximity with an eye of Observation or perhaps some combination of both? Twelve wooden grain eyes now cover the head of the staff. Merely cosmetic or something different?

"It is different from what my menu is telling me."

Either the menu isn't omnipotent or . . .

"The effect is so small it doesn't think it should be displayed," I finished. I noticed it previously, how there were tiny quirks about my race that weren't explicitly displayed on my character sheet. Stuff like how I felt pain differently or how the world was slightly duller.

Or both, Declan suggested, *the fact it isn't displaying the Holder of the Discovery Shard class supports the first.*

I closed my eyes. "**Analyze.**"

Dustin Analyze Character Sheet

Name: Dustin

Classes: Traveler Level -, Fungalmancer Level 3, Holder of the Discovery Shard Level 1?

<u>Body</u>

Strength: 8

Agility: 7

Dexterity: 6

Constitution: 18

Stamina: 10

Vitality: 12

<u>Mind</u>

Intelligence: 16

Wisdom: 18

Charisma: 6

<u>Soul</u>

Will: 10

Psyche: 10

Perception: 10

Racial Abilities: Superior Darkvision, Fungal Body, Sun Sickness, Mana Dependency, Pacifying Spores, Innate Magic

Class Skills

Traveler: Learn, 'Respawn Ability'

Fungalmancer

Path: Symbiosis

•　　Grow Sporage (Visual, Proximity), Sporage Wisp Symbiosis, Bracken Polypores

Holder of the Discovery Shard

Path: Analyze

•　　Analyze [Passive]: You passively absorb the information you gather. Learn the exact parameters of that which you observe and translate them to a form understandable to you. This information exists in a database and can be called on at any time.

•　　Observation Link [Passive]: You are linked to a user of Observe. Your minds are linked, and they may share all they see through Observe. Through you, they may also mark other willing creatures to have their vision be seen through Observe as well.

•　　Et Non-Discent [Passive]: This class was not sourced from the system, thus it does not benefit from the system either.

• Progress in this class does not rely on Traveler Experience, but on your own proficiency.

• You may not invest levels in this class.

• This class and its progress will not be displayed on your character sheet.

• Raising this classes' level will not affect your Traveler Level.

Spells

T0: Balm Spores, Light Spores, Sneezing Spores, Acid Spit

T1: Mushroom Meal, Poison Spores

T2: Bark Skin

Languages

Common

Undercommon

Compared to . . .

Dustin Level 3 Character Sheet

Name: Dustin

Race: Magic Myconid

Classes: Fungalmancer Level 3

Body

Strength: 8

Agility: 7

Dexterity: 6
Constitution: 18
Stamina: 10
Vitality: 12
Mind
Intelligence: 16
Wisdom: 18
Charisma: 6
Soul
Will: 10
Aura: 10
Perception: 10
Racial Abilities: Superior Darkvision, Fungal Body, Sun Sickness, Mana Dependency, Pacifying Spores, Innate Magic
Class Skills: Fungalmancer:
Path: Symbiosis

• **Grow Sporage (Visual) [Active]:** You may create a mushroom capable of storing a Spore based spell. These Sporages can be activated on visual contact. They glow faintly and last your myconid level in hours.

• **Grow Sporage (Proximity) [Active]:** Upgrade to Grow Sporage. You obtain the option to grow Sporages with a different activation type. The Sporage lets out a thin layer of mycelium around it that acts as a pressure detector. When sufficient weight is applied to any part of the fungus, the Sporage will explode. You and targets of Symbiosis do not detonate these Sporages.

• **Sporage Wisp Symbiosis [Active]:** Wisps have lived comfortably in your cap and have created a wonderful home there, now to teach them the wonders of rent. You may create pygmy myconid bodies for your non-corporeal Wisps to inhabit. They are considered tiny creatures and are capable of following simple commands. They possess all the qualities of Sporage, however, they can choose to self-detonate.

• **Bracken Polypores [Passive] [Active]:** A species of symbiotic fungus are seeded underneath your skin. They rely on you for food and in return can instantly grow into durable mycelium plates that can cover your entire body. The hardness and weight may vary depending on how much Satiety you feed them at any moment. Will gain defensive bonuses if used in conjunction with Bark Skin.

Spells
T0: Balm Spores, Light Spores, Sneezing Spores, Acid Spit
T1: Mushroom Meal, Poison Spores

T2: Bark Skin
New Available Spell Slots
T0: 2
T1: 1
T2: 2
Languages
Common
Undercommon
"And the fact Analyze has 'Traveler' as an actual class with skills compared to the menu."

"Possibly because we see it as something that should be."

"That is a certainty," I answered with conviction. Declan me didn't personally touch the Discovery Shard, the *only* reason it put Traveler as a class was because I thought it so.

"Go through the other stuff."

Issue of the Historia (Artifact)

A copy of the Historia, a constantly updating book that keeps a record of the entire world by the hand of the Historian.

All is Writ [Active]: Once per day, you may learn of up to ten minutes worth of events that occurred in the past and within the immediate vicinity of yourself. The information is near perfectly accurate. Destruction of the Issue or the Historia will interrupt this skill.

"That was a fucking magic item?!"

"Damn," I muttered, "I would've been fine with just this."

"But not happy. Goddamn, we got lucky."

"Yeah . . ."

"I don't trust it," he asserted.

"Took the words right out of my mouth."

"Or is it my mouth?"

"Better not question it."

"You probably die every time you log off, how could you not?"

"I'm fine with it."

"Huh," Declan replied with mock surprise, *"same here."*

"Analyze."

Issue of the Historia (Artifact)

A copy of the Historia, a constantly updating book that keeps a record of the entire world by the hand of the Historian.

All the text inside is gibberish. Might be a cipher of some kind but you are not certain.

All is Writ [Active]: Once per day, you may learn of up to ten minutes worth of events that occurred in the past and within the immediate vicinity of yourself. The information is near perfectly accurate. Destruction of the Issue or the Historia will interrupt this skill.

"Wait a minute."

"What?"

"Check the next with Analyze first, the information you're getting from the menu is affecting it."

"Huh, good catch."

Magician Tarot Card (Artifact)

A Tarot card displaying the Magician. It represents you, but its meaning escapes you as you haven't read up on esoterica. What you do know is that it somehow allows you to gain . . . "stuff" easier, so long as they are related to the five tools represented within. It is implied this card and the divined fate cannot be avoided unless you destroy the card.

Tools:

Scroll. (Filled): Unknown.

Wand (Filled): Magic.

Lens (Filled): Observation and Analysis. Perhaps the gate as well?

Chalice (Empty): Unfilled, thus variable.

Key (Empty): Unfilled, thus variable.

Magician Tarot Card (Bound Artifact)

One of Twelve Artifacts created by the Diviner Goddess, Misses Fortune. This item is Bound to you and cannot be destroyed or stolen by any other. You will find it in your possession no matter where you lose it.

Analyze quickly updated to include the menu's description of the card, but didn't replace any of the original descriptions. This was just the surface level of the ability though.

"We still need more testing."

"Took the words right out of my mouth."

"Yeah—" Declan froze as realization dawned on him. *"My mouth! How did I not catch that?"*

"Cause we're idiots?"

"Fair."

Then I respawned.

4.10

———

"And he said: 'This chest definitely has treasures in it,' and then I ate him! Hahaha!"
> —*Mimicron the Living Dungeon recounting its early years*

Noam punched the air.
Strength: 7-10
"Again, and as hard as you can."
Strength: 11-14
"Is it thirteen?"
Noam wiped some sweat off his face.
Stamina: 8-11
"Close," he answered as Greenie bought him a waterskin. "It was twelve."
Strength: 12
"Stamina ten," I guessed.
"Right on," he answered sounding impressed.
Stamina: 10
I opened my vision. My back was turned to Noam, but I could still see him clearly through Greenie.
"Good thing, too, otherwise I would've gotten traumatized for nothing."
"Your sacrifice was worth it," I drily said.
"Fuck you—Why am I insulting myself!?"
Ignoring my—Declan—whatever's outburst, I stood up. Feeling the soft sand underneath me. The sun had set some time ago, so the beach was safe for me. Annoyingly, even when I wore three layers worth of protection, heavy sunlight still got to me.
"Why does my mouth suddenly feel like it's burning?"
Strange, so was mine. "Probably nothing."
"You are literally talking to yourself now," Noam said as he stood next

to me. "I'm kinda impressed you lack so many friends you've made one with yourself."

"The guy's an asshole though," I said.

"The guy's an asshole though," he said at the same time.

"Wait, he can't hear me."

"Other Dustin said Dustin was an asshole," Yellow helpfully supplied.

Noam looked at me strangely for a moment, before shaking his head. "Don't comment on it," he muttered. "Let him figure it out himself."

"Mental stats are harder to figure out," I said as I leafed through my notepad. "Especially Charisma."

I quickly wrote something down on my notepad, before tearing the page.

"Noam, solve this differential equation, would you?"

He stared at me, eyes darting between my extended hand and my face. He pointed at himself.

"Yes," I impatiently said, "you."

He grumbled something before taking the page.

"You, too, Declan," I said. "You can see it from Greenie's perspective."

"Ah, you're using me as another measuring stick since Eve confirmed my intelligence to be fifteen. Smart."

"I gotta be, otherwise I dumped these points into wisdom for nothing."

"Most of it was from your racial bonuses though."

"Only four, which admittedly is a large amount relatively."

"Done," Declan said. I briefly checked his vision, seeing the notepad display where he solved the problem.

"Done," Noam said after a moment, handing the page back to me.

I quickly checked the answers between them, finding both to be correct.

Intelligence: 8-14

"Needs something with more challenge, doesn't it?"

"Yep," I answered.

I began writing another question. "Can you—"

"It's twelve," Noam gave up.

Intelligence: 12

"Got it." I didn't need to write it down. The information was already stuck in my head and not something I would forget. That was the main strength behind Analyze.

It's something that is initially rather useless, but with every encounter, the more I will know about my opponent.

"Don't forget my contribution," Declan said.

And yeah, Observation buffed it by an incredible amount. It doesn't have to be me that sees it. Since I can remake Greenie and Yellow as many times as I needed so long as I have the mana. I effectively had access to four separate perspectives from which I can gather information from.

"The information game is the most important, after all."

"You going to use that thing on me, anyway?" Noam asked.

"Oh yeah, almost forgot." I raised a hand, placing it on his shoulder.

"Observe," Declan said through me.

A new set of vision opened up in my mind.

"Unfortunately, I can't share what I'm seeing with you," I said, somewhat annoyed.

"Probably wishing for too much."

"What level are you anyway?" I asked. "Your stats are pretty low."

"Three," Noam said.

"Huh?"

"Huh?"

"Open your character sheet for me?"

Name: Noam

Classes: Skald Level 3

Body

Strength: 12

Agility: 14

Dexterity: 10

Constitution: 9

Stamina: 10

Vitality: 8

Mind

Intelligence: 12

Wisdom: 10

Charisma: 14

Soul

Will: 10

Psyche: 10

Perception: 10

Racial Abilities: Darkvision, Hellish Resistance

Class Skills: Breathless

Proficiencies

Polearms: Novice

Martial Arts: Swift Strike

Spells

T0: Biting Words, Vicious Mockery

Available Spell Slots

TO: 2
T1: 1
<u>**Languages**</u>
Common
Infernal

Oh. Of course, his race didn't automatically make him min/max.

"Our mistake."

Damn though, is this what a normal character sheet looks like? I just realized we have four stats in the negative.

"Subject Noam has been promoted to meatshield."

Noam kicked me. "You were insulting me somehow, weren't you?"

I hastily shook my head. "Nope, just wondering why you haven't taken a Path yet if you dinged Level Three."

"I dinged it at the restaurant, haven't gotten around to getting one yet."

What restaurannnnnnnnnnnnnnnnnnnnnnnnnnn—

"Abort that thought process!"

"Huh, what are you waiting for, then?" I asked as I bent down slightly, just in time to avoid his roundhouse.

"You, idiot," he said. "I'm thinking of doing a restat somehow. A halberd was a decent weapon, but it lacked short range," he continued, gesturing to the broken weapon head on his belt.

"I see no problem with just taking a close melee weapon," I answered. "You already have spells for ranged."

"I can't just fire them off willy-nilly, you know?"

"He can't?"

"You can't?"

"Yeah," Noam answered, "I could, but it wouldn't hurt as much."

"I have to offend my target on a *deep* and *personal* level for them to deal the most damage," he stressed. "How is someone supposed to take damage from insults if they aren't insulted!?"

Ah. Those were annoying conditions. "But you can still spam it, right?" He did so at the forest, after all.

"Yeah, but it wastes a lot more mana as I'm shotgunning it, then. With small effect other than making them pissed."

"He really is suited for a meatshield."

I absentmindedly dodged Noam's punch. "That is annoying."

"Yeah," he agreed.

"Make a new character?"

"And miss out on *this*?" he gestured to himself.

"Hmm. . ."

"Dave?" Greenie suggested.

"Huh, that could work actually," I said as I took out a Gold Coin.

"Oooh! Let me," Noam said, snatching the coin from my hand.

He rolled it between his fingers for a moment, before flicking it upward.

The coin soon landed, creating another door to Daves. Noam walked in, only pausing briefly to pick up the coin. I followed behind him.

Dave's store was still the same as ever, though it felt . . . *larger* compared to before.

"God, there's three of you now," Noam joked, gesturing to the other Dave taking my appearance, albeit with a monocle.

"Welcome, whatever you want or need, you can purchase here," all three Daves said.

"Okay, that is creepy," Noam said.

"It's routine by now." The Tiefling Dave chuckled. "You are looking for a way to fix your long range and short range problems?"

"Huh, they really can mind-read."

"May I suggest this?" with a dramatic flourish, the Dave gestured toward a display case, showing two . . . very strange swords.

"Those have to be fantasy weapons."

Inside were two . . . "swords" but with some extremely strange characteristics. For one, the tip of the blade was bent forward in a hook, leaving a rounded point, there was a spike on the hilt and another sharp crescent blade acted as a hilt guard.

"These are Hook Swords, very difficult to master, however as you see—"

Noam pushed the Dave aside. "The guard can act like a knuckle duster in a pinch, and the hooked ends are meant to hook enemies into close range."

"Also, it may be used similarly to a whip if you hook both ends," Dave continued.

"Allowing it to be used at a decent range as well!"

Noam turned to Dave. "How much?"

"Thirty Traveler Gold, however, I can also give it magical properties for an additional five gold cost."

"Such as?"

"I can make the hooked ends magnetize with each other with a command or input of some kind, you may customize, allowing you to extend your range farther and use something like a short polearm."

"Would my polearm proficiency count toward it, then?"

"In that form, absolutely. Though the rest will need—"

"I'll buy it!"

I coughed. *"He forgot who actually holds the money."*

"Dust Decs, I will beat the shit out of you IRL if you don't buy this for me."

"I can just wait till after you do it to log off," I answered.

"Hey!"

"I can do it right now as well," he said, rolling up his sleeves.

I raised an eyebrow, before turning to the weapon.

"This thing just looks fake."

"It's an actual weapon," myconid Dave interjected. "You can search it up."

"Holy shit it actually is."

"Did people actually use it though?" I asked Declan.

"Ancient China did, it would fix Noam's problems."

"Can you use this correctly?"

"Easy! I'll get the hang of it after a few tries!" he boasted.

"He probably can."

"Yeah, unlike me he's actually insane."

I sighed. "Wait here, I'll get the money."

Noam whooped as I turned to leave.

"What about your eye?" Dave suddenly asked.

"Wha—" Both wisps jumped up to shush my mouth.

"Oh, that sly—-"

"You cunning bastard," I replied, impressed, "still not a question."

The myconid Dave shrugged. "Had to try, though seriously, what's with your eye?" he asked, finger gesturing to his left eye crevice.

I raised my hand to touch it . . . and felt a sphere inside, held by several strands of . . . something.

"You didn't tell me about this?" I directed to both Noam and myself.

"I thought you knew."

"Same here."

For now, I just got my Polypores to cover that crevice up, hiding the eye. I'll examine it in detail later. "I'll be back soon."

"Hurry up!"

Weapons bought for Noam, we left the shop with him absolutely giddy.

"That reminds me of something," I started as we headed to the Way-shard so I could swap back to my Dustin body. "Have you logged off yet?"

"Umm . . ." he began nervously.

I rolled my eyes, of course not. Taking advantage of my now superior height, I bonked him on the head, which he strangely didn't dodge. "Hurry up and log off."

"Absorbing you disorientated me for a solid five minutes, and that was just two days."

"For your own health and safety, get your Path and log off for the night," I said. "Nothing else to do anyway."

Noam rolled his eyes. "Sure mom."

Regardless of his sarcasm, he still touched the Wayshard and disappeared. Hopefully logging off soon after.

I changed back to my Dustin body.

"You can't really log off, can you?"

"Not yet," I answered, *"not when we don't know what will happen with Observe inside your head."*

There was the heart of the problem. If I had Observe in the real world and it was coded into my very head, then, when my virtual self logged off and merged back, would I get a copy of Observe once I logged back on?

"Better not test it."

What the Historian said was still fresh in my mind. Taking a power currently beyond me would only lead to some kind of calamity in the future. I cheated to get both Observe and Analyze, but if I rejoined with myself and got another Observe in this world . . .

"Let's hope whatever it is, it won't be too bad."

Back off for now. Accept what I've gotten without overstepping until I've seen what a calamity could mean.

"Slow and steady . . ."

"Wins the race."

I was about to head to sleep when I got a video call request from Matt.

Curious, I accepted.

"What could he want at this hour?" Dustin asked.

On-screen, Matt had his trademarked shit-eating grin, before putting both his hands to his mouth and "BOOTS TI TI! BOOTS TI PSH!"

"Are you beatboxing?" I asked him.

Still smiling, Noam declared, "I learned how to beatbox!"

"Uhh. What's so special about that?" Dustin's thoughts must've shown on my face, because soon, Matt messaged me something.

Path: Spitfire

Beatbox [Passive] [Active]: You gain knowledge of how to beatbox alongside proficiency at the Adept level. You may also, as a free action, lock up to 5 seconds of beatboxing in a loop, where it'll continuously emanate from you at the original volume at a negligible mana cost per loop.

Fire [Passive]: When verbal-based attacks land a critical hit, the target is set alight by non-magical flame.

Catch These Hands! [Active]: Once per day, you may activate this skill to gain bonus stats to Agility, Dexterity and Charisma for every person around you currently irritated, angered, generally pissed and/or displaying hostility toward you. Stats disappear when the cooldown has ended or when hostile individuals leave your range or cease being hostile to you.

"Did he just–"

"I chose that so I could learn to beatbox!"

I didn't even need Observe to know both of me facepalmed.

"Wait a moment," I directed to Dustin, a sudden moment of clarity descending upon me, *"does that mean if you learned thermodynamics I would als—"*

"Not you, too! Me, too? Why is this so confusing!"

Guess I still had to do homework the hard way.

4.11

———

"I never knew how blind I was till I walked a mile in another's shoes."

—*The 187th Anointed Thief Lord, John Johnson the Prolific Shoe Thief (note: he stole the shoes right off the feet of the transcriber who was documenting him and is now pestering famous people for their life stories)*

Here are your registration papers," the receptionist professionally said, handing us each a sheet of paper. "Both of you are now officially registered and may take up quests as Freelance Mercenaries or as a part of a Mercenary Band. The Administrative Guild shall keep a copy of your registration papers, though you will still be required to present your papers to take up a quest unless you gain identification as a Plated Mercenary."

"Plated Mercenary?" Noam asked as he examined his paper.

"A higher ranked Mercenary, who has accomplished numerous quests, they are given a metal plate as identification as well as other benefits," she answered.

"Such as?" he continued

"Easier access to certain cities, along with the right to start and lead Bands and Guilds." She looked at us from side to side. "Are there any other questions?"

"Nope."

"*No input?*" I asked my other.

His reply was curt: "*Studying. Be quiet.*"

Briefly changing to his vision, I caught a glimpse of several dozen opened snack bags before it looked up to see lines upon lines of alien code. Several dozen tabs opened to various Wikipedia articles, coding forums and online teaching classes. Dissecting whatever "Discovery" was no doubt and trying to extrapolate more things from it.

"Keep at it," I encouraged.

I shook my head.

Satisfied, the receptionist let us go. Sneakily, I grabbed a pamphlet that was stacked on the side of the desk.

"What kinda quest should we start with?"

Unfolding the pamphlet, I answered, "No clue."

I quickly perused the pamphlet. "They recommend Plateless mercs go for something easier."

"Such as?"

"Daily quests," I answered as I got to that section. "I won't recommend it for you, it's mostly just gathering quests for items that have a constant demand but don't require a skilled person to gather."

"So, chores pretty much?" Noam deduced as we reached the quest board.

Folding the pamphlet into one of my pockets, I quickly scanned the board. It was rather barren, with daily quests sequestered to the side to leave a mostly empty board.

"This and this," I pointed to two sheets. "Those you shouldn't be bored with."

Noam followed my finger, before grinning. "You know me so well," he said as I moved my leg before he could kick it.

A Raid quest posted by a Mercenary Guild, Ivory Tower. They'd managed to corner a cultist who'd been creating and releasing chimeras and needed people to clear the caves before they could launch a full raid on the cultist. They were accepting Plateless, so it was probably a low-level quest. Five gold upfront for venturing in the caves with a party, with remaining payment determined by contribution.

"Seems kinda low, doesn't it?"

"Not really." If we were assuming one-to-one conversion of currency to Traveler Gold, then it was one-seventh of the cost of a decent weapon. Though Traveler Gold had the inherent value of being usable literally everywhere.

"It isn't?"

Oh, I forgot to say it, I quickly explained my reasoning.

Next was a subjugation quest to control the growing infestation of "Bilge Rats." Judging by the picture it was some kind of ugly, fish-like rodent covered in scales. They seemed to grow up to the size of a large dog.

"We've seen them before!" Yellow pointed out.

"Really?" Noam asked.

"Really?" Greenie chimed in.

Yellow bonked Greenie on the head. *"Of course! After we left Noam."*

There was a sentence classifying the Wharf Rats as only going up to CR 3 but going as high as 7 if a horde gathered. I flicked open the pamphlet again. CR means Combat Rating, they classified each level as . . . Bah, their description of each level just listed creatures of that level. Creatures that sounded strong, but I had no idea what their exact capabilities were.

"Were they strong?" I asked when research failed.

"Yeah! There were lots. One smart big one. Buncha weak small ones."

I should probably be effective against them, then. Horde strategies failed against any constant area of effect attacks. They paid a gold per hundred rats killed, so the real difficulty would be massing that number for me to go ham on.

Noam pointed to another quest. "This looks good as well."

Killing a manticore? Those were classified as CR 20, now *that* was definitely out of our league.

Reading more of the description, I argued, "Its location is way too vague." Hunting anywhere around the roads of the nearest three towns? Way too wide an area for two people to search. "And those things can fly. Not something we can quickly deal with even if we caught it."

The two-hundred gold bounty was nice, but not worth it.

"Aww. Killjoy."

"Let's try to not die, we've had, what? Eight deaths between us already?" Still didn't know if we could earn back any experience we lost, for all I knew every death could be lowering our maximum possible level.

He shrugged. "I lost count."

Noam casually dodged my attempt at bonking him with my staff. "We should go for a quest that's just hard enough for us to do, but not difficult enough that we could fail."

"Where's the fun in that?"

"Living," I drily answered.

"But we can't die?" Greenie squeaked.

I gently patted Greenie. "We *can* die, it's just that we come back."

"If I asked that question you would've hit me."

"If I tried to hit you, you would've dodged."

"True."

Shaking my head, I continued, "Back on track, where'd you want to go?"

Noam pursed his lips. "Hmm . . . what about this?"

A quest asking for spare hands on a whaling ship. "You know how to help out on a ship?"

"Nope."

*Tsk*ing in annoyance, I said, "If we don't have the relevant skills, then we're gonna be annoyances more than actual help."

"Gotta start somewhere," he playfully replied.

"And that somewhere is not here," I said, grabbing his chin and pointing it at the other listed quests. "These two are the only ones we can actually do in our current state."

"Hmm . . ." he murmured as he pushed my hand off. "Cave quest?"

Nodding, I agreed, "Cave quest it is, then."

In truth, I was hoping he picked that one. The quest was time-sensitive by its nature, and the fact it was underground meant I could operate freely. I was also curious to see how a guild operated in this world.

Noam moved back to the receptionist desk. "Hey, how do we accept a quest?"

The receptionist, having overheard us, swiftly pulled out another document. "For Ivory Tower's quest, you will need to sign these papers and present it to our guild's representative at the location."

Our as in the Administrative Guild's? "Are they present to ensure we don't get shortchanged for the contribution-based payment?"

"Among other things," she absentmindedly replied as she wrestled a few pages out of a stack.

Glancing at us from side to side, she asked, "Do either of you need directions to the location?"

"Please."

Dustin walked forward with his nose buried in the map. At first glance, he wasn't paying the slightest attention to his surroundings, but both Greenie and Yellow were on the top of his cap. Somehow managing to fashion the hard brown fungus into a balcony circling his cap from front to back.

Noam knew Dustin was seeing through his eyes, too, so he did his best to make sure he was looking everywhere except for where the Shroomy Bois were looking. Which he hoped Dustin would end up making their official name, though Noam also thought them being called 'THE SQUAD!' with full reverb and some sound effects would be cool as well.

He wasn't keeping a wide view to help shore up Dustin's blindspots, well, he was but not in a combat sense.

Noam was sightseeing.

A glance to the left and he saw a shop that seemed to be crafted from the overturned hull of a ship. Though the doorways and windows looked like a recent addition, Noam could see dozens of brutish lines of different coloration in the wood. Some kind of glue, hurriedly used to cover up scars of numerous encounters, until the ship was disabled by something which took a chunk out of the keel. A wound that remained there until this day.

To the right, he saw an open warehouse, where there were people of numerous races butchering the bloody corpse of some kind of shark-like beast that had hairless and muscled limbs that reminded him of a bear.

Even if he looked to the ground, he could see that the road was cobblestone, hundreds of stones placed haphazardly in a ditch before the gaps were filled with concrete. He knew that these types of roads were uneven by nature. But here they were flat, and unlike with a normal game, Noam could tell that the small indentions on the sides that were carved by years of carts traveling the road, rather than game convenience.

Even a "starter" town oozed history, and that was just what he saw!

Taking into account the ever-present smell of sea salt, he could practically taste the mix of the metallic smell of blood as people butchered huge ocean beasts along with the myriad of strange scents that came from cooking stalls.

This was a living world.

Sure, Eve tried to market it as a game, but Noam knew he could talk to anyone in this town, become friends or enemies with them like any other person.

Noam truly felt he was alive in a living world.

Something that Declan would not really understand on his own. Declan could take in more information at once, keep track of multiple factors and variables once he knew them, but he did this by simplifying them.

Noam realized long ago that this drifted into his daily life. Whenever he tried to get Declan to describe a past event, he would describe it by its most notable aspects and little else, if not outright forgetting it. Declan became better the more interactions he had with something, but Matt had figured out a long time ago, if something was not relevant, it was forgotten.

He chuckled, taking in the world so hopefully his friend would get something more than the bare minimum.

The caves were actually pretty close.

A brisk walk through the town, past the first wall that encircled the Wayshard, then the actual walls that marked the end of the town, where Noam managed to catch us a farmer who brought us the rest of the way by cart.

He exchanged farewells with the man after signaling me that I didn't need to pay for the trip. Apparently, the stories he shared were interesting enough.

Noam seemed to be more affable here than in the real world, or were people just friendlier to him? He told me that his Charisma automatically rose per level, similar to how my race had Wisdom rise automatically.

I knew that mental stats actually affected you, something I should've caught on way earlier with the rats manipulating what's his face and Peps. Was Noam better at making friends compared to Matt because Noam had a higher Charisma?

A question for later. Charisma was one of those harder to measure stats, I theoretically should be able to figure out the stats of a person in the real world with Analyze. I quickly made a mental note to get my real-world counterpart to do some exercise so I could figure my own exact stats. Pure physical stats seemed easy to figure out, and Eve was kind enough to make a judgement of my Mind stats, so that just left whatever the hell "Soul" stats were.

Speaking of, I checked up on what Declan was doing.

My vision was shaking.

Bags of chips were strewn about as my real-world counterpart was keeled over, his vision violently shaking as he clutched his chest.

"What is happening?" I tested.

Declan, who had remained silent on the entire journey, finally transmitted what was on his mind.

Hysterical laughter.

It filled my head and deafened my own voice. I waited until he calmed enough for me to ask again.

"What is happening?"

He chuckled, his breathlessness somehow transmitting in my mind: *"I realized something."*

Declan was me, or at least close enough that differences didn't really matter. What did he realize that made him laugh so violently?

"What?"

Somehow, I could feel his lips curl in a smile. *"I am never going to be able to read this, to solve this, or understand it in any meaningful way."*

His eyes rose, till they settled back on the myriad of screens before him.

"You won't get it, not yet. But I've scraped enough to realize something simple."

There was no defeat in his voice as he announced, *"This is beyond me, code made by a genius and further sharpened by thousands of years of refinement by something beyond human-level intelligence. It is a simple fact, that I will never ever reach a point where I can match what I see before me."*

There was no defeat in him, no anger, no real emotion other than simple acceptance. Similar to how one would accept that an object dropped would fall to the earth because of gravity, *I* accepted that this was beyond what I could reach.

"Understanding," he sat back down on his chair. *"That is one of the Paths that made up Discovery. One of three. What we got Analyze from."*

"Do you know why I know this?" he asked.

"No."

"The damn thing realized I was studying it, with no sign other than the fact I managed to lay its code bare. It realized it was being studied, and started teaching me."

I didn't speak, instead letting him continue.

"It told me the basics of what it was. But I learned enough code that I knew I would never hope to reach this level." His voice was dead calm now. Simply reciting a fact.

"And what will you do?"

He giggled, the action descending into another hysterical fit. *"I will continue because this interests me."*

Threads of clues finally gathered into a coherent theory, no, a certainty because I knew myself better than anyone else.

What Declan was laughing at was himself.

There was no part of himself that believed he could reach what he wanted, yet he would try anyway. Declan laughed for the same reason I would laugh at a Darwin Award, he was laughing at an idiot doing something incredibly stupid. Declan knew his actions were incredibly idiotic and pointless, but still wanted to try anyway for a reason as shallow as interest.

"Pitiful, isn't it?" he asked. *"You'd think we would learn by now."*

I looked through his eyes and strangely felt that they weren't mine.

As I heard him descend into another fit of mad giggling, the word I thought was not "pitiful."

4.12

————

The path to the caves followed a rough, rocky outcrop situated on a large plateau bordering the beach. Greenie sniffled a bit at the heavy salt smell, letting out a cute sneeze.

"Sunny," it complained, shading its eyes. Yellow nudged the bracken polypores under my skin to grow into a roof over their similarly made balcony. Were they always able to do that? Either it was another thing that was too minor for my menu to see or my choices were paying off.

I originally picked Symbiosis, because of all the other Paths, it was the option that helped deal with the sun, but in hindsight, I might've picked one of the best options. The multitude was always better than the individual, and one day I simply won't be able to progress in level. But *I* don't have to be the strong, so long as I had an army of familiars and summons to back me up, my level became pretty meaningless.

In comparison to Noam though, I was a tad overpowered.

Currently, I was a hard-to-kill status effect machine, with specs in information gathering and area control. I could very effectively hold an area so long as I had prep time, the problem was if I got disrupted early on, and my lack of close-range combat. Noam was a bard that happened to have a melee weapon but he could easily wreck me at close range. A person who was actually fully spec'd in melee combat should be able to take me out quickly or at least keep me crowd controlled enough that I won't be able to do anything.

Just from a game balance perspective, this had to be true. Eventually, I'll have to transition to a more supportive build that relied on summons and familiars, which had fewer weak points compared to my current build, or at least that type of build's strengths covered some of its weak points.

Noam, though, seemed mainly like a damage-focused skirmisher for quick but large encounters. Biting Words and Vicious Mockery gave him a degree of utility because he could effectively "taunt" people into focusing on him, so he could fill in as an off-tank. And despite the fact he had two useless abilities, his build was far more well-rounded than mine.

Noam said something, breaking me out of my thoughts.

"Sorry, what was that?"

He stopped as he glanced back at me, there was a good amount of distance between us now. Perhaps due to our wildly differing Agility?

"I said!" he yelled over a crashing wave. "Do you think there are beaches like this back home!?"

"What do you mean!?" I yelled back. Greenie and Yellow's vision jerked as I ran to catch up to him.

"Like this clean, or just the general feeling you know?" he yelled back.

"Probably not!" When I got close to him, I replied, "Any beach in our world is probably fucked by now."

Noam didn't look at me, simply staring out into the ocean. "You sure about that?"

I shrugged. "There might be, but what point is there in finding one?" I gestured to the sea. "There's one right there."

"I guess," he quietly replied, voice so low I almost missed it.

I raised an eyebrow, before slapping him on the back. "Quiet brooding doesn't fit you."

He scratched the back of his head. "Yeah . . ."

I gave him a moment, before starting back on the path. "C'mon."

Noam's boots scraped against the rough gravel as he caught up.

"What do you mean quiet brooding doesn't fit me?" Noam asked from behind me.

"Well, generally it's for quiet badasses with tragic backstories," I answered. Bending down to dodge his roundhouse.

"Screw you," he playfully replied, "I have an awesome tragic backstory!"

"Really?" I challenged. "What?"

He held his chin in a thoughtful gesture. "Entire village got massacred by someone and I'm out looking for vengeance?"

"Overdone," I critiqued. "Everyone knows that story so it's not special. Add a twist or two."

"Ah"—he smiled—"but what if the twist is that I have no tragic backstory?"

"Then you're just a gag character with a weird bit."

"Gag characters can be serious!" he defended.

"But not always."

Our destination was in sight now, a collection of squat, white huts, created from some kind of uniform stone.

"Okay, hear this." Noam gestured to his head. "What's a calm badass? Cowboys, so how 'bout I start wearing a cowboy hat."

I made sure to stare at his extremely prominent horns. "Sure." My hand caught his incoming punch.

"It can be one that has holes in it," he argued as we neared the camp, "for my horns to go through."

"I mean," I started. "Calm badasses generally don't talk aloud about how to make themselves badass."

Noam raised a finger, about to argue before shutting up, just when we stepped into the camp.

Arranged before us were dozens of small huts, built of some kind of clean white material. What was strange was their exact uniformity. Every hut looked exactly the same to an almost creepy degree. Like someone had just copy-pasted one 3D asset.

We drew some attention, but they all quickly returned to their previous task, either maintaining weapons or chatting to another. Some eyes lingered, with a start, I realized they were lingering on me.

Huh, I guess I did look a bit weird.

"Excuse me," I asked one of the people staring, "we're here for the Ivory Tower quest; where can we find the Administrative Guild representative?"

The man's face took on an indescribable expression. "You both plateless?"

"Yeah," Noam replied.

"You'll find the MAG rep in there." He gestured backward, toward a hut with a symbol etched on it. "Logo of Sword and Charter, you can't miss it."

I nodded, noting a necklace that had a bronze plate threaded in it. On it was a logo of a tower, along with some lines of writing.

"Curious, eh?" The mercenary chuckled. "Feel free to take a look," he said as he pulled out his plate.

His name was etched in it, RANDIAM OF GREYVAULT. Along with more information underneath.

CAMP 6

MAGE (BATTLE) 5

SKIRMISHER 2

"What do the classes mean?" I asked. Well, they were somewhat self-explanatory, but it didn't hurt to ask.

"MAG keeps us mercs classified in nice little bits so everyone knows what we each can do." He thumbed the first line. "Battlemage means I can hurt and heal things. Name's a bit redundant though since every mage in this business battles." He gestured to a sword hanging by his belt. "Skirmisher is a general catch-all for people that specialize in mundane weapons, though you'd be hard pressed to find a weapon that hasn't been enchanted in one way or another."

Finally, he swept his arm wide. "And camp means I can make stuff like this," he said, gesturing to the numerous squat stone houses around us.

"You made this camp?" Yellow asked.

The mage glanced at the wisp in confusion. "It asked if you made this camp Mr. Randiam," I clarified.

"Yes, I did. Smart little bugger, isn't he?" he replied in a contemplative tone. "Also in charge of feeding all these IDIOTS!" he raised his voice for the last bit, clearly talking to the people around us.

"Yeah, yeah we get it," another person, whose plate showed her as another of the Ivory Tower, tiredly said. "You're an important asset to the guild and we can't be here without you."

"Utility is good," I said. "Can't fight if you're hungry."

Utility tended to outpace both damage and durability at higher levels. Though I might be biased about that. Since people tended to like flashy damage more, I often found myself the lone utility caster in any party. Which ironically made every damage-based player I've met seem utterly normal, as they were one amongst a thousand. Whereas anyone who mained a healer or tank class was practically seen as an endangered species to be scooped up.

Good thing was I've never had to suffer through long matchmaking queues when I played with Matt.

"Damn straight," he agreed, nodding his head.

"Anything you can tell us about the guy inside?" I asked, going to what I wanted from the beginning.

"The cultist?" I nodded. "Don't know where that one popped up, he's one of the Damned—sorry about that," he said to Noam, almost as a side note—"so half of us expect devils to start spewing out."

"Should we expect to fight devils?" I asked, they were supposedly a tier below demons but still considered nasty to fight.

"Nah," he replied. "If fiends start dropping, we'll notice and start storming the caves in force."

"What should we expect to fight, then?"

"Chimeras," he replied. "'Bout as varied as fiends but his aren't nearly as strong. The shit ones don't live long, slapdashed together so some don't have all the important bits to survive."

Frankenstein-like, then, and missing vital organs as do most living weapons.

"If you're a fighter"—he nodded to Noam—"you're gonna have a hard time; you don't know where their vital organs are or if they even *have* any. Though generally they still have heads you can cut off."

Noam nodded.

"And you"—he looked at me—"can't tell what you can do. But you look like a mage so keep blasting them till they go down."

"I see," I replied. I briefly contemplated telling him what I could do. He seemed experienced and could probably help me figure something out. Probably not worth it. The information he gave was rudimentary, basic weaknesses, and nothing much to look out for. If chimeras were as varied as he was implying, then I was better off figuring a game plan on how to deal with them on a case-by-case basis.

Now, to ask the question I've been wondering since I saw the quest: "Is there a reason why you don't just go root this cultist out?" I originally thought they didn't have the manpower, but seeing the actual camp there were at least a hundred people here. Assuming half were utility or non-combatants, there were still fifty people who should be able to put up a fight.

"Ah, so you noticed." He smiled. "Truth is rather simple; most of Ivory Tower are mages."

Mages? How did that affect things?

"What's the problem with that?" Yellow asked.

I asked the same thing, to which the Randiam furrowed his eyebrows in confusion. "You don't have mana problems?"

Ah. So, that was it. "You're worried that if you go in en-mass, your forces will exhaust their mana before you can meet the cultist?"

"Indeed." He nodded. "That's why you're here, to clean out the chimeras before we go in and deal the finisher."

Looking to the long term and outsourcing the labor. "I see. And you're not afraid the cultist will run before you do?"

"If he does, we'll notice, we have people covering every cave exit with wards to detect planar magic."

"And you can pay for everyone that comes?" The quest was pretty generous compared to all the other stuff available. Most only gave payment after the task had been completed.

Randiam smiled cryptically. "It pays for itself."

Pays for itself? Were there quests that I wasn't aware of? "Pays for itself" implies that hiring outsiders was a net neutral or positive.

"What do you mean by that?"

"The chimeras," he began, "are slapdash creations made from whatever is available. Though some incorporate some rather rare parts."

"Material harvesting," I realized.

He smiled. "This is a small gamble on our part, we've confirmed some rather exotic pieces that can still be sold for a good price even if they were mangled a bit."

He added, almost as an afterthought, "Of course, if you take this quest on our behalf, you surrender the rights to any corpses you'll be making."

"And if we came, killed the chimeras, and took the loot without taking your quest?"

His smile didn't waver, but in a moment, his eyes turned cold. "That would be highway robbery, because the people doing the quest for the cultist is the Ivory Tower."

Ah, so it was looked down upon, then, or perhaps illegal.

"Got it," I said, turning to leave, "thanks for the info."

Noam followed after me, his steps sounded a bit more hurried than usual. Once we were a far enough distance, he grabbed my shoulder. "Shit, did you feel that?" he whispered.

I raised an eyebrow. "Feel what?"

"Scary," Greenie said. I saw from its view that Yellow was nodding in agreement beside it.

"Right?" Noam agreed. "That old man was scary. It felt like someone had shoved an icicle up my ass when you asked that."

"Descriptive."

He sighed loudly. "Man, I was trying to keep up this quiet and calm badass look as well. He definitely saw me flinch when he did that."

Wait, what?

"So, what do you think Maz?" Randiam directed to the woman who had tiredly replied to him earlier.

"Six out of ten, information gathering was decent, but they didn't ask in-depth," she replied. The MAG Vice-Guild Master wore a rather basic disguise, hiding inside his guild.

Randiam chuckled. "Eight out of ten, I figured it was trying to keep its own abilities hidden."

Maz moved to his side. "It?"

"Him, her?" He shrugged. "Does it matter? All myconids look the same anyway."

"That one was pretty distinct."

"Hmm."

There was a brief flicker of light, followed by the smell of smoke. "Are the wards all okay?"

"Of course!" Randiam replied, vaguely offended. "I set them myself."

The light of her smoke briefly reflected on his plate, piecing the bronze illusion and revealing a silver glint.

"Hey, keep off." He brushed off the small mote of mana. "Illusions are hard to maintain."

Maz chuckled.

"You said they were Travelers," he said after repairing his illusion. The one with a capital. The type that didn't truly die. Randiam heard of them as a child, stories of people and things constantly coming back regardless of what killed them.

"Yep," the drow agreed.

"They automatically succeed this exam, don't they?" he said. "They don't die so even if they were killed, they come back and get a plate."

"Indeed."

"Then why bother? They're already pretty lucky to immediately stumble here for their first quest."

"Because we would know what they're capable of."

The idea was simple enough. Know the enemy, though Randiam would rather not fight a Traveler. Unlike Revenants who tended to be driven by a singular and all-encompassing desire for something, or Fae who were stuck to the stories they gave them, Travelers were practically normal people, they didn't have convenient behaviors that could be predicted and exploited.

Few Travelers became truly dangerous or did heinous things, but the danger of something that won't die, something you can't easily remove from the world, one day just up and deciding they wanted to burn a town down? Then another and another?

Someone needed to deal with things like those, and though Randiam did it for a paycheck, he was still one of those people that dealt with monsters.

"What of the others?" he asked, there were normal people in this test as well. Twelve others.

"Complaining to the rep about the stringent rules."

He felt a nudge on his shoulder, seeing an unlit cigar between Maz's fingers. "No thanks," he replied.

The drow shrugged, before she blew out another line of smoke. "They seem like an interesting lot as well."

"I hope as many survive as possible."

4.13

———

What do you mean we require a 'party'!" a rough voice yelled from within.
A calmer voice answered, "It was in the . . ."

A different voice interrupted, but the tone was lower, so I couldn't hear it properly.

"Sounded like an insult," Noam supplied, hand falling to his "sword," before quickly retracting as he remembered there was a spike on the hilt.

There was a low growl. The first voice.

God, why did it have to be so troublesome?

Noam glanced at me, then upward toward Yellow. I shrugged. A conversation between us completed in a moment.

We could probably avoid a fight, but it didn't hurt to be prepared. "On Noam," I told Yellow as I presented my finger as a perch, before depositing it on Noam's shoulder.

"Why Yellow?" Greenie asked as Yellow crawled onto a comfortable spot on Noam's head.

"Yellow will be more useful with Noam," I answered. Noam was an opportunist, he seized mistakes by the balls and never let them go. The ability to crowd control the opponent for even the slightest moment would work far better with him. I already had enough.

Noam patted the mushroom on his head. "Watch my back, Yellow."

"Got it!"

"Hopefully you won't need to act much," I said to Greenie. It was mainly a damage dealer; if we were going for non-lethal, then Greenie's role should only be as a threat.

"Roo?" Noam asked.

"A bit of Poker as well," I answered. We'd run like he suggested if things turned south, but if we could observe, then we should.

Noam pushed open the swinging doors of the hut, revealing a much larger space within. Briefly pinning the bigger on the inside than the outside shenanigans on magic, I walked in after Noam, into what appeared to be a standoff.

Twelve people inside, all of whom turned to stare at our interruption, I was, in turn, examining them. Two groups in a standoff, three people to the left, two to the right. Rest were spectators, milling along the fringes.

The left group consisted of a human, a lizard-like person with vibrant red scales and small horn-like protrusions on their temple, and one that was either a halfling or gnome. Her hand was on the hilt of a short sword, but her height made her range limited so she was a low threat until proven otherwise. The human was dressed like a normal fighter archetype, but the lizard looked the most troublesome, handling a dark wood staff engraved in the shape of a dragon head.

The right group only had two, but they looked stronger. The one in front looked like a genetic engineer having a field day in creating an Olympic weight lifter. Tall and wide with the majority of his bulk in muscle, it would've been difficult to pass him as human even without the rough grey skin and the two tusk-like teeth peeking from his jaw. An orc. Damn, even his face looked like a brick. Behind him was a lizard-like humanoid, similar to the one from the other group, but there were some differences. This one had no horns, had dull green scales and was sparsely dressed, only a few belts and harnesses with pouches. An axe—no, a tomahawk of bone was holstered on their hip.

"We're here for the raid quest?" Noam began, glancing toward the edge. My eyes followed his, toward a man dressed in a uniform similar to the desk receptionist at the guild.

"Four meters to the right of him," my other self sent. My vision split to have Greenie's in parallel, it was staring at a hooded figure. I briefly caught the sight of a bandolier of something, dolls? There was a bird on their shoulder covered in a black cloth, when it turned to face Greenie, I realized that it was just a skeleton.

"There is no need to fight," the green lizard-like humanoid said to the orc, revealing sharp, needlepoint teeth. "There is nothing to be gained."

The orc snorted, spitting loudly onto the floor.

"Ew. Also, eight meters to the left, that guy is drawing a weapon."

"This one insulted your honor," the orc rebutted, pointing to the other lizard.

"I see him," I answered myself.

"Pfft. What did I do but speak but the truth? An uncivilized barbarian should go return to the jungle."

"Huh? Did I hear that right?"

"You did." Huh. I guess in the end this really was a fantasy world. I've read about racism in textbooks before, but I've never seen it in person before.

"And what would a damn lizard like you know!" the orc snarled, before quickly flitting back to *his* lizard companion. "Not directed at you, by the way."

The green lizardman remained silent.

"Am I blind or do both of them look like the same race?" Noam loudly "whispered" next to me.

I glanced at him. Oh no. *"I know that look."*

"You must be blind, then," the red lizard replied. "A dragonborn like me could not possibly be mistaken as one of the savage lizardfolk."

"I can't see a difference," Declan thought.

"At least I have the excuse of not having eyes," I added.

"Really?" Noam "incredulously" asked. "I really couldn't tell, what's so different about you lot?"

"Your education must be lacking to an egregious degree if you really think that."

Noam shrugged and his eyes flickered to me for the briefest moment.

Goddamnit. Well, if he picked this hill to die on, then I best make sure he digs someone else's grave.

"You see! A dragonborn is born with . . ."

As he began rambling, my mouth opened by the barest fraction. A strange quirk we've discovered was that my mouth doesn't actually need to move when I'm speaking.

". . . and not to mention the achievements of the Platinum . . ."

Very quietly, I began whispering. My voice was low enough that only Greenie heard me, but that was enough.

"Repeat after me."

Greenie did, and I began summarizing what I've read from one of the bestiaries I've read.

"Dragonborn seems to be descended from dragons shapeshifting and fucking with humanoids. Their abilities vary but generally, they're tougher than the average humanoid with innate magical abilities and elemental breath depending on their—"

Noam clicked his tongue. "That's all a fine and long-winded explanation, but you really aren't proving that superiority you're talking about," he said while facing the trio.

Not what he was looking for?

"This is a verbal battle," Declan pointed out.

Then what can I get?

The gnome was uneasy, she kept checking her weapon. The human didn't speak, but his pose was aggressive. Noam was in his element but still outnumbered.

The orc stepped forward. "Thank you for speaking in our defense, but I am not without fangs." He snarled as he said that, baring some rather impressive tusks.

Two to three, still not enough. I couldn't help notice that the lizard they were defending held a rather apathetic attitude to all of this.

The dragonborn began to speak up. I spoke first.

"There's no point to this."

Noam's eyes flitted rapidly to me.

"We should aim for de-escalation, not further antagonization," I had Greenie communicate to him.

"One more minute," he mouthed.

I mentally sighed. This idiot.

Verbally, I loudly said, "This lizard is all talk and no action, there is no point to arguing with someone who clearly can't back up their claims."

Noam turned to me, his back to the trio so that they couldn't see his mischievous smile. "I suppose you're right. No matter how much you teach a parrot to talk it's still just a parrot."

"Are you two daft! I'm clearly a dragon!"

Noam turned to the guild rep. "Anyway, we just need to hand you these papers, right?"

"Hey? Did you actually turn daft?"

"Indeed," the rep serenely replied. "However, due to the specific nature of the quest, we only accept completions with a 'party'."

"Groups of five or more?" I asked. "That could complicate matters."

"Hellooo?!"

"We're already here so it would be a bit late to call our own friends," Noam carefreely said. He turned to the orc and lizardman. "What about you two?"

"We are . . ." the orc uncertainly began, before he made eye contact with Noam. A glint of realization passed through them, and he cheerfully said, "Without a party as well!"

"Hey! I swear if you're ignoring—"

"We'll just need a fifth, then," I said over him.

"I said did you hear me!" the dragonborn moved forward, hand reaching for us.

"Torrin!" a female voice yelled. The dragonborn paused, glancing back at his gnome companion. She shrank back slightly but still firmly said, "Let's drop it."

"But—"

"*Please.*"

Torrin looked back at us, before letting out an indignant grunt. "You side with cannibals and savages."

I made a clicking noise, and from Yellow's perspective, I could see a brief spark of flame as Noam *tsk*ed. Quickly scanning around, I could see the room cooling down, the neutral parties remaining neutral. Discreetly, I stored the Sporage I had prepared at the start of the encounter.

"Pick your battles better," I muttered.

"I was about to light that fucker up," Noam replied.

"*So?*"

"But for what point?"

"He pissed me off," Noam quietly answered.

I mentally sighed. If only I could be as carefree as him.

"*That road died for us a long time ago,*" my other commented. "*I'll be gone, call if you need me.*"

"Got it."

"Thank you for your assistance." The orc smiled. "You enraged him far better than I would have."

Noam slapped the orc's back. "No problem," he cheerfully answered, "I have a natural talent for stuff like this."

"Utoqa"—the orc glanced at his companion—"you thank him as well."

"Thank you," he simply replied.

"No problem," Noam answered. "Umm . . . there's no easy way to ask this"—he nervously ruffled the back of his head—"but you're not actually what he said, right? Cause that would be . . . *awkward.*"

"I have not eaten another lizardfolk in my life," Utoqa answered. "Though I may be considered a savage."

The orc snorted. "Savage my goat. Take no heed to such insults, they place that label to any race with mhurran fangs."

The orc extended his hand. "I am Naukoth Stoneback."

Noam clasped it. "Noam."

"Dustin," I answered when he glanced at me.

He nodded in approval as I spoke. "You have good teeth for a plant."

"Umm . . . Thanks?"

"There is no problem. Noam, you spoke of partying, we are happy to join you."

"Sweet."

"What can the both of you do?" I asked. "I'm a mage, these are my familiars." I gestured to Greenie and Yellow. "Noam's a bard."

Naukoth perked up. "A bard? I am one as well. Where is your instrument?"

"I just use my words, man," Noam cheekily replied.

The orc nodded contemplatively. "Hmm. That does seem much more convenient."

"You have an instrument?" I asked. In all likelihood he did, but it did not hurt to check.

Naukoth nodded. "I do, I left it outside. Come! I'll show you."

Why would he leave it outside? If instruments are basically to bards what wands are to mages, then he should've carried it with him.

"Utoqa, introduce yourself as well, it is rude otherwise."

The lizardman nodded. "I am Utoqa. I can fight."

Well, that was informative.

"How?" I asked. "Are you melee or long range?"

"Melee," he simply answered.

"Using your tomahawk?" Noam asked as we left the hut.

"Yes."

The orc rounded around the hut. Must've left it behind there.

As we followed Naukoth, his "instrument" came into view.

"This is it!" the orc proudly presented.

What?

Noam rubbed his eyes. "Are you serious?"

I did a quick double-take. Yep, still the same thing.

"He plays a grand piano?" Greenie excitedly asked.

I stared at the grand piano. It was literally a grand piano, one made with polished dark wood . . . I couldn't describe it any way other than it was literally just a grand piano. There was a tiny stool next to it made with a weaved web of reeds and leather capping the top, but other than the fact it clashed with the overall design of the piano, there was nothing noteworthy.

"How do the logistics of this work?" Noam asked after some hesitation.

"I carry it!" Naukoth declared as he flexed his muscles.

"How *well* do the logistics of this work?" I stressed.

"Not very well," Utoqa drily answered.

Naukoth looked at his friend, betrayed. "Hey, hey! I can play it better than the best of them!"

Utoqa's glassy eyes met his. "You are loud, you cannot get through gaps, and you tune it every day."

The orc snarled, muttering something in a guttural language, before turning to us. "Are you fine with this?"

I looked the orc up and down once again. "Honestly, given your build, I would prefer you just carry a club." The orc began a rebuttal: "But, play it, let's see what you can do."

The orc claimed he was a bard, and while carrying a piano would be . . . suboptimal for a fight, especially one in a cave, it wouldn't hurt to evaluate his actual ability first, before deciding which to pick.

Naukoth visibly lit up at my suggestion. "Finally! A chance to show my true talents!" he declared as he rubbed his thick shovel-like hands together.

Wait . . . "Your fingers are too big for the keys," I stated. It was a grand piano but one clearly made for human proportions.

"No," Noam rebutted, his eyes glimmering with interest. "You are too confident," he said to the orc.

The orc barred his tusks, a gesture I realized with a start was a smile, before he pulled out the stool and squatted on it, his huge frame towering over the thing. I realized with slight annoyance that even sitting he was almost twice as tall as I was.

"First Melody, War of Drums."

Then he began to play.

The first song was brusque, loud and rhythmic. It felt at odds with the classical instrument it was played on, but as he played, I could feel a difference within myself.

Strength and agility buff, both by *four*. I didn't need to test it, my Analysis of myself simply updated with the new stats.

Then his song started to slow, before stopping.

"Second Melody, Ilneval's Edge."

He said as he began anew. The song sounded slower, his hands were sluggish—No. My mind and perception were getting faster. At least by twenty percent.

"Third Melody, Axe in Motion."

The third buff I didn't recognize. The song was something of constant buildup, and my body began to stir. What was this feeling? I could not recognize it, but it felt like . . . I could do anything and succeed at it. A willpower or motivation increase?

He finished the song, and turned around expectantly.

"Amazing," Noam breathed.

"Are those all you can manage?" I asked.

The orc's brow furrowed slightly. "Yes, unfortunately, those are the only complete melodies I know."

The first song increased my stats by eight total. That was four levels. "Your first song—"

"Melody," he corrected.

"Whatever. Is the strength and agility increase a flat increase or a percentage one?"

"Percentage?"

"Does your first melody increase a person's strength by a flat amount or is it dependent on how strong the person you affected was?" I simplified.

Naukoth's forehead furrowed in thought. "I am unsure."

"Noam?"

"No clue," he replied, making a fist. "I didn't get to move around, but it was more than a quarter but less than fifty percent."

"Can you play the first song again?" I asked.

"Melody," he corrected before playing again.

As he started, Noam did a few starting stretches, going through all his muscles. Yellow's eyes on him, I got back the stats I needed.

Strength: 12 (+4)

Agility: 14 (+4)

"Flat increase of four," I muttered. "What level are—" Wait, no, are levels even a concept for them?

Regardless, a plus-eight stat buff was insane for our level. Even looking back, I don't think I've seen a player with a stat surpassing twenty. This orc was either high-level or had an insanely lucky find.

"How long can you keep your songs going and how many can you affect?"

"I can play for a whole day if needed!" the orc boasted. "As for people, I do not know, but I can easily keep up for five."

"Can you selectively affect only allies?"

The orc looked at me as if I were stupid. "Of course, all bards can do that."

"Just making sure," I absentmindedly replied. "Do you require a piano to play these songs?"

"If I want to keep it at the same strength," Naukoth replied. "Regardless, I do not know other instruments."

A piano would be far too obvious and unwieldy, but the effect it could have was far too tantalizing to pass up. He said he can easily play for five, that was *forty* free stats at *least*. And they weren't random stats we weren't going to use. Noam was a mid-front line gish fighter, even if his spells scaled off Charisma he would need physical stats to stay relevant. The lizardman didn't give much away, but he was clearly also a front-liner.

Strength and agility were both dump stats for me but with the song up I could theoretically fill as an off-tank/mid-line combatant. In fact, the person whom this song would be least beneficial for would be the orc himself. Since any sane party would have him sequestered at the back constantly keeping his buffs up.

Not to mention, he could play two other songs. Yes . . . I can see it now. It can work. The unwieldiness of the piano can be accounted for. At the very least, playing around a piano will be an interesting challenge.

The pros outweigh the cons.

"You're grinning," Noam pointed out. "It's Goddamn terrifying."

"As any good smile should," Naukoth commented.

"Oh, I know," Noam replied with his own grin.

"We'll need a fifth." Ideally a healer of some kind. I could fill in for small wounds with Balm Spores, but it wasn't ideal. My build should focus on area control and damage per second.

"Would the hooded one do?" Utoqa spoke, glancing toward our midst.

Our eyes followed Utoqa's, to a hooded figure standing right between all of us.

What the—

"Ah!" a deep voice yelled as Naukoth fell out of his seat.

"None of you saw that!" Naukoth yelled.

"Yo," Noam welcomed. "How'd you get around all of us without us noticing?"

That was the same person who I noted earlier. The similarly cloaked bird skeleton on their shoulder looked around in a jerky manner.

"A necromancer," the orc snarled. "Blood brother, you cannot be serious about this."

"We require a fifth," Utoqa stated.

I had a better view of them now. A rogue type? Had to be, they didn't just get around the three of us without notice, but the *six* of us, counting Greenie, Yellow, *and* Declan.

"To be fair I wasn't paying attention," my other self's voice came through, somehow muffled by the sound of chewing even though it was purely in our heads.

"Still. That was Noam, Naukoth, the wisps, and me."

And what kind of stats did Utoqa had, that he noticed what five others could not?

Perception: >10

Still needed more information.

"Umm . . ." a soft, distinctively female voice shyly sounded out as she pulled back her hood, revealing juniper dark hair, ". . . I'm just good at blending in."

". . . And I would . . . umm . . . also like to join your party."

"What can you do?"

The woman glanced down toward me, though her eyes remained nervous. She appeared human, with a normal height of around one hundred and seventy centimeters and without the sharp ears that made me think of an elf.

Conventional wisdom placed her face somewhere between seventeen to twenty years old, though there were unknowns. I don't know if my knowledge of human ages would translate well here.

"For one, humans aren't the only race in this world, and breeding between species seems to occur on a regular occurrence."

"Which indicates that either genetics are screwed here, or most species belonged to the same taxonomical family," I replied to my Declan self. Pale skin was somewhat normal, but green hair, no matter how dark was not a natural human hair color. Unless you considered genetic or cosmetic implants to fall under the definition of natural, but few people did.

Wait, I was rambling again.

"Is it really rambling if someone responds?"

Probably not.

The woman began talking, nervous at first, but slowly gaining stride. "I umm . . . am an alchemist. I have prepared potions and know some spells." She pulled back her cloak, revealing a bandolier of potions.

Those weren't there before. She swapped them out?

"Do you remember what she had there before?" I asked Declan.

"I do," he replied. *"Weird looking dolls. Like voodoo or something."*

"What kind?" I asked her.

"There are multiple types of alchemists. See if she's a combat one."

"Don't backseat game," I chided. So annoying.

"I heard that."

"You were supposed to."

"Erm . . . I specialize in herbalism, though I do dabble in some primal material transmutation. Of course of the Trizian School, with some small inspirations from Gimetris! I like how they handle complete transmutation of non-pure materials and their theories on balancing equivalent exchange in favor of the transmuter. Of course only minor inspiration, otherwise the Gimetris Law of Bellariuan Disposition would clash with the Trizian's Theory of—"

She slowed her passionate speech as she looked around, realizing that none of her audience were looking at her with comprehending eyes—not that I had any. "If that's satisfactory!"

I shrugged. "It's fine. How do you manage in a fight?"

"Oh . . . Umm . . . I can throw and supply potions?"

"What kind?" I asked.

"Don't those cost money?" Naukoth interjected at the same time.

The three of us glanced at each other, and I shrugged. "Him first."

"They do . . . but I gather most of my own ingredients and I usually get by with just spells."

"But you still pay out of your own pocket for them?" I asked incredulously. She shouldn't be able to break more than even, then. Unless potions were ridiculously cheap.

She hesitantly nodded.

Naukoth bared his teeth as he growled, "And what of the undead?"

She noticeably seemed to flinch. "It's my familiar . . ."

"It's been cleared . . ." she hesitantly added in response to Naukoth's bared tusks.

"Few things are clear with necromancy," the orc snarled.

Utoqa placed his hand on Naukoth's shoulder. "If the legalities do not believe it a threat, then it should not be."

Interesting.

So undead could be cleared with law, hmm . . . That opened up several class skills I had dismissed before . . . but back to the conversation at hand.

The orc simply snorted in response, crossing his arms. His teeth stayed bared in an animalistic display of displeasure, but he did not contradict what was said.

Noam curiously leaned in.

"So, are undead a big deal?"

Surprise flickered across the face of the alchemist for the briefest moment.

"They are," Naukoth answered, still glaring at the alchemist. "How are you not aware of it?"

"I'm a Traveler, so I only got around here recently."

There was a brief moment before their brains caught up with capital in the word. I sighed, there wasn't a need for him to pass that along. It wasn't a big deal but it was another hidden card revealed for no gain.

"Traveler. . . as in the Grashetars?" Naukoth asked in awe.

Noam awkwardly rubbed the back of his head. "Erm . . . I don't know what that means."

"The Khartoci word for Stubborn One. I've heard tales of your kind."
The orc shuddered. "Great songs of warriors who refused death. I am glad
to have one with us."

"Does that mean you are one too?" the alchemist asked me.

My vision shifted to her. Ah, so that was what Noam wanted. Naukoth
had shifted out of his aggressive stance, his curiosity of Travelers outstripping his hostility toward the undead. Overall not a complete loss, I just
need to play along to move the subject away from her familiar.

That idiot with his bleeding heart, I thought with a smile.

"Yes," I answered, reaching out with a hand. "My name is Dustin; yours?"

"Celine," she accepted my hand with some hesitation. "Celine Kakoph."

Noam smiled, also reaching out for a handshake. "Noam."

"Utoqa," the lizardfolk said as she took it.

The orc grunted, crossing his arms before saying, "Naukoth Stoneback."

"Great," I began. "Now, onto what I can do . . ."

The Traveler group was the last to set off, having spent the time discussing
what they were each individually capable of. Maz noted with some approval
that they each seemed to keep a card hidden.

Dustin's familiars scanned the surroundings with cognizance that was
. . . unusual for what should be low-level magical constructs, and his staff
had changed since she last saw him. Motes of divine energy, not enough
to conceptualize but enough to hint at something. Most notable however
were his eyes, which he now covered completely with the strange fungus
growing on him in an odd woody mask.

The tiefling Noam spoke easily amongst strangers and moved quickly
to defend others. He carried the unmistakable aura of someone experienced. For one, when they first entered the building and encountered the
hostile environment. He disappeared. His heartbeat slowed, his footsteps
no longer made a sound and his presence seemed to fade. As another one
skilled in hiding, Maz recognized that this was near the peak of what could
be achieved without dipping into magic, aura, or having an innate gift like
the alchemist seemed to have.

Naukoth, that unreasonably strong orc, who was casually lugging around
a grand piano that was at minimum five hundred kilograms like it were an
empty travel sack, was a demented man seeking a fool's quest. What a waste
of such a sculpted body. In terms of physicality, he would rival even a Silver
Plater.

The last two were the strangest. The lizardfolk Utoqa was tough like
most of his race, but even from her perch, he was grating on her senses.

That lizard carried enough magic to fit out an entire adventuring party and wasn't particularly good at hiding it. You'd think he was about to face an entire raider encampment by himself.

Whereas Celine . . . she was an alchemist for sure, but it was not her primary Path. Not a necromancer, those had a distinct feeling which she lacked. Maz didn't think she'd ever even encountered her type of school. It was grasping . . . cursed . . . threading and . . . incomplete?

What Maz wouldn't have done to gain an aspect of divination right now, but then she would be too scattered. While it was nice to have multiple focuses, the universe will always get its due.

Instead, she weaved a working. The illusion milling around the camp was set to a pattern to repeat, and Maz soundlessly fell from her perch. Following the group a few dozen steps behind as they entered the caverns.

The first enemies the group encountered were utterly eviscerated.

4.14

———

With barely a grunt, Naukoth lifted the piano with a single hand.

"Hey, Decs?" I called out to my other.

"Yeah?"

Everyone except for Utoqa wordlessly gawked in awe as the orc easily shouldered the grand piano. *"How much does a grand piano weigh?"*

"Why— Holy shit!"

Understandable reaction.

"Okay, I'm googling it . . . Holy— Three hundred to five hundred KILOGRAMS!?"

Strength: >30

"Jesus Christ!" Noam exclaimed.

The orc smiled as he shouldered the piano between his shoulder and forearm. It clearly didn't even bother him, as he gave a thumbs up with his free arm. "I'm ready."

"Does that piano have some kind of magic lessening its weight?" I asked.

"Nope." The orc chuckled, clearly drinking in our shock.

"Erm, let's go, then . . ." I muttered. Turning around. The rest fell in step behind me, though they slowly overtook me. Naukoth, being well over two meters tall, had naturally long strides no matter how much he was encumbered, which he clearly wasn't, as he was holding a Goddamn five-hundred-kilogram piano like he was a waiter serving drinks.

"Lemme guess, you didn't actually expect him to be able to lift that?" Declan asked, to which I didn't bother to answer. He was right, after all.

"What's the human weight-lifting record?"

"Six hundred kilograms if you count purely genetic modifications. Eight hundred if you also count cybernetic. But—"

"None of them did it easily," I interrupted. If that piano weighed as much as it should, then Naukoth would be leagues ahead of anything a normal human can accomplish. Was this due to him being an orc or could anyone reach that strength here?

"The existence of our stats is in favor of the latter."

"Indeed. We both saw the base human stat block." Humans started at eleven for all stats. If they invested all their three stat points into a single stat, then they would reach thirty by level eight.

"Of course, racial benefits exist as well," he added. *"It'll only take three more levels for you to hit thirty Wisdom."*

"Though we're a bit forced into that, aren't we?" I quietly muttered.

Celine glanced at me, having fallen behind next to me.

"Just mumbling to myself," I answered. Technically the truth. While it was nice to be able to know all your teammate's abilities, there wasn't the pressing requirement to go all the way with a pick-up group. All you really needed to do was establish a baseline.

"Oh . . ." she hesitantly said, "I see."

Shy? *"Or is she hiding something?"*

"Could be both, it's a bit weird when you meld thoughts with me though."

"I know, I know, it's just when I'm paying attention I hear everything and it all sounds the same."

That . . . I was not a big fan of, but technically he was me, or at least close enough that it didn't matter. *"Keep at it, I suppose, wouldn't do if we became too different."*

"We theoretically already are. You're technically smarter and wiser than me, ya know? That can't be for nothing."

"Respects your betters, then."

"Nah. I've seen what I'm capable of and I'm not impressed."

That traitor, I'll make sure to impress upon him my intellect.

"And I'll beat you." He chuckled. *"Hey, quiet, I wanna hear what they're saying in front."*

I focused back on reality. Hearing the conversation the two in front had begun while I had my own.

"You carried rocks since you were four?" Noam asked, impressed.

"Da. It's why I'm called Stoneback," the orc answered. "Dwarves paid good money, and my Na couldn't support us both with another in the womb."

"That's still amazing though!"

"Really?" the orc asked with a slightly confused expression. "I've been told I was lucky. Orc children are already brought on hunts when they could walk."

Huh. He genuinely didn't seem to think it was a special thing. A difference in cultures I suppose. *"More importantly."* Yes, yes, I'll ask him. "So, you're so strong because you trained?"

The orc pursed his lips in thought. "Not so much trained . . . I just kept carrying the stuff they mined, and it kept slowly increasing till I was hauling enough for several mine carts."

Hmm . . . *"So, it increased as he used it,"* we thought at the same time.

That raised an interesting question. Traveler's increase their stats through level-ups . . . but if the people here could train and naturally become stronger similar to how I would IRL, were their stats linked to a level or other discreet value?

"Latter is obviously true. Don't forget you're in a computer. Everything has a value."

Noam talked, interrupting my thoughts. "So, why do you use a piano?" That one I strained my ears—or whatever the myconid equivalent was—to hear.

"It is an old story," he began, his voice shifting to a slightly more guttural accent. "A year ago, my friend Terrance dug into something. Some kind of instrument room, with a dusty piano in it."

Celine leaned in a bit, likely also curious about it. Only Utoqa remained as he were, keeping at the same pace, seemingly not interested.

"There was an undead sitting by it. A natural Skeleton, I was told later. Who remained because of regret. It didn't look up at us but was staring so intensely at a sheet of parchment that we didn't notice it was undead before it moved."

"But it didn't move until I neared it." His brows furrowed. "It was just . . . the piano looked so beautiful, I didn't think I'd seen anything more beautiful in my life. It was a gem shining in dust and dirt. I neared it, perhaps I was enchanted, but I played it. I touched the keys."

He paused for a moment before Noam spoke up. "What happened next?"

"What I played was absolutely shit," he said, a nostalgic smile on his face. "Terrance was knocked unconscious and the undead looked at me like I was some kind of freakish monster!" said the orc who was casually shouldering five hundred Goddamn kilograms. *"Whilst talking and walking!"*

Noam chuckled. "Was it really that bad? You're pretty amazing now."

"It was," the orc solemnly admitted. "It was my first time playing, so of course I would be bad! Everyone would be bad at something they tried the first time, right?" he asked, glancing around for confirmation.

Celine nodded in understanding, whilst Noam just scratched his head. "I can sorta get that."

The orc shook his head as he continued the story. "The damned undead didn't even consider that! It called me some dak like 'crime against decency!'" he vehemently ranted. "It even started crying on the ground!"

"He made a skeleton cry?"

"Yes, you heard that right."

Noam began laughing. "Did the skeleton even have eyes to cry?"

"It didn't!" Naukoth exclaimed incredulously. "But it still did it! The nerve of the thing!"

"It didn't have nerves though," I pointed out, for which I was rewarded with several amused snorts.

"What happened next?" Celine asked.

The orc's steps slowed as she asked that, I peeked around him, seeing the large entrance of the cave we were supposed to enter. By a silent agreement, we stopped just in front.

"The skeleton cried about how we weren't the 'prophesied ones,'" Naukoth quietly continued, his formerly boisterous energy dimmed as we stared at the gaping maw of the cavern. "The ones who will complete the song."

"I was still pissed as hell at it at the time, so I threw the piano at it"—he chuckled a bit at the memory—"and swore that I would do it *just to prove it wrong.*"

"What song was it?" I asked.

He set down the piano and fished inside of his tunic, withdrawing a rolled-up ancient sheet of parchment.

"This one," he said as he handed it to me. "Be careful, it's a bit head screwy."

Noam's eyebrow rose. "You sure about handing it to us?"

He chuckled. "Don't worry, I memorized it a long time ago."

I unfurled it and stared at the notes.

Similar structure to the sheet music I'd seen before, the lines are in the same places. Unfortunately, I never learned to read sheet music, so I wouldn't be able to—No.

"What?"

I could read it.

The notes weren't the ones I was used to or have ever seen in fact. Eldritch symbols that seemed to move in spite of their stillness. They seemed to hop out of the page. Worming its way into my mind till I heard the song.

A procession of a thousand lights. A dance through the darkness. A thousand predetermined paths. Yet they all moved toward the same place, but that place . . . it was empty. There was no end, the lights danced eternally without a conclusion to grace them. It desired an end. It needed it.

"*A memetic,*" Declan muttered.

I glanced away from the parchment, the action oddly easy despite how it had drawn me in. Celine was beside me, pale green eyes on the parchment.

"This is strong magic," she muttered quietly. "If even the formula is magical . . ."

I handed it to Noam's outstretched hand and rubbed my head as he examined it.

"*That affected me,*" Declan quietly said.

My eyes widened. "You mean—"

"*A thousand dancing lights, searching for an end that will never come,*" he said. "*Kinda poetic, but it is a song.*"

"*You sure it was because it affected you, or was it a secondary splash from—*"

"*Yes,*" Declan answered with certainty. "*But it can be tested. Look at it again and I'll screenshot it.*"

"*If even the still screenshot has the same effect . . .*"

"*Then it can be safely concluded that this is a set of patterns that could work on a person in the real world,*" I finished.

A memetic hazard huh. I thought those were a myth.

"*Oh? Didn't I tell you yet?*" Declan asked ponderously.

"*What?*"

"*That code of a 'God' in our house.*"

"*It's the same as this, it's a memetic.*"

The eccentric group stood in front of the cavern entrances.

"We ready?" the tiefling asked.

The orc snarled, his piano held above him like a serving platter. "Born ready."

The lizardfolk unsheathed his tomahawk of bone and drew a furred object from a pouch. "I am prepared."

The alchemist checked her pouches and potions, before nervously nodding.

Noam gave a quick glance to Dustin and received a curiously raised eyebrow in response. *Do you even need to ask?* He seemed to say.

"I'm heading in first," Noam declared, stepping onto the sandy cave floor. The rest followed in single file, Dustin, his blue glow becoming more pronounced in the dark, Naukoth, angling the piano so that it won't hit the jagged stalactites, Celine checking her potions once again and Utoqa quietly holding the rear.

The air was cold and damp, and Noam took care to watch his step. In the dark, he could only see shades of black and white—

"Umm . . . I can't see . . ." Celine nervously spoke out.

"Neither can I," Utoqa said.

Dustin *tsk*ed, the soft blue glow of his cap blinking out for a moment. "Damn, forgot about that."

"Oh, you races without Dark Vision." Naukoth rolled his eyes.

"Sorry."

"No problem," Dustin muttered as several softly glowing mushrooms grew from his arm, illuminating a few meters. "I'll have to spam this, won't I . . ." he softly muttered as more grew from his body.

"Ha!" Naukoth chuckled as he nudged his friend. "How are your scales helping now?"

"I have always said my scales are better than yours as a defense. How does this apply?" the lizardfolk asked.

"I can cast Dancing Lights," Celine helpfully supplied. She raised her hand, and four glowing balls of light appeared, revealing the spacious caverns, high and wide enough that they could walk abreast comfortably.

"Do that, I'll mark our path," he replied as he put his hand on a nearby stalagmite, a glowing mushroom popping out as he removed it.

"It is a joke," the orc said as Dustin set down some Light Sporages. "You always say we are compensating for having flesh weaker than mail."

"But you are," Utoqa stated as they moved forward, Dustin setting down another light mushroom every few meters. "Why else would you wear armor?"

"Why don't you wear armor?" Dustin curiously asked. "An additional layer of defense over your already tough scales could not hurt."

"I did not accumulate the metal pieces required to exchange for such a thing."

The orc bent down to whisper to Dustin, "Money. He's talking about money."

"It is . . . what is the word? Sad, that you are not born with armor and weapons."

"He doesn't mean it," the orc whispered.

"The mushroom creature has armor," Utoqa interjected, "the rest of you do not."

"Not natural," I said, "they're skills I got later on."

"Better than without."

The orc *tsk*ed. "None would sell my size."

"I'm broke," Celine quietly added.

"I don't really need it," Noam muttered before he suddenly dropped to the ground. "Tracks."

"What kind?" he and Dustin said at the same time.

Noam held his hand behind him, to which Dustin instantly handed him a light mushroom. The group behind shuffled forward to look at it.

"Can't tell," Noam admitted. "Too muddled."

"Shoe tracks," Utoqa said. "From many."

"The group before us probably," Dustin noted.

"Didn't they enter from a different hole?"

"Must've been connected," Naukoth growled. "Let us not meet them."

Suddenly, Utoqa's slitted eyes flicked to the darkness around them.

"Guys," Dustin started, Yellow urgently knocking his cap, "we're surrounded."

Noam and Utoqa moved first. Utoqa, having seen movement beforehand, Noam trusting his friend entirely. They moved opposite of each other, each at one side of the group.

"Finally!" the orc yelled, setting down his grand piano with a loud thud. "Battle!"

Dustin threw a clump of Sporages over Utoqa.

"Thank you," the lizard said as the light sources fell with a plop, revealing the nature of the enemies they were facing.

Shambling arrays of stitched up creatures. Remnants of life thrashed together to form dog-size mockeries lurking in the dark.

Dustin's did a quick count around them. *"At least ten."*

"War of Drums please," Dustin requested.

"Gladly."

The moment his hands touched the keys, the abominations attacked as if a starting pistol was fired. Four rapidly rushed at Utoqa's side. Amalgamations of different beasts moving with limbs not entirely theirs.

Dustin, his back turned to them, switched his vision to Greenie staring at the clump of Sporages. *"Poison Spores,"* it chirped, and one exploded in green dust.

Two chimeras were caught in the blast. Screeching as their flesh contorted in unnatural ways.

Two more hopped around the poison. One with rabbit-like legs twisting as it bared large sabre fangs at Utoqa.

He cleaved clean through the creature, then swiftly reversed the swing to catch the other beast. A hard crunch echoed as he batted it several meters.

"Two," Dustin softly muttered.

On the other side, Noam fought back three chimeras. His blades biting but not killing. Suddenly as he parried a demented otter-like chimera, the creature's skin caught on his sword's hook, and in a flash of brilliant stupidity, he swung his now weighted club at another encroaching beast.

A swing too wide, as the new weight dragged him forward. A clawed foot slashed at his now exposed back, but Dustin was faster. A glob of acid splashed onto the panther-like chimera, causing it to recoil back, attack abandoned as Noam's punched it with his crescent guard, drawing blood and blinding it.

Yellow threw its spores in the air, blinding another chimera on the ceiling. Through its eyes, Dustin saw two more lurking around the piano's exposed end.

"Right switch!" he yelled, and immediately Noam pivoted, turning to the direction of the orc. His arm in a wide swing as he catapulted the hooked chimera into another one.

"Three."

His old foe slashed out blindly, but Dustin swiftly took Noam's place. A swung staff cracked against the chimera's nose, bloodying it further.

From behind him, Celine threw a ceramic ball into the two disorientated chimeras, upon cracking it unleashed an expanding pink foam, encasing them both before it hardened.

"Got 'em!"

"Help Noam!" Dustin yelled as he slammed the butt end of his staff into the chimera's mouth. Using it as a fulcrum, he wedged open the things grotesque mouth. "Acid Spit." Burning acid fell into the creature's throat as Dustin drew back his staff. It scratched uselessly against his Barkskin as it gurgled in agony.

"Four," he muttered as he stared down the other one. The chimera slowly backed away, cautiously lurking.

Celine's skeletal familiar jumped from her shoulder and flew. It gliding over Noam's head before diving to peck the eyes of some frog weasel hybrid.

Giving up all pretense of being a swordsman. Noam used his weapon guard as knuckle dusters as he punched and slashed at two chimeras on his side, drawing a bloody line across the throat of one creature.

"Five."

The remaining chimera fell back, clawing at the pecking undead. It didn't notice the glowing blue rope until it whipped around its stitched belly. Celine pulled the animated rope, dragging it to fall onto the floor.

Noam punched down. A brutal squelch and crack as the beast's head was crushed into the floor.

"Six," Dustin said. The chimera he was staring down slunk back into the dark, disappearing and far out of range.

He quickly scanned the area, Greenie and Yellow covering his blind spots. Briefly, he noted that Utoqa was doing the same.

Neither of them saw any more enemies, save for the two still trapped in the pink foam.

"Injuries?"

"None!" Noam answered as he flicked off gore.

"I—I'm good!"

Naukoth slowed his song. "I have none."

"I am well."

Dustin pointed at the trapped chimeras with his staff. "Finish those two off."

"Now," he thought.

"Where did the last two go?"

4.15

Two got away."

Naukoth turned at the announcement, the rag he was fussily wiping away blood and gore from his piano with temporarily stilling.

"Two?"

"Three," Utoqa corrected. "I sensed the movement of two on the ceiling."

I raised an eyebrow and patted the pouting Yellow. "It's fine," I whispered, "you caught one, that was better than me."

Turning to the lizardfolk, I asked, "I counted ten at the start, you?"

"Thirteen," the lizardfolk muttered as he curiously examined the remaining two chimeras struggling in the pink foam. "Two ran at the start."

Noam gestured for Naukoth's rag. "You said you had no Dark Vision?" he asked as he started wiping his poor excuse of a melee weapon.

"I used my nose and ears." He raised his tomahawk and in a swift motion, cleaved cleanly through the head of one of the chimeras.

"Seven."

The other chimera, which happened to have the head of a large pug, stared at its cleanly decapitated companion before its cute large eyes began to tear up.

"Aww . . ." Celine said beside me.

'Eight,' I mentally counted as Utoqa swung again.

"Ahh!" she immediately screamed. "Why did you do that?!"

"It was an enemy."

She looked like she wanted to say something further but shrunk back slightly as she looked at Utoqa.

Turning back, she quietly muttered in a low voice, "You really don't feel anything huh . . ."

"Hmm?" Declan thought.

No one else seemed to hear her, Naukoth was still wiping off gore while grumbling to Noam for leaving a mess and Utoqa was . . . holding the pug head with a strange expression I couldn't read.

"Would it be fine if I ate this?"

Ah.

Naukoth shrugged. "You killed it, so it is yours."

So, this is what culture shock feels like. Is this normal? No can't be, Celine was making a strange expression as well.

"Didn't the guild say that all the hunted parts would go to them?" she cautiously said. Throw his attention somewhere else, huh.

"Good point," I said as Noam made a *That's what you're worried about!?* look.

"I'm tempted to join him," Declan muttered.

"What would a pug head taste like?" I asked.

"I will not grace that question with an answer."

"When in Rome. . ."

Utoqa tossed the bloodied pug head, shame. I kinda wanted to see him eat it. "I'm pretty sure they only care about the rare valuable parts. They probably won't care if a few random trash pieces were gone."

His gaze lingered on the head for a moment. Strange slitted eyes considered the action, before leaving it.

"Is it done?" Declan asked. *"Can I look without scarring my eyes now?"*

"Liar, there wasn't a single point where you looked away." This guy was filled with the same morbid curiosity I was. Stop pretending to have decency.

"Don't even think about it," Noam said as he neared us.

I exaggeratedly shrugged. "Whatever are you talking about dear Noam."

"Aww," my real-world self said, abandoning decency as usual, *"no dog tonight."*

"Probably would've tasted like a bitch either way."

"Ha," he drily laughed at my pun.

Celine nervously spoke up, "What were you guys talking about with the running chimeras?"

"Now I might be an antisocial . . ."

"But I recognize when someone desperately wants to change the subject," I finished.

"They were probably programmed with different instincts," I said.

"Probably ran back to report intruders," Noam followed up.

"If it was a scouting party, then it means they have a lot of chimeras to waste."

"The ones that left bought time for them to run."

"How do we know this?" Celine asked.

"Well. . ." Noam thumbed toward me. "It's what he would've done in the same situation."

"What a horrible accusation," I replied. "If I sent scouts, we would've never seen them, and they would run at first sight. Utoqa, did you catch anything when we entered?"

He shook his head.

"So, either we missed the scouts," Noam said in a pretty accurate parody of my voice, "or that wasn't a scouting party."

And given the presence of the previous party ahead of us, then there were some unfortunate implications. Either the party ahead were already beaten and these were the dregs that got past them, or they were an ambush party sent to encircle them from behind. The former was unlikely, as I didn't notice any recent damages on their bodies.

If this was a scouting party, then it meant that the cultist had chimeras to waste and/or a lack of effective information gathering types. If we assumed the runners were special or different somehow, then the fact that they had such a large contingent of other chimeras meant that they weren't confident in the information gathering types abilities, either in combat or escape. The presence of the other party muddied this theory a bit since they would've likely cleared as they moved forward, but given the abnormal size of the cavern to the point that even a two-meter tall orc can walk around and carry a grand piano without much trouble means there's room to out-maneuver, which would indicate an even higher degree of intelligence. At the very minimum threat assessment—

I felt a strong poke on my cap, almost tipping me over.

"Are you well?" Naukoth asked. "You went still."

I blinked back to reality. "It's fine, I was just thinking."

I quickly explained my train of thoughts, to which Naukoth just asked incredulously, "You gleaned all of that after one encounter?"

"You'll get used to it," Noam tiredly muttered from the side.

I shrugged. "It's all speculation and until we confirm more information it'll remain so."

"So, there's only one path."

He stared deeper into the dark caverns.

"Once more," the orc said, his eyes far, "into the fray."

I whispered a command to Yellow, and it deftly hopped off my cap. "To be safe, Yellow will scout ahead for now." Glancing at Celine, I asked, "Can your familiar accomplish a similar task?"

She hurriedly shook her head. "Nappy doesn't have Dark Vision and she can't be far from me anyway."

Nodding, I said to Yellow, "Run when you meet an enemy." We had Observe on it, so Yellow didn't need to worry about reporting.

It did a salute, this time with the correct arm. "*Yessir!*"

"Forty meters," I muttered, "remember it."

Yellow nodded before it waddled off. Its dim yellow glow disappeared as he left my sight.

"Get any preparation you need done," I said aloud. "I'll keep watch for now."

Noam sat down crosslegged, leaning on a stalagmite. Bored now that combat was over.

Utoqa began rifling through the corpses of the chimeras, sorting them with some sort of system, while Celine looked around with a flustered expression, before finally settling around Noam.

Naukoth clicked his tongue as he stared at his piano, pulling back the lid and adjusting the strings.

As for me, I was deepest into the cave. Keeping watch of what was deeper while Declan was watching through Yellow's eyes.

First off, I used my class skill, creating another Wisp body, just in case Yellow got taken out and needed a quick body to return to. Then I started preparing more Sporages. The damn problem was that I had very few places to store them. I left my backpack to my alt, a poor decision in hindsight but even if I filled it with Sporages, I wouldn't be able to access them quickly.

"*You can use your head,*" Greenie lazily chirped.

"I am but there isn't a way I can do it right now," I answered. I needed a satchel of some kind, maybe get a Bag of Holding—

"*No! I meant use your head!*" Greenie corrected as it slapped my cap. "*This boi can fit so much in it!*"

Oh God, they found Matt's history reference memories.

Greenie slid off my cap and dropped onto my shoulder before it began crawling up my neck and into my cap.

Feeling a tickling sensation as it climbed through my gills, I quickly swapped my vision to it.

"What?" I muttered in surprise.

The inside of my head was a roomy penthouse suit. The furniture Yellow and Greenie had bought earlier were decorating the place and while there were no windows, the natural blue glow along with the randomly floating motes of mana gave the place an ethereal and fairytale-like look.

Raising an eyebrow, I reached into my cap with my hand. It came up with the same relative size to Greenie . . . but significantly smaller compared to what the insides of my cap should be.

"So, it's bigger on the inside than the outside huh," I thought, mind drifting to the famous blue police box. "How long has it been like this?"

"Since we got back!" Greenie cheerfully answered. It raised an arm, pointing upward to what appeared to be a wizard hat hanging from a stray bony-like protrusion.

Looking closer at the thing, I realized from the exposed stitching that the hat was actually inverted so that it was hung from the inside out.

"Where did you get this?"

"Zoe!" the wisp answered as if it would answer everything. Very briefly, my mind flashed with images of a magical white cat, floating and . . . turning lizards into eating utensils?

I need to get the story of this Zoe out of them, but for now, I won't look a gift cat in the mouth.

"Help me sort this stuff out, then," I said as I pushed my prepared Sporages into my head, along with Yellow's back up body.

Greenie swiftly went to work, its previous lethargy disappearing as it was newly enriched by my mana. It sat the back up along one of the walls and under my instruction, piled the Sporages in places my hand could easily reach.

"*Yo,*" Declan suddenly called.

"*Update?*"

"*Yellow found them.*"

Yellow rushed through the dark empty caverns.

The path ahead was eerily silent, to the point that Yellow's felt its light and short steps sounded like booming stomps slamming into the floor.

Still, it persisted. Stopping only every few dozen meters to scan around like its Master would do.

Until it came to a point where it heard the faint sounds of metal clanging against metal and its steps fastened.

With hastened steps, Yellow began passing numerous corpses, most were the same dog-size chimeras they had easily dealt with earlier, but some were significantly larger.

It kept running, dodging corpses when it needed.

Before it suddenly heard movement.

Yellow hurriedly hid behind a stalagmite as a lumbering creature passed it.

"It's time to leave," its sensible side said.

"But I wanna keep going!" its dominant side said.

So, it kept going, and it passed more and more chimeras, all rushing toward the same place.

It hid, again and again, every time it did so, images flashed through its mind.

A man in desert camo surveyed a dusty battlefield covered in numerous jagged ruins, he took out some kind of small circular device with several digital green rings on a black background. A radar, but it was completely frozen.

Declan tsked. "Interference."

"Problem?" a distorted voice answered back.

"None," he answered, placing the device back in his pocket. "I've already marked the possible hiding spots on the map. There's also a Cloaker somewhere, need me to find it for you?"

Matt chuckled. "What do you take me for? A Goddamn casual?"

The memory ended, with Declan alone on a dusty dune as gunfire sounded through the desert.

To hide, you simply need to be outside their sight. They knew this, so they attacked everywhere they couldn't see.

Yellow was being taught how to catch hiders, but it also learned how to avoid catchers.

It dashed from one hiding spot to another. Unnoticed despite its natural glow, going deeper and deeper until the clash of metal was no longer a faint noise in the background. Until the sparse chimeras were no longer sparse, but a thick stream rushing into a single cavern.

Yellow climbed onto the wall, edging over the constantly rushing chimeras before it saw them.

A group of people pushed back to the edge of the wall. Desperately battling against the endless horde. Three people held the line, the ones that Dustin insulted earlier, they worked together noticeably better than with the other three remaining survivors.

Numerous corpses piled everywhere as blade and magic flew, but the group was failing, tiredness was setting in and they were becoming slower in front of the encroaching horde.

With a morbid fascination, Yellow noticed two humanoid corpses, scattered and broken on the ground.

Far away, Declan crossed his brow. "This could be annoying."

4.16

—————

*"Near the later stages of the Siege of Frost Wall, Bracktor the
Daring charged his company of a hundred heavy dwarf infantry
through the surrounding forces of over seven thousand undead
to reach the Frost Wall Fort. Reinforcing the fortress militia,
it allowed them to last another four months before greater
reinforcements arrived."*

—*Excerpt from* The Historia

Rapidly I stood up, jerking Greenie as it was drawing faces on the spare fungal body. "We found them," I said aloud.

Damn, they were in a bad situation, too.

"They're currently surrounded," I quickly relayed.

There were nine other people who entered. "Two are down, probably still alive." Their bodies were being protected by those still standing. "One is missing, the remaining six are backed up against a wall."

I eyed backward, toward my party.

"Shit," Noam muttered, catching on to my unspoken question. "That bad?"

Celine quickly stumbled up. "It sounded bad enough just from the—"

"No, no," Noam interrupted. "When he's giving that look it means he needs a decision made."

"In the next few moments ideally," I replied, my focus still firmly on Yellow's side of things. "The majority could probably survive until we get there, but the longer we take, the more casualties they'll have."

We only had two effective options. Rush to assist or double back and try to get support from the force outside.

"I'm going," Noam answered immediately.

"Does the group have the dragonborn within it?" Naukoth asked.

"Yes," I answered quickly. Wait, shit. *"Mistake."* I quickly swapped back to my own vision, seeing the complicated look on his face. I should've thought that through, did he still have enmity with—

"Even if he is abhorrent, no creature deserves to die honorless," the orc said with a solemn look. "I'll come."

He glanced at the lizardfolk. "You, too, Utoqa."

"I—I'll come as well!"

"There may be a problem with that, Naukoth," I replied. "There is a constant flow of chimeras toward their location, Yellow is scoping it out, but it looks like we'll have to fight through the chimera waves to get to them."

I wasn't sure of Naukoth's direct fighting strength, especially when he was carrying that piano, but the practicalities of bringing that thing safely inside was . . . "You'll have to ditch the piano."

"No matter how good your wide scales buffs would be once we met up with the other group, it would be moot if we can't get through safely."

Currently, he and Celine were the two people we could afford to cut. Utoqa and Noam were both close range fighters who'd be needed for breaking through and I'm required as an area of effect damage dealer and crowd controller, but Celine's worth was largely in her consumables, which we could just carry ourselves, and Naukoth was simply too impractical to get through with his grand piano unless we focused solely on defending him. Not only that, he would only be useful if we were stuck in a drawn out battle, when we should be aiming for a quick extraction.

The orcs face scrunched up into a grim expression. "I cannot fight without my piano."

"It is fine," I replied, bringing him would only be plan B. "Return to camp and get the message back. Tell them we require—"

"How durable is your piano?" Noam suddenly asked, his hand thoughtfully stroking the instrument.

"It is dwarvishly enchanted and enhanced for structural integrity and durability," he answered quickly, with a hint of pride. "Other than the fact I have to regularly tune the strings, it won't break from a few scuffles."

"Do you suppose we can all fit behind it, if we flipped it?" Noam casually asked.

Huh? *Oh.* Noam wanted to use it as a blocker. That could work. Naukoth still needed to carry it, but it could effectively turn the thing into a benefit instead of a liability. Nullifying one attacking angle would do wonders. Yes, instead of him being a burden on the off chance we fail the better plan, he could contribute while retaining his worth as our plan B.

Naukoth's face was contorting, going through dozens of expressions at once.

"Huh, so that was what true horror and rage looked like."

"No, no, and *no*. By Ilneval's cataract-filled eyes! I did not spend a dwarven fortune for it to be used as a . . ."

Golkean Torrin wiped sweat away from her horned forehead. Flame spewed forth from her raised dragonhead staff, burning away another row of monstrosities. There was cheering behind her as the creatures burned, yet the spell took its toll. A fresh burst of pain stabbed into her head, worming its way through a mind already racked with pain.

Remember the numbers, she thought. *Two. Three. Five. Seven. Eleven. Thirteen. Seventeen . . .*

Prime numbers. Like a dragon, solitary, divisible only by itself and one. They gave her strength, and her headache worsened, but she had mana now. Mana was a byproduct of thought, and so only such can restore it.

Nineteen. Twenty-three . . .

Clawed hands prepared to weave another spell, only to let out a pained gasp as she tried to draw on already depleted mana reserves.

Twenty-nine. Thirty-one. Thirty-seven . . .

Not fast enough. It was not a method for combat.

"Fall back Torrin!" Elucidatium Swindoobly Vulgopopopot yelled, her shortsword parrying a claw aiming for Torrin. "Get your mana back! We can't have you dropping now!"

"I can't wait!" she replied to the gnome. "There's too many!"

They were barely keeping up *with* her slinging spells. Two had already fallen, and she was not the only one tiring. She was a dragonborn, it was her *duty* to lead. To be the best one here, to be the last to fall, to be—

"What is that sound?" Mehens said from her side. The human eyed the singular entrance to the cavern.

"Does it matter!?" one of the mercenaries yelled as he stabbed another chimera with a spear. "Focus on the fight!"

"Shut up!" Torrin yelled at the mercenary, having learned a long time ago not to dismiss Mehens's senses. "What do you hear!"

The human's face scrunched up in focus. "Many footsteps, flesh crashing onto wood . . ."

"Wood?"

"It's coming closer," he answered.

Soon enough, Torrin heard it, too. Under the constant rush of dozens of monstrosities, was a slowly rising sound, of something heavy crashing and pushing. The sounds of crashing slowly rose.

Thump.

"Is that some kind of beast?"

Thump!

"No, some heavy kind of shield," Mehens answered.

THUMP!

A horrific roar echoed through the caves. Dozens of small, dog-size chimeras were forcibly pushed to the side as a huge chunk of carved, polished wood slammed through.

With a great pained cry, Naukoth pushed through.

"We're in!" I yelled, Yellow's vision having sighted us a long time ago.

Utoqa and Noam ran at the left and right sides respectively, taking pot shots at the passing beasts. Celine had her eyes closed, her face terrified as she simply held onto the orc's large back as we ran forward. I finished my first part as I dropped another Poison Sporage on the trail.

Yellow dropped down from the ceiling, landing deftly on the rim of the piano. "Look ahead!" I yelled.

"Twenty meters," Declan measured for me. Twenty more meters of monsters to push through, but Naukoth had something those things didn't. Over five hundred kilograms of pure muscle, polished wood, and ivory keys.

Chimeras that did not get out of the way slammed into the front of the piano and like water freshly parted, many were hit with enough force that they were thrown to the side or overhead.

Naukoth easily shoved through the remaining few meters, before I yelled, "Slow!"

Like we discussed, he braked. Slowed down and turned to the side with great difficulty. Now came the deciding part.

Noam split to the side, Utoqa following after a moment's hesitation. Celine let go of Naukoth and threw her foam bombs, while I threw all my remaining Sporages in a wide arc. Screams, wails, chirps, growls, you name it, they sounded off in a multitude as green and yellow spores mixed with pink foam in a series of colorful explosions.

"Crowd control set."

Noam and Utoqa hunted the remaining chimeras that were in our small circle. The six mercenaries, seeing us, were shocked for a moment but swiftly doubled their efforts to help us.

We got our brief respite.

"Get on!" Naukoth yelled to the six mercenaries.

"We need to get a final push out!" I yelled, eyeing the small pathway of poison spores I had left. "It's now or never!"

There was a moment of pause, but thankfully that dragonborn was half-way competent and recovered quickly. "We cannot! Not while someone is still trapped!"

"Sure, we can!" another mercenary yelled from behind him. Earning a dirty look from the dragonborn.

"We can't just leave her!"

I spat acid toward a chimera that made it through the dust. It was thinning too quickly, I didn't have time to get a good stash. If I had a few more hours . . . farther past the wall of spores was an empty trail of carnage we had left. Every few meters was a single Poison Sporage I left on the ground. A clear path that was ever shrinking.

"The window is closing," I told them. I spent my entire stash for the screen and to create a trail we can push through later. Naukoth didn't lack strength but like a bear he needed space to build momentum. Space that was shrinking.

"Just hurry up and run!" the human beside the dragonborn yelled.

The dragonborn's face scrunched up in a tense expression. Despite not having any human features, I could tell he was tense.

"I will stay," he finally answered. "Go and get help."

"Are you insane!?" the female gnome beside him yelled.

"Great! See you later!" the mercenary from before said before getting behind Naukoth.

I paused. In the midst of this active battlefield, as the people we were saving devolved into arguments, I stared at the dragonborn. He did not have human facial features, but Eve herself said that insight was Wisdom-based, and at this moment, I felt he was serious. A glance toward Noam confirmed it. He nodded, and I felt a bit of relief as he reached the same conclusion I did.

The way they were arguing revealed two sides. The two that stood with the dragonborn before stood with him now, a bit apprehensive but willing to stay. The remaining three wanted to grab the bodies of their comrades and escape.

Two options once again. Run and leave a few behind or stay and hope help gets here in time?

"Cowards," Naukoth spoke, revealing his tusks in a predatory manner. "Cowards, you lot are."

Noam smiled, the decision made. "You heard the orc." He shrugged. "He's the only one who can carry the piano, so if he's staying ya'all are staying."

"But—"

Naukoth gave the mercenary a hard look and she stopped talking.

"You can still take your chances," Noam suggested with a devilish smile, his thumb pointing toward the shrinking path.

Gruffly, Naukoth set the piano down.

"Around him," I said. The barrier was shrinking rapidly. "Our best hope to survive is to keep the bard playing."

"Can he really do it?"

"Yes," Noam said with a chuckle as Naukoth shifted his instrument closer to the wall. "Yes, he fucking can."

"How well can you six still fight?" I asked as we turned outwards.

"Fine—" the dragonborn began, before her human companion cut him off: "She's mana empty."

She? "Then stay back; do you have any way of quickly regenerating?"

An out of mana mage was pretty much useless. Though that applied to any resource-based build that ran empty.

"Decs," Noam interrupted my thoughts. "They won't be able to do it."

"Nonsense," the dragonborn interrupted, "I am still perfectly capable of . . ."

I ignored her. Took a good look at the six-man group.

They were bedraggled, I didn't need a fancy sight power to recognize that. They weren't that damaged, but the state of their armor was incredibly poor. Slashed, crushed, and broken almost everywhere. They had a single healer, a man wearing white robes that had been stained with blood. He stood behind, his eyes closed and hands clasped in what I assumed was prayer. I knew due to Yellow that he'd been doing an extremely good job up till now, but judging from the wounds the two lying on the ground suffered, he could not fix death.

"Healer"—I pointed—"how long can you keep going?"

The man's eyes fluttered open. "I am almost out of prayers to give, but War is my god's domain, so I will last the battle."

"Good enough," I said as parts of our crowd control screen were starting to get bypassed.

Noam grinned, his smile excited with anticipation. "He's going to do the thing!"

A few questions were thrown out, but I wasn't paying attention to them.

"You can't seriously be thinking about this," Declan said. *"You know our max is five people."*

"But there are two of us now," I answered. *"And my mental stats are theoretically twenty percent higher."*

I felt him blink, before letting out a sigh. *"You don't know if stats scale linearly; for all we know they are logarithmic, and you are barely smarter than I am."* He shook his head. *"I need to grab snacks."*

"Hurry up," I said as I turned my attention to the slowly encroaching horde.

"Until we get out of this, I require all of you to follow my orders to the best of your ability."

More questions, spoken over each other.

"We're Travelers," Noam said, his face still carved in a smile. "We're probably the most battle experienced here."

For the first time since I gained **Observe** and **Analyze**, I fully stepped back from my vision. Instead of being immersed in a singular perspective, I now viewed all of them as if they were many different screens placed in front of me. Greenie, running to the entrance of the cave to get reinforcements, Noam, convincing the rest of the group, slowly easing them into the idea of accepting my command. He was always better at that stuff than I ever could be. Yellow, still sitting on Naukoth's piano, silently watching the proceedings, and finally, my real-world half, ripping open our house's snack drawer, and shoving four chocolate bars down his throat.

They were always present at the back of my mind, and there lay the true value of my Analyze passive. It was near worthless if I used it actively, since if I was actively gauging the stats of an enemy, Analyze would only show the exact things I was measuring. Its strength lay in the fact it measured *everything* I saw as if I was paying full attention to it, even if it was the peripheral of my vision, or say, a different perspective that was at the back of my mind.

Declan shifted his perspective with mine. I already had a good idea of what everyone in this group was capable of thanks to Yellow, and he was quickly reading all that it had learned.

"You take half, I'll take the other," I softly whispered to him.

"I don't know if our snack stash can last the fight."

"At least you have one."

No one knew me as well as I did, and I knew perfectly well what I was good at. It wasn't mechanics, physical skill, reactions or split-second decision making, Noam had that more than covered. No, one of the very few things I excelled at was figuring out optimal party usage, positioning, and long-term macro strategy.

The greatest thing Observe gave me was enabling me to have an overhead view of every field.

The chimeras finally broke through, and Noam laughed. "Strap in! You're about to meet the shot caller who beat pre-nerf mythic Vek'Na!"

* * *

There was once a boss named Watcher of Death Vek'Na in the popular MMORPG Yggdrasil. Released upon the game's eighteenth expansion, Shadows of Nilbog, the boss was the only side boss in the dungeon Tomb of Nilbog, it was entirely possible for the dungeon to be beaten without fighting him, but for many, it was a priority to make sure he was the first boss killed.

For Vek'Na possessed a unique aura, Eyes of Death. If at any time a player character fell below a quarter of their health within the dungeon, Vek'Na would unleash a blast from his chambers and instakill them, no matter where they were or any obstacles in the way. Thus, it was a priority to swarm him as quickly as possible; as many other bosses possessed high damage area of effects, Vek'Na made the dungeon harder by just existing.

He was not an easy boss to take down, possessing high base stats even amongst dungeon bosses along with powerful abilities. Carrion Call, a powerful area of effect that leaves behind an incurable percent health damage over time that lasted until he was dead. His weapon, Scythe of Ruin, did 400 percent extra true damage to health shields. The boss room itself was dangerous as well, having multiple environmental effects. Grated pits of necromancy and skulls spewing green corruption constantly drained health but also periodically interrupted ability casts and animations.

Then there was his aura.

When fighting him, Eyes of Death would have other effects, when it was activated there was an uninterruptible zero point five second cast time where he would stop and stare at the target before the effect activated. Once his target was dead, Vek'Na would completely reset his aggro chart, as well as healing him for a percent of the damage Eyes of Death deals.

It was an extremely difficult boss to face which tested a party's healers and tanks. Healers needed to ensure all party members were above his execution threshold, and if his aura does activate, then tanks will be forced to quickly redo aggro. If at any time they made a mistake, it was entirely possible for it to snowball to a wipe.

However, since it was a dungeon that had no player limit on the instance encounter, most people just swarmed him. Brute forcing the dungeon with dozens, sometimes hundreds of players. At the time, it was thought to be the best strategy.

That was until one of the top raiding guilds unlocked Mythic Difficulty. The highest difficulty of any instanced encounter.

When in Mythic Difficulty, Vek'Na gained several new effects.

Blessing of Death, with every player takedown, he'll gain a huge damage buff, which will keep stacking until the dungeon is reset.

Clarion Call gained a buff, the longer the fight drags on, the more percent health damage it'll deal. Along with Scythe of Ruin, which now dealt 800 percent more damage to shields.

Final Pass, his new enrage ability. When Vek'Na himself falls below 25 percent health, he'll lose all damage resistances, cleanse, and become immune to all crowd control and taunting effects along with quadrupling the damage buff of Blessing of Death.

But the most ludicrous change was his Eyes of Death Aura. The ability's health threshold now scaled with the number of players in the dungeon. Dead or alive.

With five players, it'll activate at 40 percent health.

With six players, 60 percent.

Seven players, 75 percent.

Ten players, 80 percent.

Here the scaling began to plateau and eventually caps out at thirty players with a 99 percent health threshold. Regardless, the new thresholds meant that, if a raid group brought ten or more players, then they would wipe from a single area of effect attack.

It was an attempt by the Developers to soft-lock higher level content from simply getting brute-forced by huge groups of people. Putting a hard number lock would be against their "freedom of choice" game design which they took pride in. So, they used Vek'Na to act as a deterrent.

It worked, people quickly discovered that five to six players were the sweet spot, and the Tomb was run multiple times by top-ranking raid guilds in Mythic.

But they never managed to kill Vek'Na. Even with top players, best in slot gear, it all went to shit when Vek'Na entered his enraged mode, his damage increases simply snowballed too quickly. Being immune to crowd control and taunting effects meant he almost always rushed a squishy healer or damage dealer, hitting them once before Eyes of Death activate, healing from killing them, and gaining an absurd damage buff from Blessing of Death. After one kill, a single one of Vek'Na's attacks will place any non-tank below 40 percent health, where his Eyes of Death will activate, giving him even more damage. Then he'll start working down the aggro charts until he actually fights the tanks again.

Other strategies were proposed, replacing pure damage classes with mix-class damage tankers that had higher survivability along with more healers to deal with his enraged state, but that had a problem. His buffed

Clarion Call ability left behind an increasingly higher damage damage over time, which wasn't alarming at first, but if dealt with within a few minutes would surpass anything healers could manage. The only way to clear the debuff would be to kill Vek'Na, but a group that dropped pure damage dealer classes could not damage him fast enough before the damage over time wiped them out.

It was a catch twenty-two. Without durable damage dealers, a party would wipe once the enraged state activated, but if they did, then they would not have the damage to reach that point. Players tried running it with larger parties, but every additional character only worked against them. Shield and damage mitigation-based supports were started to be run to bypass the execution threshold, but due to Scythe of Ruin, it was even less effective against Vek'Na than healing.

When the difficulty of it was brought up, a developer simply said this:

"Mythic Tomb of Nilbog could be run with more than ten people."

The words—*"No, it fucking couldn't. You delusional detached piece of shit-stain game developer. When was the last fucking time you even played the game? It is literally impossible to beat Mythic Tomb of Nilbog with more than six people, you inherently brain dead gamer ass stain spawned by the hate farts of basement dwellers,"* though significantly censored—summarized the community response rather well.

"Pfft . . . As if players know anything. Yggdrasil's dev team has OVER TWO-HUNDRED years of game development experience combined. Obviously, I know better than you."

The community response to that was . . . well, there was no point in relaying it, as it would be A, incomprehensible, and B, so full of expletives that censoring to make it match this site's values would leave literally nothing behind.

Regardless, these were MMORPG players, one of the most stubborn and deranged groups of people on earth. Only beaten by serial killers, mass murderers, and MOBA players. "Gracefully" accepting that the Developers were once again fucking useless, they cleared Mythic Tomb of Nilbog. Always skipping Vek'Na and running health shield classes since he was the only one that dealt increased damage to shields.

The dungeon's end boss was beaten multiple times, yet the Mythic full clear achievement never happened. Until the game's PR team caught wind of the developer's comments and forced the idiot to stay up for three days in a row to program the nerfs to Mythic Vek'Na.

The nerf would've significantly lowered Vek'Na's Eyes of Death kill range along with nerfing Scythe of Ruin's damage buff against shields.

Players rejoiced after enforcing their "objectively correct" opinion and top-level guilds waited for the nerf to come out before rushing to clear the dungeon and get the First Full Clear.

Everyone had given up beating Mythic Vek'Na before his nerf.

But merely an hour before the scheduled server maintenance to update Vek'Na, something unexpected occurred.

!!Server Announcement!!

!!MYTHIC RAID FIRST FULL CLEAR!!

!!TOMB OF NILBOG!!

Players:

Aban Twice Crowned

HitZaDecs

Mattmanfoo

Mortimer Memento

Silv3r_Belle

Something thought impossible had occurred.

A group had beaten Vek'Na on Mythic difficulty.

4.17

———

"Strategy is simple. If you have more than one soldier on the field to the enemy's zero then you have won."
—*Madelyn the Skull Rain, the Great, the Conqueror, the Extremely Beautiful and Eligible Bachelorette and the please don't execute this scribe for not appropriately listing all your titles*

Noam," Dustin said. "Be annoying."

"Finally, my time has come," Noam replied with a grave face.

Stepping forward, Noam brought his twin hook swords out to bare and loudly said, "Aren't you an ugly lot?"

The tiefling almost staggered when the mana left his body.

"Did Frankenstein have a field day fucking the zoo or something?"

The second cast, the headache was almost a palpable force, yet he stood. Half of communication was body language, and his was cocksure, languid and lazy. One blade rested on his shoulder, the other held low as if he didn't see the enemy as a threat.

Vicious Mockery was not a costly spell, its effect was weaker than Biting Words and it didn't actually do damage, but there was a wonderful benefit to it. As dozens, hundreds of stitched together monsters who shifted their eyes to him demonstrated, they didn't have to understand him to feel the sharp feeling of irritation to the speaker.

"Think I got all of them?" he asked aloud.

"Two hundred and eleven out of two hundred and eight-four," he answered without pausing in his scanning gaze. "It is good enough."

Disappointment briefly flickered across his face, but his smile soon returned as he lowered his weapons.

"Now Catch These Hands," he quietly said.

. . .

Finally, Matt was somewhat serious.

Despite his best attempts to smother his smile, I could practically feel the eagerness as he raised his strange blades. I still thought those things weren't real weapons, but when he rushed forward at a speed I could barely see, blood sprayed, none of it his.

"He doesn't have any strength buffs so he must be cleaving them purely through the momentum of his buffed agility."

"Focus," I chided. I didn't need to bother with him for a few moments, he knew me enough to know the plan.

I raised a hand, stopping a few that wanted to go with him. He wouldn't appreciate people stealing his show.

"Naukoth, play Ilneval's Edge, Utoqa, catch the stragglers Noam isn't taking, Yellow will direct you."

Both quickly complied, Utoqa silent as Yellow got on his shoulder and Naukoth grumbled something about scratches.

My mind quickly sped up. A few extra seconds to consider variables. Invaluable.

"Attrition," Declan assessed.

"Agreed."

I began growing a bunch of Sporages in my hand. "Celine, do you have any stamina and energy restoring potions?"

"I do!" she quickly answered, hurriedly fumbling them out. She wasn't used to thinking faster. Her hands weren't as fast as she expected them to be.

"Pass them around and get used to this speed of thought," I said aloud. "I'll get you up to speed."

"Heh."

Assume authority, and people assume you have it.

"I require a general overview of your abilities. As quick and as concise as possible."

I already had an idea of a few of them just from Yellow observing. The brown-haired priest of war could heal with a touch, but I saw him raising a hand a few times and attacks that would've missed suddenly connected.

The dragonborn, Torrin something, used a lot of wide area of effect fire-based spells. She pretty much singlehandedly held off hordes of enemies for a while, but I have to assume she would be out of mana for now. Her two allies, the gnome and human, appeared to both be melee fighters who still seemed relatively topped up. The human was also the first to notice us coming. Something to remember.

The girl who wanted to run away used daggers and a crossbow, evoking the idea of a rogue. Just based on classical weapon conventions she wouldn't be very useful. The last was a red-haired spear user armored in decent mail and I didn't catch much other than that.

The replies given between sips of stamina potions quickly confirmed what I observed. Torrin had a trick that could **Prime** a spell to gradually grow in power and hit a lot harder, but out of her three prepared she had already used two.

The brown-haired healer could offset tiredness and fatigue for only himself when in battle, but would get them all dealt back to him later. That was how he managed to keep up until now. He would collapse once the battle was done, though I wanted to ask what constituted a "battle" ending we didn't have the time. For now, he's just a heal bot with a gimmick.

The others had a variety of useful mid-close combat abilities. The human with the dragonborn, Mehens, had sensory passives, a scout. The rogue was a hit and runner who can double herself for a short time but was better in taking down singular targets. The spear user Gohod could make his spear disappear from sight.

Ultimately minor in this sort of encounter, but something to keep track of.

"Stave em off until the dragon recharges?"

"We'll need to keep a constant rotation."

"Just need to grind it down," we said at once.

"Rogue girl." I pointed at a large trunk-like stalagmite with a broken-off tip about twenty meters from us. "Go there, don't bother with the riff-raff, aim for any that look particularly strong with your bow."

"My name is Rivita!" she yelled. "And isn't that a bit far off?!"

That spot was indeed a bit far from the main group, but ultimately, "We will be taking the main aggro of the enemies, you should be able to fight any stragglers that head your way."

She still looked unconvinced, and time was running out. My main focus was still on Noam as he used the head of an ape-like chimera as a foot-hold to jump into a perfect somersault before landing like a spinning top, decapitating and wounding several chimeras.

"Show off."

"Stupidly effective though."

But he was slowly but surely slowing. Every marked enemy he killed decreased his buff, and he'd eventually reach the point where he can't style on them with superior stats. He was already five percent slower than when he had his full buff. Not to mention how he still had a limited pool of stamina, and judging by how his mouth was constantly moving, he was still spewing insults as he did so, adding another strain to his stamina.

"Simply speaking, I wouldn't bet he'll last the next two minutes, let alone the day needed to finish his cooldown."

"If he played fully defensively, we wouldn't have this problem."

I smiled. *"But it wouldn't be the same."*

Focusing back on the rogue girl, I drily replied, "Worst comes to worst and we die, they will spend a few minutes eating us and you will be able to get a head start on running."

Surprisingly, that didn't seem to fill her with great confidence, but she did move eventually.

"Torrin, keep back, recover your mana and be prepared to use your last Primed spell, I'll tell you when to." The dragonborn nodded, likely too busy regening mana to formulate a proper answer.

"Utoqa, head back or get caught in the AOE!" I yelled. "Mehens, Gohod, gnome, form a perimeter behind me and Utoqa, with the piano behind you."

"What's AOE?" the gnome asked.

"Shorthand for area of effect," I replied, glancing at the slowly growing cluster grenade in my hand. The edges of my vision were slightly darkening, I was straining my mana. "Naukoth, prepare to swap to strength song. Utoqa, prepare to extract Noam."

In the distance, Noam was practically buried in the number of enemies. But for the briefest moment, he jumped, head poking out of the horde that was almost a singular writhing mass.

We exchanged glances.

"Naukoth, switch to your strength song *now*."

He did, and as he did so, three things happened. Noam threw out one of his blades, hooking unto the shoulder of a tall chimera, using it as leverage to throw himself over. I yelled for Utoqa to grab Noam and threw the bundle of Sporages I grew toward the airborne tiefling.

In midair, Noam swung the blunt side of his blade, batting it into the mass of enemies, before crashing into a group of peripheral chimeras.

Utoqa, the moment he saw Noam leap over, rushed forward, bone axe swinging out with deadly efficiency, carving his way to the fallen tiefling.

In front of them, the cluster Sporage grenade began to detonate as it banged into dozens of chimeras. Over the sound of dozens of creatures screaming in pain, there was the faint sound of Noam's laughter.

Here, the enormity of the cave worked against us, though the enemies were many they were spread out. The dragonborn was no slouch in terms of pure area of effect damage, at least four times better than me, but the *efficacy* of her usage was suboptimal. Often times she had wasted an entire area of effect spell on only one or two enemies.

It was a simple problem to fix. One of the first things a raiding party learned.

Noam gathered the crowd, and I killed it.

How many did I get? *"One-twenty? One-thirty?"*

Now to repeat a few more dozen times.

The ensuing conflict was not a fight, Elucidatium Swindoobly Vulgopopopot, called "Lucy" by her friends, decided.

It wasn't a massacre either, for when the strange myconid called her forward, she could see that it was tiring as well.

There was a pattern, alternating between Torrin and the myconid. The melee moved to hold the front, but also to herd the monsters into a single spot for the mages to destroy. When one tired, they swapped to regain mana.

The myconid was not as good as Torrin at destroying masses, it left creatures alive for a few moments to suffer the poison, so the more durable melees had been on his rotation, the savage lizardfolk and Gohod.

On the other hand, the tiefling was on the rotation Torrin, Mehens, and herself were on. Clearly more used to this form of combat, he yelled magical insults to draw them around him and he didn't care if he got singed by Torrin's runoff.

All the while, Rivita sniped tough-looking creatures that survived magical attacks, Lehems the cleric and the alchemist girl curing all manners of minor wounds and the large orc who was comically hunched over the relatively small grand piano kept everyone stronger during the battle.

Elucidatium Swindoobly Vulgopopopot frowned, this still wasn't a battle. It wasn't the desperate fight within an inch of her life she had just experienced. The myconid's constant call for rotations even allowed for everyone to take short rests! As the bodies piled up, it even started to become easier as the creatures had fewer angles to attack from.

This wasn't a fight at all. It was as if . . . as if . . . they were farmers harvesting crops.

Harvesting wasn't easy, it was tiring backbreaking work and there was still the chance of injury.

Yet . . .

If one kept a regular, almost casual pace, there was no chance of failure or death.

The myconid continued his orders, speaking in an almost bored yet firm tone like he'd done this hundreds of times. Making minute adjustments to everyone's position and ability usage. Pacing everyone with a calm she could not hope to muster even at her best.

Though Lucy tired as she fought, her strength sapped even when with regular rest. She slowly started to see it, through the constant grind and battle.

She could see the entire field harvested.

And soon enough.

It was.

Though it was fun at first, it slowly turned into the same grind all fights involving Decs had.

Dustin gave Noam the first initial hurrah to get everything started off, but by the time everyone started to collapse in relief and exhaustion, Noam's enthusiasm had dimmed completely as he and Utoqa finished off the last few stragglers. Strange one, that lizard, he did everything with unerring efficiency and followed orders to the letter. He felt blank in the same way Declan used to.

Oh well.

When Dustin took command, victory was assured in a way Noam never could've had. There needed to be a lot more than mere *numbers* to be any real difficulty for him. This was the same madman who calculated the exact amount of damage, time, character builds, and items it would take to kill several dozen Mythic tier raid bosses, each with unique abilities and phases that could wipe an unprepared party.

Declan believed these weren't that big a deal because anyone could make the same calculations and reach the same conclusions, but the problem was just that. Plenty of people *could*, but Declan was the one who *did*.

Noam could've kept the creatures off them for a long while, but not kill them. He'd been around Declan's rambling long enough that he could figure out how his build was *supposed* to work. Even when it was really more of a joke build.

"We need to hurry up and get out," Dustin said, barely standing as he leaned on his staff. "We can't stay here for long."

Noam frowned, Dustin looked worried, more than usual. "What's wrong?"

Dustin glanced at him before his eyes darted back to the entrance. Hundreds of bodies practically buried the way, yet his eyes jumped around as if expecting something *more*.

"Greenie died halfway through the encounter," he quietly answered. "He has yet to come back."

"Ah." Of course, that freaked him out more than hundreds of enemies could have. The thing Declan could never get over was the fear of not knowing.

Almost on cue, a huge creature burst through the entrance, throwing back hundreds of limp bodies.

"Finally." Noam smiled. There was the raid boss.

4.18

"Fifty-eight. The best thing about Shadesmar is that no matter what pit of despair you find yourself in, you always know there is an even deeper, even darker pit of despair you didn't realize existed."

—*Excerpt from* Ethanial's Enchiridion of Encounters

I couldn't decide if it was easier or harder without numbers.

On one hand, I don't need to keep accurate track of health, mana, and stamina points.

On the other hand, I *can't* keep accurate track of health, mana, and stamina points.

Without exact calculations, everything had to be estimated and horrifically, that meant *inaccuracies.*

So, when half the group fell down in exhaustion, I knew we reached the fourth-worst outcome.

Two of my safety nets were gone. The potions we had were exhausted in order to keep optimal rotations and Greenie was MIA.

Which made the current situation trickier.

As the great beast shoved aside a pile of bodies, some people hurriedly stood back up.

"But not enough," my other grumbled.

Very annoying. The cleric was completely unconscious, and while the spear user and the gnome with the absurdly long name were still conscious, they were clearly very tired.

Noam was still somewhat fresh, given his Breathless skill and just being more used to pacing himself than the others.

Utoqa was already up, that guy didn't seem to tire at all.

The dragonborn Torrin stood but there was blood flowing down her nose and she wobbled slightly. Unfortunate.

Her companion Mehens was doing a lot better, tired but had gotten a lot of time to rest.

Celine and the rogue, Rivita, were still fresh given that they stayed out of the main fight.

Naukoth was still playing his song so—

My brows crossed.

Naukoth is tired.

I saw it now that I looked at him closely, his back was hunched, his head hanging low, and his fingers moved with far more care than before.

"*Shit,*" we both thought. "*He's the important one.*"

"It is a miracle," a voice called out, "how you managed to hold out this long."

I didn't turn so much as I shifted my attention back to the beast. The thing was huge, at least five meters tall and wide. A hairy beast made the base, eight crustacean-like appendages shot out from each side, hair obscuring the base where they connected. It had three heads, a blue gecko-like head on the left, a craggy, rock-like feline head, and an eyeless beak on the right.

I was on the last rotation, so bubbles of poisonous spores still permeated the air, yet it shoved through them as if they were nothing.

"Yellow," I whispered, "tell Torrin to prepare her Prime spell."

From the back of the chimera, parting the long sinuous hair, a figure rose. Demon-like horns and red skin. A tiefling similar to Noam, he wore baggy olive-green robes which obscured most of his body. Adorned on the robes were green symbols of a water spring and he wore a sash across his chest, holding three crystalline test tubes filled with a foggy liquid.

Wait.

"*Shit.*"

I recognized that symbol, I read about it as the one representing the Oasis. Did that mean those test tubes . . .

"Has the Ivory Tower finally started to take this seriously? You are not riff-raff, yet you are not that powerful either. Some elite group sent to scout?"

There was a pause, before Noam spoke up: "We're not really a part of the Ivory Tower."

"Huh?" the cultist spoke with a bit of confusion. "You are not whelps from the Ivory Tower?"

"We were paid to help out," Noam added carefully.

To the right of us, Rivita was shuffling down the broken stump, did she plan to run? I can't assume she will be of any help soon.

"Which guild are you part of?"

"I'm not with anyone, other than the mushroom over here." Noam gestured toward me.

Good timing. Torrin flinched a bit when Yellow touched her foot, but his attention was on me for the brief moment.

"Are any of you part of a guild? Or a band?"

"I'm not."

"Did they just pay *random* people to throw themselves in here?"

There was a brief exchange of awkward glances.

"You're saying," he began in disbelief, "that their three-year-long pursuit of me from the edges of Madelyn's Cease to the Whispering Mountains and finally to the shores of the Tyrian, where I have decided to hold my final stand. They surrounded me on all sides and spent weeks to assemble a force, *and they decided to outsource our final battle to random people on the street!?*"

"That's capitalism for you."

Noam laughed, as well as someone behind me, Mehens? Huh, I took him to be the quiet badass type.

The cultist didn't seem to think I was as funny.

"You will die first," he snarled, "then your friends. Then those *fools* outside!"

"These people aren't really my friends—" in the middle of my sentence, I thought, *"Now."*

As Yellow made the signal, Torrin's arms were wreathed in flame, before they shot out. Fire splashed onto the Chimeric creature, lighting it aflame in a burst of light!

"—so you won't have to kill them."

The cultist fell off the writhing and burning creature with a scream, giving me a few seconds to cobble a plan together.

"Noam," I said, "Knife situation, go for the mage seriously."

"And if he has a decent defensive spell?"

"We're fucked."

"Buy time for us to take out the chimera."

"Prepare to fight!" I yelled. "Focus on the big one first!"

Wasted words as it turned out, as they were already moving to action. Utoqa rushed forward, his body low to the ground; in moments, he was under the flaming creature, his axe swinging wide and slashing its underbelly.

The creature roared in pain, three heads united in agony, but instead of blood, a pure black ichor dripped out. Utoqa rushed out before it fell on him, but there was a great sizzling as the ichor burned the ground.

Behind me, Mehens was helping Torrin and the gnome up. Naukoth gritted his teeth and continued his strength song.

Right now we had to bust down the chimera. Torrin used her last spell for the fight, so I remained the last active mage on the field. I swiftly reviewed my options, I was at around eighty percent mana, my high Wisdom giving me enough mana regen to last with a bit of decent parceling. The creature was on fire which was actually detrimental to me, spores would burn up and my acid would extinguish the fire. For now, I should focus on utility support. Flinging my arm out, I used my third contingency. Two Mushroom Meals grew out of my arm, the pancake-like brown mushroom sprouting out swiftly. A costly spell that was, only two casts and I lost a third of my max mana. My vision shook slightly, I was at half mana now, a bit more and I would be past my mana dependency threshold.

However, trading my combat effectiveness for two other combatants was worth it.

I began moving, pulling the meals off.

Utoqa was rushing in out of the creature's range, exchanging axe swings with shelled appendages, he wouldn't need it and I shouldn't break his rhythm.

Rivita and Mehens were still fresh, Rivita seeing the tide turn seemed to have overcome her cowardice and she was shooting arrows toward where Noam ran circles around the mutating cultist.

Naukoth needed one; if he stopped, our combat efficacy would fall dramatically. Next had to be one of the tired melees, the gnome and spear user, and while I would love to get the cleric back up, he was unconscious.

I moved to them. "Eat this!" I yelled, throwing one toward Mehens. "They restore stamina!"

Next was Naukoth. "Open your mouth!" I threw it directly in, the orc started chewing furiously, sweat dripping from his forehead.

"We need to free the other!" Torrin yelled, leaning on Mehens, she was clutching her head.

"Which one!" I yelled, glancing toward the two already downed bodies on the ground. I checked them already, concussion on one and blood loss for the other. Both were beyond my power.

"Not them," the gnome yelled as she pointed behind Naukoth. "The wall is an illusion, there's a person trapped behind it!"

She rushed toward me, taking bites of the mushroom as she did so. "We need to get her out!" grabbing my hand, she dragged me directly into the stone wall.

We passed through it harmlessly, entering a small crack in the stone.

"You guys left this perfectly good choke point!" I yelled as she dragged me through.

"We had to!" she replied, before dragging me a few meters where the crack opened up, revealing a room approximately four meters in length and diameter. In front of us were dozens, hundreds of vines coiled lazily at the back of the room. In the center, a girl in leather armor was trapped, practically subsumed into the endless vines.

Her eyes were open, but not seeing, and I soon realized why. The vines ended in serrated, lamprey-like mouths and they fed on her, biting onto any piece of exposed skin, leaving small red dotted circles wherever they drank.

I saw why they abandoned this spot, they wouldn't have fit and the vines would've attacked them.

"Can you get her out without harming her?"

The dragonborn must've been unable to help as well, the girl must've already been trapped before she could do anything. Her flames would've burned the victim as well.

"Unlikely, but I'll try," I said as I stepped up, raising both arms. "Step back and be prepared to catch me, this will be the last of my mana."

My eyes followed the vines trapping the girl back to their roots, and I sprayed. These vines were vulnerable to them, their shape meant more surface area was exposed. As the Poison Spores touched the vines, they shook and died. Low health creatures, lucky for us.

I fell to a knee, the gnome catching me before I fell further. My mind was fading. I blinked in and out of consciousness.

"Don't fall asleep here."

"Get her," I muttered through gritted teeth.

She did, using her sword to cut away the remaining vines still stuck on the trapped person. As the girl fell the gnome caught her, a lot taller than her but the gnome held on.

The formerly trapped girl was breathing; as she fell, I noticed three swords on her belt. "Hurry up," I muttered. The gnome slumped her over her shoulder, bringing her toward me, giving her bites of the meal as the girl gaped her mouth.

"Where . . ."

"You're not dead," I muttered, "which, depending on your outlook, could be a good or bad thing."

The gnome grabbed my hand and dragged me outwards. My main vision was fading in and out of black, but my other eyes were still active.

The chimera had ceased burning, revealing underneath the fur a battered and burned body covered in scars and stitches. It opened one of its mouths, the blue gecko head, and sprayed out a white frost. Utoqa reached into his pouch and pulled out a furred cloak much larger than anything the pouch should've held, before covering himself in it.

The cold touched the cloak, stopping as Utoqa reached into his pouches again. He pulled out a white fibrous sac before throwing it overhead like a grenade. The thing exploded into a fine black dust that fell onto the creature. When the dust moved I realized with slight disgust that each speck of "black dust" was actually a tiny spider. Dozens of them skittered into the exposed wounds created by the stitches and scars and the chimera screamed again as it closed the gecko and opened the beak head.

Utoqa discarded his cloak, reaching into his pouches again as we burst through the wall illusion.

The brown-haired girl was fully conscious now. "What the fuck . . ."

"Wake up and fight," I said, before adding, "or run; that is an option, too."

She stood up, getting off the gnome before drawing one of her swords, a curved sabre.

The gnome let me go, and I fell onto my staff, leaning on it. *Send the gnome to help against the big one. Torrin and the cleric are inactive, figure out what the girl can do,* my other ordered.

"I need to regen mana. Gnome, go help Mehens and Utoqa on the chimera, brown-haired girl, tell me what you can do."

"I can swing a sword," she said.

"Good enough, the chimera only has heads on one side, while Utoqa keeps them busy hit it from its left, right and back."

I couldn't finish, as I saw Noam lose an arm.

Hook swords were hard to use.

They were clearly designed with flair and style, but retained function and quality, at the cost of usability.

They were hard weapons to use. At first, Noam used them like he would normal dual swords, but that didn't work. The hooked ends meant that, if he didn't cut clean through something, then it would catch and he'd need to deal with his weapon inside his opponent. Normally not a problem, but if you were dealing with multiple enemies, then it was pretty annoying.

So, Noam did what he did best. He learned.

As he rushed the red-skinned cultist, he hooked them by the ends and threw it out like a whip. The crescent hilt drew a bloody line across the cultist's face before it was thrown back. The ends threatened to unhook, to fall apart, but with a thought, they magnetized together into a straight blade.

The weight wasn't right, but it didn't matter. Using the leftover momentum, Noam smoothly transitioned into a twirl, spinning the long halberd-like weapon almost three-hundred degrees before he came at the cultist from the other side!

But the cultist was prepared now, throwing up his right arm to block, his skin swiftly calcified into a hardened exoskeleton.

Yet the crescent hilt still slammed into the exoskeleton with great force. The red-skinned tiefling yelped in surprise as the armor cracked, simple physics making the head much stronger than anything Noam could've managed.

The cultist staggered back, trying to create distance. *Mistake,* Noam thought. He only dealt such devastating damage *because* of distance. The end of his weapon traveled a far greater distance than at the base where he held it, and the nature of the hilt also meant more energy was directed into a small surface area. That's the reason polearms were the premier weapon before firearms.

Yet the cultist was not done, he took out his other hand, green energy weaving in between his fingers.

"A mage, huh." Noam rushed in, forced to close the distance. His weapon unhooked back into a pair of swords. Five meters between them and the cultist finished his spell, a ball of fire thrown directly at him.

But Noam tanked it directly, his fire resistance meant it was naught but a warm breeze. Yet even then, he closed his eyes for the briefest moment as the light seared him.

In that brief moment, the cultist stepped to the side, his armored hand thrown out to smash into Noam's face.

With his eyes still closed, Noam tilted back and like a professional limbo player he went under the cultist's arm, scoring another slash as his blade bit into the cultist's exposed side!

The cultist snarled as he leaped back, but the blade was hooked, and the maneuver only served to impale him from the back!

"Gotta do better than that," Noam taunted with a smile. "Decs loves that trick."

"You will pay for that!" the cultist snarled in a language like crackling fire.

Noam smirked, and in Infernal, he replied, "I can afford it!"

"Damn, I always wanted to use that comeback."

The cultist snarled, his armored hand tried to unhook himself, but Noam simply dragged him closer.

He swung his free blade, a Swift Strike aiming for the cultist's neck!

In panicked desperation, the cultist blocked with his unarmored arm, trying to catch it.

Yet it did nothing, as the hook sword bit into his hand, right in between the middle and ring fingers, spliting it open down the middle!

Slowly, the blade traveled up his arm, and the split continued upward toward his chest!

"Wait."

The split in the cultist's arm was perfectly down the middle and traveling farther than the blade.

Noam's eyes widened as the cultist's left arm opened into two perfect halves, revealing teeth. His blade was still inside. Noam tried to withdraw his blade, but with unnatural elasticity, the cultist brought his own arm past his blade, past his wrist until Noam's arm was in between the two split halves.

With great force, the two halves bit together, severing Noam's arm above the elbow.

"ARRRGGHH!"

Noam fell backward, his right arm severed completely as blood flowed, yet as he found his footing, his grip on the other weapon remained.

The cultist snarled. With a step forward, he push kicked Noam, trying to dislodge his grip.

Noam gritted his teeth, trying to pull the enemy closer, yet his grip was weak now and the cultist remained standing.

Another powerful push kick slammed into his stomach and Noam vomited what little remained in his stomach.

A third kick slammed into his chest, winding him. Noam lost his breath and finally, he let go and fell to the ground.

He tried to get back up, but the cultist simply stepped forward, stomping on his chest. With his armored arm, the cultist grabbed his head by the horn, before slamming it down!

Noam felt his mind waver as his head was slammed into the ground again. The stone cracked beneath him, and blood flowed.

It took five slams, each shattering the ground, for Noam to stop moving.

The cultist let go, spitting on the unconscious tiefling, before turning his attention to his battling minion.

4.19

"Fifty-nine. My expectations for the next pit were low, but holy fuck."

—*Excerpt from* Ethan's Enchiridion of Encounters

K nife situation had failed.

"Scratch that," I said to the girl, who I absentmindedly realized was an elf. "Follow me to keep the weirdo busy."

She helped me up. "Are you sure?"

"It's that or we let him take out our bard," I said. The red-skinned tiefling was already walking toward us. The giant piano wasn't exactly hidden.

"Feel that extra strength and speed?" I asked. "That's him." I thumbed toward the sweating orc.

Utoqa was managing the large one, but only *just*. He was only one lizard and while Mehens, Rivita, and the gnome were helping him out, they were only dealing surface wounds. Only Utoqa's bone tomahawk was dealing any significant damage through the thing's tough hide, and he was distracted fending off the bursts of cold frost dealt by the gecko head.

That chimera hadn't used its two other heads yet. It almost used the beak but closed it when its master finished off Noam.

More worryingly, Utoqa threw away his trinkets right after using them, including the cold-resistant fur cloak. Those things had to be one use, or close enough that it didn't matter to keep them.

The tiefling was only a few dozen meters from us now. His left hand was split into two halves, one grabbing a foggy test tube, the other picking up a chimera corpse—a turtle-like creature with a green shell and a dog head.

Throwing both in the air, the two halves of the arm slammed together, eating them. The lump of the corpse moved up the arm and into his body.

"His right arm is armored, but not by a lot. Left arm splits into two, each highly dexterous and has at least enough force to cleanly remove an arm."

As the corpse piece was consumed, a foggy, dirty glow seemed to emanate from him. Green liquid seeped out of his right arm and the cracked armor was covered by a green shell. The cut on his face healed as a line of brown shaggy fur.

"He's wearing baggy clothing; assume he has hidden weapons underneath."

The tiefling paused as I said that, before hurrying.

I cast Balm Spores on the girl, healing the bleeding wounds.

"Don't get grappled."

His arms split into two and the elf rushed forward.

He began with a right, the large shelled fist aiming for the elf's face. She managed to parry it, the blow sliding off her blade, but his two split hands came from behind, more like tentacles than arms.

I spat a glob of acid, splashing at the base where they split. The arm screeched as it spasmed, but the man seemed unaffected. A separate entity from him perhaps?

The elf stepped forward, her blade aiming for the man's neck. Yet when it hit the exposed piece, only the sound of metal clanging could be heard as the blade rebounded back.

She was surprised for a second, an unintentional step back. Just long enough for him to draw back his arm for a grapple.

A bright yellow cap appeared over the edge of the elf's shoulder as Yellow threw Sneezing Spores directly into his face.

The tiefling's face scrunched up as he sneezed, long enough for the girl to jump out of the damage range.

"Tank, highly variable weapons and likely has all important organs protected."

"Do you have another way to deal damage to him, girl!?" I yelled as I threw Poison Spores onto him. Hacking coughs came out as he tried to wave away the green spores.

"Noam still managed to deal damage to his sides and face. Non-essential parts may not be protected."

"Other than stabbing!?"

"Yes!"

The cultist recovered, throwing out his left arms like whips. The girl dodged, jumping just out of the way. I wasn't as fast, taking a stance, the two limbs slammed into me, the teeth raking through my bark armor. They held, but my footing didn't. I was thrown off the ground, even with extra strength I simply didn't have the weight to leverage it. *We really need to fix that.*

The elf yelled in worry as I crashed, "Are you—"

"Murder him!" I yelled as I struggled back up.

The tentacle hands curled around me, I smiled and let out a burst of Poison Spores. The things fell away, writhing in pain.

Right in front of me, the elf clashed with the cultist again. A glowing sword blow blocked by an armored hand, and the armor *gave*. The exoskeleton cracked, drawing blood. The cultist switched tactics—with a spin he tripped the elf, and a glint of metal was revealed underneath his clothing. One headed straight to me.

I raised my right arm to block as a long, wicked needle stabbed into it. I felt something thick and viscous injected. A scorpion tail, some kind of venom was given to me. I flung away my arm, the tail swiftly skulking away before I could attack.

The situation in front went to shit, the girl fell to the ground and the cultist was rearing up to mete out a powerful blow. No time to deal with the venom, I had to hope my racial skill would cover it.

I raised my right arm, aiming a bit higher so as to not hit the prone swordswoman, and cast Poison Spores.

There was a crackling sound as my arm screamed in *strangeness*. I couldn't see what happened underneath the bark, but my arm split and bent as there was a sound like popcorn popping.

Multi-colored dust sprayed harmlessly out of a dozen new openings in my arm, just as the cultist punched the girl and threw her several dozen meters.

The cultist spoke again as the girl landed with a *thump*. Waving, in smugness and triumph, the scorpion tail that glinted of metal, he said, "You *think* I didn't prepare for mages?"

Of course he did. That guy said Ivory Tower was a mainly mages guild.

The hunt was going well.

Utoqa landed the fourth blow on the creature's front right leg, finally severing it. He jumped back, from his pouch he retrieved a claw as the creature breathed ice again.

Throwing the claw to the ground, it grew gigantic and he hid behind it.

The creature could not keep its breath on him for long, for other hunters wounded it. The bow user split in shadow, one jumping onto the creature's back and severing stitches, while the bow kept firing. Short soft skin and soft skin sword user darted in and out, not doing damage but being a nuisance. Soft skin sword user seemed to know attacks before they saw them, a useful ability.

Frost breath was off him now, Utoqa jumped out of cover, Gift in hand, he slashed at the flesh, drawing black ichor. He avoided that blood, soft skin spear user already lost an arm to it.

The hunt was going well, but he was running out of Crafts. He cannot **Scavenge** more from this hunt. The metal pieces soft-skins used had better be worth it.

There was a hard crack toward Utoqa's left, one of his eyes turned to it. The red horned skin had punched another soft skin with enough force to send it flying.

Red horned skin had more limbs now, two where his left arm was supposed to be, and a tail. He laughed at the bark mushroom—Dustin, before his split arms took a crystal vial from his hand, and threw it toward them.

Utoqa jumped back, was it like the cloaked stalker- Celine?

No, the creature opened its third mouth. The one that was a large bird beak, revealing rows and rows of serrated teeth, and there was a sound.

Sucking.

Utoqa jumped farther away as a great force began drawing him toward the creature. He slammed Gift into the ground, anchoring himself.

The thrown vial flew in, along with many of the dead prey. The teeth he hid behind. All flew into its mouth before it closed.

There was a sound, grinding. The beak seemed to rapidly spin. It was chewing.

A dirty fog began emanating from the creature. Its cuts healed, burned skin calcified into bone some places and grew fur other places. A dozen different heads sprouted from its back and four different tails shot out. Shadow tried to swipe at it, only for a newly sprouted head to shatter it.

Its front right leg grew back.

Hunt wasn't going well.

Noam's body lay unmoving, a web of broken stone around his body.

Slowly, unnoticed on the battlefield, a shadow walked to him.

Celine pulled off the hood of her cloak as she kneeled by the body.

"Baba said that Travelers disappear if they give up," she whispered. "You haven't yet."

Her dark ratty cloak shifted and twirled, almost like a living being. The things strapped to her body were changed. From empty potion bottles to dolls, save for two straps, where glowing red and blue potions lay. The cloak handed her the red potion, and she poured it down Noam's throat.

There was a hacking cough as Noam returned to consciousness, small scratches and scars healed. His stump of an arm ceased bleeding.

He tried to rise, but he was coughing too much. Celine held him to stabilize him, helping him sit.

"Ah . . . let me at him again, Decs . . . I can murder that fucker . . ."

"You can't! Your arm's off!" Celine urgently whispered. Glancing around in fear, trying to avoid notice from the battle behind her.

"'Tis but a . . . scratch . . . wound . . ." he muttered as he slowly regained consciousness.

His eyes finally regained lucidity as the potion coursed through him.

"Ah shit, my arm is actually gone," he disappointedly muttered as he held the stump.

"It's here," Celine said, her cloak moving the severed arm to her side. It was cut cleanly and still bled slightly. "I can fix it."

"How?" Noam asked, a gentle curiosity on his face.

The girl had a complicated face, but carefully she said, "I will need some things."

"What things?" Noam asked, seeing her hesitate.

"Blood and hair, best given freely—"

Noam raised his remaining arm, pulling a bit of hair from his head, as well as cupping a bit of leftover blood from his stump.

"Hurry up, please," Noam said, his eyes glancing at the fight. "Dusts will give me a shit time otherwise."

With a slightly surprised face, Celine took a dusty, brown doll from her belts, and carefully, she let the blood drip onto the doll, as well as dipping her fingers in it.

Quickly, but with great proficiency, she drew a circle of blood on the ground, the bloodied doll in the center, she took the hair and scattered it around the doll.

Holding her hands together, her fingertips touching each other to form a triangle, she quietly chanted in a language old and ancient—one simultaneously incomprehensible and understandable:

Bind the flesh, bind the bone.

The blood writhed as if living, rising, and spinning.

Form the link to make like-kind.

The sprayed hairs moved, weaving themselves into the doll, stitching cloth together.

So, bleed as one, heal as one.

The doll began to shake violently, writhing. The right arm exploded off, white fluff flowing like blood. The doll's head was slammed into the ground, five times, not more, not less.

Now one fate, forever twined.

The spinning blood fell onto the ground, and the doll ceased moving.

"Well, that was intense," Noam muttered casually.

Celine let out a tired gasp, catching her breath before her cloak handed her a needle, threaded with a white silvery thread.

"Now, this might hurt," she said as she held the needle.

She placed Noam's arm by his side, before picking up the doll and its severed arm. Carefully, she stabbed the needle through the arm stump of the doll. Noam felt a pinching feeling, the same spot as the doll.

Celine threaded silver thread through the doll, and a phantasmal silver thread appeared through Noam's arm stump.

Carefully, she pulled the thread through, before joining it with the severed doll arm.

The silver thread on Noam's arm mimicked the action, stabbing itself into the severed arm.

She repeated the action, using the silver thread to create another connection. Each time, the phantasmal thread on Noam's actual arm mimicked the action, and slowly, the silvery thread stitched Noam back together.

"Now that," Noam said with a smile, "is awesome."

He looked at his weapons, thrown on the ground. Dual swords didn't work, neither did polearms.

"Wait."

The weapons handles were pointed away from him, from that perspective . . .

"I have an idea, do you have any cloth?"

Shit.

The cultist rushed toward Naukoth, I had to stop him, but my magic was disabled. Of course antimagic measures existed! This was a fucking high fantasy world! What kind of venom did he use? Why did the possibility never cross my mind!?

"Shut up and stop him!"

"How!?" I yelled back as I stepped in between them.

The cultist splayed out his tentacle arm, the insides of it were coated with sharp knife-like teeth.

I had no options. *"I lose a contest of strength due to lack of weight. I have no magic. What could I do!? How do I Analyze my way out of this!?"*

"Just block the way for a few seconds!" my other yelled.

The tentacle arms flew toward me, faster than a whip and twice as dangerous. Could I use Pacifying Spores? No, that thing definitely had a higher Constitution than me. I braced myself for impact, knowing full well it'd do nothing.

There was a whirring sound as something metallic spun through the air and severed the mouth arm.

Both pieces fell, just as the weapon hit the ground with a thump and I saw what it was.

Noam's hook sword, the crescent guard embedded into the ground.

The cultist turned to see Noam standing, his left arm forward in the motion of throwing while his severed right arm attached by ethereal silver string held a glowing blue potion as he chugged it. His remaining hook sword was stabbed into the ground from the hilt end.

He threw the empty bottle to the ground, the glass shattering.

"Now," he began, taking a deep breath, "*now,* you have my attention, you pajama-wearing goat-fucking goblin-smelling pussy-armed son of clype acne-ridden red-faced baboon-assed worthless bag of filth pissed from the bleeding dickhole of a gonorrhea-suffering murloc spawned from the sniveling worm eyes of a bleating foal. I'd insult you but Mother Nature has clearly beaten me to the punch, or was it your own mother? You curdled staggering mutant dwarf insult to decency, richly suffused with offal and the drool of sewer slimes so deficient in basic human cognitive function that it goes beyond understanding."

He took another deep breath.

"I've seen fungi more charming than your backstabbing ass stitched from whatever good looking parts you could beg from a butcher's store to compensate for your negative charisma. And how the fuck are the sperm that *won?* I don't think I've ever seen someone actually look *better* with a knife in their face! I'd call you dung but that'd be an insult to dung! You micropenis bobby dipshit pillock lickspittle gremlin milksop, have some decency and at least try to hide your face! And no, I am not insulting you, but describing you!"

The cultist shook as if physically wounded. Words beat on his body and his face contorted in anger as he turned to Noam. All reason and sense lost.

"And I bet your mother was a hamster and your father smelled of elderberries!" he yelled.

That was the final straw, as the cultist charged, screaming in a blind rage, his body afire, but my attention wasn't on him.

I looked at Noam. He leaned slightly forward, his eyes never left his opponent. He picked up his hook sword, holding it by the blade. The hook was underneath his pinky and the guard held up in a way that looked like an axe.

"Celine fixed him up."

He was no longer smiling.

Noam nodded, knowing I was looking, before rushing the maddened and on fire cultist, an axe in hand.

"That is dealt with," we both thought at once.

I rushed to check the elven swordswoman; a pile of bodies broke her fall. I quickly checked her pulse, bark moving away to reveal my bare fingers. Still alive, I grabbed her eyelids, forcing them open. Movement. She winced slightly, still conscious.

"She's still conscious," a voice muttered from beside me.

"Can you help her?" I asked Celine.

"I have some herbs that can help . . . but I gave my emergency health and mana potion to Noam . . ." she replied apologetically.

"Stabilize her," I said. "Guard her, at the very least. I need to help out on the other side." Not that I knew how.

Yellow had jumped off her at the moment of impact and was surveying the battlefield as I instructed. The chimera fight was going poorly. That thing was faster and possessed far more limbs after drinking what I was sure was some version of Oasis Water. Had to be diluted or weakened somehow, the mutations were far too random.

If that was the same Oasis Water I had read about, the only thing we could've done was run.

Noam was handling the cultist, now purely focused on taking down the opponent instead of dragging it out for fun.

He still needed his other weapon.

I ran, grabbing his thrown weapon with my remaining left hand, raising it much like he did. "NOAM!!"

He gave me a grateful look, which quickly turned sour as the throw went completely wide.

"Great aim."

Ah shit, I still had trash Dexterity.

Nonetheless, Noam jumped toward it, catching it in mid-air by the handle. The cultist tried a swing at him, but he was too blinded by rage to calculate the distance correctly, his arm fell just short.

"DON'T LET HIM DRINK THE OTHER POTION!" I yelled. That last potion remained the most dangerous factor in this battle.

Almost as if reading my mind, he used his twinned weapons to slash at the cultist's sash. Cutting it off, before kicking it toward me.

Oh Goddamnit! That idiot! It can't crack onto the ground!

I rushed to grab it, jumping forward with my arms outstretched. Crashing into the ground just as the sash hit my face, the tube still safely sealed. With great care, I stuffed it into my cap, before turning my attention away and rushing toward the chimera. The cultist was far too blinded by rage now to do anything that could harm Noam.

Right now, I had to stabilize the other situation.

The chimera had grown several times uglier if that was even possible. Rivita was in shock—Yellow saw her eyes go blank when her shadow got chomped, what an annoying drawback. Utoqa no longer attacked, instead focusing purely on defense, while Mehens and the gnome were completely off to the side, Mehens trying a crossbow that failed to pierce that thing's skin.

They needed either another damage dealer or a tank.

I didn't know when the venom would cease working, for all I knew it would last for hours. We didn't have that.

Right now wasn't the worst situation possible. Utoqa kept its attention, but we didn't have an effective damage dealer except him, and he could only fill one role at a time. Torrin had been ineffectively trying to cast spells since the battle began. I needed to tank it and let Utoqa act as our damage dealer. Yellow was running toward us now, and Noam had the cultist handled. We had no healer, but if we could pull off the classic trifecta-

"Grrf!"

The music stopped. Something I had slowly, but surely, put at the back of my mind.

Both Yellow and I turned toward Naukoth, to see the severed mouth arm of the cultist coiled around him like a demented snake. His own shovel-like hands were straining against them, trying to pull it off, but the thing contracted and Naukoth's head popped like a grape.

"*Shit.*"

Behind us, Utoqa became *just slightly* too slow and was hit by a tail. He was sent flying before crashing into me.

My vision became rolling earth, but I could still see through Noam and Yellow. On the other side, there was the sound of clanging metal as Noam slammed his axe into the cultist's neck. It didn't cut, but he hit it with his other blade, forcing it into through the cultist's skin. Drawing blood.

Noam slammed into the sword again, finally forcing the guard halfway into the neck! Once more and blood sprayed as he decapitated the cultist.

There was a horrific scream and Yellow turned to see the chimera crying out in pain. Only one head cried out, and it was the middle one. The stone feline head.

We crashed into a large stalagmite. Utoqa slammed into me, his fall was cushioned, but he fell off, spitting blood.

I tried to stand, only to fall again and realize the ground was shaking. *"No, the whole cavern is shaking."*

Everywhere I looked, stone shook violently as the middle head screamed. Ah.

So that was what the middle head did.

The cavern collapsed, and rocks fell upon us all.

"Wake up!"

Darkness.

"I said wake up!"

There was a voice screaming in my head.

"Get up you dropped child!"

My return to lucidity was sudden. One moment there was darkness, the next, I found myself in a small, darkened crevice.

"WAKE UP!"

"I heard you!" I yelled back in frustration.

My body felt sore. My right arm felt strange, as if someone had rewired every nerve along it. It was bleeding as well. Viscous brown blood fell from it.

I tried to stand up, and stone debris fell off me, including the stone that had knocked me unconscious. My hand fell on something.

It was the Magician card, and it was pointed away from me, so I saw it was downside up.

"Where did that come from?" Regardless, I put it into my cap, before surveying the place.

The stalagmite me and Utoqa fell against—a single large stone slab stabbed into its tip, creating a ceiling that shouldered the worst of it. Where was Utoqa?

I saw him. He lay next to the stalagmite, slightly obscured by a pile of stones. There was a large stone shard protruding from his gut.

"Shit."

I hurried toward him, my soft blue glow lighting up the darkness somewhat. Kneeling beside him, I brushed away the loose stone and dirt to check him over.

The shard was approximately seven centimeters in diameter and four centimeters in width. Stuck inside where the intestines should be.

"He's a lizard folk, would they even have similar anatomy?"

"Be useful and search up lizard anatomy," I shot back.

"Fuck . . . I'm not sure. These diagrams don't translate well to a biped form."

I was more worried about blood loss. Even now the liquid pooled into an ever-growing pond.

What could I do? *"You can't remove the shard, that would exacerbate the bleeding."* I had no health potions, nor could I use magic. Wait, no—I had to check.

I tried casting Light Spores with my broken arm, but nothing except ineffective dust sprayed out of the shattered remains.

"Was it just localized to that arm?" It didn't matter, I shouldn't risk destroying my operational arm. My only healing spell was Balm Spores and this was beyond its ability to fix. Maybe it could stop the bleeding, but that wasn't a surety, not with a wound this big.

What kind of venom was injected into me? Had to be specialized in magic disruption, I was feeling no other side effects. Unless they were extremely subtle.

"Wasn't your blood yellow?"

Yes, it should be. *"It only appears brown because it's under blue light."*

"Mixing yellow and blue doesn't yield brown, but green," he shot back.

"Then what—"

"Orange," he quickly answered. My vision swapped to his, a google search page. *"Complimentary colors."*

Then whatever venom it was, it made my blood orange. Made it a darker hue.

"One. Darker hues, toward red."

Two. Magic disruption effects.

My mind connected the dots.

"Iron!" we both thought at once.

The cultist injected pure iron into my system. Likely in a dust form. That was why magic failed.

"But how does that help?" I asked.

"It opens up the other option."

Oh.

Yes, that remained an option.

Utoqa stirred, and I leaned down beside him. "Who is there?" he weakly called out.

"Me, Dustin," I replied.

"I am . . . hurt . . ."

"I don't really have the means to fix that," I replied, slightly apologetic. "My magic is disrupted, and I don't have a good healing spell, regardless."

He gasped in pain, straining to speak. "No . . . no way?"

"There is one way," I said. "But I would prefer your agreement on the matter."

"I agree," he instantly said.

"I—I didn't even—"

"I agree, Dustin," the lizardfolk repeated, his reptilian eyes strained on me, the only source of light in the room. "I will survive." He spoke with a monotone and . . . almost fanatical type of certainty. "Survive, no matter what."

I looked him in the eye.

There it was.

The madness that made people want to live.

I sighed. "Very well, then."

From the inside of my cap, I pulled out the crystalline test tube holding the Oasis Water, putting it to the side, I picked up his tomahawk with my left hand.

With only the slightest bit of hesitation. I cut two fingers off my useless right hand.

"Let us be logical about this. It wouldn't do to find out halfway I'm poisonous."

4.20

———

"And so, the Princess saw the great suffering of her peasants and farmers and did nothing. Then came the ledgers for this month's tax collection. And she declared war on the Plague Dragon."
—*Excerpt from* The First Princess

While I didn't understand the exact mechanics of Traveler death, there were some certainties.

One, a Traveler will die if their body is compromised and damaged beyond what was capable of keeping stable operations. However, the exact time when the body begins to disintegrate is unknown, some begin at the moment of death, others way before that. There are likely factors I am not yet aware of playing into it.

Two, while a Traveler's body disappears upon death, certain conditions can be met to ensure it remains in the world.

Conditions which I am hopefully fulfilling.

For this, there are three notable instances of Traveler death that I have observed.

First was the player killing I was a part of, with that gnome . . . Valhouse, was it? Anyway, that one resulted in nothing of the dead players remaining.

Second was one of Matt's deaths, the one in which he lost a magic item he got from the tutorial. A whistle that greatly increased speed if I remembered correctly.

Third was my own death, in which my corpse was left behind after being infested by maggots.

Originally, I assumed Traveler's worked similar to classic MMORPGs, where upon death there was a random chance of an item dropping and Noam through sheer number of deaths managed to hit one where he lost an item. That would also explain why we didn't get any drops when we first killed other players. If a random drop probability existed, then it was often tuned down to cater to those more casual players or had some conditions, such as a bounty system. We simply weren't lucky or didn't fulfil the conditions.

But that explanation strained to explain why my body remained after I was killed by maggots. For one, did the system consider a corpse an "Item"? It was plausible, a corpse could be counted as a type of material to be used in crafting. My race of myconid was also considered innately magical, which flagged it as a potential crafting material for magical items. If you could make a weapon from the bones of a mob, couldn't you do the same with a person?

Or did I unwittingly fulfill the conditions in which a Traveler's corpse remained regardless of death?

It was an uncertainty, but the most notable thing that differentiated my death and Matt's was that my body was in the midst of being infested. He dropped an item while I dropped a body.

There were alternative explanations, both of us had killed players previously, so there may have been a bounty-based drop table implemented—that would also explain why the first party didn't drop anything, assuming they were clean.

However, the purpose of a bounty system was to *punish* a player for player killing. My body was regained upon respawning, and the remaining corpse was even a benefit to me. Its random floppings wouldn't have triggered the proximity-based Sporages I planted, so it made an excellent carrier.

Thus, the only notable variable remaining was that my body was infested at the moment of death, perhaps even post-death if the Poison Spores took its time getting to the maggots.

So, at the very least, I can assume a Traveler's body will remain if a portion of it was "ingested," or perhaps "possessed." If this extended to the items carried by a Traveler, then that opened a lot of looting options.

Either way, my time was running out.

I wiped away the warm liquid trickling out of my mouth and eyes. Internal bleeding. If my iron dust hypothesis was true, then it was likely shredding up my veins with each pump of my heart. My slower heart rate and myconid biology likely held it back somewhat, but time took its toll.

"Utoqa."

The lizardfolk tilted his head—around him was a dirty, grey fog that seemed to cling to his skin. Healing him took my damaged arm and both my legs. This Oasis Water solution was definitely inefficient, it didn't translate my mass one to one to his, or perhaps a portion of my mass was being burned for energy to fuel the regeneration? Who knows. This world only follows pseudologic, so the scientific method might not even work.

"Do me a favor, take the dagger on my belt."

He did.

My vision darkened again. The room was swirling. I had long ceased glowing. Declan was muttering something, but it was far away, so far away that I could barely make it out. Did the iron finally make its way to my brain or the myconid equivalent?

"When you get out of this, find me and tell me if my body and dagger remained."

That would hopefully prove my hypothesis.

You have died.

I awoke on the island.

"Think it paid off?"

I checked my belt, finding one of the daggers missing. *"That is a good sign."*

"At the very least, a degree of conversion might've made it so that it wasn't a 'Traveler,' so it wouldn't disappear alongside us."

"Indeed," I spoke, instead of thought, before looking at the scores of announcements before me.

You have leveled up!

You have unlocked Multiclassing.

You may invest your level in either Fungalmancer or Warlock (Gift of Discovery)

Note: Investing in Warlock (Gift of Discovery) will remove the [Et Non-Discent] skill

Impact Point Summary

+10 for leveling up

+5 for witnessing the birth of a sun

+50 for obtaining a Mythic Grade Artifact [The Magician Tarot]

+100 for obtaining a Deific Grade Artifact [Left Eye of The Historian, Deity of History Writ and Recorded, Lord of Wisdom, He Who Wars Against the Unknown, One Who Remembers All]

+150 for helping The Historian and acting as the conduit to send Discovery to your world

+25 for rescuing the trapped mercenary group

+5 for rescuing [Tai Gnari, Sword Apprentice of the Gnari]

+20 for playing a major role in the demise of [Giatan Xienne the Priest of Life]

+15 for saving the life of [Utoqa the Tribeless]
Impact Points: 398
You have unlocked the qualifications for the following Feats and may unlock them at the cost of Stat Points
Mysterious Sustenance Provider
Magician Tarot
Dimensional Gate
Keen Mind
Strategician
War Caster
Sacrifice

We both took a moment to read over the text.

"Is it too late to play as a dragon?"

No, definitely not. The amount of Impact Points I possessed definitely placed me in the range of unlocking a dragon character, not the shit halfie that the dragonborn was, but a *motherfucking dragon.*

We had checked over the starting dragon stat line, and those weren't the weak fire-breathing lizards that some games tried to pass off as dragons, but actual *fucking dragons.* They were humongous statistics sticks with premium growth stats, up to thirty extra stat points each level, as well as powerful racials, elemental breaths, damage resistances, and even immunity in some cases.

"The only caveat is that they cannot take classes and rely entirely on their innate Dragon class."

Which, while it scaled powerfully, was unique in the way it didn't use Experience, but time. To get a single level, dragons had to wait for years, which scaled the same way Experience did. To get from levels three to four would take decades, and five to six was centuries. This was real-world time I had to spend as the character. My real-world counterpart could very well die of old age before I even ticked level four.

"Which sucks."

No, there were alternatives. Didn't we get the Holder of the Discovery Shard as a class not originating from the system? Which the system classified as a Warlock class.

"But we didn't get stat points from getting it. I feel like if we invested a level into it, we would get the stat points, but it isn't worth it."

Yes. Indeed, the whole reason we took it was as an alternative to the exponentially scaling Experience system. If it was made into an actual "Level," then it would defeat the whole purpose.

What other races did that leave? I swiftly opened the Impact Point store. Magic Myconid was already an extremely good race, but the weaknesses were crippling, which was the point of a system designed to balance on itself. I had extremely good strengths while having crippling weaknesses, however, with this amount of Impact Points I could very well get a—

"No."

I scrolled through the dozens of listed races, only to realise something I had forgotten in my excited fervor.

Every race was balanced in some way.

Myconids had their crippling weaknesses. The elemental Genasi were weak to their opposing elements. Dragons needed time. Base humanoids like humans, elves, and dwarves had their lack of innate specialty.

At best, getting a new character with a new race was just picking up another set of strengths and weaknesses.

"Not to mention another thing."

Indeed.

My hand reached for my left eye crevice, feeling the artifact that was melded into my very skull. I would lose **Observe** and **Analyze**. As demonstrated by my elven alt, those don't carry over. While I could theoretically get another alt, the commitment would mean abandoning the progress I made on this character, which unless the Historian was willing to give me another eye, was not an ideal option.

"Hells, just having the fucking eye got us a hundred Impact Points."

It was indeed valuable, however . . .

"What else could we spend these Impact Points on?"

The answer as it turned out, was nothing. Once I had determined that switching to another race wasn't optimal, at least at the current time, there were very few things I could actually do with the Impact Points.

I *could* buy a shit ton of invites and bring a lot of people here but . . .

"Other than Matt we don't have a single real friend."

So, in effect, the treasure of Impact Points I sat on was nothing more than a large number. Impressive, but ultimately useless. Honestly, I would've preferred I gotten paid out in Traveler's Gold because at least I could shop at Daves.

However, the Impact Points helped me realize another thing.

I had obtained significant amounts of Impact Points just from saving and murdering people. Much more than in Gaia despite my longer time spent there.

These were Impact Points, a numerical measure of the effect my actions had on the world. It made sense. Saving a party of Travelers didn't mean much if they would get back up after a few minutes.

But a person whose death meant that they stayed dead? Saving their life meant I unlocked the potential their entire natural lifespan had. Ending someone else's meant I ceased all the impact they had.

Impact that would get translated to Impact Points for me.

"The problem is we have little reason to farm Impact Points."

Indeed. Other than buying more invites, which four hundred Impact Points was more than enough for, we had no reason to get more Impact Points.

Unless more options were opened up in the Impact Point store, there was little reason for me to use it and thus, little reason to get more Impact Points.

The number was impressive and nothing more.

Next up, were these "Feats."

Mysterious Sustenance Provider (3 Stat Points): You gain +1 to Constitution and gain proficiency and knowledge with the Cooking Skill.

Magician Tarot (3 Stat Points): You select from the Tarot Spell List and learn 2 Tier 0 and 1 Tier 1 Spells of your choice. They do not take up existing spell slots.

Dimensional Gate (9 Stat Points): You gain +3 to Intelligence. You select from the Interweaved Dimensions Spell List and learn 2 Tier 2 and 1 Tier Conjuration Spells of your choice. They do not take up existing spell slots.

Keen Mind (3 Stat Points): You gain a +2 to Intelligence. You always know which way is North, the exact time before sunrise or sunset and may accurately recall anything you have seen or heard within the past month.

Strategist (3 Stat Points): You gain a +1 to Wisdom and gain proficiency and knowledge with the Martial Skill. (Note, as you already have proficiency, your current proficiency will receive a minor bonus.)

War Caster (6 Stat Points): You gain +2 to any Body or Mind stat of your choice. You can choose to remove one required spell component of your choice (Somatic, Verbal, or Material) when casting a spell in exchange for a higher mana requirement. (This does not apply to Ritual Spells.)

Sacrifice (3 Stat Points): Once per day, you may remove one instance of damage on another. An equivalent amount of damage will be inflicted upon yourself.

Yet another level of absurd customization.

If the developers of Yggdrasil saw this, they would be desperately trying to hide it from the Design Director to ensure he didn't get any more weird ideas on "Freedom of Choice."

Annoyingly these things cost actual stat points. Meaning I had to invest points that could've gone to raising my numbers. The only feats I could purchase currently were Mysterious Sustenance Provider, Keen Mind, and Strategist. Keen Mind was just an assorted amount of utility effects, the usefulness of which should be rarely needed.

"Though we will be kicking ourselves if we ever need to know where North is, or the exact time to sunrise."

Hmm. Good point, knowing when sunrise is could be really useful, though I already have a layer of coverings.

"Practically speaking, Mysterious Sustenance Provider would be most useful. I've been meaning to learn how to cook."

"Just do that normally, idiot," I casually retorted.

Though this gave a good reference to how much proficiency a skill was worth. Two stat points, not a large investment but also not a negligible one. Another interesting thing was that the system counts that I already had Martial proficiency.

"If that shit show could be counted as strategizing."

Indeed, all I really did was implement net positive energy to enemy trading. It wasn't strategy, but arithmetic.

"People really need to learn the difference."

Oh well. "No need to look a gift horse in the mouth."

It was another option that I could take. Though realistically it was a toss-up between Magician Tarot, Dimensional Gate, and War Caster.

"Sacrifice is interesting as well."

More interesting perhaps was that this acts as a pseudo achievement system. Mysterious Sustenance Provider was likely due to me umm . . . serving people 100 percent legal edibles.

"Can't be illegal if there aren't any laws."

Magician Tarot was self-explanatory, Dimensional Gate I assumed had something to do with helping the Historian. I really got lucky with that one. Even now I'm getting massive dividends from it.

Keen Mind, Strategist, and War Caster I assume were unlocked in the last encounter, with Sacrifice for fixing Utoqa.

"I almost always save for Gate or War Caster, correct?" I asked my other. Whether you liked having bigger numbers or more abilities depended on your own personal playstyle, but I preferred having more options on the table as opposed to being able to swing a stick better.

"Indeed." War Caster's ability didn't seem like much, but if I ever faced an intelligent enemy, then they were going to notice me yelling Poison Spores every so often.

Problem is, to get them both I'm going to have to have to wait another three levels. So, which one to get first?

"Eh, decide when we're there."

Damn, I should've saved some Stat Points.

"Too late now, they don't sell Stat respecs."

Wait a minute.

"I'm waiting?"

"Do you suppose War Caster's free stats are subject to my racials lowering the value of the stat points?" I asked.

There was a moment of silence as we both considered it.

"I'm not sure," Declan answered.

"But if I had to lean toward a side . . ." I prompted.

"It would be no," we both said at once.

I opened up the page indicating my natural stat growth.

Growth:

+1 Wisdom per level

+1 Intelligence per 2 levels

+1 Free point that can be spent on Constitution or Vitality per 2 levels

2 Stat Points required to raise Dexterity

5 Stat Points required to raise Agility

5 Stat Points required to raise Charisma

"It says Stat Points . . ." I muttered.

"It is rather specific wording."

So, theoretically, if I took War Caster and put the free points into agility . . .

"There would be a net increase of four Stat Points and the War Caster ability."

That raised its value significantly.

"However, this is two points in Agility or Charisma. Agility is a useful stat, but is it worth it to spend the points rounding out our bases instead of min/maxing?"

That was the question, wasn't it?

It would only raise Agility to nine points.

But looking at it another way, it was a thirty percent increase to my agility.

"We'll have to think about it on the way."

My respawn timer ticked to zero and though the Impact Point rewards gave me an idea, I had to confirm with my own eyes whether they made it out alive.

4.21

*"People point to a Traveler's immortality as the greatest reason to
fear them. Once upon a time, I thought so, too, but speaking with
them and hearing their tales, I have learned better. Travelers
battle undying monstrosities, have warred across countless realms
for reasons inane, and have created and mastered more types
of weapons and styles than one can even conceive. They thrive
in a world wrecked and destroyed long ago. Nay, I do not fear
Travelers because they cannot die.
I fear them because they are insane even without it."*
—Verron Pluton the Suffering Sage

I had accepted the outcome.

Checking my friend's list before I set out, I learned that Noam had survived somehow. He was far enough away that he could've gotten out when rocks started falling.

It seemed the others were not as fortunate.

Naukoth's body was laid on the ground outside the cave, near the camp. His head was popped, and Analyze told me most of his bones were broken.

The healer was dead as well, his blood unseen on his red robes.

The rogue girl, Rifter was it? Her corpse only had a small blanket, not enough to conceal a shard of stone lodged inside her head. An unfortunate side effect of her skill, getting stunned.

Torrin's body was slightly better, in well enough form a healer had to declare her dead instead of knowing at a look. Her friend with the absurdly long name cried while the other one was still receiving treatment.

The bodies of the last two were splayed out next to the others. Dead long before I got to them.

It was a strange thing, looking at corpses.

Intellectually, I understood the normal reaction would be weeping, some type of sadness, anything really.

But I barely knew them, not even a few hours, so why cry at a stranger's death?

And even if I did cry, what was the point of it, if it does not change anything?

Crying for crying's sake? A good enough reason for some, but not for me.

Inside me, there was only a familiar emptiness.

Still, I kneeled over Naukoth's corpse. Just the feeling of needing to do *something* moving my actions.

"You were the most useful there," I whispered.

It was not a lie, a plus-four buff to Strength and Agility was a significant enough amount to our front line that I relied on a damage cycling method, rather than riskier approaches. Thanks to him I only needed minor corrections to maintain an effective frontline. I also learned through his buffs that stats indeed grew linearly, something that would've taken much longer if I had relied on natural leveling or comparing different people when different factors such as weight or race affected the effectiveness of stats across people. For example, the translation of strength between Noam and I was not linear, since I lack so much weight I could not hold my ground the same way he could even if I had the same amount of strength.

I stood up, a slight clamor had occurred as a woman in robes embroidered with a golden symbol of a coin stood up. Her hand was raised, an uncut diamond held within.

"Raise Dead."

The diamond disappeared, breaking into dust and one of the corpses breathed once more. He was one of the already dead ones who contributed nothing to the fight.

The woman bowed. "Welcome back to the living realm Master Tagron. The bill will be sent to your father."

She left, leaving the dead man rasping on the ground. Not even a glance toward the other corpses.

"That was a priestess of Ethelinda I believe."

One of only two religions with access to resurrection magic, the other being Light.

"It is a rare thing to resurrect the dead," the grey-skinned Vice Guildmaster said behind me. "Probably less so for people like you who get it for free."

Her tone was not accusing, simply stating a fact.

"Indeed."

The resurrected man finally got his bearings; he stood up, face filled with shock and relief, before it turned to anger as he looked at the other person.

"Piece of shit!" he kicked the corpse. "Some bodyguard you are!"

It took him a moment to stop, angrily huffing and puffing. His maddened eyes passed us for a moment before he scoffed and began to walk away. Though not before spitting on Naukoth's corpse once.

He did not get far, as Noam's blade was held to his neck.

His breath hastened, panic set in. He wasn't a combatant, his armor was well made, but new and barely used. He had a holstered weapon on his belt, but his hand did not immediately go to it.

"Wha—What do you want! Are you going to assassinate the son of a noble in broad daylight?"

Noam didn't answer, instead, looked questioningly at me.

"Getting a murder charge isn't worth it," I answered.

Noam withdrew his sword, sheathing it before spitting at the noble.

"Gaah! Disgusting hellspawn, tame your attack dog you creature—"

"Would you shut up?" I asked, taking a step forward, slowly closing in on him.

"My current interactions with you only include you being a useless corpse and you spitting on someone who gave his life to defend yours."

I stopped, directly in front of him. I was short enough that I had to look up, but still, I locked eyes with him.

"All of which points to you being a net negative on existence," I said, my tone cold and calm. "And the most logical way to deal with those is to *remove* them. So please leave before I decide you're my problem."

What a useless thing. How much air and resources were wasted on this creature? He opened his mouth to speak, but he saw something in me and he ran.

"Hmm, not bad," the Vice Guildmaster said. "I always thought they were full of it."

"Do you have anything relevant to add, Ms. Guildmaster?" I asked.

"Nope, just want to give you two some things," she cheerfully said. "I saw some great things today, so I hurried it up."

The drow Vice Guildmaster gestured to the two of them to follow. To a quiet place, before throwing two bronze objects at them. Noam caught his in the air, whereas the other bronze plate slapped Dustin's face before falling to the ground.

Noam glanced at his while Dustin picked his up.

Noam (Traveler)

Skirmisher 6

Voice 3

"Saw?" Dustin asked as he brushed off his tag.

"Yep," she answered, "you may not know this, but every now and again we hold promotion tests. The tell is the upfront payment. Mercs who've already done it know to avoid it."

"So, that cultist in there was one of yours?"

She chuckled. "Oh, no. The quest was real, one of the guilds just applied to put it as the test. They get some cheap labor and you guys get work experience. Win win."

"I see." Dustin sighed. "I suppose there is still much to learn."

"There's always something," she agreed. "You guys did a lot more than was expected. Killing that guy was considered a Challenge 20 quest, you just needed to kill a few chimeras and get back."

"I see."

Almost absentmindedly, she added, "Oh, yeah, and I almost forgot to give this back."

The drow reached into her robes, pulling out a bag. Opened it and passed something to Dustin.

Dustin froze as he received it. Greenie, asleep and unmoving.

"Is he . . ." Noam began.

"Yes," Dustin answered, pushing the small mushroom into his cap. "It is just sleep."

Dustin's tone swiftly turned frigid as he asked the next question: "Did you interfere with it getting assistance?"

She mulled it over for a moment. "Yes, I suppose, but it wouldn't have come either way."

"Why is that?"

Noam recognized Dustin's anger. Not the fake anger, where he yelled and acted angrily, but the real one, where he was cold, and any emotion he felt was crushed and made to fuel a logical purpose. Unlike most, when Declan was truly angry, he did not feel a single sliver of wrath.

"It was your test, and I would've liked to see how far you would've gotten on your own."

"By your own admission, we had already surpassed whatever expectations you held. That should've proved sufficient for the test."

"And did you want to *settle* on that?" she asked. "Have the moment of excellence stolen from you?"

"Less people would've died. It would've been a significantly better use of human resources."

"Truly? You just saw the fool over there, blaming others for his mistake—would it have been better to use one life to save him? If a person deserved their life saved, then they would do it *themselves*."

"You are utilizing a straw man argument; tell me, would it have been worth it to save one of the other corpses?"

She considered it for a moment. "Perhaps the sorcerer, but she was not good at using her power. You, a stranger was better at managing her mana than she was, and she died because of it."

"She could've improved."

"But she didn't when it mattered," she answered. "So, she died. Understand that, if a creature doesn't get past their own weakness, then they can't improve. The betters evolve and surpass."

For a moment, Dustin just stared at her, before his mouth opened and a laugh sounded out. Hearty and mirthful and so very fake. Even in real life, his laugh was slightly fucked up. Bit too guttural and insane.

He abruptly stopped as he slammed his staff into the ground.

"Evolution is a *flawed* method of improvement. It creates organisms that fit a particular niche, with overspecialization leading to a weakness to change. After a significant amount of environmental change, the whole ecosystem will collapse. Leaving only generalists, which leads to the whole thing repeating as *they* take up different niches. I don't know how or if evolution here works similarly to my world, but the greatest thing it has done is create generalists and *that is not a particularly great achievement*."

"So, tell me, if you have a single *good* reason for wasting these people?"

For the first time, the drow began to frown, before her presence expanded and darkness seemed to wrap all around them.

Noam's eyes widened, his breath quickened as he dipped to a combat stance, ready to fight or run.

Next to him, Dustin staggered. "Wha—what is that?"

He needed a distraction. In a single smooth motion he drew a dagger and threw it at the drow. It passed through her harmlessly. There was a point directly behind him where he felt no threat, that was the safe path. He willed his legs to run, but they *refused to move*.

"Answer me!"

Noam knew, he'd felt this before. "You know how I described the other guy as an icicle up your ass?"

"Yes?"

"Dis is the whole focking freezer."

Dustin's body was almost frozen. "Your tell is showing. Your accent."

Speak for yourself, idiot, Noam thought, noting his sudden over analyzation.

The presence withdrew, leaving only the drow. She didn't look intimidating, being shorter and less muscular than him, yet Noam regarded her with renewed caution. This was an opponent that needed that to be beaten.

She spoke again, her tone quiet and threatening: "In those five seconds I could've killed the both of you."

Neither of them said anything, for it was true.

"How many of you would it have taken to land even a scratch on me? Numbers would not have mattered. It is simply a question of *strength*. If you don't have it the moment it matters, then it simply *won't matter*. So, think before you speak, you *spoiled immortals*, who get to try again and again, what point is there in saving people who don't have power when it *matters*."

"I thought you were cool, but you're just a bitch aren't you?"

"Six people."

Both Noam and the drow blinked as Dustin said that.

"Naukoth with his area buffs was worth at least six other people." When he spoke, it was a calm and calculated thing. With no emotion, as if simply speaking fact. "He had power at a place where it was sorely needed. If he were not there, we would not have held as we did without six other people."

"An extreme specialist like him I agree had severe weak points. *But* the whole point of moving in groups is to make up every member's collective weak points, and you actively impeded that."

"Then get stronger and make it up yourself." She shrugged as if it were the most obvious thing.

Noam paused, looking at the drow while she and Dustin went back and forth. *Extreme specialist . . .* Dustin mentioned something about a balanced system, where conditions mattered more than strengths. There was a strange thing when she expanded her presence. Slowly, and carefully, he drew a dagger.

God, I hope I am right.

"If you cannot put your own beliefs to work, then why spout them?"

"Do I literally need to shove Plato's Republic up your—"

"Hey," Noam interrupted. "Remember that question you asked?" he directed to the Vice Guildmaster.

"What question—"

Before she could finish, Noam in a swift and smooth motion threw the dagger directly behind himself.

There was a sound like fizzling mist as the illusion shattered, revealing an exact copy of the drow behind them. *No, not copy. That is the original one.*

Genuine surprise was on her face as the dagger thudded into the ground behind her, leaving a shallow cut on her robes.

"Your question on how many of us it would take to put a scratch on you."

The illusion behind them disappeared as Noam spoke to the real one this time.

"The answer is two."

She blinked back surprise and shock. "How?" she asked, tone disbelieving. "Neither of you should be capable of seeing through illusions."

There was surprise on Dustin's woody face, but it quickly receded as he too turned around fully. *Deliver the one-liner! Deliver the one-liner—*

"Do you know the term, crouching tiger, hidden dragon?"

Yes!

"Well"—Noam smiled, face smug—"say hello to the tiger."

The Vice Guildmaster left soon after, leaving me to my thoughts.

Noam spoke first: "Well, she's a bitch."

"Understatement of the century," I replied.

"But more importantly . . ."

"How did you know she was really behind us?"

Noam shrugged. "It was a hunch—isn't she an illusionist? I figured it was strange her fear thing covered every direction *except* directly behind us. Like she was just asking someone to run there."

"I see."

Noam's eyes looked distant for a moment, staring toward the direction of Naukoth. "So he's . . ."

"Dead. I have confirmed it," I answered.

He sighed. "That sucks, he was cool as well. Stupid, bringing a big ass piano into battle, but I could respect that."

"Wait a moment," I said.

My arm fumbled into my cap, looking for something, before withdrawing it, a single golden coin.

"Let's exhaust our options first."

I flicked the coin, and the door appeared.

We entered, a Dave appearing for each of us. Noam, the unconscious Greenie, and me. He didn't bother with theatrics this time, simply showing us a scroll.

T5 Raise Dead (One use)

Returns a dead creature to life, provided that it has been dead no longer than 10 days and if the creature's soul is both willing and at liberty to rejoin the body.

8,000,000,000 Gold

"Jesus Christ that is a high ass cost."

"Impossible, then," I muttered, "we cannot realistically raise the funds within ten days."

And why should we? I left unsaid.

"Why is the cost of that so fucking high, mate?" Noam demanded.

The tiefling Dave sighed sadly. "The rules are I have to keep to what the prices most realistically are. It is simply because the cost of resurrection has been greatly inflated."

"Why?"

I knew the answer to that. "Only two groups have access to resurrection type spells. Three if you count Druidic reincarnation. But the only group willing to share are the Mercantile Church, who charge a premium. Not only that, it consumes a diamond and those are artificially made valuable by the Deep Imperium, who control the flow of them to the surface world."

"In short," I summarized, "controlled by both those capable of doing it, and those capable of supplying the needed materials."

The myconid Dave nodded. "Osshiven'Kai could provide resurrection."

I raised an eyebrow. *"I did not know that."*

That would be interesting, but not what we needed. Shaking my head, I said, "No, that isn't a good method, the last time a major follower of Osshiven'Kai was found the Inquisition burned down everything within a twenty kilometer radius, and frankly that wasn't an overreaction if what I read was true."

"So, you're saying it's impossible without a diamond?"

Myconid Dave raised an eyebrow. "I believe the Magus Smar Da Ten Yu figured out a method without using them, but she was assassinated shortly after, so the knowledge is lost."

Noam didn't even react to the stupid pun that made every Magus's title. "What about Wayshards?"

"Not diamond," I answered. "Believe me, much smarter people than either of us have tried."

Despite this world's magic system being rather soft, *costs* and *conditions* are literally hard-coded into it. It wouldn't be easy to overcome them. At the very least, not something we could accomplish within ten days.

Noam sighed, before lethargically punching my arm. "Thanks for raising my hope asshole."

I didn't answer.

"Perhaps the Adept Battle Caster feat?" Declan posed. *"You could realistically level and buy that feat within ten days."*

"Raise Dead is a ritual spell, same with Reincarnate. Even if it did work, we don't know the mana increase for removing a vital component of a spell. There is a very possible chance that we straight up won't have the mana for it. Not to mention both are tier five spells, something we don't even have access to yet. At level four our class still only has tier two spells, realistically we need to get to level nine to even access them. By then, the ten-day time limit would have passed."

Declan, too, went silent after that.

"Let's leave, Matt."

His face was in his hands, but when I spoke, he answered, "Give me a moment."

He pushed his hands up until they went over his forehead. Slicking his hair back, Noam smiled weakly at me. "Let's go."

I made toward the door, knowing better than to look at him.

"Wait a moment." Noam stopped me again.

"How much does *this* cost?" he asked, holding up another scroll.

We both left, though only Noam bought something. Pocketing the spell scroll, he had an evil, scheming look to his face. I had a fairly good idea on where he wanted to use it and had already made preparations for it.

But until then, we were both free.

"Noam?"

"Yeah?" he asked, an eyebrow raised.

I looked to the sky, it was noon now and the sun was passing. Even now, I could see stars blinking in the sky.

"You know what I think about doing things."

"—Yeah?" he answered with hesitance.

"So, I want to ask you this again," I said, repeating an old question. "Is there any worth in doing anything?"

At a base, logical, and materialistic level, nothing a single sapient creature does will ever truly matter. I could disappear from this world and all traces of me would be removed and the world would keep moving on. Even if I accomplished great things, there would come a time where it would not matter. Where it would be forgotten or gone. Perhaps the Deadhand finally destroys the world, or maybe our sun explodes, or maybe even the heat death of the universe or a million other things. There will come a point where anything humanity has ever achieved will not matter. So why achieve anything at all?

"Of course, there is," he replied patting me on the back.

I did not believe him, but still I spoke. "I see, then . . ."

I paused, thinking for a long moment as I stared at the sky.

Nothing I do in my time will matter in the end. I have no reason to try, no reason to be here, no reason to be friends with people. All I have is some vague animalistic instinct that I pleasure occasionally by gaining money, min/maxing, and outsmarting idiots.

I enjoy those things, but if all I wanted was to satisfy my desire, I could be like 60 percent of the population and permanently strap on a VR helmet, living off a Universal Basic Income for the rest of my life.

So why am I here?

For a moment, I felt there was another hand on my shoulder.

"The only reason that seems to matter," Declan said, sympathetic in a way no one else could ever be.

"I feel . . ." I thought about my words, whether I truly felt what I was feeling before carefully, I spoke. "I believe I feel motivated now."

"Or at the very least annoyed."

"I disagreed with her," I continued, my voice quiet and introspective. "On a fundamental level, I cannot agree with that sort of ideology, so I wish to prove her *wrong*."

There was a slow, pregnant pause as Noam simply stared at me, wide eyed. Then, slowly, he laughed, the sound long, sharp and loud.

He heartily slapped me on the back. "Finally! I thought you went off and died on me already! What are we doing? Clearing an impossible boss? Beating the shit out of someone we don't like?"

"Getting influence, power, ideally some that aren't just from the innate fact we are Travelers."

"How are we gonna do it?" he asked, poised, relaxed, yet anticipating.

"What can two idiots who are only particularly good at playing games, particularly MMOs, do to gain real influence?" I asked, only half rhetorically.

Noam furrowed his brow, thinking about it for a moment. "Killing stuff . . .? No, too obvious, unless . . ." his lips parted into a wide smile. "How many?"

I thought about it for a moment, trying to think of the optimal number. "At the very minimum, a full raid."

Noam chuckled. "Aiming to be the best, are we?"

"Only needs to be above average. A passing score worthy of imitation," I replied. I don't need to do it well, or perfectly, just good enough.

We don't have to be better, we just had to set a trend that others will imitate.

"Still gotta aim for the best!" he cheered, slapping me on the back once again. "You aren't allowed to half-ass this now!"

He looked around us, at the moving pieces of the Ivory Tower guild around us. Before, it was mostly a glance of curiosity, but now, there was a new look.

Now, he saw them as competition.

"Indeed. A guild shouldn't be half-assed."

Journey Part 1

"World might be fked but at least we still have memes."
—*Anon, 5:36 UTC, March 7, 2034, on the popular messaging board '6tan' nine minutes before the first Solar Flare hit*

Harsh winds whipped across the harsh desert expanse, hurling sand and dust through the shattered and desiccated ruins of a city. In this blinding sandstorm, several barely visible dots struggled through.

Heavily armed, they wore thick desert camo, faces obscured by gas masks. Despite their attire, they seemed unbothered by the heat.

"This is Charlie," their shared coms buzzed. *"How much farther is B? Over."*

"Few more minutes," his coms answered.

"Hurry up, this sandstorm won't last forever."

"Damn campers," the fourth soldier muttered, before absentmindedly adding, *"Over."*

"More reason to hurry—bzzzzzzzzzzzz—"

Suddenly, one of the soldiers dropped, a spray of blood erupting from the back of his head, before it was lost in the desert wind.

"—zzzzt."

"Sniper!" Charlie yelled as he fell to the ground, taking shelter behind the broken husk of a car.

"WHAT THE FU—bzzzzzzt," another soldier foolishly yelled instead of getting to cover, leading to a rather predictable result.

"Duh!" the other living soldier replied as he got behind a wall. *"Cover me!"* With practiced ease, he kneeled on the ground, one hand rapidly tapping a holographic device on his arm, before one of the pouches on his belt shot out, landing on the ground before unfurling into a mechanical drone.

Using the holographic device, he controlled the drone, piloting it out of the alleyway. *"It's just one guy, gimme a moment to—"*

The drone caught sight of one shadowy figure before a bullet pierced its camera.

"Shit! This fucker isn't—"

"Fuck he's here!"

He couldn't finish his sentence, as he heard the spray of bullets from Charlie's weapon before it abruptly stopped.

"Oh fuck."

The remaining soldier's breath hastened, he held his rifle tight. His eyes darted around rapidly like a hunted dog.

"He's just one guy . . ."

"Yo."

His reaction was instant, the voice came behind him, from within the alley. In less than a breath, his rifle was aiming at the enemy behind him.

. . . Only to see a near-exact replica of the drone he used, save for the darker coloring.

From both the drone and behind him, a voice laughed.

"Haha, you thought."

The first bullet hit the back of his head; stopped by his helmet, the soldier fell forward, but the shooter's aim was true.

The second bullet entered the hole made by the first, pushing both into his skull.

Mattmanfoo sniped xXDPS_KINGXx with the Operator
Mattmanfoo sniped COD_was_BETTER with the Operator
Mattmanfoo silenced charliewastaken with the Ghost
Mattmanfoo silenced ValorantMan with the Ghost

Matt removed his VR helm, his lips curling with a mischievous and smug glee that can only be obtained when two-thirds of the game lobby just accused you of hacking.

Oh, and the cheering crowd around him also helped.

He rose from his machine, hands thrown in the air.

"EASY!" he declared, reveling in the cheers. "Now pay up!"

"Oy you fucking cheated, you asshole!" One of them yelled, tearing off their helmet, the thing clanged onto the floor as he jumped up. "I know you fucking cheated! How the fuck did you managed to snipe us at the start?"

He shrugged. "I only cheated as much as you did damage . . . Oh wait?" he paused for effect, tapping into the holoboard.

The game statistics showed up on the viewer screen, and with exaggerated surprise, Matt slapped his face. "You didn't do any damage! Guess I didn't cheat, *DPS King.*"

The crowd laughed, shouting insults at the guy as his face reddened.

One of his friends, Charlie, put his hand on his shoulder. "Knock it off, Jared—"

"Oy, fuck off!" Jared yelled, throwing off his arm. "I ain't you paying a cheater nothin'!" The tall, high school boy stormed toward Matt.

His friends tried one last attempt to stop him. "He ain't worth it, Jared!"

Jared stopped, only a few steps from Matt, even he could see that Jared was significantly taller and bulkier than him. He took a deep breath, before saying, "You're right, this kid isn't worth it, let's leave. I need to make an appointment with my anger management—"

"Well, I guess these little bitches can't keep a promise," Matt interrupted the near one-hundred and ninety centimeters tall high schooler. The crowd, mostly composed of other middle schoolers, booed around him. "I beat all you weak tiny shits in a one-versus-four like I said, so pay up!"

Whatever rational breakthrough Jared was having, he stopped at Matt's words. As the high schooler, approximately fifty centimeters taller than him, reddened once again and stomped those last few steps.

"I'LL SHOW YOU WHO'S A LITTLE SHIT!"

His friends jumped forward, trying to grab him, but Jared had a head start, and grabbed Matt by the collar, lifting the smug boy off the ground.

"WHO'S THE LITTLE SHIT NOW!" he yelled as he shook Matt like a rag doll, spittle flying everywhere.

Matt responded, putting a hand on his nose, "Still you! Also, brush your teeth!"

"AHH!" Jared's grip tightened, threatening to choke him.

He raised a fist, slamming it into Matt's mouth, his knuckle leaving a gash on his lip.

Matt's head spun, a brief moment of disorientation quickly passing as he licked the cut on his lip. "Savor this moment! This will be the deepest you'll ever be in a person!"

"I'LL FOCKING MURDER YOU AND SHIT DOWN YOUR THROAT!"

"STOP YELLING IN MY STORE OR I'LL DO IT FIRST YA GITS!"

And there's the cavalry, Matt thought as Angelo pushed away the gawking crowd recording the whole encounter on their phones.

The other three idiots he had beaten were crowding around them, more concerned for their friend than Matt, and they readily stepped away as Angelo's huge bulk dwarfed the high schooler.

"YA GIT! DAFUQ DID YOU DO TO MY MACHINE!"

Matt smiled as Jared simply looked confused for a moment before he fully took in the leering figure two heads taller than him. The reddened face paled quickly. Matt was never worried about his situation because the moment Jared had thrown the headset he was *fucked*.

With slow, deliberating words, Angelo spoke, "Get. Out."

Jared dropped him and legged it, his friends following him.

The crowd around them cheered as the high schoolers ran out, but Angelo simply gave a stern look before they legged it as well.

Leaving only a grinning Matt on his ass.

"Afternoon Angelo!" He cheerfully waved. "How's business—WOAH!" Matt yelled as Angelo grabbed him by his collar, lifting him up.

"I swear to God that, if you keep doing this, then I'll kick you out of my store!"

"You won't do that, Angelo," he smugly replied, before gesturing around. "Look at how much business I always bring."

The crowd may have dispersed, but they dispersed into other parts of the gaming cafe, gleefully wasting money on all manner of things Angelo managed to scrounge up.

Angelo looked cross for another moment, before he gruffly set Matt on the ground. "I know you would—Ow!"

Locking him into a headlock, Angelo gave him a noogie. "Do you give?" he asked.

"I give! I give!" Matt yelled, slapping him on his beefy arm. He knew this was more for his pride than anything—Angelo wouldn't let him have the last word here.

With one final playful rap on the head, Angelo let him go. "You gotta stop getting into trouble kid, what if your mothers find out?"

"Don't worry man, I can handle myself," Matt replied, rubbing his head.

"What were you doing playing this?" He gestured to the Virtual Reality machine. "You know you aren't old enough—"

"Meh"—Matt shrugged—"I'm only two years off the PG-Fifteen rating anyway, it's fineeeee."

Angelo gave him a hard look, before he shook his head. "Get moving, scamp. Sarah called, she needs you back for something. Both of them."

Matt paused slightly at that; if both ma and mum needed him, then it had to be important . . . Not too subtly, he looked at the clock: 5 P.M. Surely he could—Angelo glared at him—never mind.

With a clumsy salute, he replied, "Got it, boss!"

Grabbing his bag, Matt made for the exit, giving one final wave. "See ya later!"

"Be safe!" Angelo replied.

He stepped out of the store and onto the graveled ground. Once upon a time, trains ran through here, providing public transport, but now the rails had been ripped off, used for material somewhere else. On both sides, the walls had been taken down and holes dug to allow for more space, where dozens more stores and other such things lined the tunnels.

From his pocket, he took out a pair of earpods and his phone, old but well maintained. Humming an old song as he passed by countless stores, lit by glaring neon and a thousand other scavenged forms of light.

Matt's home was three stations south and as he walked, he passed through the Metrocity with a used familiarity. Waving at those he recognized as he passed them, sometimes they returned waves, other times middle fingers. He gleefully returned those, angered shouts and greetings drowned out by music and the general bustle of humanity.

But when he reached the second station, his eyes perked up in curiosity as he saw the four stooges he beat earlier loitering around.

It could've been nothing, but Matt liked to think he was better than that, so a fight was definitely on the table.

He glanced around; he was near his home turf but he couldn't see any of his friends nearby. He had no backup. That put a slight wrench in his plans, as good as he was at games, he was still a skinny—and very handsome teenager in real life.

There were four of them, each physically larger and older than Matt.

He could probably take them.

But as he moved to declare himself, a thought nagged at his mind.

Sarah and Denise still needed him for something, something important enough Angelo seriously glared at him.

Now, he *could* fight these four idiots, but he would definitely come home late or bruised, probably both.

Carefully hiding himself again, he considered for a moment.

Enjoy a small moment of victory over idiots he already beat?

Or don't get a three-hour lecture by mum?

"Next time," he whispered, making a note to gather his crew and jump them later.

Until then, he faded into the crowd, making his way to a nondescript alleyway between someone's house and a seemingly dismantled part of the subway wall. After making sure no one was looking, he kicked aside a pile of trash, revealing a small passageway.

Once again making sure no one was looking, he entered, dragging the trash back into place as he did.

It was completely dark in the tunnel, but he knew his way. After giving his eyes a moment to adjust to the dark, he began walking again. His hand was on the wall, feeling the roughly hewn concrete.

Turn right here . . .

Slowly, the sounds of the main tunnel faded as he walked deeper into the darkness. There was a slow incline as he followed a path downward.

One more left here . . .

But slowly, he began to hear the sounds of life flare up again. Walking toward the sound, he turned a right, and to his destination.

His hole was a dozen meters off ground, so he had a good view of the place as the small tunnel opened up to a massive chamber, La Sous-Terre or whatever the snobs called it. Most people just called it Sous. A ceiling almost forty meters high, held up by countless enormous concrete pillars placed at regular intervals, numerous holes drilled into them to form a ventilation system that didn't require energy. Underneath them was a sprawling metropolis. Near the actual entrance underneath the station, there were hundreds of squat concrete apartments, built almost to the height of the ceiling. Their base was completely uniform white concrete, but over the years most people had settled in, painting over the boring white with graffiti, art pieces, anything really. Their individual lights brought the only glow in this place and added a much-needed splash of color to whatever drab thing people of the past erected.

As Matt turned his gaze farther left, the squat concrete apartments began to disappear, slowly replaced by things less solid. Though the underground chamber stretched many kilometers, the apartments did not. The lights became less common, the apartments there were half-constructed, and the roofs and walls later covered up by scrap metal and whatever material the denizens could find. Even farther to the left, there were no more of the uniform houses, just huts formed of dozens of different scavenged materials. Few lights appeared there, and though he wanted to explore it one day, Denise would surely do worse than just a lecture if someone ever snitched.

He shrugged, no time for sightseeing today. He edged to the side of the hole and found numerous handholds chipped into the concrete, used by whoever dug the tunnel from the ventilations to the subways. With practiced ease, he grabbed onto them and made his way downward, even skipping a few holds as he did. Once he was only a meter off the ground, he let go, sliding on the slope at the base of the pillar.

Once on the ground, he quickly made his way back home to one of the many concrete apartments scattered in the middle area. He knocked on a metal bin outside, just once, and his brother heard it.

Max peeked out from the window, hearing the sound. His younger brother gave him a conspiratorial look, before holding his hand in a thumbs up with a shrug.

So, probably not me, huh?

He got on the concrete stairs, quickly climbed to their level. Opening the door, he raised it slightly so that it didn't scratch on the ground like it always did and quietly entered. Shushing Max who was giggling at a corner.

Already he heard hushed voices of argument.

"Max is only six, do you think he could make it?" Matt recognized Denise's voice, soft-spoken like usual.

"But we've been waiting for a spot for years, it's supposedly pretty easy. So long as we stick with the guide." The second voice was Sarah's, uncharacteristically hushed and strangely cheerless.

He tiptoed into the main room, and though both his parents were facing the entrance they were too engrossed in their conversation. Quiet like a shadow, he crept behind Sarah and . . .

"Guess who?"

He saw the slight smile quirk on Sarah's lips as he put his hands over her eyes.

"Heya, Matt," she answered tiredly, "sorry but I'm gonna need you to sit down for this."

A slight feeling of unfamiliarity washed over Matt. He'd been doing that ever since they got adopted, yet Sarah never answered as if she was tired. It was always full of cheer and infectious energy.

He shook off the feeling, taking a seat next to them.

"What's up?"

"This . . . might be hard to swallow," Sarah began. "But we're thinking of leaving the Metros."

Matt's brow furrowed slightly. "The Metros . . . as in underground? I thought topside wasn't safe for living? Perimeter and SANS and all that."

"It isn't," Denise answered, "but it's possible to travel through. If you keep to guides, then you can get to ports and leave Europe."

"And right now is an opportune time!" Sarah cut in. "Right now the Equator is calm over the Mediterranean, so they're running planes over it again. It won't be like this for another four years!"

Denise shook her head. "I don't know, Sarah. If we wait one or more decades, then Oceania would finally get the underground rail complete. Then we can safely travel regardless."

"They've been saying that for years!" she hissed. "It always gets held up by something or other. This might be our chance, Denise! A better life for all of us." She clasped her wife's hands. "Please? If not for me, then for them."

Hesitantly, Denise brought their hands to her forehead. "I don't know. . . that's why I wanted to ask you, Matt." She turned to him, Sarah following suit. "Max said he wants to stay with us no matter where . . . but . . ."

"What do you want?"

"One final run down," the guide, Alex, said.

Max checked his pack again, his hands shaking somewhat. In a few moments, he'd be on the surface. A place he'd been warned against since childhood.

"If you see the sun, then run—"

"We've made it as far as we can underground," the other guide, Jeremy, said as he checked his pack, a heavy automatic rifle strapped to it. "Now we'll have to surface. To confirm, we'll be surfacing in Old Paris, and make the remaining trip on foot until we reach the military base in Rouen."

"The trip should take two days, but we've made allowances for three." Alex gruffly said, "Be sure you memorize the map given to you."

"Run back to your holes, that is your goal—"

Denise opened the map again, staring at it intensely. As if trying to physically burn the images into her memory.

"If we follow the normal route along with the *exact* times, then we'll be fine. But the slightest deviation could cause us to get caught by the Perimeter. If a deviation occurs, then make sure you stick by us. We've got the patrol routes and times memorized, so we can avoid most detection."

"For with Peri, we will never be merry—"

Alex kneeled down, pulling out several black bags. "Any electronics you have you need to shut down and leave them inside. We'll be passing through several EMP zones and I don't want Perimeter to catch any transmissions. That means complete radio silence."

Sarah kneeled down, helping an almost crying Max part from his phone. *He wasn't even that sad when we left home.*

"Are you all ready?" Jeremy asked.

Max nodded eagerly.

And if you have SANS, you can only pray to St Anne's!

There were hesitant nods all around.

With a sigh, Alex stood up. "Then follow."

Journey Part 2

Matt took his first breath of outside air. It felt . . . dirtier, unfiltered by ventilation. Yet it wasn't dusty, there were no particles in it like the air in less ventilated areas, but it was still dry and alien.

The air wasn't clean, but it also wasn't stale.

He looked up and . . . was shaken a bit. Matt thought he was prepared or at least didn't think it would be that big of a deal, but for the first time in his life, he stared at a ceilingless sky and comprehended its vastness in a way Virtual Reality with its limited render distance never could. A burning bright orb illuminated an indigo purple sky as sickly looking black clouds lazily floated. He kept looking, expecting an end to the horizon, a wall, an unrendered chunk . . . but he never found it.

"It used to be blue . . ." Denise quietly muttered as she tightly clutched Max's hand.

"Is everyone out?" Alex asked, their eyes scanning the skies. Matt's eyes followed theirs, unlike him, Alex's eyes were searching. For the drones, he thought, Peri was a bitch to fight even in-game.

Matt turned his gaze down. He recognized some parts of the city: the abandoned bombed-out buildings, leaving little but blackened frames. Old Paris was a pretty open area for a city, making it a bitch to keep when he played defense on the map. If it wasn't a national symbol of the old nations, then it would've fallen a lot quicker.

"I'm good," Matt said. The rest of the group quickly sounded off, with Jeremy the last.

"About time?" the soldier asked, checking an analog watch on his wrist.

"Yes," Alex said, just as loud sirens began to blare. They signaled to the rest of the group and began hurrying forward, taking point. Matt followed behind, his steps passively adopting the soundless movement he was used to. Sarah and Denise were behind them, each holding one of Max's hands, they weren't fast, but Alex was keeping pace. Jeremy was last, watching the group like a wolf with his pack.

They managed to jog past several streets before the bombs started dropping. The aftershocks shook the ground, powerful winds whipped at them. Matt barely managed to brace for it—he was almost knocked off his feet, but Alex caught him.

"Thanks." Alex wasn't looking at him, instead, they stared to the southward end as numerous explosions bloomed from small black dots dropped from the sky. As the explosions moved away from them, they gestured to keep going.

Here laid the core of the plan. Whenever the Perimeter bombed a location, it withdrew most of its forces. This allowed small gaps where one could slip through its security.

They jogged past abandoned streets and bombed out buildings, with the heavy smell of gunpowder and acrid stench permeated throughout the city; they made good time. A few minutes and the remains of the Eiffel Tower was in sight; passing under the Seine River through an out of use sewer tunnel, they were allowed their first moment of rest.

Matt breathed in and out deeply as he leaned by the brick wall. He was fit so it wasn't as hard on him. He could've gone for another two hours at least, he decided. Alex and Jeremy were barely even huffing, while Sarah and Denise were in relatively similar shape to him. His mums weren't as fit but they were also older, had longer legs, and took fewer steps compared to him. They stopped for Max, who didn't complain, but was clearly slowing and fell to the ground almost immediately.

"Deep breaths," Denise said as she gently ruffled his brother's hair. "Take deep breaths."

"I'm . . . *huff* . . . fine!" Max defiantly said, pushing Denise's hand off him as he shakily stood. "Let's keep going!"

"*Shh,*" Jeremy shushed from the back, his gaze still focused on the outside.

"Ah . . . sorry." Quieter this time, he said, "Let's keep going . . ."

"Rest for the moment," Alex said. "There aren't a lot of shelters the Perimeter won't check. But we only have another ten till we need to be moving again."

"I feel a bit tired as well," Sarah said, squatting down next to Max. "Can you wait a moment for me?"

Max *hmmphed* and sat down with all the patience of a ten-year-old. Matt smiled, and the next few minutes passed in comfortable silence—well, as silent as they could with the constant sound of bombs dropping just a few kilometers from them. They had sparse conversation other than Jeremy reporting what he saw at the edge of the tunnel to Alex.

"Time," Alex said, and everyone quietly stood back up. Outside, Jeremy checked his watch. "Accurate to the second once again."

The sounds of bombings had long since dimmed, still noticeable if you strained your ears, but now far off.

"We'll keep following the Seine," Alex said as they shuffled outside.

Max looked at the river. "Can't we boat?"

Jeremy shook his head. "Can't, the entire stretch of river was mined after Paris fell."

"Couldn't have given them that easy of a time," Matt muttered. "Can't have them launching attacks to the other bases from the river."

Jeremy cocked a brow. "You're pretty knowledgeable kid."

"I play PoW," he answered.

The soldier nodded. "The river won't be safe till Poses," he continued, "and by that point, we'll be in the home stretch."

"We need to hurry and move," Alex said. "There are only a few more minutes of error we can afford."

With that, everyone began moving again.

They had passed the remains of Cergy when something happened. Max, who was now being piggybacked by Jeremy, as a soldier can't have his hands occupied, spotted it first. He raised a small hand and pointed to the sky.

Alex saw it next, their eyes enhanced beyond what mere genetics could give, and they quietly swore as they brought their rifle up in the air.

"Jeremy, visual on canary, broken wing two-two."

Then Matt saw it, a small shape in the sky. A quadcopter drone flying fifty meters above as if drunk, before Matt realized the propeller on its back right wasn't moving.

It stopped, turned toward them.

Jeremy put Max down and pulled out his own weapon. "Wet Peter?"

No, Max thought. It wasn't a white phosphorus drone.

"Negative," Alex replied, weapon still trained on the drone, just barely hovering. "It's an eye."

Their weapon fired and the working propeller on the drone's right blew off. It went spiraling down, but as it did, there was a slowly mounting sense of realization.

They were detected.

"This is Jumbo Four," Jeremy said into comms as they rushed through the forest, uncaring of the radio silence they'd previously held. "Situation Tango One-One. I repeat, Tango One-One."

The device blared to life. *Has an Eight-Six Scheduling Shift scenario occurred? Over.*

"Negative," the soldier answered. "Wounded Canary, Eunuch Alpha suspects it wasn't able to follow evac protocol."

Wear and tear, Matt thought. Alex examined the drone when it fell and concluded the rotor broke from years of cold exposure and small accumulating damage. No matter how sturdy the Russians made their toys, the decades wore on them and thus it wasn't able to follow the normal, *predictable* routes Peri had.

"Copy," the comms said. *"Hunting Dog?"*

"Negative," Jeremy answered as he helped pull Sarah over a ledge. "No Tango yet. We have Metros, requesting Helivac ASAP."

"Are you currently in an EMP Field?"

Jeremy slowed to a stop, the old soldier staring at his communicator. "I want you to take a moment and think about what you just asked."

The comms were silent for a moment.

"Understood," it said, dodging the subject, *"sending a B-Eagle to—BZZZZZZZZZT"*

Jeremy swore and ripped off the communicator, tossing it to the ground, the thing fizzling with smoke and sparks before it popped, its circuits now fried and useless.

"Shit," Alex swore, "contact imminent."

"What do we do?" Sarah asked, panic filling her eyes as they darted around wildly, while Denise tightly hugged the both of them.

"Calm down," Alex said with forced composure. "There is an average of three minutes once an EMP field is set before the drones make contact. More so since they still haven't reestablished their presence here."

"But . . ." Sarah began with hesitation. Denise's arm tightened around Matt. He knew what was left unsaid, the problem was *them.* Peri's drones were tireless and would eventually wear them down. They might get out in the short term but eventually, they'd be hunted down. With an EMP field up, they don't even have the chance of an air evac. Both soldiers could probably make it out safely *if* they didn't have them four slowing them down.

"No, no, no, no!" Alex said, violently shaking their head. "I'll get you guys out! There are ways, but it'll be risky. We can move westward toward Évreux. It's out of Perimeter's range, so we'd have a head start before the wolves are after us."

"Are there subways we can use to move underground?" Sarah asked.

"None that are usable," Jeremy answered with barely veiled frustration. "Trust me, the Greens were thorough in making sure nothing can be used anymore."

The soldier turned to Alex. "Isn't the route to Évreux just as dangerous?"

Face still scrunched up in thought. "It is, the area between Évreux and the Seine was where the fighting was most fierce. But Évreux itself should remain relatively intact, there may still be underground routes, and Peri is unlikely to pursue us past the lines."

There were a few small nods of agreement, but Matt was looking at the two soldiers. Jeremy spoke, "Only problem is the area is probably mined to all hell."

"Both paths are risky," Alex agreed, "but moving as we are now means the wolves will catch up to us eventually. I have a field map of the area memorized, so I can direct us to some relatively safe—"

They froze, the soldier's ears perked up, hearing something they couldn't. Jeremy raised his rifle as his partner did theirs.

"Move," Alex quietly whispered in urgency, "now!"

They began running, Alex in the lead. From behind, Matt heard the deafening sound of gunfire as Jeremy covered their back.

The trees rushed past them in a blur. Matt ran, in his element. The only sound in the dusk was gunfire, explosions, and their thudding footsteps. In front, Alex paused for the slightest moment to fire two shots into the sky. Matt only saw the two smoking trails as the drones fell from the sky before Alex rushed them to keep going.

Their head turned to the woods on their left and Matt couldn't help but follow, only to see a fast-moving blur.

Bipedal, its sleek body painted in camouflage long flaking. Its "head" was a black glass surface containing a camera. The machine spoke first in French, a phrase spoken endlessly in PoW, Matt only now hearing it in person. "CITIZEN! YOU ARE ATTEMPTING TO BREACH UNION BORDERS! SUBMIT YOURSELF FOR CAPTURE AND BE DIRECTED TO THE NEAREST CORRECTIONAL FACILITY!"

It began to speak again in English, but Alex shot it in the head, breaking the glass and knocking it away as it crashed into a tree.

From above, he heard another drone shout, "CITIZEN! YOU ARE COLLABORATING WITH AN ENEMY OF THE PEOPLE! THIS IS YOUR FINAL WARNING OR YOU WILL BE FORCIBLY DETAINED—" Alex was faster now, whipping their weapon immediately to the other drone.

"Keep running!" Alex yelled as a smoke trail fell from the sky.

"NO NEED TO TELL US TWICE!" Matt yelled.

Four more wolf drones on the right, keeping up easily with them. Their sides popped open but Alex was faster, shooting one before it could launch its net, while a grenade landed in between the rest. The resulting explosion knocked them away slightly.

"BAD NEWS, ALEX!" Jeremy yelled from behind as he caught up with them.

"There are *worse* news!?" Sarah yelled back, just as Alex's weapon whipped up to take out another two aerial drones.

"There's a crab in the area! We gotta get out *now*—"

There was a low thrumming sound, a sensation which Matt felt in his very *bones*. Jeremy jumped and pushed Sarah out of the way before the roar of thunder deafened them. Jeremy's right side was torn off and the ground beside Matt exploded as the slug blasted it apart.

They were thrown to the ground, while Jeremy *flew*. Alex swore and turned around, guns blazing. Denise rushed to Sarah, and Matt was only dimly aware she was piggybacking Max. He turned around and for a brief moment, Matt was stunned.

A shadow, about twenty meters away but not at all hidden. It loomed in the trees. Six insectoid-like legs, supporting an armored hull with machine guns attached on both sides, and an additional Gauss cannon on its "head" that he learned about from encountering it in PoW. But this thing, it was ancient, something VR could never simulate. The machine gun on its right was blown off, scorch marks still present on the metal, its other was trying to spin but was jammed. Its camouflage coating was rife with scarring and damage. Three of its legs seemed damaged in some small way, and one was being dragged uselessly behind it. All proof that this machine was older than him, fought wars longer than he had been alive.

The only weapon that was functioning was the Gauss cannon. A magnetic slingshot firing devastator slugs the size of soda cans. The only thing it needed to kill all of them.

Alex was firing at it, their bullets not even scratching its armor. Matt knew only anti-tank weapons would get through it. But Alex achieved something else, the crab turned toward him as they ran and a piece of ground exploded as it fired, not because the slugs were explosive, but due to the *sheer* force they were shot with. The crab moved with impossible speed, unexpected of something of that size. Tearing through trees as if they weren't there, chasing the soldier.

As Matt moved to action, he turned to see Denise lift Sarah up. In the distance, he heard Jeremy swear as he applied medspray to his blown off torso. He knew the crab wasn't moving as fast as it could, that the machine's max speed was ninety-six kilometers an hour, but it was ancient. Alex could buy time, but it will catch up, damage or not.

"We can't beat that thing!" he yelled as he scrambled back to the group. "Alex's gonna die at this rate!"

Sarah was simply staring off into space, her body covered in Jeremy's blood and flesh. "I'm sorry. I'm sorry. I'm sorry. I'm sorry. I'm sorry . . ." Max was tightly gripping onto Denise, eyes shut tight and small tears coming out of his eyes.

Matt turned to the soldier, hoping he could give *anything* to help, a speech, confidence, experience, just *something*. But Jeremy was leaning on a tree, heavily breathing, the right side of his torso blown open revealing his ribs jutting out as he pushed his intestines back into himself, blood dripped from yellow fat as he desperately applied nanite gels and medsprays. His entire side was gone and that was what happened when the crab *missed*. There was no help there, he was dealing with their own problems, how could—

Denise slapped Sarah on the face.

"I'm mad at you," Denise said with forced calm, "but I would much rather be mad at you when we're all safe. So, *stop* apologizing and get out of here!"

Sarah looked stunned for a moment before shame and embarrassment filled her face. "I'm—I'm sorry."

Denise hugged her, Max's own stubby arms reaching around her neck to wrap around Sarah's.

Jeremy spoke, his voice hoarse with pain, "If you're all done, we need to keep moving."

They turned to him, suddenly realizing he was there. "Oh my God are you—"

"No," the old soldier replied—Matt could see his lungs expand behind the blue gel, the bloody blots where his intestines were torn and a piece of dark red flesh that might've been his liver poking out—"but us fuckers are expected to take on shit like that without any help, so I'll be fine."

"The crab's hunting Alex right now," Matt urgently relayed, "they can't last long." Even here, they could hear the thundering roars as the Gauss cannon fired its shots. It kept firing, which meant Alex was still alive, but for how long?

"No," Jeremy replied with a pained groan, "but the lad will buy us enough time to cross the river, run and try to get into a heavily covered area, it's our only—"

He paused as a single wolf drone stepped over a hill next to them. The thing turned to them, its side blowing open. Jeremy couldn't raise his weapon in time and Matt saw the electrified net fly out—

The launcher of the drone dented as Sarah shot at it, knocking it aside just enough that they managed to jump out of the net before it fell.

Sarah gripped her pistol, even as the drone fell to the ground she kept shooting at it until it finally stopped moving.

She let out a sigh of relief. "Papa always said to keep a gun under the mattress . . ."

"Your father is a smart man," Jeremy said, still barely standing but slowly getting his bearings as the anesthetics kicked in. "I would like to meet him."

Sarah let out a nervous laugh as she helped him lean on her. "Oh, he got his head bashed in by gangbangers when I was seven." She waved the pistol above her. "But hey, at least I still have his Glock!"

"Was that what was under the mattress?" Denise asked, shaking her head with disbelief. "I thought it was a dil—" she shook her head, remembering who was still on her back. "Never mind."

Despite the situation, a smile cracked on Matt's face and he let out a giggle. Denise looked embarrassed while her wife simply smiled. Jeremy tried to chuckle, but instead it came out like a pained cough. Max smiled as well, not knowing the joke but doing so because everyone else did.

In a land of death, hunted by one of the most dangerous military systems out there, it was a moment of vapid bullshit. But weren't these the moments that made life worth living?

Jeremy straightened his back, not quite okay, but close enough to muster his voice: "We need to keep moving. Alex bought us time, but it won't be enough."

The drone Sarah shot was one of many. Everything they'd encountered was just the scouting party. Other than the crab, all of them were meant for non-lethal takedowns. Staying here meant they wouldn't be as lucky.

"I'm not sure we can run," Matt said.

They turned to him, and he continued, "After the crab is done with Alex, it's gonna chase after us next. We need to take it down, one way or another."

Denise shook her head. "No, no! It's too dangerous! How can we—"

"What's your idea, kid?" Jeremy asked, his face thoughtful. "We don't have anti-tank weapons. I'm carrying some grenades and plastic explosives but it won't be enough."

Matt told them.

Within the depths of a military base, a screen flickered on, lighting up a dark room. A hundred processes, a hundred actions, all done within the span of a moment by the Perimeter.

Intruders detected. Sector FP1407.

Three Civilian Non-Combatants

One Civilian Combatant

Two Enhanced Combatants

Apprehension was attempted and failed.

Requiring Input.

Nothing moved in the room.

Requiring Input.

The screen sat as it had for decades, untouched as age old dust settled on it in a thick blanket.

Requiring Input.

Revealed by the light: splayed out messily onto the keyboard was a military uniform. The back of the uniform faced upward, but the imprints of many military medals could be seen, along with stripes that placed it as a general's uniform.

Requiring Input.

There was nothing inside the uniform, save for a thick grey goo.

Requiring Input.

In another military base, the uniforms of dozens of soldiers lay in their barracks, their uniforms fallen on top of their weapons, the same grey goo oozing out like a viscous slime.

Requiring Input.

In the depths of a large sealed bunker, civilian clothes were spread everywhere, over earthly possessions, on empty beds, and on dirty toilets. A grey goo within all of them.

Requiring Input.

Above ground, a wolf drone passed by a preschool. Its camera passed over the inside of a large gym, where there lay a pile of clothes for young children, old, dirty and frayed from weather and time, all containing or covered in grey goo.

Requiring Input.

The Perimeter did not receive an order, and it had not received one in decades.

No Input Received.

Activating Automatic Response.

One log added to countless others of the same nature.

Accessing threat level.

Threat level 1.

Protocol 6 has been activated.

In the darkness, it spoke, a mechanical voice, devoid of emotion, meaning, or reason. A machine bent to a purpose long lost, waging a pointless war because it knew nothing else.

"GLORY TO THE UNION. MAY HER PEOPLE LIVE FOREVER."

Matt stood at the end of an old bridge. Early twenty-first century by the design, he idly analyzed. He was waiting, spinning a pin around his finger and anticipating as the sounds of thunder came ever closer.

Then he saw it, a figure running toward him. Alex.

Behind them was the crab, tearing through trees and tirelessly chasing the soldier. He felt it now, that thrum which seemed to shake his very bones as the weapon powered up. Alex felt it, too, so they jumped to the side, just as the slug tore through scores of trees, annihilating them to sawdust.

The soldier jumped out of the treeline and onto the road, sharply turning toward him. The crab shot out a moment later, but its turn was slow. Alex managed to destroy one of the legs somehow. Its turret turned to them, but it was slow, and once more Matt was reminded: no matter how terrifying something was, time got to it eventually.

As Alex stepped onto the bridge, Matt kneeled down with both arms raised. A gesture of surrender, one that the Perimeter was programmed to respect.

The Gauss cannon depowered as Alex ran near him.

In the end, it was still just a machine. It would wait till Alex was away from him, to avoid hurting a non-combative civilian. Alex stopped near him, appearing to fall down tired, and the crab stepped onto the bridge with its Gauss cannon still pointed at them.

One wrong move, one single sign of aggression, and both of them were dead.

It inched closer to them, its pace slowed. After all, it had all the time in the world. The wolf drones were coming, they had non-lethal means of subjugation, before they dragged their prisoners deeper into the Perimeter, until they were brought into the SANS infected area.

Matt was suddenly aware of his heart. It beat loudly in his chest, as if it were a caged animal—it clawed at his rib cage, begged to be freed. A single wrong move and he would be turned to pink mist. The Gauss cannon almost killed Jeremy, a heavily enhanced soldier, with a slug that missed. It was a weapon that could've been used to take down tanks, much less squishy human flesh.

He could die here and he was enjoying every moment of it.

"You're crazy," Alex muttered as they pushed themselves up, "smiling in a place like this."

Was he? He didn't realize until Alex mentioned it. He felt it now, and his grin grew wide as the crab stepped onto the midpoint of the bridge.

To the left, he saw a small black object thrown from where Jeremy was hiding. Toward the bridge but not over it. The grenade landed in the Seine river under the bridge and Matt laughed as it detonated, triggering the sonic mine in the water.

There was a thunderous ringing sound, as if a bell larger than mountains was being struck. The concrete foundations of the bridge were *crushed* as it started to collapse inward. A sickening sense of nausea filled him as Alex grabbed him and ran. Underneath, it looked like the water was rippling in countless places as the mine went off. The water shook and droplets shot from the river in a mad dance to the endless cacophony of sound. The crab fell into the water, not even a moment of movement allowed before its armored shell buckled as if it were mere tinfoil. At that moment, it was as if *God itself* kicked the machine in the balls.

Matt barely noticed them reaching the other side, onto solid ground, nor the fact he was still laughing. His ears were ringing, the world was shaking and he felt vomit come up his throat, but still, he *laughed*.

The soldier let go of him, crashed into a tree, barely able to stand themself. Matt fell to the ground. He didn't know how long passed as the world shook. Seconds? Minutes? Hours? Did he laugh the entire way? He didn't know, but when he came to, he was out of breath, coughing out vomit with a massive smile on his face.

Shakily he stood up, Alex beside him. His idea worked, *he* won a great victory here. Perimeter couldn't produce more crabs without humans assisting it. Peri may have tens of thousands of them but he just made it have one less permanently.

"You're fucking insane, kid," Alex muttered or maybe yelled. He couldn't tell. Everything sounded slightly quiet to him. The soldier turned to him. "Good job—" Their eyes widened in panic. "Calm down and don't mo—"

It was too late, still elated from the victory, his ears deafened, Matt didn't hear the click as he stepped off the landmine.

Journey Part 3

"Fuck it! I give up! Next flare hmu!"
—Anon, 3:57 UTC, March 18, 2034, on the popular messaging
board "6tan" two minutes before Yellowstone erupted

Her ears still ringing with shock, Denise first glanced at Max to make sure he was okay, then frantically turned her head to where Matt was. *"It had to be me,"* he had argued. *"Jeremy's in no condition. Sarah's recognized as a combatant and Peri might mistake you for her. We need Alex to get back."*

God, why did she listen to him?

She saw it unfold, almost in slow motion. Matt stepped toward the soldier and a cloud of orange exploded from the ground and enveloped both of them.

She screamed and her voice fell on deafened ears. No one heard her, for no one could hear. She scrambled toward her son, tears dripping from her eyes.

But where hearing failed, sight succeeded. Jeremy grabbed her with the one good arm he had left. He shouted something as he pulled her back, moving in front of her. Something was hastily shoved into her face, plastic—no, a gas mask. She tore at it, her *son* was in there! Yet as she scratched and kicked at the old soldier, he remained standing and his grip didn't waver. Jeremy simply stared at the same place she was. As the smoke dispersed, she saw her son on the ground, a mask shoved into his face, held on firmly by a gloved hand. Alex was over him as if attempting to shield his tiny body with their own.

The ringing in her ears was lightening, and she started to hear words.

"Alex!" Jeremy yelled beside her. "Speak to me!"

"Don't come close!" they yelled back. "It's the stripes!"

Jeremy gripped tightened on her shoulder, he swore but Denise couldn't hear it. "MATT!" she finally yelled. "MATT!"

Jeremy grabbed her by both shoulders. "Ma'am I need you to calm down now!"

"Denise calm down!"

"But—but," she blubbered. Her son was hurt! She needed to—

There was a feeling of something. A rattle that permeated within her very bones. She barely saw the barrel of the crab in its death throes, its head just barely poking above the water, before she was shoved away. The three of them fell to the ground in a tangle but in his haste, Jeremy let a single arm poke out behind them.

Sarah's arm turned to pink mist and the crab was finally consumed by the dancing waters.

Red splattered on her face. *Her* red. Sarah's. And with it, a moment of clarity. Denise made this happen. She was the cause of this. If she wasn't screeching like an idiot they might've noticed that the crab still barely functioned. They could've gotten out if it *weren't for her.*

Above her, blood leaked from Jeremy's mouth. The soldier fell forward, landing between them.

There was swearing somewhere. Alex. She noticed them standing, but didn't come near them.

"Denise, I need you to listen very carefully," the soldier said. "There's medspray and gel in his belt, but it's likely not enough. You should have some in your own pack. Take it out and tend to his back."

She sat up, finding the aforementioned gels. She saw the torn remains of Jeremy's back with a blank expression. Her mind and body went suddenly numb. Simply *tired* as she used the gel. She shouldn't have relented to Sarah. Even if living in the Metros was hard, it was *doable.* Even if it was no place to raise children, it could be *done.* She shouldn't have relented to Matt. Even if making it out was harder, it was still *possible.*

She was a pushover, dragged along by other people's dreams of a better path. And what did that lead to?

They lay halfway across a ruined continent, the soldier who led them here missing two sides and his spine exposed. Sarah lost an arm while Matt lay infected with an unknown weapon. Meanwhile, Max was quietly huddled in the background, crying or paralyzed with fear.

Denise numbly applied the same medspray to Sarah's arm.

"...Mum?" she heard Matt weakly call. "Are you okay?"

She didn't know what to answer, because she didn't want to hurt him with truth or lie.

"Don't move, Matt," Alex said. "I can't look after your foot, I don't know if the nanites in the spray might have a reaction with the one in you."

That stirred something within her.

"There's a stim in his leftmost pouch," the soldier continued, voice forcefully calm. "Take it out and inject it into his neck."

She pulled out the cylindrical object. She noticed her hands were shaking in the same way a person might note the weather was cloudy. Denise put the stim next to Jeremy's neck and pressed the button.

The soldier let out a hacking cough and pushed himself up. ". . . Alex . . ." He spat out blood. ". . . Fuck . . . Status, Alex!"

"Stripes landmine," the other soldier muttered, his eyes glued to the shallow river. "Crab is gone, visual confirmation."

"Is it SANS?" Matt asked, his voice trembling.

Alex shook their head. "Unlikely, that was an old mine, markings say it's at most from the fifties, way before SANs usage."

"Infection status?" Jeremy rasped.

"Both of us at least," Alex said, and Denise felt her heart clenched. "You're upwind from us so you're unlikely to be infected."

The soldier pulled out a small rectangular device with three glass bulbs and buttons. They pressed one of the buttons and the bulb lit up for a brief moment before the glass exploded. "Still within Perimeter range," they said with clenched teeth. "Jeremy, you need a medivac."

"I'll be—" he groaned, his arms giving out under him as he fell. Sarah caught him, catching him by his still present side. A normal person would've died thrice over by now, but no living soldier was still normal. It was a statement of the effectiveness of the modifications, that flesh and blood humans held off the Perimeter for so many years with little more than analog equipment.

Alex stood, the orange smoke long dissipated, gently they picked up Matt. "We can't stay here, Jeremy," he said, not unkindly. "My database on pre-sixties nanite weapons is incomplete, but trends and design philosophies make it unlikely for it to be infectious unless in close contact. Either way, we need to split up."

Denise noticed Matt's left foot was a mangled mess. No blood because it was scorched, he was missing toes. Could he ever walk again? If he made it out, then probably. They needed to make it out.

"Jeremy, we needed to get out of Perimeter range *yesterday*."

"Give me another stim," the soldier said, his breathing heavy and laden, "and a pain killer."

Sarah looked at her, still supporting the old soldier from falling down completely. Even if her arm was gone, she didn't cry, she was holding it in, Denise realized. Max was curled up, appearing so . . . small. She heard soft sobbing coming from him. And what was in her? Numbness even as her family bled and cried?

Why was she here?

She knew.

When Sarah talked with her, all she could think of was something that happened several months ago. A video she saw passed from a friend.

It showed Matt and a gang of older boys beating a man till he had to be admitted to what passed as a hospital down there.

She never confronted him about it. He never changed at home, he was as kind to them as he always was. Some days he came back home with some bruises, other days he left money on the table and it . . . helped. It helped when the jobs they worked weren't enough. Sarah probably knew about it, she still had her family, which helped her out in small ways, even if she said she cut ties.

Denise had no illusions of what the Metros were. It wasn't the last remnants of a defiant Europe, it wasn't one of the last bastions of freedom in the world. They were an unorganized and terrified mob clinging to old ideals and artifacts as the world above them burned. Hiding in massive bunkers never meant to be lived in. Matt took to it like a fish to water: he was liked, he had connections even as a child, she'd seen him dismantle people with smug casualness and some days he brought back more money than either of them earned working a nine-to-five. They would've cracked ages ago if it weren't for him. Matt was born and *thrived* in a world like this.

And yet, at night Denise couldn't help but think, what kind of person was she, to let Matt, a boy who she called her son, walk this path? The same path that killed Sarah's father, that killed so many more before they grew old.

What kind of person was she?

She didn't know, but she knew one thing.

They could do *better* than this.

She took the stim and pain killer, injecting both into the old soldier's arm.

"Thank you," Jeremy rasped, his breath stabilizing.

"We need to split up, I can't risk you guys as vectors of an unknown nanite," Alex said, piggybacking Matt. "I can lead you to Évreux but I can't risk close quarters in a place like a tunnel. You guys need to take a route down there and call a medivac with Jeremy's spare—"

"What about Matt?" Denise cut in.

"I'll have to get him out myself," the soldier replied. "We're both infected and I don't know how long we have but I swear to God I will."

She let go of the other soldier, standing tall and calmly, but firmly demanded, "Swear to me."

The soldier stopped.

Alex's old and hard eyes met hers, a moment of silence passed, only the wind howling in this godforsaken place. The soldier stared into Denise's eyes and found them harder than their own.

"I swear, ma'am," they replied, putting a hand on their heart. "Even if I have to die trying."

Denise nodded. She turned, kneeling next to Max, and gently ruffled his hair. "Are you okay?" she quietly asked.

"No."

"It'll be alright."

He turned his small face to hers, wet tears drawing small lines in the grime. "And if it isn't?"

"Then we can only hope for the best."

Matt gave one last wave as he watched the far-off forms of the others walk away. Only the light of the glowstick signaled they were there at all.

Next to him, Alex sorted a bag. Taking what they could from supplies Jeremy couldn't use and left behind. Ammo, rations, water and . . . medspray.

He unintentionally glanced at his foot. His shoe was destroyed, leaving only a hastily wrapped mess covered in gel.

"I'm sorry about that," Alex said, standing back up.

Matt tried to get up on his one good foot, not finding leverage until Alex brought him up. Where he balanced with his hurt foot's heel.

"Don't be," Matt answered. It wasn't their fault anyway.

"I still am," they replied, taking the rectangular device out of their pocket. Two bulbs left. Alex flicked the switch, and the light was only on for a moment before popping. One.

"I'll carry you again," the soldier said, glancing at the darkening skies. "I fear we'll have to make the journey topside. I don't want to contaminate what usable tunnels are left for other people."

Matt agreed in theory, but who cared about the people that came after? Only the thought that his family would have to turn back into tunnels that they might've infected stilled his tongue.

"You still have no clue what it could be?"

The soldier shook their head, Matt examined their face closely and found little. That was the problem with people like Alex, a bunch of unnecessary facial muscles were removed so they became a lot harder to read.

Alex passed their largely emptied pack to Matt and kneeled down. Matt put it on and wrapped his arms around the soldier's neck. He tucked his legs around Alex's waist as they stood up. What a stupid pair they made. A kid barely older than twelve clinging to a grizzled veteran like a koala.

Every now and again, Alex looked up to the sky. Matt tried to follow it the first few times but found that his eyes were significantly worse than Alex's since he never saw anything. Regardless, Alex kept on, they followed a route only they seemed to know. Sometimes they walked on clear paths and roads, sometimes they pushed through destroyed or hollowed-out buildings. They never seemed to rest. Matt only had the vaguest idea of what soldiers of that era were capable of.

As they walked, Matt inadvertently became a tourist, his eyes wide as he stared at the world they passed. That horizon that never seemed to end. Here and there were patches of red and violet plants. He'd heard of green plants before but hadn't seen them on the way here. Some were an extremely dark sort of green, but he felt it was different from the much lighter colors from before the twenty-first century he sometimes saw in pictures.

He was surprised when he heard his first bird. Eyes turned almost in panic at the chirping sound, before the small greyish bird that made it quickly flew off. The flutter of its wings was still in his mind long after it left.

"We've left most of the bioweapon territory," Alex began. "Life isn't as dead here."

"You think it's still chasing us?" Matt asked.

The soldier shook their head. "Unlikely, even if we took out a crab we're both low priority targets. It has a drone on us but that's fine."

He felt the hairs on his neck rise, he resisted the urge to look into the sky again. "Fine?"

"If the Perimeter knows where we are," the soldier began slowly, "it knows we aren't near anywhere important to mount an actual response. The drone will eventually withdraw. If I shot it down, then it would just start sending wolves to sniff us out."

Matt nodded. "And what about Max? Sarah and Denise and your partner?"

"They're off the grid," the soldier answered. "The Perimeter was never tasked with taking care of the tunnels, only their entrances. If the subways are still intact, they should surface in Rouen, far from its defensive border."

The soldier turned slightly to him, dark black eyes met his. "Don't worry about them. They are a lot stronger than you think."

"I know Sarah is," he answered, a bit of pride swelling in his chest. She never told him she was such a good shot.

"The other, too," Alex answered.

Denise? "How?"

The soldier answered, their eyes no longer staring at him, but instead at a far-off place. "It is easy, so easy . . . to lose resolve. To simply pass the days following whatever ordered you first."

Alex shivered slightly, and Matt became aware of just how grey their short hair was. They spoke quietly, voice a whisper in the quiet wasteland, "It takes something else, to not lose it."

They passed into silence. Matt wanted to ask the soldier to elaborate further but . . . it seemed a sensitive topic. Something he shouldn't prod at. Not for someone who risked life and limb to help them.

After a while, when the sun started to set again, on the second day of their journey, from Paris to Évreux and eventually to Rouen, Alex spoke.

"Tell me about them."

"Who?" Matt asked, not sure who Alex was referring to at first.

"Your family," Alex replied, "and how you met them."

Matt thought about it for a moment, that was a long time ago. Back when Max was still an actual baby rather than the metaphorical one he was now.

"I . . ." he hesitantly began, recalling memories a bit too far out of his reach, "it was at an orphanage. They came in looking for a child to adopt, but for some reason . . . they took both of us."

"I thought they were pretty cool, and they fed us . . ."

". . . This one time when a guy broke into our house, Sarah hid us in a closet."

". . . she makes the best mushroom stew ever . . ."

"Denise always passes portions to us saying she wants to keep thin, even when she's really hungry. Don't tell her I know this by the way."

"Sarah taught me how to get good at racing games . . ."

". . . once Max got sick and Sarah did overtime for four days to pay for the medication. . ."

"Apparently they didn't know each other was gay until way later and just got into an extended game of gay chicken."

". . . some asshole was harassing Mrs. Jones who lent us her washing machine, and Denise put the fucking idiot in his place!"

". . . she can't tell a lie to save her life though . . ."

". . . and Sarah just kicked him right in the balls! That idiot was feeling it for four generations."

"They don't appreciate some of my friends, though, but that don't matter . . ."

"Denise is really good at making Max feel safe."

". . . and I beat the shit out of that guy who was shit-talking my 'rents!"

Before Matt knew it, the sun had risen all the way till midday. A night and a half, where he just talked, spoke stories, and laughed and cried. The stone-faced Alex lightened somewhat, their face seemingly without the tiredness and hardiness Matt saw before.

When the sun began to set again, they saw it.

Lights in the distance, a city still intact.

As they walked, Alex took out that rectangular device and lit the final bulb. It activated and most importantly, stayed on.

There was a melancholic smile on Alex's face as they pulled out their comms. "It was fun, kid. Let's hope we make the next part."

Matt was confused. "Hope?"

But the soldier simply kept walking as their communicator blared to life. "Mayday! Mayday!" they yelled. "Three-four unknown bioweapon! Mayday!"

Matt suddenly noticed his legs were numb, not the sort of numb from inactivity, but one that seemed to keep clawing at him. Like a cold wind that permeated throughout his entire body.

"Immediate quarantine and medivac! Two infected! One's a civilian!" Alex coughed, blood coming out. They stumbled, three steps, four steps, before falling to the ground.

As Matt fell off them and rolled onto the ground, he noticed he could not move. His body refused to answer. As if he were trapped in an inanimate doll. He could still move his neck slightly, his head flopped to the side, and he saw it.

Alex's feet, still on the ground, the joint that connected them with his legs covered in a dark black, almost crystal-like substance.

Nanites, he realized, and complex ones at that. Ones that would've been shut down by the constant EMP the Perimeter emitted, either destroyed completely or made dormant. But not new enough to be immune to it like the later versions were.

And they were now outside the Perimeter.

Matt felt his sight slowly blot out as helicopters came with figures in white.

Journey Part 4

"FUCKING HELL 2034 WORST YEAR!!!!!1!!!11!!!!!!!11!!!
LITERALLY NO GOOD OPTIONS!!11!!!1!!1!!!!1!!!!!1!!1"
—Anon, 3:57 UTC, March 18, 2034, on the popular messaging
board '6tan'

Kevin Lu rubbed his brow, tiredness setting in from the late night. His steps were the only sound in the sterile white halls of the hospital. A nightly walk: humans were always meant to be active creatures, and though his body felt like collapsing, the walk served its purpose, reinvigorating him enough to stay awake to pass the night.

The department he was currently in was a quiet one, after all, the hundreds and thousands of "patients" here didn't do much. Opening a random door, he was greeted by the sight of dozens of rows of tubes, each housing a single person. A helmet connected to breathing and feeding tubes kept them alive. Occasionally, it would send a nerve signal, making them jerk in the nanite fluid to ensure their muscles did not atrophy.

Every one of them was healthy and would likely remain so for decades with the support they were getting. They were, nicely put, passive income for the hospital to milk. Connected to life support and VR helmets, they spent their entire lives in virtual worlds, living out whatever dream they wanted. All costs paid for by the government's Universal Basic Income.

It was a dream for many, but as Kevin Lu stared at the seemingly unending rows of people, he could not help but feel despair as his mind recalled a certain statistic.

Right now, twenty percent of people in Oceania lived like this, and the number had been rising for the past decade.

Not for the first time, Kevin Lu felt the slowly crushing realization that he might be part of the last generation of doctors, of people who actually bothered to educate themselves, understand how the world works. Eventually, even his job would become automated, the future of a world where man lay dreaming in billions of tubes while AI tended to their every need outside of it. What was a pipe dream a century ago seemed so very close.

They abolished homelessness, got rid of poverty, and made the concept of hunger alien, and this was all they had to show for it? People quitting life the moment their high school education ended, the moment they started receiving their Universal Basic Income, and sequestering themselves in different worlds. They never bothered to even attempt to progress and reach the same heights their species once did, for the simple reason they no longer *needed* to.

For the first time, he felt his heart clench as he wondered if his own child would go down this path. If one day he'd be looking after a tube, only interacting with him through a virtual world.

A message pinged at the edge of his vision as he was called back to work.

The doctor activated an augment in his brain, melatonin blockers flooded his system, and he was once again wide awake.

". . . only so much time," he muttered as he left to do his job.

"Two patients," an assistant AI said next to him, "paramedic initial diagnosis is B199, unknown mass replicating nanite."

"Skip to current diagnosis," the doctor replied.

"Understood," it replied in its robotic tone, "Dr. Auburn diagnosed it as B212, Frasier R3C2-AP Nanobots used in Anti-Personnel Landmines by the former United States of America, currently in Stage Three."

The doctor would've sworn if it wasn't unprofessional; the Greens made the worst nano weapons.

"Load the details of the nanite in written form," he replied. "Location of operation?"

"Rouen University Hospital, current latency is 3.68ms to 6.24ms."

Not the worst and the hospital was well equipped to deal with most things, but lag of just a few moments could cause death. "Kill code?"

"Not available," the assistant returned. "The current patent holder of the nanite, Mcdothra Biomedicals, claims that knowledge was lost during the Civil War."

Figures, they wouldn't have called him if it was that simple.

He reached his office and sat down in the pod already waiting for him; as it closed, a dozen new heads-up displays opened.

"Dr. Lu," a figure in scrubs said, "we currently have the patients iced; you should be seeing their statuses right now."

He nodded, eyes glancing over the various metrics, along with quickly scanning the details. Two males, one a kid that couldn't have been older than his son, the other an enhanced. They were already very far gone, the enhanced was missing all his extremities but the child still looked relatively healthy, if not for the fact his entire nervous system was paralyzed. "You attempted a localized EMP burst for treatment?"

The other doctor nodded. "It failed," she answered as another video popped up. A foot, detached, likely one from the soldier, was covered entirely in the nanites. *"Begin initial test,"* her voice said as an EMP was used, and there was a horrendous popping sound as the foot dissolved into sludge. "By the point of retrieval we were too late; the nanites had already passed into Stage Two by then."

At that point, deactivation meant self-destruction. "How much time do I have?"

"Preservation was successful," the other doctor answered, a feed of both patients suspended in cryo appearing. "Nanite activity has lowered to 1.6 percent. We have time for the child, but the nanites are reacting violently with enhanced's immune system—at best six hours."

"Are the Sub-0-C1s available for use?"

Dr. Auburn nodded.

"Not the worst situation, then," he muttered. Those ones were one of the few models that can operate in cryo with complex control. "Then let me—" Dr. Lu paused as he looked at the second patient, the enhanced soldier.

He glanced back at the biometrics sent to him. "That one's listed as genderless?"

The other doctor glanced at the biometrics on her side. "Yes," she confirmed.

"Run a pupil scan," he said as he prepared to connect to the nanites on his side.

She looked confused for a moment, before doing as told, then surprise flickered on her face as the image returned to him. It confirmed his suspicions. Imprinted on their left eye was a line code that translated to "PEOPLE'S REPUBLIC OF CHINA. 克隆人 920008."

"It's one of the Eunuch clones?"

"They," he absentmindedly corrected. "Don't forget the Amendments; they are a person, and we must treat them as such."

Dr. Auburn shook her head. "Sorry, just surprised. I thought they only had a lifespan of twenty years or so. I didn't expect to ever see one, much less operate on one."

They might have undergone telomere regeneration to stay alive this long. Dr. Lu shook his head, that didn't matter much here.

"We'll begin on them," Dr. Lu said. "Assistant, pull up modification data for China's Eunuch Units. Dr. Auburn I have connected with the S0s, prepare the injection."

She nodded. In the background of the patient's room, several delicate robotic arms moved as Dr. Auburn manipulated them.

"Injection here, here, and here," Dr. Lu said as he marked the spots on the body. Two locations in the head and neck, one in the left upper arm and another in the chest, into the lungs where the nanites were most dense.

Dr. Auburn made the injection, and multiple feeds appeared in his vision.

He *tsk*ed in annoyance—the lungs and arms were lost. At the microscopic level, he could see the soldier's own immune system fighting a war in slow motion, and they were unfortunately winning. Every modified phage that successfully ate a nanite almost immediately underwent apoptosis, except they were now carrying volatile nanite which let out a mild chemical acid upon death. Not that dangerous to the body on its own, but they signaled other nanites to increase reproduction, and as Lu watched the capillaries burst and melt away from literally *millions* of dying nanites, he remembered that quality did not always trump quantity.

The soldier's own modified and improved immune system made them extremely susceptible to these kinds of weapons. They had to operate on the soldier first, otherwise they would be dead before anyone knew it.

"His lower body is unsalvageable," he declared, activating the self-destruct on his controlled nanites, before turning his attention to the ones in the neck region. There were fewer here. "We need to focus on preserving the brain. Dr. Auburn, can you begin amputation of the infected locations?"

"On it," she answered as she manipulated several robotic limbs.

"Remember to incinerate them," he absentmindedly added as he surveyed the brain.

"I'm not new to this," she curtly replied.

The brain was . . . it was salvageable, there were clusters of nanites mostly on the cranium, but a few stragglers were on the brain cells. "I'll begin extraction."

Here came the hardest part of his job. Dr. Lu only directly controlled a large observer nanite capable of receiving his signals, every other one had to be programmed and commanded through the observer nanite. He put simple commands into the nanites on the neck, attacking and disassembling the infectious nanites. Forming a small perimeter, those didn't need advanced commands, they just needed to reinforce the blood-brain barrier and stop more from entering the brain. Even if they lost the neck while they were at it, they just needed to prevent the brain from dying and they could regenerate the man completely from it.

It was the brain that was the problem. Regularly glancing at the R3C2-AP's schematics, he went about reprogramming his own nanites for safe disassembly. He added a chemical marker so that the neuroimmune system wouldn't target them. He couldn't afford to be rough or suffer any distraction here, every cluster of brain cells lost was a memory gone, a learned skill forgotten. Basic human functions they could repair, but if he failed, then the soldier would almost have had a factory reset done on them.

Dr. Lu was one of the few people who could operate nanomachines with extremely sought-after precision. He coupled macro- and micromanaging with a beyond solid grasp of both practical and theoretical biomechanics and nanorobotics. In all of Earth and Mars, there were less than eight thousand people capable of this.

Three clusters of nanites safely removed from the hippocampus, he gritted his teeth as the last one self-destructed. What was lost there? The ability to form new memories?

In the Amygdala, there were six clusters separated on each part. Four were successfully and safely removed, the last two clusters damaged the left hemisphere.

His programming wasn't succeeding, he felt his hands tighten as he had a deactivated nanite brought to the observer nanite and scanned it. Different, these nanites were visually the same as the R3C2-AP but had minor differences that made them more active in sub-zero temperatures.

He began reprogramming the S0s—different operations were required, but the blood-brain barrier was getting breached again, the S0s he left there weren't enough. He divided his attention between programming on each front, but it wasn't enough.

The soldier's heartbeat flatlined. Was it finally destroyed? Or did Auburn remove it? It didn't matter, the blood flow to the soldier's brain stopped and with it the tide of nanites. He was on limited time now, but he could finally focus on safely preserving the brain.

Cingulate gyrus, all clusters successfully removed.

Temporal lobe, he gritted his teeth as the auditory complex was damaged, but otherwise, all clusters were removed.

Occipital lobe, all clusters removed.

Parietal lobe all clusters . . .

Frontal lobe . . .

Cerebrospinal fluid cleared. He had his nanites make another two scans of the brain, but the cerebrum was completely cleared, the remains were being safely deconstructed by his own nanites.

He had another set move down and began clearing the cerebellum.

Cerebellum cleared.

Onto the brain stem now, his teeth clenched as he saw the amount there, a field of black covering the world, but he could do it, he *had* to—

"Doctor," a voice suddenly interrupted him, shaking him out of his concentration.

Dr. Lu shook his head. "Sorry Auburn . . . I forgot you were there . . ."

She didn't seem to react to this. "We can't save the brain stem, I'll begin removal. Just having the brain saved is enough."

The doctor blinked away tiredness, concentration now slipping. "Yes . . . yes, I'll leave that part to you, then."

She nodded. "Take a nap, you look horrible, Lu."

He nodded in return. "Yes, maybe I will."

He moved the nanites to a safe spot and had them all safely self-destruct. The remains were relatively non-toxic, and the body's own system could flush them out with no significant long-term problems. Before disconnecting, the pod opened up back into his office. He kept a feed of Auburn's surgery up though, despite his promise he couldn't sleep now, not yet.

He rubbed his brow, only noticing just how much sweat had accumulated. His clothes now wetly clung to him.

It was only when Dr. Auburn finished her part, that he finally fell asleep.

"I'm afraid it won't be so simple," the doctor before Denise explained. "The surgery we did on Alex was a last resort measure."

The Asian-looking doctor on the screen added, "I took into account their enhanced status; they were most likely to survive even if a catastrophic mistake occurred. Even then, Alex still suffered irreparable damage to many parts of their brain." With a defeated look, Dr. Lu said, "I'm afraid if we go for the same operation on your son, there is a forty to fifty percent chance he won't come out the same person."

Sarah's hand tightened around her arm. "What are the other options?"

"We can store him in advanced cryo until a suitable and safe solution is found, but Rouen doesn't have the infrastructure for it. He'll have to be moved to a hospital somewhere else." He looked hesitant for a moment. "I can recommend a hospital over here, but you'll have to apply for citizenship."

"We'll have to speak with the Department of Immigration for that?"

He nodded.

"The nanovirus, tell us about it again."

"Nanovirus is actually the incorrect term to describe a nanobot." He paused, remembering his audience. "*Ahem,* specifically it seems to be a modded variant of the R3C2-AP nanite, but the modifications are not enough that it greatly strays from its original purpose. Which is generally not to *kill,*" he emphasized, "but to permanently cripple the infected by attacking their nerve cells. So that they are, to put it kindly, a constant drain of resources. It is, thankfully, not infectious."

It was, as Denise understood, something meant to fulfill the original purpose of an Anti-Personnel Landmine in a war where someone could be regenerated from only a head and torso.

"People infected with it will slowly enter a vegetative state through three stages. The violent reaction it had with Alex's body was due to their greatly enhanced immune system, which was successful enough that it killed a majority of the nanites initially, greatly speeding up the stages and causing a cascade of replication signals that led to Alex almost being killed by it."

By good or bad luck, it meant Matt had more time.

"The stages are as follows: Stage One, the nanite propagates and replicates in the body, it is relatively harmless at this point. However, once it has propagated throughout the entire body, it progresses to stage two."

"In Stage Two, the nanite detects that it has spread throughout the entire body by latching onto and piercing cells. Each detects certain DNA phenotypes, causing it to release certain chemical signals related to them. Once a nanite not attached to a cell has received a signal of each type, it activates and begins attacking the nervous system."

A video appeared, showing the nanite replicating to two, the original latched onto and pierced a cell, before producing a colored circle which attached to the second nanite.

He paused for a moment. "It is around here that the immune system begins to heavily intervene, but the nanites are designed to self-destruct upon getting phagocytosed or otherwise damaged. Leading to a chemical spill that damages the body and signals other nanites to increase replication, which caused the cascade that almost killed Alex. This is the stage Matt is currently in and why he is prescribed several immune suppressors. Most damaging, the nanites would be in his brain by now and have latched onto several brain cells."

Denise listened intently, as if there was a single thing she could get, a miracle solution that could be gotten just by hearing *harder.*

"And in Stage 3 . . ." he trailed off, sighing before saying, "he will technically not die, but so long as the nanites remain in his system, he'll be unable to move a single muscle, meaning he'll require constant life support just so his heart can keep beating. It is by this point, that the affliction is considered terminal."

They were quiet, not a sound was made. The simple *weight* of the decision that lay before them. One, they put Matt into cryosleep for who knows how long until an actually safe cure or solution could be found, or they gamble with their son's life and person.

There was a third option, but neither of them would choose St. Anne's.

"This is . . . a heavy decision," he said. "Regardless, both of them are best solved with the higher-tech support in Oceania. The probability of either option working would be greatly increased with better equipment. I would suggest at least getting in contact with the Department." Dr. Lu turned to the side of the screen. "Dr. Auburn, I have another appointment, can you take the rest?"

"Yes, I can, Lu," the female doctor replied.

He nodded. "Thank you," he said before the screen closed.

There was only silence between the women, before Dr. Auburn spoke up. "You may want to sleep on this. It is a hard decision."

Denise mutely nodded.

"Refugees are always welcome here; you can stay for as long as you want . . . but your son will need a decision soon. We can keep him in cryo, but we don't have the right equipment to fully prevent brain damage."

"We understand," she quietly said as they left.

Sarah's hand shook slightly as she read the papers.

"Installation of a brain chip and the signing of an NDA program stopping us from speaking about Europe?" she asked, almost in shock at the incredulity of it.

The official shook her head. "No, you misunderstand, you may still speak about it, in fact, we are recommending you go on several talk shows to speak of your simply *harrowing* experience. You don't have to if it is too much, but it is, of course, recommended you share your experience."

But no matter how she put it, the NDA would prevent them from speaking of certain aspects of the Metro Cities, the Perimeter and even SANS.

"And the brain chip?"

"A Somatic Implant is vital to modern life," she answered. "Without it and an AAD, that is, an Auxiliary Augment Device, you won't be able to use most technology or obtain a job. They are vital for modern life in Oceania. It monitors your health and returns them in real-time so you can be made aware of any problems you have before they become problems."

She shrugged. "I am sure I am coming off as authoritarian, however, I assure you that this is just fact. Everyone in Oceania has a Somatic Implant and their life has been made better for it. It may be some culture shock to you, but you simply must get with the times."

Perhaps what was most unsettling for Sarah, was that the official did not seem to speak with malicious intent, no, she was acting as if *Sarah* was the crazy one here. She looked at her with pity, as if she'll *learn*. It was like the time Sarah spoke to a flat-earther except *she* was the flat-earther and the official was Sarah, tired of explaining facts for the tenth time.

"I . . . I need to think about this," she said as she stood.

The official nodded. "Take your time, lady, I was already informed of your situation and have sped everything as much as possible, but . . ."

She let the sentence drift, but Sarah wasn't an idiot. She was on a time-line. But at the very least, they had to explore other options, perhaps the Federation was better.

"I hope you find the solution you need, even if it isn't with Oceania," the official said as Sarah left.

"Thank you," she replied, and meant every word.

Sarah was rather puzzled, asking about the Federation didn't bring her into an office like the last, but rather one that made her think of a CEO's office. A large study with a mahogany desk situated in front of the window and before it was a pair of tasteful lounging couches with a coffee table in the middle. The young man behind the desk smiled as she entered, putting away some papers. "Ah, welcome . . . Mrs. O'Sullivan?" he glanced at her to confirm the paper was correct.

"Yes, and you?"

"Mr. Reese, but please just call me John, take a seat," he said, gesturing to a chair facing his desk.

Cautiously, she sat down, not too sure what to make of this, but John kept smiling. He poured some tea from a kettle into a cup. "Would you like some tea?"

She shook her head. "Not really."

"Your loss," he said as he took a small sip. "You must be wondering why you are here instead of with a government official," he said. Not even both-ering to wait for an answer, he continued, "Well, I'm here on behalf of the Carolina Republic to smooth over your process of immigration."

"I am sure you've already received an offer from Oceania, which I must suggest you reject." He shook his head. "Oceania is an authoritarian hellscape; it is no place to raise children."

"I've heard rumors in the Metros, yes," she replied.

John nodded. "I'm afraid most of them are true. You can't take a shit in there without the *government* knowing, but don't worry." He shuffled some papers in front of her. "As you can see, I am with Guilliman Pharmaceuticals, which is a subsidiary company of Mcdothra Biomedicals, the company who has the . . ." He paused. "Hmmm . . . I suppose, *owns* the Frasier R3C2-AP Nanobots that have . . . unfortunately infected your son." His face seemed greatly saddened by the fact.

Sorrowfully, he orated, "It is greatly unfortunate that the foolishness of our forefathers has led to harm to your son's beautiful soul, however, we would like an opportunity to remedy this, and are willing to lend you the money and company resources to allow for your son Max's full recovery."

One of Sarah's fingers twitched. "Lend?"

"Of course, we can't be expected to give things away for free," he replied, apparent sorrow on his face. "It is no way to run a business, that is why it'll take the form of a loan. Don't worry about the small stuff, Guilliman Pharmaceuticals is the most apt in the world for solving your son's affliction."

"Tell me more about the loan," she cautiously asked, "and how you expect a pair of recently jobless individuals to pay it back. After all, giving things away is no way to run a business."

The man seemed to beam. "Well, it's a rather simple matter: we are currently offering employment; we have many factories across the Americas that are largely automated, but a human touch is needed to keep things smoothed and geared."

"How much is the loan and what's the interest?"

John shrugged. "Such small details can be fleshed out later—"

Sarah's arm moved and grabbed the paper the man was trying to hide, bringing it to her face to take a long, long look at it.

"Do you take me for an idiot?" she very, very quietly asked. "These terms are unpayable. The position you offer and the wages *mathematically* cannot pay it off. The interest grows faster than what could be earned."

The man's face was unchanged. "It is only an initial position, which you may bargain from, and even then, that's not accounting for the many raises and promotions which you may—"

Sarah slammed the papers onto the desk. "I'm done here." She stood and began to leave.

"Wait a moment."

She paused at the door, turning to the man who only looked smug. "I said before that we are the best option to treat your son."

Sarah scoffed. "From what I've heard, the Federation is severely behind Oceania in tech level; if they can't do it, then you expect me to believe you can?"

"Ah, but there's the trick," the man said. "We are the ones who *made* the product, of course, we are the ones most . . . 'knowledgeable' about its ins and outs."

Sarah had a blissful moment in which she didn't understand what the man was saying. But then she did, and she grit her teeth. "Are you saying that you have the deactivation codes for the nanites?"

The man smiled. "I am very *specifically* not saying that. I am, however, saying that we are best suited to save your son Max."

"After all, don't you want to speak to your—"

Sarah wasn't listening, she walked up to the man, grabbed him by the collar and slammed his fucking face into the desk.

There was a satisfying crack as his nose broke.

"His name," she spoke slowly, quietly, and deliberately as she held his head down, "is Matt."

Slowly, Sarah let go and headed for the door.

"Gurrgh," the man groaned as he clutched his broken nose. "You'll pay for that!" he screamed. "You know what just did you stupid woman! We bought your fucking migration rights! You can't get into the Federation without going through us!"

"Shove a dick up your nose, it might straighten it," she coldly replied as she slammed the door behind her.

Sarah walked for a long time, fueled by more things than rage. It was only after a while that she slowed and stopped. The realization of what she'd done slowly hitting her.

The American Federation was a bust if everything he said was true. That left Oceania and the People's Republic, but there was no way they could go to Mars, so Oceania remained the only option. With a shaky hand, she brought out her phone.

She dialed Denise's number and panicked for a moment when the call didn't go through, before she remembered she needed to swap services to above ground. This time, she picked up on the third ring.

"Denny-boo," she quietly said into the phone.

"*Yes?*" her wife asked.

"I may have ruined our chances with the Federation and . . . a one-hundred percent way to save Matt." Her voice broke as she admitted this.

There was only a quiet sigh. *"Tell me about it when you're back, but for now, I just want to know—was it worth it?"*

She thought about it for a long moment, before replying, "Yes."

"Then I'm not worried," Sarah could hear the tired smile on the other end. *"C'mon back. We haven't eaten a proper meal for three days now . . ."*

Journey Part 5

"Yo, don't be so negative anon, we got dis."
—Anon2, 3:58 UTC, March 18, 2034, in response to Anon, on the popular messaging board '6tan'

Matt woke up in a strange place, nothing but white stretching out as far as the eye could see, then reality began to shift and he recognized the telltale signs of a VR world loading.

He did not wait long, because he was soon inside a dinky looking office. Plentiful computer screens covered a desk, and bible-thick pages were stacked everywhere. There was a VR pod next to a cot, both seemed well used. Behind the desk, a man loaded; in front, two women and Matt recognized them.

"Sarah? Denise?" He glanced around. "Where's Max!?"

"He's safely sleeping at our new home," Denise said, reaching out for him before . . . stopping. "We didn't want him to hear this."

"What do you mean? What happened?" he asked. He furrowed his brow, the last thing he remembered was . . . Alex saying something to him. "Are Alex and Jeremy okay?"

"They are," the man behind the desk said. "They went through some life-threatening danger, but both are safely regenerating back in Europe."

Matt's brow furrowed harder. "Back?"

Sarah coughed. "Well, this isn't how we wanted to tell you this, but . . . welcome to Australia!" She threw her arms outwards in a sort of explanatory gesture.

"This is a shitty office."

"Sorry," the man said, scratching the back of his head. "I've been meaning to clean up, but then I'll lose where I kept everything."

"Can we get back to the topic?" Denise asked, and Matt realized her hand was shaking slightly. "Dr. Lu, please tell him what you've discussed with us."

The man nodded. "Greetings, Matt Nguyen. I am Dr. Kevin Lu, and I'm your doctor for your current affliction."

He figured it out. "That black crystal. The nanites Alex told me about." Matt felt at that moment his heart should've clenched, or maybe his would hand tighten, but none of that happened. He wasn't in his real body.

Dr. Lu nodded. "As I am led to understand it, you triggered an Anti-Personnel Mine in the Paris Theatre and were infected with a nanite weapon." He moved a hand and a video popped up on one of the screens.

"The nanite that has infected you is a modified version of the Frasier R3C2-AP Nanobots, which is used in Anti-Personnel weapons . . ."

The doctor explained it to him. The three stages, how the nanites slowly brought a person to a vegetative state. His two options.

"So, it's difficult to remove the nanites?" he asked.

Lu shook his head. "Difficult it is not." His hand moved in the air, and the screen changed to another video. It showed one of the nanites attached to a cell and producing a circular chemical. "The nanites attach to your cells to progress from Stage one to two, physical *removal* of the nanites is not difficult, the problem, however." He moved his hand again, and this time it showed another nanite ripping the previous one out of the cell. The cell's wall burst and its inside leaked out. "Is preventing cell lysis, which will happen if the nanite is removed from your cell. It isn't a problem for your normal cells but . . ."

On-screen, it showed a diagram of his body and the infected portions. His brain was highly infected.

"If your brain is damaged, you may lose memories and I'm afraid that is irrecoverable."

"And my other option," Matt slowly asked, "is to be put on ice for how many years?"

"My most generous projections say at least a decade," the doctor frankly answered. "Removing the nanite is not the problem, it's finding a method to prevent the lysis of your brain cells."

"I'll take the gamble," he replied.

"Matt!" Denise yelled, she reached to grab him but . . . her hand passed through him. She flinched, her hand clenching into a ball. "Matt, don't make a decision that fast. This is life and death here."

"I just made my decision mum," he replied, his head turning between her and Sarah. "Ten years is a long time." He stared at his hands. "Max hasn't even been alive that long. After ten years would you all be the same people? Would Max even *remember* me?" Matt asked, his eyes pleading for an answer.

Would you still love me? Would I still be welcome in your home? Those questions he didn't ask, the fear of a loving lie outstripped the hope of a heartful truth.

"I would rather get it over and done with than let it drag out," he said. "Alex went through it fine, didn't they?" he asked with a small hope.

The doctor shook his head. "They're in therapy to find out exactly what memories they're missing and how to deal with them . . . It is. . ." He sighed. "If I was a gambling man, I wouldn't bet on you coming out the same person."

Matt's hand clenched. That was fine, even if he forgot Denise, Sarah and Max he could learn to love them again. Perhaps he was selfish, choosing this path because he didn't want the pain of seeing them forget him, who could tell?

"Regardless of your choice, it will take some time to have everything prepared," the doctor said. "You're hooked up with the Hospital's server, I suggest you three . . . speak about it among yourselves."

They nodded, and as they filed out of the office, they found themselves in a place more private.

What was spoken between them that night is not something we should intrude on.

Matt wandered the quiet halls of the hospital. Even from his brief looks outside, Oceania seemed so alien to him. The people were nice, they smiled to him as he walked past, the walls were clean and devoid of graffiti and . . . he stopped himself from instinctively avoiding another camera. From how he understood it, the places where the camera was watching were the only places where he could interact with people in real-world. What was slightly distressing was just how many of these locations existed, even in places where he was *sure* there wasn't a camera nearby.

Sometimes other virtual people passed him, but everything about them seemed . . . too perfect. Even people in the real world, he couldn't see any kind of physical deformity, skin blemish, or even overweight or underweight! Practically everyone looked like some variant of a model and he'd been instinctively trying to avoid them.

Which led him to here.

He was on the top floor of the hospital, on a long flight of dusty stairs that led to a door. It wasn't locked, and when he pushed it open he was outside. He tried to breathe in the outside air, only to remember he couldn't do that, so instead, he just looked around.

A wide area, with boxish tubes coming out of the floor signifying the numerous ventilators and fans that moved air throughout the hospital. There was a thin wire fence several times taller than him covering the entire edge of the roof. As his eyes moved toward the center of the roof, he saw something he didn't expect.

A kid, about the same age as him, black-haired and most surprisingly, kinda pudgy. Like not obesely fat, but enough that there was a noticeable potbelly. He was sitting on a ventilator and pulling fries out of a paper fast food bag with a giant M on it. He turned and apparently saw him, but didn't comment, instead of turning back and eating his fries.

"You're from here?" Matt asked as he walked closer. This kid was the first person he saw that was even slightly deviant from the "model" or "supermodel" theme he'd been seeing in the people here, well other than Dr. Lu and even the doctor would look pretty good if he just took a five-month nap.

The boy sighed. "Where else could I be from?" he tiredly replied.

"I dunno," he answered as he sat on the ventilator next to him. "Europe? America? Some other part of Oceania? Maybe even Mars?"

"Never been anywhere but here," the boy answered.

"Eating dinner?"

"On the off chance you are not capable of sight, I'll answer with a yes," the boy sarcastically replied. "And yes, I am aware I am extremely fat," he added as he pulled another handful of fries.

Matt chuckled. "Nah, I've seen worse, this guy Angelo for one is so big you have to wonder how he even fits in his pods."

"Huh," the boy simply answered.

"What do you do around here?"

"Eat."

Matt shook his head. "Nah, I mean what do you do for fun? Bit new here and I'm getting stir crazy. Got any games or something?"

The boy stared at him as if he were an idiot. "You're on the hospital server, just open a tab and swipe to them."

Matt was about to ask how but thought better and decided to find them himself before the other child had a chance to look at him as if he were stupid, *again*. Shortly, he found it, and with only slightly faked annoyance, he said, "Nah, this shit is all kid's games!"

Wasn't even a lie, was he supposed to play *Sudoku* to pass time?

The boy sighed. "I can link you up with my AAD if you can stop bothering me?"

"What's on it?" he asked, slightly intrigued.

The boy swiped the air. "Ygg, Arrowed, PoW . . ."

"Wait did you say PoW?" he intruded.

He nodded. "Yeah, Path of War, want that one?"

"Sure, sure! How do you link me?" Matt asked, feet swinging from the ventilator.

"Your name?" the boy asked.

"Matt Nguyen."

"Found you," he replied as he tapped the air a few times.

Declan Lu has opened a LAN, do you wish to—

Matt barely even read the message before he hit yes, and with a cheer he watched the PoW menu load in front of him.

"Finally! I've been going crazy doing nothing but walk around and watch videos!" They used a weird site called "Ustube" here, most of the shit on it was boring trope vomits that seemed mindlessly designed to appeal to people. Sure, it had higher quality than the stuff in the Metros but it was just shit in a different way.

With glee, he hit the matchmaking queue only for—

Hospital Server has disabled this due to Age-Restricted Content.

"What the fuck!?"

There was a smirk on the other kid. "Yeah, I'm connected to the Hospital net right now and they have blocked a bunch of online shit." He shrugged. "Guess you can't play."

"Ahh!" he yelled in disappointment, before falling to the ground. "Goddamnit, that sucks."

"Mmhmm," the other boy murmured in agreement, before tossing another handful of fries into his mouth. "Does, doesn't it?"

"Yeah . . ." Suddenly, Matt shot up. "Hol'up, this is a LAN right?"

The other boy nodded, mouth too busy chewing chips to talk.

"Can't I play with you, then?"

The boy shrugged. "Probably," he replied, before manipulating his own menu. "Hmm. . ." He raised an eyebrow. "Huh, there is such a feature."

"You didn't know that?" Matt asked. He'd used it plenty of times when connection was spotty. "Never used it with friends or something?"

"Never had friends," the boy drily answered.

"Yeesh, you're depressing," Matt replied as he accepted the invite.

The boy hopped off the ventilator, sitting in a more comfortable position where he was leaning against it and he, too, accepted the game.

Reality bled out around them as the world slowly loaded.

"Just a warning, I am very good at this."

"Heh." The other boy smirked.

* * *

In a frozen wasteland, a figure squatted down and with an annoyed huff began operating a holographic device on his arm.

Had to be the freezing cold map, Declan thought as he got to the tool he wanted. Opening up the thermal imaging tool, he began to survey the area—

A hand pressed down on his shoulder. "Huh, a full scout spec? You came prepared."

"What the fuck?" he practically jumped as he realized his opponent was right behind him. "How'd you get—"

"Walked," Matt casually answered.

Mustering himself, Declan asked, "Then how'd you find—"

"Looked," Matt casually answered, gesturing at a barely visible line of footprints leading up to him.

"What the hell?" They were in white-out conditions and he managed to catch *that*? "What kind of eyes do you have?"

He shrugged. "I mean you get used to it after playing on the map so many times."

Declan regarded his opponent with a newfound wariness. "And you didn't just shoot me?"

"Naaaah," he replied as he began walking, "too boring. Was just saying hi. Imma find a new spot and let's restart."

Declan didn't reply, instead, his eyes were glued to the floor as he watched Matt walk away.

No sound, he noted, *and the footwork seemed to minimize the weight he was moving with. He barely left any footsteps . . .*

"Dangit," Declan muttered. He didn't put stock in the rumors and memes of people who played PoW so much they accidentally became super-soldiers, but unless that guy knew an exploit he didn't, then that was very much the real deal. After all, Path of War's original code was from a VR program the Chinese used to quickly train their clone soldiers. It only became a game after it became apparent that it was the best VR experience in existence from all the bankrolling their military did.

Declan stood and began to move; after all, this might actually be somewhat difficult.

Matt ran through the frozen expanse, quickly dashing between massive supply crates to minimize exposure. The trail went cold, pun intended, the moment the other player began to move. He paused at a bit of snow that looked like someone had swept it. *Covering your tracks or . . .*

Suddenly Matt leaped backward, just as a bullet flew through where his head had been and embedded itself in the crate next to him. He swiftly took cover just as the second bullet missed him and loaded his own gun.

Sniper, huh? This'll be fun.

Still behind cover, he began to move. Opening the holographic device on his arm, he quickly selected an option that expelled a drone from his belt, then another that caused climbing spikes to pop out of his glove. Holstering his weapon, he grabbed onto the wall of a crate and climbed.

Lost him again, Declan thought as he opened his wrist device. His opponent was good, good enough he didn't miss a small detail like swept snow. *Did he jump knowing it was a trap or was it just a lucky guess?* Didn't matter. He stared at the tracker; if his opponent used any electronics, then he would know. There was a ping south of him; he brought up his sniper rifle facing that direction and—

A small, tube-like object was suddenly thrown in front of him.

Flashbang! Declan fell to the ground, minimizing his exposed area as bullets flew overhead. It came from west of him. The flash barely lasted a second, but Declan was already forced into a disadvantageous position. The bullets stopped, and he heard the sound of a magazine being ejected.

Declan jumped up, sniper rifle raised, only to see a silenced pistol pointing at him.

Both fired, but Matt was faster.

The map was called Nuclear York, an island filled with bombed out buildings and the husks of hundreds of vehicles, based on an actual place like most maps. Matt moved as he usually did, completely silent on the dust and asphalt, before stopping as he saw the casing of a stim pack on the ground. Immediately he jumped back, getting behind a car and dodging the bullet.

"Again," he muttered in annoyance. Matt activated the same options on his wrist, before moving again undercover.

Once again, the drone pinged them the wrong location while Matt threw a flashbang into the room where he saw the sniper muzzle. Once again, he laid down fire with his rifle before the other player jumped out to capitalize on the reload.

Once again, Matt had his pistol pointing at them. The bullet struck him in the head, but they shot another into Matt and killed him.

What?

From the death replay, Matt noticed his bullet didn't penetrate and that his opponent was no longer holding the high-powered sniper rifle from before.

"Shit, you respec'd, didn't you," he muttered as the other shrugged beside him. They swapped out their rifle for maxed body armor; that's why they survived the first shot.

"Again."

A different map, but a similar paradigm. His opponent was holed up again and Matt had to flush him out.

This time, he threw the flash then immediately went in. Only three bullets in his rifle and it was one too many.

Again, they played.

The other player was on the move this time; Matt was able to track them, but he left mines in his path and he was forced to take detours. It was when he was running through an alley that he saw a grenade being thrown into it.

Again.

Matt learned his tricks, and this time shot him from behind where he was planning to throw the grenade.

Again.

Matt kicked down the door, only to pull several springs, causing a dozen clicks. His opponent survived the grenade blast by the skin of his nose.

Again.

He realized something as they fought, his opponent had a worse reaction time than him, not bad enough it was obvious, but enough that when he dragged him into an open gunfight he emerged victorious.

Again.

They took a drone spec this time; as Matt was distracted by the drones, he was finished off with a pistol from behind . . .

Again.

Matt managed to snipe him even when harried by . . .

Again.

Fucker blew up the building . . .

Again.

Again.

Again.

Again.

Again . . .

Matt didn't know when he began grinning through every match. Nor when he started slapping his opponents back and chatting amicably with him in the downtime between. He just did.

For how long did the two of them play? Time bled away as they both fought their tiny war. In the middle of it, Matt realized with surprise that he had altered his strategy and build dozens of times just in the past hour to match with the other. A constant battle of one-upping, Matt was faster and better in terms of all physical mechanics, but his opponent seemed to know every weapon and build combination like the back of his hand. Constantly pulling out increasingly strange and unexpected combinations. Each time Matt tried to smash through them, and he did not always succeed.

Then came the last match.

Declan scoffed as he put away the scrambled wrist device. "Fucking horrible map," he muttered as he stared at the blank desert-like expanse, only a line of blackened rods breaking up the scenery.

"Yeah, sucks, doesn't it." Declan wasn't even surprised that his opponent had managed to sneak up on him again. Leaning on one of the rods, he said, "Mongolian Border's a bitch to play with any high-tech build."

Specifically, the rods that went in a line as far as the eye could see. They were irradiated thorium rods constantly emitting radiation which screwed up most signaling devices. Their actual purpose was to act as a barrier against SANS, the radiation was enough that the nanite got scrambled into a more useless form if it ever came near, not that it mattered in-game of course.

"How 'bout this?" Matt began as he pulled out a small, timed explosive. "Let's do this old-west style. I'll set a timer and we move away; on the explosion we shoot each other."

"Why the sudden need for theatrics?" Declan asked. Every other fight they had barely been aware of each other until too late.

Matt shrugged. "Got a message calling me back, gonna be my last game tonight. Want it to be a bang."

"Oh."

"Or I suppose morning," Matt said as he laid the bomb next to the rod.

"Jesus, time passed that fast?" Declan asked as he swiped open a menu.

"Yeah," Matt fondly said, "passes fast when you're having fun, doesn't it?"

The other boy seemed taken aback for a moment. "I . . . yeah, I suppose."

"One-twenty seconds alright?"

"Sure," he answered, and Matt started the count. Cheerfully hopping back up, he said, "Let's take our places."

But the other boy was already moving away.

"Gee could've waited for me," Matt muttered as he began moving.

Both were moving away. Both had their hands on their weapons.

In the past, a pro-gamer said this, that to become a pro, you needed two things.

One, the pure and raw mechanical skill that if a battle ever comes down to the coin flip, when the odds were against you, you won every time.

I've seen this guy move, he's definitely slower than me, Matt thought as he strode away.

Two, the planning, knowledge and tactical acumen, to make situations where the odds were against you, the coin flip, never happen. To stack the coin so much it is never flipped.

Eighty-six, eighty-five, eighty-four . . . Declan counted as he walked away. The moment the bomb was set, he began counting. *Be the first to know when the bomb detonates. Move to the left to use the small smoke cover of the explosive. Bank on those heartbeats of advantage . . .*

If a player had both, then they were a pro.

The bomb exploded and both players instantly turned and raised their weapons.

Two shots were fired.

"Aaah!" the other boy yelled as he rubbed his head. "Goddamnit, why do I need to leave!?"

Declan didn't answer, instead, sitting listlessly behind them, mind engrossed in thought.

"Oh well." The boy shrugged. "Hey, you better be here tomorrow!" he said, pointing directly at him.

"It is tomorrow," Declan answered as he gestured at the rising sun.

"You know what I mean!" the other boy exasperatedly said. "Either way see ya! I have a damn doctor's appointment to be at."

Declan mutely nodded as the other boy began to leave, but he stopped a few moments before the door. "Oh, shit, I forgot to introduce myself, I'm Matt Nguyen! Good to see ya!"

"Declan Lu," he said, but Matt was already gone.

The boy sat there for a long time, the fries by his side already cold.

"Fun huh . . ." he quietly said. Declan hopped off the ventilation tube and simply stared at the morning sky.

Slowly, he began walking toward the square-ish box that led downstairs, but instead of going in, he went around, to behind it, where the wire fence was only a few centimeters away.

There, in the wire fence, behind the door, hidden from the cameras, was a perfectly cut hole.

Slowly, Declan sat, staring at the thing he made, he didn't do it all in one sitting, even if he could've. It was the work of months, some days where he just *snipped* a part off, until they added up, leaving nothing but a hole.

Wrist cuts wouldn't have done the trick, any kind of slow death would've led to his Somatic Implant alerting an ambulance. A hanging wouldn't have worked, even if he choked to death so long as his brain remained he could be fully revived. And he couldn't get ahold of a weapon capable of destroying his brain quickly.

That was why he made the hole. A fall from eight stories high. If he aimed it right, nothing could be retrieved.

As for *why* he did this. He no longer remembered exactly. Could he even give a single reason, if he knew them?

There was one thing, however, he knew.

How many times had he come up to this roof? How many times other people had seen him come up here. Yet how many of them have joined him up here? How many of them have found the hole?

No one. He simply didn't matter enough for people to bother, and every day this hole went unnoticed was another day that proved it. That in the end, no one cared. No one would care.

"Tomorrow huh . . ." he muttered. Slowly he shrugged and moved away from the hole in the fence, pulling open the doors and entering the hospital.

It doesn't matter either way.

Matt once again stood in Dr. Lu's office. Eyes engrossed on the animatic on the screen, showing the nanite replicating.

The nanite split in two, one entrenched itself into a cell and began producing signals, the other received them and began attacking a nerve. When it was destroyed, it released an acid that damaged nearby cells and signaled other free-floating nanites to replicate.

"Are you sure of your decision, Matt?" the doctor asked.

"Yes," he answered.

The doctor only sighed. "May I at least know why, before your parents come?"

Matt stared at the video, thinking for a long moment before speaking: "I just believe something."

The doctor waited on him to elaborate.

"I feel like . . ." He paused, thinking of the right words. "That every moment we have matters. Every moment means something, and if I don't make the most of it, if I don't enjoy it as much as I can, do I even deserve it?"

The doctor was silent, but after a while, he nodded. "I understand where you're coming from. Somedays I wish I could clone my mind a dozen times just so that one could be active even when I sleep."

"We never have enough, do we?" Matt said quietly. That was why he didn't want to be put in stasis, all the time he would lose. All the ties he had made. Friendship, family, they were like a garden, requiring constant care, but withering with a season of negligence.

"No," the doctor answered, a sad smile on their own face, "we don't."

A moment of silence passed, before Matt spoke again. "Hey doc?"

"Yes?"

"Radiation therapy won't work right?"

The doctor shook his head. "You still have the problem of the nanites attached to your brain cells, except now I can't use my own to try to patch up any damage."

Matt stared silently at the video.

"I have a question."

"Ask away."

"These nanites," he said, turning to the doctor, "the new replicated ones aren't in an activated state, are they?"

"No, they aren't." The doctor shook his head. "If you're thinking of using some kind of signal disrupter, know that the signals used to activate the nanite are all similar to chemicals and proteins your body heavily needs. Disrupting even one could outright kill you. An identical inhibitor could be used, but according to this it would still activate off that."

Matt stared at the doctor. Thinking. Last night, he fought a person that needed constant adaptation, a constantly shifting perspective just to keep up with them.

To face the Declan, Matt had to learn to use and counter things that he *couldn't* expect. He had to learn the unlearnable. He had to deeply understand his opponent and their intentions. It was a first for him, for before everyone else rolled over with his simple skill.

"I have an idea," he slowly began, the smallest fear that what he was proposing was dumb. "If the nanites only produced the signals upon scanning and attaching to certain cells, then . . . why don't we just remove every cell that creates a signal?"

The doctor stared at him dumbstruck for a single moment before he jumped out of his seat. Hands moving frantically over his virtual interface.

"Why didn't I think of . . . No, the better question is why isn't it in the records the company gave us?" he muttered. He grabbed a blank page and pen and began furiously scribbling on it. "Mcdothra didn't give us full treatment records . . . Doesn't fucking matter, which cells need to be removed? Fingers and toes at least, maybe up to the entire limb . . . Liver and heart? Fuck—can't remove bone marrow or blood . . . or bone for that matter . . ."

The doctor was like that for a few frantic moments, before he finally said, "I don't know, I'm going to need to call in some special help with prosthetics and this isn't a permanent solution but . . ."

"I think it might work, at least, till we find a permanent safe solution."

Matt turned and looked at the video, seeing it once again from the perspective of the nanite maker.

The purpose of the nanite was to cripple, not to kill.

So, why not become a cripple? After all, *Every moment matters, even those where I'm not fully there. So long as some part of me is there.*

"Let's try it, then."

Blue

———

"To deal with fiends is like splattering your own blood against a canvas. Intentional, and you may paint a great work, involuntary, and all you have is a dirty sheet. Regardless, you will bleed."

    —The Thaumaturge, current ruling head of Var'Ah'Bwek

You've been to the Ardere Lands haven't you?" Leo conversationally began.

Helen sleepily blinked open her eyes as she floated out of the coral bed. "Yeah?"

"I've always wondered something," he began, "we've heard of tales of those mad cities bordering the Canal. They apparently commercialized demon summoning have they not? If so—"

Leo could not finish, as the other triton leaped from the coral bed and hushed the male. "Don't say that! What if they hear you? You'll get demoted or worse!"

The male simply smiled. "Pfft, as if they won't already do that if they realize I'm laying with you."

Helen's cheeks reddened. Though they were childhood friends and hatch mates, their current difference in rank made things . . . difficult. Even if discovery meant they would both be punished, Helen would get off easier, being a trained Magus, while Leo was a mere sergeant. One would get a slap on the wrist, the other would see court marshalling and reassignment.

"Not only that," Leo pressed, "you may be the only one I am able to ask this question to, any other Magus or Pontiff would only give me a lecture on how dealing with fiends of any sort is wrong. Regardless of how they make it work in the surface world."

Helen puffed, a spray of bubbles exiting her mouth and gills.

"Even so, it is a stupid thing to ask, you know how they deal with anyone who even *thinks* about fiend contracting. By the Blue you are stupid."

Leo simply shrugged in a way Helen could tell was brushing off the danger. She briefly thought about withholding the information but reasoned knowing it would shy the young triton from searching deeper.

"The answer is rather simple, fiends, and specifically demons, are not made equal."

Her back straightened, an unintentional habit she gained from surface teachers. She had learned much from them during her short few years in the Ardere, from reading notes left behind by Diabolists of old to attending a lecture from *The* Thaumaturge.

"Though many demons are capable of reason and forming contracts with people, the desire to do so seems to diminish the higher the Hell Circle the demon originates from."

"The Circle?"

"Yes."

Leo was confused, as was she when she first learned it. "But why though?"

"There are no concrete reasons known, but it is believed it is related to how old the Hell Circle is."

"Hell Circles are numbered by how easily accessible they are from our world. The first Hell Circle is the easiest to access, the second being the next easiest and so on and so on. The farther a Hell Circle is, the older it is, thus it is assigned a higher number."

"The older a fiend is, the more dangerous it will be," she said, despite knowing that every Triton child was taught this from birth. "It is speculated that while devils will retain their willingness to form contracts with people, demons seem to lose this desire as they age. Thus, it is a simple leap to think that the older a Circle is, the older its resident demons will be."

The next part she made sure to heavily stress: "The fiends the landers make contracts with *only* go up to the Fifth Circle, but it becomes impossible to make a contract with a demon from Circles above the Third."

"Because they become too unreasonable?"

"Exactly," Helen answered. It was rumored that the Thaumaturge managed to bend a demon from the Fourth Circle to his service, but it was an exception rather than the rule. "The Hell Circle the Gate is connected to is at *least* the Eighth."

She gently knocked Leo on the head. "So, make sure not to ever think about such foolish things again, or at least keep it to yourself."

"Understood, mother," Leo cheekily said.

"Who are you calling mother—"

Helen could not finish, because at that moment the scrying pearl in her room lit up.

"ATTENTION ALL CREW SHIP MEMBERS! CODE BELUA! A DEMON HAS TRIGGERED PRELIMINARY WARDS! I REPEAT! CODE BELUA! A DEMON HAS TRIGGERED PRELIMINARY WARDS!"

Both tritons moved, surprise having long been trained out of them. Hastily they threw on uniforms, assigned protection wards.

"Any idea what's going on?"

"About as much as you," Helen answered as she grabbed her staff. "We got to get to our stations quickly, a Code Belua means at least a Greater."

They were at the door of Helen's quarters in mere moments.

"Make sure you survive," Helen said. "You're assigned to one of Pistris Ships, you *will* be on the front."

"Pistris Four," Leo answered mildly, "and I will, there is no need to worry." Leo clasped her hand. "Remember your promise for me to take you on a proper date."

Glacies Testudo was what the structure covering the Hell Gate was called. It consisted of four walls, each arranged in an ovoid surrounding the Trench. The walls were seventy percent ice, maintained through an elaborate web of computational pearls that took the place of traditional wizards. With a fifty kilometer gap between each wall. Covering the entire thing was a frozen ceiling approximately five hundred meters thick.

Overall, the structure was approximately two thousand kilometers long and eight hundred kilometers wide.

It was a structure meant to contain, and as Helen swam through the living corridors of the Leviathan Ship Cetus, she could not help but feel slightly nervous.

This was her first Breach. She studied lesser fiends, but at best they were from the Second Circle. Not impressive things all things considered.

She swiftly reached the heart of Cetus, where the main computational pearl was stationed. The heart was alive with activity, numerous high-ranking tritons swam around. Many of them magically inclined, peering over numerous measure devices and scrying pearls.

She quickly saluted the Senior Staff Mage who noticed her presence. "Magus Helen."

The Mage grunted. "Magus, take your station with Magister Rhea."

"Understood."

She moved to take her spot next to the Magister. "Teacher Rhea, what is the situation?"

The older triton briefly looked up from the array of pearls in front of her. "Minimum—one Greater Demon. Entropy judging from the damage the wards sustained. Sonar arrays are picking up strange fluctuations though. There may be—"

The triton cursed as she as several new readings appeared on the displays. "Fuck! Staffer! It is a duo event!! Another demon has appeared on sonar!"

In the depths of the Trench, affectionately named the Abyssal Scar by the tritons, a figure emerged from the Hell Gate.

As the thing passed through the Gate, dozens of magical formations lit up, before they *broke*. Intricate and ordered webs of magic, in an instant, became chaotic. Corrupted to meaninglessness.

Its body was humanoid, ape-like if you ignored the fins, but its head was that of an eyeless fish, opening up to a massive gaping mouth without teeth. Within this mouth, several dozen serpents slithered out, tasting the water.

The demon took its first look into reality, and something approximating a wicked smile carved its toothless jaw.

It unleashed its aura, and the world turned to chaos. Entropy ran rampant as all order gave way to chaos.

Wards broke, their complex machinery altered beyond usage. Only several remained. The most ancient and made to withstand the passing of time.

During all this, the demon saw above the Scar several dark dots up high above release something. Swiftly, huge pillars of ice and frost descended upon it. Striking the ocean bed like thunder, crackling tubes of ice swiftly spreading. Forming a labyrinth of ice. The demon's aura struck it but did not affect it.

It leaped back, dodging the swiftly spreading ice before all the ice stopped.

As one, the many serpentine heads of the demon turned to the Hell Gate, they saw that nothing had passed, yet *something* had passed.

Several stones on the ocean bed rose, they spun, until they orbited the largest amongst them, a boulder. The stone of the boulder warped, shaped like clay until it was covered with dozens of tortured faces. As the mouths of these faces opened to scream, they revealed a human eye, held delicately between their lips.

"You cannot affect it, Babon," the faces spoke in Abyssal.

The many snakes hissed back. A question.

The stones moved forward until one of the orbiting rocks touched the ice.

"I see. They are dumping sub-zero brine. I see. It has a lower freezing temperature, but it is cold enough to cause the seawater to freeze on contact. I see." The many faces of the demon spoke, *"No doubt they intend to freeze us. I see. Stop us in place until a greater weapon descends. I see. And what is this?"*

The faces lit up in an expression of supreme pain. *"There are bubbles of super-heated water. I see. Maintained by hidden wards. I see. We have adjusted to this freezing temperature. I see. But if we touch this heat, then thermal shock shall break us. I see. Ingenious."*

"You cannot affect the ice, for they are drawing on a lesser aspect of Entropy. The equalization of heat and energy. You cannot add disorder to the temperature any more than it is already."

Then every face screamed and the eyes bled. *"They truly are intelligent, to exploit the laws of their world to this extent. But laws will be amended. Exploits covered up."*

The main boulder did not move from its position, but the orbiting stones rose. *"I shall correct these oversights. Your hand, Babon?"*

Babon lifted an arm and touched the boulder.

At that moment.

Entropy reversed.

Helen stared in horror as she read the divination pearls.

An extremely hot mass was forming in the hand of the Entropy demon. Energy was getting drawn toward it, but no matter how hot it became, the water around it only seemed to get colder.

Rhea cursed next to her. "Order is also of the Greater classification! Has the ability to alter abyssal aspects!" she yelled. "Entropic ability has been reversed; energy is no longer dispersing down the energy gradient but upward to where more energy is placed!"

A star was forming in the hands of the Entropy demon.

"Senior Staff"—Helen's voice broke—"the average temperature of the Testudo is going down! Heat from up here is being drawn to them!"

Frost began snaking out of the Trenches. The nearby Concha Vessels were able to get out after dropping their payload but the ice continued to snake out, and ever so slightly, Helen began to feel colder.

"Prepare to go in!" the Senior Legate ordered. "Take them out before—" He could not finish, as at that moment, the demons released the energy. Creating a bubble of superheated gas which slowly floated up. Boring a hole through the frozen labyrinth.

"Breaking through the first layer!" Rhea yelled.

"Entropy demon moving up!"

The commanding Legate screamed orders through the pearls.

"Ten thousand meters till emergence!" Helen yelled.

The Leviathan Cetus took its place circling the trench. Its starboard side opened to reveal numerous mage emplacements.

"Eight thousand meters!"

Concha Vessels reloaded, arming themselves with concussive drops.

"Six thousand meters!"

The mages of Cetus's sister ship, Hydra, were a quarter of the way finished on their attack spell.

"Four thousand meters!"

Surrounding Pistris Ships prepared their weapons.

"Two thousand meters!"

"Emerging!"

The ball of gas broke through the frozen ceiling covering the Trench. Mages aboard Cetus fired a flash freeze spell, cooling the superheated gas before it could damage the ice ceiling above. A hundred different ships fired concussive drops, magical propulsion torpedoes and a dozen other things.

When the demon emerged, they all broke.

Magical shells, torpedoes, all their intricate and ordered wiring, that would've each taken an industrial mage a full day to create, they were all corrupted to meaninglessness.

When the weapons hit it, they were naught but mundane stones.

"Concha Vessels retreat!"

"Mages switch to attack pattern six! Status on Hydra's ritual!"

"Fifty percent!"

"Forward Hastati deploy!"

Infantry spearmen shot out of their hiding spots. Swift swimmers, trained for delaying actions, to slow down the demon until mages could destroy it.

Unfortunately for them, the demon was faster.

It opened its great maw, revealing a writhing mass of serpents. Each serpent shot out with impossible elasticity, biting onto the exposed spearmen. Almost immediately, the tritons began to crumble into dust from the bitten point.

"Fire!" the Legate ordered over the pearls.

Helen's eyes widened. "There are still—"

Pistris Ships, the fighting Leviathan, the mages on board all of them fired a simple spell. A small, directed explosion that created a wave of force in a certain direction.

Water is extremely close to a concussive superconductor, it is near incompressible, so force was conducted easily in it.

Anything inside the water, however, would not fare nearly as well.

The demon began to contort as white waves of force struck it.

"Confirmed hit!"

"Prepare for the second volley!"

Helen stared uncomprehendingly at the readings, several Hastati got out but many more were simply . . . flattened, and yet, the remainder kept going.

She felt a hand on her shoulder. Magister Rhea wasn't looking at her, still staring at the devices, she whispered, "We are Tritons, Defenders of the Ocean Blue. To hesitate is to sign the death of more than us."

Not unkindly, she said, "Take over monitoring on the Order demon, it has yet to make another move."

Helen mutely nodded.

Outside, the battle raged on. Most of the Hastati had fallen back, attacking only occasionally when they saw the chance. Leaving only their captain, Caligula, to face the demon head on.

Whenever Caligula moved, he pushed several tons of water with him. Even when the demon dodged by large margins, the following shockwave from Caligula's movements hit it with secondary damage.

The demon was battered. It was time for the finisher.

"Status on Hydra's ritual?"

"Ninety-eight percent! Hydra is moving in to cast!"

"Move in! Prepare for secondary volley!"

Cetus circled above the trench, a dozen other Pistris ships with it.

"FIRE!" the Senior Legate ordered.

Then it all went to shit.

When the mages prepared their spells, the force of the explosion multiplied. Backfiring on them and each unleashing a force wave several dozen times stronger.

Entropy was the spreading of energy. That was what the mages were doing. A controlled explosion that unleashed a wave of energy in a specific direction. So, the Entropy demon *enhanced* it by several times. Within the sea, where water already enhanced concussive wave effects by several times?

The results were disastrous.

The sides of every ship facing the demon dented as the extreme force pushed them all back by several hundred meters. The surviving Hastati were obliterated in an instant and every Pistris Ship within two hundred meters were torn to pieces.

The demon did not escape unscathed. It had somehow lowered the forces on it, but still, there was little left of it. Only its upper torso and head were left, the rest mangled beyond recognition. Yet, when its maw opened, one could not help but think it was smiling.

That smile soon disappeared as Caligula shot out of the white foam and stabbed the demon with his lance.

Both his arms and a leg were simply crushed. His chest was flattened, so his body could no longer take in air. He held his lance with only his teeth.

A dead man still swimming. Yet in defiance, he clenched his teeth and held even when dozens of serpents swept out and bit onto him. His body crumbled, but he kept the demon in place.

Just as the Hydra came.

A ritual that took the entirety of the battle and several of the finest mages Tritus can offer. One that would only target demons and not affect others.

Banishing Smite was cast at Eighth Level. The maximum which mortals can reach.

The demon did not even get to scream as its remains were compressed into a cube, only a centimeter wide.

"Confirmed hit!"

Caligula finally let go. He died when he stabbed the demon. Only Will kept him in place.

"Remaining Pistris to the Trench!" the Legate ordered. "Cetus retreat to supporting position! Hydra take point!"

There was no rest. No moment of celebration.

"Order is making a move!" Helen yelled.

The remaining sonar wards detected that the clump of stones the demon had possessed were moving. In a rhythmic up and down motion.

"Press the attack! Do not allow it to entrench itself!"

The Hydra swam toward the breach. The Pistris ships that were still in a relatively functioning state followed it. A single Pitris ship left it to retrieve the corpses of Caligula and the demon as Cetus retreated.

Then the attacking force stopped. Frozen as they entered the Trench.

"Hydra report!" the Senior Legate yelled. When no answer came, he yelled again, "Hydra!"

"Communications are still online," Rhea said. "The attacking force is frozen . . . How?"

"Isn't time stop," another Magus called out. "This isn't the first Order Demon Hydra has dealt with, it should have anti-time-stop measures."

"No activity on any ship, everyone is frozen."

"What the Blue is it, then?" the Legate yelled.

Magister Rhea left her position next to Helen to stand next to the Senior Staff Mage. Bringing out a variety of measuring implements. Muttering things to each other as they read the readings.

Slowly, the discussions rose in urgency. Until it finally fell to disbelief.

"Senior Legate Ajax, we believe that . . . the Order demon didn't stop time but has made movement impossible."

"Explain."

The entire room craned their necks as the Staff Mage continued, "Are you aware of the Twelve Giottian Paradoxes?"

"No, but how are they relevant?"

"Paradox Six posits that if you cut a brick in perfect half, you cut the half in another perfect half and continue this pattern forever, creating infinitely smaller pieces of the brick."

"By this logic, Paradox Six claims that movement is impossible," Rhea continued, "because things travel half the distance between it and something, then travel another half of that remaining distance."

"And you are claiming?"

"We believe that the Order demon has made this true."

"But for what purpose? It is affected as well, isn't it?"

"Yes, it is. A spell of this scale and speed, it might be able to take it down but that is it."

"The wards," Helen blurted out, "what do the wards on the other side of the Hell Gate say?"

They checked and, horrifyingly, saw the gathering horde of fiends.

"By the Blue, we barely survived that," Leo said in a light-hearted tone he didn't truly feel. Instead, he directed it to his squad of five. All of them were newbies like him, and more than slightly shaken at the experience. "I don't know about you guys but I'm getting laid after this."

Agata punched his leg. "Who would want to lay with you?" she replied drily.

"No daydreaming Leo, we have a job," Alcaeus seriously said, but more cheekily added, "but do invite me once we're finished with this."

Leo smiled as the previous oppressive silence melted away. "Please, women are simply fighting to get to lay me!"

"You sure they aren't fighting for the privilege of being the first to lynch you?"

Leo chuckled at Agata's dry humor.

"No, that honor would go to my mother!" he laughed aloud but did not let it overly distract him. Alcaeus made sense, their squad of four needed to check up on what happened to one of the mage emplacements. Winning back morale should not take the place doing their mission.

"What do you think happened anyway?" Cyrus asked.

"The emplacement was aimed at Entropy when it screwed everything up," Agata answered. "It wouldn't be surprising if it were destroyed in the process."

"Still, it's strange they only sent three of us," Cyrus said.

Yeah, it was strange, Leo had to admit. Even if he skimmed through the Manuals, he knew the protocol was to send at minimum a squad of five in a situation like this.

"They were shorthanded," Agata answered, "a lot of tritons fell. That was why they could only spare the two of us."

"Yeah," Leo answered as the mood dimmed again and they reached the end of the hallway.

He would be alone. They couldn't spare any more tritons to check up on every little bit of damage dealt to the ship.

When he saw the doorway that led to the mage emplacement, he lifted his spear. The door was opened.

There was a slight amount of force damage on the interior, but it likely wasn't what pushed it open. The damage wasn't enough. The door was opened by something.

Slowly, he swam inside the emplacement. Clean, there were no bodies here.

Then he suddenly heard a clicking behind him.

Instantly he turned around, spear pointed, only to see *something*.

The bodies of seven tritons, three mages and four infantry units of a lower rank than him, floating in the water. No, not floating. They were attached to something, numerous holes bore through their bodies, and Leo could see thin scratches left on the wall as the bodies moved.

With horror, he began to realize that the bodies were attached to something invisible that impaled them with long spikes to hold their corpses in place. He realized at almost the same time, that the water around him was not clear.

It was a dirty red. Dirtied with blood.

Slowly, Leo began to back off. He did not recognize the infantry but the mages were likely from this emplacement. How did he not notice the thing following him? A thousand questions and fears warred in his mind, but a single order took precedent.

There was a scrying pearl behind him, farther into the emplacement.

He needed to get to it and report the breach. Leo could not face this thing, not when it clearly killed seven others.

Unfortunately, the demon seemed to have come to the same conclusion.

Leo could not see it move, but the corpses slightly shifted as whatever was the head of the thing turned to the scrying pearl.

The scrying pearl shattered. Something like a long spike piercing its side. In that moment, Leo bolted. There was another door leading outside the emplacement. He swiftly reached it, his own swimming speed outstripping anything the demon seemed to be able to muster.

A demon was loose on the ship. Leo *had* to warn Command about it.

He swam through the corridors of the Pistris Four. There should be another patrol or scrying pearl around here, he had to quickly reach them.

To his relief, he saw another patrol, headed by Euripides, a sergeant senior to him.

"By the Blue, I am glad to see your ugly face!" he exclaimed. "There's a breach on the ship, we have to report it!"

The patrol passed him.

Leo spent a solid second frozen in shock before he hurriedly turned and swam toward them. "Are you daft! Can't you hear me yelling!"

They continued. Eyes scanning the area around them. One of them passed by Leo, but he did not acknowledge him.

"Hey! Has old age finally gotten to you!?" Euripides did not respond.

Half in anger, half in desperation, Leo punched the other sergeant, knocking him back.

Euripides looked dazed for a moment before he swam back to the patrol.

None of the five acknowledged the punch or the brief moment Euripides was gone.

Their eyes were seriously scanning every nook and cranny of the hallway. Prepared for potential attacks. Yet they did not seem to realize Leo was here or his attack.

"Hey! Hey! C'mon, there has to be a limit to how deaf you are right!?" Leo yelled, he yelled as loud as he could.

No one heard him.

Click.

Leo turned and saw clouds of blood. The demon was not visible to him even now, save for the clicking it made as it moved.

"Hey! Can't you see that!" he screamed. "IT'S RIGHT FUCKING THERE!"

Leo grabbed the shoulders of the farthest back patrol guard. "DON'T

GO THERE!" he screamed till his throat became hoarse. Holding the guard back and turning him directly to him.

The guard—Homer, if Leo remembered correctly—looked at him and saw past him.

"Hurry up, Homer," Euripides called.

Leo turned to see that the demon was right in front of them. It pushed the group to the side, Euripides even hit the head of one of the corpses laying on its back.

It was not acknowledged.

Even when it pushed them aside. Even when the patrol group was on high alert. None of them saw the demon.

Homer brushed off Leo. "Sorry, the wall appeared strange to me."

As Homer passed the demon, one of the spikes sliced his arm, yet he continued, unheeding of his bleeding.

Leo realized what demon this was.

Absence.

"What happened to Pistris Four?" Helen asked as she looked at several record pearls.

"What about it?" Rhea asked as she sorted a dozen other records. "Hmm ..." she muttered as she got to the record. "Apparently it never left the dock. It was kept by the Outer Wall."

Helen furrowed her brows. "Odd ..."

"Do not be distracted," Rhea said. "Thoroughly check through the records. We have to observe Absence Protocols."

"I know," she answered.

Helen just felt like she should've remembered something.

Character Sheets

Name: Dustin
Race: Magic Myconid
Classes: Fungalmancer Level 3, Holder of the Discovery Shard Level 1

<u>Body:</u>
Strength: 8
Agility: 7
Dexterity: 6
Constitution: 18
Stamina: 10
Vitality: 12

<u>Mind:</u>
Intelligence: 16
Wisdom: 18
Charisma: 6

<u>Soul:</u>
Will: 10
Aura: 10
Perception: 10

<u>Racials:</u>
  • **Superior Darkvision** [Passive]: You can see in dim light within forty meters as if it were bright light, and in darkness as if it were dim light. You cannot discern colors in darkness, only shades of grey.
  • **Fungal Body** [Passive]: Innate resistance to poisons.

- **Sun Sickness** [Passive]: Being in direct sunlight will drain your stamina, this effect can be mitigated by raising Constitution.
- **Mana Dependency** [Passive]: Taking physical actions with low mana will drain additional stamina.
- **Pacifying Spores** [Active]: Eject spores at a creature within five meters of you; if the target fails a Constitution Save, then it is put to sleep. This skill scales with your Constitution and Vitality.
- **Innate Magic** [Passive]: Gain two Tier 0 Spells from the Magic Cap Myconid Spell List.

Class Skills:
Fungalmancer:
Path: Symbiosis
- **Grow Sporage** (Visual) [Active]: You may create a mushroom capable of storing a Spore based spell. These Sporages can be activated on visual contact. They glow faintly and last your myconid level in hours.
- **Grow Sporage** (Proximity) [Active]: Upgrade to Grow Sporage. You obtain the option to grow Sporages with a different activation type. The sporage lets out a thin layer of mycelium around it that acts as a pressure detector. When sufficient weight is applied to any part of the fungus, the Sporage will explode. You and targets of Symbiosis do not detonate these Sporages.
- **Sporage Wisp Symbiosis** [Active]: Wisps have lived comfortably in your cap and have created a wonderful home there, now to teach them the wonders of rent. You may create pygmy myconid bodies for your non-corporeal Wisps to inhabit. They are considered tiny creatures and are capable of following simple commands. They possess all the qualities of Sporage, however, they can choose to self-detonate.
- **Bracken Polypores** [Passive] [Active]: A species of symbiotic fungus are seeded underneath your skin. They rely on you for food and in return can instantly grow into durable mycelium plates that can cover your entire body. The hardness and weight may vary depending on how much Satiety you feed them at any moment. Will gain defensive bonuses if used in conjunction with Bark Skin.

Analyze Additions:
Holder of the Discovery Shard:
Path: Analyze
- **Analyze** [Passive]: You passively absorb the information you gather. Learning the exact parameters of that which you observe and translating

them to a form understandable to you. This information exists in a database and can be called on at any time.

   • **Observation Link** [Passive]: You are linked to a user of Observe. Your minds are linked, and they may share all they see through Observe. Through you, they may also mark other willing creatures to have their vision be seen through Observe as well.

   • **Et Non-Discent** [Passive]: This class was not sourced from the system, thus it does not benefit from the system either.

   • Progress in this class does not rely on Traveler Experience, but on your own proficiency.

   • You may not invest levels in this class.

   • This class and its progress will not be displayed on your character sheet.

   • Raising this class's level will not affect your Traveler Level.

<u>Spells:</u>
T0: Balm Spores, Light Spores, Sneezing Spores, Acid Spit
T1: Mushroom Meal, Poison Spores
T2: Bark Skin

<u>Available Spell Slots:</u>
T0: 2
T1: 1
T2: 2

<u>Languages:</u>
Common
Undercommon

Name: Noam
Race: Tiefling
Classes: Skald Level 3

<u>Body:</u>
Strength: 12
Agility: 14
Dexterity: 10
Constitution: 9
Stamina: 10
Vitality: 8

<u>Mind:</u>
Intelligence: 12
Wisdom: 10
Charisma: 14

<u>Soul:</u>
Will: 10
Aura: 10
Perception: 10

<u>Racials:</u>
Darkvision, Hellish Resistance

<u>Class Skills:</u>
Skald:
Path: Spitfire

- **Breathless** [Passive]: Your body no longer needs to breathe, but you retain maximal efficiency of aerobic respiration.
- **Beatbox** [Passive] [Active]: You gain knowledge of how to beatbox alongside proficiency. You may as a free action, lock-up to 5 seconds of beatboxing in a loop, where it'll continuously emanate from you at the original volume at a negligible mana cost per second.
- **Fire** [Passive]: When verbal-based attacks land a critical hit, the target is set alight by non-magical flame.
- **Catch These Hands!** [Active]: Once per day, gain bonus stats to Agility, Dexterity and Charisma for every person around you currently irritated, angered, generally pissed and/or displaying hostility toward you. Stats disappear when the cooldown has ended or when hostile individuals leave your range or cease being hostile to you.

<u>Martial Arts:</u>
Swift Strike

<u>Spells:</u>
T0: Biting Words, Vicious Mockery

<u>Available Spell Slots:</u>
T0: 2
T1: 1

<u>Proficiencies:</u>
Polearms: Novice
Beatboxing: Novice

<u>Languages:</u>
Common
Infernal

Name: Naukoth Stoneback
Race: Orc
Titles: Stoneback, 'Another Mentally Deficient Orc'

<u>Classes:</u>
Haulier Level 2
Virtuoso Level 3

<u>Body:</u>
Strength: 25
Agility: 11
Dexterity: 16
Constitution: 16
Stamina: 23
Vitality: 18

<u>Mind:</u>
Intelligence: 12
Wisdom: 8
Charisma: 13

<u>Soul:</u>
Will: 22
Aura: 12
Perception: 9

<u>Racials:</u>
Darkvision, Powerful Build

<u>Class Skills:</u>
Haulier:
Path: Resolute

Carrying Capacity Increase, Endurance

<u>Virtuoso:</u>
Path: Requiem (Incomplete)
Erudite Dexterity, Battle Inspiration, Solo Opera

<u>Guild Report:</u>
Mercenary Combat Rating: 20

Boss Sheets

GIATAN XIENNE
THE PRIEST OF LIFE

<u>Class:</u>
Priest (Life Domain) Level 3
Chimerist: Level 5

<u>Body:</u>
Strength: 19
Agility: 12
Dexterity: 13
Constitution: 23
Stamina: 19
Vitality: 18

<u>Mind:</u>
Intelligence: 19
Wisdom: 11
Charisma: 12

<u>Soul:</u>
Will: 13
Aura: 18
Perception: 13

<u>**Traits:**</u>
Martial Novice: This creature is an inexperienced martial combatant.
Magic Adept: This creature is a magical combatant.
Recovery: This creature is capable of healing itself by a significant amount.

Devour: This creature may consume an opponent. Keeping it inside its stomach and potentially eating killed opponents for benefits.

Lord: This creature utilizes additional creatures to aid itself on the battlefield.

Bond: This creature has a long-time bond with a companion, it has certain abilities based on this bond.

Faith: This creature is a servant of a god that may participate in the fight.

Hidden:

Silence: This creature has abilities that may seal an opponent's ability to cast magic.

Basic Combat:

Command Pheromones: This ability was never identified but was used in combat.

Hardened Fist: Giatan's right fist has been augmented with the skin of the Vulcanos Raptor. It may rapidly harden to a toughness akin to volcanic rock. Attacks done with this fist deal bludgeoning damage.

Spell Caster: Giatan Xienne knows the following spells:
- T0: Sacred Flame, Mending, Control Flame, Druidcraft, Guidance, Thaumaturgy
- T1: Healing Word, Cure Wounds, Animal Friendship, Speak with Animals
- T2: Animal Messenger, Locate Animals and Plants
- T3: Plant Growth, Revivify
- T4: Dominate Beast

Aura User: Giatan Xienne knows the following martial arts:
Enhance Ability: Fox Cunning, Protection from Poison

Altered Tiefling: Giatan Xienne is a tiefling with an altered form, as such, he has the following resistances:
- Damage Resistances: Bludgeoning, Piercing, Slashing, Fire
- Condition Resistances: Charmed, Exhaustion, Paralyzed, Unconscious

Integrate:

Create Chimera (Ritual): This ability was never identified or used in combat.

Integrate Form (Ritual): This ability was never identified or used in combat.

Distilled Waters of the Oasis (Item): Giatan Xienne possesses a unique concoction made in part of the water from the Oasis. He possesses three such mixtures encased in salt crystal tubes blessed with desiccation and necrotic properties to prevent mutation. Upon consumption of this concoction, the drinker will experience rapid metabolism and regeneration. However, this regeneration still relies on the creature's natural metabolic processes and as such still needs swift consumption to fully activate. Failure to consume may result in the swift autophagy of random 'unessential' organs.

"This right here... we can save so many people with this."—Giatan Xienne.

Hidden:

Basic Combat:

Mimic Arm: Giatan's left arm has been replaced with flesh from Mimicron The Living Dungeon. It is extremely dexterous and has enough biting force to break steel plate. It acts as a pseudo-separate entity from Giatan similar to an octopus arm.

Mage Slaying Tail: Giatan has grafted the tail of a Magebane Scorpion's tail onto his body. When wrapped around him it acts as pseudo-armor against physical attacks and its metallic nature disrupts spell casting near him. It has a stinging tip which injects fine iron dust into the body of an enemy. This greatly disrupts their spellcasting and may permanently damage their abilities to spell cast.

Life:

Disciple of Life [Passive]: This ability was never identified or used in combat.

Channel Divinity, Enhance Life [Active]: This ability was never identified or used in combat.

Dead God [Domain]: This ability was never identified but was used in combat.

Bond:

Beast Bond [Passive]: This ability was never identified but was used in combat.

Cries of the Master [Triggered]: This ability was never identified or used in combat.

Weaknesses:

Inexperienced Combatant: Giatan is not an experienced combatant, as such he tends to leave the fighting to his creations. Solving most problems by just swarming enemies with endless chimeras.

Thin Skin: Giatan responds easily to any provocation, given or perceived.

One Way Communication: Giatan cannot receive information from the majority of his creations unless they directly return to him. This has one exception in CH-067.

Magical Nullification: Giatan's **Mage Slaying Tail** disrupts his own spell casting, when it is wrapped around him, he gains armor akin to full plate mail but can only cast T0 spells.

Loyal till the End: This weakness was never identified or used in combat.

Bounty Notice:

Giatan Xienne is an intelligent magic caster who possesses dangerous amounts of the Class I Restricted Object: Oasis Water. His own chimeric skills allow him to greatly augment himself for any sort of situation and his heretical worship of his god gives him great healing abilities. Though the base chimeras are weak, he makes up for it in huge quantities and usually implements swarm tactics. It is not recommended you face him without a way to clear his swarm.

His crimes include: Heretical Worship, Human Experimentation, Unnatural Treatment of Living Creatures, Possessing Class I Restricted Objects.

CH-067 "TODD"
THE CHIMERIST CREATION

Racial:
Chimera Level 2

Body:
Strength: 25
Agility: 8
Dexterity: 7
Constitution: 28
Stamina: 24
Vitality: 12

Mind:
Intelligence: 4

Wisdom: 3
Charisma: N/A

<u>Soul:</u>
Will: 2
Aura: 2
Perception: 8

<u>Traits:</u>
Overwhelm (Physical): This creature has abilities that can overcome physical resistance.
Devour: This creature may consume an opponent. Keeping it inside its stomach and potentially eating killed opponents for benefits.
Bond: This creature has a long-time bond with a companion, it has certain abilities based on this bond.
Enrage: This creature enters a new phase after certain conditions are met.

<u>Basic Combat:</u>
Frost Breathe: CH-067 has the head of a minor frost elemental, granting it a breath weapon. It may breathe frost in a large cone, dealing cold damage.
Stone Speaker: CH-067 has the head of a minor stone elemental, granting it control of all stone nearby when it sings.
Vacuum Crush: CH-067 has the mouth of a Deep Devourer Otter-Squid, granting it extreme suction power and a grinding mouth.

Hidden:

<u>Bond:</u>
Beast Bond [Passive]: This ability was never identified but was used in combat.
Cries of the Beast [Triggered]: Should Giatan Xienne perish in battle, CH-067 will scream in anguish, attempting to destroy all nearby creatures in vengeance.

<u>Weaknesses:</u>
Unintelligent: CH-067 is incapable of thinking for itself, as such it follows its master's orders completely.
Restricted: CH-067 has been instructed to not use **Stone Speaker** or

Vacuum Crush due to the large amount of collateral damage they cause to Giatan's experiments and furniture.

Puppy: CH-067 can be temporarily distracted by calling it by its nickname "Todd." When done so, it will excitedly look at the caller and expect a treat to be thrown. This was used by Giatan to feed it **Distilled Waters of the Oasis**.

Loyal till the End: Should Giatan Xienne fall, CH-067 will fall into a depressive state after **Cries of the Beast,** it is completely unresponsive even to harm and will wait for orders that will never come. CH-067 was later euthanized by the Ivory Tower when discovered in this state.

Afterword

Man, it's so strange to be here. Hello, everyone, I'm Sir Nil (aka Eric Lin), writer of this story. When I started Mycology, I never really expected it to be anything more than a niche indie webnovel sequestered in some unknown corner of the internet. In fact, I was so sure of my mediocrity that when I received an offer from a publisher, I really couldn't believe it, almost ignoring the offer because it was just so incomprehensible to me. Everyone, my peers, my readers, and even my parents, who haven't read this novel, all tell me this is a great achievement, yet some nagging part of me is still just . . . awestruck, I suppose.

It's not without any sense, since I started writing Mycology all the way back in 2019. So much has happened, and even though I keep writing, I've changed a lot as an individual from the day I began. I'm still rather embarrassed reading the things the younger me had written; the techniques, ideas, and themes that I once thought clever seem so clumsy to me now.

In many ways, I was limited by my format. Being a webnovel writer often means chapter-by-chapter releases, meaning I didn't think much from chapter to chapter, I wrote freely of whatever came to my mind and thought not much of what happened afterward, yet I was still able to tie it all together. In the end, the webnovel format of my story informed the theme that I had thought of for this story. Originally, I had written an afterword for the webnovel version, and wanted to change it to fit the differing release methods of a full book release; however . . . I realized I don't want to. I don't want to remove the afterword I wrote back then and replace it with something else, yet I felt that a fresh comment from the author was necessary. So in order to preserve the authenticity of my original writing, I have added this short introduction here, and I saved the original text from back then for your perusal below.

Thanks to my original readers back on Royal Road for sticking with me through multiple writing hiatuses. Thanks to my friends for telling me to take this offer, and thanks to the people at Podium Audio for helping me publish this. And most importantly, thank *you* for reading.

I began writing this story on November 18, 2020, initially releasing it on Royal Road.

I'm writing this note at the same time as 4.15, though it doesn't really matter, does it? In the end, this is going to be shipped out the same time as the interlude. I'm not sure what to say, honestly, I'm not sure why you all are still reading. I can come up with plenty of explanations, entertainment, boredom, the need to simply burn time, but I never *know*.

When I set out to write this story, I had only a few things, a D&D character sheet for a canceled campaign, a shit ton of notes for a VRMMO world and the desire to try my hand once again at writing after I burned out on "WTF I'm a Dungeon."

So I sat down and wrote.

Mycology is the fourth iteration of a list of VRMMO stories, I can't remember the exact order but there was a necromancer BBEG, murder hobo party and a steampunk story before it. The murder hobo party story had four different chapter ones, each slightly different. Even not considering the VRMMO stories, I had three different dungeon core stories, a modern superhero, meta isekai, and even a jojo fanfic written down.

I'm rambling again it seems. Well, they don't really matter, since they probably won't ever see the light of day, I'm just trying to show how much work happens behind the scenes in the hopes my effort will receive a small bit of validation.

Now, I'll inform you of the purpose, or perhaps the structure I've been keeping to this story.

Originally, I didn't want to post this, let the readers figure it out themselves, or maybe let them think it's all the result of a strange stylistic choice.

But I didn't want the work and thought I put in to go unnoticed, never known, or even worse, mistaken for something unintentional.

So here I am, writing.

Thus far, I have tried to keep to a writing style of absurd realism, with emphasis on the absurd. I've made it a personal challenge to give the phrase "Reality is stranger than fiction" a huge middle finger. I'm probably failing, but still making a good effort.

I've told you all that from the beginning that Declan and Dustin were my self-inserts and by now you should have a deeper understanding of them. For the sake of convenience, I shall just refer to them as Declan. 4.21 was meant to definitively fill in that final gap you probably guessed, but didn't know for sure.

Declan relies on logic, he hates acting on negative emotions no matter how justified they are, but he is a purposeless character stuck in the monotone of existence.

He has no true reason or motivation to ever act. Reading back you will notice that most of his important actions occur because someone *else* asked him to do it. Declan is a character with nearly no autonomy or care for his life. Even in the sole danger situation, the beginning of the story, did Declan actually ever *say* he was afraid for his life?

He didn't, did he?

Something so simple and taken for granted. Not having it mentioned.

How does one write such a character into a story? Not to mention a main character? They refuse to engage in anything like a plot and would be perfectly content living like a river rock. Most stories have a monotony at the start, before something happens which drags into the plot. Something that forces them to act.

In a darker story, Eve's call would've led to some horrible sci-fi shit. Declan's opponent is an AI far above anything he can intellectually match. Even if it was programmed to act juvenile, even human, it is a dangerous entity capable of freely hijacking people's minds.

In a lighthearted story, he would've gone on an adventure with the first friends he meets. Discovering some bastardized Machiavellian plot including rats, a mastermind raccoon, and way too many moving parts to not fail.

But none of them happen, because Declan simply *does not care*. I've been hinting at this, and have pretty much confirmed it when I released Journey, but Declan's world is fucked on an irrevocable level, but he is a teenager, how is he supposed to deal with that? How is he supposed to fight off Skynet or solve a global crisis? There's some kind of strange and fun plot with the players at spawn, but why should he care? It affected him somewhat but not unduly and the rats paid him well enough. If he's capable of fixing it, why can't someone else deal with it?

Why do anything at all?

Why even bother living?

I'm not sure myself, I can't answer that question, but perhaps I can pose this question to you, dear reader.

Why did you keep reading?

This is a purposeless story, one that meanders, one that drops plot points and interesting characters, one that doesn't have a clear goal until nearly 600 pages in. There is no reason for you to be here, so *why* are you here?

Why do you check the story for updates, why do you open the page when there's a new release, why are you still here?

I think, whatever answer you give, will be as good a reason as any.

And so, I hope you understand now, why I have been writing this way.

The purpose of this story thus far, is to be purposeless, to not have a point, to not have a central "plot" to make a reader continue. To just be a realistic, if insane story where the world will continue to move regardless of the actions of the characters. More a report or biography than a driven story with a central plot.

I sacrificed the story for the character. A realistic story isn't about consequences for your actions, it isn't Grimdark like most would have you believe, it is fun and enjoyment, chaos and order, horrors and sadness, simple inanity and boredom. That is why a realistic story does not always make for a good story, because unlike a story, real life does not have to make coherent sense, it doesn't follow central themes or characters, just a report of the everyday.

I've accepted that because of this, this story will forever be considered to have a "slow start" at best or a 'doesn't go anywhere in 10 chapters 0.5 stars' at worst. I've accepted that because of what I've done this story will never rise above a 3/10 as a story, for the simple reason I killed the story for this long, probably pointless message.

All of you who've read up till this point, probably understand what it means to be purposeless, to not have a good reason to do anything. But *you are still here.* Any reason is better than none. Or maybe I'm just being a pretentious idiot rationalizing bad writing, who knows? Does it matter either way? If you are still here, it meant that some part of you enjoyed what I wrote, and honestly, before deep and great meanings, that simple fact is good enough for me. Reality is stupid, brutal and a thousand other bad things, but that doesn't mean it can't be enjoyed.

Though, the story sacrificed cannot be gone for long. That is why now was the end of the Prologue, because until now, the story hadn't started. Many people spend their entire lives without purpose, and I would like to write a story like that one day, but in this one a purpose is found, even one made in pettiness. A reason to continue is found, an eventual reward for staying by and congratulations my friend, you made it.

I will still be here, for as long as I want, maybe for as long as I can. I already have several thousand pages worth of future events jotted down in notes and wriggling inside my head, they only need to be written down. If

I could instantly write and release all my ideas, Mycology would probably end with a lot of pages, but I'll brag about that whenever I reach that point, but I'll say this, *relatively* speaking, it makes sense for the prologue to be this long.

I'm in it for the long haul and will take breaks if I need them, I won't make the mistakes of my past but I will not be afraid to experiment.

I hope you all do well, this is far from a perfect story, probably far from a good one as well. A 3/10 on my scale is the question of plot, and I've already fucked that up. Intentionally or not an artist who rips up the canvas still ruins the piece.

But in the end, I hope in this purposeless story, one that has no point or meaning, I hope you find something you can invest in or take away.

In the end, it's up to you.

Sir Nil out.

About the Author

Sir Nil is an Australian author who got really bored one afternoon in high school and decided to vomit out a piece of brain-melting word soup he called a "story," dragging the poor netizens of a certain webnovel site through a truly horrific experience. He didn't even compose it on a typewriter, but on a smartphone—the absolute gall! Some say he's gotten better as a writer since then, having started multiple highly rated webnovels, one of which you may be reading as a published series, but he personally denies such allegations.

Sir Nil studies biotechnology, though is not particularly good at it, and his personal writing motto is: "The secret to being original is copying so many people that your detractors give up pointing it out," which he encourages everyone to shamelessly steal without crediting him.

If ever you may face Sir Nil in battle or debate, simply bring up his first webnovel and he will shrivel up like an embarrassed prune, guaranteeing your victory through tried-and-true ad hominem attacks.

Podium
DISCOVER
STORIES UNBOUND
PodiumAudio.com